A Treasury of AMERICAN MYSTERY STORIES

ABOUT THE EDITORS

FRANK D. MCSHERRY, JR., is a noted mystery authority and bibliophile. He has written numerous essays for "The Armchair Detective" and with Charles G. Waugh and Martin H. Greenberg is an editor of *Baseball 3000*.

CHARLES G. WAUGH is a leading authority on science fiction and fantasy and has collaborated on more than 100 anthologies and single-author collections with Frank D. McSherry, Jr., Martin H. Greenberg, and assorted colleagues.

MARTIN H. GREENBERG, who has been called "the king of the anthologists," now has some 305 books, 240 of them anthologies, to his credit. He is also co-editor, along with Frank D. McSherry, Jr., and Charles G. Waugh, of *A Treasury of American Horror Stories*.

A Treasury of
AMERICAN
MYSTERY
STORIES

Edited by Frank D. McSherry, Jr., Charles
G. Waugh, and Martin H. Greenberg

BONANZA BOOKS
New York

A detailed list of acknowledgments begins on page v.

Copyright © 1989 by Martin H. Greenberg, Charles G. Waugh, and Frank D. McSherry, Jr.

First published in 1989 by Avenel Books, distributed by Crown Publishers, Inc., 225 Park Avenue South, New York, New York 10003

Printed and bound in the United States of America

Library of Congress Cataloging-in-Publication Data

Treasury of American mystery stories.

   1. Detective and mystery stories, American. I. McSherry, Frank D. II. Waugh, Charles.
III. Greenberg, Martin Harry.
PS648.D4T74   1989   813'.0872'08   88-24190

ISBN 0-517-67657-5

h g f e d c b a

ACKNOWLEDGMENTS

Grateful acknowledgment is given to the following sources for permission to reprint the material listed below.

"The Vital Element" copyright © 1989 by Talmage Powell. A version of this appeared in *Alfred Hitchcock's Mystery Magazine,* © 1967 by H.S.D. Publications. Reprinted by permission of the author.

"Whippin' Wildcats" copyright © 1987 by Davis Publications, Inc. From *Ellery Queen's Mystery Magazine.* Reprinted by permission of the author.

"The Sleeping Dog" copyright © 1965 by The Margaret Millar Survivor's Trust u/a 4/12/82. First published in *Argosy.* Reprinted by permission of Harold Ober Associates, Inc.

"Graveyard Shift" copyright © 1953 by Steve Frazee. Reprinted by permission of the Scott Meredith Literary Agency, Inc., 845 Third Ave., New York, NY 10022.

"The Old Barn on the Pond" copyright © 1965 by Davis Publications, Inc. Reprinted by permission of Brandt & Brandt Literary Agents, Inc.

"The Washington, D.C., Murders" copyright © 1963 by Patricia McGerr. Reprinted by permission of Curtis Brown, Ltd.

"Hijack" copyright © 1972 by Robert L. Fish. Reprinted by permission of Richard Curtis Associates, Inc.

"The Sky Pirates" copyright © 1983 by Donald Jordan. From *Alfred Hitchcock's Mystery Magazine.* Reprinted by permission of Alex Jackinson.

"Scrimshaw" copyright © 1979 by Brian Garfield. From *Ellery Queen's Mystery Magazine.* Reprinted by permission of the author.

"Bull and Bear" copyright © 1989 by Edward D. Hoch. An original story by arrangement with the author.

"A Debt to Be Paid" copyright © 1980 by Dick Stodghill/Davis Publications, Inc. From *Ellery Queen's Mystery Magazine.* Reprinted by permission of the author.

"The Happy Days Club" copyright © 1963 by James M. Ullman. Reprinted by permission of the author.

"Kansas in August" copyright © 1989 by Edward D. Hoch. An original story by arrangement with the author.

"Hunter and the Widow" copyright © 1984 by Davis Publications, Inc. Reprinted by permission of the author.

"Colt .24" copyright © 1987 by Rick Hautala. Reprinted by permission of the author.

"Will You Always Be Helping Me?" copyright © 1956 by Thomas Walsh. Reprinted by permission of Thomas Walsh, Jr.

"A Case of Innocent Eavesdropping" copyright © 1978 by Helen McCloy. From *Ellery Queen's Mystery Magazine.* Reprinted by permission of Richard Curtis Associates, Inc.

CONTENTS

vii

THE MYSTERY TOUR

The doors are opening.

The Mystery Tour is about to begin—a tour of murder and mystery, magic and suspense. Sit down. Be comfortable. Let me hold your hand—and jugular vein. Don't worry—I have a firm grip. . . .

Here is a volume chock-a-block with mystery stories, one set in each of the fifty states in the Union, plus a story for the District of Columbia—a murderer's tour not only of the entire country but also of the capital.

And more than that—it's a tour through the annals of the American mystery, too.

It was in fact an American who created the modern mystery story. Edgar Allan Poe, one of the first Americans to gain international recognition as a writer, was born in 1809 in Boston, and was raised by an actress mother and a businessman stepfather who never understood his genius. After brief studies at the University of Virginia and West Point, Poe embarked on a poorly paid career in journalism, and in *Graham's Magazine* for April 1841 wrote the world's first modern detective story, "The Murders in the Rue Morgue." Poe died in 1849 in circumstances as mysterious as any in his stories: he disappeared for five days and was found in a coma from which he never recovered.

In a mere handful of short stories, one of which is included here, Poe created not only the mystery story itself but also most of its variations and plot devices, such as the "impossible crime," the "least suspected person," the eccentric detective and his sidekick, and many others. Poe's idea of a mystery story was a series of sinister, eerie, inexplicable events which the major character eventually shows to be understandable after all.

Out of darkness, light . . .

The stories in this volume have been chosen for their drama, color, and variety. In "The Sun-Dog Trail," Jack London's great story of crime and pursuit set in the frozen white wilderness of Alaska's snow country, an Eskimo guide wonders why a teenage brother and sister are willing to die of the cold if they can first find and kill the person they're hunting.

In "The Jabberwocky Murders," set in the green pine forests of Vermont, robbery and murder get mixed up with a peculiar organization devoted to the literal interpretation of Lewis Carroll's *Alice in Wonderland*. Before its publication in this volume, "The Jabberwocky Murders" had been available only in an expensive limited edition.

In "Scrimshaw," by Brian Garfield, murder comes to Hawaii, gem of the Pacific. Erle Stanley Gardner, creator of Perry Mason, takes us on a manhunt through the mountains of Idaho, while the late John D. MacDonald offers an impossible crime committed in the depths of a Nebraska winter.

Murder often arises out of current social problems, too—a battered wife commits murder in New Jersey; a white-collar criminal steals computer secrets in Minnesota; a social outcast commits Jack-the-Ripper-type murders in Detroit.

Stories about America's rich, historic past are also included here. There's midnight murder as wreckers lure ships onto the rocks off the colonial Rhode Island coast; an impossible crime is committed in broad daylight as the Wright brothers plan the world's first powered flight at Kittyhawk, North Carolina. In pre-Civil War days a teenager accidentally kills a local bully, and his penniless mother calls on an important Illinois lawyer and political figure named Abraham Lincoln for help. Echoes of the Civil War resound in "The Gettysburg Bugle," as detective Ellery Queen probes past and present in a case that is linked to that famous battle.

And there are many more wonderful stories here, as well.

Join us now in our trip through America's mysteries from past and present, about her land and heart and history and people. Settle down in your most comfortable chair and dig in. There are lots of surprises in store.

The Editors

A Treasury of AMERICAN MYSTERY STORIES

Alabama

THE VITAL ELEMENT
by Talmage Powell

I WOULD NEVER again love the warm water of Lake Boniface . . . never find beauty in its blue-green color . . . never hear music in its rustling surf . . .

The dead girl had been hurriedly buried in the lake. She was anchored in about thirty feet of water with a hempen rope that linked her lashed ankles to a pair of cement blocks.

I'd stirred the water, swimming down to her depth. Her body bobbed and swayed, with her bare toes about three feet off the clean, sandy bottom. It was almost as if a strange, macabre new life had come to her. Her long blonde hair swirled about her lovely gamine face with every tremor of the water. A living ballerina might have enjoyed her grace of motion, but not her state of being. I wept silently behind my face mask.

A single stroke sent me drifting, with my shoulder stirring silt from the bottom. I touched the rope where it passed into the holes in the cement blocks and out again. A natural process of wear and tear had set in. The sharp, ragged edges of the blocks were cutting the rope. In a matter of time, the rope would part. Her buoyancy would drift her toward the sunlight, to the surface, to discovery.

I eeled about, careful not to look at her again, and plunged up toward the shadow of the skiff. My flippers fired me into open air with a shower of spray and a small, quick explosion in my ears.

I rolled over the side of the skiff and lay a moment with my stomach churning with reaction. Sun, blue sky, the primitive shoreline of mangrove and palmetto, everything around me was weirdly unreal. It was as if all the clocks in the world had gone *tick,* then forgot to *tock.*

"You're a too-sensitive, chicken-hearted fink," I said aloud. I forced myself to peel out of my diving gear, picked up the oars, and put my back into the job of rowing in.

I docked and tied the skiff, then walked to the cottage with my gear slung across my shoulder. Sheltered by scraggly pines, the lonely cottage creaked tiredly in the heat.

I stood on the sagging front porch. For a moment I didn't have the strength or nerve to go inside.

The Alabama heat was a cloying shroud lined with a film of ice. Make sense? Perhaps not. It was such a day, insects humming, birds singing joyously, life seething, in the black-hole emptiness of death.

Movement came to me with a twitch. I turned and went inside. The cottage was its usual mess, a hodgepodge of broken down furniture, dirty dishes, empty beer bottles and bean cans, none of which bothered me. But *she* was strewn all over the place, the dead girl out there in the water. She was portrayed in oil, sketched in charcoal, delicately impressed in pink and tan watercolors. She was half finished on the easel in the center of the room, like a naked skull.

Shivering and dry-throated, I slipped dingy ducks over my damp swim trunks, wriggled into a tattered T-shirt, and slid my feet into strap sandals. The greasy feeling was working again in the pit of my stomach as I half-ran from the cottage.

Palmetto City lay like a humid landscape done with dirty brushes as my eight-year-old station wagon nosed into DeSota Street. Off the beaten tourist paths, the town was an unpainted clapboard mecca for lantern-jawed farmers, fishermen, swamp muckers.

I looked at the street scene, trying to make some reality take shape in the day. Black man in laborer's jeans coming out of Jack's Eatery picking his teeth . . . same front door his daddy had not dared to enter . . . same pinpoint on a map of muggy lowland where a long-deceased fellow had located a cotton gin and mule-powered wagons had hauled the bales to the port of Mobile, and a few tradesmen had optimistically called their burgeoning village a city.

Echo from the miasma of the past. You are not quite real, Palmetto City. Alabama is the science of Huntsville, the steel of Birmingham, a Crimson Tide and ghost of Bear Bryant. It's a George Wallace today unrecognizable by the young governor reared in defiance. It's blacks in high elective offices putting the memories behind of police dogs and cattle prods in Selma.

But you must be real, like all the other Palmetto Citys lurking in the concrete, glass, and steel hustle of the New South. You are as real as the covert lingering KKK whispers in decent, Bible-reading country. You are as real as death. . . .

I angled the steaming wagon beside a dusty pickup at the curb and got out. On the sidewalk, I glimpsed myself in the murky window of the hardware store: six feet of bone and cartilage without enough meat; thatch of unkempt sandy hair; a lean face that wished for character; huge sockets holding eyes that looked as if they hadn't slept for a week.

Inside the store, Braley Sawyer came toward me, a flabby, sloppy man in his rumpled tropical weight suit. "Well, if it ain't Tazewell Eversham, Palmetto City's own Gauguin!" He flashed a wet, gold-toothed smile. "Hear you stopped in Willy Morrow's filling station yestiddy and gassed up for a trip to Mobile. Going up to see them fancy art dealers, I guess."

I nodded. "Got back early this morning."

"You going to remember us country hoogers when you're famous, Gauguin?" The thought brought fat laughter from him. I let his little joke pass and in due time he waddled behind the counter and asked, "You here to buy something?"

"Chain." The word formed in my parched throat but didn't make itself heard. I cleared my throat, tried again, "I want to buy about a dozen feet of medium weight chain."

He blinked. "Chain?"

"Sure," I said. I had better control of my voice now. "I'd like to put in a garden, but I have stump problems. Thought I'd dig and cut around the roots and snake the stumps out with the station wagon."

He shrugged, his eyes hanging onto me as he moved toward the rear of the store. "I guess it would work—if that bucket of bolts holds together."

I turned and stared at a vacant point in space as the chain rattled from its reel. "Easier to carry if I put it in a gunny sack, Gauguin," Sawyer yelled at me.

"That's fine." I heard the chain clank into the sack.

Seconds later Sawyer dropped the chain at my feet. I paid him, carried the gunny sack out, and loaded it in the station wagon. Then I walked down the street to the general store and bought a few things—canned goods, coffee, flour, and two quarts of the cheapest booze available, which turned out to be a low-grade rum.

I'd stowed the stuff beside the gunny sack, closed the tailgate, and was walking around the wagon to get in when a man called to me from across the street. "Hey, Taze."

The man who barged toward me looked like the crudest breed of piney woods sheriff, which is what Jack Tully was. Big-bellied, slope-shouldered, fleshy faced with whisky veins on cheeks and nose, his protruding eyes searched with a sadistic hunger. His presence reminded me that not all Neanderthals had died out ten thousand years ago.

He thumbed back his hat, spat, guffawed. "Kinda left you high and dry, didn't she, bub?"

An arctic wind blew across my neck. "What are you talking about, Sheriff?"

He elbowed me in the ribs; I recoiled, from his touch, not the force behind it. "Bub, I ain't so dumb. I know Melody Grant's been sneaking out to your shack."

"Any law against it?"

"Not as long as the neighbors don't complain." He gave an obscene wink. "And you got no neighbors, have you, bub?"

His filthy thoughts were written in his smirking, ignorant face. No explanation could change his mind, not in a million years. Might as well try to explain a painting to him.

"Maybe she ain't told you yet, bub?"

"Told me what?"

"About young Perry Tomlin, son of the richest man in the county. She's been seeing him, too, now that he's home with his university degree. Going to marry him, I hear, honeymoon in Europe. Big come-up for a shanty cracker girl, even one as pretty as Melody. I reckon that shack'll be mighty lonesome, knowing you'll never see her again."

"Maybe it will, Sheriff, maybe it will."

"But . . ." We were suddenly conspirators. He gloated. ". . . there's one thing you can waller around in your mind."

"What's that, Sheriff?"

"Son of the county's richest man is just getting the leavings of a rag-tag artist who's got hardly a bean in the pot." Laughter began to well inside of him. "Bub, I got to hand you that! Man, it would bust their blood vessels, Perry's and the old man's both, if they knew the truth."

Raucous laughter rolled out of him, to the point of strangulation. When I got in the station wagon and drove off he was standing there wiping his eyes and quaking with mirth over the huge joke.

Back at the cottage, I opened a bottle of the rum, picked up a brush, and stood before the easel. I swigged from the bottle in my left hand and made brush strokes on the unfinished canvas with my right. By the time her face was emerging from the skull-like pattern, the rum had begun its work. I knew I wasn't cut to fit a situation like this one, but the rum made up a part of the deficit.

I dropped the brush and suddenly turned from the canvas. "Why did she have to leave me? Why?"

She was, of course, still out there when the gunny sack dragged me down through thirty feet of water. Her thin cotton dress clung to her as she wavered closer. Behind and beyond her a watery forest of weed dipped and swayed, a green and slimy floral offering.

I felt as if my air tanks were forcing raw acid into my lungs as I spilled the chain from the gunny sack. My trembling hands made one . . . two . . . three efforts . . . and the chain was looped about her cold, slender ankles.

I passed the chain through the holes in the cement blocks, and it no longer mattered whether the hempen rope held. The job was done. No risk of floating away.

In the cottage, I picked up the rum jug and let it kick me. Then I put on a clean shirt and pants and combed my hair nice and neat.

I went to the porch and took a final look at the bloodstains on the rough planking. My eyes followed the dripping trail those blood droplets had made down to the rickety pier and the flatbottom skiff. Before my stomach started acting up again, I dropped from the porch, ran across the sandy yard, and fell into the station wagon.

I pulled myself upright behind the wheel, started the crate. Through the non-reality of the day, the wagon coughed its way over the rutted, crushed seashell road to the highway. Trucks swooshed past and passenger cars swirled about me.

On the outskirts of Palmetto City, I turned the wagon onto the private road that snaked its way across landscaped acreage. The road wound up a slight rise to a colonial mansion that overlooked half the county, the low skyline of the town, the glitter of the Gulf in the far distance. A pair of horse-sized Great Danes were chasing, tumbling, rolling like a couple of puppies on the vast manicured lawn.

A lean, trim old man had heard the car's approach and stood watching from the veranda as I got out. I walked up the short, wide steps, the shadow of the house falling over me. The man watched me narrowly. He had a crop of silver hair and his hawkish face was wrinkled. These were the only clues to his age. His gray eyes were bright, quick, hard, as cold as a snake's. His mouth was an arrogant slit. Clothed in lime slacks and riotously colored sport shirt thirty years too young for him, his poised body exuded an aura of merciless, wiry power. In my distraught and wracked imagination he was as pleasant as a fierce, deadly lizard.

"Mr. Tomlin?"

He nodded. "And you're the tramp artist who's become a local character. Didn't you see those no trespassing signs when you turned off the highway?"

"I've got some business with your son, Mr. Tomlin."

"Perry's in Washington, tending to a matter for me. He flew up yesterday and won't be back for another couple days. You call, and make a proper appointment. And get that crate out of here—unless you want me to interrupt the dogs in their play."

My stomach felt as if it were caving in, but I gave him a steady look and said in an icy voice, "If Perry's away, you must be the man I want to talk to. Sure. Perry wouldn't have killed her, but you didn't share your son's feeling for her, did you?"

"I don't believe I know what you're talking about." He knew, all right. The first glint of caution and animal cunning showed in his eyes.

"Then I'll explain, Mr. Tomlin. Yesterday I went to Mobile to interest an art dealer in a one-man show. When I got back this morning I found some bloodstains. They led me to the water. I spent the morning diving, searching. I found her in about thirty feet of water."

I expected him to say something, but he didn't. He just stood there looking at me with those small, agate eyes.

"It wasn't hard to figure out," I said. "She'd come to the cottage to tell me it was all over between us. The shanty cracker girl was marrying the richest son in the county. But you didn't cotton to that idea, did you?"

"Go on," he said quietly.

"There's little more. It's all very simple. You sent Perry out of town to give you a chance to break it up between him and the cracker girl. Not much escapes your notice. You'd heard the gossip about her and the tramp artist. When you couldn't find her in town, you decided to try my place. I guess you tried to talk her off, buy her off, threaten her off. When none of it worked, you struck her in a rage. You killed her."

The old man stared blindly at the happy Great Danes.

"Realizing what you'd done," I said, "you scrounged a rope, couple of cement blocks, and planted her in thirty feet of water." I shook my head. "Not good. Not good at all. When the blocks sawed the rope in two, a nosy cop might find evidence you'd been around the place; a tire track, footprint, or maybe some fingerprints you'd left sticking around."

He studied the frolicking dogs as if planning their butchery. "You haven't named the vital element, artist; proof of guilt, proof that I did anything more than talk to her."

"Maybe so," I nodded, "but could a man in your position afford the questions, the scandal, the doubts that would arise and remain in your son's mind until the day you die? I think not. So I helped you."

His eyes flashed to me.

"I substituted a chain for the rope," I said. "The cement blocks will not cut that in two." I drew a breath. "And of course I want something in return. A thousand dollars. I'm sure you've that much handy, in a wall safe if not on your person. It's bargain day, Mr. Tomlin."

He thought it over for several long minutes. The sinking sun put a golden glitter in his eyes.

"And how about the future, artist? What if you decided you needed another thousand dollars one of these days?"

I shook my head. "I'm not that stupid. Right now I've caught you flat-footed. It's my moment. Everything is going for me. You haven't time to make a choice, think, plan. But it would be different in the future. Would I be stupid enough to try to continue blackmailing the most powerful man in the county after he's had a chance to get his forces and resources together?"

"Your question contains a most healthy logic, artist."

"One thousand bucks," I said, "and I hightail it down the driveway in the wagon. Otherwise, I'll throw the fat in the fire, all of it, including the chain about her ankles and my reason for putting it there. And we'll see which one of us has most to lose."

Without taking his eyes off my face, he reached for his wallet. He counted out a thousand dollars without turning a hair; chicken feed, pocket change to him.

I folded the sheaf of fifties and hundreds, some of them new bills, and slipped it into my pocket with care. We parted then, the old man and I, without another word being spoken.

The station wagon seemed to run with new life when I reached the highway. I felt the pressure of the money—the vital element—against my thigh.

The chain on her ankles had lured Tomlin, convinced him that he was dealing with a tramp interested only in a thousand bucks, so he had signed his confession of guilt by putting his fingerprints all over the money.

I didn't trust the gross sheriff in Palmetto City. I thought it far better to take the vital element and every detail of the nightmare directly to the state's attorney in Montgomery.

I was pretty sure the battered old station wagon would get me there.

ALASKA

THE SUN-DOG TRAIL
by Jack London

SITKA CHARLEY SMOKED his pipe and gazed thoughtfully at the *Police Gazette* illustration on the wall. For half an hour he had been steadily regarding it, and for half an hour I had been slyly watching him. Something was going on in that Indian mind of his, and, whatever it was, I knew it was well worth knowing.

We had struck this deserted cabin after a hard day on trail. The dogs had been fed, the supper dishes washed, the beds made, and we were now enjoying that most delicious hour that comes each day, and but once each day on the Alaskan trail—the hour when nothing intervenes between the tired body and bed save the smoking of the evening pipe. Some former denizen of the cabin had decorated its walls with illustrations torn from magazines and newspapers, and it was these illustrations that had held Sitka Charley's attention from the moment of our arrival two hours before. He had studied them intently, ranging from one to another and back again, and I could see that there was uncertainty in his mind.

"Well?" I finally broke the silence.

He took the pipe from his mouth and said simply, "I do not understand."

He smoked on again, and again removed the pipe, using it to point at the *Police Gazette* illustration.

"That picture—what does it mean? I do not understand."

I looked at the picture. A man, with a preposterously wicked face, his right hand pressed dramatically to his heart, was falling backward to the floor. Confronting him, with a face that was a composite of destroying angel and Adonis, was a man holding a smoking revolver.

"One man is killing the other man," I said.

"Why?" asked Sitka Charley.

"I do not know," I confessed.

"That picture is all end," he said. "It has no beginning."

"It is life," I said.

"Life has beginning," he objected. "No, I do not understand pictures."

Sitka Charley's disappointment was patent. It was his desire to understand all things that white men understand, and here, in this matter, he failed.

"Pictures are bits of life," I tried to explain. "We paint life as we see it. For instance, Charley, you are coming along the trail. It is night. You see a cabin. The window is lighted. You look through the window for one second, you see something, and you go on your way. Maybe you saw a man writing a letter. You saw something without beginning or end. Nothing happened. Yet it was a bit of life. You remember it afterward. It is like a picture in your memory. The window is the frame of the picture."

For a long time Sitka Charley smoked in silence. He nodded several times, grunted once or twice. Then he knocked the ashes from his pipe, carefully re-filled it, and, after a thoughtful pause, lighted it again.

"Then have I, too, seen many pictures of life," he began; "pictures not painted, but seen with the eyes. I have looked at them like through the window at the man writing the letter. I have seen many pieces of life, without beginning, without end, and without understanding."

With a sudden change of position he turned his eyes full upon me and regarded me thoughtfully.

"Look you," he said; "you are a painter-man. How would you paint this which I saw, a picture without beginning, the ending of which I do not understand, a piece of life with the northern lights for a candle and Alaska for a frame?"

"It is a large canvas," I murmured.

But he ignored me, for the picture he had in mind was before his eyes and he was seeing it.

"There are many names for this picture," he said. "But in the picture there are many sun-dogs, and it comes into my mind to call it 'The Sun-Dog Trail.' It was a long time ago, the fall of '97, when I saw the woman first time. At Lake Linderman I had one canoe, very good Peterborough canoe. I came over Chilkoot Pass with two thousand letters for Dawson. I was letter carrier. Everybody rush to Klondike at that time. Many people on trail. Many people chop down trees and make boats. Last water, snow in the hair, snow on the ground, ice on the lake, on the river ice in the eddies. Every day more snow, more ice. Maybe one day, maybe three days, maybe six days, any day maybe freeze-up come, then no more water, all ice, everybody walk, Dawson six hundred miles, long time walk. Boat go very quick. Everybody want to go boat. Everybody say, 'Charley, two hundred dollars you take me in canoe,' 'Charley, three hundred dollars,' 'Charley, four hundred dollars.' I say no. I am letter carrier.

"In morning I get to Lake Linderman. I walk all night and am much tired. I cook breakfast, I eat, then I sleep on the beach three hours. I wake up. It is 10 o'clock. Snow is falling. There is wind, much wind that blows fair. Also, there is a woman who sits in the snow alongside. She is white woman, she is young, very pretty, maybe she is twenty years old, maybe twenty-five years old. She look at me. I look at her. She is very tired. She is no dance-woman. I see that right away. She is good woman, and she is very tired.

" 'You are Sitka Charley,' she says. I get up quick and roll blankets so snow does not get inside. 'I go to Dawson,' she says. 'I go in your canoe—how much?'

"I do not want anybody in my canoe. I do not like to say no. So I say, 'One thousand dollars.' Just for fun I say it, so woman cannot come with me; much better than say no. She look at me very hard, then she says, 'When you start?' I say right away. Then she says all right, she will give me one thousand dollars.

"What can I say? I do not want the woman, yet have I given my word that for one thousand dollars she can come. I am surprised. Maybe she make fun, too, so I say, 'Let me see thousand dollars.' And that woman, that young woman, all alone on trail, there in snow, she take out one thousand dollars, in greenbacks, and she put them in my hand. I look at money, I look at her. What can I say? I say, 'No, my canoe very small. There is no room for outfit.' She laugh. She says, 'I am light traveler. This is my outfit.' She kick one small pack in the snow. It is two fur robes, canvas outside, some woman's clothes inside. I pick it up. Maybe thirty-five pounds. I am surprised. She take it away from me. She says, 'Come, let us start.' She carries pack into canoe. What can I say? I put my blankets into canoe. We start.

"And that is the way I saw the woman first time. The wind was fair. I put up small sail. The canoe went very fast; it flew like a bird over the high waves. The woman was much afraid. 'What for you come Klondike much afraid?' I ask. She laugh at me, a hard laugh, but she is still much afraid. Also is she very tired. I run canoe through rapids to Lake Bennett. Water very bad, and woman cry out because she is afraid. We go down Lake Bennett, snow, ice, wind like a gale, but woman go to sleep.

"That night we make camp at Windy Arm. Woman sit by fire and eat supper. I look at her. She is pretty. She fix hair. There is much hair, and it is brown, also sometimes it is like gold in the firelight, when she turn her head, so, and flashes come from it like golden fire. The eyes are large and brown, sometimes warm like a candle behind a curtain, sometimes very hard and bright like broken ice when sun shines upon it. When she smile—how can I say?—when she smile I know white man like to kiss her, just like that, when she smile. She never do hard work. Her hands are soft, like baby's hand. She is soft all over, like baby. She is not thin, but round like baby; her arm, her leg, her muscles, all soft and round like baby. Her waist is small, and when she stand up, when she walk, or move her head or arm, it is—I do not know the word—but it is nice to look at, like— maybe I say she is built on lines like good canoe, just like that, and when she move she is like the movement of good canoe sliding through still water or leaping through water when it is white and fast and angry. It is very good to see.

"Why does she come into Klondike, all alone, with plenty of money? I do not know. Next day I ask her. She laugh and says: 'Sitka Charley, that is none of your business. I give you one thousand dollars to take me to Dawson. That only is your business.' Next day after that I ask her what is her name. She laugh, then she says, 'Mary Jones, that is my name.' I do not know her name, but I know all the time that Mary Jones is not her name.

"It is very cold in canoe, and because of cold sometimes she not feel good. Sometimes she feel good and she sing. Her voice is like a silver bell, and I feel good all over like when I go into church at Holy Cross Mission, and when she sing I feel strong and paddle like hell. Then she laugh and says, 'You think we get to Dawson before freeze-up, Charley?' Sometimes she sit in canoe and is think-ing far away, her eyes all empty. She does not see Sitka Charley, nor the ice, nor the snow. Sometimes, when she is thinking far away, her face is not good to see.

"Last day to Dawson very bad. Shore-ice in all the eddies, mush-ice in the stream. I cannot paddle. The canoe freeze to ice. I cannot get to shore. There is much danger. All the time we go down Yukon in the ice. That night there is much noise of ice. Then ice stop, canoe stop, everything stop. 'Let us go to shore,' the woman says. I say no, better wait. By and by, everything start down-stream again. There is much snow. I cannot see. At 11 o'clock at night every-thing stop. At 1 o'clock everything start again. At 3 o'clock everything stop. Canoe is smashed like eggshell, but is on top of ice and cannot sink. I hear dogs howling. We wait. We sleep. By and by morning come. There is no more snow. It is the freeze-up, and there is Dawson. Canoe smash and stop right at Dawson. Sitka Charley has come in with two thousand letters on very last water.

"The woman rent a cabin on the hill, and for one week I see her no more. Then, one day, she come to me. 'Charley,' she says, 'how do you like to work for me? You drive dogs, make camp, travel with me.' I say that I make too much money carrying letters. She says, 'Charley, I will pay you more money.' I tell her that pick-and-shovel man get fifteen dollars a day in the mines. She says, 'That is four hundred and fifty dollars a month.' And I say, 'Sitka Charley is no pick-and-shovel man.' Then she says, 'I understand, Charley. I will give you seven hun-dred and fifty dollars each month.' It is a good price, and I go to work for her. I buy for her dogs and sled. We travel up Klondike, up Bonanza and Eldorado, over to Indian River, to Sulphur Creek, to Dominion, back across divide to Gold Bottom and to Too Much Gold, and back to Dawson. All the time she look for something, I do not know what. I am puzzled. 'What thing you look for?' I ask. She laugh. 'You look for gold?' I ask. She laugh. Then she says, 'That is none of your business, Charley.' And after that I never ask any more.

"She has a small revolver which she carries in her belt. Sometimes, on trail, she makes practice with revolver. I laugh, 'What for you laugh, Charley?' she ask. 'What for you play with that?' I say. 'It is no good. It is too small. It is for a child, a little plaything.' When we get back to Dawson she ask me to buy good revolver for her. I buy a Colt's .44. It is very heavy, but she carry it in her belt all the time.

"At Dawson comes the man. Which way he come I do not know. Only do I know he is *che-cha-quo*—what you call tenderfoot. His hands are soft, just like hers. He never do hard work. He is soft all over. At first I think maybe he is her husband. But he is too young. Also, they make two beds at night. He is maybe twenty years old. His eyes blue, his hair yellow, he has a little mustache which is yellow. His name is John Jones. Maybe he is her brother. I do not know. I ask questions no more. Only I think his name not John Jones. Other people call him Mr. Girvan. I do not think that is his name, either. I do not think her name is Miss Girvan, which other people call her. I think nobody know their names.

"One night I am asleep at Dawson. He wake me up. He says, 'Get the dogs ready; we start.' No more do I ask questions, so I get the dogs ready and we start. We go down the Yukon. It is nighttime, it is November, and it is very cold—sixty-five below. She is soft. He is soft. The cold bites. They get tired. They cry under their breaths to themselves. By and by I say better we stop and make camp. But they say they will go on. Three times I say better to make camp and rest, but each time they say they will go on. After that I say nothing. All the time, day after day, is it that way. They are very soft. They get stiff and sore. They do not understand moccasins, and their feet hurt very much. They limp, they stagger like drunken people, they cry under their breaths; and all the time they say, 'On! on! We will go on!'

"They are like crazy people. All the time do they go on and on. Why do they go on? I do not know. Only do they go on. What are they after? I do not know. They are not after gold. There is no stampede. Besides, they spend plenty of money.

"We make Circle City. That for which they look is not there. I think now we will rest, and rest the dogs. But we do not rest, not for one day do we rest. 'Come,' says the woman to the man, 'let us go on.' And we go on. We leave the Yukon. We cross the divide to the west and swing down into the Tanana Country. There are new diggings there. But that for which they look is not there, and we take the back trail to Circle City.

"It is a hard journey. December is most gone. The days are short. It is very cold. One morning it is seventy below zero. 'Better that we do not travel today,' I say, 'else will the frost be unwarmed in the breathing and bite all the edges of our lungs. After that we will have bad cough, and maybe next spring will come pneumonia.' But they are *che-cha-quo*. They do not understand the trail. They are like dead people they are so tired, but they say, 'Let us go on.' We go on. The frost bites their lungs, and they get the dry cough. They cough till the tears run down their cheeks. When bacon is frying they must run away from the fire and cough half an hour in the snow. They freeze their cheeks a little bit, so that the skin turns black and is very sore. Also, the man freezes his thumb till the end is like to come off, and he must wear a large thumb on his mitten to keep it warm. And sometimes, when the frost bites hard and the thumb is very cold, he must take off the mitten and put the hand between his legs next to the skin, so that the thumb get warm again.

"We limp into Circle City, and even I, Sitka Charley, am tired. It is Christmas Eve. I dance, drink, make a good time, for tomorrow is Christmas Day and we will rest. But no. It is 5 o'clock in the morning—Christmas morning. I am two hours asleep. The man stand by my bed. 'Come, Charley,' he says, 'harness the dogs. We start.'

"Have I not said that I ask questions no more? They pay me seven hundred and fifty dollars each month. I am their man. So I harness the dogs, and we start down the Yukon. Where do we go? They do not say. Only do they say, 'On! on! We will go on!'

"They are very weary. They have traveled many hundreds of miles, and they do not understand the way of the trail. Besides, their cough is very bad—the dry cough that makes strong men swear and weak men cry. But they go on. Every day they go on. Never do they rest the dogs. Always do they buy new dogs. At every camp, at every post, at every Indian village, do they cut out the tired dogs and put in fresh dogs. They have much money, money without end, and like water they spend it. They are crazy? Sometimes I think so, for there is a devil in them that drives them on and on, always on. What is it that they try to find?

"We pass Fort Yukon. We pass Fort Hamilton. We pass Ninook. January has come and nearly gone. The days are very short. At 9 o'clock comes daylight. At 3 o'clock comes night. And it is cold. Will we go on forever this way without end? I do not know. But always do I look along the trail for that which they try to find. Sometimes we travel one hundred miles and never see a sign of life. There is no sound. Sometimes it snows, and we are like wandering ghosts. Sometimes it is clear, and at midday the sun looks at us for a moment over the hills to the south. The northern lights flame in the sky, and the sun-dogs dance, and the air is filled with frost-dust.

"I am Sitka Charley, a strong man. I was born on the trail, and all my days have I lived on the trail. And yet have these two made me very tired. If I am lean like a starved cat, they are lean like cats that have never eaten and have died. Their eyes are sunk deep in their heads, bright sometimes as with fever, dim and cloudy sometimes like the eyes of the dead. Their cheeks are hollow like caves in a cliff. Sometimes it is the woman in the morning who says, 'I cannot get up. I cannot move. Let me die.' And it is the man who stands beside her and says, 'Come, let us go on.' And they go on. And sometimes it is the man who cannot get up, and the woman says, 'Come, let us go on.' But the one thing they do, and always do, is go on. Always they go on.

"Sometimes, at the trading posts, the man and woman get letters. I do not know what is in the letters. But it is the scent that they follow. One time an Indian gives them a letter. I talk with him privately. He says it is a man with one eye who gives him the letter, a man who travels fast down the Yukon. That is all.

"It is February, and we have traveled fifteen hundred miles. We are getting near Bering Sea, and there are storms and blizzards. The going is hard. We come to Anvig. I do not know, but I think sure they get a letter at Anvig, for they are much excited, and they say, 'Come, hurry, let us go on.' But I say we must buy grub, and they say we must travel light and fast. Also, they say that we can get grub at Charley McKeon's cabin. Then do I know they take the big cut-off, for it is there that Charley McKeon lives, where the Black Rock stands by the trail.

"Before we start I talk maybe two minutes with the priest at Anvig. Yes, there is a man with one eye who has gone by and who travels fast. And I know that for which they look is the man with the one eye.

"We leave Anvig with little grub, and travel light and fast. There are three fresh dogs bought in Anvig, and we travel very fast. The man and woman are like mad. We start earlier in the morning, we travel later at night. I look sometimes to see them die, these two baby wolves, but they will not die. They go on and on.

"Even I, Sitka Charley, am greatly weary, and I think seven hundred and fifty dollars is a cheap price for the labor I do. We take the big cut-off, and the trail is fresh. The baby wolves have their noses down to the trail, and they say, 'Hurry!' All the time do they say, 'Hurry! Faster! Faster!' It is hard on the dogs. We have not much food and we cannot give them enough to eat, and they grow weak. Also, they must work hard. The woman has true sorrow for them, and often, because of them, the tears are in her eyes. But the devil in her that drives her on will not let her stop and rest the dogs.

"And then we come upon the man with one eye. He is in the snow by the trail, and his leg is broken. Because of the leg he has made a poor camp, and has been lying on his blankets for three days and keeping a fire going. When we find him he is swearing. He swears like hell. Never have I heard a man swear like that man. I am glad. Now that they have found that for which they look, we will have rest. But the woman says, 'Let us start. Hurry!'

"I am surprised. But the man with the one eye says, 'Never mind me. Give me your grub. You will get more grub at McKeon's cabin tomorrow. Send McKeon back for me. But you go on.' Here is another wolf, an old wolf, and he, too, thinks but the one thought, to go on. So we give him our grub, which is not much, and we chop wood for his fire, and we take his strongest dogs, and go on. We left the man with one eye there in the snow, and he died there in the snow, for McKeon never went back for him. And who that man was, and why he came to be there, I do not know. But I think he was greatly paid by the man and the woman, like me, to do their work for them.

"That day and that night we had nothing to eat, and all next day we traveled fast, and we were weak with hunger. Then we came to the Black Rock, which rose five hundred feet above the trail. It was at the end of the day. Darkness was coming, and we could not find the cabin of McKeon. We slept hungry, and in the morning looked for the cabin. It was not there, which was a strange thing, for everybody knew that McKeon lived in a cabin at Black Rock. We were near to the coast, where the wind blows hard and there is much snow. Everywhere there were small hills of snow where the wind had piled it up. I have a thought, and I dig in one and another of the hills of snow. Soon I find the walls of the cabin, and I dig down to the door. I go inside. McKeon is dead. Maybe two or three weeks he is dead. A sickness had come upon him so that he could not leave the cabin. The wind and the snow had covered the cabin. He had eaten his grub and died. I looked for his cache, but there was no grub in it.

"'Let us go on,' says the woman. Her eyes were hungry, and her hand was upon her heart, as with the hurt of something inside. She bent back and forth like a tree in the wind as she stood there. 'Yes, let us go on,' says the man. His voice was hollow, like the *klonk* of an old raven, and he was hunger-mad. His eyes were like live coals of fire, and as his body rocked to and fro, so rocked his soul inside. And I, too, say, 'Let us go on.' For that one thought, laid upon me like a lash for every mile of fifteen hundred miles, had burned itself into my soul, and I think that I, too, was mad. Besides, we could only go on, for there was no grub. And we went on, giving no thought to the man with the one eye in the snow.

"There is little travel on the big cut-off. Sometimes two or three months and nobody goes by. The snow had covered the trail, and there was no sign that men had ever come or gone that way. All day the wind blew and the snow fell, and all day we traveled, while our stomachs gnawed their desire and our bodies grew weaker with every step they took. Then the woman began to fall. Then the man. I did not fall, but my feet were heavy and I caught my toes and stumbled many times.

"That night is the end of February. I kill three ptarmigan with the woman's revolver, and we are made somewhat strong again. But the dogs have nothing to eat. They try to eat their harness, which is of leather and walrus-hide, and I must fight them off with a club and hang all the harness in a tree. And all night they howl and fight around that tree. But we do not mind. We sleep like dead people, and in the morning get up like dead people out of their graves and go on along the trail.

"That morning is the first of March, and on that morning I see the first sign of that after which the baby wolves are in search. It is clear weather, and cold. The sun stay longer in the sky, and there are sun-dogs flashing on either side, and the air is bright with frost-dust. The snow falls no more upon the trail, and I see the fresh sign of dogs and sled. There is one man with that outfit, and I see in the snow that he is not strong. He, too, has not enough to eat. The young wolves see the fresh sign, too, and they are much excited. 'Hurry!' they say. All the time they say, 'Hurry! Faster, Charley, faster!'

"We make hurry very slow. All the time the man and the woman fall down. When they try to ride on sled the dogs are too weak, and the dogs fall down. Besides, it is so cold that if they ride on the sled they will freeze. It is very easy for a hungry man to freeze. When the woman fall down, the man help her up. Sometimes the woman help the man up. By and by both fall down and cannot get up, and I must help them up all the time, else they will not get up and will die there in the snow. This is very hard work, for I am greatly weary, and as well I must drive the dogs, and the man and woman are very heavy with no strength in their bodies. So, by and by, I, too, fall down in the snow, and there is no one to help me up. I must get up by myself. And always do I get up by myself, and help them up, and make the dogs go on.

"That night I get one ptarmigan, and we are very hungry. And that night the man says to me, 'What time start tomorrow, Charley?' It is like the voice of a ghost. I say, 'All the time you make start at 5 o'clock.' 'Tomorrow,' he says, 'we will start at 3 o'clock.' I laugh in great bitterness, and I say, 'You are dead man.' And he says, 'Tomorrow we still start at 3.'

"And we start at 3 o'clock, for I am their man, and that which they say is to be done, I do. It is clear and cold, and there is no wind. When daylight comes we can see a long way off. And it is very quiet. We can hear no sound but the beat of our hearts, and in the silence that is a very loud sound. We are like sleep-walkers, and we walk in dreams until we fall down; and then we know we must get up, and we see the trail once more and hear the beating of our hearts. Sometimes, when I am walking in dreams this way, I have strange thoughts. Why does Sitka Charley live? I ask myself. Why does Sitka Charley work hard, and go hungry, and have all this pain? For seven hundred and fifty dollars a month, I make the answer, and I know it is a foolish answer. Also is it a true answer. And after that never again do I care for money.

"In the morning we come upon the last-night camp of the man who is before us. It is a poor camp, the kind a man makes who is hungry and without strength. On the snow there are pieces of blanket and of canvas, and I know what has happened. His dogs have eaten their harness, and he has made new harness out of his blankets. The man and woman stare hard at what is to be seen, and as I look at them my back feels the chill as of a cold wind against the skin. Their eyes are toil-mad and hunger-mad and burn like fire deep in their heads. Their faces are like the faces of people who have died of hunger, and their cheeks are black with the dead flesh of many freezings. 'Let us go on,' says the man. But the woman coughs and falls in the snow. It is the dry cough where the frost has bitten the lungs. For a long time she coughs, then like a woman crawling out of her grave she crawls to her feet. The tears are ice upon her cheeks, and her breath makes a noise as it comes and goes, and she says, 'Let us go on.'

"We go on. And we walk in dreams through the silence, and we see the snow and the mountains and the fresh trail of the man who is before us, and we know all our pain again. We come to where we can see a long way over the snow, and that for which they look is before them.

"A mile away there are black spots upon the snow. The black spots move. My eyes are dim, and I must stiffen my soul to see. And I see one man with dogs and a sled. The baby wolves see, too. They can no longer talk, but they whisper, 'On, on. Let us hurry!'

"And they fall down, but they go on. The man who is before us, his blanket harness breaks often, and he must stop and mend it. Our harness is good, for I have hung it in trees each night. At 11 o'clock the man is half mile away. At 1 o'clock he is a quarter mile away. He is very weak. We see him fall down many times in the snow. One of his dogs can no longer travel, and he cuts it out of the harness. But he does not kill it. I kill it with the axe as I go by, as I kill one of my dogs which loses its legs and can travel no more.

"Now we are three hundred yards away. We go very slow. Maybe in two, three hours we go one mile. We do not walk. All the time we fall down. We stand up and stagger two steps, maybe three steps, then we fall down again. And all the time I must help up the man and woman. Sometimes they rise to their knees and fall forward, maybe four or five times before they can get to their feet again and stagger two or three steps and fall. But always they fall forward. Standing or kneeling, always they fall forward, gaining on the trail each time by the length of their bodies.

"Sometimes they crawl on hands and knees like animals that live in the forest. We go like snails that are dying, yet we go faster than the man who is before us. For he, too, falls all the time, and there is no Sitka Charley to lift him up. Now he is two hundred yards away. After a long time he is one hundred yards away.

"It is a race of dead men and dead dogs. I want to laugh, it is so funny.

"The stranger-man who is before us leaves his dogs behind and goes on alone across the snow. After a long time we come to the dogs. They lie helpless in the snow, their harness of blanket and canvas on them, the sled behind them, and as we pass them they whine to us and cry like babies that are hungry.

"Then we, too, leave our dogs and go alone across the snow. The man and the woman are nearly gone, and they moan and groan and sob, but they go on. I, too, go on. I have but one thought. It is to come up to the stranger-man. Then it is that I shall rest, and not until then shall I rest, and it seems that I must lie down and sleep for a thousand years, I am so tired.

"The stranger-man is fifty yards away, all alone in the white snow. He falls and crawls, staggers, and falls and crawls again. He is like an animal that is sore wounded and trying to run from the hunter. By and by he crawls on hands and knees. He no longer stands up. And the man and woman no longer stand up. They, too, crawl after him on hands and knees. But I stand up. Sometimes I fall, but always do I stand up again.

"It is a strange thing to see. All about is the snow and the silence, and through it crawl the man and the woman, and the stranger-man who crawls before, looking back over his shoulder.

"After a long time the stranger-man crawls no more. He stands slowly upon his feet and rocks back and forth. Also he take off one mitten and wait with revolver in his hand, rocking back and forth as he waits. His face is skin and bones and frozen black. The eyes are deep-sunk in his head, and the lips are snarling. The man and woman, too, get upon their feet and they go toward him very slowly. And all about is the snow and the silence. And in the sky are three suns, and all the air is flashing with the dust of diamonds.

"And thus it was that I, Sitka Charley, saw the baby wolves make their kill. No word is spoken. Only does the stranger-man snarl with his frozen face. Also does he rock to and fro, his shoulders drooping, his knees bent, and his legs wide apart so that he does not fall down. The man and the woman stop maybe fifty feet away. Their legs, too, are wide apart so that they do not fall down, and their bodies rock to and fro. The stranger-man is very weak. His arm shakes, so that when he shoots at the man his bullet strikes in the snow. The man cannot take off his mitten. The stranger-man shoots at him again, and this time the bullet goes by in the air. Then the man takes the mitten in his teeth and pulls it off. But his hand is frozen and he cannot hold the revolver, and it falls in the snow. I look at the woman. Her mitten is off, and the big Colt's revolver is in her hand.

"Three times she shoot, quick, just like that.

"The hungry face of the stranger-man is still snarling as he falls forward into the snow.

"They do not look at the dead man. 'Let us go on,' they say. And we go on. But now that they have found that for which they look, they are like dead. The last strength has gone out of them. They can stand no more upon their feet. They will not crawl, but desire only to close their eyes and sleep. I see not far away a place for camp. I kick them. I have my dog-whip, and I give them the lash of it. They cry aloud, but they must crawl. And they crawl to the place for camp. I build fire so that they will not freeze. Then I go back for sled. Also, I kill the dogs of the stranger-man so that we may have food and not die. I put the man and woman in blankets and they sleep. Sometimes I wake them and give them little bit of food. They are not awake, but they take the food. The woman sleep one day and a half. Then she wake up and go to sleep again. The man sleep two days and wake up and go to sleep again.

"After that we go down to the coast at St. Michaels. And when the ice goes out of Bering Sea, the man and woman go away on a steamship. But first they pay me my seven hundred and fifty dollars a month. Also, they make me a present of one thousand dollars. And that was the year that Sitka Charley gave much money to the Mission at Holy Cross."

"But why did they kill the man?" I asked.

Sitka Charley delayed reply until he had lighted his pipe. He glanced at the *Police Gazette* illustration and nodded his head at it familiarly. Then he said, speaking slowly and ponderingly:

"I have thought much. I do not know. It is something that happened. It is a picture I remember. It is like looking in at the window and seeing the man writing a letter. The picture is as I have said, without beginning, the end without understanding."

"You have painted many pictures in the telling," I said.

"Ay," he nodded his head. "But they were without beginning and without end."

"The last picture of all had an end," I said.

"Ay," he answered. "But what end?"

"It was a piece of life," I said.

"Ay," he answered. "It was a piece of life."

ARIZONA

WHIPPIN' WILDCATS
by Jane Bosworth

IT GETS PLUM lonely settin' on the porch rocking in the night with nothin' to keep you company but the rustlin' a critters in the sagebrush and the howl a distant coyotes. Sets the mind to rummaging through memories that's best left forgotten, an' it makes the heart ache for them what's passed on to a better place. Aging brings on that kind of aloneness 'cause sometimes us oldsters get too tired a chasing the merry-go-round to ever get on.

Reckon it was that aloneness what made my ticker skip a beat when Jake McEwan phoned an' invited himself over. Had to be the aloneness what done it, 'cause Em Grady here ain't dumb enough to get herself snared by the gigolo a the senior citizen's set. No, siree—Jake McEwan may be a heartthrob to many a old minx, but he ain't one to me. Never will be, neither.

You best keep that in mind, Em Grady, I says to myself, 'cause the gigolo just arrived.

I stood an' watched Jake's car pull into my driveway an' park. And when I seen that tall, lean man emerge from it the breath caught in my throat so's I couldn't even get my howdy out.

Jake sauntered up my steps, wrapped both arms round me, and give me a kiss that set my head to spinning. Then he turned loose a me an' stepped back so's he could see iffen he had any effect or not. "Turn you on, old girl?" he asked.

Danged iffen them words didn't putty my brain an' chase the words from my mouth so's I just stood there blushin' like a schoolgirl. But then Jake started chucklin' an' that got my dander up.

"Think you're purty good, don't ya?"

He stretched a might taller, thumbed his belt loops, an' shed a smug look my way. "I don't just think so, old girl, I know I am."

I wanted to bust that all-knowin' smile right offa his mouth an' pound it clear down to his toenails, but he give me one a them shoulder rubs that seemed to say, "Calm down, Emily, I didn't mean no harm," an' the anger melted right outa me.

That all-knowing smile a his give way to his old salt's grin an' I knowed he was up to somethin' ornery. "Emily, my love, it pleases me to be allowed to spend the night with you again." He laughed, pullin' me close an' huggin' me. "I've missed you. More than you'll ever know. Tell me, did you miss me, too?"

I caught the scents a soap, shampoo, an' aftershave, all minglin' together with just a hint a sweat. Strong masculine scents, comfortin' scents.

"Did you miss me, Emily?" he prodded.

"Reckon I did, Jake," I admitted.

His arms tightened round me and then relaxed. He give me a peck on the cheek an' broke the embrace. "Let's go inside," he said. "I've somethin' important to show you."

I led the way into my rock shop and on back to my livin' quarters, where I settled into my Elmer's easy chair. Jake sat on the sofa across from me. I looked at his weathered face an' marveled at how the years had sculpted his wrinkles to give him a dignified handsomeness all his own.

"It's been almost four months since we last saw each other," he said.

"Three months, fifteen days, to be exact." The words just escaped 'fore I could get my mouth shut. Way to go, Em, I says to myself. That's like exposing cards in a poker game.

A smile wriggled loose at the corners a Jake's mouth, but he didn't up the ante any. A gentleness settled in his eyes an' somethin' comfortable passed from him to me. Then I seen seriousness drift onto his face an' I knowed he was here for somethin' more than visitin'.

"Ella Mae Fitzhugh's in trouble," he said, an' dug some papers outa his coat. "I figured you'd like to know about it."

"What kinda trouble?"

He leaned forward an' handed the papers to me. "These will explain it," he said.

I read the title a one a them papers an' I suspicioned just what kinda trouble Ella Mae was in. *Transglobal Resources, Inc. Lease Purchase Agreement*, it read. By the time I finished readin', I realized that she was in a heap a trouble. She'd invested $75,000 in a share of a oil lease out near Weaver, Arizona.

"Weaver! Weaver! Why there's nothin' out there but ruins, rattlesnakes, an' a old graveyard!"

I reckoned her Homer musta been doing flip-flops in that grave a his right 'bout now 'cause the money she'd invested had come from the insurance policy he'd left her.

"Used to be," I said to Jake, "that us decent folks could tar an' feather crooks that sold worthless paper to widows like Ella Mae."

"Used-to-be's aren't going to help your friend." Jake's voice was gentle. "And neither will anger, old girl."

The sense a them words lowered my blood-pressure some an' set my mind to ponderin' ways a gettin' Ella's money back.

"Maybe Sheriff Bill could help," I said.

"Emily, I know how these outfits work," Jake said. "At the first sign of trouble, the company will fold up and disappear."

I set the papers down an' looked at him. "What can you tell me 'bout this here Transglobal Resources?"

"The parent headquarters for the company is in Laguna Hills, California, but it's got temporary offices in Wickenburg," he said. "The owner, J. Norton Mailer, is working out of those offices. Ella Mae gave me his phone number.— Emily, what are you thinking?"

"I'm thinkin' that the first thing we got to find out is iffen there really is a well at Weaver. Iffen it ain't there, Sheriff Bill will arrest Mailer before he can run away. At first light tomorrow, you an' me is goin' for a spin in the desert. . . ."

I'd a bet my last dollar there was no drillin' rig at Weaver—an' iffen I'd a made that bet, I'd a lost. It was there, all right. Settin' smack dab in the middle of a third of a acre a graded land just south a the old graveyard was one a them portable drillin' rigs mounted on the bed of a huge semi. Whoever had done the gradin' had been careful not to bother the old rockhouse ruins just west a the mud pits or the stream that trickled out natural spring near the house.

I expected Jake to say somethin' 'bout the rig, but he didn't. He just sat there starin' at it.

"Emily, do you know anything about drilling?" he asked.

"Reckon I picked up some when my Elmer wildcatted the McKitrick fields in 'thirty-six. Why?"

"Because, my dear Emily, I know absolutely nothing about drilling for oil."

I parked Old Lizzy beside a pair a battered jeeps in front a the rig an' Jake an' me got out. I could hear the steady hummin' a the mud pumps an' I seen the mud line jumpin' as it pumped mud into the hole they was drilling, but the kelly wasn't turnin' an that seemed a mite peculiar. It meant that the bit wasn't turnin' against the bottom a that hole.

"Why would anyone pump mud down through a bit that wasn't turnin'?" I asked myself.

"Mud?" Jake caught the word.

"Mud's a mixture a chemicals that gets pumped into the hole through the drillin' pipe an' out the drillin' bit," I said. "It brings rock an' debris outa the hole and keeps the bit from gettin' stuck. But that bit ain't turning 'cause the kelly up there ain't rotatin' that pipe one inch."

"Emily," he said, "that makes no sense at all."

"It would iffen they weren't drillin' at night, an' it looks like that's what they're doing, 'cause there ain't a soul in sight up there on that rig. You go on up there an' see iffen you can find anyone. I'm goin' over to the mud pits an' have me a look at the tailin's to see what's been comin' outa that hole they're supposed to be drillin'."

Jake went on up the stairs onto the substructure a the rig whilst I moseyed off to the left where the mud pits was.

I reckoned pits had been modernized some since Elmer's day 'cause they weren't just holes dug in the sand. They were two huge steel containers set on top a the sand. Mud is pumped outa one side a the pits an' down the drillin' pipe, where it collects debris. It flows up outa the hole an' over the shaker tables, where debris is screened out an' dumped onto the ground whilst the mud goes down into the pit to be used again. I had me a look at that debris.

They was mighty peculiar tailin's—bone-dry an' layered in the order they'd been drilled outa the earth. Sand on the bottom, shale in the middle, an' quartz, epidote, an' actinolite on top. They'd drilled from soft to hard rock.

I had me a look at the mud in them pits an' seen that it still had the pinkish tinge a baroid, just like it wasn't gettin' dirtied by whatever the bit was cuttin' into. I was standin' there ponderin' on clean mud an' hard rock when a gruff voice yanked me upright an' spun me around. I come nose to nose with a bearded prospector who looked for all the world like Ian McFarland. I ain't seen Ian in thirty years.

"Ian McFarland?" I asked.

The look on his face told me he was diggin' through his memory for my name an' couldn't find it. "It's me, you old hound," I said. "Em Grady."

He stood there looking 'bout as foolish as a greenhorn that'd just laid claim to a stake chock full a nothing but fool's gold. He didn't have a word to lay on me.

"Last time I heard from you," I said, "you was workin' a claim in Alaska. What are you doin' back here?"

"Government bought me out," he said, " 'cause my claim's on the east corner of a new national park. I packed up my nuggets, took out ten sacks a quartz-laden ore to remind me a my luck up there, an' came back here to search for another vein. I was prospectin' out here when I met up with this Mailer fellow. He offered me fifty dollars a day plus a trailer to live in if I'd keep the rockhounds off his lease. I didn't have anythin' better to do so I took his offer. You rockhoundin' out here, Em?"

"Nope, Ella Mae Fitzhugh's got a interest in this here lease," I said, "an' I come out here to see iffen there really was a well at Weaver."

The mentionin' a Ella Mae set the spark of affection to smoldering in them grey eyes a Ian's. Everybody in Jerome knowed they was high-school sweethearts. Then outa the blue, she up an' married Homer. Ian left town the day a the weddin'.

"How come Homer's not checkin' it out?" he asked.

"Homer died last year," I said. "It's his insurance money that's invested out here. Iffen it gets lost, Ella May's got nothin' left to live on."

Ian scratched that thought into his beard whilst he stood there rummagin' through my words, filin' away Homer's death an' Ella Mae's vulnerability.

"Mailer don't seem like the kinda man that'd steal from widows," he said.

I ignored his words. "How come there ain't no crew out here?"

"Crew's here, Em," he said. "They been here since five this mornin'. That's when they start drillin' for the day."

I looked up an' seen that somebody had started the kelly to turning, but I didn't see a soul on the rig. "I don't see nobody on that rig," I said.

"They're probably eatin' pie and drinkin' coffee in the doghouse, Em. Leastways that's what they do most of the day. That rig just don't need a crew to do much more than check the pumps once in a while."

I knowed that drillin' had modernized a lot since my Elmer first wildcatted, but nothin' could convince me that one a them rigs could up an' do the drillin' all by itself whilst the crew sat chewin' fat inside a steel outbuilding used to shelter 'em.

"Mind iffen I have me a look at some a the gauges on the rig?" I asked.

"Course not, Em. I'll even take you up there."

Ian an' me walked over to the rig an' climbed the stairs to the substructure. We popped our heads into the doghouse, where we found Jake jawin' with three bearded longhairs that looked for all the world like pirates. One of 'em even wore a rhinestone plug in his left nostril. Jake looked mighty outa place in their company. "Emily," he said. "I hope you haven't been looking for me."

"Reckon I was lookin' for you," I said. "Iffen you're through gabbin', I got to get home before noon."

Jake said his goodbyes, an' stepped outside. I introduced him to Ian McFarland, then we found the gauges I wanted to see. They read 'bout as I expected they would, with the needle of the Martin-Decker Drill weight gauge a little to the right a zero an' the needle of the rotary torque gauge settin' smack dab on zero.

"Well, what do you think?" Ian asked.

"I'm thinkin' that we got to find us some way a whippin' these no good wildcatters out here," I said. "There's no pressure on the rotary torque gauge an' the Martin-Decker gauge shows only enough pressure to account for the mud being pumped in an' outa the hole. All they're doing out here is fannin' the bit above the hardrock they hit a while back. Oil pools on top of hardrock, not underneath it. I figure they'll keep fannin' that bit long enough to bilk Joe Public for all they can get, then they'll light on outa here."

Ian McFarland looked like you coulda blowed him over just by breathin' hard. Then I seen the cheeks above his beard redden with anger. "Mailer's bringin' the payroll out tomorrow," he said. "Maybe we oughta just steal it, along with that brand-new jeep he drives."

"Ain't enough money in that payroll to account for what Ella Mae invested," I said. "Besides, all that'd do is land us in the poky an' that ain't gonna do nobody no good."

"Maybe I oughta put a slug in Mailer's fat gut."

"Ian McFarland, you got to quit thinkin' physical an' start thinkin' smart. Greed is what runs Transglobal Resources an' we got to think a some way to use that greed."

Then it hit me that everythin' about Weaver, from its founding to its death, had to do with that peculiar kinda greed that drives men to spend a lifetime searching for that pot a gold at the end a the rainbow. "You ever do any serious prospectin' in Weaver?" I asked Ian.

" 'Course I did," he said. "Most everybody that knowed the history a Weaver went lookin' for the vein a gold that fed her placer claims."

"You got any a that Alaska quartz you mentioned out here?" I asked.

"Sacks a it. Why?"

" 'Cause I got me a idea 'bout whippin' wildcats," I said.

I told Ian an' Jake my idea an' each a them added a touch or two of his own. We come up with a plan that was based on good old-fashioned tried-an'-proven greed. Jake an' me was to work outa my place. Ian had to wait for them wildcatters to go home for the night 'fore he could bait the trap to catch Mailer in.

Jake an' me got to my place in the early afternoon. Whilst he went inside to call the number Ella Mae give him, I went out back an' dug up my Elmer's money jar. They was two pouches a gold dust, a pouch a nuggets, three one-carat diamonds, and fifty thousand in cash in that jar. I took out the money an' pouches a gold, then I reburied the jar. On the way back to the house, I stopped at the old tack shed to pick up Elmer's prospectin' gear. I put the gold an' the gear inside a Lizzy an' went inside to check on how Jake was doin'.

He was jawin' on the phone when I come into the living room. "That's right, Mr. Mailer," he was sayin'. "I did say she keeps a money jar buried in her back yard. Of course, I know how dangerous that is. Banks! Pshaw, why, Emily hasn't trusted banks since she lost nine-tenths of her money in the Great Depression. This will have to be a cash deal, Mr. Mailer.—How much cash?" He looked at the wad of money in my hand. "I'd guess about fifty thousand dollars," he said.

Silence.

Jake cupped his hand over the mouthpiece. "I think he fell over in his chair. I heard a thump and—

"Yes, Mr. Mailer," he said. "We are free today. One hour sounds fine. Coming from Wickenburg, you take Highway 89 to Congress. Go about a mile, and you'll come to a rock shop on the left. That's my sister's place. We'll see you soon."

He hung up and grinned at me. "Our wildcat is on his way to the whipping post," he said.

J. Norton Mailer arrived sooner than expected, apologized for being early, an' then walked right in an' settled into my Elmer's favorite chair just like he belonged there. He wiped the sweat from his fat brow and shed a benevolent smile into the room. Settin' there like that, grinnin' like a saint, Mr. J. Norton Mailer looked more like a fat preacher than a crook. He had a soft, plump body an' eyes that drilled into your very soul. It was his eyes that bothered me most. They were icy blue eyes that appraised your every weakness.

He asked us all about how we heard 'bout his company, 'an then he got to the business a selling up a line a goods 'bout his philanthropic interests in my money.

"You see, Mrs. Grady, I have a soft spot in my heart for widows." He slapped at the flab on his chest to punctuate his words. "After I was orphaned at the tender age of three, my Grandmother Mailer, God bless her sweet soul, took me in and raised me. And she did it on a Social Security pension!

"Why, I can remember times when she went without food—without food, mind you—so she could save enough to buy shoes for me to wear to school. It was hunger that sent Grandma to an' early grave. Black ugly hunger."

He punctuated them last three words with a fist in the air. Then the fist fell into his lap, his fat face transformed from anger into sadness. "You look like dear—old—grandma." His voice broke with emotion.

He took out a handkerchief an' mopped his eyes. Then he tooted his nose and studied the effect he'd had on us. His eyes bulged from under his lids an' flicked from Jake to me an' back again.

"I've spent a lifetime repaying grandma." His voice took on a revivalist's lilt. "A lifetime, I tell you. Dedicating my very soul to searching out and helping deserving widows. God gave me—me! J. Norton Mailer!—the mission to seek out and help deserving widows. Now I've found another one for my parish!"

He looked ceilingward to see iffen anyone up there had heard. Then he nodded to himself an' shed a lovin' look on me.

"Amen," I said.

"I can tell by just lookin' at you, Mrs. Grady, that you are a deserving woman. So how much money can I triple for you?"

I dug my wad outa my pocket an' handed it over.

"Fifty thousand dollars," I said.

He cupped that money in both hands an' stared at it like it was some kinda holy relic.

"You can count it iffen you've a mind to," I said.

He stuffed the money into his pocket an' dug out a set a papers identical to the ones Ella Mae had signed. He handed them over to me along with a pen. The amount was filled in an' the papers signed in silence. Then he give me my copy an' pocketed his. He hauled himself to his feet an' started for the door. Jake an' me moseyed along after him as far as the porch, where we stopped an' watched him squeeze his mass in behind the wheel a his car an' drive off.

"Once he's got your money, he don't mince with any more words," I said to Jake.

"J. Norton Mailer only *thinks* he's seen the last of you, Emily Grady," he said. "By this time tomorrow afternoon, he'll be wishing he wasn't such a charitable man."

Three hours before sunrise the next morning, I loaded Jake an' me into Lizzy an' drove out to the rig in Weaver where Ian was waiting. I parked near the foot a the substructure an' Jake an' me got out. Ian greeted us.

"I shut off them mud pumps soon as the crew left yesterday," he said, "an' did what needed to be done. If we're lucky, the crew will get so interested in what we're doin' they'll forget to turn 'em on when they come in.''

"Reckon we'll just have to make sure they forget," I said.

Jake an' Ian carried my prospectin' gear an' pouches a dust an' nuggets over to the stream just west a the tailin's from the mud pits. I scooped up a pan full a tailin's, sprinkled 'bout a fourth a the dust an' seven nice nuggets into it. Then I handed the rest a the gold over to Ian an' Jake, who worked it into the tailin's. By the time them wildcatters come in, all three a us had the beginnin's of a nice stash a gold in our pans. Sure enough them wildcatters got so interested in our pannin' they plumb forgot 'bout the pumps.

"Who'd a ever thought?" the biggest one scratched his head.

"Thought, hell," the one with the rhinestone in his nostril said. "I want to get me some a that before Mailer shows up with the payroll."

"But what are we gonna use for pans?" the third one asked.

"Pie tins," I said. "I think I seen a few pie tins in that doghouse a yours."

All three a them run up to the doghouse an' come back with a tin. Pie tins ain't the best pans in the world, but they was so much gold in them trailin's it weren't long till each a them had a little show in the bottom a his pan. They got so interested in pannin' that they didn't even notice when Mailer drove in an' parked.

I watched him get outa his jeep an' waddle over to us.

"What the hell are you people doing?" he bellowed.

"Numbin' the arthritis outa our hands," I said.

I was gettin' more than show now, 'cause the nuggets was coming into view. I stopped my swirlin' long enough for Mailer to get a good look at that yeller. Mailer leaned over so's that his hot breath warmed my neck. "What's that?" His fat finger pointed to the nuggets.

"Gold," I said.

"We struck it rich, boss!" Rhinestone Nostril shouted. "We hit us a vein down there!"

Next thing I knowed, Mailer was runnin' his fingers through the show in my pan. I had a nugget in there the size of a marble.

I finished my pannin', tweezered the flakes into my glass vial, an' put the nuggets into my pouch. Then I got up, walked over to them tailin's, scooped up another pan, an' come back to the stream. I knelt down an' started pannin' again. Mailer never said nothin' but I could feel his eyes borin' into my back. Didn't take me long before another nugget started shinin' through the rock. It was 'bout the size a the fingernail on my little finger. I was gettin' plenty a show a flakes, too.

I finished my pan, stood, an' offered it to Mailer. He poked at the gold. Then his eyes met mine.

"Looks like you drilled right into the vein that fed the placer claims a Rich Hill, Mr. Mailer," I said. "An' from the looks a what's coming outa them tailin's, I'd say I got me seventy-five percent of a fortune. At least, that's what my contract offers. Seventy-five percent a all mineral rights."

Mailer's eyes shifted from me to Jake to Ian McFarland. It didn't take him long to put two and two together an' come up with a snake. "You're all in this together," he said.

"Reckon you could say that," I said. "Ian McFarland there use to prospect this here desert with my late husband."

Iffen looks coulda killed, Ian McFarland woulda been struck dead by Mailer. Then somethin' else settled onto Mailer's fat face, somethin' I couldn't quite put a finger on.

"Maybe," he said, "the gold's only in those tailings. Maybe, you salted the tailings."

"Iffen you believe that," I said, "then start drillin' in that there well an' see what comes outa her."

Mailer accepted my challenge an' ordered his crew to start drillin'. Didn't take long before the mud started bringin' up quartz-laden ore. Mailer waddled over to the tailin's an' rummaged through them like a hungry pig. When he found a nugget, he liked to went crazy.

"Ain't no purtier sight in the world than that," I said.

Them words had a peculiar affect on Mailer. Iffen I didn't know better, I say they up an' slapped him a good one 'cause he just stared at me like he was in shock. Then them pig's eyes a his narrowed on me an' he licked his lips.

"I'll write you a check right now for seventy-five thousand dollars for your share," he said.

I looked to Ian for help.

"Developing a mine can take years, Em," he said. "An' none a us is gettin' any younger."

"I ain't plannin' on dyin' just yet," I told him.

"Emily," Jake took over, "twenty-five thousand dollars is not a bad return on your investment."

I rubbed the numbers into my chin. Then I looked from Ian to Jake to Mailer.

"I don't deal with no bank checks," I said. "It's strictly cash with me."

Mailer looked like them words had hit him in the middle of his fat gut.

"I don't keep that much cash lying around," he said. "I'll have to telex my headquarters in California for the money. And I'll have to go to Phoenix in order to find a bank with that much cash in it. It will take all day."

"You make that a hundred and seventy-five thousand dollars," I said, "an' I won't call my friend who works for the *Sedona Sentinel Newspaper* to tell him 'bout my good fortune."

Mailer looked downright confused.

"I reckon you could buy back all them contracts you sold on this here lease at cost iffen this was kept under the hat, so to speak," I added.

Understandin' passed from him to me an' back again. He knew I had a hold a him where it hurts an' he also knowed they was no way a gettin' free without a lot a pain. He agreed to my terms.

* * *

J. Norton Mailer was as good as his word. Right 'bout three in the afternoon, he showed up at my place with a briefcase full a money. I handed him my contract and Ella Mae's contract. Surprise settled on his face.

"I ain't a greedy woman," I said. "The extra hundred thousand is for Ella Mae Fitzhugh. I figured that was fair."

"More than fair." Mailer was thrilled. "More than fair."

He left with a empty briefcase an' two canceled contracts.

That night Ian, Jake, Ella Mae, an' me celebrated with a champagne dinner at the El Bayou in Sedona. Ella Mae couldn't believe her good fortune.

"But how do you know there *really* isn't gold there?" she asked. "After all, you did say that nuggets and quartz-laden ore started coming out of the well just after they started drilling again. Didn't you?"

"Ella Mae," Ian said, "last night when I shut off the mud pumps to the well, I put ten full sacks a quartz-laden ore an' one pouch a nuggets down that hole. It all sank to the bottom. When Mailer ordered the drillin' to start again, the mud brought it up."

"But where did all the gold come from?" she persisted.

"From my claim in Alaska," he said. "I brought it with me for luck when I came home."

"And now it's gone," she said. "All because of me. Ian, how will I ever repay you?"

Ian reached over an' give her hand a lovin' pat. I seen the spark a affection begin to sputter in them eyes a Ian's an' I seen the look in her eyes fan it to life. Then I looked across the table at Jake an' seen somethin' more than warmth in them blue eyes a his. He raised his glass for a toast an' we all followed suit.

"Here's to good friends," he said an' looked at me. "Because good friends, like good wine, keep getting better with age."

The glasses clinked.

The wine was drunk.

The meal was eaten.

I went home with Jake McEwan.

ARKANSAS

A RETRIEVED REFORMATION
by O. Henry

A GUARD CAME to the prison shoe-shop, where Jimmy Valentine was assiduously stitching uppers, and escorted him to the front office. There the warden handed Jimmy his pardon, which had been signed that morning by the governor. Jimmy took it in a tired kind of way. He had served nearly ten months of a four-year sentence. He had expected to stay only about three months, at the longest. When a man with as many friends on the outside as Jimmy Valentine had is received in the "stir" it is hardly worth while to cut his hair.

"Now, Valentine," said the warden, "you'll go out in the morning. Brace up, and make a man of yourself. You're not a bad fellow at heart. Stop cracking safes, and live straight."

"Me?" said Jimmy, in surprise. "Why, I never cracked a safe in my life."

"Oh, no," laughed the warden. "Of course not. Let's see, now. How was it you happened to get sent up on that Springfield job? Was it because you wouldn't prove an alibi for fear of compromising somebody in extremely high-toned society? Or was it simply a case of a mean old jury that had it in for you? It's always one or the other with you innocent victims."

"Me?" said Jimmy, still blankly virtuous. "Why, warden, I never was in Springfield in my life!"

"Take him back, Cronin," smiled the warden, "and fix him up with outgoing clothes. Unlock him at seven in the morning, and let him come to the bull-pen. Better think over my advice, Valentine."

At quarter past seven on the next morning Jimmy stood in the warden's outer office. He had on a suit of the villainously fitting, ready-made clothes and a pair of stiff, squeaky shoes that the state furnishes to its discharged compulsory guests.

The clerk handed him a railroad ticket and the five-dollar bill with which the law expected him to rehabilitate himself into good citizenship and prosperity.

The warden gave him a cigar, and shook hands. Valentine, 9762, was chronicled on the books "Pardoned by Governor," and Mr. James Valentine walked out into the sunshine.

Disregarding the song of the birds, the waving green trees, and the smell of the flowers, Jimmy headed straight for a restaurant. There he tasted the first sweet joys of liberty in the shape of a broiled chicken and a bottle of white wine— followed by a cigar a grade better than the one the warden had given him. From there he proceeded leisurely to the depot. He tossed a quarter into the hat of a blind man sitting by the door, and boarded his train. Three hours set him down in a little town near the state line. He went to the café of one Mike Dolan and shook hands with Mike, who was alone behind the bar.

"Sorry we couldn't make it sooner, Jimmy, me boy," said Mike. "But we had that protest from Springfield to buck against, and the governor nearly balked. Feeling all right?"

"Fine," said Jimmy. "Got my key?"

He got his key and went upstairs, unlocking the door of a room at the rear. Everything was just as he had left it. There on the floor was still Ben Price's collar-button that had been torn from that eminent detective's shirt-band when they had overpowered Jimmy to arrest him.

Pulling out from the wall a folding bed, Jimmy slid back a panel in the wall and dragged out a dust-covered suitcase. He opened this and gazed fondly at the finest set of burglar's tools in the East. It was a complete set, made of specially tempered steel, the latest designs in drills, punches, braces and bits, jimmies, clamps, and augers, with two or three novelties invented by Jimmy himself, in which he took pride. Over nine hundred dollars they had cost him to have made at——, a place where they make such things for the profession.

In half an hour Jimmy went downstairs and through the café. He was now dressed in tasteful and well-fitting clothes, and carried his dusted and cleaned suitcase in his hand.

"Got anything on?" asked Mike Dolan, genially.

"Me?" said Jimmy, in a puzzled tone. "I don't understand. I'm representing the New York Amalgamated Short Snap Biscuit Cracker and Frazzled Wheat Company."

This statement delighted Mike to such an extent that Jimmy had to take a seltzer-and-milk on the spot. He never touched "hard" drinks.

A week after the release of Valentine, 9762, there was a neat job of safe-burglary done in Richmond, Indiana, with no clue to the author. A scant eight hundred dollars was all that was secured. Two weeks after that a patented, improved, burglar-proof safe in Logansport was opened like a cheese to the tune of fifteen hundred dollars, currency; securities and silver untouched. That began to interest the rogue-catchers. Then an old-fashioned bank-safe in Jefferson City became active and threw out of its crater an eruption of banknotes amounting to five thousand dollars. The losses were now high enough to bring the matter up into Ben Price's class of work. By comparing notes, a remarkable similarity in the methods of the burglaries was noticed. Ben Price investigated the scenes of the robberies, and was heard to remark:

"That's Dandy Jim Valentine's autograph. He's resumed business. Look at that combination knob—jerked out as easy as pulling up a radish in wet weather. He's got the only clamps that can do it. And look how clean those tumblers were punched out! Jimmy never has to drill but one hole. Yes, I guess I want Mr. Valentine. He'll do his bit next time without any short-time or clemency foolishness."

Ben Price knew Jimmy's habits. He had learned them while working up the Springfield case. Long jumps, quick getaways, no confederates, and a taste for good society—these ways had helped Mr. Valentine to become noted as a successful dodger of retribution. It was given out that Ben Price had taken up the trail of the elusive cracksman, and other people with burglar-proof safes felt more at ease.

One afternoon Jimmy Valentine and his suitcase climbed out of the mailhack in Elmore, a little town five miles off the railroad down in the black-jack country of Arkansas. Jimmy, looking like an athletic young senior just home from college, went down the broad sidewalk toward the hotel.

A young lady crossed the street, passed him at the corner and entered a door over which was the sign "The Elmore Bank." Jimmy Valentine looked into her eyes, forgot what he was, and became another man. She lowered her eyes and colored slightly. Young men of Jimmy's style and looks were scarce in Elmore.

Jimmy collared a boy that was loafing on the steps of the bank as if he were one of the stockholders, and began to ask him questions about the town, feeding him dimes at intervals. By and by the young lady came out, looking royally unconscious of the young man with the suitcase, and went her way.

"Isn't that young lady Miss Polly Simpson?" asked Jimmy, with specious guile.

"Naw," said the boy. "She's Annabel Adams. Her pa owns this bank. What'd you come to Elmore for? Is that a gold watch-chain? I'm going to get a bulldog. Got any more dimes?"

Jimmy went to the Planters' Hotel, registered as Ralph D. Spencer, and engaged a room. He leaned on the desk and declared his platform to the clerk. He said he had come to Elmore to look for a location to go into business. How was the shoe business, now, in the town? He had thought of the shoe business. Was there an opening?

The clerk was impressed by the clothes and manner of Jimmy. He, himself, was something of a pattern of fashion to the thinly gilded youth of Elmore, but he now perceived his shortcomings. While trying to figure out Jimmy's manner of tying his four-in-hand he cordially gave information.

Yes, there ought to be a good opening in the shoe line. There wasn't an exclusive shoestore in the place. The dry-goods and general stores handled them. Business in all lines was fairly good. Hoped Mr. Spencer would decide to locate in Elmore. He would find it a pleasant town to live in, and the people very sociable.

Mr. Spencer thought he would stop over in the town a few days and look over the situation. No, the clerk needn't call the boy. He would carry up his suitcase himself; it was rather heavy.

Mr. Ralph Spencer, the phoenix that arose from Jimmy Valentine's ashes—ashes left by the flame of a sudden and alterative attack of love—remained in Elmore, and prospered. He opened a shoestore and secured a good run of trade.

Socially he was also a success, and made many friends. And he accomplished the wish of his heart. He met Miss Annabel Adams, and became more and more captivated by her charms.

At the end of a year the situation of Mr. Ralph Spencer was this: he had won the respect of the community, his shoestore was flourishing, and he and Annabel were engaged to be married in two weeks. Mr. Adams, the typical, plodding, country banker, approved of Spencer. Annabel's pride in him almost equaled her affection. He was as much at home in the family of Mr. Adams and that of Annabel's married sister as if he were already a member.

One day Jimmy sat down in his room and wrote this letter, which he mailed to the safe address of one of his old friends in St. Louis:

DEAR OLD PAL:

I want you to be at Sullivan's place, in Little Rock, next Wednesday night, at nine o'clock. I want you to wind up some little matters for me. And, also, I want to make you a present of my kit of tools. I know you'll be glad to get them—you couldn't duplicate the lot for a thousand dollars. Say, Billy, I've quit the old business—a year ago. I've got a nice store. I'm making an honest living, and I'm going to marry the finest girl on earth two weeks from now. It's the only life, Billy—the straight one. I wouldn't touch a dollar of another man's money now for a million. After I get married I'm going to sell out and go West, where there won't be so much danger of having old scores brought up against me. I tell you, Billy, she's an angel. She believes in me; and I wouldn't do another crooked thing for the whole world. Be sure to be at Sully's, for I must see you. I'll bring along the tools with me.

Your old friend
JIMMY.

On the Monday night after Jimmy wrote this letter, Ben Price jogged unobtrusively into Elmore in a livery buggy. He lounged about town in his quiet way until he found out what he wanted to know. From the drugstore across the street from Spencer's shoestore he got a good look at Ralph D. Spencer.

"Going to marry the banker's daughter are you, Jimmy?" said Ben to himself, softly. "Well, I don't know!"

The next morning Jimmy took breakfast at the Adamses. He was going to Little Rock that day to order his wedding suit and buy something nice for Annabel. That would be the first time he had left town since he came to Elmore. It had been more than a year now since those last professional "jobs," and he thought he could safely venture out.

After breakfast quite a family party went down town together—Mr. Adams, Annabel, Jimmy, and Annabel's married sister with her two little girls, aged five and nine. They came by the hotel where Jimmy still boarded, and he ran up to his room and brought along his suitcase. Then they went on to the bank. There stood Jimmy's horse and buggy and Dolph Gibson, who was going to drive him over to the railroad station.

All went inside the high, carved oak railings into the banking room—Jimmy included, for Mr. Adams's future son-in-law was welcome anywhere. The clerks were pleased to be greeted by the good-looking, agreeable young man who was going to marry Miss Annabel. Jimmy set his suitcase down. Annabel, whose heart was bubbling with happiness and lively youth, put on Jimmy's hat and picked up the suitcase. "Wouldn't I make a nice drummer?" said Annabel. "My, Ralph, how heavy it is. Feels like it was full of gold bricks."

"Lot of nickel-plated shoehorns in there," said Jimmy, coolly, "that I'm going to return. Thought I'd save express charges by taking them up. I'm getting awfully economical."

The Elmore Bank had just put in a new safe and vault. Mr. Adams was very proud of it, and insisted on an inspection by everyone. The vault was a small one, but it had a new patented door. It fastened with three solid steel bolts thrown simultaneously with a single handle, and had a time-lock. Mr. Adams beamingly explained its workings to Mr. Spencer, who showed a courteous but not too intelligent interest. The two children, May and Agatha, were delighted by the shining metal and funny clock and knobs.

While they were thus engaged Ben Price sauntered in and leaned on his elbow, looking casually inside between the railings. He told the teller that he didn't want anything; he was just waiting for a man he knew.

Suddenly there was a scream or two from the women, and a commotion. Unperceived by the elders, May, the nine-year-old girl, in a spirit of play, had shut Agatha in the vault. She had then shot the bolts and turned the knob of the combination as she had seen Mr. Adams do.

The old banker sprang to the handle and tugged at it for a moment. "The door can't be opened," he groaned. "The clock hasn't been wound nor the combination set."

Agatha's mother screamed again, hysterically.

"Hush!" said Mr. Adams, raising his trembling hand. "All be quiet for a moment. Agatha!" he called as loudly as he could. "Listen to me." During the following silence they could just hear the faint sound of the child wildly shrieking in the dark vault in a panic of terror.

"My precious darling!" wailed the mother. "She will die of fright! Open the door! Oh, break it open! Can't you men do something?"

"There isn't a man nearer than Little Rock who can open that door," said Mr. Adams, in a shaky voice. "My God! Spencer, what shall we do? That child—she can't stand it long in there. There isn't enough air, and, besides, she'll go into convulsions from fright."

Agatha's mother, frantic now, beat the door of the vault with her hands. Somebody wildly suggested dynamite. Annabel turned to Jimmy, her large eyes full of anguish, but not yet despairing. To a woman nothing seems quite impossible to the powers of the man she worships.

"Can't you do something, Ralph—*try*, won't you?"

He looked at her with a queer, soft smile on his lips and in his keen eyes.

"Annabel," he said, "give me that rose you are wearing, will you?"

Hardly believing that she heard him aright, she unpinned the bud from the bosom of her dress, and placed it in his hand. Jimmy stuffed it into his vest-pocket, threw off his coat and pulled up his shirtsleeves. With that act Ralph D. Spencer passed away and Jimmy Valentine took his place.

"Get away from the door, all of you," he commanded shortly.

He set his suitcase on the table, and opened it out flat. From that time on he seemed to be unconscious of the presence of anyone else. He laid out the shining, queer implements swiftly and orderly, whistling softly to himself as he always did when at work. In a deep silence and immovable, the others watched him as if under a spell.

In a minute Jimmy's pet drill was biting smoothly into the steel door. In ten minutes—breaking his own burglarious record—he threw back the bolts and opened the door.

Agatha, almost collapsed, but safe, was gathered into her mother's arms.

Jimmy Valentine put on his coat, and walked outside the railings toward the front door. As he went he thought he heard a far-away voice that he once knew call "Ralph!" But he never hesitated.

At the door a big man stood somewhat in his way.

"Hello, Ben!" said Jimmy, still with his strange smile. "Got around at last, have you? Well, let's go. I don't know that it makes much difference now."

And then Ben Price acted rather strangely.

"Guess you're mistaken, Mr. Spencer," he said. "Don't believe I recognize you. Your buggy's waiting for you, ain't it?"

And Ben Price turned and strolled down the street.

CALIFORNIA

THE SLEEPING DOG
by Ross MacDonald

THE DAY AFTER her dog disappeared, Fay Hooper called me early. Her normal voice was like waltzing violins, but this morning the violins were out of tune. She sounded as though she'd been crying.

"Otto's gone."

Otto was her one-year-old German shepherd.

"He jumped the fence yesterday afternoon and ran away. Or else he was kid-naped—dognaped, I suppose is the right word to use."

"What makes you think that?"

"You know Otto, Mr. Archer—how loyal he was. He wouldn't deliberately stay away from me overnight, not under his own power. There must be thieves involved."

She caught her breath. "I realize searching for stolen dogs isn't your métier. But you *are* a detective, and I thought, since we knew one another. . . ."

She allowed her voice to suggest, ever so chastely, that we might get to know one another better.

I liked the woman. I liked the dog, I liked the breed. I was taking my own German shepherd pup to obedience school, which is where I met Fay Hooper. Otto and she were the handsomest and most expensive members of the class.

"How do I get to your place?"

She lived in the hills north of Malibu, she said, on the far side of the county line. If she wasn't home when I got there, her husband would be.

On my way out I stopped at the dog school in Pacific Palisades to talk to the man who ran it, Fernando Rambeau. The kennels behind the house burst into clamor when I knocked on the front door. Rambeau boarded dogs as well as trained them.

A dark-haired girl looked out and informed me that her husband was feeding the animals. "Maybe I can help," she added doubtfully, and then she let me into a small living room.

I told her about the missing dog. "It would help if you called the vets and animal shelters and gave them a description," I said.

"We've already been doing that. Mrs. Hooper was on the phone to Fernando last night." She sounded vaguely resentful. "I'll get him."

Setting her face against the continuing noise, she went out the back door. Rambeau came in with her, wiping his hands on a rag. He was a square-shouldered Canadian with a curly black beard that failed to conceal his youth. Over the beard, his intense dark eyes peered at me warily, like an animal's sensing trouble.

Rambeau handled dogs as if he loved them. He wasn't quite so patient with human beings. His current class was only in its third week, but he was already having dropouts. The man was loaded with explosive feeling, and it was close to the surface now.

"I'm sorry about Mrs. Hooper and her dog. They were my best pupils. He was, anyway. But I can't drop everything and spend the next week looking for him."

"Nobody expects that. I take it you've had no luck with your contacts."

"I don't have such good contacts. Marie and I, we just moved down here last year, from British Columbia."

"That was a mistake," his wife said from the doorway.

Rambeau pretended not to hear her. "Anyway, I know nothing about dog thieves." With both hands he pushed the possibility away from him. "If I hear any word of the dog I'll let you know, naturally. I've got nothing against Mrs. Hooper."

His wife gave him a quick look. It was one of those revealing looks which said, among other things, that she loved him but didn't know if he loved her, and she was worried about him. She caught me watching her and lowered her eyes. Then she burst out, "Do you think somebody killed the dog?"

"I have no reason to think so."

"Some people shoot dogs, don't they?"

"Not around here," Rambeau said. "Maybe back in the bush someplace." He turned to me with a sweeping explanatory gesture. "These things make her nervous and she gets wild ideas. You know Marie is a country girl—"

"I am not. I was born in Chilliwack." Flinging a bitter look at him, she left the room.

"Was Otto shot?" I asked Rambeau.

"Not that I know of. Listen, Mr. Archer, you're a good customer, but I can't stand here talking all day. I've got twenty dogs to feed."

They were still barking when I drove up the coast highway out of hearing. It was nearly 40 miles to the Hoopers' mailbox, and another mile up a black-top lane which climbed the side of a canyon to the gate. On both sides of the heavy wire gate, which had a new combination padlock on it, a hurricane fence, eight feet high and topped with barbed wire, extended out of sight. Otto would have to be quite a jumper to clear it. So would I.

The house beyond the gate was low and massive, made of fieldstone and steel and glass. I honked at it and waited. A man in blue bathing trunks came out of the house with a shotgun. The sun glinted on its twin barrels and on the man's bald head and round, brown, burnished belly. He walked quite slowly, a short heavy man in his sixties, scuffling along in huaraches. The flabby brown shell of fat on him jiggled lugubriously.

When he approached the gate, I could see the stiff gray pallor under his tan, like stone showing under varnish. He was sick, or afraid, or both. His mouth was profoundly discouraged.

"What do you want?" he said over the shotgun.

"Mrs. Hooper asked me to help find her dog. My name is Lew Archer."

He was not impressed. "My wife isn't here, and I'm busy. I happen to be following soy-bean futures rather closely."

"Look here, I've come quite a distance to lend a hand. I met Mrs. Hooper at dog school and—"

Hooper uttered a short savage laugh. "That hardly constitutes an introduction to either of us. You'd better be on your way right now."

"I think I'll wait for your wife."

"I think you won't." He raised the shotgun and let me look into its close-set, hollow, round eyes. "This is my property all the way down to the road, and you're trespassing. That means I can shoot you if I have to."

"What sense would that make? I came out here to help you."

"You can't help me." He looked at me through the wire gate with a kind of pathetic arrogance, like a lion that had grown old in captivity. "Go away."

I drove back down to the road and waited for Fay Hooper. The sun slid up the sky. The inside of my car turned oven-hot. I went for a walk down the canyon. The brown September grass crunched under my feet. Away up on the far side of the canyon an earth mover that looked like a crazy red insect was cutting the ridge to pieces.

A very fast black car came up the canyon and stopped abruptly beside me. A gaunt man in a wrinkled brown suit climbed out, with his hand on his holster, told me that he was Sheriff Carlson, and asked me what I was doing there. I told him.

He pushed back his wide cream-colored hat and scratched at his hairline. The pale eyes in his sun-fired face were like clouded glass inserts in a brick wall.

"I'm surprised Mr. Hooper takes that attitude. Mrs. Hooper just came to see me in the courthouse. But I can't take you up there with me if Mr. Hooper says no."

"Why not?"

"He owns most of the county and holds the mortgage on the rest of it. Besides," he added with careful logic, "Mr. Hooper is a friend of mine."

"Then you better get him a keeper."

The sheriff glanced around uneasily, as if the Hoopers' mailbox might be bugged. "I'm surprised he has a gun, let alone threatening you with it. He must be upset about the dog."

"He didn't seem to care about the dog."

"He does, though. *She* cares, so *he* cares," Carlson said.

"What did she have to tell you?"

"She can talk to you herself. She should be along any minute. She told me that she was going to follow me out of town."

He drove his black car up the lane. A few minutes later Fay Hooper stopped her Mercedes at the mailbox. She must have seen the impatience on my face. She got out and came toward me in a little run, making noises of dismayed regret.

Fay was in her late thirties and fading slightly, as if a light frost had touched her pale gold head, but she was still a beautiful woman. She turned the gentle force of her charm on me.

"I'm dreadfully sorry," she said. "Have I kept you waiting long?"

"Your husband did. He ran me off with a shotgun."

Her gloved hand lighted on my arm, and stayed. She had an electric touch, even through layers of cloth.

"That's terrible. I had no idea that Allan still had a gun."

Her mouth was blue behind her lipstick, as if the information had chilled her to the marrow. She took me up the hill in the Mercedes. The gate was standing open, but she didn't drive in right away.

"I might as well be perfectly frank," she said without looking at me. "Ever since Otto disappeared yesterday, there's been a nagging question in my mind. What you've just told me raises the question again. I was in town all day yesterday so that Otto was alone here with Allan when—when it happened."

The values her voice gave to the two names made it sound as if Allan were the dog and Otto the husband.

"When what happened, Mrs. Hooper?" I wanted to know.

Her voice sank lower. "I can't help suspecting that Allan shot him. He's never liked any of my dogs. The only dogs he appreciates are hunting dogs—and he was particularly jealous of Otto. Besides, when I got back from town, Allan was getting the ground ready to plant some roses. He's never enjoyed gardening, particularly in the heat. We have professionals to do our work. And this really isn't the time of year to put in a bed of roses."

"You think your husband was planting a dog?" I asked.

"If he was, I have to know." She turned toward me, and the leather seat squeaked softly under her movement. "Find out for me, Mr. Archer. If Allan killed my beautiful big old dog, I couldn't stay with him."

"Something you said implied that Allan used to have a gun or guns, but gave them up. Is that right?"

"He had a small arsenal when I married him. He was an infantry officer in the war and a big-game hunter in peacetime. But he swore off hunting years ago."

"Why?"

"I don't really know. We came home from a hunting trip one fall and Allan sold all his guns. He never said a word about it to me but it was the fall after the war ended, and I always thought that it must have had something to do with the war."

"Have you been married so long?"

"Thank you for that question." She produced a rueful smile. "I met Allan during the war, the year I came out, and I knew I'd met my fate. He was a very powerful person."

"And a very wealthy one."

She gave me a flashing, haughty look and stepped so hard on the accelerator that she almost ran into the sheriff's car parked in front of the house. We walked around to the back, past a freeform swimming pool that looked inviting, into a walled garden. A few Greek statues stood around in elegant disrepair. Bees murmured like distant bombers among the flowers.

The bed where Allan Hooper had been digging was about five feet long and three feet wide, and it reminded me of graves.

"Get me a spade," I said.

"Are you going to dig him up?"

"You're pretty sure he's in there, aren't you, Mrs. Hooper?"

"I guess I am."

From a lath house at the end of the garden she fetched a square-edged spade. I asked her to stick around.

I took off my jacket and hung it on a marble torso where it didn't look too bad. It was easy digging in the newly worked soil. In a few minutes I was two feet below the surface, and the ground was still soft and penetrable.

The edge of my spade struck something soft but not so penetrable. Fay Hooper heard the peculiar dull sound it made. She made a dull sound of her own. I scooped away more earth. Dog fur sprouted like stiff black grass at the bottom of the grave.

Fay got down on her knees and began to dig with her lacquered fingernails. Once she cried out in a loud harsh voice, "Dirty murderer!"

Her husband must have heard her. He came out of the house and looked over the stone wall. His head seemed poised on top of the wall, hairless and bodiless, like Humpty-Dumpty. He had that look on his face, of not being able to be put together again.

"I didn't kill your dog, Fay. Honest to God, I didn't."

She didn't hear him. She was talking to Otto. "Poor boy, poor boy," she said. "Poor, beautiful boy."

Sheriff Carlson came into the garden. He reached down into the grave and freed the dog's head from the earth. His large hands moved gently on the great wedge of the skull.

Fay knelt beside him in torn and dirty stockings. "What are you doing?"

Carlson held up a red-tipped finger. "Your dog was shot through the head, Mrs. Hooper, but it's no shotgun wound. Looks to me more like a deer rifle."

"I don't even own a rifle," Hooper said over the wall. "I haven't owned one for nearly twenty years. Anyway, I wouldn't shoot your dog."

Fay scrambled to her feet. She looked ready to climb the wall. "Then why did you bury him?"

His mouth opened and closed.

"Why did you buy a shotgun without telling me?"

"For protection."

"Against my dog?"

Hooper shook his head. He edged along the wall and came in tentatively through the gate. He had on slacks and a short-sleeved yellow jersey which somehow emphasized his shortness and his fatness and his age.

"Mr. Hooper had some threatening calls," the sheriff said. "Somebody got hold of his unlisted number. He was just telling me about it now."

"Why didn't you tell me, Allan?"

"I didn't want to alarm you. You weren't the one they were after, anyway. I bought a shotgun and kept it in my study."

"Do you know who they are?"

"No. I make enemies in the course of business, especially the farming operations. Some crackpot shot your dog, gunning for me. I heard a shot and found him dead in the driveway."

"But how could you bury him without telling me?"

Hooper spread his hands in front of him. "I wasn't thinking too well. I felt guilty, I suppose, because whoever got him was after me. And I didn't want you to see him dead. I guess I wanted to break it to you gently."

"This is gently?"

"It's not the way I planned it. I thought if I had a chance to get you another pup—"

"No one will ever take Otto's place."

Allan Hooper stood and looked at her wistfully across the open grave, as if he would have liked to take Otto's place. After a while the two of them went into the house.

Carlson and I finished digging Otto up and carried him out to the sheriff's car. His inert blackness filled the trunk from side to side.

"What are you going to do with him, Sheriff?" I asked.

"Get a vet I know to recover the slug in him. Then if we nab the sniper we can use ballistics to convict him."

"You're taking this just as seriously as a real murder, aren't you?" I observed.

"They want me to," he said with a respectful look toward the house.

Mrs. Hooper came out carrying a white leather suitcase which she deposited in the back seat of her Mercedes.

"Are you going someplace?" I asked her.

"Yes, I am." She didn't say where.

Her husband, who was watching her from the doorway, didn't speak. The Mercedes went away. He closed the door. Both of them had looked sick.

"She doesn't seem to believe he didn't do it. Do you, Sheriff?"

Carlson jabbed me with his forefinger. "Mr. Hooper is no liar. If you want to get along with me, get that through your head. I've known Mr. Hooper for over twenty years—served under him in the war—and I never heard him twist the truth."

"I'll have to take your word for it. What about those threatening phone calls?
Did he report them to you before today?"

"No."

"What was said on the phone?"

"He didn't tell me."

"Does Hooper have any idea who shot the dog?"

"Well, he did say he saw a man slinking around outside the fence. He didn't
get close enough to the guy to give me a good description, but he did make out
that he had a black beard."

"There's a dog trainer in Pacific Palisades named Rambeau who fits the description. Mrs. Hooper has been taking Otto to his school."

"Rambeau?" Carlson said with interest.

"Fernando Rambeau. He seemed pretty upset when I talked to him this
morning."

"What did he say?"

"A good deal less than he knows, I think. I'll talk to him again."

Rambeau was not at home. My repeated knocking was answered only by the
barking of the dogs. I retreated up the highway to a drive-in where I ate a torpedo
sandwich. When I was on my second cup of coffee, Marie Rambeau drove by in
a pickup truck. I followed her home.

"Where's Fernando?" I asked.

"I don't know. I've been out looking for him."

"Is he in a bad way?"

"I don't know how you mean."

"Emotionally upset."

"He has been ever since that woman came into the class."

"Mrs. Hooper?"

Her head bobbed slightly.

"Are they having an affair?"

"They better not be." Her small red mouth looked quite implacable. "He was
out with her night before last. I heard him make the date. He was gone all night,
and when he came home he was on one of his black drunks and he wouldn't go to
bed. He sat in the kitchen and drank himself glassy-eyed." She got out of the
pickup facing me. "Is shooting a dog a very serious crime?"

"It is to me, but not to the law. It's not like shooting a human being."

"It would be to Fernando. He loves dogs the way other people love human
beings. That included Otto."

"But he shot him."

Her head drooped. I could see the straight white part dividing her black hair.
"I'm afraid he did. He's got a crazy streak and it comes out in him when he
drinks. You should have heard him in the kitchen yesterday morning. He was
moaning and groaning about his brother."

"His brother?"

"Fernando had an older brother, George, who died back in Canada after the
war. Fernando was just a kid when it happened and it was a big loss to him. His

parents were dead, too, and they put him in a foster home in Chilliwack. He still has nightmares about it."

"What did his brother die of?"

"He never told me exactly, but I think he was shot in some kind of hunting accident. George was a guide and packer in the Fraser River valley below Mount Robson. That's where Fernando comes from, the Mount Robson country. He won't go back, on account of what happened to his brother."

"What did he say about his brother yesterday?" I asked.

"That he was going to get his revenge for George. I got so scared I couldn't listen to him. I went out and fed the dogs. When I came back in, Fernando was loading his deer rifle. I asked him what he was planning to do, but he walked right out and drove away."

"May I see the rifle?"

"It isn't in the house. I looked for it after he left today. He must have taken it with him again. I'm so afraid that he'll kill somebody."

"What's he driving?"

"Our car. It's an old blue Meteor sedan."

Keeping an eye out for it, I drove up the highway to the Hoopers' canyon. Everything there was very peaceful. Too peaceful. Just inside the locked gate, Allan Hooper was lying face down on his shotgun. I could see small ants in single file trekking across the crown of his bald head.

I got a hammer out of the trunk of my car and used it to break the padlock. I lifted his head. His skin was hot in the sun, as if death had fallen on him like a fever. But he had been shot neatly between the eyes. There was no exit wound; the bullet was still in his head. Now the ants were crawling on my hands.

I found my way into the Hoopers' study, turned off the stuttering teletype, and sat down under an elk head to telephone the courthouse. Carlson was in his office.

"I have bad news, Sheriff. Allan Hooper's been shot."

I heard him draw in his breath quickly. "Is he dead?"

"Extremely dead. You better put out a general alarm for Rambeau."

Carlson said with gloomy satisfaction, "I already have him."

"You have him?"

"That's correct. I picked him up in the Hoopers' canyon and brought him in just a few minutes ago." Carlson's voice sank to a mournful mumble. "I picked him up a little too late, I guess."

"Did Rambeau do any talking?"

"He hasn't had a chance to yet. When I stopped his car, he piled out and threatened me with a rifle. I clobbered him one good."

I went outside to wait for Carlson and his men. A very pale afternoon moon hung like a ghost in the sky. For some reason it made me think of Fay. She ought to be here. It occurred to me that possibly she had been.

I went and looked at Hooper's body again. He had nothing to tell me. He lay as if he had fallen from a height, perhaps all the way from the moon.

They came in a black county wagon and took him away. I followed them inland to the county seat, which rose like a dusty island in a dark green lake of orange groves. We parked in the courthouse parking lot, and the sheriff and I went inside.

Rambeau was under guard in a second-floor room with barred windows. Carlson said it was used for interrogation. There was nothing in the room but an old deal table and some wooden chairs. Rambeau sat hunched forward on one of them, his hands hanging limp between his knees. Part of his head had been shaved and plastered with bandages.

"I had to cool him with my gun butt," Carlson said. "You're lucky I didn't shoot you—you know that, Fernando?"

Rambeau made no response. His black eyes were set and dull.

"Had his rifle been fired?"

"Yeah. Chet Scott is working on it now. Chet's my identification lieutenant and he's a bear on ballistics." The sheriff turned back to Rambeau. "You might as well give us a full confession, boy. If you shot Mr. Hooper and his dog, we can link the bullets to your gun. You know that."

Rambeau didn't speak or move.

"What did you have against Mr. Hooper?" Carlson said.

No answer. Rambeau's mouth was set like a trap in the thicket of his beard.

"Your older brother," I said to him, "was killed in a hunting accident in British Columbia. Was Hooper at the other end of the gun that killed George?"

Rambeau didn't answer me, but Carlson's head came up. "Where did you get that, Archer?"

"From a couple of things I was told. According to Rambeau's wife, he was talking yesterday about revenge for his brother's death. According to Fay Hooper, her husband swore off guns when he came back from a hunting trip after the war. Would you know if that trip was to British Columbia?"

"Yeah. Mr. Hooper took me and the wife with him."

"Whose wife?"

"Both our wives."

"To the Mount Robson area?"

"That's correct. We went up after elk."

"And did he shoot somebody accidentally?"

"Not that I know of. I wasn't with him all the time, understand. He often went out alone, or with Mrs. Hooper," Carlson replied.

"Did he use a packer named George Rambeau?"

"I wouldn't know. Ask Fernando here."

I asked Fernando. He didn't speak or move. Only his eyes had changed. They were wet and glistening-black, visible parts of a grief that filled his head like a dark underground river.

The questioning went on and produced nothing. It was night when I went outside. The moon was slipping down behind the dark hills. I took a room in a hotel and checked in with my answering service in Hollywood.

About an hour before, Fay Hooper had called me from a Las Vegas hotel.

When I tried to return the call, she wasn't in her room and didn't respond to paging. I left a message for her to come home, that her husband was dead.

Next, I called R.C.M.P. headquarters in Vancouver to ask some questions about George Rambeau. The answers came over the line in clipped Canadian tones. George and his dog had disappeared from his cabin below Red Pass in the fall of 1945. Their bodies hadn't been recovered until the following May, and by that time they consisted of parts of the two skeletons. These included George Rambeau's skull, which had been pierced in the right front and left rear quadrants by a heavy-caliber bullet. The bullet had not been recovered. Who fired it, or when, or why, had never been determined. The dog, a husky, had also been shot through the head.

I walked over to the courthouse to pass the word to Carlson. He was in the basement shooting gallery with Lieutenant Scott, who was firing test rounds from Fernando Rambeau's .30/30 repeater.

I gave them the official account of the accident. "But since George Rambeau's dog was shot, too, it probably wasn't an accident," I said.

"I see what you mean," Carlson said. "It's going to be rough, spreading all this stuff out in court about Mr. Hooper. We have to nail it down, though."

I went back to my hotel and to bed, but the process of nailing down the case against Rambeau continued through the night. By morning Lieutenant Scott had detailed comparisons set up between the test-fired slugs and the ones dug out of Hooper and the dog.

I looked at his evidence through a comparison microscope. It left no doubt in my mind that the slugs that killed Allan Hooper and the dog, Otto, had come from Rambeau's gun.

But Rambeau still wouldn't talk, even to phone his wife or ask for a lawyer.

"We'll take you out to the scene of the crime," Carlson said. "I've cracked tougher nuts than you, boy."

We rode in the back seat of his car with Fernando handcuffed between us. Lieutenant Scott did the driving. Rambeau groaned and pulled against his handcuffs. He was very close to the breaking point, I thought.

It came a few minutes later when the car turned up the lane past the Hoopers' mailbox. He burst into sudden fierce tears as if a pressure gauge in his head had broken. It was strange to see a bearded man crying like a boy. "I don't want to go up there."

"Because you shot him?" Carlson said.

"I shot the dog. I confess I shot the dog," Rambeau said.

"And the man?"

"No!" he cried. "I never killed a man. Mr. Hooper was the one who did. He followed my brother out in the woods and shot him."

"If you knew that," I said, "why didn't you tell the Mounties years ago?"

"I didn't know it then. I was seven years old. How would I understand? When Mrs. Hooper came to our cabin to be with my brother, how would I know it was a serious thing? Or when Mr. Hooper asked me if she had been there? I didn't know he was her husband. I thought he was her father checking up. I knew I shouldn't have told him—I could see it in his face the minute after—but I didn't understand the situation till the other night, when I talked to Mrs. Hooper."

"Did she know that her husband had shot George?"

"She didn't even know George had been killed. They never went back to the Fraser River after nineteen forty-five. But when we put our facts together, we agreed he must have done it. I came out here next morning to get even. The dog came out to the gate. It wasn't real to me—I'd been drinking most of the night— it wasn't real to me until the dog went down. I shot him. Mr. Hooper shot *my* dog. But when he came out of the house himself, I couldn't pull the trigger. I yelled at him and ran away."

"What did you yell?" I said.

"The same thing I told him on the telephone: 'Remember Mount Robson.'"

A yellow cab, which looked out of place in the canyon, came over the ridge above us. Lieutenant Scott waved it to a stop. The driver said he'd just brought Mrs. Hooper home from the airport and wanted to know if that constituted a felony. Scott waved him on.

"I wonder what she was doing at the airport," Carlson said.

"Coming home from Vegas. She tried to call me from there last night. I forgot to tell you."

"You don't forget important things like that," Carlson said.

"I suppose I wanted her to come home under her own power."

"In case she shot her husband?"

"More or less."

"She didn't. Fernando shot him, didn't you, boy?"

"I shot the dog. I am innocent of the man." He turned to me. "Tell her that. Tell her I am sorry about the dog. I came out here to surrender the gun and tell her yesterday. I don't trust myself with guns."

"With darn good reason," Carlson said. "We know you shot Mr. Hooper. Ballistic evidence doesn't lie."

Rambeau screeched in his ear, "You're a liar! You're all liars!"

Carlson swung his open hand against the side of Rambeau's face. "Don't call me names, little man."

Lieutenant Scott spoke without taking his eyes from the road. "I wouldn't hit him, Chief. You wouldn't want to damage our case."

Carlson subsided, and we drove on up to the house. Carlson went in without knocking. The guard at the door discouraged me from following him.

I couldn't hear Fay's voice on the other side of the door, too low to be understood. Carlson said something to her.

"Get out! Get out of my house, you killer!" Fay cried out sharply.

Carlson didn't come out. I went in instead. One of his arms was wrapped around her body, the other hand was covering her mouth. I got his Adam's apple in the crook of my left arm, pulled him away from her, and threw him over my left hip. He went down clanking and got up holding his revolver.

He should have shot me right away. But he gave Fay Hooper time to save my life.

She stepped in front of me. "Shoot me, Mr. Carlson. You might as well. You shot the one man I ever cared for."

"Your husband shot George Rambeau, if that's who you mean. I ought to know. I was there." Carlson scowled down at his gun and replaced it in his holster.

Lieutenant Scott was watching him from the doorway.

"You were there?" I said to Carlson. "Yesterday you told me Hooper was alone when he shot Rambeau."

"He was. When I said I was there, I meant in the general neighborhood."

"Don't believe him," Fay said. "He fired the gun that killed George, and it was no accident. The two of them hunted George down in the woods. My husband planned to shoot him himself, but George's dog came at him and he had to dispose of it. By that time George had drawn a bead on Allan. Mr. Carlson shot him. It was hardly a coincidence that the next spring Allan financed his campaign for sheriff."

"She's making it up," Carlson said. "She wasn't within ten miles of the place."

"But you were, Mr. Carlson, and so was Allan. He told me the whole story yesterday, after we found Otto. Once that happened, he knew that everything was bound to come out. I already suspected him, of course, after I talked to Fernando. Allan filled in the details himself. He thought, since he hadn't killed George personally, I would be able to forgive him. But I couldn't. I left him and flew to Nevada, intending to divorce him. I've been intending to for twenty years."

Carlson said, "Are you sure you didn't shoot him before you left?"

"How could she have?" I said. "Ballistics don't lie, and the ballistic evidence says he was shot with Fernando's rifle. Nobody had access to it but Fernando—and you. You stopped him on the road and knocked him out, took his rifle, and used it to kill Hooper. You killed him for the same reason that Hooper buried the dog—to keep the past buried. You thought Hooper was the only witness to the murder of George Rambeau. But by that time Mrs. Hooper knew about it, too."

"It wasn't murder. It was self-defense, just like in the war. Anyway, you'll never hang it on me."

"We don't have to. We'll hang Hooper on you. How about it, Lieutenant?"

Scott nodded grimly, not looking at his chief. I relieved Carlson of his gun. He winced, as if I were amputating part of his body. He offered no resistance when Scott took him out to the car.

I stayed behind for a final word with Fay. "Fernando asked me to tell you he's sorry for shooting your dog."

"We're both sorry." She stood with her eyes down, as if the past was swirling visibly around her feet. "I'll talk to Fernando later. Much later."

"There's one coincidence that bothers me. How did you happen to take your dog to his school?"

"I happened to see his sign, and Fernando Rambeau isn't a common name. I couldn't resist going there. I had to know what had happened to George. I think perhaps Fernando came to California for the same reason."

"Now you both know," I said.

COLORADO

GRAVEYARD SHIFT

by Steve Frazee

DOZING IN FRONT of the microphone in the radio dispatcher's office, Joe Crestone blinked groggily when one of the heavy side doors downstairs whushed open and then started rocking back to center. Since midnight the building had been dead still.

The footsteps swung out briskly on the tiles of the lobby. They made quick taps on the steel steps leading up towards the dispatcher's room. Crestone was wide awake. The clock on the radio reeled up another minute. It was 2:17. He swung his chair to face the counter.

She was close to six feet. Her hair was dark, her eyes soft brown. She wore a fur jacket and under that a green woolen dress caught high at her neck with a silver clasp. Her smile was timid. "I—I thought Mr. Walters would be here again." She studied the work schedule of the Midway police department on the board.

"He's got the flu. It was my day off so I'm sitting in for him."

"I see." She stared at the maps on the wall. "I—I just don't know exactly how to start it."

She was white and scared. Crestone let her make up her mind. On the model side, he thought, the kind who pose in two-thousand-dollar dresses. Plenty of neck above the silver clasp, more gauntness in her face than he had observed at first.

"Hit and run deal?" he asked, eyeing her sharply.

Before she could answer, state patrol car 55 checked in from Middleton, eighteen miles north on Highway 315. A woman dispatcher in Steel City read a CAA flight plan to Bristol for relay to Cosslett. Webster came in with a pickup-and-hold on a 1949 blue Chev with three men. Crestone sent out the information on the pickup-and-hold.

When he swung to the log sheet in the typewriter at his left, she asked, "Do

47

the state cars patrol the old highway from the boarded-up brick works east toward Steel City?"

"State 7? No, not unless there's a crash out there." He wrote a line on the log. "Did you have a wreck?"

She hesitated. "In a way."

He turned back to the desk and pulled a pad to him. "Name?"

"Judith Barrows."

"Address?"

When she did not answer he twisted his head to look at her. He looked into a snub-nosed .38. For one fractured moment the bore was big enough to shoot a golf ball. Crestone sucked in his breath.

"Give me the log sheet," she said. "Don't even brush your arm near the mike or you'll get it in the liver."

He stripped the log sheet from the machine and put it up on the counter. She drew it to her with long, thin fingers that bent into carmine-tipped hooks. "Now, a copy of the code sheet, and not the old one with blanks behind some of the numbers."

Crestone took a code sheet from a folder. When he put it on the counter he saw that she had shrugged out of her fur jacket. He heard the power hum and then Bud Moore said in his bored after-midnight voice, "Seven fifty." Crestone started to reach toward the microphone and then he stopped.

"Acknowledge it," she said softly.

He stared at the .38. She was resting her hand on the counter. The gun looked down at his mid-section. He gripped the long bar of the mike switch on the stem of the instrument. Under *Transmit* on the face of the radio a purple button lit up like an evil eye glaring at him. "Seven fifty," he said, then automatically released his grip on the switch.

"Going 10-10 at Circle 7365," Moore said, which meant that he and Jerry Windoff were going out of service temporarily to get a cup of coffee at the Mohawk Diner out on Sterling Pike.

Crestone's mind froze on 10-19: *report back to this office.* But then she would read it on the code sheet and—His head rocked sidewise. His left elbow jammed against the typewriter. There was a thin crack of tension in her voice when she said, "Answer the car, Buster."

He was still half stunned from the crack on his head when he said, "Seven fifty, 10-4." *Okay, 750.*

"Give me the local code sheet now, Crestone."

He gave that to her. It held sixteen messages for local use, and then there were four blanks. She said, "Don't get any ideas about using Code 17 or any other blank."

Code 17 was unlisted, strictly a private deal between Bill Walters and all cruiser cops: *Bring me a hamburger and a jug of coffee.* She had found out plenty from old Bill, a friendly, trusting guy who liked to talk about his work.

"Face the radio, Crestone. Don't worry about me."

He turned around, staring at a transmitter which controlled all law enforcement in the area. It was worthless unless he had the brains and guts to figure out something.

"Where's state patrol 54?" she asked.

"After a 10-47 on State 219." It was on the log; there was no use to lie. He heard papers rustle.

"That's right," she said. "Chasing a possible drunk. Keep everything you say right, Crestone, especially when you talk into that microphone."

The right-hand reel of the clock put up three more minutes. Now it was 2:25. She made no sound behind him. After another minute he could not stand it any longer. He had to look around. She was still there. The gun was still there too, slanted over the edge of the counter.

"Face the radio."

He hesitated, and then while he was turning, the gun bounced off his head again. He sucked air between his teeth and cursed. For a tick of time his anger was almost enough to make him try to lunge up and reach her; but his sanity was greater. She struck him again, sweeping the barrel of the gun on the slope of his skull.

"Don't curse me!" she said.

After a foggy interval Crestone was aware of the messages coming from both channels. Two stolen cars from Bristol. He added them to a list of twenty others stolen that day. Steel City sent a car to investigate a prowler complaint. Seventy miles away state patrol car 86 stopped to pull a dead pig off the highway. The dispatcher in Shannon sent a car to a disturbance at Puddler's Casino. York asked Webster for a weather report on Highway 27.

Then there was just the hum of the radio and the silence at his back. Where was it, one of the banks? No, blowing vaults was a worn-out racket. A payroll at one of the mills or at the automobile assembling plant? Wrong time of week. Besides, that stuff went from the banks by armored cars in daytime.

At the other end of the narrow slot where he was trapped there was a desk, a big steel filing cabinet, and a rack with four sawed-off shotguns. The shells were in a drawer in the bottom of the rack. In another steel cabinet that he could almost reach with his right hand were five pistols and enough ammunition to last a year.

The whole works was as useless now as the radio.

Car 54 asked Shannon for an ambulance at the cloverleaf on State 219. "Two dead, two injured. Didn't catch up with the *dk* soon enough."

"What's *dk?*" Judith Barrows asked quickly.

"Drunk." Crestone's head was aching. "Car 54 will be back here in about an hour. He'll come in to write a report." That was not so, but Crestone wanted to judge her reaction to the time. He leaned toward the radio and twisted his neck to look at her. The one-hour statement had not bothered her.

When he straightened up, he ducked quickly. She laughed. When he raised his head again the gun banged against it. He rolled his head, grinding curses under his breath.

Car 751 came in. Sam Kurowski said, "Any traffic? We've been out of the car a few minutes."

"Where are they?" the woman asked.

Crestone pressed the mike switch. "10-20, 751?"

"Alley between Franklin and Madison on Tenth Avenue."

When the transmitting light was off she said, "Code 6 them to the corner—the southeast corner—of River and Pitt."

Code 6 was boy trouble, kids yelling, throwing rocks—any of a hundred things. They could spot a cruiser a mile away. When Kurowski and Corky Gunselman got way out north on River and Pitt and found nothing, they would think nothing of it. Crestone followed the woman's orders.

Car 752 came alive. Dewey Purcell said, "Going east on Washington at Sixth Street after *dk*. Give me a 10-18 on K6532."

That does it, Crestone thought. Purcell was hell on drunken drivers. He and Old McGlone would be coming in with a prisoner in about five minutes.

"Give him the registration he asked for, Crestone."

He pulled the vehicle registration book to him. *K6532, 1953 Cadillac cpe., maroon, J. J. Britton, 60 Parkway.* Jimmy Britton, the Hill itself. Damnation! You didn't dump guys like him in the tank overnight; but he took hope from knowing that Purcell was in 752 tonight.

"Give him the 10-28, Buster."

"When they stop. Old McGlone can hardly write, let alone in a car doing eighty after a stinking *dk*."

Purcell called again from Washington and Trinity. "We got him." A woman's shrill voice came from the background before the car mike was closed. Crestone gave Purcell the registration information.

Crestone stared at the radio. Jimmy Britton would be drunk, affable, mildly surprised at being picked up. Among other things, when he fumbled out his driver's license, he would show his honorary membership in the Midway Police Department. Old McGlone would say, "Ah now, Dewey, let's take the lad home, shall we? No harm's been done, has it?"

But Purcell was tough and he did not give a damn for the social register and he hated drunken drivers. Crestone had been the same way too, and now he was working for a year as a dispatcher.

It was Old McGlone who spoke the next time. "We'll be going up the hill now to 60 Parkway."

No lucky breaks tonight, Crestone thought. Tomorrow he would think of a dozen things he could have done, and every man out there in the cars would do the same. That was tomorrow. The gun was behind him now. She could reach him when he swung, and she could not miss if she shot.

There was a drawer in the desk full of stories of tough private-eyes who took bushels of guns away from dames clad in almost nothing, and then slapped them all over the joint or made love to them. Joe Crestone sighed. His head was aching brutally. He did not feel like taking any guns away from any dames.

Car 750 came back into service. Moore and Windoff had drunk their coffee.

Then 752 went out of service temporarily at the Sunset Drive Inn. Crestone knew how Purcell was feeling now, the to-hell-with-it attitude. Old McGlone would be telling him, "There's some things, Dewey boy, that you've got to learn about being a cop." Old McGlone knew them all.

Car 751 signalled arrival at River and Pitt. A few minutes later Kurowski said, "10-98." *Assignment completed.* There was no use to elaborate on nothing.

Judith Barrows said, "Send 751 to the Silver Moon on Oldtown Pike to look for a '49 green Ford sedan with front-end damage."

Crestone obeyed. He studied the map. She wanted 751 north and east all the time. Then where in the southern or southeastern part of Midway was any heavy money? There was a brawl at the Riverview country club tonight, maybe a few thousand loose in pockets and a handful of jewelry, but—

The phone at Crestone's elbow and the extension on the desk near the big filing cabinet spilled sound all over the room.

"Don't touch it until I say so!" the woman said.

She went around the counter and backed into the chair at the other desk. She crossed her legs and steadied the .38 on her knee. She raised the phone and nodded.

"Police station, radio dispatcher," Crestone said.

"Ten cents, please," the operator said.

Crestone heard the pay phone clear. A man asked, "You got a report on State 312?"

"Just a minute." Crestone had never heard of 312.

"Just tell him it's all clear, Buster." Judith Barrows was holding the mouthpiece against her thigh.

"All clear." Crestone held on to hear a jukebox, the clatter of a cafe—anything to help position the call. The man hung up. A booth, Crestone thought. He put his phone down, staring at the woman's legs. They were beautiful. He did not give a damn. She got up carefully, standing for a moment in a hip-out-of-joint posture. A model, he thought. It was in her walk too when she went around the counter again.

So they knew this end of it was set now. Where was the other end? Somewhere in the southern part of the district covered in normal patrol by Car 751. Anybody could read the red outlines on the map. It struck him then: the Wampum Club. Big business, cold and sure, with a fine patina of politeness, free drinks, free buffet and other incidentals for the regular suckers. The green-and-crackly on the line at Sonny Belmont's Wampum Club. Let the cops take Jimmy Britton home and tuck him in, but Belmont never took his check, drunk or otherwise.

The job would take at least four fast, tough men. Making Sonny's boys hold still for a deal like that was not for amateurs. There was a lot of dough around the Wampum; the income tax lads had been wondering how much for a long time.

So I think I've got it doped, and what good does it do? Belmont could stand the jolt. Why should men like Corky Gunselman and Sam Kurowski risk catching lead to protect money in a joint like the Wampum?

That was not the answer and Crestone knew it.

He looked at the last two stolen cars on the list. A '52 blue Mercury and a '53 green Hornet. That Hudson would go like hell and the Mercury was not so slow either. Both cars stolen around midnight in Bristol. He wondered which one was outside right now. He could be way off, but he had to figure he was right.

Since the Hornet and the Merc were already aired as hot, they would probably be used only to make the run to another car stashed close. East was the natural route. Old State 7 was narrow and twisting, but the farmers who used it would all be sleeping now. Say a half hour to reach the web of highways around Steel City, and then road blocks would be no more than something to annoy whiz kids on their way home with the old man's crate. She had asked about State 7.

Car 751 came in. Kurowski said, "Nothing at the Silver Moon with front-end damage. What's the dope on it?"

"Code 4," Judith Barrows said. "The Ford was last seen going north on Pennsylvania at Third Avenue."

Code 4, *hit and run.* Crestone obeyed the .38.

Kurowski said, "10-4. We'll swing up that way."

She was keeping 751 north, sure enough. The phone exploded. Judith Barrows went around the counter again to the extension. She nodded.

From the background of a noisy party a man said, "Somebody swiped my car." A woman shouted. "Tell 'em it's even paid for!"

Crestone wrote down the information. A '52 cream Cadillac sedan, R607, taken sometime between 12:30 A.M. and 1:30 A.M. "It was right in the damned driveway," the owner complained. "We're having a little party here and—"

"Keys in it?" Crestone asked.

"Sure! It was in my own driveway."

"We'll get on it right away." Crestone hung up.

The woman said, "You won't put *that* one out, Buster."

So he was guessing right. They had a cream Cad waiting. If they planned to use State 7, the quick run for the crew at the Wampum was up the county road past the country club and then on out Canal to where it intersected across the river with State 7 near the old brick plant. Barrows could shoot straight north on Meredith to Glencoe, turn east—Why hell, she would strike State 7 just a hundred yards from the old brick works. The Cad was waiting out there now!

She was behind him once more. As if she had read his thoughts she asked, "What's in your little round head now, Buster?"

"I'm wishing you'd beat it."

She laughed but there were little knots of tension in the sound. The deal must be on at the Wampum now. Before she left she would have to level him. She would swing lower and harder then. The thought made Crestone's headache worse. He hoped she knew the bones on the side of a man's skull couldn't take it like the thick sloping top. She might stretch him so he never got up. He could smell his own sweat.

Before the clincher came he would have to run a test on her. The next time she was in the chair.

One of the side doors made a whushing sound and then a voice boomed across the lobby. "Hey there, Bill, how's the peace and dignity of the community?" It was old Fritz Hood on his way home from the power company's sub station. He always stopped to bellow at Bill Walters.

"Hello, Fritz!"

"You, Joey! Where's Bill tonight?"

"Sick."

"The old bastard! I'll go see him before he dies." The door rocked back to center. Hood was gone.

Judith Barrows was in the chair, with her jacket across her lap and the code sheets on the desk. Crestone rose slowly. The fur jacket slid away and showed the .38. Something dropped out of one of the jacket sleeves. He made another step. She tilted the muzzle, resting the edge of her hand on her knee. She cocked the gun then. Her face was white.

Crestone tried to talk himself into it; but he knew she was too scared. An excited or scared dame with a gun. Murder. He backed up and sat down. His head was pounding. On the floor at her feet lay a piece of doubled wire, the raw ends covered with white tape.

The phone sang like a rattlesnake. The woman made a nervous stab at it before she gained control and nodded at Crestone. Mrs. John Slenko, 3648 Locust, had just seen a man in her back yard. She wanted the police.

Judith Barrows' vigilance wavered while she was fumbling her phone back into the cradle. Crestone used his phone to push the *Gain* dial of the radio down to *One* while he was putting the instrument away. He dispatched 750 to Mrs. Slenko's home.

The big dame was in a knot now and Crestone was coming out of it. She had grabbed at the phone because she was expecting a call to tell her that the job at the Wampum was done. She was staying in the chair to be near the phone.

When York and Shannon began to talk about a revoked driver's license, the sounds came faintly.

"What did you do to the radio!"

"Nothing."

The .38 was on his stomach. "What did you do?"

"Nothing, damn it! We get a split-phase power lag on the standby tower every night." He hoped she knew as little of radio as he did. "The reception fades, that's all."

"You're lying! You did something, didn't you?"

"No! You've been watching me every second."

"You're going to get it, Crestone, if anything goes wrong." She was wound-up but the gun was easy.

Car 752 came in, so faint that only "seven-fift'" was audible, but Crestone knew Purcell's voice and he could guess the message. Purcell had sulked in the Sunset Drive Inn, dwelling on the inequalities of traffic code enforcement, but now he and Old McGlone were on their way again.

The woman's voice was a whip crack. "What was it?"

"I'll have to get it on the other mike."

"What other mike?"

Crestone kept his finger close to his chest when he pointed. "On a hook around at the side of the radio."

The faint call came again.

"All right," Judith Barrows said.

There was dust on the curled lead of the hand mike. Crestone said, "Car 750, I read you 10-1. The standby trouble again, as usual." 10-1 meant: *receiving poorly.* From the corner of his eye he saw the woman grab the code sheet to check on him.

Car 750, which had not called, now tried to answer at the same time 752 came in. Crestone said, "Standby, 751. 10-6." *Busy.* Now he had them all confused. He called for a repeat from Car 750 to make it more confused. During the instant Judith Barrows was checking the code number he had used, he turned transmitting power to almost nothing.

Faint murmurs came from the radio as the three local cars asked questions Crestone could not hear. The woman did not like her loss of contact. She got out of her chair. "Where's 751?" she demanded.

Into a dead mike Crestone asked the location of the car. He pretended to hear the answer from the receiver against his ear. "He's trailing a green Ford toward the Wampum Club."

"Get him away from there!" She was panicked for a moment and then she got hold of herself. She grabbed the local code sheet. "Code 9 him to the Silver Moon."

Code 9 was a disturbance. Crestone went through the pretense of calling 751. There was still enough flow of power to light the purple eye.

"Tell him to disregard the Ford," she ordered.

"10-22 previous assignment, 751. Code 9 at the Silver Moon."

When the next small scratch of sound came from the speaker, he said, "Midway, Car 55. Go ahead." He began to write as if he were taking a message: *'52 cream Cadillac sedan, R607, State 7 near old brick plant. Driver resisted arrest.*

She came out of her chair. "What's the message?"

"Car 55 just picked up a guy in a stolen car near the brick works."

It struck her like death. "Give me that paper!"

He tossed it toward her. She raked it in with her heel, and picked it up without taking her eyes off him. She read it at a glance and cursed.

The phone rang. She had it without making her signal to Crestone. He lifted his receiver. A tense voice said, "All set here."

"No!" she cried. "The state patrol just got Brownie and the car!"

"You sure?"

"It just came in on the radio."

"The other way then. You're on your own, kid, till you know where." The man hung up.

Crestone said into the hand mike, "10-4, Car 750." He swung to face the woman when she went around the counter. "Car 750 is four blocks away, coming in."

She raised the gun. "They're coming in," he said. A man might have done it. She broke. It was her own safety now. Her heels made quick taps on the steel steps, a hard scurrying on the lobby tiles.

Crestone loaded the shotgun as he ran. The blue Mercury was at the first meter south of the police parking zone. She spun her wheels on the gutter ice and then the sedan lurched into the street. He put the muzzle on the right front window. Her face was a white blur turned toward him. He could not do it. He shot, instead, at the right rear tire and heard the shot rattle on the bumper.

He raced back to the radio and put the dials where they belonged. He poured it out then in crisp code. All cars, all stations. First, a '53 green Hudson sedan, K2066, possibly four men in car. Left Wampum Club, Midway, two minutes ago. Armed robbery. Dangerous. Second, a '52 blue Mercury sedan, K3109, last seen going north on Meredith one minute ago, possibly shotgun marks on right rear fender.

The phone blasted. "This is Sonny Belmont, Bill. We've had some trouble down here. Four men in a late Hudson tudor, a light color. They cut toward town on Market. The license was a K2—something."

"K2066, a green '53 Hornet, Belmont."

"Who is this?"

"Crestone. What'd they look like?"

Belmont's descriptions were sharp. "I slipped, Joey. They nailed me opening the safe."

"How much?"

"About eighty grand." Belmont said the amount reluctantly. It would be in the papers and he knew it. "How'd you boys get hot so quick, Joey?"

"Luck." Crestone hung up. Car 750 reported that a speeding Hornet sedan had outrun the cruiser and was headed north on 315. Crestone sent that information to all cars north of Midway.

Car 752 came in. "We're on the blue Mercury with the woman," Purcell said. "She's got a flat rear tire."

"She's got a .38 too," Crestone said.

Three minutes later Purcell called from Glencoe and Pitt. "We got her. Car 751 is here with us."

Crestone dispatched Car 751 to the old brick works with the dope on a cream Cadillac sedan. Car 55 came in from Highway 315. "The green Hudson got past me, Midway. I'm turning now to go north. Tell Shannon."

The Shannon dispatcher said, "10-4 on that message, Midway." A moment later he was talking to a sheriff, and then state patrol 54 came in.

When the channels were clear again Crestone called Steel City to cover State 7 from the east, just in case. He called the police chief and the sheriff by telephone. The chief said he would be down at once. Crestone was still talking to the sheriff when Car 751 reported. "We got the cream Cadillac sedan at the brick plant," Kurowski said. "The guy scrammed into the weeds and took the keys with him."

The message went into the mouthpiece of the telephone. The sheriff said, "I'll be down there with a couple of boys in ten minutes." Crestone hung the phone up. He told Car 751 to stand by at the brick works.

Everything was set now. There would be a tough road block at the Y on State 20 and Highway 315. If the Hudson got around that, there would be trouble on ahead, piling up higher as more cars converged.

Crestone lit a cigarette. The phone rang. A man asked, "You got my car yet?"

"What car?"

"My Cadillac! My God, man! I just called you."

"The only stolen car in the world," Crestone said. "Yeah, we got it. You can pick it up at the police garage in the morning. Bring your registration and title and five bucks for towing charges."

"Towing! Is it hurt?"

"No keys."

"Oh," the man said. The party was still going on around him. "Look, officer, I've got an extra set of keys. If you'll send a car around—"

"Get it here in the morning."

"Okay then." The man hung up. Crestone decided that his skull was breaking. He punched his cigarette out and tried to swallow the bad taste it had left in his mouth.

They brought her in, Purcell and Old McGlone. The tension was gone from her now; she looked beaten down and helpless.

"Cute kid." Purcell held up the .38. "She put a couple of spots on 752 by way of greeting us. Is the chief on his way?"

Crestone nodded. The woman looked at him and said, "I'm sorry I kept hitting you."

"Yeah."

"She was here?" Purcell asked. "She slugged you?"

"She did."

Old McGlone needed a shave as usual. He was staring at Judith Barrows. All at once he asked, "When did you leave Pulaski Avenue, Zelda Tuwin?"

Her eyes jerked up to Old McGlone's face. "Five years ago. It was raining."

"I remember you. You were a chubby kid, Zelda. You—"

"I was a big fat slob!"

"You been a dress model?" Crestone asked.

"Yeah! Big stuff! I got tired of parading in front of bitches and their men. I couldn't eat what I wanted to. I had to walk like I was made of glass. I got tired of it."

Old McGlone nodded. "Sure, sure. So you wanted to have the money like them you pranced in front of. You were doubtless making plenty yourself—for a kid from the Polish section of Midway. You'd have been better off staying on Pulaski and marrying a good boy from the mill, Zelda Tuwin."

Old McGlone looked sad and wistful. He never did want to believe the things he had been seeing for twenty-five years. He was tough but not hard. He understood and he deplored but he never could condemn. Zelda Tuwin watched him for several moments and seemed to recognize those things about him.

And then she stared at the floor.

The chief tramped in. Crestone gave him the story. The chief nodded, watching Zelda Tuwin. He tilted his head toward his office and clumped down the steps. Old McGlone and Purcell took her out, Purcell walking ahead. Old McGlone said, "Watch them steel steps there, Zelda."

After a while the sheriff's car came in. He had Brownie, who had tried to jump a canal and nearly drowned. Car 54 was on the air a moment later.

"We got the Hornet, Midway. Four men. What's the authority?"

"Midway PD. Bring 'em back, and everything they have with them."

"They got it too. Cars 55 and 86 are coming in with me."

Crestone sent out a cancellation on the two stolen cars. He could hear the chief talking to Zelda Tuwin downstairs. He knew how Old McGlone felt about some things there seemed to be no help for. It was 3:41 A.M.

Joe Crestone had a hell of a headache.

CONNECTICUT

THE OLD BARN ON THE POND
by Ursula Curtiss

HE CAME BACK on a raw, darkly glistening day in March, but it was not at all the triumphant return he had planned. It was a hasty, off-balance thing, like being pushed rudely onto a stage before the raised trumpets had blown a single note.

Conlon's letter—the letter that had brought him tumbling up from New York to this inhospitable part of the New England countryside—was still in his pocket. He had never liked Conlon, but the architect was Marian's cousin and it would have looked odd, when he had the old barn remodeled, to have given the job to someone else. And now here was Conlon writing ". . . have been approached by friends about the possibility of renting your property here for the summer, with an option to buy. As they have a young child, they would like to drain the pond, and although I told them I was certain you would not permit this—"

For a moment the typed lines had blurred before Howard Hildreth's eyes—except for that one staring phrase.

Drain the pond.

"Not yet," he thought lucidly—"not after only six months." Anonymous in the Forty-second Street Library, he had read up on the subject, and learned that under certain conditions—depth of water, amount of rainfall, and other climatic factors—this kind of soil might have sucked its secret under at the end of a year, provided there was no extensive digging.

But not yet. He had sat down at once to write a brief note of refusal, but another phrase struck up at him from Conlon's letter. ". . . I was certain you would not permit this—"

A deliberate challenge? Bill Conlon was Marian's cousin, remember, and had been away at the time. Better go up there, stay a week or two, establish the impression of keeping the place as a country retreat upon which he might descend at any time. It was only necessary for Conlon; the townspeople, he was sure, accepted his remodeling of the barn as proof of his faith that his missing wife would some day return.

58

At that thought, alone in his comfortable apartment, Howard Hildreth shuddered. . . .

On the station platform there were gratifying little whispers and stirs of recognition—"Isn't that Howard Hildreth, the playwright? I'm sure it is"—and a turning of heads which he pretended not to see. He could hardly pretend not to see Conlon, striding across the platform toward him with his fair head a little cocked. Conlon had Marian's eyes, light gray with a peculiar curl of lid; but that was the only physical resemblance between them.

Hildreth put out a hand and said with an air of geniality, "Well, this is kind. I hope you haven't been meeting trains all day?"

Conlon sent one of his roving glances around the platform. "Matter of fact, a fellow in our office was supposed to catch this one but he seems to have missed it. Come on, I'll give you a lift."

After his first annoyance at Conlon's balloon-pricking, Hildreth was pleased; this would give him a chance to demonstrate his calm. He said as they got into the car, "I can see how you thought I wouldn't be using the place this summer. I'd have been in touch with you sooner about coming up but we've had a little trouble in the cast."

He waited for Conlon to show interest, but the other man only said, "Too bad. Play still going well?"

"Very, thanks."

"I particularly liked"—Conlon turned a sharp corner with care—"the third act. It packs quite a wallop. Are you working on a new play?"

"I am, as a matter of fact, and I thought a little peace and quiet . . . You know New York," said Hildreth resignedly. In his tone were autograph hunters, sheaves of fan mail, a telephone carrying an invitation with each ring.

And part of it was true. *The Far Cry* was that rarest of things, a hit first play, and the playbill's revelation that it had been eight years in the writing had given an additional fillip. Eight years—what constancy! No wonder that superb third act expertly shivered like a diamond. Here was no glib young creature with a gift for bubbling out dialogue but a major talent who cut his work like a precious stone.

So the critics said, and the important hostesses, and Howard Hildreth, who had been laughed at in this little town, and had his credit refused and his electric light turned off, found his champagne all the winier and forgot those few hours of frantic typing. . . .

". . . not a word," Conlon was saying, and Hildreth wrenched his attention from his play, his other self. They were out of the town now, rising into little hills and woodland, puddled and glinted yellowly by a sky which, having rained earlier, was now gloating over it.

Hildreth's mind spun back and recaptured the sense of his companion's words. He said, "Nor I. But I refuse to believe . . . you knew Marian—"

"I think she's dead," said Conlon bluntly without turning his head. "I think she was dead all the time the police were out looking for her."

"But . . . where—?" said Hildreth in a shocked voice.

Conlon waved a hand at the dimming landscape. "There's almost as much water as there is land around here," he said. "Lake, marshes, even quicksand. She had such a horror of things eaten up in the water, remember?"

"Stop!" said Hildreth with genuine violence. "You mustn't talk about her as though— Besides, Marian was happy, she would never have—"

"Committed suicide, or disappeared on purpose?" said Conlon when it was apparent that Hildreth was not going to finish. "Oh, I never thought she had. As you say, I knew Marian . . . here we are."

The car had descended a gentle twisting curve. At the bottom, opposite a stand of birches and set perhaps a hundred feet in from the road, was the pond, as round and clear as a wondering eye, lashed by willows that looked lamplit in the approaching dusk.

On the far side of it, on a slight rise, stood the creamy new structure, the remodeled barn, which six months ago had been weather-beaten planks and a wobbly brown-painted door. There was no breath of wind; the house and reflection met themselves in a mirror stillness.

Howard Hildreth gazed, and his heart raced with such horror that he wondered if he was about to have a stroke. He wrenched at his horn-rimmed glasses with a trembling hand, and heard Conlon say curiously, "Are you all right, Howard?"

"Yes. These damned glasses—the doctor warned me that I needed new ones." Even the effort of speaking calmly seemed to put a nutcracker pressure on his heart. "You've done a beautiful job of remodeling the barn, Bill. The photographs you sent didn't do it justice. Shall we go on in?"

The drive up to the house itself was screened by willows. By the time Conlon had helped him inside with his bags, Hildreth was able to say almost normally, "Well, here we are. You'll have a drink, won't you?"

Conlon shook his head. He said with a hand on the doorknob, "Sarah—Sarah Wilde, you know—ordered a few essentials for the kitchen, so you ought to get through the night without starving. Well—"

Hildreth did not press him to stay. He said, standing in the open doorway, "These friends of yours that I had to disappoint—do I know them? What's their name?"

"Pocock," said Conlon promptly, and it was so unlikely a name that Hildreth had to believe him. Or was it meant to be a shortened version of poppycock?

He did not even look around at the long studio that took up most of the lower front of the house. He waited tensely for the final retreat of Conlon's motor, and when even the echoes were gone he opened the door and walked the length of the driveway in the lonely frog-sounding dusk.

And there was light enough—just enough—to show him the same sickening apparition. On the far side of the pond stood the new barn, radiantly pale, bearing no resemblance to its former weather-beaten brown. But at his feet, glassily etched on the surface of the water, lay the old barn, with its knotholes and weather stains and the wide brown-painted door.

Hildreth drew a long uneven breath. There was no one to see him step squash-
ily to the reed-grown edge of the pond and dip a hand in the icy water. The old
barn quaked under the willows, and shook and was presently still again—but it
was still the old barn. . . .

He did not drink—Marian had—but he took a tranquilizer and headed for his
reviews like a child to its mother's skirts. The *Times, Tribune, Daily News*, the
out-of-town papers. "Last night at the Odeon Theatre this critic was refreshingly
jolted. . . ."
    "*The Far Cry* is just that in a season so far noted for its weary offerings. . . ."
"Let us hope we do not have to wait another eight years for the next Hildreth
play. . . ."
    And presently he knew what had happened to him out there at the pond's edge.
Autosuggestion, hallucination—at any rate, there was an accepted term for it; if
beauty lay in the beholder's eye, so did other things. He knew what was under
that pleasant and pastoral surface, and at the subconscious tension of his mind,
because Conlon had been with him, his retina had produced the appropriate
setting.
    But not for Conlon, with all his suspicions—and in retrospect, the man had
exuded suspicion. Conlon had looked at the pond and seen nothing amiss; for
him, the still water had reflected only his personal creation of shored-up beams
and plaster and creamy paint and whatever else went into his remodeling of an
old structure. The thought gave Hildreth a satisfaction that, keyed up as he was,
bordered on triumph.
    What a joke on them all, he mused as he broiled the steak Sarah Wilde had left
in the refrigerator, if only he, Hildreth, could see this watery witness, gaze at it in
their presence, say casually, "Lovely day, isn't it?"—and stand there calmly and
casually in the midst of their blindness.
    Not that the reflection would be on the pond in the morning. Tonight it had
simply been a product of nerves and fatigue, and a good night's sleep would
erase it. Still, he was shaken, and he prudently avoided his after-dinner coffee.
He darkened the downstairs, flipped on the staircase switch, and went up to his
bedroom.
    And came face to face with a portrait of Marian which he never knew had been
taken.
    As the blood came and went from his heart more slowly, he realized that the
matted and mounted photograph on the bureau was not a portrait but an enlarged
snapshot; on closer inspection it bore a telltale grain and blurriness. It was in
color and it showed Marian laughing. There was a halo of sunlight on the close
curls that scrambled over her beautifully shaped head, and the same light picked
out the comma of mirth beside her mouth although her short, soft, full white
throat was in shadow.
    Marian laughing . . .
    . . . laughing at his play, which she was not supposed to have seen at all until

he had written the final word—*Curtain*. Managing to say through the laughter, "My dear playwright, you don't mean to say you've been muddling around with this thing for eight years and missed the whole *point?* It ought to be satire at the end, don't you see, and you fox the audience in the third act instead of this heavy Russian gloom going on and on? It would have such a wonderful, final crack-the-whip effect, and you could get rid of Anna coming in and saying"—she draggled at her hair, which was much too short and curly for draggling—"whatever that long lugubrious speech is."

Her face was brilliant with excited laughter. "Oh, *wait* till I tell Bill and Sarah we've found a way to finish the Odyssey at last! They'll be so—Howard, for heaven's sake, I'm only—*Howar*—"

For such a full throat, it was as soft and weak as a child's. . . .

In the morning Hildreth looked at the pond, and the old weather-beaten barn was still there, shaken and distorted under a gently falling rain. Disturbingly, he was not terrified or shocked or even very surprised; it was as though, at some point during his sleep, his brain had accepted this phenomenon as readily as the pond had accepted Marian.

After breakfast he made arrangements for renting a car, and then he called Sarah Wilde.

It was through Sarah, who also had an apartment in the building on East Tenth Street, that he had met Marian Guest. Sarah and Marian were copywriters in the same advertising agency, and although Hildreth had a sober loathing of advertising copy and all the people who wrote it—there was a flippancy about them that appalled him—Sarah was well connected. An aunt of hers was a best-selling novelist, and it had never harmed any hopeful playwright to have even a hearsay acquaintance with a publisher. He had cultivated Sarah in the elevator, lent her an umbrella one day, and ultimately wound up at a party in her apartment.

And there was Marian, sitting on the floor although there were chairs available. She wore black slacks and an expensive-looking white silk shirt with a safety pin where a button should have been, and, profile tilted in the lamplight, she was explaining with zest how she had come by her black eye and scraped cheekbone. She had been walking her dog George and had fallen over a sheep on a leash. "The man said it was a Bedlington but he was obviously trying to cover up his own confusion. Poor George bit him, not the man, and I think he's got a hair ball."

Although there were two or three other girls present, all with a just-unboxed Madison Avenue attractiveness, the attention seemed to cluster about Marian. She said presently to Howard Hildreth in her boyish and uninhibited voice, "You look terribly broody. What are you hatching?"

"A play," he told her distantly, and it might have been the very distance that attracted her, as it was the attention focused on her that attracted him. At any rate, he ended up taking her home to her apartment on Barrow Street, drinking innumerable cups of black coffee, and telling her about his play. He began challengingly, prepared for amusement when she learned that he had already been working on it for three years; but she listened, her light clear eyes as wide and sober as a child's.

She said, "What do you do—for an income, I mean?"

When he said flatly, "I'm a shoe clerk," she stared past him with a kind of wondering sadness.

"How marvelous," she had said, "to give that much of a damn about anything."

There was Marian, summed up in a single sentence; even after they were married she never told him anything as self-revelatory as that. And under the influence of her respect for his dedication, his work, which had always been his Work to him, was able to come out in the open with its capital letter. Until she had defected—

But Hildreth had learned to discipline his mind, and he did it now.

He said into the telephone, "Sarah? I'm an ingrate for not calling you last night to tell you how much I like the way you've done the place—as well as providing my dinner—but. . . ."

Sarah Wilde cut him off easily. "Do you like it? I'm glad. It's rather a lot of lavender, but you did specify—"

"Yes," Hildreth gazed, secretly entertained, at the lavender draperies, the lavender cushions, round and square and triangular, piled on the black tweed couch. Lavender—Marian's favorite color. Any doubters close to Marian could not help saying to themselves, "Well, if he can live with that. . . ."

"It's very soothing," he said to Sarah with the defensive air of a husband standing up for his wife's vagaries. "Very restful. I like the picture on my bureau, by the way."

It was as though the telephone cord had been pulled taut between them. "It is a good one, isn't it? I took it—oh, some time last summer, I think, and I'd forgotten all about it until Bill Conlon happened to see it and thought you'd like an enlargement."

"It was very thoughtful of you both," said Hildreth with perfect evenness. "That's the way I think of her, you know. Laughing. I suppose Bill's told you that I haven't given up hope."

"Of course you haven't," said Sarah, bright and artificial.

Between them, in the small silence that followed, lay the many trips that he and Conlon had taken to view unidentified female bodies which corresponded even roughly with Marian's age and height. It was grim work, which helped; he was always a thoroughly pale and shaken man. And with each fruitless trip, because of the very nature of such an errand, the official belief that Marian Hildreth was dead had grown. Hildreth could tell that Sarah believed it too—in which, of course, she was quite right.

She was veering quickly away from the subject now, saying something about dinner this week. Hildreth accepted for Thursday evening, adding with a deprecating little laugh that he trusted it wouldn't be an Occasion; he'd come up here to get started on his new play.

"No, just two or three people," Sarah assured him. "I did tell you, didn't I, how much I liked *The Far Cry*? I thought I knew what was coming in the third act, but it was one time I loved being made a fool of."

Hildreth thanked her, a trifle aloofly, and there was not the smallest alarm along his nerves. He suspected that Sarah and Conlon, mere acquaintances six months ago, would be married before the year was out, but the fact that they had undoubtedly seen the play together didn't matter. They could not say, "That last act sounds like Marian," because as far as they knew Marian had never laid eyes on the script—she had said wryly, in fact, two or three days before that last night, "Howard thinks I'll mark his baby, like a gypsy. . . ."

(What a very tellable joke it would have been, what an irresistible nugget for gossip columns, because Marian's was not a secret-keeping nature: that Howard Hildreth had toiled unremittingly over his play for eight years, and in the space of a single hour his wife, who had never written anything but tongue-in-cheek praise of vinyl tile and slide fasteners, had offhandedly supplied the satirical twist that made it a success.)

Even at the thought Hildreth felt a qualm of nausea. Although his portable typewriter stood ready on the desk at the far end of the studio, with a fresh ream of yellow paper beside it, he let himself out the front door into the falling rain and walked to the pond's edge. There was the old barn, shaking dimly under the falling drops, and he knew that in some terrible way he was drawing strength from this private vision, locked under the willows for his eyes, and apparently for his alone. . . .

A notion of incipient madness slid across his mind, but he looked quickly about him and everything else was sane and clear. If Marian thought to retaliate after death. . . .

He drew himself up sharply.

In the afternoon he was gracious to the editor of the local newspaper, with the result that his favorite publicity picture appeared in the next morning's issue. He was holding his horn-rimmed glasses with one earpiece casually collapsed, and the three-quarter turn of his head almost concealed the double chin developed since those lean days.

". . . seeking inspiration for his new play," said the account below, proudly, and, "Residents will recall the still-unresolved disappearance of Mrs. Marian Hildreth six months ago. Mrs. Hildreth, 38, told her husband late on the evening of October 4, 1963, that she was going out for a walk. She did not return, and no trace of her has since been found. Mr. Hildreth maintains his staunch belief that his wife is still alive, possibly suffering from a loss of memory. . . ."

Hildreth read with calm pleasure the rest of the telling—how the pond on the property had been dragged without result. The police had indeed dragged it over his demurs—"Oh, come now, she wouldn't fall into a pond she's lived beside for five years"—and then came the heavily tactful, "Mr. Hildreth, your wife wasn't—er . . . ?"

Because Marian's more madcap exploits were not unknown to the local police. They viewed her with a tolerant and even an indulgent eye—that was the effect she had on people; but under the circumstances they could not rule out a tragic and alcoholic whim.

"No," Hildreth had said with transparent stoutness. "Oh, she may have had a highball or two after dinner. . . ."

He knew, he had known at the moment of her death, that the marital partner was usually Suspect Number One. But that had not actually held true in little Ixton, Connecticut. If there had been any whisper of discord, any suggestion of dalliance by either party, any prospect of inheriting money—or even if Marian's life had been insured—the police might have looked deeper than they did. As it was, they walked past the burlaped yew, the burlaped roses, Marian's burlaped body, and then announced that they would drag the pond.

This procedure netted them two ancient inner tubes, a rotted and hinged object which had once been the hood of a convertible, and a rust-fretted oil drum which seemed to have spawned a great many beer cans. If the police had returned at just after dark, when one particular piece of burlap among the yews had been lifted free of its stiffened secret, and the secret transferred to the now officially blameless water . . . but, predictably, they had not.

They could have no further reason for dragging the pond now—indeed, thought Hildreth, they would need a warrant. And for a warrant they would need evidence.

That was the safety element in a spur-of-the-moment murder. The cleverest planners—Hildreth rejected the word *killers*—had come to grief over elaborate timetables, unsuspected correspondence, a hint of fear dropped somewhere. There could be none of that in this case. Neither he nor Marian had known what was coming until that moment of her crowing laughter, that intolerable tearing-down of the secrecy and seriousness of his Work.

It was not so much that Marian had burst the bonds of curiosity and somehow contrived to unlock the desk drawer which housed his script, nor even that she had slipped at least temporarily into the ranks of the people who found him clownishly amusing. It was that she was right. Like someone engaged on a pains-taking tapestry, he had been following stitch after stitch and lost sight of the pattern, which had leaped at once to Marian's unbothered and mischievous eye.

It was as if . . . he could not say at the time, because his logic had smoked away like cellophane in a flame. Later, more calmly, he could compare himself to a woman who, after a long and difficult labor, watches the doctor merrily bearing the infant off to his own home.

But there was no evidence, and he would not be tricked or trapped. His visit here—the first since the five weeks or so after he had reported Marian missing—would proclaim his innocence. Not to the police—he wasn't worried about them—but to Bill Conlon and Sarah Wilde, the only people who, close to Marian, might just possibly. . . .

Hildreth arranged yellow paper beside his uncovered typewriter in the white-walled lavender-and-black studio, but he did not, that morning or the next or the one after that, commence even the roughest work on a new play.

He told himself defensively that he had spent several months under considerable strain; a man didn't bounce back from that right away. And critical success was paralyzing in itself: there was the inevitable restudying of the first work in search of the magic ingredient, and the equally inevitable fear of comparison with a second.

At no time did he allow it to cross his mind that there were one-play playwrights as there were one-book novelists, and that his one play would still be in various stages of rewriting except for Marian's unruly wit. But there was a moment when, seated blankly at the typewriter, he thought, *Do I look like the pond?* and got up and crossed the room to examine himself in a mirror.

But no; he hadn't changed at all in spite of his damp little tremor of fright. And if he could see the truth on the pond's surface, surely he could see it on his own? There was the gained weight, granted, but his dark eyes gave back their old serious look, his eyebrows were forbiddingly level, a lock of hair—now pampered by his New York barber—still hung with dedication.

But when he stared long enough and hard enough, moving his face to within an inch or two of the mirror, tiny little Howard Hildreths peeked out of the pupils, and behind them—

Ah, behind *them*. . . .

He developed a kind of triumphant passion for the pond. He watched it ballooned with clouds, or covered with nervous little wrinkles under a sudden wind. He saw the weather-beaten planks and the brown door warp and fly to pieces under the miniature tidal waves caused by water bugs or perhaps frogs. Pretending to enjoy a cigarette in the course of a stroll, he took note of the passing cars that slowed for an admiring view of the clean creamy little house behind the willowed pond, and no car jerked to a shocked halt, no one screamed.

Hildreth had a Polaroid camera, and one afternoon, in a fascinated test, he took a picture of the pond. Conlon's photographs had shown no abnormality, but this time it was he who was pressing the shutter. The day warranted color film— the willows dripped and candled about the round eye of water, enameled so perfectly that it might have been a brooch.

Wouldn't it be odd, thought Hildreth, counting excitedly to sixty, if only the camera and I—?

He was peeling the paper shield away when Sarah Wilde's voice said at his shoulder, "Oh, may I see?"

The print and its fluttering attachment dropped to the ground.

Hildreth got only a swinging glimpse of Sarah's slanted white cheek, caught only the beginning of the rueful, "I'm sorry, I didn't mean—" before he bent, barely circumventing her; if necessary he would have put his shoe on the print.

As it was, he snatched it up and turned away, manufacturing a cough, while he finished stripping the shield. He said a second later, turning back, "Not bad, is it?" and handed the innocent color print to Sarah. No, not the camera and himself—only himself.

Sarah, he thought watchfully, was a remarkably beautiful young woman. Her dropped lashes were a thick unretouched silver-brown, her polished hair a slightly deeper brown; her gaze, when she lifted it, would be gray. With the suave red lipstick to counterpoint the water-color effect, she was quietly startling in any gathering.

"Very good indeed," she said, handing the print back by its edges. "The pond's so pretty, isn't it? Especially now."

She glanced at the circle of water and then back at Hildreth, who following her gaze had still seen the placidly mirrored old barn. A tremble of nerves ran along his throat. To control a wild impulse toward laughter he said in a considering, landownerish way, "It seems quite full, but you've had heavy rains this month, haven't you?" and he slid the print casually into his coat pocket.

"Yes, it is full," said Sarah in his own considering tone, and there was no doubt about it; the eyes that moved from the pond to his face held some kind of— doubt? Challenge? Hildreth said coolly, "Well, if you'll excuse me, it's back to the typewriter," and he took a step away.

"Wait, I almost forgot what I came for." Sarah was dipping into her calf handbag. "Here—the mailman put this in my box instead of yours. Wonderful to get fan mail. Don't forget about dinner tonight—cocktails at six thirty."

It wasn't fan mail which Hildreth opened when the red Volkswagen had disappeared over the hill, but one of the many letters which, the police had told him, always arrived in the wake of a disappearance. This one was from "Someone Who Can Help," and in exchange for two hundred dollars mailed to an enclosed box number in Vermont the writer would put him in touch with his missing wife.

The maddening part of these communications was that they could not be ignored—at least, not by a man in whom hope supposedly sprang eternal. Hildreth, sitting down to write the form reply that thanked the writer and said he was turning the letter over to the officers in charge of the investigation, thought angrily that there ought to be a law.

The afternoon passed slowly. Conlon telephoned to say that there would be a plumber coming over to do something to the downstairs bath, and Hildreth said pettishly, "Really, Bill, forgive me, but I thought all that had been taken care of. One doesn't greet plumbers in the middle of Scene One, you know."

He was mollified a little later by a delegation from the local high-school magazine, asking humbly for a "Best Wishes from Howard Hildreth" to be photostated for the graduation issue. One of the shiny-haired, wide-eyed girls ventured close to his typewriter, in which Hildreth foresightedly kept a typed yellow sheet—the opening scene of The Far Cry—and he said at once, austerely, "Please don't—I have a 'thing' about work in progress."

It only added to their awe. But he had had it, thought Hildreth, presently seeing them to the door; he had had all the local adulation he wanted. Imperiously buying delicacies at the only market that carried them, he had seen the fawning face of the manager who only a year ago had told him that if his bill wasn't settled promptly he would find himself in the small-claims court.

He had been pointed out respectfully on the main street, and had declined invitations from the town's reigning hostess. More importantly, he had been accepted everywhere without a trace of suspicion; if there was any sentiment in the air, it was one of embarrassed pity for a man who so courageously continued to hope.

In a day or two he could go back to New York, having established to Bill Conlon and Sarah Wilde and everybody else that there was no question of his selling or even renting the property with its pretty, deadly pond.

He was all the more shocked, in the midst of these comfortable reflections, when at a little after three he had a call from a Sergeant Fisk at the police station. Some little girls looking for pussy willows in a field on the outskirts of the town had discovered a woman's leather handbag and part of a dress with some suggestive stains; would Hildreth please come down and see if he could identify them?

"Certainly," said Hildreth, staring angrily out the window. "Of course, being out in the weather, I imagine they're pretty well—?"

"No, sir, they were stuffed in the remains of an old stone wall and they're still in fair condition. Recognizable, anyway."

"I'll leave right away," said Hildreth, tempering his eagerness with the right amount of dread.

At the police station he was asked to wait—Sergeant Fisk would be right with him.

By four o'clock Sergeant Fisk still was not with him; at four thirty, fuming, Hildreth walked up to the uniformed man at the switchboard and said sharply, "I came here at the request of Sergeant Fisk to look at some objects for identification, and I cannot wait any longer. Please leave a message—"

"Just a minute, sir," said the policeman unruffledly, and slipped a plug into its socket and inquired for Sergeant Fisk. "There's a Mr. Hildreth here, been waiting since—okay, I'll tell him to go right in."

But the handbag and dress fragment, when Hildreth reached Sergeant Fisk's office, had been transferred to Lieutenant Martin's office, where there was some question as to their possible connection with the vanishing of a Colorado couple making a cross-country tour four months ago. Hildreth contained his temper as he went with the sergeant to Martin's office; he was, he remembered, a man who would do anything to find a clue to his wife's fate.

He was badly tempted when, at after five o'clock, he surveyed a rotted and mildewed navy calf handbag, empty, and the sleeve and half the bodice of what had once been a yellow wool dress. Why not say, "Yes, they're my wife's," and bury his face in his hands and be done with it?

Because, he thought with a feeling of having stepped back from the edge of a cliff, Marian had never worn yellow—she said it made her look like a two-legged hangover; and there was a suggestion of something on the leather lining of the bag that could easily be a nearly obliterated name or monogram. Hildreth had read what modern police laboratories could do with things like that. So he shook his head and said, "They're not my wife's," and with a shudder at the stains on the rotting yellow wool, "Thank God."

Three hours, he thought as he drove home seething in the rainy dusk; three hours on a fool's errand which he could not have risked refusing. Just barely time to dress for dinner at Sarah Wilde's—and then get out of here, tomorrow.

He was restored at the thought, and at the glimpse of the old barn quivering on the pond in the last of the light as he drove to Sarah's. His temper was further improved by Sarah's big, casually gay living room—two rooms thrown together in a very old saltbox—and the contrast between an open fire and a cold rattling rain on the windows.

The other guests were already established with drinks—Conlon, a Mr. and Mrs. Slater, and Mrs. Slater's decorative visiting sister.

Hildreth thawed, physically and temperamentally. He felt a slight jar of recognition when he was introduced to the Slaters, but he had undoubtedly encountered them on the station platform at some forgotten time, or in a local store. He noted with approval that Sarah had obviously got someone in for the evening, because there were sounds of kitchen activity while Sarah sat on the couch, in black and pearls, beside Conlon.

On the rare occasions when he and Marian had entertained, Marian had charged in and out like a demented puppy, crying, "My God, who's been watching the beans? Nobody!" Or, abashedly, "We all like nutmeg instead of pepper in our mashed potatoes, don't we?"

Sarah had turned her head and was gazing at him; somebody had clearly asked a question. Hildreth used a handkerchief on his suddenly damp forehead and temples and said, "I got wetter than I thought—that's really quite a downpour," and he got up to stand by the fire.

And the bad moment was gone, further wiped out by Sarah's "You said you mightn't be here long on this visit, Howard, so we're having your favorite dinner—you know, what you won't eat in restaurants."

"Don't tell me . . . ?" said Hildreth, delighted, but it was: trout, a crisp deep-gold outside, succulent white within, delicately enhanced by herbs that only hinted at themselves. He ate with deliberate pleasure, not succumbing until close to the end of dinner to his habit of providing backgrounds for people.

The extraordinarily good-looking sister from New Haven—her name was Vivian Hughes—seemed the kind of young woman who, convinced in her teens that she could have any man she wanted, had ended up with none; there was a kind of forced grace to the frequent turn of her head, and lines of discontent around her really striking green eyes.

Mrs. Slater wasn't a fair test, because she had ticketed herself earlier by a reference to the young twins they had left with a baby-sitter, and by her very casualness she had given herself away. She was the new and on the whole the best breed of mother, thought Hildreth approvingly; slender, amiable, intelligent, she kept her maternal dotings strictly for hearth and home.

Slater? Hildreth gazed obliquely through candlelight at the other man, perhaps a year or two younger than his own forty. The lean, polished, ruddy face suggested an outdoorsman, but everything else pointed to an executive. He went on gazing, and like an exposed print washed gently back and forth in developer, outlines began to emerge.

A desk, not executive grain, but scarred oak. Two telephones on it. A uniformed man in a far doorway saying, "Yes, sir, right away," then disappearing down one of a warren of corridors.

Yes, Slater was a police officer of some sort, or a detective, glimpsed or perhaps even talked to in the first stages of the investigation six months ago. And Sarah and Conlon hoped that he would be terrified by this recognition, and go to pieces. That was the whole point of this friendly little gathering.

How very disappointed they must be. Hildreth stirred his coffee tranquilly, because no motive for murder had existed until sixty seconds before Marian died, and there wasn't a single clue. In an enjoyment of the attention he now knew to be trained on him he said in a well-fed voice, "Marvelous dinner, Sarah. I don't know when I've had trout like that," and Sarah said, "As a matter of fact, you never have."

She was leaning forward a little in the candlelight, her gaze cool and removed. "The trout were from your pond, Howard, and they were caught this afternoon while you were down at the police station. You didn't know that Marian had had the pond stocked for you, as a birthday present, just before she—disappeared, because you love trout but never trust it in restaurants. We didn't know about it either until the friend who did it for her stopped by to see Bill a couple of weeks ago."

Hildreth's neck felt caught in one of those high white collars you saw on injured people; he could not turn it even when he heard Conlon's, "Nice fat trout, I thought, but lazy. They bite at anything."

. . . while he had sat in the police station, decoyed there by a telephone call.

"You all ate it," said Hildreth triumphantly, in a candlelight that had begun to tremble and dampen his face. "You all—"

"No. Ours was perch from the Old Town Fish Market," said Sarah, and although she continued to hold his gaze, her forehead had a cold glimmer and her mouth seemed clenched against a scream.

Hildreth lost them all then. He dropped his eyes, but instead of his dessert cup he saw his dinner plate, with the neat spiny bones from which all the succulent white flesh had been forked away. Marian's soft white throat, and the busy, inquisitive, nibbling mouths at the bottom of the pond, and the plump things placed on his plate—

He heard his chair go crashing back, and the gagging cry of horror that issued from his own throat as he plunged blindly for somewhere to be sick; and, from a mist, Slater's voice saying, ". . . looks like it. Very definitely. We'll get at it first thing in the morning. . . ."

DELAWARE

TOM CHIST AND THE TREASURE BOX

by Howard Pyle

1

To TELL ABOUT Tom Chist, and how he got his name and how he came to be living at the little settlement of Henlopen, just inside the mouth of the Delaware Bay, the story must begin as far back as 1686, when a great storm swept the Atlantic coast from end to end. During the heaviest part of the hurricane a bark went ashore on the Hen-and-Chicken Shoals, just below Cape Henlopen and at the mouth of the Delaware Bay, and Tom Chist was the only soul of all those on board the ill-fated vessel who escaped alive.

This story must first be told, because it was on account of the strange and miraculous escape that happened to him at that time that he gained the name that was given to him.

Even as late as that time of the American colonies, the little scattered settlement at Henlopen, made up of English, with a few Dutch and Swedish people, was still only a spot upon the face of the great American wilderness that spread away, with swamp and forest, no man knew how far to the westward. That wilderness was not only full of wild beasts, but of Indian savages, who every fall would come in wandering tribes to spend the winter along the shores of the fresh-water lakes below Henlopen. There for four or five months they would live upon fish and clams and wild ducks and geese, chipping their arrowheads, and making their earthenware pots and pans under the lee of the sandhills and pine woods below the Capes.

Sometimes on Sundays when the Rev. Hilary Jones would be preaching in the little log church back in the woods, these half-clad red savages would come in from the cold, and sit squatting in the back part of the church, listening stolidly to the words that had no meaning for them.

But about the wreck of the bark in 1686. Such a wreck as that which then went ashore on the Hen-and-Chicken Shoals was a godsend to the poor and needy

71

settlers in the wilderness where so few good things ever came. For the vessel went to pieces during the night, and the next morning the beach was strewn with wreckage—boxes and barrels, chests and spars, timbers and planks, a plentiful and bountiful harvest to be gathered up by the settlers as they chose, with no one to forbid or prevent them.

The name of the bark, as found painted on some of the water barrels and sea chests, was the *Bristol Merchant,* and she no doubt hailed from England.

As was said, the only soul who escaped alive off the wreck was Tom Chist.

A settler, a fisherman named Matt Abrahamson, and his daughter Molly, found Tom. He was washed up on the beach among the wreckage, in a great wooden box which had been securely tied around with a rope and lashed between two spars—apparently for better protection in beating through the surf. Matt Abrahamson thought he had found something of more than usual value when he came upon this chest; but when he cut the cords and broke open the box with his broadax, he could not have been more astonished had he beheld a salamander instead of a baby of nine or ten months old lying half smothered in the blankets that covered the bottom of the chest.

Matt Abrahamson's daughter Molly had had a baby who had died a month or so before. So when she saw the little one lying there in the bottom of the chest, she cried out in great loud voice that the Good Man had sent her another baby in place of her own.

The rain was driving before the hurricane storm in dim, slanting sheets, and so she wrapped up the baby in the man's coat she wore and ran off home without waiting to gather up any more of the wreckage.

It was Parson Jones who gave the foundling his name. When the news came to his ears of what Matt Abrahamson had found he went over to the fisherman's cabin to see the child. He examined the clothes in which the baby was dressed. They were of fine linen and handsomely stitched, and the reverend gentleman opined that the foundling's parents must have been of quality. A kerchief had been wrapped around the baby's neck and under its arms and tied behind, and in the corner, marked with very fine needlework, were the initials T.C.

"What d'ye call him, Molly?" said Parson Jones. He was standing, as he spoke, with his back to the fire, warming his palms before the blaze. The pocket of the great-coat he wore bulged out with a big case bottle of spirits which he had gathered up out of the wreck that afternoon. "What d'ye call him, Molly?"

"I'll call him Tom, after my own baby."

"That goes very well with the initial on the kerchief," said Parson Jones. "But what other name d'ye give him? Let it be something to go with the C."

"I don't know," said Molly.

"Why not call him 'Chist,' since he was born in a chist out of the sea? 'Tom Chist'—the name goes off like a flash in the pan." And so "Tom Chist" he was called and "Tom Chist" he was christened.

So much for the beginning of the history of Tom Chist. The story of Captain Kidd's treasure box does not begin until the late spring of 1699.

That was the year that the famous pirate captain, coming up from the West

Indies, sailed his sloop into the Delaware Bay, where he lay for over a month waiting for news from his friends in New York.

For he had sent word to that town asking if the coast was clear for him to return home with the rich prize he had brought from the Indian seas and the coast of Africa, and meantime he lay there in the Delaware Bay waiting for a reply. Before he left he turned the whole of Tom Chist's life topsy-turvy with something that he brought ashore.

By that time Tom Chist had grown into a strong-limbed, thick-jointed boy of fourteen or fifteen years of age. It was a miserable dog's life he lived with old Matt Abrahamson, for the old fisherman was in his cups more than half the time, and when he was so there was hardly a day passed that he did not give Tom a curse or a buffet, or, as like as not, an actual beating. One would have thought that such treatment would have broken the spirit of the poor little foundling, but it had just the opposite effect upon Tom Chist, who was one of your stubborn, sturdy, stiff-willed fellows who only grow harder and more tough the more they are ill-treated. It had been a long time now since he had made any outcry or complaint at the hard usage he suffered from old Matt. At such times he would shut his teeth and bear whatever came to him, until sometimes the half-drunken old man would be driven almost mad by his stubborn silence. Maybe he would stop in the midst of the beating he was administering, and, grinding his teeth, would cry out: "Won't ye say naught? Won't ye say naught? Well, then, I'll see if I can't make ye say naught." When things had reached such a pass as this Molly would generally interfere to protect her foster son, and then she and Tom would together fight the old man until they had wrenched the stick or the strap out of his hand. Then old Matt would chase them out of doors and around and around the house for maybe half an hour, until his anger was cool, when he would go back again, and for a time the storm would be over.

Besides his foster mother, Tom Chist had a very good friend in Parson Jones, who used to come over every now and then to Abrahamson's hut upon the chance of getting a half dozen fish for breakfast. He always had a kind word or two for Tom, who during the winter evenings would go over to the good man's house to learn his letters, and to read and write and cipher a little, so that by now he was able to spell the words out of the Bible and the almanac, and knew enough to change tuppence into four ha'pennies.

This is the sort of boy Tom Chist was, and this is the sort of life he led.

In the late spring or early summer of 1699 Captain Kidd's sloop sailed into the mouth of the Delaware Bay and changed the whole fortune of his life.

And this is how you come to the story of Captain Kidd's treasure box.

2

Old Matt Abrahamson kept the flat-bottomed boat in which he went fishing some distance down the shore, and in the neighborhood of the old wreck that had been sunk on the Shoals. This was the usual fishing ground of the settlers, and here old Matt's boat generally lay drawn up on the sand.

There had been a thunderstorm that afternoon, and Tom had gone down the beach to bale out the boat in readiness for the morning's fishing.

It was full moonlight now, as he was returning, and the night sky was full of floating clouds. Now and then there was a dull flash to the westward, and once a muttering growl of thunder, promising another storm to come.

All that day the pirate sloop had been lying just off the shore back of the Capes, and now Tom Chist could see the sails glimmering pallidly in the moonlight, spread for drying after the storm. He was walking up the shore homeward when he became aware that at some distance ahead of him there was a ship's boat drawn up on the little narrow beach, and a group of men clustered about it. He hurried forward with a good deal of curiosity to see who had landed, but it was not until he had come close to them that he could distinguish who and what they were. Then he knew that it must be a party who had come off the pirate sloop. They had evidently just landed, and two men were lifting out a chest from the boat. One of them was a negro, naked to the waist, and the other was a white man in his shirt sleeves, wearing petticoat breeches, a Monterey cap upon his head, a red bandana handkerchief around his neck, and gold earrings in his ears. He had a long, plaited queue hanging down his back, and a great sheath knife dangling from his side. Another man, evidently the captain of the party, stood at a little distance as they lifted the chest out of the boat. He had a cane in one hand and a lighted lantern in the other, although the moon was shining as bright as day. He wore jack boots and a handsome laced coat, and he had a long, drooping mustache that curled down below his chin. He wore a fine, feathered hat, and his long black hair hung down upon his shoulders.

All this Tom Chist could see in the moonlight that glinted and twinkled upon the gilt buttons of his coat.

They were so busy lifting the chest from the boat that at first they did not observe that Tom Chist had come up and was standing there. It was the white man with the long, plaited queue and the gold earrings that spoke to him. "Boy, what do you want here, boy?" he said, in a rough, hoarse voice. "Where d'ye come from?" And then dropping his end of the chest, and without giving Tom time to answer, he pointed off down the beach, and said, "You'd better be going about your own business, if you know what's good for you; and don't you come back, or you'll find what you don't want waiting for you."

Tom saw in a glance that the pirates were all looking at him, and then, without saying a word, he turned and walked away. The man who had spoken to him followed him threateningly for some little distance, as though to see that he had gone away as he was bidden to do. But presently he stopped, and Tom hurried on alone, until the boat and the crew and all were dropped away behind and lost in the moonlight night. Then he himself stopped also, turned, and looked back whence he had come.

There had been something very strange in the appearance of the men he had just seen, something very mysterious in their actions, and he wondered what it all meant, and what they were going to do. He stood for a little while thus looking and listening. He could see nothing, and could hear only the sound of distant talking. What were they doing on the lonely shore thus at night? Then, following a sudden impulse, he turned and cut off across the sand hummocks, skirting around inland, but keeping pretty close to the shore, his object being to spy upon them, and to watch what they were about from the back of the low sand hills that fronted the beach.

He had gone along some distance in his circuitous return when he became aware of the sound of voices that seemed to be drawing closer to him as he came toward the speakers. He stopped and stood listening, and instantly, as he stopped, the voices stopped also. He crouched there silently in the bright, glimmering moonlight, surrounded by the silent stretches of sand, and the stillness seemed to press upon him like a heavy hand. Then suddenly the sound of a man's voice began again, and as Tom listened he could hear some one slowly counting. "Ninety-one," the voice began, "ninety-two, ninety-three, ninety-four, ninety-five, ninety-six, ninety-seven, ninety-eight, ninety-nine, one hundred, one hundred and one"—the slow, monotonous count coming nearer and nearer—"one hundred and two, one hundred and three, one hundred and four," and so on in its monotonous reckoning.

Suddenly he saw three heads appear above the sandhill, so close to him that he crouched down quickly with a keen thrill, close beside the hummock near which he stood. His first fear was that they might have seen him in the moonlight; but they had not, and his heart rose again as the counting voice went steadily on. "One hundred and twenty," it was saying—"and twenty-one, and twenty-two, and twenty-three, and twenty-four," and then he who was counting came out from behind the little sandy rise into the white and open level of shimmering brightness.

It was the man with the cane whom Tom had seen some time before—the captain of the party who had landed. He carried his cane under his arm now, and was holding his lantern close to something that he held in his hand, and upon which he looked narrowly as he walked with a slow and measured tread in a perfectly straight line across the sand, counting each step as he took it. "And twenty-five, and twenty-six, and twenty-seven, and twenty-eight, and twenty-nine, and thirty."

Behind him walked two other figures; one was the half-naked negro, the other the man with the plaited queue and the earrings, whom Tom had seen lifting the chest out of the boat. Now they were carrying the heavy box between them, laboring through the sand with shuffling tread as they bore it onward. As he who was counting pronounced the word "thirty," the two men set the chest down on the sand with a grunt, the white man panting and blowing and wiping his sleeve across his forehead. And immediately he who counted took out a slip of paper and marked something down upon it. They stood there for a long time, during which Tom lay behind the sand hummock watching them, and for a while the silence was uninterrupted. In the perfect stillness Tom could hear the washing of the little waves beating upon the distant beach, and once the far-away sound of a laugh from one of those who stood by the ship's boat.

One, two, three minutes passed, and then the men picked up the chest and started on again; and then again the other man began his counting. "Thirty and one, and thirty and two, and thirty and three, and thirty and four"—he walked straight across the level open, still looking intently at that which he held in his hand—"and thirty and five, and thirty and six, and thirty and seven," and so on, until the three figures disappeared in the little hollow between the two sand hills on the opposite side of the open, and still Tom could hear the sound of the counting voice in the distance.

Just as they disappeared behind the hill there was a sudden faint flash of light; and by and by, as Tom lay still listening to the counting, he heard, after a long interval, a far-away muffled rumble of distant thunder. He waited for a while, and then arose and stepped to the top of the sand hummock behind which he had been lying. He looked all about him, but there was no one else to be seen. Then he stepped down from the hummock and followed in the direction which the pirate captain and the two men carrying the chest had gone. He crept along cautiously, stopping now and then to make sure that he still heard the counting voice, and when it ceased he lay down upon the sand and waited until it began again.

Presently, so following the pirates, he saw the three figures again in the distance, and, skirting around back of a hill of sand covered with coarse sedge grass, he came to where he overlooked a little open level space gleaming white in the moonlight.

The three had been crossing the level of sand, and were now not more than twenty-five paces from him. They had again set down the chest, upon which the white man with the long queue and the gold earrings had seated to rest himself, the negro standing close beside him. The moon shone as bright as day and full upon his face. It was looking directly at Tom Chist, every line as keen cut with white lights and black shadows as though it had been carved in ivory and jet. He sat perfectly motionless, and Tom drew back with a start, almost thinking he had been discovered. He lay silent, his heart beating heavily in his throat; but there was no alarm, and presently he heard the counting begin again, and when he looked once more he saw they were going away straight across the little open. A soft, sliding hillock of sand lay directly in front of them. They did not turn aside, but went straight over it, the leader helping himself up the sandy slope with his cane, still counting and still keeping his eyes fixed upon that which he held in his hand. Then they disappeared again behind the white crest on the other side.

So Tom followed them cautiously until they had gone almost half a mile inland. When next he saw them clearly it was from a little sandy rise which looked down like the crest of a bowl upon the floor of sand below. Upon this smooth, white floor the moon beat with almost dazzling brightness.

The white man who had helped to carry the chest was now kneeling, busied at some work, though what it was Tom at first could not see. He was whittling the point of a stick into a long wooden peg, and when, by and by, he had finished what he was about, he arose and stepped to where he who seemed to be the captain had stuck his cane upright into the ground as though to mark some particular spot. He drew the cane out of the sand, thrusting the stick down in its stead. Then he drove the long peg down with a wooden mallet which the negro handed to him. The sharp rapping of the mallet upon the top of the peg sounded loud in the perfect stillness, and Tom lay watching and wondering what it all meant. The man, with quick-repeated blows, drove the peg farther and farther down into the sand until it showed only two or three inches above the surface. As he finished his work there was another faint flash of light, and by and by another smothered rumble of thunder, and Tom, as he looked out toward the westward, saw the silver rim of the round and sharply outlined thundercloud rising slowly up into the sky and pushing the other and broken drifting clouds before it.

The two white men were now stooping over the peg, the negro man watching them. Then presently the man with the cane started straight away from the peg, carrying the end of a measuring line with him, the other end of which the man with the plaited queue held against the top of the peg. When the pirate captain had reached the end of the measuring line he marked a cross upon the sand, and then again they measured out another stretch of space.

So they measured a distance five times over, and then, from where Tom lay, he could see the man with the queue drive another peg just at the foot of a sloping rise of sand that swept up beyond into a tall white dune marked sharp and clear against the night sky behind. As soon as the man with the plaited queue had driven the second peg into the ground they began measuring again, and so, still measuring, disappeared in another direction which took them in behind the sand dune where Tom no longer could see what they were doing.

The negro still sat by the chest where the two had left him, and so bright was the moonlight that from where he lay Tom could see the glint of it twinkling in the whites of his eyeballs.

Presently from behind the hill there came, for the third time, the sharp rapping sound of the mallet driving still another peg, and then after a while the two pirates emerged from behind the sloping whiteness into the space of moonlight again.

They came direct to where the chest lay, and the white man and the black man lifting it once more, they walked away across the level of open sand, and so on behind the edge of the hill and out of Tom's sight.

3

Tom Chist could no longer see what the pirates were doing, neither did he dare to cross over the open space of sand that now lay between them and him. He lay there speculating as to what they were about, and meantime the storm cloud was rising higher and higher above the horizon, with louder and louder mutterings of thunder following each dull flash from out the cloudy, cavernous depths. In the silence he could hear an occasional click as of some iron implement, and he opined that the pirates were burying the chest, though just where they were at work he could neither see nor tell.

Still he lay there watching and listening, and by and by a puff of warm air blew across the sand, and a thumping tumble of louder thunder leaped from out the belly of the storm cloud, which every minute was coming nearer and nearer. Still Tom Chist lay watching.

Suddenly, almost unexpectedly, the three figures reappeared from behind the sand hill, the pirate captain leading the way, and the negro and white man following close behind him. They had gone about halfway across the white, sandy level between the hill and the hummock behind which Tom Chist lay, when the white man stopped and bent over as though to tie his shoe.

This brought the negro a few steps in front of his companion.

That which then followed happened so suddenly, so unexpectedly, so swiftly that Tom Chist had hardly time to realize what it all meant before it was over. As the negro passed him the white man arose suddenly and silently erect, and Tom Chist saw the white moonlight glint upon the blade of a great dirk knife which he now held in his hand. He took one, two silent, catlike steps behind the unsuspecting negro. Then there was a sweeping flash of the blade in the pallid light, and a blow, the thump of which Tom could distinctly hear even from where he lay stretched out upon the sand. There was an instant echoing yell from the black man, who ran stumbling forward, who stopped, who regained his footing, and then stood for an instant as though rooted to the spot.

Tom had distinctly seen the knife enter his back, and even thought that he had seen the glint of the point as it came out from the breast.

Meantime the pirate captain had stopped, and now stood with his hand resting upon his cane looking impassively on.

Then the black man started to run. The white man stood for a while glaring after him; then he, too, started after his victim upon the run. The black man was not very far from Tom when he staggered and fell. He tried to rise, then fell forward again, and lay at length. At that instant the first edge of the cloud cut across the moon, and there was a sudden darkness; but in the silence Tom heard the sound of another blow and a groan, and then presently a voice calling to the pirate captain that it was all over.

He saw the dim form of the captain crossing the level sand, and then, as the moon sailed out from behind the cloud, he saw the white man standing over a black figure that lay motionless upon the sand.

Then Tom Chist scrambled up and ran away, plunging down into the hollow of sand that lay in the shadows below. Over the next rise he ran, and down again into the next black hollow, and so on over the sliding, shifting ground, panting and gasping. It seemed to him that he could hear footsteps following, and in the terror that possessed him he almost expected every instant to feel the cold knife blade slide between his own ribs in such a thrust from behind as he had seen given to the poor black man.

So he ran on like one in a nightmare. His feet grew heavy like lead, he panted and gasped, his breath came hot and dry in his throat. But still he ran and ran until at last he found himself in front of old Matt Abrahamson's cabin, gasping, panting, and sobbing for breath, his knees relaxed and his thighs trembling with weakness.

As he opened the door and dashed into the darkened cabin (for both Matt and Molly were long ago asleep in bed) there was a flash of light, and even as he slammed to the door behind him there was an instant peal of thunder, heavy as though a great weight had been dropped upon the roof of the sky, so that the doors and windows of the cabin rattled.

4

Then Tom Chist crept to bed, trembling, shuddering, bathed in sweat, his heart beating like a trip hammer, and his brain dizzy from that long, terror-inspired race through the soft sand in which he had striven to outstrip he knew not what pursuing horror.

For a long, long time he lay awake, trembling and chattering with nervous chills, and when he did fall asleep it was only to drop into monstrous dreams in which he once again saw ever enacted, with various grotesque variations, the tragic drama which his waking eyes had beheld the night before.

Then came the dawning of the broad, wet daylight, and before the rising of the sun Tom was up and out of doors to find the young day dripping with the rain of overnight.

His first act was to climb the nearest sand hill and to gaze out toward the offing where the pirate ship had been the day before.

It was no longer there.

Soon afterward Matt Abrahamson came out of the cabin and he called to Tom to go get a bite to eat, for it was time for them to be away fishing.

All that morning the recollection of the night before hung over Tom Chist like a great cloud of boding trouble. It filled the confined area of the little boat and spread over the entire wide spaces of sky and sea that surrounded them. Not for a moment was it lifted. Even when he was hauling in his wet and dripping line with a struggling fish at the end of it a recurrent memory of what he had seen would suddenly come upon him, and he would groan in spirit at the recollection. He looked at Matt Abrahamson's leathery face, at his lantern jaws cavernously and stolidly chewing at a tobacco leaf, and it seemed monstrous to him that the old man should be so unconscious of the black cloud that wrapped them all about.

When the boat reached the shore again he leaped scrambling to the beach, and as soon as his dinner was eaten he hurried away to find the Dominie Jones.

He ran all the way from Abrahamson's hut to the parson's house, hardly stopping once, and when he knocked at the door he was panting and sobbing for breath.

The good man was sitting on the back-kitchen doorstep smoking his long pipe of tobacco out into the sunlight, while his wife within was rattling about among the pans and dishes in preparation of their supper, of which a strong, porky smell already filled the air.

Then Tom Chist told his story, panting, hurrying, tumbling one word over another in his haste, and Parson Jones listened, breaking every now and then into an ejaculation of wonder. The light in his pipe went out and the bowl turned cold.

"And I don't see why they should have killed the poor black man," said Tom, as he finished his narrative.

"Why, that is very easy enough to understand," said the good reverend man. " 'Twas a treasure box they buried!"

In his agitation Mr. Jones had risen from his seat and was now stumping up and down, puffing at his empty tobacco pipe as though it were still alight.

"A treasure box!" cried out Tom.

"Aye, a treasure box! And that was why they killed the poor black man. He was the only one, d'ye see, besides they two who knew the place where 'twas hid, and now that they've killed him out of the way, there's nobody but themselves knows. The villains—Tut, tut, look at that now!" In his excitement the dominie had snapped the stem of his tobacco pipe in two.

"Why, then," said Tom, "if that is so, 'tis indeed a wicked, bloody treasure, and fit to bring a curse upon anybody who finds it!"

" 'Tis more like to bring a curse upon the soul who buried it," said Parson Jones, "and it may be a blessing to him who finds it. But tell me, Tom, do you think you could find that place again where 'twas hid?"

"I can't tell that," said Tom, " 'twas all in among the sand humps, d'ye see, and it was at night into the bargain. Maybe we could find the marks of their feet in the sand," he added.

" 'Tis not likely," said the reverend gentleman, "for the storm last night would have washed all that away."

"I could find the place," said Tom, "where the boat was drawn up on the beach."

"Why, then, that's something to start from, Tom," said his friend. "If we can find that, then maybe we can find whither they went from there."

"If I was certain it was a treasure box," cried out Tom Chist, "I would rake over every foot of sand betwixt here and Henlopen to find it."

" 'Twould be like hunting for a pin in a haystack," said the Rev. Hilary Jones.

As Tom walked away home, it seemed as though a ton's weight of gloom had been rolled away from his soul. The next day he and Parson Jones were to go treasure-hunting together; it seemed to Tom as though he could hardly wait for the time to come.

5

The next afternoon Parson Jones and Tom Chist started off together upon the expedition that made Tom's fortune forever. Tom carried a spade over his shoulder and the reverend gentleman walked along beside him with his cane.

As they jogged along up the beach they talked together about the only thing they could talk about—the treasure box. "And how big did you say 'twas?" quoth the good gentleman.

"About so long," said Tom Chist, measuring off upon the spade, "and about so wide, and this deep."

"And what if it should be full of money, Tom?" said the reverend gentleman, swinging his cane around and around in wide circles in the excitement of the thought, as he strode along briskly. "Suppose it should be full of money, what then?"

"By Moses!" said Tom Chist, hurrying to keep up with his friend, "I'd buy a ship for myself, I would, and I'd trade to Injy and to Chiny in my own boat, I would. Suppose the chist was all full of money, sir, and suppose we should find it; would there be enough in it, d'ye suppose, to buy a ship?"

"To be sure there would be enough, Tom; enough and to spare, and a good big lump over."

"And if I find it 'tis mine to keep, is it, and no mistake?"

"Why, to be sure it would be yours!" cried out the parson, in a loud voice. "To be sure it would be yours!" He knew nothing of the law, but the doubt of the question began at once to ferment in his brain, and he strode along in silence for a while. "Whose else would it be but yours if you find it?" he burst out. "Can you tell me that?"

"If ever I have a ship of my own," said Tom Chist, "and if ever I sail to Injy in her, I'll fetch ye back the best chist of tea, sir, that ever was fetched from Cochin Chiny."

Parson Jones burst out laughing. "Thankee, Tom," he said, "and I'll thankee again when I get my chist of tea. But tell me, Tom, didst thou ever hear of the farmer girl who counted her chickens before they were hatched?"

It was thus they talked as they hurried along up the beach together, and so came to a place at last where Tom stopped short and stood looking about him.

" 'Twas just here," he said, "I saw the boat last night. I know 'twas here, for I mind me of that bit of wreck yonder, and that there was a tall stake drove in the sand just where yon stake stands."

Parson Jones put on his barnacles and went over to the stake toward which Tom pointed. As soon as he had looked at it carefully he called out: "Why, Tom, this hath been just drove down into the sand. 'Tis a brand-new stake of wood, and the pirates must have set it here themselves as a mark, just as they drove the pegs you spoke about down into the sand."

Tom came over and looked at the stake. It was a stout piece of oak nearly two inches thick; it had been shaped with some care, and the top of it had been painted red. He shook the stake and tried to move it, but it had been driven or planted so deeply into the sand that he could not stir it. "Aye, sir," he said, "it must have been set here for a mark, for I'm sure 'twas not here yesterday or the day before." He stood looking about him to see if there were other signs of the pirates' presence. At some little distance there was the corner of something white sticking up out of the sand. He could see that it was a scrap of paper, and he pointed to it, calling out: "Yonder is a piece of paper, sir. I wonder if they left that behind them?"

It was a miraculous chance that placed that paper there. There was only an inch of it showing, and if it had not been for Tom's sharp eyes, it would certainly have been overlooked and passed by. The next windstorm would have covered it up, and all that afterward happened never would have occurred. "Look, sir," he said, as he struck the sand from it, "it hath writing on it."

"Let me see it," said Parson Jones. He adjusted the spectacles a little more firmly astride of his nose as he took the paper in his hand and began conning it. "What's all this?" he said; "a whole lot of figures and nothing else." And then he read aloud, " 'Mark—S.S.W.S. by S.' What d'ye suppose that means, Tom?"

"I don't know, sir," said Tom. "But maybe we can understand it better if you read on."

" 'Tis all a great lot of figures," said Parson Jones, "without a grain of meaning in them so far as I can see, unless they be sailing directions." And then he began reading again: " 'Mark S.S.W. BY S. 40, 72, 91, 130, 151, 177, 202, 232, 256, 271'—d'ye see, it must be sailing directions—'299, 335, 362, 386, 415, 446, 469, 491, 522, 544, 571, 598'—what a lot of them there be—'626, 652, 676, 695, 724, 851, 876, 905, 940, 967. Peg. S.E. by E. 269 foot. Peg. S.S.W. by S. 427 foot. Peg. Dig to the west of this six foot.' "

"What's that about a peg?" exclaimed Tom. "What's that about a peg? And then there's something about digging, too!" It was as though a sudden light began shining into his brain. He felt himself growing quickly very excited. "Read that over again, sir," he cried. "Why, sir, you remember I told you they drove a peg into the sand. And don't they say to dig close to it? Read it over again, sir—read it over again!"

"Peg?" said the good gentleman. "To be sure it was about a peg. Let's look again. Yes, here it is. 'Peg. S.E. by E. 269 foot.' "

"Aye!" cried out Tom Chist again, in great excitement. "Don't you remember what I told you, sir, 269 foot? Sure that must be what I saw 'em measuring with the line."

Parson Jones had now caught the flame of excitement that was blazing up so strongly in Tom's breast. He felt as though some wonderful thing was about to happen to them. "To be sure, to be sure!" he called out, in a great big voice. "And then they measured out 427 foot south-southwest by south, and they then drove another peg, and then they buried the box six foot to the west of it. Why, Tom—why, Tom Chist! if we've read this aright, thy fortune is made."

Tom Chist stood staring straight at the old gentleman's excited face, and seeing nothing but it in all the bright infinity of sunshine. Were they, indeed, about to find the treasure chest? He felt the sun very hot upon his shoulders, and he heard the harsh, insistent jarring of a tern that hovered and circled with forked tail and sharp white wings in the sunlight just above their heads; but all the time he stood staring into the good old gentleman's face.

It was Parson Jones who first spoke. "But what do all these figures mean?" And Tom observed how the paper shook and rustled in the tremor of excitement that shook his hand. He raised the paper to the focus of his spectacles and began to read again. " 'Mark 40, 72, 91—' "

"Mark?" cried out Tom, almost screaming. "Why, that must mean the stake yonder; that must be the mark." And he pointed to the oaken stick with its red tip blazing against the white shimmer of sand behind it.

"And the 40 and 72 and 91," cried the old gentleman, in a voice equally shrill—"why, that must mean the number of steps the pirate was counting when you heard him."

"To be sure that's what they mean!" cried Tom Chist. "That is it, and it can be nothing else. Oh, come, sir—come, sir; let us make haste and find it!"

"Stay! stay!" said the good gentleman, holding up his hand; and again Tom Chist noticed how it trembled and shook. His voice was steady enough, though very hoarse, but his hand shook and trembled as though with a palsy. "Stay! stay! First of all, we must follow these measurements. And 'tis a marvelous thing," he croaked after a little pause, "how this paper ever came to be here."

"Maybe it was blown here by the storm," suggested Tom Chist.

"Like enough; like enough," said Parson Jones. "Like enough, after the wretches had buried the chest and killed the poor black man, they were so buffeted and bowsed about by the storm that it was shook out of the man's pocket, and thus blew away from him without his knowing aught of it."

"But let us find the box!" cried out Tom Chist, flaming with his excitement.

"Aye, aye," said the good man; "only stay a little, my boy, until we make sure what we're about. I've got my pocket compass here, but we must have something to measure off the feet when we have found the peg. You run across to Tom Brooke's house and fetch that measuring rod he used to lay out his new byre. While you're gone I'll pace off the distance marked on the paper with my pocket compass here."

6

Tom Chist was gone for almost an hour, though he ran nearly all the way and back, upborne as on the wings of the wind. When he returned, panting, Parson Jones was nowhere to be seen, but Tom saw his footsteps leading away inland, and he followed the scuffling marks in the smooth surface across the sand humps and down into the hollows, and by and by found the good gentleman in a spot he at once knew as soon as he laid his eyes upon it.

It was the open space where the pirates had driven their first peg, and where Tom Chist had afterward seen them kill the poor black man. Tom Chist gazed around as though expecting to see some sign of the tragedy, but the space was as smooth and as undisturbed as a floor, excepting where, midway across it, Parson Jones, who was now stooping over something on the ground, had trampled it all around about.

When Tom Chist saw him he was still bending over, scraping sand away from something he had found.

It was the first peg!

Inside of half an hour they had found the second and third pegs, and Tom Chist stripped off his coat, and began digging like mad down into the sand, Parson Jones standing over him watching him. The sun was sloping well toward the west when the blade of Tom Chist's spade struck upon something hard.

If it had been his own heart that he had hit in the sand his breast could hardly have thrilled more sharply.

It was the treasure box!

Parson Jones himself leaped down into the hole, and began scraping away the sand with his hands as though he had gone crazy. At last, with some difficulty, they tugged and hauled the chest up out of the sand to the surface, where it lay covered all over with the grit that clung to it. It was securely locked and fastened with a padlock, and it took a good many blows with the blade of the spade to burst the bolt. Parson Jones himself lifted the lid. Tom Chist leaned forward and gazed down into the open box. He would not have been surprised to have seen it filled full of yellow gold and bright jewels. It was filled half full of books and papers, and half full of canvas bags tied safely and securely around and around with cords of string.

Parson Jones lifted out one of the bags, and it jingled as he did so. It was full of money.

He cut the string, and with trembling, shaking hands handed the bag to Tom, who, in an ecstasy of wonder and dizzy with delight, poured out with swimming sight upon the coat spread on the ground a cataract of shining silver money that rang and twinkled and jingled as it fell in a shining heap upon the coarse cloth.

Parson Jones held up both hands into the air, and Tom stared at what he saw, wondering whether it was all so, and whether he was really awake. It seemed to him as though he was in a dream.

There were two-and-twenty bags in all in the chest: ten of them full of silver money, eight of them full of gold money, three of them full of gold dust, and one small bag with jewels wrapped up in wad cotton and paper.

" 'Tis enough," cried out Parson Jones, "to make us both rich men as long as we live."

The burning summer sun, though sloping in the sky, beat down upon them as hot as fire; but neither of them noticed it. Neither did they notice hunger nor thirst nor fatigue, but sat there as though in a trance, with the bags of money scattered on the sand around them, a great pile of money heaped upon the coat, and the open chest beside them. It was an hour of sundown before Parson Jones had begun fairly to examine the books and papers in the chest.

Of the three books, two were evidently log books of the pirates who had been lying off the mouth of the Delaware Bay all this time. The other book was written in Spanish, and was evidently the log book of some captured prize.

It was then, sitting there upon the sand, the good old gentleman reading in his high, crackling voice, that they first learned from the bloody records in those two books who it was who had been lying inside the Cape all this time, and that it was the famous Captain Kidd. Every now and then the reverend gentleman would stop to exclaim, "Oh, the bloody wretch!" or, "Oh, the desperate, cruel, villains!" and then would go on reading again a scrap here and a scrap there.

And all the while Tom Chist sat and listened, every now and then reaching out furtively and touching the heap of money still lying upon the coat.

One might be inclined to wonder why Captain Kidd had kept those bloody records. He had probably laid them away because they so incriminated many of the great people of the colony of New York that, with the books in evidence, it would have been impossible to bring the pirate to justice without dragging a dozen or more fine gentlemen into the dock along with him. If he could have kept them in his own possession they would doubtless have been a great weapon of defense to protect him from the gallows. Indeed, when Captain Kidd was finally brought to conviction and hanged, he was not accused of his piracies, but of striking a mutinous seaman upon the head with a bucket and accidentally killing him. The authorities did not dare try him for piracy. He was really hanged because he was a pirate, and we know that it was the log books that Tom Chist brought to New York that did the business for him; he was accused and convicted of manslaughter for killing of his own ship carpenter with a bucket.

So Parson Jones, sitting there in the slanting light, read through these terrible records of piracy, and Tom, with the pile of gold and silver money beside him, sat and listened to him.

What a spectacle, if anyone had come upon them! But they were alone, with the vast arch of sky empty above them and the wide white stretch of sand a desert around them. The sun sank lower and lower, until there was only time to glance through the other papers in the chest.

They were nearly all goldsmiths' bills of exchange drawn in favor of certain of the most prominent merchants of New York. Parson Jones, as he read over the names, knew of nearly all the gentlemen by hearsay. Aye, here was this gentleman; he thought that name would be among 'em. What? Here is Mr. So-and-so. Well, if all they say is true, the villain has robbed one of his own best friends. "I wonder," he said, "why the wretch should have hidden these papers so carefully away with the other treasures, for they could do him no good?" Then, answering his own question: "Like enough because these will give him a hold over the gentlemen to whom they are drawn so that he can make a good bargain for his own neck before he gives the bills back to their owners. I tell you what it is, Tom," he continued, "it is you yourself shall go to New York and bargain for the return of these papers. 'Twill be as good as another fortune to you."

The majority of the bills were drawn in favor of one Richard Chillingsworth, Esquire. "And he is," said Parson Jones, "one of the richest men in the province of New York. You shall go to him with the news of what we have found."

"When shall I go?" said Tom Chist.

"You shall go upon the very first boat we can catch," said the parson. He had turned, still holding the bills in his hand, and was now fingering over the pile of money that yet lay tumbled out upon the coat. "I wonder, Tom," said he, "if you could spare me a score or so of these doubloons?"

"You shall have fifty score, if you choose," said Tom, bursting with gratitude and with generosity in his newly found treasure.

"You are as fine a lad as ever I saw, Tom," said the parson, "and I'll thank you to the last day of my life."

Tom scooped up a double handful of silver money. "Take it, sir," he said, "and you may have as much more as you want of it."

He poured it into the dish that the good man made of his hands, and the parson made a motion as though to empty it into his pocket. Then he stopped, as though a sudden doubt had occurred to him. "I don't know that 'tis fit for me to take this pirate money, after all," he said.

"But you are welcome to it," said Tom.

Still the parson hesitated. "Nay," he burst out, "I'll not take it; 'tis blood money." And as he spoke he chucked the whole double handful into the now empty chest, then arose and dusted the sand from his breeches. Then, with a great deal of bustling energy, he helped to tie the bags again and put them all back into the chest.

They reburied the chest in the place whence they had taken it, and then the parson folded the precious paper of directions, placed it carefully in his wallet, and his wallet in his pocket. "Tom," he said, for the twentieth time, "your fortune has been made this day."

And Tom Chist, as he rattled in his breeches pocket the half dozen doubloons he had kept out of his treasure, felt that what his friend had said was true.

As the two went back homeward across the level space of sand Tom Chist suddenly stopped stock-still and stood looking about him. "'Twas just here," he said, digging his heel down into the sand, "that they killed the poor black man."

"And here he lies buried for all time," said Parson Jones; and as he spoke he dug his cane down into the sand. Tom Chist shuddered. He would not have been surprised if the ferrule of the cane had struck something soft beneath that level surface. But it did not, nor was any sign of that tragedy ever seen again. For, whether the pirates had carried away what they had done and buried it elsewhere, or whether the storm in blowing the sand had completely leveled off and hidden all sign of that tragedy where it was enacted, certain it is that it never came to sight again—at least so far as Tom Chist and the Rev. Hilary Jones ever knew.

7

This is the story of the treasure box. All that remains now is to conclude the story of Tom Chist, and to tell of what came of him in the end.

He did not go back again to live with old Matt Abrahamson. Parson Jones had now taken charge of him and his fortunes, and Tom did not have to go back to the fisherman's hut.

Old Abrahamson talked a great deal about it, and would come in his cups and harangue good Parson Jones, making a vast protestation of what he would do to Tom—if he ever caught him—for running away. But Tom on all these occasions kept carefully out of his way, and nothing came of the old man's threatenings.

Tom used to go over to see his foster mother now and then, but always when the old man was away from home. And Molly Abrahamson used to warn him to keep out of her father's way. "He's in as vile a humor as ever I see, Tom," she said; "he sits sulking all day long, and 'tis my belief he'd kill ye if he caught ye."

Of course Tom said nothing, even to her, about the treasure, and he and the reverend gentleman kept the knowledge thereof to themselves. About three weeks later Parson Jones managed to get him shipped aboard of a vessel bound for New York town, and a few days later Tom Chist landed at that place. He had never been in such a town before, and he could not sufficiently wonder and marvel at the number of brick houses, at the multitude of people coming and going along the fine, hard, earthen sidewalk, at the shops and the stores where goods hung in the windows, and, most of all, the fortifications and the battery at the point, at the rows of threatening cannon, and at the scarlet-coated sentries pacing up and down the ramparts. All this was very wonderful, and so were the clustered boats riding at anchor in the harbor. It was like a new world, so different was it from the sand hills and the sedgy levels of Henlopen.

Tom Chist took up his lodgings at a coffee house near to the town hall, and thence he sent by the postboy, a letter written by Parson Jones to Master Chillingsworth. In a little while the boy returned with a message, asking Tom to come up to Mr. Chillingsworth's house that afternoon at two o'clock.

Tom went thither with a great deal of trepidation, and his heart fell away altogether when he found it a fine, grand brick house, three stories high, and with wrought-iron letters across the front.

The counting house was in the same building; but Tom, because of Mr. Jones's letter, was conducted directly into the parlor, where the great rich man was awaiting his coming. He was sitting in a leather-covered armchair, smoking a pipe of tobacco, and with a bottle of fine old Madeira close to his elbow.

Tom had not had a chance to buy a new suit of clothes yet, and so he cut no very fine figure in the rough dress he had brought with him from Henlopen. Nor did Mr. Chillingsworth seem to think very highly of his appearance, for he sat looking sideways at Tom as he smoked.

"Well, my lad," he said, "and what is this great thing you have to tell me that is so mightily wonderful? I got what's-his-name—Mr. Jones's—letter, and now I am ready to hear what you have to say."

But if he thought but little of his visitor's appearance at first, he soon changed his sentiments toward him, for Tom had not spoken twenty words when Mr. Chillingsworth's whole aspect changed. He straightened himself up in his seat, laid aside his pipe, pushed away his glass of Madeira, and bade Tom take a chair.

He listened without a word as Tom Chist told of the buried treasure, of how he had seen the poor negro murdered, and of how he and Parson Jones had recovered the chest again. Only once did Mr. Chillingsworth interrupt the narrative. "And to think," he cried, "that the villain this very day walks about New York town as though he were an honest man, ruffling it with the best of us! But if we can only get hold of these log books you speak of. Go on; tell me more of this."

When Tom Chist's narrative was ended, Mr. Chillingsworth's bearing was as different as daylight is from dark. He asked a thousand questions, all in the most polite and gracious tone imaginable, and not only urged a glass of his fine old Madeira upon Tom, but asked him to stay to supper. There was nobody to be there, he said, but his wife and daughter.

Tom, all in a panic at the very thought of the two ladies, sturdily refused to stay even for the dish of tea Mr. Chillingsworth offered him.

He did not know that he was destined to stay there as long as he should live.

"And now," said Mr. Chillingsworth, "tell me about yourself."

"I have nothing to tell, Your Honor," said Tom, "except that I was washed up out of the sea."

"Washed up out of the sea!" exclaimed Mr. Chillingsworth. "Why, how was that? Come, begin at the beginning, and tell me all."

Thereupon Tom Chist did as he was bidden, beginning at the very beginning and telling everything just as Molly Abrahamson had often told it to him. As he continued, Mr. Chillingsworth's interest changed into an appearance of stronger and stronger excitement. Suddenly he jumped up out of his chair and began to walk up and down the room.

"Stop! Stop!" he cried out at last, in the midst of something Tom was saying. "Stop! Stop! Tell me; do you know the name of the vessel that was wrecked, and from which you were washed ashore?"

"I've heard it said," said Tom Chist, " 'twas the *Bristol Merchant*."

"I knew it! I knew it!" exclaimed the great man, in a loud voice, flinging his hands up into the air. "I felt it was so the moment you began the story. But tell me this, was there nothing found with you with a mark or a name upon it?"

"There was a kerchief," said Tom, "marked with a T. and a C."

"Theodosia Chillingsworth!" cried out the merchant. "I knew it! I knew it! Heavens! To think of anything so wonderful happening as this! Boy! Boy! Dost thou know who thou art? Thou art my own brother's son. His name was Oliver Chillingsworth, and he was my partner in business, and thou art his son." Then he ran out into the entryway, shouting and calling for his wife and daughter to come. So Tom Chist—or Thomas Chillingsworth, as he now was to be called— did stay to supper, after all.

This is the story, and I hope you may like it. For Tom Chist became rich and great, as was to be supposed, and he married his pretty cousin Theodosia (who had been named for his own mother, drowned in the *Bristol Merchant*).

He did not forget his friends, but had Parson Jones brought to New York to live.

As to Molly and Matt Abrahamson, they both enjoyed a pension of ten pounds a year for as long as they lived; for now that all was well with him, Tom bore no grudge against the old fisherman for all the drubbings he had suffered.

The treasure box was brought on to New York, and if Tom Chist did not get all the money there was in it (as Parson Jones had opined he would) he got at least a good big lump of it.

And it is my belief that those log books did more to get Captain Kidd arrested in Boston town and hanged in London than anything else that was brought up against him.

DISTRICT OF COLUMBIA

THE WASHINGTON, D.C., MURDERS

by Patricia McGerr

THERE ARE TWO schools of thought on the best way to begin a murder story. One says it must open with a bang—a beginning like, "A shot rang out, a woman screamed, and a man, blood dripping from a dozen wounds, staggered off the roof." For advocates of that school, this story should begin, "The first body was discovered in the Lincoln Memorial, stretched in back of the huge Lincoln statue, a bullet through the heart."

There is, however, a more leisurely method, designed to lead to the murder through a description of events far from the scene of the crime—as, for example, "Holmes drew the bow lightly across the strings of his violin, producing a plaintively melodic accompaniment to Watson's account of his trip to Surrey." Perhaps this would be a better type of opening for an account of the sensational series of murders that terrorized the residents of Washington, D.C., and made sightseers tremble with fearsome anticipation as they made the rounds of its historic spots.

Let us then settle for the indirect approach and begin the story in the city room of the *Washington Daily Comet,* a tabloid with a small circulation and an even smaller reputation, but with aspirations surpassing its strongest competitor.

City Editor Stan Morris was reading his morning mail, the calm of the spring morning disturbed only by the rattle of dice in a far corner and the mumblings of a copy boy laboriously working the daily crossword puzzle with a stub pencil. One by one, Morris dropped announcements of an artists vs. writers ball game, a lecture on mental health, and an outdoor concert into his already overflowing wastepaper basket. From the last envelope he drew a narrow slip of paper bearing only the words, *Sic semper tyrannis.* His eyebrows slightly raised as he read it a second time, shrugged, and tossed it, too, toward the basket. Fingering the change in his pockets meditatively, he rose and moved in the direction of the dice game.

Two hours and one edition later, he was back at his desk working on his assignment sheet when the phone rang.

"Yeah," he said into the mouthpiece. "Yeah. The Lincoln Memorial, you say? Sure. Yeah. Right away. Thanks for the tip, Chief. Sure, any time."

Banging down the receiver, he shouted across the room, "Get moving, Jimmy. Some guy's been killed in the Lincoln Memorial. A busload of school kids on tour found the body. Take Walter and get some angle shots of the corpse with the statue."

Jimmy and Walter had been gone almost half an hour before Morris had the thought that sent him diving toward his basket and scattering its papers in a frenzy of activity that made the copy boy stare in amazement. The return of the reporter and photographer found him in a state of high excitement.

"Not much in it, Morris," Jimmy announced, unaware of the other's agitation. "They've identified the fellow. Nobody important. Worked in the National Archives. I've got all the dope."

"Not much in it!" Morris' voice was almost trembling. "We're holding the presses, Jimmy. This is the yarn of the year. Look what came in the morning mail."

Without much interest Jimmy accepted the crumpled paper and envelope.

"You know what that means?" Morris demanded. "That's what John Wilkes Booth shouted at Lincoln just before he shot him. It means the killer planned to reenact the assassination and he sent the *Comet* an advance announcement. Give the story all you've got."

Jimmy caught some of his editor's fervor and wrote a great story but the reaction of the public was disappointing. They were, to put it mildly, skeptical. Their attitude was summed up in an editorial in the *Comet*'s morning competitor headed *How Yellow Can You Get?* and denouncing the *sic semper tyrannis* note as an unethical invention designed to create sensation and to boom circulation. Even the police, usually friendly to Morris, laughed in his face when he suggested lab study of the note and envelope. Since both were block-printed on plain cheap stationery, it was perhaps not a serious oversight.

Investigation of the murder drew blanks for two days and even the *Comet* relegated the "police baffled" story to page nine. Then, on the third day, Morris was electrified to find on his desk, postmarked the night before, an envelope which in appearance was a twin of the earlier anonymous note. Opening it with trembling fingers, he again found a single slip of paper. This one bore the words: *An old place to pay new debts.* He stretched his hand toward the phone, but before he could lift the receiver, it rang piercingly.

"Yeah," he growled impatiently, "Morris here."

He listened a minute, his eyes widening.

"At the entrance to the Treasury, you say? Good Lord, Chief, listen to this. I just got another note—no, take it easy. Chief, this is on the level. But you've got to listen . . . Okay, Chief, I'll send a man over."

His spirits slightly dampened, Morris sent Jimmy out again to collect details.

This time the victim was an employee of the Government Printing Office. He too had been shot and his body had been found by a guard at the Treasury Department shortly after the doors opened for the day. The second murder, coming so closely on the heels of the first, made the public more receptive to the *Comet*'s style, and its story drew a parallel between this new homicide and the shooting of Alexander Hamilton, first Secretary of the Treasury.

The police, however, remained dubious and the paper's most dignified evening competitor carried an editorial on the ethics of journalism. Without mentioning the *Comet* by name, it suggested that one newspaper that resorted to forgery and the fabrication of evidence could degrade the entire body of the press. Morris writhed a little as he read it, since he yearned for prestige almost as much as for a soaring circulation. He began to wish that the unknown murderer had chosen some other paper for his gratuitous predictions.

Police Still Baffled, the headlines read the next day, and the next. No connection had been found between the two victims and none between the two crimes, except the use of a gun and the tie-in of each with a historical personage who had died violently. It was probably the desperate need of doing *something* that led the police to accept Morris' suggestion that a man be assigned to the main post office to intercept all letters addressed to the *Comet* city editor—on the chance that, if the killer intended to strike again, his intent might be determined in advance. And late on the third night this precaution bore fruit.

Into the hands of the policeman at the post office came one of the familiar block-printed envelopes, with its slim contents.

This time the words asked simply, *Did George Washington sleep here too?*

There was activity in the Capital City that night. At least a dozen policemen were hidden in strategic spots around the Washington Monument. One manned the elevator, one waited in the tower, and two more lurked in the reception room. Jimmy covered this point for the *Comet* but Morris himself joined the detail that sped to Mount Vernon to patrol the house and grounds. The all-night vigil in both places ended without event, except that the city editor had to be forcibly restrained from striking a rival reporter who sneered, "Going home to write yourself another letter, Morris?"

Vindication for Morris and the *Comet* was not long in coming. And when it came it left Washington in a state of shaking horror unmatched since Jack the Ripper roved the streets of London.

An early morning hiker, striding along the highway that skirted the Tidal Basin, found a dead man lying at the foot of one of the cherry trees—a dead man with a hatchet in his skull.

Not everyone in Washington was interested in the *Comet*'s interpretation of the cherry-tree-and-hatchet legend, but everyone was appalled by the possibility that he might be next. The minority of Washingtonians allied with private business drew minor comfort from the fact that the newest victim was on the payroll of the Department of Health, Education and Welfare. "You see," they reminded each other in tones that lacked conviction, "the killer only attacks government workers. These mad murderers always run true to form."

The police now kept a constant watch on the *Comet,* staying in continual consultation with Morris. His glory was marred by only one touch of ignominy: they insisted on fingerprinting not only him but the entire newspaper staff.

"Of course we know you wouldn't go that far." The police lieutenant tried to laugh it off. "But the department's been getting some phone calls. And you can't deny that this has been mighty good for your circulation. Anyway, no harm in checking, is there?"

So they compared the *Comet* fingerprints with those on the handle of the hatchet and gave the paper a clean bill of health. It was the only decisive action taken in the two days before the policeman in the post office intercepted a fourth note. This one said cryptically, *SO LONG!*

Bafflement was gross understatement as a description of the police at this point. The two words told them nothing. They had no idea where to go. The general public, on the other hand, were much more interested in which places to stay away from, but the note gave them no clue. Optimists drew comfort from its apparent finality. "It's a suicide message," they insisted. "The killer has finished his job and he's saying goodbye."

"He's saying goodbye, all right," pessimists countered, "but we're the ones who are going. Could be he's triggered some device that will blow the whole town off the map."

The night passed without developments. State Department cipher experts were put to work trying to decode the new note. The Secret Service doubled its guard around the White House. Absenteeism in all government bureaus reached record heights. The morning wore on and no fresh corpse was discovered. But no one relaxed.

In the City Room of the *Daily Comet,* Jimmy's desk was piled high with files. Through long nerve-wracking hours he'd sat up reading the victims' mail, seeking a link between them. It was a tedious assignment, but at last the hunch paid off. Like cards drawn to a straight flush, he slapped three letters down in front of the editor.

"I've got it, Morris!" Excitement overrode the fatigue in his voice. "Almost missed it because the letters seemed so routine. But he's the only man who wrote to all three and when you read them over they have a fanatic ring."

"O. O. Smith." Morris read the signature. "What's his angle?"

"He's a small town schoolteacher who's written a book on American history. Worked on it for twelve years, then couldn't get it published. No wonder he cracked up. See—" Jimmy's forefinger underlined a key sentence. " 'I have original material and a new approach that will make all other texts obsolete and will revolutionize teaching methods. Therefore, the publishers are in league to suppress my work.' "

"Then what's his grudge against civil servants? Why didn't he go to New York and start mowing down publishers?"

"He wanted the government to take it over, print it, and put copies in every public school and library. Each of these fellows got a letter from him and answered with a polite brushoff. He decided they were all part of the conspiracy.

And he'd been living so long with history—don't you get it? He started reliving it!"

"Sounds logical," Morris nodded grimly. "The question is, how many other government offices did he write to? Who's next on his list of victims?"

Jimmy shook his head. "There could be a hundred answers. Maybe some general at the Pentagon refused to use his book for basic training. Or he might have asked the Information Agency to send it overseas. Name any department and I'll give you a tie-in. The only thing to do is headline the story and urge everyone who's had correspondence with Smith to get under cover and ask for protection."

"Yeah, that could work, so long as he hasn't already—" Morris broke off in mid-sentence, repeated his own words. "So long as—*so long*—all his other notes had a meaning, this one must too. So—long. Wait a minute." He pressed his fist hard against his forehead as if to force thought. "Sic—Sic—"

"You bet he's sick," Jimmy agreed. "The guy's a real psycho."

"I don't mean that. I'm thinking of the first message. *Sic semper tyrannis.* We translated it 'thus always to tyrants.' But we could have used 'so' instead of 'thus'—so always to tyrants. And now, 'so long'—Good Lord, of course, that's what he means! Why didn't I think of it before? What time is it?"

"Twenty to twelve."

"And the Senate meets at noon. Come on, let's get out of here!"

He pulled Jimmy after him to the door where they collided with the police lieutenant who was just coming in. They dragged him back to his car, scrambled in beside him, and ordered the driver to head for the Capitol at top speed.

"What the devil—" began the lieutenant.

"If we're lucky," Morris said breathlessly, "you'll have the murderer in a few minutes. If we're unlucky, you'll have a dead senator to explain. Fill him in on the Smith letters, Jimmy."

The officer listened noncommittally.

"Sounds screwy enough to be true," he conceded. "But what's this chase we're on now? You know the next one he's after?"

"I don't know who," Morris admitted, "but I know *where* and how."

The car pulled up before the Capitol and Morris sprinted ahead of the others up the stone steps. Outside the Senate chamber there was the usual bustle of a session-about-to-begin, but it seemed today somewhat subdued. A cluster of high school students listened to a guide's lecture.

Morris stood for several seconds blinking at the change from bright sunlight. Then an elevator door opened and an elderly gentleman stepped out, flanked by document-bearing aides. Morris made a quick identification—Chairman of the Senate Appropriations Committee. Scheduled to speak on federal aid to education. Naturally Smith wrote to him, too.

Morris' eye caught a flick of movement from behind a pillar and he made a flying leap for the startled Senator, toppling him to the floor beneath him.

"It's the mad killer!" the students shouted gleefully, surging toward the fallen pair. "We've caught the mass murderer!"

A shot froze them to silence. As Morris dove at the Senator, Jimmy had sprung in the opposite direction toward the little man emerging from the shelter of the pillar. He reached him just in time to knock his gun arm upward so that the bullet lodged harmlessly in the molding above the elevator.

Almost simultaneously the police lieutenant, his own gun unholstered, moved in. Together they hustled Smith into one of the small private rooms before the spectators could sort out who was attacking whom.

The aides helped the Senator to his feet and he felt gingerly for bruises.

"It appears that you saved my life, young man," he told Morris. "But I don't think I could survive many such rescues."

"Sorry to be so rough, sir." Morris identified himself, then added, "I hope you'll give the *Comet* an exclusive on how it feels to be shot at."

"You're entitled to that," the Senator agreed. "But what gave you the idea you'd find the assassin here?"

"He spelled it out in his last note," Morris explained. *"So long* didn't mean goodbye. The word 'so' means 'in that or like manner.' Here's the way the meaning works out: so long—like long—like Long—*like Huey Long."*

"Poor Huey," the Senator said. "I knew him well. It must be twenty-five years since he was killed."

"That's right," Morris said. "Shot to death in the capitol at Baton Rouge on his way to address the Senate. And you were here in the Capitol on your way to address the Senate. . . . Again he was making history repeat—in his fashion."

FLORIDA

HIJACK

by Robert L. Fish

FIVE O'CLOCK ON a late-summer afternoon, a warm hazy day with only a faint cloud line at the distant horizon hovering over the low Tennessee mountains sloping toward flatness to the west, and the plane—a 727 tri-jet—at 28,000 feet approaching the Tennessee River Valley on a south-southwestern heading from Kennedy in New York to New Orleans, with the sun quartering in on the copilot, sinking fast.

The radioman pushed himself into the cockpit through the narrow door from the cabin, adjusting his trousers, nodding comfortably to the captain. He settled himself at his desk again, putting his earphones back in place, reaching to fiddle with knobs. The captain studied him a moment, reading nothing in the even expression, and then glanced over his shoulder, looking below. Sunlight winked from water. The captain reached for his microphone, switching off the soft cabin music to gain priority, pressing the button that transferred the intercom system from tape to voice.

"Ladies and gentlemen, this is your captain speaking. To the right of the plane and almost directly beneath us is Watts Bar Lake, a part of the TVA project. Those passengers on the left can see the Watts Bar Dam and Lake Chickamauga beyond. In the distance to the east, for those with sharp eyesight, there are the Great Smoky Mountains. . . ."

He replaced the microphone neatly and flipped the switch; the music returned. Almost in the same instant a light flashed on his intercom panel. The captain leaned over and pressed a button.

"Yes?"

"Captain, this is Clarisse. We've got trouble."

"Trouble?"

"A passenger is locked in the washroom with Milly." The stewardess' voice hurried on, anxious to avoid misunderstanding. "It isn't a pass, Captain. It's a hijacking." Her voice, striving for steadiness, echoed metallically in the crowded cockpit.

The radioman stared; the copilot started to come to his feet. Captain Little-john's restraining hand motioned him to sit down again.

"Where are the air marshals?"

"One of them is here with me now—"

"Before you put him on, what about the passengers?"

"They don't know a thing yet."

"Good. Let's keep it that way. Now, let me talk to the marshal."

There was a brief pause and then a man's low voice was heard in the cockpit.

"Hello, Captain. Apparently what happened was the man walked back to the lavatory, nobody paying any attention to him, and when he got there he pulled a gun on the girl and forced her into the washroom. I've spoken to her through the door. So far she's all right, but she says he's got a gun and a knife, and also a bottle he claims is nitro. She says it looks oily and yellow." The sky marshal cleared his throat. "What do you want us to do?"

"Nothing," the captain said quickly and firmly. "Go back to your seat. He's having Milly talk because he has her between him and the door. Go sit down. Let Clarisse handle any communication. I'll get through to New Orleans for instructions."

The radioman was already at work, calling the New Orleans tower. The captain's face was stiff. He spoke into the microphone.

"Clarisse?"

"Yes, Captain?"

"Put an OUT OF ORDER sign on the washroom door. And keep the curtain drawn. Is Milly still all right?"

"Yes, sir. Wait a second—she's saying something"—there was a pause. "Hello, Captain? She says he wants the plane diverted to Jacksonville. To refuel."

"Where does he want to go? We have more than enough fuel for Cuba. Better have Milly remind him this isn't a 747, however."

"Yes, sir. She didn't say anything else."

"Who is he, do you know?"

"He's on the seat chart as a Charles Wagner from Hartford. He was in seat sixteen C, on the aisle. I served him lunch when we left Kennedy—"

"What did he look like?"

Clarisse sounded unsure of herself. "Like—like anybody, I guess. Middle thirties, hair a little long but getting thin. . . ."

"How much did he have to drink?"

"Just a beer. I'm sure he wasn't drunk. What should I do?"

"Nothing. Try to look busy back there, in case anybody wonders why you're hanging around there. Get that sign up right away. And remember the curtain. And let me know if—"

The radioman swung around. "New Orleans tower. I've already identified."

"Mayday here," the captain said into the microphone. "We've got a hijacker on board."

"What condition?"

"He has one of our stewardesses locked in a washroom. Armed. Several times. Maybe with nitroglycerin, too. It sounds like it."

"Where does he want to go?"

"So far, just to JAX. For refueling, he says."

"Hold it," said the voice. "I'll contact higher up and be back."

The captain stared ahead, his face a mask. Under his hand the wheel held steady. The shadows ahead deepened. The wait seemed endless, filled with niggling static. Then the static cleared; a different voice was on the radio. It sounded more assured, more authoritative.

"Captain Littlejohn? This is Security, New Orleans. Permission granted to change course to Jacksonville."

The copilot was already digging into his map bag for routing maps. Captain Littlejohn's hand was already swinging the wheel, banking gently. A thought came to him to explain away any of his passengers' doubts.

"Ladies and gentlemen," he said into the cabin intercom, "to give the people on the other side of the plane a chance to see what little can be seen of the TVA project at this late hour. . . ."

He continued on a wide banking circle, coming out of it gently with the nose pointing now to the southeast and the growing darkness there. The voice of Security came on.

"Good work, Captain. Eventually, of course, they're going to have to know. In the meantime, tie into Jacksonville Security. They've been informed. We'll be on, too."

"Roger," Littlejohn said, and he peered over the copilot's shoulder at the air map. Clarisse's voice came back.

"Captain?"

The captain straightened up from the folded map almost reluctantly.

"Yes?"

"He wants money. A ransom for the passengers and the plane. He wants it waiting for him when we get there. Otherwise, he says he'll take Milly first and then blow up the plane."

"How much ransom?"

Clarisse swallowed. "A—a quarter of a million dollars."

Captain Littlejohn's expression didn't change in the least. He picked up his microphone.

"New Orleans Security? Do you still read me?"

A different voice answered. "This is JAX. We read you loud and clear."

"The hijacker wants a quarter of a million dollars."

"We heard. Who is he?"

"He's listed as a Charles Wagner, from Hartford, Connecticut."

"What else does he want?"

"One second." The microphone was laid aside temporarily, the intercom button pressed. "Clarisse—anything else?"

"Yes, sir. A whole flock of things. I guess he's had time to think. I scribbled them down." Clarisse referred to her paper; her tone changed abruptly. "I'm sorry, sir, that lavatory is out of order. No, the other one is fine. Yes, sir." Her voice dropped again. "A passenger. I put the sign up, but some people—"

"Never mind. Go on."

"Yes, sir. Here's what he wants. The money in an overnight bag, nothing smaller than fifties, nothing bigger than hundreds, banded in twenty-five-thousand-dollar bundles. He wants the plane to land at the end of runway 725 at Jacksonville, as far from the terminal as possible—"

"Hold it," Captain Littlejohn said and spoke into the mike. "Security, did you get that?"

"We got it. Go on."

"Go ahead, Clarisse."

"Yes, sir. He doesn't want anyone to come near. He says the passengers can get off. After that, he will come out of the washroom. The money will be delivered, but no one can enter the plane. And he wants—two parachutes. . . ."

"Two of them?"

"That's what he said. A sports model and an Army standard."

Security could be heard, speaking in an aside to someone. "Get a fast check on Charles Wagner through the U. S. Parachute Association right away, hear?" It came back full. "What else, Captain?"

"Clarisse?"

"That's all, Captain. So far. He says further instructions will be given when we're on the ground."

"Right." The intercom button was depressed; the captain spoke into his mike. "Security? We'll want to be cleared for landing on 725 regardless of wind direction."

"Roger."

"And what about the money he wants?"

"It'll be there. I don't know how long he'll keep it, but he'll get it. As well as the parachutes."

"Good," Captain Littlejohn said. "I'd hate to lose Milly. Not to mention a plane full of passengers."

There was no reply. The mike was switched off, attention given to flying the plane. The sunset was almost behind them now, the shadows of the Smokies creeping beneath their wings. The Knoxville-Jacksonville beam was intercepted; the plane banked smoothly into the air corridor, its heading now nearly due south. The engines droned in the deepening darkness; the cockpit lights showed the strain on the faces of the men within. At last the lights of Jacksonville could be seen, together with the feathery trail outlining the beach down toward St. Augustine. The plane began losing altitude. With a sigh, Captain Littlejohn turned over the plane to the copilot, who immediately began speaking with the tower. Captain Littlejohn took over the task of informing the passengers. He pressed the proper button. His voice was completely impersonal.

"Ladies and gentlemen, this is your captain again. Due to adverse weather conditions, we are forced to make our landing at the Jacksonville, Florida, airport. A company representative on the ground will explain the delay and arrange any necessary transportation. We regret this inconvenience. Now, please fasten your seat belts, bring your seats to the vertical position and observe the NO SMOKING SIGN. . . ."

The last grumbling passenger had filed from the plane, surprised to find himself forced to take a waiting bus to the distant terminal building, unaware that very shortly he and his fellows would be in the envious position of being able to tell their friends of their adventure. Gasoline trucks were completing their refueling operation; a small station wagon took the place of the departing bus and two men got out.

One brought a small parachute in one hand and an overnight bag in the other; the second man carried a more cumbersome parachute. They climbed the aluminum steps, placed their loads on the floor of the plane without entering, nodded to a pale Clarisse, merely glanced in the direction of the washroom door and made their departure. They looked like FBI, and were. From the cockpit window, Captain Littlejohn watched them climb into their car and back off. He raised his microphone.

"Clarisse?"

"Yes, Captain?"

"Where do we go from here?"

"Just a second"—there was a long pause. On the ground, the fuel lines were being sucked into the trucks like monsters consuming outsized spaghetti. Clarisse was back. "Captain, he says first head toward Miami. He wants you to maintain minimum flying speed, he says two hundred knots will do, and to stay at two-thousand-feet altitude. And he wants the rear passenger entrance door left unlatched from the outside—"

Security in the tower had heard. It cut in.

Captain, is it possible to jump from your plane?"

"It is from this one," Littlejohn said. "He obviously selected a 727 on purpose. He couldn't do it with a 707 or a 747. Either he must know something about flying or he studied up for this caper."

"For a quarter of a million dollars," Security said dryly, "I imagine a man would be willing to study. Or even to make his first parachute jump. There's no record of him in any sky-diving group we've dug up so far."

"If it's his real name."

"As you say, if it's his real name. Any danger of depressurization at that altitude with the door being opened?"

"Not at two thousand feet. And Florida's flat. And if we didn't leave the door unlatched, he could still always use one of the emergency doors." Captain Littlejohn's voice was getting tight; the wait was making him nervous. "Well, what do we do?"

There was a pause. A new voice came on.

"Captain? This is Major Willoughby of the Air Force. Do you have any suggestion?"

"Well," Littlejohn said slowly, "I suppose we could keep over water; he wouldn't jump there. It might give you time to scramble a few planes and meet us somewhere. He won't stand still for that water bit very long, but if you have a few planes follow, it might help."

The copilot cut in, a boy with much wartime experience.

"If he free-falls even five hundred feet, they'll never see him at night."

"At least they could try."

"I'll buy that," Major Willoughby said. "I'll get you cleared for following the coast as long as you can; we'll get other aircraft out of the way, although you'll be flying far below anything commercial until you get near airports. Try to hold over water until Daytona, if you can. We'll be with you by then at the latest. All right?"

"Fine."

"Captain," Clarisse said in a tight voice. "He's getting nervous."

"Tell him we're on our way," Littlejohn said, and he pressed the first of the engine starting buttons.

The plane swung about; the engine whine built up, and then they seemed to leap free. The large plane raced down the runway, gathering speed, and then seemed to raise itself slightly. They swooped up vertically; the city lights fell away, twisting as they banked. Littlejohn leveled off, following the coast a mile offshore. Security came back on the radio.

"What's our boy doing now?"

"God knows," Littlejohn said. "He'll undoubtedly be coming out of his little washroom soon and he'll see we're over water. Then"—he shrugged; the shrug was reflected in his voice. "Well, then we'll see."

"Keep this radio link open."

"Don't worry."

"Captain—"

"Yes, Clarisse?"

"He's going to come out—"

Littlejohn spoke rapidly:

"Clarisse! That microphone cord should reach to the next seat. I want you to strap yourself in and I want Milly to strap *herself* in as soon as she comes out. That nut can jump or fall, for all I care, but I don't want either of you girls to take any chances near that open door. Do you hear?"

"Yes, sir. Just a second"—there was a short pause. "I'm strapped in, Captain." The timbre of her voice changed. "Captain—they're out. . . ."

"How's Milly?"

"Pale as a ghost, and I don't wonder. Milly, sit down. Strap yourself in"—a brief pause, with everyone in the cockpit staring intently at the small cloth-covered speaker. "Captain, he's looking down at the water. He says either you turn overland right now or he'll kill Milly and then me. Captain—I—I think he means it. . . ."

"Turn," Security said at once.

"It's all right, anyway," Major Willoughby's voice said. "We just picked you up."

Littlejohn instantly put the plane into a bank; the lights of Crescent Beach fled beneath them, a cluster with Route A1A etched on either side.

"Captain—"

"Yes, Clarisse?"

"He says—"

"Let me talk to him."

"Just a second." Silence. "Captain, he won't talk into the microphone. But he says fly to Ocala and then turn straight south for Naples, same speed, same altitude as now. He says you can come out of the cockpit by Naples; he'll be gone by then."

Security cut in:

"Do it his way, Captain. Don't take any chances. The major's planes have you in sight and we've also got every town's police notified to be on the lookout for a chute. He won't get far."

"There's a lot of empty space in central Florida, but whatever you say," Littlejohn said. "In that case, why not get us cleared from Naples over to Miami at a reasonable altitude and make us some hotel reservations there for tonight?"

"Will do."

Clarisse came back on, nervous.

"Captain, he wants us to get up into the cockpit before he jumps, doesn't want us to see. . . ."

Littlejohn sighed. "All right, but hang on. I'll bank slightly to keep you away from that door. Come ahead."

The men waited impatiently; at last there was a tap on the door. It opened and two very nervous stewardesses sidled into the cramped space, shutting the door behind them. Milly was pale from her ordeal; Clarisse was partially supporting her. Littlejohn looked at them questioningly.

"She'll be all right," Clarisse said.

Littlejohn set his jaw and stared down. Beneath their steady nose, Dade City came and went, and then the vastness of southwestern Florida, inching past at the maddeningly slow speed of 200 knots. At long last the lights of the west coast could be seen in the still night. The radioman looked up.

"Naples coming up," he said.

They stared down, watching the lights pass them, and then they were out over the Gulf. Littlejohn turned to the copilot.

"Mike, want to take a look? Be careful."

"Right," said the copilot, and he pushed past the stewardesses and into the empty corridor of the plane. He walked to the other end of the plane and back, hanging onto the seats as he passed the cabin door, swinging back and forth, clanking as it struck each time. He came back into the cockpit and closed the door.

"All clear."

"We missed him," Major Willoughby's voice said, disappointed.

"We'll pick him up. Don't worry," Security promised. "We've got the whole state covered under your route. Well, Captain, you're cleared to Miami. Good night and good luck."

"Thanks," Littlejohn said, and he switched off the microphone. His hand pressed the engine throttles forward. "Well, children," he said, "it's been a long day. Let's go get some rest."

The maps from the map bag were piled to one side. Captain Littlejohn was reaching into the bag.

"Fifty thousand each," the captain said softly. "Not bad for a few hours' work, plus a little careful planning. Especially considering that it's tax-free."

"I ought to get more," Milly said sullenly. "Five long damned hours crammed into a tiny washroom with a dead man!"

"You?" Clarisse said. "What about me? I had to push him out of that damn door. Even though I was fastened in with the harness and the rope, I was scared silly that I'd go out of the plane with him."

"I had to kill the poor bastard," the radioman said.

The copilot was paying no attention to the complaints. He was neatly putting his share in his attaché case.

"Charles Wagner . . ." he said to no one in particular. "The hard-luck guy who went to the john at the wrong time. I wonder what he did for a living."

GEORGIA

THE
SKY PIRATES
by Donald Jordan

IN THE AFTERNOON of each weekday, the helicopter for the S&D Bank left its pad atop the Atlanta center and sprang into the air like an odd looking insect given a sudden burst of energy. Taking a southerly course, it proceeded to fly in a rough circle, dropping down upon the helipads on top of S&D's branch banks or subsidiaries. Hovering over each pad, it ingested several sacks of cash and paper transactions representing the bank's daily receipts. The helicopter was small, not much more than a bubble with props, and was fondly referred to as the Jolly Green Pea. On any given day its return to the home bank found its belly engorged with bags of money, checks, and bonds—and receipts which hitherto would have taken at least forty-eight hours to transfer were turned over within the day of the transactions.

The protection of the chopper in its speedy collection of funds and paper rested with S&D's security chief, Sidney Longhorn Hammer. An ex-FBI agent, Hammer was a tough and meticulously careful security officer, with an eye for loopholes and vulnerable areas. He was a stocky man, not tall, with a thick torso and short-cropped, graying hair, stern and somewhat suspicious eyes, a no-nonsense air, and the movements of authority. He often chewed on the butt of an unlit cigar and from his left ear a small piece was missing, the result of an engagement with drug smugglers when he had been with the FBI. Hammer was well liked by the officers of the bank, demanded and earned confidence, and under his authority the exposure of the bank to theft and fraud, beginning at the home office and continuing through each of its vast network of branches and subsidiaries, had been all but eliminated. A restless and untiring man, he spent his days refining the bank's security, and extending this protection to the branches throughout the state.

The Jolly Green Pea was a fast little chopper and skimmed over the countryside like a bee. To reach the several cities it visited in a day, it crossed a great deal of open and forested land, sometimes no more than a speck in the sky, sometimes skimming the treetops. Its efficiency had been honed to a science, and as it settled onto the top of a bank building, one, two or three officers emerged as though on signal, threw their sacks into the bubble, and sent the aircraft on its way in a matter of seconds. But for occasional sick leave or time off, the pilot was a young man named Griggs who flew with confidence and ability and enjoyed his job immensely. The helicopter service had become so integrated into its system of accounting that it was scarcely noticed. On any given day, the Jolly Green Pea flew around the state, dropped down onto banks' roofs like a praying mantis, stuffed its belly with currency, and returned to the Atlanta nest like a full and satisfied insect.

In a little clearing deep into a pulpwood forest, far from any farmhouse, highway, or road, two men sat in another helicopter. The first was a young man with serious gray eyes, a strong jutting Dick Tracy chin, a face perhaps too lean and angular to be considered handsome, loosely groomed light hair, and a cool and quiet voice which, though sometimes icy, usually held a note of humor. His name was William Dailey. The second was a little older, shorter, and heavier, with thick, powerful legs that appeared incapable of the agility with which they could negotiate a wall or an obstacle course, eyes equally serious but in a different way—eyes that had seen the worst in men and what could happen to men, eyes that could not be shocked. His name was Holmes Fitzpatrick. They sat quietly, hardly speaking. In the copter were two radios, and, to be as certain as possible, each was monitoring a separate frequency. The hands and fingers of both men were sheathed in thin surgical gloves.

Bill Dailey glanced at his watch. "It's about time."

Without responding, Fitzpatrick gave him a look that asked silently: how could they know this would be the route chosen today?

"His navigation varies," Dailey said. "But I've watched Griggs too long. Today he'll be right on us." He'd hardly spoken when they heard the Jolly Green Pea contact the Atlanta tower. Dailey tightened his gloves and started the rotors. "Ready?"

"Yes, sir," Fitzpatrick said.

The chopper rose, attained visible altitude, and hovered just above the treetops. In minutes they saw the Pea; it was at about three o'clock, exactly as Dailey had calculated. Dailey swung around, flew low, then rose and shadowed the S&D copter for a few miles. At precisely three forty-five he looked at Fitzpatrick.

"I'm ready, captain," Fitzpatrick said. From beneath his legs he drew an automatic rifle. He inserted a clip, and braced himself into the door. Dailey increased speed, gained altitude, and flew in close and slightly above the Pea. The pilot, surprised, gave them a hard look, then with a flash of perception called the tower. "This is SD one-five-niner-two-seven. I got a chopper on me. . . ."

Dailey broke into this transmission with authority. "SD one-five-niner-two-seven, change to frequency two thirty-seven."

There was a moment's hesitation, then on this new frequency Griggs said tersely, "All right, what do you want?"

Dailey jockeyed into a position which made Fitzpatrick, sitting in the door with the automatic, clearly visible. "Remain on this frequency," he ordered. "Do not contact the tower. Now, Mr. Griggs, in approximately one minute I want you to get that chopper down."

There was another second's delay, then Griggs' voice from the Pea blurted, "You're crazy! What the hell do you—"

Fitzpatrick leaned forward. He lifted the automatic rifle so that Griggs could easily see what he intended to do. Fitzpatrick fired three rounds in front of the Pea. The pilot saw the recoil and he could hear the rat-tat-tat of the report. The second radio, sitting between Fitzpatrick's legs, was tuned in to the Atlanta tower. On this radio they heard Griggs' urgent call, "Mayday! Mayday! This is SD one-five-niner-two-seven. I'm being hijacked—"

Fitzpatrick, an expert marksman, steadied himself and fired one round at the Pea. It entered one side of the bubble and passed cleanly through the other. The pilot's recoil was easily visible; the Pea took a dip, then went into a series of evasive actions. Dailey, the better pilot, stayed with him, perhaps fifty feet away. Fitzpatrick, his legs braced against the sides of the cockpit, took the shock without lowering the rifle. The little chopper leveled off and Dailey said coolly, "Return to frequency two thirty-seven."

The unnatural, mechanical movements of the young pilot were evident, his anger at being cornered almost palpable. Then on the radio he said tersely, "All right, you got me. What do you want?"

"I want you to put that chopper down," said Dailey. "I do not wish to shoot you down but I will if necessary. Turn right ten degrees. In one minute you'll see an open field."

The chopper responded. In seconds the field appeared and the Jolly Green Pea settled upon it as neatly as a bird alighting. Dailey followed closely.

"Cut your engine," Dailey ordered. "Get out of the chopper."

Griggs did not respond. Dailey tapped Fitzpatrick on the shoulder and the latter lowered the rifle and placed it between his knees.

"Mr. Griggs," said Dailey, "get out of the chopper. You will not be harmed. Walk away. Don't look back."

"Listen," Griggs said. "You'll never get away—"

"You have ten seconds," said Dailey.

Griggs swore and climbed out of the Pea. He gave them one quick furtive look, then turned and began to walk. He walked slowly at first, glancing over his shoulder, then suddenly he began to run, darting, as though to evade the bullets he expected. He ran until he reached the woods.

"All right," said Dailey.

Fitzpatrick put down the rifle and walked to the Pea. He removed the bank bags and loaded them into their copter. He then decommissioned the Pea's radio and tore out the ignition. To Dailey he said, "I'll cut the fuel line, just to be safe."

"Make sure he can see it," Dailey said. "I'd hate for him to take off without fuel."

Fitzpatrick cut the line, then climbed back in. As they rose they saw Griggs running back to the Pea, looking up at their rising chopper. Turning south, they flew until they were beyond Griggs' hearing, then they turned east and north. Within minutes Dailey brought the chopper down again, this time in an open area not far from a secondary road. They got out and removed the sacks from the chopper. Two cars sat in the shade of an oak grove.

"You're sure you don't want to take the bags?" Fitzpatrick said.

"No, Just the cash."

Methodically, they cleared one sack, then placed in it the currency extracted from all the others. The remaining documents were left undisturbed. "How much do you think?" said Fitzpatrick.

"I don't know," Dailey replied. "But whatever—here." He counted out roughly one hundred thousand dollars from packages of large bills. Fitzpatrick put this in a suitcase retrieved from his car.

"Put everything back into the chopper," Dailey said.

They stacked the bags neatly in the aircraft. Fitzpatrick hesitated, as though reluctant to abort a mission. "You're sure about the chopper?"

"Yes," Dailey said. "Leave it. They'll find it easily. It can be flown out of here. The key is in the ignition."

He took his sack and threw it into the trunk of his car. They looked at one another, then shook hands. "Good luck, captain."

"Good luck to you, Holmes. You know the rules."

"I know them. If I never see you again. . . ."

"I know." Fitzpatrick gave a little salute, got into his car, and drove off. Dailey waited five minutes, then started his car.

Behind them they left a rented helicopter, fully operational and unscathed; bank bags with all receipts and records intact and, but for the missing currency, apparently untouched; the tracks of two rented cars and oversized boots; and no more prints than are made by surgical gloves. With them they took just under two million dollars in unmarked bills.

Except for a young helicopter pilot who had no transportation and no radio and who would have to walk two or three hours to find help, an aviation rental service who had to bring in a pilot to fly their chopper out, and several sacks of bank transactions temporarily diverted, William Dailey's sky piracy of S&D's Jolly Green Pea had been accomplished with little inconvenience to anyone. Ex-combat veteran Holmes Fitzpatrick had, as a good tactical man will, questioned the validity of this maneuver but had accepted it totally when he agreed to his part in the mission. Ex-military pilot William Dailey had always been inordinately considerate, had always taken risks for the protection of others, but had never been known to fail. Fitzpatrick trusted him completely, would follow the strategy they'd agreed on for the dissemination of his part of the money, and would die protecting the secret.

Dailey drove north, parked the rented car in a ten acre parking lot where his own car was waiting, left the keys under the floor mat, and continued driving until he reached a motel where he had reservations. Both the car and the copter had been rented with documents he'd spent a year compiling—ersatz policies, a false address, counterfeit licenses, several previous legitimate rentals, and a beard, a wig, and a slight accent that distanced the fictitious Lawrence Price from himself, William Dailey. The year of research and planning had required the patience, intelligence, and resolve of a man dedicated to triumphing over an unseen enemy.

In his Holiday Inn room, Dailey arranged the money in stacks of one hundred thousand dollars each, which he placed in legal sized envelopes brought along for this purpose. He slept, but in the morning he did not return home. He embarked on a week-long automobile tour through four states and nearly twenty cities. The ingenuity with which he conducted this phase of his plans was not derived from experience. Dailey's record was clean. He knew, however, that sudden and unlimited cash had been the undoing of many a well-planned operation, and for the dissemination of the S&D money he had constructed a background over a long and painstaking period. In cities in Florida, Tennessee, the Carolinas, and Georgia he'd visited banks and made himself known to one or more of the officers. He told the bankers that he and his wife were thinking of retiring nearby, since his wife's people were from the area. This might be several years off, but in the meantime he wanted to establish credible banking contacts. He was expecting to come into some money, and perhaps he would be making a deposit in the bank. Of course at each bank he received a warm reception. On one or two subsequent visits he repeated the casual but carefully schemed contact.

Now, perhaps a year later, as Dailey drove through the four states, returning to some twenty or so banks, he said to each of the bankers in turn, "My uncle died recently and I've come into the inheritance I mentioned to you. I'd like to buy a savings certificate." He then handed over the envelope containing a hundred thousand in cash. The bank officers expressed surprise and not a little consternation that he carried cash. "Well, it's kind of a joke," Dailey said. "That was so much money that when the will was probated, my wife and I asked for cash, just so we could look at it for a day or two. I know that's foolish but we really got a kick out of touching all that money, you know. Actually, it wasn't quite a hundred thousand but I put a little with it to make a nice round number."

The bankers were eager to get the deposit, and raised no fuss when Dailey asked if the interest could be mailed to him at his present address.

Within a week, Dailey had deposited something under two million dollars in savings certificates in nearly twenty cities, with arrangements for interest to be mailed to him monthly. His annual projected income was approximately a quarter of a million dollars.

During his travels, Dailey read several reports about the skyjacking, described as a "daring daylight robbery" or "the space-age pirate's raid" but there was nothing in the papers to indicate that the police expected to break the case.

When he returned home he was tired, but his wife Gloria and his daughters Norma and Ellie greeted him with love and affection. "Daddy! When are we going to move?"

"Soon," he told them. "We're going to get a new start and some new friends."

Dailey had prepared his family to move to a new town as soon as his "inheritance" came through. Beginning a new life with a lot of money would not arouse the suspicion of old friends exposed to their sudden wealth. "Bill's expecting to receive an inheritance," Gloria had told her neighbors, "and when he does, he wants us to move to a place where he thinks he can take advantage of it."

For Gloria's benefit Dailey had arranged several telegrams through the year reporting his Uncle William's illness and, finally, months ago, the telegram announcing William's death. His week-long trip was ostensibly to assist in the final probation of his uncle's estate and the collection of his own patrimony. On the phone he'd told Gloria, "We'll get some cash but most of what I receive will be in securities. We'll get a nice monthly income, though."

So proficient had Dailey been in preparing his wife for these events that the final news of their wealth was no shock to her.

After he'd given the girls some presents and seen them off to bed, Dailey called his wife into their bedroom. "I want to show you something."

"What?" Gloria was excited. She was like a little girl, bright-eyed and flushed.

He took her into his arms. "We've got some money now. For the first time in our lives—we're rich!"

"Bill—oh, Bill, rich! We can't be rich!"

"I thought of getting you a little something special," he said. "Then I decided what the heck, we may as well treat ourselves to one big splurge. Here." He dumped the contents of his last envelope on the bed. She gave a cry. With noises of excitement, somewhere between laughter and crying, Gloria handled the money, felt it, smelled it, spread it out on the covers.

Then she jumped up and smothered him with kisses. "Oh Bill! I wish I had known your uncle!"

Sidney Longhorn Hammer received his first call from pilot Griggs some three hours after the Jolly Green Pea had been forced to land in the little clearing deep into the Georgia woodlands. Griggs called from a farmhouse that he'd reached after a hike of several miles over rough terrain. Hammer said, "I'll be damned." He obtained the location of the Pea and notified the authorities. By the time he informed the president of the bank, conferred with the federal agents, awaited the bank's decision on procedure, and decided to drive down and pick up Griggs himself, it was dark. Not until the following morning was the Pea located by air, when another chopper was used to fly in repair parts, along with Hammer, FBI agents, and Griggs. All the necessary ground investigations were made but in the heavily weeded field there was virtually no evidence that a second helicopter had ever been near the area. Griggs flew the S&D copter out. The sky was a clear cloudless blue and the first as picturesque as a postcard.

During the drive back to Atlanta, Hammer had interrogated Griggs and received an account of what had happened; his swift and shrewd mind, however, had already formed a pretty accurate conception before he heard the pilot's report. The sky pirates had evidently monitored the Pea's activity so long and thoroughly that a pattern had been surmised. The criminal chopper had obviously been piloted by an expert, which narrowed the range of suspects—considering the training facilities within a three hundred mile radius and the last decade's buildup of helicopter pilots—to several thousand.

In the next few days the investigations of federal agents, agents for the insurance companies, and Hammer tracked one another, but even after the authorities decided that there were no holes in the execution of the robbery and that only a long process of elimination might produce a lead, Hammer dogmatically pursued the case. It was his bank, his baby—almost his money. His professional competence had been attacked, and a fierce competitive instinct was aroused.

Hammer climbed into the Pea and had Griggs fly the route he'd taken on the day of the robbery. He hated flying, suspected that his bridges were going to be shaken loose, felt as exposed in the little bubble as a man taking a shower in public, and had to steel himself against the low altitude, the somewhat woozy sensation of treetops whizzing past fifty feet beneath like an exaggerated early movie clip of a comic car chase. From the S&D helipad they took off at precisely the same time Griggs had on the day of the robbery.

"I want you to fly as closely as possible over the route you took and do it in approximately the same time frame. Touch down on every bank."

Hammer kept his eyes on the ground, noting anything that might be of value, monitoring the time and questioning Griggs to help him recall anything extraordinary.

"You're always on the frequencies with the control towers, right? Do you remember any kind of transmission with another helicopter?"

"No, but these people would never have contacted the controllers and they wouldn't have had to reach an altitude that would put them on radar."

"That means that wherever they came from, somebody might have noticed them."

"I doubt it," said Griggs. "There's a lot of military chopper activity in this area. Chances are, nobody gave it a second thought."

"Let's say he flew the thing in, maybe from another state. Would he have had to fuel up?"

"That depends. Maybe not. I don't think he was on me very long." Doubtless feeling his own sense of responsibility and outrage, the young pilot set his jaw. "Maybe he was sitting quietly somewhere," Griggs said. "He heard my transmission or got a visual reading on me. Then he lifted off." Griggs' tone assumed a professional respect. "He could cowboy that chopper, I'll say that for him. It was like he anticipated every move I made."

Hammer made a note of that. Perhaps the skyjacker was a stunt helicopter showman; an aerial trapeze artist.

"About here's where he first intercepted me," Griggs said. "I doubt that he'd been shadowing me very long, but I can't be sure." They turned right and flew to the field where the Pea had been forced to land. "Want to sit her down?"

"No, we've trampled those weeds to death," said Hammer. "All right, they flew south, probably for your benefit. Then turned and went—where?"

"Probably not too far without refueling."

They returned to home base to refuel their own machine, but were in the air again when they learned, almost simultaneously, that a rented helicopter was missing, and that a farmer had discovered one. The chopper was located by air no more than ten miles northeast of the clearing where the Pea had been relieved of its cargo. This was forty-eight hours after the robbery, during which time Hammer realized the thieves could easily have reached Europe or Central America. He joined the feds in their site investigation, which proved about as frustrating as the previous one. Obviously the helicopter had been abandoned for cars; tracks were found, more or less obscured by the farmer's tractor tires. In the aircraft were all but one of the banks' bags, the contents, but for the currency, unmolested. The copter was in good flying condition. Hammer noted the neatness, the thoughtfulness with which the criminals had left all they couldn't use, and was struck with the sense of a personality who didn't wish to displease or harm—a personality almost apologetic in its criminality.

The aviation rental service brought in fuel and a man to fly the abandoned helicopter home. Hammer drove over and talked with the owners—Benning Aviation, Inc., a small partnership air service which owned only the one helicopter.

"Sure, this guy's rented our aircraft three, four times," Benning said. "No problems at all, paid in cash as I recall."

"Show me your documents," said Hammer.

"They're all here, believe me. We don't rent to anybody who's unqualified."

All the necessary records were in order. Benning described a man with a beard and blond hair who, though Hammer didn't know it, was totally unlike William Dailey. Though the authorities had gathered copies of the document as well as handwriting samples, Hammer asked for a few of his own. Already he knew that the previous helicopter rentals were contrived simply to lay the groundwork for the robbery.

As Hammer left, Benning added, "He had an accent, that I can tell you. Maybe European. Or Oriental."

"I'll bet he did," said Hammer.

A day later, a missing Hertz was found by the local police. It had been rented at the busy Atlanta airport with similar documents. The tank was half full and the key easily located.

To his wife, Mary, Hammer said, "These guys should have blown up the helicopter, destroyed the bank bags. Instead they went out of their way to be neat." He pulled on the ear lobe missing one small piece. "It doesn't fit the mode. What does that tell me?"

"I don't know, dear."

"Neither do I—yet."

He retreated to his overstuffed chair where he could chew on his cigar and brood in privacy. It seemed the skyjackers, infallible in their strategy, neat in their execution, had relieved the bank of a great sum of money and disappeared, as it were, into thin air.

Norma and Ellie Dailey squealed. They ran in circles and jumped up and down. "It's finished! It's finished!"

Gloria Dailey clapped her hands. "That's the most beautiful doll house I've ever seen."

Bill Dailey smiled faintly, pleased. "I've always wanted to do things like this," he said.

"It's having the time to put your mind on it," said Gloria. "And that handsome shop you've set up: Are you going to make the miniature furniture?"

"I think you should buy the furniture. Good stuff, though," Bill said. "Nothing cheap. Remember, this could be an heirloom."

Beyond their windows the picturesque Tucson mountains were etched against a sky brilliantly blue. The fully equipped shop was one Bill had ordered when he purchased the house. Gloria was right; having the time to devote himself to handicrafts made a difference. For one thing, it established the impression of a man of leisure. Dailey had hardly done anything more than work in his new shop, prepare his wife and daughters for a lifestyle of relative wealth, and wait.

Dailey left his family and walked outside. He himself was not utterly acclimated to luxury and the indulgence of it left him with a faint sense of guilt. Though he loved flying, since moving into their new house he had not flown; nor would their slowly developing circle of new friends know he had been a pilot. For his aircraft he had substituted something he'd always thought he would like, a sleek and expensive car. In his garage sat a white and blue Mercedes. It was part of their one-time "splurge."

Prior to robbing the S&D bank, Dailey had committed no crimes. He had been a good student and had graduated from college. He'd served his country. He had been a dedicated family man. After finishing his tour of duty he'd found that, like so many others, he could not get a job as a pilot, and had tried to make it in some of the technological fields in which he had some expertise. Times were hard, jobs were scarce, and even when he had tried moonlighting as a computer operator there was hardly enough money to guarantee his family the things they needed.

To his wife, Dailey had often said, "What happened to the dream? I must have been some kind of moonstruck college kid."

"Things will work out," Gloria said. "We have each other." Her faith in him was compelling.

"It seems all I do is work," Dailey said. "If I'm not working I'm looking for ways to get ahead. I hate it. And if I hate it, how are you and the kids ever going to be happy?"

Dailey considered himself a victim of circumstances. He evidently could not do what he had expected to be able to do with his life. Dedication to patriotism, morality, and uprightness had been a disaster. He saw corruption in government, criminal infiltration into law enforcement, men in high places succeeding in shady deals for a quick buck, the triumph of criminality and crime, which seemed to receive protection from a mantle of respectability. He saw his family deprived while those who had contributed nothing fed on the vulnerability of others. And he was outraged.

Dailey actually had an Uncle William who was very much alive. Dailey's parents had died in an accident when he was a child and his father's brother Bill had taken him. Uncle William had administered the estate, providing for Dailey's needs and his education. The bulk of the money, however, he had invested in long term bonds which would not mature until Dailey was in his forties. It was foolish to so restrict the estate during a period of life when Dailey would need it most, and when Dailey had found out about it, at about age twenty-three, he and his uncle had had harsh words. He moved out, joined the service, and ceased to have contact with his uncle except concerning matters of the estate. Now that he was independently wealthy, he saw no point in advising Uncle William of his whereabouts; when it was occasionally necessary for them to discuss business he handled this on the phone. It would be impossible to permit Gloria to know, ever, that he had any family.

Dailey took a look at his Mercedes, wiping a spot with his handkerchief. Then he walked back into the house to share the happiness of his family. As he reached the door a small plane flew overhead, and a twinge of apprehension and regret swept through him. He forced this aside by reminding himself that he was a man of wealth, that he had used his mind to establish his family for life without seriously injuring anyone, and that he had gotten away with it.

Sidney Hammer was not intimidated by the meeting that had been called by S&D's president but he knew that in the final analysis it was his scalp that would be shaved. The butt of the cigar jammed between his teeth was no less than a week old and had acquired something of the aroma of a rotted swamp log. Though no flame burned at its tip, the sign on the conference room door that said "Thank You For Not Smoking" would not have compelled him to extinguish the flame had he chosen to smoke.

The bank's president was a man named Gliglow, a *wunderkind* of the banking industry with an aggressive format, an impressive history, and an almost uncanny grasp of the legal and physical aspects of running a bank. Local law enforcement officials, agents for the FBI, insurance investigators, and most of the bank's security force—Hammer's people—attended the meeting, along with selected bank officers indoctrinated in the necessity for secrecy. Though Gliglow's questions were probing and enlightened, the result of the two hour meeting was a report which Hammer could have provided him with in five minutes: the well-executed robbery left them with no early leads; none of the money surfaced, and the freely flowing arteries of police information had received no injection of covert information.

As expected, Gliglow, who above all else was a man of responsibility, addressed himself to the weaknesses of the bank. "We evidently opened ourselves to exposure," he said. "How do you think this happened, Sidney?"

Out of respect, Hammer removed the cigar butt before answering. "At all the points of ground contact the helicopter was secured. We have a contingency plan in case of motor failure or forced landing. An in-air commandeering wasn't programmed."

"Not programmed, but it happened," said Gliglow. "Evidently we have some gaps in our security."

"Yes, sir."

"What've we done to correct this?"

"The weakness appears to have been in navigation procedures. We've briefed our pilots on the uses of a highly varied circuit."

"You're convinced this couldn't happen again?"

"No, sir," Hammer said. "I wouldn't say it couldn't. There's no absolute security against people who have the ingenuity and the resources. Not even for Brink's."

Gliglow knew, of course, what any street cop could tell him: that beyond a certain point there was nothing you could do to prevent robbery by someone determined enough and bold enough.

"Getting hit is one thing," Gliglow said. "Making no arrest is another. I'd hate to discontinue the helicopter service."

"We won't," Hammer said. "We'll find them."

The president gave him a chilly look. "I hope it's before all the money's gone."

Over and over, Hammer reviewed his sketchy evidence. The driver's and pilot's registrations used in the renting of cars and chopper were issued to a state resident, obviously an alias. Did this mean the impostor lived out of the state? Not necessarily. He might live around the corner from the temporary address used. Instead of the time-consuming process of obtaining false registrations, why hadn't the pirate simply used forged documents? Perhaps because he hadn't had a source of forged papers; perhaps because he wished to involve no one else in his scheme, or simply because he chose to keep things orderly and neat.

Hammer sent the driver's license number to the motor vehicle unit and received in return a picture of Lawrence Price, whose beard and blond hair matched the description offered by the personnel at Benning Aviation. He didn't think there was a prayer, but he took the picture out to the address that Price had used, an apartment complex called the Village Green on Piedmont. It was a somewhat seedy, low rent project, a quadrangle of two story brick buildings with exterior steel stairs, flaked and unpainted cornices, and concrete walks so cracked by roots and weather that every step was a danger. He found the resident manager in E-5, an athletic, vivacious little woman wearing jeans and stripping down an antique china cabinet which stood on newspapers on her patio. He showed her the picture.

"I guess you don't remember this tenant. He used to live in—let's see—A-7."

From a chain attached to her collar dangled a pair of glasses and she put these on. "You know, I do remember him. And you know why? I think he was the neatest single man we've ever had here."

"What do you mean neat? Personality?"

"No, I mean *neat*. His apartment." She lowered her voice. "Not very many of the people we get here care much about how the place looks, you know? It's low rent, comparatively. You go into any one of these apartments and—well, a mess. That's why the man who owns them never does any painting or repair that isn't necessary. This Mr.—what was his name?"

"Price?" asked Hammer.

"Price. That's it. Mr. Price moved in and right away fixed his apartment up. I mean, he straightened drapery rods, put screws in the door hinges, mended the furniture—he didn't have any of his own furniture—that sort of thing. Neat."

"How long's he been gone?"

"Oh, several months. He signed a year's lease but left before his time was up. That's pretty unusual, too."

"Did you get to know him, talk to him?"

"We hardly spoke at all," she said. "He had a funny little accent. The only thing I can remember is when I asked him what sort of business he was in he told me he was a geologist. He flew planes or something with all this exploration equipment. I couldn't imagine what they thought they'd find in this part of the world, but you know, he looked exactly like a geologist!"

Hammer thought about this a minute. The best lie was a half truth. Price evidently was not worried about letting it be known he was a pilot. Why should he be? It was the purpose for his establishing a false residence.

"Maybe I could see Mr. Price's apartment," he said.

She returned the picture, removed her glasses, and said, "Someone else lives there now. Why do you want to?"

Hammer gave her a brief glimpse of his I.D.—just enough to let her know he carried a badge. "Mr. Price seems to have disappeared. It could be he left something behind that would give us some lead as to his whereabouts."

"Not a chance," she said. "He hardly even had any clothes. All right, I'll let you see it. The tenants are at work. I'll have to go in with you."

She accompanied him to A-7. It now was occupied by a couple with two small children. Not very tidy. Of course all evidence of the previous tenant had been eradicated. The chance of undisturbed prints was nil. As they left, the manager said again, "Mr. Price simply didn't talk much. Any time he wanted anything he'd leave me a note. Like when he'd be back for his mail."

"Notes, huh?" said Hammer. "Not a chance you'd have kept any of these?"

She gave him a bright, efficient look. "Before I retired and took this job I was a secretary for a man who was always writing me notes on anything he could find—envelopes, pieces of magazine covers. I'd always follow the instructions, then file the notes. You'd be surprised how many times I had to prove to him I'd done what he told me. Yes," she said, "I probably have Mr. Price's notes in my correspondence file."

Hammer grinned. "How sweet you are. Dig them out for me, will you?" He gave her his address. "Drop them in the mail, huh?"

A day or two later he received a couple of notes that Price had written the apartment manager. They were in the same neat printing used on the rental forms—hardly identifiable—though the signature *Lawrence Price* was freer and perhaps that of a man not expecting scrutiny. Hammer sent copies to the lab on the hopes that a handwriting analysis might provide him a hint. The result was negative.

He took another drive out to the Village Green for a second look around and to ask the energetic manager, "Do you remember ever noticing the car Price drove. Make, model? County?"

"Gosh no," she said. "I couldn't tell you right now what any tenant drives or even if they have a car. I remember one other thing, though. The day he fixed my cabinet, I asked Mr. Price about his family. The only thing he said was that they lived in another state and in a few months he was going to join them."

"He fixed a cabinet in his apartment?"

"No, in my laundry room. Out by the pool. We have a cabinet where I keep my supplies. One of the doors had warped so badly it had twisted the hinge, you know? Every time I locked it, I had to lift up one side. I think Mr. Price just looked at that lopsided door until he was sick of it."

"Let me take a look, will you?"

She led him to the laundry room and the cabinet. It was inside, not exposed to weather. He could see that the door had been removed, trimmed and new hinge holes aligned.

"He borrowed my tools and fixed it in a jiffy."

"You've done no painting since then?" said Hammer. "Cleaning?"

"All I do out here is sweep up the chewing gum and cigarette wrappers."

"How about letting me borrow your door for a couple of days? I'll need a screwdriver."

She gave him a look. "I guess I could take my supplies inside. Not that there's anything worth stealing. You will bring my door back."

"For sure," he said.

Using her screwdriver Hammer carefully backed out the screws and removed the cabinet door. He took this in to the lab. Chances were good that no one else had touched the hinge side of the door and that, out of the weather, the slick plywood held a removable print.

It was a hunch—and the first stroke of luck—a hunch that paid off. The lab picked up a couple of clean prints. The data went out and Hammer waited.

Within twenty-four hours he had his answer. Nobody could identify the finger-prints. Alias Mr. Price had no record.

The preparations and subsequent movements of Holmes Fitzpatrick were not, by necessity, as dramatic as those of Dailey. Holmes would have done almost anything Dailey requested of him. The captain had once saved his life when Fitzpatrick's gunship went down and Dailey literally darted in through the trees to pluck Holmes and his buddies out of the jaws of the enemy. After that Holmes insisted on, and was granted, assignment with Dailey's crew.

Holmes' part in the robbery was simple enough. Other than a short briefing he knew nothing of the details. On a specified day he was picked up, told his assign-ment, jockeyed into position to fire on the Jolly Green Pea, and returned safely to his car. Not bad for a hundred thousand grand.

Holmes was a single man and had no family to whom to explain anything. He elected not to dispose of his money but to secrete it discreetly in his home. Just as discreetly, he used small amounts of currency at will. He was an expert marks-man and followed the shooting circuits. At gun and skeet clubs he won many a bet, which would explain extra funds if the question ever arose. The worst that could happen was an investigation of unreported income by the IRS.

Fitzpatrick had no desire to be caught and imprisoned for robbery; but he had seen worse things—much worse. He had an attitude of inevitability, perhaps fatalism, that endowed him with a certain freedom. He did what he wished when he wished it. He gambled for high stakes on his marksmanship, and when he lost, he paid off with fairly large sums of cash. He did not worry about implicat-ing Captain Dailey, for no matter what happened to him, he would never reveal the identity of his collaborator.

Hammer knew that a man who could fire a missile through a moving aircraft, doing harm to neither pilot nor machine, would have to be an expert marksman. He might be military or ex-military. He might be civilian, a sportsman and gun enthusiast, a top-notch rifleman. He might even be a police sharpshooter. Pilot Griggs, in fleeing to the cover of the trees, had had a distant glimpse of but one of the two robbers, and he appeared to be a man of average height and build, mid-thirties, who worked swiftly and confidently around choppers with spinning ro-tors. This perhaps implied familiarity with the aircraft, or ignorance of its dangers. All possibilities were fed into police profile computers with negative results. There were hundreds of skeet and gun clubs, branches of the riflemen's associations and shooting ranges, and the process of elimination, with limited police forces, could take forever.

Hammer racked his brain for a shortcut. The lack of a discoverable police record implied that these two men had come together to execute an isolated crime. What had brought them together? What did they have in common? One was a skilled pilot, the other an expert marksman. Where would two such profi-cient craftsmen merge? The only answer Hammer could think of was the military—helicopter gunships perhaps. Both military helicopter training and marksmanship were taught within two hundred miles of Atlanta.

With cooperation from the military and throwing all available personnel behind the effort, Hammer began to explore the records with emphasis on army sniper training. He received the dossiers on dozens, hundreds of men. The range of personalities he uncovered was varied: the street kid from Chicago, the Mexican-American who had been known to sit for three days on a trail waiting for a shot at the enemy. Griggs was shown as many photographs as possible. When current servicemen were exhausted, Hammer started working back for ten years.

The seemingly pointless task took an upswing when he talked to a colonel who headed up sniper training at Fort Benning. Not crazy about the direction of Hammer's pursuit, Colonel Slyke scoffed.

"You won't find any helicopter gunners in my outfit. That kind of weaponry resembles what we do like an elephant resembles a cobra."

"I may be dead wrong," said Hammer, "but somehow I keep getting flying and shooting together."

The next time he approached Slyke, the colonel was less adamant. "I happened to mention this to one of my officers. He remembered a man who came to us from a chopper assault outfit. Made a damn top sharpshooter."

"Who was he?"

"My officer couldn't recall the name. We'll find it. Can tell you this, though. The man hasn't been in the service for years."

"Okay. Who knows? It's all we've got," said Hammer. "Find it for me, will you?"

A few days later the colonel gave Hammer a name.

Moving at a fast pace, William Dailey took a mountain curve and felt the power, the performance, of his sleek Mercedes. He found a straight decline and gave it thrust, sliding into the inside as the blacktop canted into a reverse curve. He waited for a couple of vehicles to pass, then made a crossover, braked, and jerked to a halt. He stepped out of the car, walked to the rail, and looked out over the stark Arizona countryside. The colors, with a purity of light, appeared cleaner, more intense: blues, burnt siennas, crimsons. The vista was as close as he'd come to an airborne perspective since his pursuit of the Jolly Green Pea. He took a deep breath, filling his lungs, letting it out slowly.

Dailey felt restless. The transition to leisure from a hectic effort to work and earn money didn't come with ease. It wasn't that he was bored; more, it was that his talent, his ingenuity, weren't taxed. But for flying, he could think of no job he desired, and, for the moment at least, he could not consider opening his own flying operation. Conforming to his plan, he could do nothing that would require an extensive outlay of cash.

He rested his foot on the rail and was shocked, suddenly, by a thought that struck him. The thought was that he could commit another robbery. The action, the risk, the danger stirred his pulses, and he was surprised at himself. Maybe crime was addictive. He forced the thought aside as a passing idiocy. He refused to believe that his perfect success had placed him in a trap.

Dailey got into his car and drove home. The important thing to remember was that his wife and children were taken care of. He must do nothing to jeopardize that. He had made his will and attached to it, locked in his safe deposit box, was a list of his securities. Even if he died, even if he were imprisoned, his family would be okay.

His arrival at home was greeted with no outcry of excitement. Gloria was sitting on the patio, drinking a cocktail and wondering what to prepare for dinner. Her cupboards were so replete that making a decision required effort—gone were the days of hamburger helper and ground steak. The girls were fussing over their homework or the doll house, he wasn't sure which. He took a seat on the patio and Gloria made him a drink.

"You know, I was just thinking," she said. "Next week's my birthday. And I can't think of a thing I want."

"What a horrible fate."

"It just means that my beautiful husband has given us everything. It's nice, really. But I can never remember having a birthday when I didn't want a million things."

Mention of her birthday reminded Dailey of his restlessness, then of the fact that the annual interest on his bonds was nearly due. He'd have to call his Uncle William. The small annuity from his father's estate seemed a pittance compared to his present income, but he had no intention of letting it go.

When Colonel Slyke gave Hammer the name of Holmes Fitzpatrick it didn't sound like much to go on. Fitzpatrick had established his credentials as an army sharpshooter following his tour with a helicopter assault unit, and that linked expert marksmanship with flying. But so what? There was no telling how many such combinations might be uncovered. Hammer had no trouble finding Fitzpatrick and monitoring his movements. Holmes worked for a construction outfit and spent his weekends on the shooting circuits. He lived a relatively quiet life, maintained a small bank balance, and had made but one discernible change in his lifestyle. This was a notable increase in the amounts of money he wagered and his payments of losses in hard cash.

Hammer requested and was granted a search warrant and, with the authorities, entered Fitzpatrick's house while the man was away. It took about three hours for them to discover the cash secreted in a concealed compartment of a handsome gun case which contained a number of fine weapons. The sum was over fifty thousand dollars, and it was returned to its place.

With this break in the case, Hammer told his wife Mary, "Fitzpatrick did it. I'm sure we can nail him. But I think he got only a fraction of the money, otherwise he'd really be using it."

"Then who was the brains?" she asked, using the vernacular of the trade.

"We're going to monitor Fitzpatrick but not touch him until we find out. That's who'll have the money."

Pushing his luck with Colonel Slyke, Hammer sought and received help in tracing Fitzpatrick's record, his background with the assault unit. Numerous missions had been flown with various gunships, but there was one item in the record that stood out: a request by Fitzpatrick to be assigned to the crew of the chopper pilot who'd rescued him when his ship went down. The pilot was Captain William Dailey.

Hammer turned his attention to Dailey. From the service, he obtained handwriting samples which he returned to the experts along with the notes Lawrence Price had left with the Village Green apartment manager. The experts reported that the samples were strikingly similar if not identical.

Hammer got fingerprint records and personally took them, along with the prints lifted from the laundry room cabinet, to the crime lab. The results: the prints from the cabinet were William Dailey's.

When Hammer heard this he performed an uncharacteristic little jig, yanked the cigar butt from his mouth, and cried, "Hot damn!" At home during the evening his wife kept eyeing him, as though she could scarcely decide what to make of him. "You look," she said, "like the cat who's eaten the mouse."

Hammer settled down to figure out what he had. Alias Lawrence Price had, with a rented chopper, robbed the S&D bank. Price had rented an apartment in the Village Green apartments. He had changed a cabinet door. The fingerprints taken from the door were those of ex-military pilot William Dailey. This proved that Dailey was at the apartments. Did it prove that he and Price were the same? The odds against such a coincidence were a zillion to one, yet the evidence was, Hammer realized, circumstantial. To prove that Dailey committed the robbery he must find the money.

Hammer searched out Dailey's old address and found that the family had moved about a week after the robbery. He spoke to one of the neighbors, a young woman named Clark. "Oh, they've been gone a while," she said. "We hated to see them go. Especially Gloria."

"Do you know why they decided to move?"

"Bill got some money—from an inheritance, I think. I guess he thought he could put it to better use with a new start."

"Where'd they go?"

"Arizona. Tucson. I really don't know their plans."

"Actually, I'm trying to run down some of Bill's family," Hammer said. "This inheritance—did they mention any details?"

"I think Gloria said an uncle of Bill's died. They'd been anticipating it for several months."

Returning to military records, Hammer found that Dailey's aunt and uncle— the Uncle William Dailey for whom Bill had been named—lived in Alexandria, Virginia. He contacted a local investigator to perform some legwork. Hammer was interested in Dailey's "inheritance." If there were any truth to it, Dailey might be able to explain the acquisition of some money; but its happening so soon after the robbery made it entirely suspect. In a couple of days the investigator, Lowery, got back to him.

"I found the elder William Dailey all right," he said. "He's alive and healthy. He took care of his nephew until young Dailey moved out. They've had little contact since."

"Is he well off?"

"I'd say not. Very moderate house, style of living. I did find out he'd been executor for the estate left to Dailey. But that's tied up for a few years yet."

"So Dailey's come into no inheritance."

"Not from these people. And as far as I can determine they're his only relatives," Lowery said.

"Where's Dailey now?"

"They didn't know. They expect to hear from him soon about the estate. Funny thing, though, Mr. Dailey wouldn't tell me anything until I explained why I was there."

"What did you explain?"

"That his nephew had applied for a job and we were running a security check. I told him it was confidential and not to mention it even to young Dailey. I think he swallowed it."

"Okay," said Hammer. "Thanks."

Hammer flew to Tucson. The evidence against William Dailey was mounting, but without the money it came down to very little. What had Dailey done with the currency? Perhaps spirited it out of the country long before now. Hammer's original enthusiasm took a downplunge. Recovery and conviction began to appear hopeless. He sat in his seat like an old mole, chewing his cigar with a vengeance. Dailey had made only one mistake, and that was to leave a fingerprint that in itself would never bring him into court. He had outwitted Hammer's security system.

In Tucson, Hammer got his first look at William Dailey. Sitting in a rented van with a pair of binoculars, he spent a morning watching Dailey putter around his yard, go in and out of his workshop. Deciding he was too old for such reconnaissance, he enlisted help from the local authorities to monitor Dailey's movements for another couple of days. The man apparently didn't work. When Dailey left the house it was for various car trips. Yet his Mercedes and his house were not the trappings of an unwealthy man. Was it possible that he had the money secreted at his residence?

Hammer had Gloria Dailey tailed. At the market and the beauty shop she was seen writing checks. Hammer used his authority to make inquiries of the Tucson banks. He easily discovered an account in the name of William and Gloria Dailey. It took a phone call from the D. A. to get him into the bank's bookkeeping department.

"I just want to look over the Daileys' transactions," he told the pretty young girl who was assigned to assist him. "Especially the deposits."

"You know, the account's pretty new," she said, frowning over the readouts. "We show that the initial deposit was a cash one. There have been one or two deposits since."

As Hammer looked at the records he suddenly yanked the cigar butt from his teeth, hunched over the table like a defensive guard, and stared. A recent deposit was a direct transferal from the First Bank of Columbia, South Carolina, evidently a payment of interest on a certificate of deposit. "My God," he cried, "the man put the money in the bank!"

William Dailey's conversation with his uncle was, as usual, reserved if not cool. They discussed affairs of the small estate, and since Dailey didn't choose to reveal his present residence he requested that interest proceeds be deposited in his account in Alexandria. And as usual his uncle said, "You know, Bill, I think you should at least bring your wife and children to see us. What do you have now, two?"

"If we're ever up that way," Dailey said.

"We all make mistakes," said William. "You lived with us half your life, you know. I'd hate for your mother and father to know—"

"So would I," said Dailey. He could not bring himself to relinquish his bitterness.

His uncle sighed finally and said, "A man came here to ask us about you. We didn't know where you were but we told him good things about you, Bill."

Dailey was calling from a pay phone. He gripped the receiver tighter. "What man?"

"Someone running a security check on you. He asked us not to say anything but I figure you're entitled to know. You applying for a new job?"

"No—yes. When was this?"

"Few days ago. Is there anything you want us—"

"No," said Dailey. "I have to go. Say hello to Aunt Bess."

As Dailey hung up, he found that in his stomach was a feeling much as he'd experienced just before he took off for a chopper assault—tension, a thrill of fear, unease. Who could have traced him to his uncle? If it were someone from his past they would not have lied about their purpose; if someone were digging into his records, it could mean he was under investigation. Why?

Instead of returning home Dailey drove around, going over and over his steps from beginning to end. Where had he made a mistake? He could think of nothing that would implicate him in the robbery—except one thing. The money. It was possible that if the authorities had his name they would also discover the bank deposits. This, he realized, was the only way they could prove anything against him. He saw suddenly that the savings certificates were a mistake. He had been so thoughtful, so neat—perhaps too neat. But if he could move fast enough, if he could get the money withdrawn. . . .

For the first time since he'd moved to Tucson, Dailey rented a small plane. He went home, packed a bag, provided Gloria with an excuse for being away for a few days, and took off.

* * *

As quickly as he could get a flight, Sidney Hammer returned to Atlanta. Though excited, he didn't wish to jump so quickly he'd make a blunder; besides, there was no reason for Dailey to know he was under suspicion. When he reached his office at S&D, the first thing Hammer did was phone the First Bank of Columbia, and when he did, he felt that he'd had his wings broken with a double load.

"Yes," the bookkeeper told him, "our records show a William Dailey as a customer but his maximum deposit has been a hundred thousand dollars."

"A hundred thousand?" Hammer was looking for about two million. His heart sank. Dailey must have deposited some money to live on and gotten rid of the rest.

"And even that's been withdrawn," the bookkeeper said.

"Withdrawn?"

"Just yesterday. Mr. Dailey paid a penalty in order to withdraw his certificate."

When Hammer hung up he let out a bellow that made several people in the outer office come running. He gave them a snarl, closed the door, broke out a new cigar—he hated having to nurse a new cigar down to the butt—and tried to recover his dignity. Where was all the money? Why had Dailey made an untimely withdrawal? Had he been tipped off or was there another explanation for it? Where the hell was the two million?

Hammer puffed furiously and, enshrouded in smoke, stared at the pigeons strutting on the ledge beyond his glass. Suddenly he slammed his fist down. Maybe Dailey had not gotten the money out of the country. Maybe he'd made deposits in five banks, ten—twenty. Of course! Except by breaking the currency down, how else could he have made unsuspicious deposits? But what banks? What city—state?

Hammer called in all available personnel. "I want you to start phoning every bank within two hundred miles. Section off the states and each of you take an area. We want to know if William Dailey is a customer and the amount of his deposits."

"You mean call every bank?" someone said.

"Every bank. Even the small towns. It'll be faster than trying to get the local authorities on it. I need this yesterday."

Before the banks closed, Hammer's people had found two banks which had held certificates for William Dailey, but both gave the same report: the deposits had been withdrawn within the last seventy-two hours. Why was the man doing this? Was it coincidental, or had Dailey been tipped off? Hammer could only assume the worst—Dailey had surmised he was under investigation and was recapturing his money with frightening speed. How was he doing this? He'd have to surrender his certificates at each bank. Of course: he was a pilot. To get to the banks so rapidly, he'd have to be flying.

Hammer called in S&D pilot Griggs and spread out a map of the southeastern states. On this he circled the towns where Dailey had made his withdrawals.

"We're still calling banks to find out where he has, or had, deposits. Take a look at this."

Griggs examined the map.

"There may be a pattern here," said Hammer. "He's hit these three banks. They aren't far apart—almost in a line. He's probably calculated his route in some kind of pattern to save time. He must be flying. What's the chance he'd file a flight plan?"

"Little to none," said Griggs.

"Okay. All we can do is find the banks he's used and try to figure where he'll go next."

"Can't you get a federal judge to freeze those certificates?"

"Yeah, maybe, when I find them. But I want Dailey."

By plotting the banks where Dailey had made deposits Hammer established some logical boundaries, and within these his staff continued their furious telephone bombardment. They had the advantage, for bookkeeping departments could be reached after floor transactions had been closed. Still, two additional accounts were discovered just after withdrawals had been made. Hammer realized that if Dailey knew they were onto him, at some point he'd take the money he had been able to withdraw and flee.

William Dailey had been only peripherally conscious of the fact that all the banks he'd chosen were in towns that had airfields, even the small ones. Now he realized that some warning system had perhaps informed him that he might need to get to his money quickly and to get away quickly.

Dailey flew into two, three, four towns, parked the plane or left it for servicing, caught a cab or rented a car, drove to the bank holding his deposit, made his withdrawal, returned to the airport and flew to the next town. The withdrawals were time-consuming and costly. For premature withdrawal, penalties were assessed, and on withdrawals of that size a bank officer always questioned the customer at length. Expecting this, Dailey had invented an elaborate explanation of his withdrawal and in the long run he received his money.

When Dailey flew into Memphis, he grabbed a cab at the airport, handed the driver a twenty-dollar bill, and told him to break the rules; nevertheless, they were late and he reached the Central Bank of Tennessee just after it had closed. For a few moments he stood at the door, trying to decide what to do. He didn't like staying anywhere long. Flying to another town at his hour would accomplish nothing. Finally he decided to wait until the bank opened in the morning, and he instructed his driver to take him to a motel.

As a rule, when Sidney Hammer confronted a problem, he terminated contact with everyone, hunched down at his desk, gnawed on his cigar butt as a canine attacks a leathery bone, and went into a trance of concentration. Now he paced the floor, disturbing the pigeons beyond his window, hands buried in pockets, the only thing characteristic about his attitude the mutilated cigar. It appeared that William Dailey had with criminal ingenuity or incredible good luck broken Hammer's security system, made off with a fortune, and, in a moment of crisis, initiated a procedure for snatching the money from under their noses for the second time. Hammer was beginning to think their time had run out when one of the girls who had been canvassing the banks walked into his office just minutes before bookkeeping operations would normally be closing down.

"I found a deposit," she said, "on the Central Bank of Tennessee. So far it's still there."

Hammer glanced at his watch, confirming the time. "Dailey can't get to it today. About a hundred thousand?"

"Yes," she said.

"Okay. Those are the deposits he's going after." Hammer drove his fist into the palm of his hand. "Hot damn, we've finally jumped ahead of him!"

He called in Griggs and they took a look at their map. "Columbia, Charlotte, Nashville, and a couple of points between. He could be making a circle, heading for Florida maybe."

"Memphis would fit in," said Griggs.

"There may be others but he could be on his way. Or he might reverse the pattern, change his procedure to throw us off."

"Or," Griggs said, "he could be headed for Memphis right now."

Hammer thought for a moment, shifted his cigar, monitored his gut feeling, and decided. "Get the helicopter ready. We're going to Memphis."

When Dailey walked into the Central Bank of Tennessee the moment the doors opened, he wasn't the only one who'd had a sleepless night. Hammer had spent the night working with the FBI and local authorities on his case. What needed to be done, when and if Dailey showed up in Memphis, was done.

Though Dailey was in a hurry, he entered the bank, suitcase and briefcase in hand, with an attitude of excitement. The only hint he'd had that he might be under scrutiny was the inquiry made of his Uncle William; how distantly or how closely he might be associated with the S&D robbery he didn't know, but there was something thrilling about retrieving the money, something akin to pulling off the robbery for the second time. He didn't know law but he assumed that if his deposits were discovered they could be frozen. Beyond all else he had to protect his wife and children. Getting money out of the banks, perhaps out of the country, required an operation of speed, cunning, and risk.

Dailey was dressed in a business suit and he kept his manner casual. He approached one of the bank secretaries, presenting his certificate, and told her, "I'd like to withdraw this deposit. I know there'll be a penalty."

The young lady looked at the certificate, noticing the sum. "For this amount we'll need one of the officers."

"All right," he said. "I'm in a hurry, if you please."

As she stood to lead Dailey into Mr. Rand's office, Sidney Longhorn Hammer, sitting casually in one of the upholstered chairs in the lobby's waiting area, spoke to an agent on his right. "That's Dailey. We've got him."

The agent nodded and gave a signal to men stationed near the front and side doors, in the event Dailey somehow became suspicious and made a run for it.

In Mr. Rand's office, William Dailey explained, "I'm sorry to say I must withdraw these funds. If you don't mind, I'd like cash."

Neither Rand nor anyone else in the bank had been told what was happening. The banker's reaction was therefore what Dailey had come to expect. "Is something wrong, Mr. Dailey? I hope you haven't found the bank inadequate."

"Frankly, I've decided to invest in a hot business venture," Dailey said. "Win, lose, or draw, I can afford it. My people want cash." He answered a few more questions, then said with a practiced degree of impatience, "Is there some problem? I have a right to withdraw my money, do I not?"

"Of course, of course," Rand said. "A bank's procedure when a large withdrawal is made is to be sure the customer isn't under some kind of duress." He gave a little laugh. "You know, we want to be sure you're not the victim of extortion or something."

Dailey smiled pleasantly, enjoying the irony of this. "I understand. I assure you everything's fine and I know exactly what I'm doing."

"All right. Sign here and we'll get your money."

Dailey endorsed the certificate, then followed Rand into a conference room where he was asked to count his money with a cashier. As he did this he placed the currency in his briefcase.

In the lobby, the agent sitting beside Hammer said, "We'll let him claim the money. There's no need to rush it now. It's that much better if he has the cash on him."

"Agreed," said Hammer. From his pocket he took a brand new cigar, removed the paper, and added, "I have all the time in the world."

William Dailey emerged from the conference room swinging his briefcase with the jauntiness of a man well acquainted with success. His intention was to catch a cab to the airport, take the plane, and fly south. He was halfway across the lobby when Sidney Hammer, smoking his new cigar, intercepted him and said with the undisguised pleasure of one who has won a difficult contest, "Mr. Dailey? So glad to meet you at last. I'm Sidney Hammer, security chief for S&D banks."

Dailey halted as if shot. It took a full moment for him to register what had been said. Before he could react, the federal agent, flashing his credentials, said, "William Dailey, you're under arrest. The charge against you is robbery."

Dailey stood still another moment, then leaned down to set the briefcase on the floor. He placed it at a precise right angle to his feet. He rose and, as if instinctively recognizing his counterpart, said to Hammer, "Where did the mission fail?"

Hammer extracted his cigar with a certain grudging respect. "You're neat, Mr. Dailey. Very neat and accommodating. You left a print on a door you repaired for your landlady."

Dailey remembered, clearly recognized his mistake, but did not flinch. "My wife and kids," he said.

"Yes, what about them?"

Dailey's look was unflagging.

Hammer thought for a moment, jammed the cigar between his teeth, and said without pity, "Maybe when they grow up they'll remember what a nice thief their father was."

He stepped aside to let the agent handcuff Dailey and lead him out of the bank.

HAWAII

SCRIMSHAW
by Brian Garfield

SHE SUGGESTED LIQUID undulation: a lei-draped girl in a grass skirt under a windblown palm tree, her hands and hips expressive of the flow of the hula. Behind her, beyond the surf, a whaling ship was poised to approach the shore, its square-rigged sails bold against a polished white sky.

The scene was depicted meticulously upon ivory: a white fragment of tusk the size of a dollar bill. The etched detail was exquisite: the scrimshaw engraving was carved of thousands of thread-like lines and the artist's knife hadn't slipped once.

The price tag may have been designed to persuade tourists of the seriousness of the art form: it was in four figures. But Brenda was unimpressed. She put the piece back on the display cabinet and left the shop.

The hot Lahaina sun beat against her face and she went across Front Street to the Sea Wall, thrust her hands into the pockets of her dress and brooded upon the anchorage.

Boats were moored around the harbor—catamarans, glass-bottom tourist boats, marlin fishermen, pleasure sailboats, outrigger canoes, yachts. Playthings. It's the wrong place for me, she thought.

Beyond the wide channel the islands of Lanai and Kahoolawe made lovely horizons under their umbrellas of delicate cloud, but Brenda had lost her eye for that sort of thing; she noticed the stagnant heat, the shabbiness of the town, and the offensiveness of the tourists who trudged from shop to shop in their silly hats, their sunburnt flab, their hapless T-shirts emblazoned with local graffiti: "Here Today, Gone to Maui."

A leggy young girl went by, drawing Brenda's brief attention: one of those taut tan sunbleached creatures of the surfboards—gorgeous and luscious and vacuous. Filled with youth and hedonism, equipped with all the optional accessories of pleasure. Brenda watched gloomily, her eyes following the girl as far as the end of the Sea Wall, where the girl turned to cross the street. Brenda then noticed two men in conversation there.

One of them was the wino who always seemed to be there: a stringy unshaven tattered character who spent the days huddling in the shade sucking from a bottle in a brown bag and begging coins from tourists. At night he seemed to prowl the alleys behind the seafood restaurants, living off scraps like a stray dog: she had seen him once, from the window of her flyspecked room, scrounging in the can behind the hotel's kitchen; and then two nights ago near a garbage bin she had taken a shortcut home after a dissatisfying lonely dinner and she'd nearly tripped over him.

The man talking with the wino seemed familiar and yet she could not place the man. He had the lean bearded look of one who had gone native; but not really, for he was set apart by his fastidiousness. He wore sandals, yet his feet seemed clean, the toenails glimmering; he wore a sandy beard but it was neatly trimmed and his hair was expensively cut, not at all shaggy; he wore a blue denim short-sleeved shirt, fashionably faded but it had sleeve pockets and epaulets and had come from a designer shop; and his white sailor's trousers fit perfectly.

I know him, Brenda thought, but she couldn't summon the energy to stir from her spot when the bearded man and the wino walked away into the town. Vaguely and without real interest she wondered idly what those two could possibly have to talk about together.

She found shade on the harbor front. Inertia held her there for hours while she recounted the litany of her misfortunes. Finally hunger bestirred her and she slouched back to her miserable little third-class hotel.

The next day, half drunk in the afternoon and wilting in the heat, Brenda noticed vaguely that the wino was no longer in his usual place. In fact, she hadn't seen the wino at all, not last night and not today.

The headache was painful and she boarded the jitney bus to go up-island a few miles. She got off near the Kapalua headland and trudged down to the public beach. It was cooler here because the northwest end of the island was open to the fresh trade winds; she settled under a palm tree, pulled off her ragged sneakers, and dug her toes into the cool sand. The toes weren't very clean. She was going too long between baths these days. The bathroom in the hotel was at the end of the corridor and she went there as infrequently as possible because she couldn't be sure who she might encounter and anyhow, the tub was filthy and there was no shower.

Across the channel loomed the craggy mountains of Molokai, infamous island, leper colony, its dark volcanic mass shadowed by perpetual sinister rain clouds, and Brenda lost herself in gruesome speculations about exile, isolation, loneliness, and wretched despair, none of which seemed at all foreign to her.

The sun moved and took the shade with it and she moved round to the other side of the palm tree, tucking the fabric of the cheap dress under her when she sat down. The dress was gone—frayed, faded, the material ready to disintegrate.

She only had two others left. Then it would be jeans and the boatneck. It didn't matter, really. There was no one to dress up for.

It wasn't that she was altogether ugly; she wasn't ugly; she wasn't even plain, really; she had studied photographs of herself over the years and she had gazed in the mirror and tried to understand, but it had eluded her. All right, perhaps she was too bony, her shoulders too big, flat in front, not enough flesh on her—but there were men who liked their women bony; that didn't explain it. She had the proper features in the proper places and, after all, Modigliani hadn't found that sort of face abominable to behold, had he?

But ever since puberty there'd been something about her gangly gracelessness that had isolated her. Invitations to go out had been infrequent. At parties no one ever initiated conversations with her. No one, in any case, until Briggs had appeared in her life.

. . . She noticed the man again: the well-dressed one with the neatly trimmed beard. A droopy brown Hawaiian youth was picking up litter on the beach and depositing it in a burlap sack he dragged along; the bearded man ambled beside the youth, talking to him. The Hawaiian said something; the bearded man nodded with evident disappointment and turned to leave the beach. His path brought him close by Brenda's palm tree and Brenda sat up abruptly. "Eric?"

The bearded man squinted into the shade, trying to recognize her. Brenda removed her sunglasses. She said, "Eric? Eric Morelius?"

"Brenda?" The man came closer and she contrived a wan smile. "Brenda Briggs? What the devil are you doing here? You look like a beachcomber gone to seed."

Over a drink in Kimo's she tried to put on a front. "Well, I thought I'd come out here on a sabbatical and, you know, loaf around the islands, recharge my batteries, take stock."

She saw that Eric wasn't buying it. She tried to smile. "And what about you?"

"Well, I live here, you know. Came out to Hawaii nine years ago on vacation and never went back." Eric had an easy relaxed attitude of confident assurance. "Come off it, duckie, you look like hell. What's happened to you?"

She contrived a shrug of indifference. "The world fell down around my ankles. Happens to most everybody sometimes, I suppose. It doesn't matter."

"Just like that? It must have been something terrible. You had more promise than anyone in the department."

"Well, we were kids then, weren't we. We were all promising young scholars. But what happens after you've broken all the promises?"

"Good Lord. The last I saw of you, you and Briggs were off to revitalize the University of what, New Mexico?"

"Arizona." She tipped her head back with the glass to her mouth; ice clicked against her teeth. "And after that a state college in Minnesota. And then a dinky jerkwater diploma mill in California. The world," she said in a quiet voice, "has little further need of second-rate Greek and Roman literature scholars—or for any sort of non-tenured Ph.D.'s in the humanities. I spent last year waiting on tables in Modesto.''

"Duckie," Eric said, "there's one thing you haven't mentioned. Where's Briggs?''

She hesitated. Then—what did it matter?—she told him: "He left me. Four years ago. Divorced me and married a buxom life-of-the-party girl fifteen years younger than me. She was writing advertising copy for defective radial tires or carcinogenic deodorants or something like that. We had a kid, you know. Cute little guy, we named him Geoff, with a G—you know how Briggs used to love reading Chaucer. In the original. In retrospect, you know, Briggs was a prig and a snob.''

"Where's the kid, then?''

"I managed to get custody and then six months ago he went to visit his father for the weekend and all three of them, Briggs and the copy-writer and my kid Geoff—well, there was a six-car pileup on the Santa Monica Freeway and I had to pay for the funerals and it wiped me out.''

Eric brought another pair of drinks and there was a properly responsive sympathy in his eyes and it had been so long since she'd talked about it that she covered her face with the table napkin and sobbed.

"God help me, Eric. Briggs was the only man who ever gave me a second look.''

He walked her along the Sea Wall. "You'll get over it, duckie. Takes time.''

"Sure," she said listlessly. "I know.''

"Sure, it can be tough. Especially when you haven't got anybody. You don't have any family left, do you?''

"No. Only child. My parents died young. Why not? The old man was on the assembly line in Dearborn. We're all on the assembly line in Dearborn. What have we got to aim for? A condominium in some anthill and a bag full of golf clubs? Let's change the subject, all right? What about you, then? You look prosperous enough. Did you drop out or were you pushed too?''

"Dropped out. Saw the light and made it to the end of the tunnel. I'm a free man, duckie.''

"What do you do?''

"I'm a scrimshander.''

"A what?''

"A bone-ivory artist. I do scrimshaw engravings. You've probably seen my work in the shop windows around town.''

Eric's studio, high under the eaves in the vintage whaler's house that looked more New Englandish than tropical, revealed its owner's compulsion for orderly neatness.

She had never liked him much. He and Briggs had got along all right, but she'd always found Eric an unpleasant sort. It wasn't that he was boorish; hardly anything like that. But she thought him pretentious and totally insincere. He'd always had that air of arrogant self-assurance. And the polish was all on the surface; he had the right manners but once you got to know him a little you realized he had no real understanding of courtesy or compassion. Those qualities were meaningless to people like Eric. She'd always thought him self-absorbed and egotistical to the point of solipsism; she'd felt he had cultivated Briggs's friendship simply because Eric felt Briggs could help him advance in the department.

Eric had been good at toadying up to anyone who could help him learn the arts of politics and ambition. Eric had always been very actorish: he wasn't real—everything was a role, a part, a performance: everything Eric did was done with his audience in mind. If you couldn't be any help to him he could, without a second thought, cut you dead.

He wasn't really handsome. He had a small round head and ordinary features. But he'd always kept himself trim and he'd always been a natty dresser. And the beard sharpened his face, made it longer, added polish to his appearance. Back on the mainland, she remembered, he'd tended to favor three-piece suits.

Eric's studio was spartan, dominated by a scrubbed-clean workbench under the dormer window's north light. An array of carving tools filled a wooden rack, each tool seated in its proper niche, and there were four tidy wooden bins containing pieces of white bone of graduated sizes. Antique inkwells and jars were arranged beside a tray of paintbrushes and other slender implements. In three glass display cases, each overhung by a museum light, lay examples of Eric's art. One piece, especially striking, was a large ivory cribbage board in the shape of a Polynesian outrigger canoe with intricate black-and-white scenes engraved upon its faceted surfaces.

"That's a sort of frieze," Eric explained. "If you follow those little scenes around the board, they illustrate the whole mythology of the Polynesian emigration that led to the original settlement of Hawaii a thousand years ago. I'm negotiating to sell it to the museum over in Honolulu."

"It must be pretty lucrative, this stuff."

"It can be. Do you know anything about scrimshaw?"

"No," she said, and she didn't particularly care to; but Eric had paid for the bottle and was pouring a drink for her, and she was desperate for company—anyone's, even Eric's—and so she stayed and pretended interest.

"It's a genuine American folk art. It was originated in the early 1800s by the Yankee whalers who came out to the Pacific with endless time on their hands on shipboard. They got into the habit of scrimshanding to pass the time. The early stuff was crude, of course, but pretty quickly some of them started doing quite sophisticated workmanship. They used sail needles to carve the fine lines of the engraving and then they'd trace India ink or lampblack into the carvings for contrast. About the only materials they had were whalebone and whales' teeth, so that's what they carved at first.

"The art became very popular for a while, about a century ago, and there was a period when scrimshanding became a profession in its own right. That was when they ran short of whalebone and teeth and started illustrating elephant ivory and other white bone materials. Then it all went out of fashion. But it's been coming back into favor the past few years. We've got several scrimshanders here now. The main problem today, of course, is the scarcity of ivory."

At intervals Brenda sipped his whiskey and vocalized sounds indicative of her attentiveness to his monologue. Mainly she was thinking morosely of the pointlessness of it all. Was Eric going to ask her to stay the night? If he did, would she accept? In either case, did it matter?

Watching her with bemused eyes, Eric went on, "The Endangered Species laws have made it impossible for us to obtain whalebone or elephant ivory in any quantities any more. It's a real problem."

"You seem to have a fair supply in those bins there."

"Well, some of us have been buying mastodon ivory and other fossilized bones from the Eskimos—they dig for it in the tundra up in Alaska. But that stuff's in short supply too, and the price has gone through the ceiling."

Eric took her glass and filled it from the bottle, extracting ice cubes from the half-size fridge under the workbench. She rolled the cold glass against her forehead and returned to the wicker chair, balancing herself with care. Eric smiled with the appearance of sympathy and pushed a little box across the bench. It was the size of a matchbox. The lid fit snugly. Etched into its ivory surface was a drawing of a humpback whale.

"Like it?"

"It's lovely." She tried to summon enthusiasm in her voice.

"It's nearly the real thing," he said. "Not real ivory, of course, but real bone at least. We've been experimenting with chemical processes to bleach and harden it."

She studied the tiny box and suddenly looked away. Something about it had put her in mind of little Geoff's casket.

"The bones of most animals are too rough and porous," Eric was saying. "They tend to decompose, of course, being organic. But we've had some success with chemical hardening agents. Still, there aren't many types of bone that are suitable. Of course, there are some people who're willing to make do with vegetable ivory or hard plastics, but those really aren't acceptable if you care about the artistry of the thing. The phony stuff has no grain, and anybody with a good eye can always tell."

She was thinking she really had to pull herself together. You couldn't get by indefinitely on self-pity and the liquid largess of old acquaintances, met by chance, whom you didn't even like. She'd reached a point-of-no-return: the end of this week her room rent would be due again and she had no money to cover it; the time to make up her mind was now, right now, because either she got a job or she'd end up like that whiskered wino begging for pennies and eating out of refuse bins.

Eric went on prattling about his silly hobby or whatever it was: something about the larger bones of primates—thigh bone, collarbone. "Young enough to be in good health of course—bone grows uselessly brittle as we get older . . ." But she wasn't really listening; she stood beside the workbench looking out through the dormer window at the dozens of boats in the anchorage, wondering if she could face walking into one of the tourist dives and begging for a job waiting on tables.

The drink had made her unsteady. She returned to the chair, resolving to explore the town first thing in the morning in search of employment. She *had* to snap out of it. It was time to come back to life and perhaps these beautiful islands were the place to do it: the proper setting for the resurrection of a jaded soul.

Eric's voice paused interrogatively and it made her look up. "What? Sorry."

"These two here," Eric said. She looked down at the two etched pendants. He said, "Can you tell the difference?"

"They look pretty much the same to me."

"There, see that? That one, on the left, that's a piece of whale's tooth. This other one's ordinary bone, chemically hardened and bleached to the consistency and color of true ivory. It's got the proper grain, everything."

"Fine." She set the glass down and endeavored to smile pleasantly. "That's fine, Eric. Thank you so much for the drinks. I'd better go now—" She aimed herself woozily toward the door.

"No need to rush off, is there? Here, have one more and then we'll get a bite to eat. There's a terrific little place back on the inland side of town."

"Thanks, really, but—"

"I won't take no for an answer, duckie. How often do we see each other, after all? Come on—look, I'm sorry, I've been boring you to tears with all this talk about scrimshaw and dead bones, and we haven't said a word yet about the really important things."

"What important things?"

"Well, what are we going to do about you, duckie? You seem to have a crucial problem with your life right now and I think, if you let me, maybe I can help sort it out. Sometimes all it takes is the counsel of a sympathetic old friend, you know."

By then the drink had been poured and she saw no plausible reason to refuse it. She settled back in the cane chair. Eric's smile was avuncular. "What are friends for, after all? Relax a while, duckie. You know, when I first came out here I felt a lot the way you're feeling. I guess in a way I was lucky not to've been as good a scholar as you and Briggs were. I got through the Ph.D. program by the skin of my teeth but it wasn't enough. I applied for teaching jobs all over the country, you know. Not one nibble."

Then the quick smile flashed behind the neat beard. "I ran away, you see—as far as I could get without a passport. These islands are full of losers like you and me, you know. Scratch any charter-boat skipper in that marina and you'll find a bankrupt or a failed writer who couldn't get his epic novel published."

Then he lifted his glass in a gesture of toast. "But it's possible to find an antidote for our failure, you see. Sometimes it may take a certain ruthlessness, of course—a willingness to suspend the stupid values we were brought up on. So-called civilized principles are the enemies of any true individualist—you have to learn that or you're doomed to be a loser for all time. The kings and robber barons we've honored throughout history—none of them was the kind to let himself be pushed around by the imbecilic bureaucratic whims of college deans or tenure systems.

"Establishments and institutions and laws are designed by winners to keep losers in their place, that's all. You're only free when you learn there's no reason to play the game by their rules. Hell, duckie, the fun of life only comes when you discover how to make your own rules and laugh at the fools around you. Look—consider your own situation. Is there any single living soul right now who truly gives a damn whether you, Brenda Briggs, are alive or dead?"

Put that starkly it made her gape. Eric leaned forward, brandishing his glass as if it were a searchlight aimed at her face. "Well?"

"No. Nobody," she murmured reluctantly.

"There you are, then." He seemed to relax; he leaned back. "There's not a soul you need to please or impress or support, right? If you went right up Front Street here and walked into the Bank of Hawaii and robbed the place of a fortune and got killed making your escape, you'd be hurting no one but yourself. Am I right, duckie?"

"I suppose so."

"Then why not give it a try?"

"Give what a try?"

"Robbing a bank. Kidnaping a rich infant. Hijacking a yacht. Stealing a million in diamonds. Whatever you feel like, duckie—whatever appeals to you. Why not? What have you got to lose?"

She twisted her mouth into an uneven smile. "You remind me of the sophomoric sophistry we used to spout when we were undergraduates. Existentialism and nihilism galore." She put her glass down. "Well, I guess not, Eric. I don't think I'll start robbing banks just yet."

"And why not?"

"Maybe I'm just not gaited that way."

"Morality? Is that it? What's morality ever done for *you?*"

She steadied herself with a hand against the workbench, set her feet with care, and turned toward the door. "It's a drink too late for morbid philosophical dialetics. Thanks for the booze, though. I'll see you. . . ."

"You'd better sit down, duckie. You're a little unsteady there."

"No, I—"

"Sit down." The words came out in a harsher voice. "The door's locked anyway, duckie—you're not going anywhere."

She scowled, befuddled. "What?"

He showed her the key; then he put it away in his pocket. She looked blankly at the door, the keyhole, and—again—his face. It had gone hard; the polite mask was gone.

"I wish you'd taken the bait," he said. "Around here all they ever talk about is sunsets and surfing and the size of the marlin some fool caught. At least you've got a bigger vocabulary than that. I really wish you'd jumped at it, duckie. It would have made things easier. But you didn't, so that's that."

"What on earth are you talking about?"

She stumbled to the door then—and heard Eric's quiet laughter when she tried the knob.

She put her back to the door. Her head swam. "I don't understand. . . ."

"It's the ivory, duckie. The best material is fresh human bone. The consistency, the hardness—it takes a fine polish if it's young and healthy enough. . . ."

She stared at him and the understanding seeped into her slowly and she said, "That's where the wino went."

"Well, I have to pick and choose, don't I? I mean, I can't very well use people whose absence would be noticed."

She flattened herself against the door. She was beginning to pass out; she tried to fight it but she couldn't; in the distance, fading, she heard Eric say, "You'll make fine bones, duckie. Absolutely first-rate scrimshaw."

IDAHO

BULL AND BEAR

by R. L. Stevens

I RAISED THE rifle to my shoulder and took careful aim. The great lumbering grizzly, with a beautiful deep brown coat and the familiar hump on its shoulders, came out from behind the shelter of the tree and started across the rocky slope to the nearby woods. There would be time for only one clean shot and I made it count. The grizzly reared up on its hind legs in anger, took a few steps and then collapsed.

I approached the big bear cautiously until I was certain it wasn't moving. At nearly five hundred pounds, grizzlies can be deadly even when they're not up to full strength, and I hadn't driven up from Idaho Falls and spent two nights in the woods to be mauled by an angry bear. I put down my rifle and unstrapped the backpack from my shoulders.

That was when I saw the bearded stranger come out from behind a boulder and start down the slope toward me. He was carrying an old 30-30 deer rifle, which wouldn't have been much good against the grizzly. "That was nice shootin', mister. Brought him down with one shot, huh?"

"Lucky shot," I answered, not liking the looks of the man. I'd heard stories of poachers who followed hunters through the woods to hijack their kills.

"What kind of rifle you use?"

I was about to reply when his jacket fell open and I saw the butt of a revolver protruding from a shoulder holster under his left arm. Some hunters carry side-arms to finish off a wounded animal at close range, but I'd never known one to wear a revolver in a shoulder holster like that. I suddenly realized who this man was. "You're Bull Marlin, aren't you?"

The bearded man threw back his head and laughed. "God, I didn't know my fame had spread this far!"

Bull Marlin had operated a garage in Boise until a year ago when he went a little crazy and pumped six bullets into his wife and another man. Rather than take his chances in a court of law he'd run off into the hills, making his way east through the Sawtooth National Forest with the police on his tail and search helicopters circling overhead. They hadn't found him, and after a few months the press more or less forgot about Bull Marlin.

But then he'd killed again, breaking into a cabin where a Vietnam vet with mental problems was hiding out from the world. This killing lost him whatever sympathy he might have had, and when he attacked and raped a girl hiker a few weeks later the law came after him in force.

They didn't find him. Bull Marlin just kept moving east, like a wandering grizzly bear, slapping down anyone that got in his way. Most lawmen figured he'd crossed into Wyoming by now, possibly heading for Yellowstone National Park, but somehow I wasn't too surprised to find him here, in the mountains near the Bear Gulch Ski Area.

"Your picture's in every government office," I told him. "I figured you were still in Idaho somewhere."

He'd come down level with me, stepping around the bear's body to get a clear shot at me with the 30-30. I knew I had to do some fast talking or I'd be a dead man very soon. "What's your name?" he asked.

"Ron Halliday."

"You a lawman?"

"No, just a hunter."

"Grizzly hunter, eh?"

"It's the biggest thing around."

"But not the smartest, Ron. I'm the smartest thing around. You shoulda come huntin' for me."

"This where you been hiding out?" I asked.

"For the summer. I figured a ski area don't attract too much attention in the summertime. Come winter I'll head over to Yellowstone."

"The bears didn't bother you?"

"Didn't know they was here. Figured Bear Gulch was just a name."

I sat down on a log. The rifle jerked but he didn't fire. Maybe after all those months alone he felt like talking to someone. "They say back in Idaho Falls that you killed three people." I didn't mention the rape.

He laughed, loud enough to echo off the hills across the gulch. Maybe he was crazy like some people said. "Four people. They ain't found the last one yet."

"I hope that's not me."

He laughed even louder. "No, you'd be number five if I decide to kill you."

"Why do they call you Bull?" I asked, trying any ploy to keep the conversation—and myself—alive.

"'Cause I got a bull neck and I'm bullheaded. Them's good enough reasons."

"Where'd you get the revolver and shoulder holster?"

"Off number four. He was a private dick my wife's family hired to track me down. God, he was good at followin' a trail. But he wasn't as good as old Bull. I got him from behind with my 30-30, and dumped his body in Mud Lake."

He was telling me too much. I knew there wasn't a chance in the world that I'd be walking away from him alive, not unless I came up with something quick. "A regular Mountain Man, aren't you?"

"I'm gettin' to be," he agreed. "Livin' off the land, takin' what I want." That reminded him of something. "You must have a car with you, Ron boy."

"I parked it at the ski area and hiked in," I told him truthfully. "I've been camped up here two nights waiting for a grizzly."

"Them's a threatened species, you know. I think it's against the law to shoot 'em except in Alaska."

"Then we've got something in common, Bull, with our law-breaking. Tell you what—neither of us can turn the other in without getting in trouble ourselves, so why don't we make a deal? We just separate and forget we even saw each other."

Bull Marlin laughed again. "You take me for a sucker, Ron? I know you're just waitin' to get back to Idaho Falls and tell the cops I'm up here. Maybe there's even a reward for me."

"I don't know. I'm not interested in any reward."

Bull glanced down along the trail. "You're alone, aren't you? Didn't bring a partner along?"

"I'm alone."

"Well, we'd better get on with it, then." He pumped a cartridge into the chamber of his rifle. "This is nothin' personal, you understand. Not like with my wife and Gregory. When I shot them, *that* was personal! I enjoyed every bullet."

"Can't we talk about this?"

"Hell, seems like we been talking the better part of an hour already!"

"Why don't you just leave me tied to a tree?"

"You might starve to death." He chuckled. "This way's more humane."

I stood up, wiping my sweaty palms against the sides of my pants. He was about eight feet in front of me. I wondered if I could cover that distance in one leap before he squeezed the trigger. Probably not, I decided.

"At least give me a minute to pray."

He raised the rifle. "One minute, buddy."

I lowered my head and said a silent prayer that the big old grizzly bear would come back to life.

"Thirty seconds."

"Just give me—"

"Time's up!"

The bear gave a startling roar as it raised itself from the dead. Bull Marlin whirled around, his terrified face twisted into a scream. The bear made a half-hearted swipe with its massive paw before I yanked him back by the collar, out of harm's way. Then I knocked the rifle from his trembling hands and pulled the revolver from his shoulder holster.

"What in hell? That bear's dead!"

"Only a little sleepy," I said, twisting his arms behind him so I could tie them with a leather thong. "I'm with the Department of Wildlife. We shoot the grizzlies with tranquilizer guns so we can attach collars with little radio transmitters. They're a threatened species, like you said, and we have to keep track of their wanderings."

"You tricked me! You kept me talkin' till that damn bear woke up."

"He'll still be groggy for an hour or two. By that time I should have you back to civilization and inside a jail cell."

ILLINOIS

THE COUNSEL ASSIGNED
by Mary Raymond Shipman Andrews

A VERY OLD man told the story. Some twenty years ago, on a night in March, he walked down the bright hallway of a hotel in Bermuda, a splendid old fellow, straight and tall; an old man of a haughty, high-bridged Roman nose, of hawklike, brilliant eyes, of a thick thatch of white hair; a distinguished person, a personage, to the least observing; not unconscious possibly, as he stalked serenely toward the office, of the eyes that followed. An American stood close as the older man lighted his cigar at the office lamp; a red book was in his hand.

"That's a pretty color," the old fellow said in the assured tone of one who had always found his smallest remarks worth while.

The American handed it to him. As he turned over the leaves he commented with the same free certainty of words, and then the two fell to talking. Cigars in hand they strolled out on the veranda hanging over the blue waters of the bay, which rolled up unceasing music. There was a dance; a band played in the ballroom; girls in light dresses and officers in the scarlet jackets or the blue and gold of the British army and navy poured past.

The old man gazed at them vaguely and smiled as one might at a field of wind-blown daisies, and talked on. He told of events, travels, adventures—experiences which had made up an important and interesting life—a life spent partly, it appeared, in the United States, partly in Canada, where he was now a member of the Dominion Parliament. His enthusiasm, it developed, was for his profession, the law. The hesitating, deep voice lost its weakness, the dark eyes flashed youthfully, as he spoke of great lawyers, of legal *esprit de corps*.

"It's nonsense"—the big, thin, scholarly fist banged the chair arm—"this theory that the law tends to make men sordid. I'm not denying that there are bad lawyers. The Lord has given into each man's hand the ultimate shaping of his career; whatever the work, he can grasp it by its bigness or its pettiness, according to his nature. Doctors look after men's bodies and parsons after their souls;

141

there's an opinion that lawyers are created to keep an eye on the purses. But it seems to me"—the bright old eyes gazed off into the scented darkness of the southern night—"it seems to me otherwise. It seems to me that the right lawyer, with his mind trained into a clean, flexible instrument, as it should be, has his specialty in both fields. I am a very old man; I have seen many fine deeds done on the earth, and I can say that I have not known either heroic physicians or saintly ministers of God go beyond what I've known of men of my own calling. In fact—"

The bright end of the cigar burned a red hole in the velvet darkness, the old man's Roman profile cut against the lighted window, and he was silent. He went on in his slow, authoritative voice:

"In fact, I may say that the finest deed I've known was the performance of a lawyer acting in his professional capacity."

With that he told this story:

The chairman of the county committee stopped at the open door of the office. The nominee for Congress was deep in a letter, and, unpretentious as were the ways of the man, one considered his convenience; one did not interrupt. The chairman halted and, waiting, regarded at leisure the face frowning over the paper. A vision came to him, in a flash, of mountain cliffs he had seen—rocky, impregnable, unchangeable; seamed with lines of outer weather and inner torment; lonely and grim, yet lovely with gentle things that grow and bloom. This man's face was like that; it stood for stern uprightness; it shifted and changed as easily as the shadows change across ferns and young birches on a crag; deep within were mines of priceless things. Not so definitely, but yet so shaped, the simile came to the chairman; he had an admiration for his Congressional candidate.

The candidate folded the letter and put it in his pocket; he swung about in his office chair. "Sorry to keep you waiting, Tom. I was trying to figure out how a man can be in two places at once."

"If you get it, let me know," the other threw back. "We've a use for that trick right now. You're wanted to make another speech Friday night."

The big man in the chair crossed his long legs and looked at his manager meditatively. "I didn't get it quite figured," he said slowly. "That's my trouble. I can't make the speech here Friday."

"Can't make—your speech! You don't mean that. You're joking. Oh I see—of course you're joking."

The man in the chair shook his head. "Not a bit of it." He got up and began to stride about the room with long, lounging steps. The chairman, excited at the mere suggestion of failure in the much-advertised speech, flung remonstrances after him.

"Cartright is doing too well—he's giving deuced good talk, and he's at it every minute; he might beat us yet you know; it won't do to waste a chance—election's too near. Cartright's swearing that you're an atheist and an aristocrat—you've got to knock that out."

The large figure stopped short, and a queer smile twisted the big mouth and shone in the keen, visionary eyes. "An atheist and an aristocrat!" he repeated. "The Lord help me!"

Then he sat down and for ten minutes talked a vivid flood of words. At the end of ten minutes the listener had no doubts as to the nominee's interest in the fight, or his power to win it. The harsh, deep voice stopped; there was a pause which held, from some undercurrent of feeling, a dramatic quality.

"We'll win!" he cried. "We'll win, and without the Friday speech. I can't tell you why, Tom, and I'd rather not be asked, but I can't make that speech here Friday." The candidate had concluded—and it was concluded.

Traveling in those days was not a luxurious business. There were few railways; one drove or rode, or one walked. The candidate was poor, almost as day laborers are poor now. Friday morning at daybreak his tall figure stepped through the silent streets of the western city before the earliest risers were about. He swung along the roads, through woodland and open country, moving rapidly and with the tireless ease of strong, accustomed muscles. He went through villages. Once a woman busy with her cows gave him a cup of warm milk. Once he sat down on a log and ate food from a package wrapped in paper, which he took from his pocket. Except for those times he did not stop, and nine o'clock found him on the outskirts of a straggling town, twenty miles from his starting point.

The courthouse was a wooden building with a cupola, with a front veranda of Doric pillars. The door stood wide to the summer morning. Court was already in session. The place was crowded, for there was to be a murder trial today. The Congressional candidate, unnoticed, stepped inside and sat by the door in the last row of seats.

It was a crude interior of white walls, of unpainted woodwork, of pine floors and wooden benches. The Franklin stove which heated it in winter stood there yet, its open mouth showing dead ashes of the last March fire; its yards of stovepipe ran a zigzag overhead. The newcomer glanced about at this stage-setting as if familiar with the type. A larceny case was being tried. The man listened closely and seemed to study lawyers and Judge; he was interested in the comments of the people near him. The case being ended, another was called. A man was to be tried this time for assault; the stranger in the back seat missed no word. This case, too, came to a close. The District Attorney rose and moved the trial of John Wilson for murder.

There was a stir through the courtroom, and people turned on the hard benches and faced toward the front door, the one entrance. In the doorway appeared the Sheriff leading a childish figure, a boy of fifteen dressed in poor, homemade clothes, with a conspicuous bright head of golden hair. He was pale, desperately frightened; his eyes gazed on the floor. Through the packed crowd the Sheriff brought this shrinking, halting creature till he stood before the Judge inside the bar. The Judge, a young man, faced the criminal, and there was a pause. It seemed to the stranger, watching from his seat by the door, that the Judge was steadying himself against a pitiful sight.

At length: "Have you counsel?" the Judge demanded.

A shudder shook the slim shoulders; there was no other answer.

The Judge repeated the question, in no unkind manner. "Have you a lawyer?" he asked.

The lad's lips moved a minute before one heard anything; then he brought out, "I dunno—what that is."

"A lawyer is a man to see that you get your rights. Have you a lawyer?"

The lad shook his unkempt yellow head. "No. I dunno—anybody. I hain't got—money—to pay."

"Do you wish the court to assign you counsel?" He was unconscious that the familiar technical terms were an unknown tongue to the lad gasping before him. With that, through the stillness came a sound of a boot that scraped the floor. The man in the back seat rose, slouched forward, stood before the Judge.

"May it please your Honor," he said, "I am a lawyer. I should be glad to act as counsel for the defense."

The Judge looked at him a moment; there was something uncommon in this loose-hung figure towering inches above six feet; there was power. The Judge looked at him. "What is your name?" he asked.

The man answered quietly: "Abraham Lincoln."

A few men here and there glanced at the big lawyer again; this was the person who was running for Congress. That was all. A tall, gaunt man, in common clothes, gave his name. Frontier farmers and backwoodsmen in homespun jeans, some of them with buckskin breeches, most in their shirtsleeves, women in calico and sunbonnets, sat about and listened. Nobody saw more. Nobody dreamed that the name spoken and heard was to fill one of the great places in history.

The Judge, who had lived in large towns and learned to classify humanity a bit, alone placed the lawyer as outside the endless procession of the average. Moreover, he had heard of him. "I know your name, Mr. Lincoln; I shall be glad to assign you to defend the prisoner," he answered.

The jury was drawn. Man after man, giving his name, and, being questioned by the District Attorney, came under the scrutiny of the deep eyes under the overhanging brows—eyes keen, dreamy, sad, humorous; man after man, those eyes of Lincoln's sought out the character of each. But he challenged no one. The District Attorney examined each. The lawyer for the defense examined none; he accepted them all. The hard-faced audience began to glance at him impatiently. The feeling was against the prisoner, yet they wished to see some fight made for him; they wanted a play of swords. There was no excitement in looking at a giant who sat still in his chair.

The District Attorney opened the case for the People. He told with few words the story of the murder. The prisoner had worked on the farm of one Amos Berry in the autumn before, in 1845. On this farm was an Irishman, Shaughnessy by name. He amused himself by worrying the boy, and the boy came to hate him. He kept out of his way, yet the older man continued to worry him. On the 28th of October the boy was to drive a wagon of hay to the next farm. At the gate of the barnyard he met Shaughnessy with Berry and two other men. The boy asked

Berry to open the gate, and Berry was about to do it when Shaughnessy spoke. The boy was lazy he said—let him get down and open the gate himself. Berry hesitated, laughing at Shaughnessy, and the Irishman caught the pitchfork which the lad held and pricked him with it and ordered him to get down. The lad sprang forward, and, snatching back the pitchfork, flew at the Irishman and ran one of the prongs into his skull. The man died in an hour. The boy had been thrown into jail and had lain there nine months awaiting trial. This was the story.

By now it was the dinner hour—twelve o'clock. The court adjourned and the Judge and the lawyers went across the street to the tavern, a two-story house with long verandas; the audience scattered to be fed, many dining on the grass from lunches brought with them, for a murder trial is a gala day in the backwoods, and people make long journeys to see the show.

One lawyer was missing at the tavern. The Judge and the attorneys wondered where he was, for though this was not the eighth circuit, where Abraham Lincoln practiced, yet his name was known here. Lawyers of the eighth circuit had talked about his gift of story telling; these men wanted to hear him tell stories. But the big man had disappeared and nobody had been interested enough to notice as he passed down the shady street with a very little, faded woman in shabby clothes; a woman who had sat in a dark corner of the courtroom crying silently, who had stolen forward and spoken a timid word to Lincoln. With her he turned into one of the poorest houses of the town and had dinner with her and her cousin, the carpenter, and his family.

"That's the prisoner's mother," a woman whispered when, an hour later, court opened again, and the defendant's lawyer came up the steps with the forlorn little woman and seated her very carefully before he went forward to his place.

The District Attorney, in his shirt sleeves, in a chair tipped against the wall, called and examined witnesses. Proof was made of the location; the place was described; eyewitnesses testified to the details of the crime. There appeared to be no possible doubt of the criminal's guilt.

The lad sat huddled, colorless from his months in jail, sunk now in an apathy—a murderer at fifteen. Men on the jury who had hardy, honest boys of their own at home frowned at him, and more than one, it may be, considered that a monster of this sort would be well removed. Back in her dark corner the shabby woman sat quiet.

The sultry afternoon wore on. Outside the open windows a puff of wind moved branches of trees now and then, but hardly a breath came inside; it was hot, wearisome, but yet the crowd stayed. These were people who had no theaters; it was a play to listen to the District Attorney drawing from one witness after another the record of humiliation and rage, culminating in murder. It was excitement to watch the yellow-haired child on trial for his life; it was an added thrill for those who knew the significance of her presence, to turn and stare at the thin woman cowering in her seat, shaking with that continual repressed crying. All this was too good to lose, so the crowd stayed. Ignorant people are probably not willfully cruel; probably they like to watch suffering as a small boy watches the animal he tortures—from curiosity, without a sense of its reality. The poor are notoriously kind to each other, yet it is the poor, the masses, who throng the murder trials and executions.

The afternoon wore on. The District Attorney's nasal voice rose and fell examining witnesses. But the big lawyer sitting there did not satisfy people. He did not cross-examine one witness, he did not make one objection even to statements very damaging to his client. He scrutinized the Judge and the jury. One might have said that he was studying the character of each man; till at length the afternoon had worn to an end, and the District Attorney had examined the last witness and had risen and said: "The People rest." That side of the case was finished, and court adjourned for supper, to reopen at 7:30 in the evening.

Before the hour the audience had gathered. It was commonly said that the boy was doomed; no lawyer, even a "smart" man, could get him off after such testimony, and the current opinion was that the big hulking fellow could not be a good lawyer or he would have put a spoke in the wheel for his client before this. The sentiment ran in favor of condemnation; to have killed a man at fifteen showed depravity which was best put out of the way. Stern, narrow—the hard-living men and women of the backwoods set their thin lips into this sentence; yet down inside each one beat a heart capable of generous warmth if only the way to it were found, if a finger with a sure touch might be laid on the sealed gentleness.

Court opened. Not a seat was empty. The small woman in her worn calico dress sat forward this time, close to the bar. A few feet separated her from her son. The lawyers took their places. The Sheriff had brought in the criminal. The Judge entered. And then Abraham Lincoln stalked slowly up through the silent benches, and paused as he came to the prisoner. He laid a big hand on the thin shoulder, and the lad started nervously. Lincoln bent from his great height.

"Don't you be scared, sonny," he said quietly, but yet everyone heard every word. "I'm going to pull you out of this hole. Try to be plucky for your mother's sake."

And the boy lifted his blue, young eyes for the first time and glanced over to the shabby woman, and she met his look with a difficult smile, and he tried to smile back. The audience saw the effort of each for the other; the Judge saw it; and the jury—and Lincoln's keen eyes, watching ever under the heavy brows, caught a spasm of pity in more than one face. He took off his coat and folded it on the back of his chair and stood in his shirt sleeves. He stood, a man of the people in look and manner; a comfortable sense pervaded the spectators that what he was going to say they were going to understand. The room was still.

"Gentlemen of the Jury," began Abraham Lincoln, standing in his shirt sleeves before the court, "I am going to try this case in a manner not customary in courts. I am not going to venture to cross the tracks of the gentleman who has tried it for the prosecution. I shall not call witnesses; the little prisoner over there is all the witness I want. I shall not argue; I shall beseech you to make the argument for yourselves. All I'm going to do is to tell you a story and show you how it connects with this case, and then leave the case in your hands."

There was a stir through the courtroom. The voice, rasping, unpleasant at first, went on:

"You, Jim Beck—you, Jack Armstrong—"

People jumped; these were the names of neighbors and friends which this stranger used. His huge knotted forefinger singled out two in the jury.

"You two can remember—yes, and you as well, Luke Green—fifteen years back, in 1831, when a long, lank fellow in God-forsaken clothes came into this country from Indiana. His appearance, I dare to say, was so striking that those who saw him haven't forgotten him. He was dressed in blue homespun jeans. His feet were in rawhide boots, and the breeches were stuffed into the tops of them most of the time. He had a soft hat which had started life as black, but had sunburned till it was a combine of colors. Gentlemen of the Jury, I think some of you will remember those clothes and that young man. His name was Abraham Lincoln."

The gaunt speaker paused and pushed up his sleeves a bit, and the jurymen saw the hairy wrists and the muscles of hand and forearm. Yes, they remembered the young giant who had been champion in everything that meant physical strength. They sat tense.

"The better part of a man's life consists of his friendships," the strong voice went on, and the eyes softened as if looking back over a long road traveled. "There are good friends to be found in these parts; that young fellow in blue jeans had a few. It is about a family who befriended him that I am going to tell you. The boy Abraham Lincoln left his father, who was, as all know, a man in the humblest walk of life, and at twenty-two he undertook to shift for himself. There were pretty pinching times along then, and Abraham could not always get work. One fall afternoon, when he had been walking miles on a journey west-ward to look for a chance, it grew late, and he realized suddenly that unless he should run across a house he would have to sleep out. With that he heard an axe ring and came upon a cabin. It was a poor cabin even as settlers' cabins go. There was cloth over the windows instead of glass; there was only one room, and a little window above which told of a loft. Abraham strode on to the cabin hopefully. The owner, a strong fellow with yellow hair, came up, axe in hand, and of him the young man asked shelter." Again the voice paused and a smile flashed which told of a pleasant memory.

"Gentlemen of the Jury, no king ever met a fellow monarch with a finer wel-come. Everything he had, the wood-chopper told Abraham, was his. The man brought the tired boy inside. The door was only five feet high and the young fellow had to stoop some to get in. Two children of five or six were playing, and a little woman was singing the baby to sleep by the fire. The visitor climbed up a ladder to the loft after supper.

"He crawled down next morning, and when he had done a few chores to help, he bethought himself to take advice from the wood-chopper. He asked if there were jobs to be got. The man said yes; if he could chop and split rails there was enough to do. Now Abraham had had an axe put into his hands at eight years, and had dropped it since only long enough to eat meals. 'I can do that,' he said.

" 'Do you like to work?' the woodsman asked.

"Abraham had to tell him that he wasn't a hand to pitch into work like killing snakes, but yet—well, the outcome of it was that he stayed and proved that he could do a man's job."

A whispered word ran from one to another on the benches—they began to remember now the youngster who could outlift, outwork and outwrestle any man in the county. The big lawyer saw, and a gleam of gratification flashed; he was proud always of his physical strength. He went on:

"For five weeks Abraham lived in the cabin. The family character became as familiar to him as his own. He chopped with the father, did housework with the mother, and tended Sonny, the baby, many a time. To this day the man has a clear memory of that golden-haired baby laughing as the big lad rolled him about the uneven floor. He came to know the stock, root and branch, and can vouch for it.

"When he went away they refused to take money. No part of his life has ever been more light-hearted or happier. Does anybody here think that any sacrifice which Abraham Lincoln could make in after life would be too great to show his gratitude to those people?"

He shot the question at the jury, at the Judge, and, turning, brought the crowded courtroom into its range. A dramatic silence answered. The tiny woman's dim eyes stared at him, dilated. The boy's bright, sunken head had lifted a little and his thin fingers had caught at a chair at arm's length, and clutched it. The lawyer picked up his coat from where he had laid it, and, while every eye in the courtroom watched him, he fumbled in a pocket, unhurried, and brought out a bit of letter-paper. Holding it, he spoke again:

"The young man who had come under so large a weight of obligation prospered in later life. By hard work, by good fortune, by the blessing of God, he made for himself a certain place in the community. As much as might be, he had—I have—kept in touch with those old friends, yet in the stress of a very busy life I have not of late years heard from them. Till last Monday morning this"—he held up the letter—"this came to me in Springfield. It is a letter from the mother who sat by the fire in that humble cabin and gave a greeting to the wandering, obscure youth which Abraham Lincoln, please God, will not forget—not in this world, not when the hand of death has set his soul free of another. The woodsman died years ago, the two older children followed him. The mother who sang to her baby that afternoon"—he swept about and his long arm and knotted finger pointed, as he towered above the courtroom, to the meek, small woman shrinking on the front seat—"the mother is there."

The arm dropped; his luminous eyes shone on the boy criminal's drooping golden head; in the courtroom there was no one who did not hear each low syllable of the sentence which followed.

"The baby is the prisoner at the bar."

In the hot crowded place one caught a gasp from back by the door; one heard a woman's dress rustle, and a man clear his throat—and that was all.

There was silence, and the counsel for the defense let it alone to do his work.

From the figure which loomed above the rude company virtue went out and worked a magic. The silence which stretched from the falling of Lincoln's voice; which he let stretch on—and on; which he held to its insistent witchcraft when every soul in the courtroom began to feel it as personally harassing; this long silence shaped the minds before him as words could not. Lincoln held the throng facing their own thoughts, facing the story he had told, till all over the room men and women were shuffling, sighing, distressed with the push and the ferment of that silence.

At the crucial moment the frayed ends of the nerves of the audience were gathered up as the driver of a four-in-hand gathers up the reins of his fractious horses. The voice of the defendant's lawyer sounded over the throng.

"Many times, as I have lain wakeful in the night," he spoke as if reflecting aloud, "many times I have remembered those weeks of unfailing kindness from those poor people, and have prayed God to give me a chance to show my gratefulness. When the letter came last Monday calling for help, I knew that God had answered. An answer to prayer comes sometimes with a demand for sacrifice. It was so. The culminating moment of years of ambition for me was to have been tonight. I was to have made tonight a speech which bore, it is likely, success or failure in a contest. I lay that ambition, that failure, if the event so prove it, gladly on the altar of this boy's safety. It is for you"—his strong glance swept the jury—"to give him that safety. Gentlemen of the Jury, I said when I began that I should try this case in a manner not customary. I said I had no argument to set before you. I believe, as you are all men with human hearts, as some of you are fathers with little fellows of your own at home—I believe that you need no argument. I have told the story; you know the stock of which the lad comes; you know that at an age when his hands should have held schoolbooks or fishing rod, they held—because he was working for his mother—the man's tool which was his undoing; you know how the child was goaded by a grown man till in desperation he used that tool at hand. You know these things as well as I do. All I ask is that you deal with the little fellow as you would have other men deal in such a case with those little fellows at home. I trust his life to that test. Gentlemen of the Jury, I rest my case."

And Abraham Lincoln sat down.

A little later, when the time came, the jury filed out and crossed to a room in the hotel opposite. The boy stayed. Some of the lawyers went to the hotel barroom, some stood about on the ground under the trees; but many stayed in the courtroom, and all were waiting, watching for a sound from the men shut up across the way. Then, half an hour had passed, and there was a bustle, and people who had gone out crowded back. The worn small woman in the front row clasped her thin hands tight together.

The jury filed in and sat down on the shaky benches, and answered as their names were called, and rose and stood.

"Gentlemen of the Jury," the clerk's voice spoke monotonously, "have you agreed upon a verdict?"

"We have," the foreman answered firmly, woodenly, and men and women thrilled at the conventional two syllables. They meant life or death, those two syllables.

"What is your verdict, guilty or not guilty?"

For a second, perhaps, no one breathed in all that packed mass. The small woman glared palely at the foreman; every eye watched him. Did he hesitate? Only the boy, sitting with his golden head down, seemed not to listen.

"Not guilty," said the foreman.

With that there was pandemonium. Men shouted, stamped, waved, tossed up their hats; women sobbed; one or two screamed with wild joy. Abraham Lincoln saw the slim body of the prisoner fall forward; with two strides he had caught him up in his great arms, and, lifting him like a baby, passed him across the bar into the arms, into the lap, of the woman who caught him, rocked him, kissed him. They all saw that, and with an instinctive, unthinking sympathy the whole room surged toward her; but Lincoln stood guard and pushed off the crowd.

"The boy's fainted," he said loudly. "Give him air." And then, with a smile that beamed over each one of them there, "She's got her baby—it's all right, friends. But somebody bring a drink of water for Sonny."

The American, holding a cigar that had gone out, was silent. The old man spoke again, as if vindicating himself, as if answering objections from the other.

"Of course such a thing could not happen today," he said. "It could not have happened then in eastern courts. Only a Lincoln could have carried it off anywhere, it may be. But he knew his audience and the jury, and his genius measured the character of the Judge. It happened. It is a fact."

The American drew a long breath. "I have not doubted you, sir," he said. "I could not speak because—because your story touched me. Lincoln is our hero. It goes deep to hear of a thing like that." He hesitated and glanced curiously at the old man. "May I ask how you came by the story? You told it with a touch of—intimacy—almost as if you had been there. Is it possible that you were in that courtroom?"

The bright, dark eyes of the very old man flashed hawklike as he turned his aquiline, keen face toward the questioner; he smiled with an odd expression, only partly as if at the stalwart, up-to-date American before him, more as if smiling back half a century to faces long ago dust.

"I was the Judge," he said.

INDIANA

A DEBT TO BE PAID
by Dick Stodghill

THE OLD MAN awoke with a start. He peered around the veranda, his eyes blinking rapidly as they skipped from one empty chair to another. Satisfied he was alone, that he had not been observed by any of his cronies, he sighed with relief.

He struggled to his feet, using both hands and arms to hoist himself out of a wicker chair. Once up, he remained still a moment, giving his blood a chance to start circulating through his shaky legs. When the tingling eased he reached out to the long wooden railing and used it for support until he got to the stairs.

He walked down them, across a wide lawn and past a barn with COUNTY HOME lettered on its cupola. He continued on to a small woods cut in half by a brook flowing along a rocky bed.

He stopped when he reached his favorite hideaway, a huge gray boulder close beside the stream. Its smooth surface was imbedded with small pebbles and he traced a pattern from one to another of them with a bony forefinger. After a few seconds he eased around the side of the boulder and faced the water, coming to the small ledge that was his usual seat. Once settled, he bent and picked up a loose pebble, tossed it in the brook, and wondered what he was going to do about the dream.

He had easily coped with it when it interrupted his sleep only three or four times a year. Then it began bothering him more and more often. Once a month, twice a month, every week until finally now it had become a nightly occurrence. It had invaded his afternoon nap for the first time a week earlier. Twice he awoke with a cry to find the others on the veranda staring at him. Had he been talking in his sleep?

The dream started to take shape in his mind just as it did in his sleep. A swirling white mist and then suddenly a starkly vivid picture. He angrily pushed it aside. Bad enough seeing it in his sleep without letting it take over his waking

151

hours. But after a minute or two it crept back again and this time caught hold. He sat glassy-eyed as it unfolded. . . .

The train was creeping into a dark freightyard as he dropped to the ground from an open boxcar door. A light rain, hardly more than a vapor in the air, dampened his face. He turned up the collar of his red-and-black plaid jacket in a futile attempt to ward off the intermittent gusts of cold wind from the west. He didn't know where he was and didn't care. The important thing was the railroad bulls were preparing to sweep the train and it was time to find shelter elsewhere.

He had jumped from the south side of the train, so he headed south. Cautiously he picked his way across half a dozen tracks to a street that ended at a guard rail where two large warehouses faced each other. He considered each of the buildings as a place of refuge but rejected them in turn. Watchmen with clubs would surely be inside.

He walked on, coming next to a long row of ramshackle houses. In the following block, the houses began to show improvement and after two more blocks he was in a neighborhood of well-maintained bungalows. Most had garages, so maybe he'd be lucky and find one with an unlocked door. The third knob he tried was unlocked.

He slipped inside, softly closed the door behind him, and stood quietly in the blackness. He reached out a tentative hand, touched a car, a sedan. It also was unlocked, so he opened a rear door and silently climbed inside.

The seat was soft. Not wide enough to stretch out full length but a lot more comfortable than his usual bed, the ground or the floor of a boxcar. Best of all, the car was warm and dry.

He reached in a jacket pocket and pulled out half a sandwich wrapped in wax paper. He chewed slowly, savoring every bite, making it last as long as possible. When the final crumb was gone he rooted around in another pocket until his fingers closed on the butt of a cigar. He put it in his mouth, withdrew a flattened box of matches from the same pocket, struck one, and drew on the dry cigar. When it was burning he relaxed on the soft seat, exhaled the smoke, and sighed contentedly.

It was October, time to think about heading south. Maybe find a job somewhere. Conditions were improving, or so they were saying around the hobo jungles. He had seen little sign of it himself but it would be nice if it were true. Life on the road seemed harder at 32 than it had even a year earlier. Yes, it would be nice if he could find a job, rent a room of his own, eat regularly . . . The cigar went out and slipped from his fingers as he fell asleep.

The florid face was only a foot from his own. Bulging eyes, bulbous nose, thick lips spread wide as angry words poured from the man's mouth. For an instant he was bewildered, disoriented, but then he sprang from the seat and out the door on the other side of the car.

The man continued to berate him. "You no-good bum! You dirty, rotten bum, I'll teach you a lesson you won't forget!"

Too late he moved toward the open double doors. The man had grabbed a heavy spade, cut off his retreat, and was advancing menacingly. As the spade descended toward his head he made a desperate lunge for the handle, wrenched it free, and kicked at his assailant's groin.

The man gasped and sank to the floor. Instinctively he raised the spade and struck. Again and again he lifted it and brought it down. At last he stopped, recoiling in horror from the bloody heap on the floor. He dropped the spade, looked around wild-eyed, and ran out into the gray light of early morning.

Once outside he hesitated, caught sight of a woman's face watching him from a window of the house, and fled down the driveway. Again he halted uncertainly when he reached the sidewalk. A man stared at him in surprise from a porch across the street, so he began running. North this time, back toward the railroad tracks.

The run was like miles instead of blocks. When at last he arrived at the warehouses he slipped out of his blood-spattered jacket and tossed it under a loading platform. He hated to part with it—he would miss its warmth and protection; but it was too distinctive, too easy to spot.

He resumed his run but after crossing several tracks he slowed to a walk and struck out east. He was nearing a dense patch of tall weeds when he heard the first siren. He recrossed the tracks, stumbled over the last rail, and fell headlong into the tall protective weeds.

The wailing of the sirens seemed interminable. He lay shivering among the weeds and knew it was not from the cold alone. At last he heard a train and carefully parted the foliage. An eastbound freight was moving through the yards, slowly gaining speed. He ran for it, climbed aboard an open gondola, and dropped down among pieces of tarpaulin-covered machinery.

He jumped from the train when it slowed just west of Cleveland, hid in a woods until darkness fell, then stumbled wearily along the tracks to a hobo camp. An old man offered him the remains of a stew and after gulping it down he slept fitfully, cold, lonely, afraid. In the morning he realized he didn't know where the nightmare had taken place. A good-sized town somewhere east of Indianapolis, but it wasn't important. He was on the run and what did it matter where the pursuers had taken up the chase?

The dream faded and the old man slowly focused on the present. Damn the dream, he thought. It was becoming an obsession. Why? Why now, after 42 years? If only it really were a dream, but of course it wasn't.

He rummaged through his pockets until he found a battered old pipe bound together at the stem and shank with friction tape. From a roll-up pouch he tamped crumbling flakes of stale tobacco into the bowl, struck a match, and puffed until it was burning well. He watched the smoke curl skyward and meditated. If he walked away from the County Home he wouldn't be able to return. Others had done so and found themselves at the end of a long list waiting for admission.

He had to do it though, he had known that for days now. Conscience, that must be it. A feeling after all this time that he had to clear the record before it was too late. There would be no worry about getting back into the County Home—he would have a new home behind high walls. At least he would be able to sleep again and that made all other considerations unimportant.

He'd leave in the morning. There was money the authorities didn't know about, concealed long ago near the gray boulder and added to from time to time. Not a lot but enough for a bus ticket west, food, and a few nights in cheap hotels.

After breakfast he gathered his meager possessions, slipped out a side door, and walked to the highway. He raised his thumb and the fourth car pulled over.

The public library in town was his first stop. A librarian directed him to a large atlas showing railroad lines. With a gnarled finger he followed the old New York Central mainline east from Indianapolis. Anderson was the first possibility, then Midland. Winchester was too small. So were Union City, Sidney, and Bellefontaine. Marion, Ohio? Big enough but too far east. No, it had to have been Anderson or Midland.

Shortly after noon he boarded a Trailways bus. The ride was long and tiring, so he kept reminding himself how much more comfortable the seat was than the floor of an empty boxcar. Still, it would be nice to stretch out. He changed buses twice, arrived in Anderson the following morning, and went directly to the library.

The librarian placed the reel on the machine, showed him how to focus it and center the pages of the *Herald* on the screen. Laboriously he studied headline after headline, page after page. Hours later, eyes burning, he switched off the machine. The librarian came over, put the reel back in the small cardboard box labeled *October 1937*. He stood up, flexed his legs, and walked slowly to the door and outside into the nippy autumn air. No, it hadn't been Anderson.

He bummed a ride to the edge of town, hitched another on to Midland. Rickety stairs led him to a flophouse over a tavern near the tracks. When the dream jerked him awake hours before dawn it had been even more distinct, more intense than usual. Despite his weariness he was unable to sleep again.

A bowl of oatmeal and a cup of coffee in a greasy restaurant was his breakfast. When the library opened he was waiting on the wide steps outside, the grocery bag containing all his earthly possessions under his arm. He pored over microfilm again until noon, then stopped when his eyes could take no more. He had covered the pages of the *Midland News-Banner* from the first to the fifteenth of the month without finding what he was looking for.

The first nagging doubt entered his mind as he got up and wandered outside. What if he had made a mistake? Suppose it hadn't been the New York Central between Indianapolis and Cleveland? But it had been, he was certain of it. Still, the knot in the pit of his stomach grew steadily larger. What if he couldn't find it? His money was getting low. Where could he go, what could he do?

He ate a sandwich, drank another cup of coffee. He wanted to lie down and rest his burning eyes, but he forced his legs to climb the steps of the library again. He had to find the place, he couldn't give in to the fatigue that engulfed his body.

It jumped out at him twenty minutes after he returned to his seat at the machine. Page one, October 17, 1937. *South Side Man Murdered, Transients Questioned.*

A 42-year-old Midland man, John J. Squires, was beaten to death early today in the garage at his home, 614 S. Dudley St. Police immediately began a roundup of transients.

The victim's wife, Anna, told police her husband went to the garage shortly before seven o'clock this morning. Several minutes later, not having heard the car start, she went to a rear window and saw a man run out of the garage.

Mrs. Squires went to the garage and found her husband lying beside the car. He had been badly beaten, apparently with the blade of a garden spade. Mrs. Squires called an ambulance and the police. Her husband was pronounced dead at the scene by Coroner Ralph T. Taylor.

Mrs. Squires said the running man appeared to be a transient. She told the police he was about 30 years old, 5-10, and 150 pounds. He was wearing a gray cap, black trousers, and a red-and-black plaid jacket.

A neighbor, Frank Edwards, 613 S. Dudley St., also saw the man run from the garage and then north on Dudley. He confirmed Mrs. Squires's description of the killer.

Police theorize the man sought shelter in the garage and was surprised by Mr. Squires. By noon more than a dozen men had been picked up and questioned at police headquarters.

Mr. Squires, an 18-year employee of Clay Brothers Co., also is survived by . . .

The old man leaned back in the wooden chair, sat quietly for a moment, then read the story again. When he reached the end he rewound the film, placed it in its box, and walked to the service desk.

The librarian looked up and smiled. "Finished?" she said.

The old man nodded his head. "Where's the jail?" he asked. The woman told him and he walked away.

He pressed the button beside the pair of heavy steel doors and looked around, puzzled, when a voice asked, "Can I help you?" Above and to the left of the doors he saw a small television camera. He looked at it and said, "I want to see the sheriff."

"What?" This time he realized the voice came from a square grating above the button, so he repeated, "I want to see the sheriff."

"He's up at the courthouse. Can I help you?"

The old man shook his head and turned away. He had passed the sprawling modern courthouse walking down from the library, so he retraced his steps and entered the white structure. He crossed the lobby to a directory, studied it a moment, then turned to the elevators. When he got off at the third floor he looked around uncertainly, finally saw a small black sign reading *Sheriff,* and shuffled toward it.

A woman seated at a desk behind a counter smiled and said, "Can I help you?" but he ignored her and walked to the open door of a small office at his right. A portly, ruddy-complexioned man in a brown uniform looked up from his desk.

"Hello," he said. "What can I do for you today?"

"You the sheriff?"

"You called it." The man stood up, walked around the desk, and extended his hand. "Joe McAuliffe. What's on your mind?"

"I killed a man."

The sheriff drew back a little and studied him from surprised eyes. "Better tell me about it, old-timer. Who'd you kill?"

"A man named Squires. John J. Squires."

"Where'd this happen?"

"At his house. 614 South Dudley Street. In the garage."

"It would be a city matter then, but I should of heard about it. Did you just come from there?"

The old man shook his head, so the sheriff said, "You're sure you killed him? How'd it happen?"

"I hit him with a shovel. It killed him all right."

"John J. Squires, you say?" The sheriff scratched his head, then shook it from side to side. "Funny, I don't remember it. When exactly did it happen?"

"October 17, 1937."

The sheriff dropped down in his chair, hard. He frowned a moment, then his face broke into a grin. "Are you putting me on, old man? That's better'n forty years ago."

"I know it. Want to get it off my chest."

A frown creased the sheriff's brow again. He studied his visitor intently for a minute before picking up the phone, dialing a number, and saying, "Detectives." After a pause he said, "That you, Charlie? Joe McAuliffe. Do me a favor, will you. See if you've got an open file on a John J. Squires." He spelled the last name, looking at the old man for confirmation, and then, "A murder victim."

The sheriff drummed two fingers on his desk and continued to stare at his visitor while several minutes passed in silence. At last he said, "You don't? No, don't bother. Thanks, Charlie."

He cradled the phone, took two cigars from a shirt pocket, and held one out to the other man. "They don't have a file on it, Pop. Think maybe you made a mistake?"

"No mistake. Not by me, anyway."

The sheriff removed the cellophane wrapper from his cigar, rolled the tip of it around his lips, and struck a match. Through a haze of smoke he said, "I don't know what to tell you, old-timer. What do you want me to do?"

"Lock me up. I told you, I killed a man."

McAuliffe chuckled a little.

He picked up the phone again, dialed, and said, "This is the sheriff. Is Phil there?" A short delay and then, "Phil, I need some help. Can you come down to my office a minute?"

The two men sat without speaking until a dark-haired man of about 30 attired in an expensive suit entered the door. The sheriff stood up again and walked to the man, put a hand on his shoulder. Turning to the old man, McAuliffe said, "This is Philip Cosgrove, the county prosecutor," and then, to the other, "Phil, we've got a little problem. My friend here says he killed a man out on South Dudley back in 1937 but the city hasn't got a file on it."

The prosecutor laughed. "Did you say 1937?" He turned to the old man and said, "That's forty-two years ago and you're just getting around to reporting it?"

"Like I told the sheriff, I want to get it off my chest."

"Better explain it."

"I was on the bum. That was back in the Depression, you know. It was cold and I needed a place to sleep, so I hid in a garage. In the morning this man found me, came at me with a shovel, and I took it away from him and killed him with it. I hopped a freight a little while later and they never caught up with me."

The prosecutor looked at the sheriff. "You say there's no record of it?"

"No active file at the city. That's all I checked."

The prosecutor looked at his watch, glanced at the old man, and shrugged. "Okay, lock him up. It's too late to do much about it now but we'll check it out in the morning. No hurry, I guess, after forty-two years."

The old man leaned back in his chair and sighed. For the first time in days he smiled.

He was given a cell to himself. It was warm; the bunk suspended from a wall was comfortable and the evening meal was tasty, better than the ones served back at the County Home. After dinner he stretched out on the bunk, lit the cigar the sheriff had given him, and reviewed it all in his mind. He had made the right move, he was certain of it. Now he was content. After a time the cigar went dead and he slept soundly, untroubled by dreams.

Late the next morning a turnkey unlocked his cell and said, "The sheriff wants to see you." He led him out of the block and down a hallway to a small room.

Joe McAuliffe was leaning back in a chair, feet on a table, a cigar in his mouth. He took another from his pocket and held it out. The old man put it away to enjoy later. "Sit down, Pop," the sheriff said and grinned at him as a clock on the wall loudly ticked away seconds that extended into minutes. Finally he said, "What's the story, old-timer? Need a place out of the cold with winter coming on, is that it?" The old man stared at him, bewildered.

The sheriff swung his feet to the floor. "Why don't you try the mission down the street? They could put you up for a night or two. Don't you have relatives somewhere, kids or anything?"

The first tremor of fear shook the old man's body. Haltingly he said, "I don't get you, Sheriff."

"I hear you were checking the old newspapers down at the library before you came in to see me yesterday. It was a good try but you didn't read far enough."

His fear intensified. "I still don't get you."

"That murder took place, all right. Just like you said but they caught the guy the same day. If you'd read one more issue you'd've known that and saved us both a lot of trouble."

The room seemed hazy before the old man's eyes. He ran the back of a hand across them but it made things even less distinct.

"But—" he began, then he hesitated, groped for words. "But I did it, I told you that. What do you mean they caught the guy? They couldn't have."

"They did, old-timer. A fella named George Prescott. Caught him in the railroad yards about six blocks away. Two witnesses identified him." The sheriff flipped the pages of a file on his desk. "An Anna Squires, the victim's wife, and a Frank Edwards."

"But how could they? It was me."

"Positive identifications. Picked him out of a lineup."

McAuliffe took a paper from the folder and read, "George Prescott, twenty-seven, no known address. Five-eleven, one hundred seventy pounds. Brown hair, brown eyes. Wearing blue denims and a red-and-black plaid jacket."

The old man brought his fist down sharply on the table. "That was it, the jacket! I threw it away under a loading dock. I knew it would be too easy to spot. He must have found it."

The sheriff grinned at him. "Give it up, Pop. Everything you know about it could have come from the newspaper. The case was closed a long time ago."

"You're not saying they convicted this Prescott?"

McAuliffe nodded.

"But how could they? He was innocent!" The old man sat down, shaking his head, staring with haunted eyes at the tabletop. Suddenly he jerked his head up and said, "What about fingerprints? On the shovel or in the car."

The sheriff leafed through the papers. "Nothing in here. No mention of finding any at the scene. Prescott's are on file, of course."

"But there had to be prints! Can't you check?"

McAuliffe chuckled. "I have checked." He pointed to the file and said, "This is it. What do you expect after forty-two years?"

The old man slumped. "This Prescott, how long did he serve?"

"Six or seven months."

"That's all?" The old man's face brightened. "Thank God for that."

"Yep," the sheriff said. "He got the chair in May of thirty-eight."

A deputy was holding smelling salts under the old man's nose when he came to. The sheriff handed him a cup of coffee and said, "Drink this, you'll feel better."

When the cup was empty, McAuliffe gave him the bag containing his possessions and walked him to the double steel doors. "How you fixed for money?" the sheriff asked and when there was no reply, took a ten dollar bill from his wallet and pressed it in the other's hand. He unlocked the door and gently nudged the old man outside.

He turned then and murmured, "I thought only one died but—" The door clanged shut behind him.

The old man remained standing there, confused, uncertain. After a time he slowly descended the stairs and shuffled away up the street. A misty rain had begun to fall. With fumbling fingers he turned up the collar of his jacket, but the cold October wind found its way inside. The frail old body trembled.

IOWA

THE HAPPY DAYS CLUB
by James M. Ullman

"TED, I'VE GOT one right up your alley," Michael Dane James announced over the telephone.

Ted Bennett, sprawled in a chair beside a customer's man in a broker's boardroom, replied without taking his eyes from the tape moving overhead. "Mickey, if it's another scheme to drift me into a Detroit tool and die plant in the guise of a laborer, climb a tree. I don't care *what* the 1965 Whozit is going to look like."

"It's a defensive assignment," James said, "and won't compromise your principles one bit. One of the nation's biggest mutual funds, with assets of half a billion dollars, thinks its secrets are being stolen by a little investment club in Iowa."

"You're kidding," Bennett chuckled.

"I'm leveling," James went on. "So meet me in front of Sam's at five o'clock. Our Wall Street friends want to talk to us there before they commute home to suburbia. They don't think it would look good for us industrial spies to be seen in their offices."

A sign in the window proclaimed *SAM'S—HOME OF THE 25-CENT MARTINI*. The price prevailed only during the cocktail hour, but as a result the place was jammed, mostly with executives from the financial district. James, a stocky man with horn-rimmed glasses riding his pug nose, and Bennett, tall, lean, and hatless, pushed through the crowd to a rear booth tagged *RESERVED FOR MR. ALLEN*.

Victor Allen, president of the Gibraltar Fund's management group, rose to shake hands. He was big and burly and in 1934 had played tackle for the Green Bay Packers. He introduced James and Bennett to the other occupant of the booth—Stuart Clark, chairman of the fund's stock selection committee.

"Mickey and I," Allen told Clark as they sat down, "banged heads one year in the old N.F.L. We both got out alive somehow. Mickey's an industrial espionage consultant now, and Bennett works for him. Sam, a couple more here."

"Is this," Bennett inquired, settling in a corner, "where you boys decide which stocks the Gibraltar Fund will buy? Booze up and then shove a pin through the Big Board listings in the *Times*?"

"Hardly," Clark smiled. "Let's just say that here we review in more relaxed surroundings decisions made elsewhere."

"Show him the clip, Stu," Allen said.

Clark drew an envelope from his pocket and removed a newspaper clipping. He pushed it across the table. A waiter brought two drinks and set them down.

"This clipping," Clark explained, "was forwarded to us by the branch manager of a brokerage house in Des Moines, Iowa. It's a story from a small daily newspaper, the Canfield, Iowa, *Gazette*. The story is the usual feature that papers print now and then about a local investment club."

"'The Happy Days Club,'" James read aloud, "'is composed of fifteen residents of the Westlake subdivision. Its members are drawn from all walks of life.'"

"They seem," Bennett observed, peering over James's shoulder, "to have done rather well."

"There's something remarkable about The Happy Days Club," Clark went on. That's why my friend in Des Moines sent me the clipping. He sells a lot of shares in our fund, you see, and knows our portfolio. And he noticed in the past eight months that The Happy Days Club has been buying or selling only those stocks which *we* bought and sold."

"It could be coincidence."

"It could be," Allen broke in, "but even more remarkable is the fact that their buying and selling took place *before* we announced we had bought or sold the stocks, and in some cases, *after* we had reached a decision but *before* we had even completed a transaction. That story gives the dates of their sales and purchases and we checked them against our records. The club didn't buy every stock we bought, of course—they don't have that much money. But there's not a single stock in their list that we didn't buy. And not a single stock we sold that, if they owned it, they didn't sell."

"Secrecy," Clark added, "is essential at a certain stage in our business, Mr. James. We're required to report quarterly on our purchases and sales. But we're allowed enough leeway so that we don't have to report on the transactions we're making *at that time*. Our minimum investment in any stock is about two million dollars. Naturally, we don't go into the market and buy two million dollars' worth of stock in one day—the purchase, or sale, is spread out over a period of weeks or months. The brokers we buy through are carefully screened for their ability to keep their mouths shut about what we're doing. Because if word got out that we were putting two million dollars or more into a company a lot of speculators would buy the stock, too, hoping for a killing."

"Secrecy isn't as much of a consideration," Allen explained, "when we buy widely held blue chips like AT&T or Jersey Standard. But it's a prime consideration when we buy into a lesser-known company which we think may become a blue chip in the future. And it's that class of stock, incidentally, which The Happy Days Club has been buying into with us."

"So you believe," Bennett said, "that The Happy Days Club has a pipeline into the innermost circles of the Gibraltar Fund."

"Exactly," Clark said. "We're not so concerned that these fifteen Iowans are stealing our judgment, so to speak, as we are with the fact there *is* a leak in our organization. If word of our decisions reaches many people before we announce them, the price of every smaller company we start buying into will be bid up to the moon. What's more, we're one of the big funds in the country. If the story ever got out that a little investment club was able to steal information from us, we'd be held up to ridicule. Someone might even investigate us. You know how things are these days."

James fingered the clipping. "Any of these names—the fifteen club members—strike a responsive chord?"

"None whatsoever."

"Well," James concluded, "I'd say the way to begin would be for Bennett, here, to go right to the source and find out how The Happy Days Club arrives at their decisions. Meanwhile, I'll have Barney, my sound man, see if your phones are being tapped or anything. And I'll run a check on the backgrounds of everyone involved in your stock transactions."

"We don't want to alarm those people in Iowa," Allen said.

"Don't worry," Bennett said. "Bennett will appear in appropriate disguise."

A day later Bennett flew to Chicago, took another plane to Davenport, and then rented a car. He drove south along the Mississippi, reaching Canfield, a river town of some 20,000 population, as dusk fell. He checked in at a motel, wolfed a paper plate of fried chicken at a drive-in, and returned to his room for a good night's sleep.

In the morning he drove to downtown Canfield. He breakfasted on tomato juice and toast, stopped at a news agency for a *Wall Street Journal,* and then, *Journal* and an attaché case in hand, entered the offices of the Canfield Savings and Loan Association. The newspaper clipping had identified the president of The Happy Days Club as Robert Gordon, a loan officer at the institution.

Gordon, a genial, portly man in his fifties, greeted Bennett with a puzzled smile.

"You say you're from New York? Are you buying real estate in our town, Mr. Bennett?"

"No," Bennett said, shaking Gordon's hand and taking a chair. "I'm a writer. Free-lance. I'm working up a magazine piece on investment clubs."

"You've come a long way for that."

"I know," Bennett explained, "but that's the point. I want to get away from the usual slick big-city and fancy suburban crowd—advertising men and sales executives and all that. I want a good part of my article to deal with the way an investment club works in small-town America, the folks right across the street." He pulled a photostat of the clipping from his pocket. "I've had a clipping service send me everything they could find on small-town investment clubs. And as soon as I read about The Happy Days Club in the *Gazette,* I knew it was the club I wanted to feature in my article."

"I'm flattered," Gordon said. "I'm sure the whole club will be flattered. In what magazine will your story appear?"

"I have a tentative commission from the editors of *View,*" Bennett said, handing Gordon a faked letter written on *View* stationery. "But if they decide they don't want it, I don't expect to have much trouble selling it elsewhere."

"Will there be pictures?"

"Of course. I have my camera at my motel."

"Well, won't that be nice," Gordon said, beaming and returning the faked letter. "Tell you what. Meet me for lunch at the American Café around the corner. Meanwhile, I'll phone the members and try to set up a special meeting as soon as possible."

Bennett walked to the Canfield *Gazette* building. He told the managing editor the same story he had told Gordon and got permission to use the newspaper's library for background material on the club and its members.

He spent two hours going over the *Gazette*'s clipping files. When at last he left the building, a police car slowly followed him around the corner and down the block to the American Café. Bennett tried without much success to pretend it wasn't there.

"All our members have been contacted," Gordon announced over coffee. "Most of them can make it at my house tomorrow night. They'll be there at eight. But I wish you'd drop in tonight and have dinner with my family."

"Delighted," Bennett said. "By the way, who makes the buying and selling decisions for your club?"

"We have a three-man selection committee—Cromie, Hubbard, and Price. When anyone has a suggestion for a stock to buy or a reason to sell a stock we hold, it's forwarded to the committee. When we were first organized, the whole membership used to vote on what purchases or sales to make. But recently we've let the committee make the actual decisions, since they say timing may be important."

"Who's chairman of the committee?"

"We have no chairman. Just the three men. But the selections they've been making lately have been doing so well that we haven't changed members of the committee in nearly a year. Before that we had an awful lot of losers."

Bennett had almost reached his car when the police car pulled up behind him and stopped. A tall, husky man in uniform emerged.

"Sir," the officer said cordially, "would you mind coming with us?"

"What's the trouble?"

"No trouble. The Chief wants a word with you."

Bennett shrugged and climbed into the back of the police car. He flipped through his *Wall Street Journal* as they rode to the station in silence.

The Chief of Police, a huge, crew-cutted man of about Bennett's age, late thirties, smiled and nodded toward a chair.

"Sit down, Mr. Bennett. I understand you're a writer."

"That's correct," Bennett said. He put his attaché case and the *Journal* on a radiator under the window and sat down. Inwardly, he debated whether to volunteer to show the Chief the faked *View* letter. Something about the Chief made him decide not to.

"What magazine do you write for?"

"I may do this story for *View*."

"Would you mind naming some other magazines where your work has appeared?"

Bennett rattled off the names of several nationally circulated publications. He felt much as he had one day in 1944, when a German officer asked why a French farm laborer who stubbed a toe should know so many American obscenities. That had been a bad day too.

The Chief wrote the names on a pad. "I don't suppose you'd mind," the Chief asked, "if we checked these out."

"Not at all," Bennett replied. "And now I'd like to know why you've taken such a sudden interest in me."

"Well, it's funny," the Chief explained, "but a lot of people from the big city think we're kind of slow out here. They try to sell our citizens traps for mortar mice and all sorts of things. And this morning one of our citizens called me and said there was a man in town from *View* who wanted to meet the members of The Happy Days Club. He said he was suspicious because he'd heard of confidence men approaching investment clubs in one disguise or another, for the very good reason that people in investment clubs have money to invest. He didn't say *you* were a confidence man, understand. He just asked us to check and make sure you're a writer."

"Who was this called?"

"I'd rather not tell you."

"You asked me in here on the basis of that?"

"Not entirely," the Chief said. "We've had writers around here before, Mr. Bennett. A year ago, when a farmer outside of town chopped up two mail-order brides and buried them in an onion patch, a lot of writers came down. I called one of those boys—he works out of New York too—and he said he never heard of you. So far nobody else he's asked ever heard of you either—including, by the way, the editor of *View*. And the librarian here has been going through the *Reader's Guide* and she can't find any record of where you ever had anything published. Maybe if you'd tell me the dates where some of your stuff ran, she could look it up, and we could both forget the whole thing."

"At the moment," Bennett said blandly, "I just don't remember."

The Chief considered this. "Well, that's too bad," he said. "Now, you haven't done anything illegal I know of yet, so I can't charge you and put you in jail. Your name *is* Theodore Bennett—we know because you showed identification when you rented that car in Davenport. We checked. We're great respecters of the law out here. We don't push people around because they're strangers. But the way it is, though, I'm afraid there'll be a squad car or a police officer at your elbow every second you're inside the city limits until I'm satisfied you *are* a writer. So if you want to operate under those conditions, you go right ahead."

Bennett managed a weak grin. "Well," he said, "I'm not going to argue. It's ridiculous. But on the other hand, I'm not going to waste my time giving Canfield and The Happy Days Club national publicity if this is the treatment I receive here." He rose. "I saw a pay phone near the sergeant's desk on my way in. I'll telephone Gordon and call the whole thing off."

"Use my phone."

"Wouldn't think of it. I don't want to waste a cent of your taxpayers' money."

Bennett left the Chief's office. He fumbled clumsily through a telephone book for Gordon's number, taking plenty of time. Then he called Gordon and abruptly informed him he was leaving town and wouldn't write a story about The Happy Days Club after all. He hung up, leaving Gordon in mid-sentence, and returned to the Chief's office for his attaché case and *Wall Street Journal*.

"A couple of my boys," the Chief said genially, "will go with you to your motel and see to it you get packed proper and on the right road back to Davenport. If you drive fast, you might reach there before dark."

Two uniformed officers drove Bennett to where he had parked the rented car, then followed him to the motel. Bennett packed in five minutes and checked out. They stayed with him to the city limits, pulling to the curb and watching as Bennett gunned the motor and roared out of sight over a hill.

Bennett drove at high speed for about five miles. In the future, he vowed, he'd provide himself with a solid cover story and appropriate supporting documents no matter how innocuous the assignment seemed. Apparently he had vastly underestimated the sophistication of Iowa investment clubs—and of the Iowa police.

When Bennett came to a strip of roadside stores and drive-ins he bounced to a stop in a gravel parking area. He hauled his attaché case from the back seat and opened it, exposing a transistorized tape recorder built into the bottom. Bennett had activated the recorder just before placing the attaché case on the radiator in the Chief's office. No matter how the conversation went, it had seemed a good idea.

Quickly Bennett reversed the tape, pushed the playback button, and lit a cigarette, listening to a recording of their conversation, to the point where the Chief had said, "Use my phone."

"Wouldn't think of it. I don't want to waste a cent of your taxpayers' money."

Then he heard the door close as he left the Chief's office to telephone Gordon. And then the Chief did what Bennett had hoped he would do. He picked up his own telephone and dialed a number.

"Hello, Mrs. Price? Chief Waner. Your husband home? Hello, Frank. You were right. He must be some kind of swindler, although I never heard of this investment club approach before. But he sure isn't a writer. Don't worry. We had a little talk and he's leaving Canfield this afternoon. He seemed sensible enough not to try to come back. Thanks. Glad you put me on to this guy before he did any damage."

The Chief hung up.

Frank Price, Bennett knew without having to check his list, was a member of The Happy Days Club. What's more, he was one of the three men on the stock selection committee.

Bennett turned the recorder off and looked around. What he needed now was a woman.

He found her behind a counter in a diner. She was reasonably articulate and, from the way she talked back to truck drivers, she seemed to have plenty of nerve. Bennett had to drink two cups of coffee before the place cleared out and he was alone with her. The cook in the back was engrossed in a telecast of a baseball game.

"Miss," Bennett asked, "can you dial Canfield direct on that pay phone?"

"Yes, sir."

"Well," Bennett said, "I'll give you twenty bucks if you make a call for me. It will take you less than five minutes."

"You're crazy," she said.

He pulled twenty dollars from his wallet and pushed it across the counter. "There it is. No fooling. In fact, I'll make it thirty." He extracted another ten.

"I don't want to get in trouble," the girl said.

"You won't."

"Why don't you call?"

"Because I want someone to impersonate a telephone operator."

"That sounds illegal." She advanced and fingered the bills.

"It is a little illegal," Bennett admitted, "but there'll be no risk for you. You've heard of private investigators, haven't you? I can't tell you any more than that. But if you make the call and hang up, nobody will be able to trace it. And even if they did trace it, you could always say some woman came into the diner and used the phone."

"What do you want me to say?"

"Say, 'This is the long-distance operator. The charge on your call to San Diego is twenty-eight dollars and nineteen cents.' I have reason to believe this party just made a long-distance call, although probably not to San Diego. The party will probably be so mad at you that he'll volunteer information about any long-distance calls he did make this afternoon. If he doesn't, ask him if he made any long-distance calls, and to where. Get the out-of-town number if you possibly can. If you can't get any information after a minute or two, say, 'This is Albany 4-5634, isn't it?' He'll say no, because his number is Albany 4-5624. Then say you're sorry you made the error and hang up."

"Albany 4-5634," she repeated, reaching for the thirty dollars. "Okay, hon. I'll go along. Got a dime?"

Twenty minutes later Bennett climbed into his car and drove to the next river town. There he turned right and crossed a bridge over the Mississippi into Illinois. The road wound down the river's foothills and then flattened out into farm country. It was dark when Bennett checked in at an eight-unit motel in a tiny junction called Blackford.

There was a telephone booth in the parking lot and Bennett called James from there.

"Where've you been?" James demanded. In the background, the roar of guns from a television set mingled with youthful screams. "I got a pack of Cub Scouts in my living room and can hardly hear you."

"I got chased out of Canfield," Bennett reported, "by the Chief of Police. He knows I'm not a writer and he thinks I'm a confidence man."

"Some industrial espionage agent you are," James said sarcastically. "What happened? Your false mustache fall off?"

"Wait a minute," Bennett said. "The Chief didn't think this up on his own. He was tipped by a club member named Frank Price. Frank Price is also a member of a three-man committee that decides what stocks the club will buy and sell."

A moment of silence ensued.

"Are you thinking," James asked slowly, "what I'm thinking?"

"It occurred to me at the time," Bennett said, "but I figured it was just one chance in a million."

"Well, the odds are shortening. I'll have Barney work on that angle first thing tomorrow. Where are you now?"

"Blackford, Illinois. I'm going to sack in here tonight."

"You'll never get back to New York the route you're taking. Drive to some place with an airport and catch a plane. I'll send another agent to Canfield with a better cover."

"I'm at Blackford because I had a girl call Price to find out if he placed any long-distance calls after I was run out of town. She pretended to be a long-distance operator. And Price did make a long-distance call this afternoon. To Eaton, Illinois, which is twelve miles from Blackford."

"It's probably a waste of time."

"Maybe. The girl couldn't get the Eaton number that Price called. But Price has a brother, William, who lives in Eaton. I learned that from some social notes about him in the Canfield *Gazette* morgue. It will only take a day to check the brother out and see if he has any connection with the Gibraltar Fund."

"Since you're there anyhow, go ahead. I'll hold up on that other agent. Come to think of it, Price called that Chief of Police so fast when he heard you were in town it's like someone pushed a button. He must have known you were coming. I got a hunch that by this time tomorrow we'll both have arrived at the same conclusion."

In the morning Bennett drove to Eaton and parked on a side street. He walked a block to the business district, entered a drug store, bought a *Wall Street Journal*, and stepped into a telephone booth. He flipped through the book to PRICE, WILLIAM J. and dialed the number.

A woman answered.

"Good morning," Bennett said. "Is your husband there?"

"He's asleep. He's always sleeping at this hour. He doesn't get in until three."

"When can I reach him?"

"Who is this?"

"I represent a firm doing market research for an advertising agency in Peoria. We're surveying all property owners in Eaton."

"Well," she said irritably, "why don't you get him at work, then? He doesn't like to be bothered at home. Call him at the restaurant this afternoon."

"What restaurant is that?"

"Why, Betty's, of course," she said, hanging up.

Bennett hung up and opened the book to the yellow pages. Under "Restaurants" he found a display ad for *BETTY'S—Steaks, Chops, Chicken, Cocktails, Open 8 A.M. to 2 A.M. Bill Price, Prop.*

He left the booth and walked back to the car. He drove to the address listed in the telephone book for the restaurant, getting directions from a small boy on a bicycle. The restaurant would be as good a place to begin an investigation of William J. Price as any.

The restaurant, a roadhouse, had been converted from an old farm building on the outskirts of town. Bennett pulled into the parking lot but didn't get out of his car. He didn't have to. Because a foot-high sign in the window proclaimed: *BETTY'S—HOME OF THE ORIGINAL 25-CENT MARTINI.*

Michael Dane James handed the report to Allen—he, Allen, and Bennett were sitting in James's office.

James explained: "Sam, the owner of that comfortable two-bit cocktail-hour martini joint across from your building, wired your reserved booth for sound. The mike was hooked to a tape recorder in his office. Barney found the mike in ten minutes when he joined us for a drink yesterday. A restaurant or bar owner bugging tables isn't unheard of, you know. Usually they say they're just checking customer reaction to food and service and whatnot. In this case it's obvious one of Sam's motives was to get tips on stocks. His location in the financial district would be a natural for that. His twenty-five-cent martini between five and six would be a lure to bring people in. And when he got the right people—like top decision-makers for one of the nation's big mutual funds—he reserved a booth for you regularly, to make sure he could hear everything you had to say."

"As I get it," Allen said, "Sam's connection with The Happy Days Club was through his brother-in-law."

"That's right," Bennett said. "Sam came from Eaton originally. He and his sister, Betty, ran a roadhouse there. After Sam left for New York, Betty married William J. Price, and he took over the roadhouse. As time went on, and Sam got established here, he started relaying some of his inside stock information to his sister and her husband, William Price. And William, in turn, passed it on to his own brother, Frank, who lived in Canfield. Frank belonged to The Happy Days

Club and got on the selection committee. Once on it, it wasn't much of a trick to control it. If necessary, he could take one of the other two committee members into his confidence, and the two of them could always outvote the third member. I'm sure most members of the club had no idea they were using information stolen from the Gibraltar Fund."

"Sam taped our conversation the day we were in his place and you gave us the assignment," James said. "He knew, then, that Bennett was going to Canfield in one role or another. And he had a brief look at Bennett when you ordered martinis for us. When Sam heard the tape he must have panicked. No doubt he called his brother-in-law, William, who in turn called Frank and warned him Bennett was on the way. So the minute Frank Price learned Bennett was in Canfield, he asked the police to check Bennett, hoping Bennett would be run out of town."

"The mystery is solved," Allen admitted, "but it does leave me with a dilemma."

"I don't think," James smiled, "that The Happy Days Club will follow the Gibraltar Fund's lead any more. This probably scared the daylights out of William and Frank Price."

"Nevertheless," Allen said, "the problem remains: What do we do about Sam? If we expose him, we may still get all the publicity we've been trying to avoid. And if we say nothing, he'll go on eavesdropping on his patrons."

"If it were up to me," James suggested, "I'd pass the word discreetly to your employees never to go into that place again because it's bugged. The news will get around the financial district fast enough, and Sam's will die a slow but certain death."

"Why," Bennett offered, "don't you just sit there, drink his martinis, and pass along tips on stocks you think will go down instead of up?"

"I like that," Allen grinned. "Between all of us, we could give Sam enough bad advice to bankrupt him in thirty days. But we don't want to hurt any innocent investors—even in Canfield, Iowa. No, I think we'll adopt Mr. James's suggestion."

KANSAS

KANSAS IN AUGUST
by Edward D. Hoch

CLARE GENTRY WAS stretched out on the hotel bed singing quietly to herself. *"I'm as crazy as Kansas in August—"*

Milt Hayes was trying unsuccessfully to adjust the room's air conditioner. "Damn it, Clare, if you're going to sing that song at least get the lyrics right!"

"I just meant I was crazy to ever come here with you, Milt. Everything's so flat, and it's so hot!"

"God's country, Clare. You think man was made to frolic in the surf at Malibu all day? These people work. They're out in those wheat and corn fields from dawn to dusk, to say nothing of the sunflowers."

"What sunflowers?"

"Hell, it's the Sunflower State, isn't it?"

Milt was a screenwriter and he was forever reeling off odd facts and statistics. That was one of the things which had first impressed her about him—that and his million-dollar home at Malibu. She'd never imagined that screenwriters earned so much money. Milt was good, of course. He kept his two Oscars on the mantel in case anyone doubted it.

They'd come to Kansas in August because Milt had an assignment to write a sequel to *The Wizard of Oz,* one in which the Wizard comes to Kansas to visit Dorothy. It wasn't a bad idea, Clare had to admit, but she didn't understand why Milt couldn't work on it at home in California. Taking a hotel room in Wichita for a week was her idea of nothing. The first night they'd made the rounds of the bars and that had been sort of fun for Clare. There were enough young guys from Wichita State and McConnell Air Force Base to make life interesting. Milt got upset when one fellow tried to pick her up, but that pleased her too.

Today they'd rented a car and just driven around past fields of corn and wheat, often stretching for miles. Milt wanted to get the feel of the place, he said, and maybe find special attractions or landmarks that could figure in the screenplay. He was good at details, which was one reason he got big money and won awards.

"Baum's book was never very specific about where in Kansas Dorothy lived," he told Clare. "I've decided it was not far outside Wichita—to the west, of course, where it's flatter."

It was flat, all right, and after a while Clare wanted nothing more than to go back to their room. The temperature was in the low nineties by late afternoon and that's when the room air conditioner started making strange noises. "For the amount we're paying we should have a cool room," she insisted, though she knew the room rate was nothing compared to hotels in New York or Los Angeles.

Milt Hayes made a few notes on the portable word processor he traveled with, then went to the hotel phone. "I'll get someone from engineering up to fix it. In the meantime let's go downstairs for a drink. The hotel bar doesn't look bad."

That sounded good. She changed into her backless dress with the flowery print and he put on a sport jacket. They sat at the bar and Clare ordered a new Mexican drink she'd tried in L.A. The bartender didn't know how to make it so she listed the ingredients for him. "I should get you a job here," he told her with a grin.

Milt had gone over to buy a pack of cigarettes from the machine and she took the opportunity to banter some more with the bartender. "I could use one this week. I'm bored stiff in this city."

A man sitting two stools away turned and studied her with an appraising glance. He was in his thirties, with a little black mustache and horn-rimmed glasses. She guessed he was probably a tractor salesman.

After one drink Milt began to grow restless. She knew the signs. "You want to get back to your word processor."

"Well, yeah. This thing's finally beginning to jell in my mind."

"Mind if I stay and have another drink?"

"No, go ahead. Give me an hour and then we'll go out to dinner."

"Fine." She smiled and gave his hand a squeeze.

When she was alone she ordered another Mexican Sunrise. "You remember how to make it?"

"Sure do!" the bartender assured her.

The man two stools away turned to Clare and asked, "That your husband?"

"No, a friend. We're here on business."

"For a whole week?"

"That's right." She looked away and began playing with her drink, fearful that he'd mistaken her for a prostitute.

"If you're really bored and you have some free time, I might be able to hire you for a few hours' work." He must have seen her expression begin to harden because he hastened to add, "I didn't mean to sound crude. It's a serious offer."

"I'm afraid I couldn't."

He moved over onto the stool next to Clare while the bartender became suddenly busy polishing glasses. "My name is Simon Lane. I need a woman like yourself—attractive and well-dressed—to accompany me to a private club. That's all you have to do."

"I'm sorry. I am here on business."

He tore a page from his pocket notebook. "Here's my name and room number.

If you should change your mind tomorrow I would like to hear from you." He left the note beside her glass, partly covered by a ten-dollar bill. "This should cover your drink too." Then he was gone.

Well, it wasn't the first time somebody tried to pick her up in a bar. As a matter of fact, she'd met Milt Hayes for the first time at a Beverly Hills night club. It only proved that Kansas wasn't that much different from California after all. She smiled and slipped the note into her purse, not really intending to do anything about it.

She awoke in the morning to find Milt already working at his word processor. "I just phoned down for breakfast," he said. "I think I'd better stick to this all day. It's coming along good right now. The Wizard has just arrived at Dorothy's farmhouse."

"That sounds great, Milt."

"I know this isn't much fun for you. Do you think you could go out and do some shopping or something today? They're supposed to have a good Indian museum here, and that Cowtown section with all the restored buildings."

"Sure," she agreed. "I'll find something to do." But from their window all she could see was a row of enormous grain elevators off in the distance.

She had breakfast with Milt and then showered and dressed for the day. After an hour or so of random shopping she wandered back to the hotel lobby and called Simon Lane's room on the house phone. "This is Clare Gentry. I met you in the bar last night."

"Yes, Clare. How are you today?"

"Fine, but I find myself with some unexpected free time. I was wondering if you still need a companion."

"I certainly do! Will you still be free tonight?"

"I could arrange to be."

"Let's meet at the bar this afternoon at four and I'll explain it to you."

He was there on schedule when she walked in, but seated in a booth this time for a little more privacy. "Clare, is it? I'm pleased you could come. What are you drinking?"

"Just a glass of white wine for now." Seeing him again, with his eyes bright and a bit frightening behind the horn-rimmed glasses, she wondered why she had come at all.

"Fine." He ordered from the waitress and then settled back. "My, you're a stunning young woman! Are you from around here?"

"California."

"I should have known! You could be the original California girl."

"Where is this place we're going tonight?"

"It's a private club called the Gypsum, after the river, but people have been known to call it the gyp-some. It's a gambling club."

"Is that legal?"

"Apparently the police don't bother it. If you're not a member you've got to have a special invitation. I have one, but it's for 'Mr. and Mrs.' and I understand they don't like people showing up alone. It's not the sort of place I could take just anyone, but you have the right look for it. You're all class, Miss Gentry."

"Call me Clare."

"There's five hundred dollars in this for you. OK?"

"You must be awfully anxious to visit this place."

"I am. Wear your fanciest dress and meet me in the lobby at eight."

Milt Hayes didn't even notice what she was wearing when she went out. Hunched over his word processor in a far-off land of wizards and witches and dogs named Toto, he might have been fourteen hundred miles away in Malibu. "I won't be late," she told him. "Maybe I'll take in a movie."

"Sure, Honey. I should finish this up in the morning. Then we can have some fun."

"My idea of fun would be to head back home."

"Whatever you say," he answered agreeably without looking up.

Clare had worn the best of her summer dresses, a glittering light green number that was sure to turn heads. She could see by Simon Lane's face that it was exactly what he wanted. "You're gorgeous!" he told her. "Come on, I've got a rental car parked outside."

They drove out Kellogg Street toward the Beech Factory Airfield. It wasn't yet dark and she could see the small private planes still landing and taking off. Then Simon Lane made a left turn and pulled up in front of a large house with a curving driveway. About a dozen other cars were already parked there. A small brass plaque on the door announced *Gypsum Club* in subdued lettering.

The man who answered the door was dressed like a butler but somehow he didn't fit the part. He inspected Simon Lane's invitation and carefully filed it away. "Welcome to the Gypsum, folks. Go right through the archway."

It was a gambling club, all right, but nothing like Las Vegas. The small individual rooms with their roulette wheels and crap tables reminded Clare of the places she'd visited with Milt in London. Many of the men wore formal clothes and some of the women had long dresses. Clare paused at a blackjack table long enough to note that the chips were ten dollars each.

Simon Lane bought a stack of them and gave her ten. "Amuse yourself," he said. "There's somebody who works here that I have to see."

He walked away from her and she noticed him gambling for a few minutes at one of the other tables. He seemed to be watching for someone. Finally a little bald man appeared, rushing in from the other room with a metal tray full of chips. Simon Lane watched him enter a small office without unlocking the door. He waited a moment and then casually followed him in.

"You come here often?" a man at Clare's side asked her.

"First time." Strangers were always trying to talk to her, even in classy places like this. She moved away from the man and checked out the tables in the adjoining room. Being alone in a place like this made her nervous.

After five minutes Simon Lane had not reappeared. She went to the office he'd entered and walked in without knocking.

Simon was standing behind a desk cluttered with mail in the process of being opened. A slim letter-opener lay among the envelopes. At his feet she saw the body of the bald-headed man. There was a black silk cord knotted around his throat.

"I told you to stay out there," he said tonelessly.

"What in hell is going on here? Did you kill him?"

"He tried to stab me with the letter-opener. I had no choice."

"But—"

"He's someone I knew long ago. He owed me money."

"We have to call the police."

"Why? I told you it was self-defense. The police will just ask a lot of fool questions. Walk out of here casually and I'll follow in a minute or two."

She put a hand on the desk to steady herself. What had she gotten herself into? Simon Lane bent down over the body. "Wait for me outside," he said.

"All right."

No one noticed her emerge from the office and walk to the roulette table, her purse held close to her side. She bet a chip at random and won two. Simon came out of the office and smiled at her. "We'd better be going, don't you think?"

"I'm trembling."

"You'll be all right. Nobody noticed."

On the way out he slipped one of his remaining chips to the doorman. "Nice place. We'll come again."

"Thank you, folks."

In the car back to the hotel Clare could hardly speak. "You killed that man."

"I told you, it was an old debt. His name was Reynolds and we had a place like this in Omaha. He cheated me out of my share and left me to take the rap with the local police. I just came here for what was mine." He took a thick wad of bills from an inside pocket. "And I got it. I'll double what I promised to give you."

"I—"

He pulled onto a side road. She had no idea where they were except that it was near one of the small airfields. "Come on, we'll settle up right now before we get back to the hotel." He stopped the car.

"I don't want any money. Just take me back."

"Sure, Clare." She saw his hands moving, twisting, and then she saw the black silk cord coming at her. She wondered if it was the same one he'd used on Reynolds.

Then she stabbed him with the letter-opener.

Clare left the car and walked to a nearby shopping center where she found a taxi to take her back to the hotel. Milt was overjoyed to see her, filled with such enthusiasm that she knew the first draft was finished and he liked it. "Let's go out for a late supper," he suggested.

"That would be great, Milt."

In the morning the double killing was front-page news. The chips in Simon Lane's pocket had linked him to the Reynolds killing at once, and police were speculating that Reynolds might have stabbed him with the letter-opener during their struggle. The Medical Examiner doubted he could have driven that far with a chest wound, but stranger things had happened. No mention was made of a woman who'd accompanied him.

Milt changed their plane tickets so they could fly back to California that evening. As the plane was taxiing for a takeoff he said, "I'll bet you're not sad about leaving this place."

"It was an experience," she said with a shrug. "Kansas in August."

KENTUCKY

HUNTER AND THE WIDOW
by D. L. Richardson

"SAY I TOLD you so and you're fired."

Tracey, my secretary, scowled at me before continuing her ministrations. The warm water in the mixing bowl beside her thigh was a weak pink. Which is exactly how I felt. Weak pink.

"Ouch!"

I jerked my head back and reached for my cheekbone, only to have my fingers slapped away and my chin clamped in her grasp. She resumed washing the blood from the gash just under my left eye, her hazel gaze scrutinizing the damage.

"If ever anyone deserved an I-told-you-so, it's you," she said. "But since you never listen to me anyway, I won't waste my breath."

"That's not true," I said between gritted teeth. "I always listen to you." I tried to pull away, but she only tightened her grip.

"Sit still!" she snapped. "And quit scrunching up your face like that. If you listened to me, neither of us would be here at three A.M. doing a bad imitation of some old movie."

She had a point. If I had listened to her, we wouldn't be watching a bowl of water turn red with my blood. She wouldn't be perched on my coffee table in jeans and an ice-blue satin pajama jacket trying to find my face amidst the cuts and scrapes and blood. I wouldn't be sitting on my couch trying to decide which hurt worse—the cheek she was cleaning or the chin she was gripping—and wondering, rather irreverently, if she was wearing anything under that blue satin.

"That cut and the one on your forehead need stitches." She surveyed her handiwork and then looked me in the eye. She scowled again. "Don't you think you've had enough trouble for one night, Adam Hunter, without asking for more?"

I had the decency to look sheepish as she gathered up the bowl and the first-aid paraphernalia and headed for the kitchen. Sometimes I had the notion that she was a witch. I mean, it wasn't natural for someone to be able to read minds the way she could read mine.

I relaxed back into the softness of the couch and closed my eyes against the dull throbbing that was steadily permeating every centimeter of my body. I could hear Tracey in the kitchen.

I hated it when Tracey was right. Probably because she was right so often.

"Here's the rough draft of your story." Tracey laid the pages in front of me. "And that phone call was your editor reminding you that he's still waiting for the last five chapters of *Murder by Yesterday*."

"He'll have to wait a little longer. I've got a job."

"Not her?" Tracey jerked her thumb in the direction of the door that, just moments before, had closed behind my new client.

"Her name is Easter Simmons, and yes, she's the one."

Tracey studied me for a moment, her lips pressed together, her eyes narrowed. With a deep breath and a single shake of her head, she left my office. I heard the rollers on her chair squeak when she sat down.

Damn! She was always doing that to me. This time I vowed not to give in. I pulled the notepad out from under the freshly typed manuscript and studied the notes I had just made. Typing sounds came from the outer office. Vicious typing sounds. Fifteen minutes later (a new endurance record for me), I was perched on the front of her desk.

"You don't think I should take the case."

"No." She pulled the page from the typewriter and scanned it.

"You don't even know what the case is."

"It's not the case that bothers me."

"What then?"

"Her."

"What about her?"

"I don't trust her."

"Why?"

She inserted a fresh piece of paper into the typewriter, the platen making clicking sounds of protest. "I never trust anyone named after a holiday." She pushed her reading glasses back up on the bridge of her nose and resumed typing without so much as a glance at me. The yellow pencil behind her ear was a sharp contrast to her short, dark hair.

Had I not known better, I would have said that Tracey's mistrust of my new client was, in actuality, a bad case of the green monsters. Easter Simmons had the looks to bring out the cat in a lot of women.

Medium height and willowy with shoulder-length, wheat-colored hair. Dazzling green eyes. Expensive clothes. The air of a woman who always got what she wanted.

Trouble was, I *did* know better, and Tracey wasn't the catty type.

"Maybe she was born on Easter and had eight or nine older brothers and sisters and her parents just ran out of favorite names," I offered.

"Maybe." She was still typing.

The subtle approach was getting me nowhere, so I reached over and flicked the switch on the electric typewriter. With a sigh, Tracey removed her glasses and swiveled her chair a quarter turn toward me. Her eyes always got to me, and the teal blouse she wore turned them a deep aquamarine that made matters worse.

"Why don't you trust her?"

"The way I understand it, she stands to lose a great deal of money if you find this long-lost stepson."

"Ah ha! You were eavesdropping."

"You left the door open."

So I had.

Tracey continued. "Her husband's been dead for over a year. Why look for the stepson now, after all this time?"

"You heard her. She *has* been looking for him. It's taken this long to get a solid lead. After all, Lexington, Kentucky, is a long way from Los Angeles." My explanation obviously didn't satisfy her suspicious mind. "What else bothers you?"

"Let's assume that she's telling the truth. That she has spent this last year looking for her stepson. That she's hired the kind of agencies only wealth can afford, agencies with lots of contacts and manpower. Why come to you now? Why not stick with the people who were able to track him down?"

"She wanted someone local who was familiar with the territory and the people."

"Then why not hire one of the larger agencies in town, like Marshall and Associates? They do security work for several of the horse farms. Why come to you, a writer, who only does this on a part-time basis?"

"If I weren't such a secure individual, I could really be hurt by that remark. Besides, you heard her. She doesn't want to make a big production out of this. She's afraid she'll scare him so far off she'll never be able to find him again."

"That simply means that she gets to keep all the money."

"Maybe, but she feels the money is his, and she can't, in good conscience, spend what isn't hers to spend."

"She said that?"

"She said that."

"And you believe her?"

"I believe her."

"I should think gullibility would be a hindrance to a private investigator."

"There's a difference between being gullible and trusting your client."

Tracey shook her head with a sigh, put her glasses on, and swiveled back to the typewriter. She flipped the switch. "Have it your way. I'm just the hired help."

I rose from the desk and headed back to my office, her voice stopping me in the doorway.

"But don't expect me to be there to put you back together again."

"Why should I need anyone to put me back together?"

"Are you forgetting that walking mountain she calls a chauffeur?"

"Lots of ladies with her kind of money have chauffeurs who double as bodyguards."

"People with bodyguards tend to draw undesirables. Otherwise they wouldn't need bodyguards."

I smiled. "It's nice to know you care."

"I just want to be sure you're around to sign my pay check at the end of the week."

I put my feet up on the coffee table, wincing at the pain in my ribs.

"You probably have two or three cracked ribs, too."

I opened my eyes to find Tracey standing in front of me, a pottery mug in her hand.

"I've already told you I'm not going to the hospital, Tracey. I'm not in the mood to make explanations."

"Suit yourself." She thrust the mug toward me. "Drink this."

I took it from her. "What is it?"

"Hemlock. It will put you out of your misery." She turned and disappeared into the kitchen.

A quick sniff confirmed it to be her special hot toddy. I took a cautious sip and welcomed the warmth that trickled down my esophagus. After two more sips, the whisky spread its own special warmth to combat the pain in my aching body.

I surveyed the mess that had been my living room. At the hospital there would be questions about my injuries, and questions meant explanations, and explanations meant lies because at this point the puzzle pieces were still scattered around the table. Hell. I wasn't too sure I even had all the pieces.

Brad Walters. Easter Simmons' stepson, Brantley Simmons, was using the name Brad Walters and had been working on a horse farm in the Lexington area for the last six months. She didn't know which one.

It wasn't much help, considering that there must be two hundred or more horse farms of varying size and prosperity within a fourteen-mile radius of Lexington. That's a lot of legwork. I decided to let my fingers do the walking and called an old friend at Marshall and Associates. They did security work for several of the local horse farms, and while finding Walters/Simmons working on one of those particular farms was a long shot, it was a place to start.

And I got lucky.

My friend had been predictably reluctant to release company information, but he owed me more than one favor, a point I was quick to make. Before long, he came up with the information I needed. Brad Walters had applied for a job at Willow Hill Farm, and a security check had netted strong recommendations from a horse breeder in Texas and a horse trainer out in L.A. As far as my friend knew, he was still there.

The next morning, after a call to the farm's manager, I left Tracey in the office and headed out Newtown Pike to Willow Hill, a small, but respected, brood mare farm a couple of miles past Ironworks Pike. It was a warm, sunny May morning, one of those days that Kentuckians dream about in February. The pastures were emerald green and lush. A few dogwoods still dotted the countryside with their white and pink lacework. A day for rolling down the car windows and inhaling the spring-scented air.

I shifted my position carefully, gritting my teeth against the pain. Another sip of Tracey's "hemlock" helped. I leaned my head back and closed my eyes.

It was hard to believe it had only been three days ago that I had bumped my way down a gravel lane to the main barn. Only three days since I had stood in the warm morning, savoring the sights and sounds of a working farm. Only three days since I had leaned against a plank fence and talked with a living, breathing Brad Walters. Too much can happen in three days.

I watched the farm manager talk to two men, point in my direction, and then disappear into the barn. I waited as the two conferred before one of them moved in my direction. With interest, I watched Brad Walters/Brantley Simmons approach.

He was about six feet tall with thick black hair, ruffled by the breeze. He wore scuffed boots, faded jeans, and a checked shirt with its long sleeves rolled up to reveal strong forearms already beginning to tan. As he got nearer, he pulled off work gloves to reveal long, blunt-ended fingers which he offered in a handshake.

"Mr. Hunter? I'm Brad Walters," he said in a clear baritone.

I returned the firm grip, studying the smooth planes of his face and the almost-black eyes. Somehow, he wasn't what I had expected.

"Mr. Trexler said you wanted to talk to me about a missing person, someone I might have met in Houston when I worked there."

"That's really only part of the truth. The person isn't actually missing. He's been found, only he doesn't know it yet. I was hired to tell him he's been found."

"I'm not sure I understand any of this, but if I can help you, I'll be glad to. Who is this guy?" he drawled.

"You."

For a brief moment he looked puzzled, and then he grinned. "Me? Who in the world would be looking for me?"

"Your stepmother."

The grin was gone, and the puzzled look was back. "My stepmother? Mr. Hunter, you must have me confused with someone else. I don't have a stepmother."

Easter's description of Brantley's departure from the Simmons household had prepared me for this reaction.

"Listen, Brad," I said, trying to maintain a friendly atmosphere by using his chosen alias, "your stepmother explained about the estrangement between you and your father that led to your leaving home. She also explained that you might be reluctant to come home."

"Wait a minute. Maybe you'd better tell me who my stepmother is."

"Easter Simmons."

I thought for an instant that something flashed in his eyes, but it was so brief that I wasn't sure.

"Easter hired you to find me?"

"Not exactly. She's been looking for you for a year, ever since—" I didn't know any better way to say it "—ever since your father died. She wasn't sure if you had even heard about his death."

"Yeah, I heard the old man got into one too many board meeting arguments and had a heart attack and died." He stuck his hands in his hip pockets. "Unless I'm badly mistaken, that makes Easter a very wealthy woman."

"It also makes you a wealthy man. Your father left a sizable portion of his estate to you. Easter hired several agencies to track you down. When they discovered that you had changed your name and were working on a horse farm in this area, she decided to come talk to you herself."

"Easter is here? In Lexington?"

I nodded. "She hired me to talk to you first. She wasn't sure you'd see her."

Brad was silent, and I gave him time to think before I continued.

"She wants you to know there are no strings attached to the inheritance. All you have to do is go back to L.A. with her to meet with the lawyers and get the paperwork taken care of."

"That's all I have to do, huh?"

Something in his voice struck a wrong chord deep in my brain, but I dismissed it. After all, I was dredging up a past he had discarded.

"That's all." I pulled a business card from my shirt pocket. "Here's my card with my office and home phones. Easter is staying at the Hyatt, and I've written her room number on the back. I won't even tell her where you work. You can call and talk to her yourself, or you can talk to her through me. It's up to you."

Brad looked at the small, buff-colored card, turning it over in his fingers and reading each side at least twice.

"When do I have to give her an answer?"

"Any time within the next two days. She said something about a clause in the will that says you have to claim your inheritance within a specific length of time or it reverts to her."

He nodded, a sardonic smile on his face. "My stepmother always did have a flair for the dramatic."

There was some bitterness in his voice. But what can you expect from someone whose stepmother is his own age?

"Don't be too hard on her. You haven't been the easiest person to find."

"Yeah. I guess not." He extended his hand again. "Thanks."

I shook his hand. "There's really nothing to thank me for."

"Oh, I don't know. You may have helped make me a wealthy man." That sardonic smile was back again. "Make sure you send my stepmother a big bill. She can afford it."

I thought about that drive back to the office. My conversation with Brad Walters had put a damper on my earlier high spirits. Something had kept nagging at me. Something I couldn't point a finger to and say, "Ah ha!"

Maybe it had been his attitude. His voice when speaking of his father's death had shown no remorse, no concern, nothing. And there had been a definite snideness in his references to his stepmother. But I didn't know the true situation. I didn't even know Brad Walters. I only knew what Easter Simmons had told me, and who was to say that was an accurate picture? No, it had to have been something else.

I had pushed it out of my mind, telling myself that I had done what I was hired for. Anything else would constitute meddling.

The sounds of Tracey moving quietly around the room broke through my thoughts. I opened one eye to see her righting a hassock. She picked up a lamp from the floor, straightened its shade, and replaced it on the table next to the chair. She disappeared down behind the chair.

"I didn't hire you to be a maid," I said.

The lamp came on.

"You didn't hire me to be a nurse either, but I seem to have done more than my share of that," she said, standing back up, hands on hips. "Besides which, this place will have to be straightened some before a maid can even get in. Most maids don't clean up after demolition derbies." She plucked a velvet pillow from the carpet.

"You could be destroying evidence, you know."

She looked me straight in the eye. "Are you planning to call the police after all?"

In the silence I regarded the score. Tyler, two; Hunter, nothing, and fading fast.

"I thought not." She returned to her self-assigned chore.

I watched her for a while. Watched her movements. Athletically graceful. No energy wasted. I found myself thinking it was a sight I could get used to and decided I must have taken a harder shot to the head than I had first thought.

I closed my eyes again only to have her image reappear in my mind. This time she was standing in front of my desk, looking too much like a knockout in red and black, a folded newspaper in her hand.

"I know you don't read the newspaper this early in the day, but I think you should make an exception today."

I looked up at her to argue but was stopped by the look in her eyes. I took the paper and began to read the story made prominent by her folding. I read the headline and lead paragraph, looked back up at her, and then finished the short item.

Brad Walters had been killed by a hit and run driver on Newtown Pike. According to coworkers, Walters, a photography buff, had walked a quarter mile up the road to photograph a dogwood. When he hadn't returned after a reasonable amount of time, one of the men had gone looking for him and found him in the ditch, dead.

"Seems hard to believe that I just talked to him yesterday morning."

"Is that all you have to say?"

"What do you want me to say? That Easter Simmons could have saved her money? Hit and run is not uncommon, Tracey. Not even here. It's just a coincidence. A rotten one, but a coincidence nonetheless."

"I don't believe in coincidences," she said in a tight voice and left, closing the door with more force than necessary.

Truth be known, neither do I. That same uneasy nagging I'd had the morning before was back. I read the article once more. Then again. And it hit me. The reason for the nagging.

According to the paper, Brad Walters was from Eagle Lake, Texas. When I had spoken with him, I had been aware that his voice hadn't sounded exactly as I'd thought it should. He had a Texas drawl, an authentic Texas drawl. The kind you don't acquire overnight. Marshall and Associates hadn't discovered that Brad Walters was Brantley Simmons either, and they were much too thorough to overlook something like that.

I grabbed my windbreaker from the antique hall tree and stepped into the outer office. Tracey was proofreading.

"I'm going to see Charlie Whisk."

"You could call him and save time."

"I need the fresh air."

I took the stairs at a half run, barely missing the guy from the pest control outfit come to check the messages on his answering machine in his tiny office across the hall from mine. When I reached the street, I turned right toward West Main Street, my back to West Vine. At the corner I turned right again. Charlie Whisk had a small work area above his cousin's camera supply store on East Main. When it came to computers, Charlie Whisk was a certified genius, and he was also a good friend. Right now I needed quick access to information from distant parts, and Charlie's computer terminal was faster than a Concorde.

I emerged an hour later and retraced my steps, having left Charlie a happy man. I had always been a little uneasy about using Charlie and had told him so once. He had laughed, rubbed his hands together, and said he could tiptoe through anybody's data banks and never leave a trace. For some reason that didn't make me feel better.

"Any calls for me?" I asked Tracey upon my return.

"No."

"None at all?"

"None."

"Are you sure?"

I recognized that look and put my hands up in surrender. "Sorry. I just expected the police to have called before now."

She followed me into my office. "Why would the police call you?"

I put my jacket back on the hall tree and sat down behind my desk. "When I talked to Brad Walters yesterday, I gave him my business card."

Tracey sat on the front of my desk. "And you think they would have checked with you even though they're calling it hit and run?"

"They should have at least been curious as to why a horse farm worker would need a private investigator."

She nodded and went off into her own thoughts.

"Do you know the number for the Hyatt?" I asked, picking up the phone.

"I'm sure it's in the book."

I ignored her sarcasm, flipped quickly through the phone directory, and penciled the number on a notepad.

"Why are you calling the Hyatt?"

I started dialing. "To see if the police have contacted Mrs. Simmons. Her room number was also on the business card."

"I'll leave the two of you alone, then," she said, slipping off my desk and out of my office, her perfume following her.

Two minutes later I was even more puzzled. The bodyguard-chauffeur had answered the phone and said that Mrs. Simmons was too upset to talk. I'd be upset, too, if I'd just inherited an extra ten million dollars. Whatever would I spend it on?

Tracey poked her head in the door. "Well?"

"The police haven't called her either."

"Curious."

"That's the word for it." I picked up the phone.

"Who are you calling now?"

"Newman."

She groaned, "I'm not here," and left.

Newman was my very limited pipeline into the Metro police department. Obnoxious and overbearing, he was not one of my favorite people, but a source is a source. Tracey didn't agree.

That uneasy feeling got worse after talking to Newman. So bad that I moved to the couch. Tracey came in and leaned against the end of my desk.

"He makes me feel the same way," she said.

"He asked for you."

"Spare me. Please."

I had to grin.

"What did you find out from Mr. Personality?"

"Zip. As far as Metro is concerned, it's straight hit and run."

"And the business card?"

I shook my head. "Nada. All he had on him was a billfold, a set of keys, and some loose change."

"Did you see where he put the card?"

"In his shirt pocket."

"Maybe it flew out when he was hit."

"Maybe."

"Or maybe he took it out before then and put it away somewhere."

"Maybe."

I looked up at her and saw that she was reading my thoughts again. I got up from the couch and grabbed my jacket.

"I'm going back out to Willow Hill. If Charlie calls, tell him I'll call him back."

I left her perched distractingly on the end of my desk.

But the trip to Willow Hill netted me nothing. Brad and two other hands shared a small house on the farm, and a search of his belongings turned up no little buff-colored card. When I got back to the office and returned Charlie's call, he confirmed my suspicions. I gave him another name to play with.

"Hunter, are you asleep?"

I opened my eyes to find Tracey leaning over me, something close to worry in her eyes, her perfume tickling my nose. Maybe the perfume was my imagination. After all, it was four A.M. Heck. Maybe the worry was my imagination.

"Just thinking." I smiled, or at least I think I did.

"I think you should go to bed and get some rest."

"You're probably right."

She frowned. "Are you all right?"

"Sure. Why?"

"Never mind. Can you manage by yourself?"

"Of course."

She stood back to give me room. She needn't have been in a rush about it. Slow was about as fast as I could manage. I finally got to my feet without too many un-macho grimaces and headed for the bedroom, grateful that Tracey was never out of reach.

"I suppose it would be chauvinistic of me to say that I don't like the idea of your driving home at this hour?"

"You should have thought of that at two A.M. when you called and asked me to come over here."

"Good point." I reached the bedroom door and stopped. "Do me a favor and be careful anyway."

"I will." There was a trace of a smile on her face.

I liked her smile. "Sweet dreams, Tyler."

The smile grew a little. "Sweet dreams, Hunter."

I entered the darkness of my bedroom, that smile following me, and made it to the bed. I managed to lower myself gently to the edge of it and shrug out of my shirt before the weariness overwhelmed me. The last thing I remember was my head hitting the pillow.

I awoke to bright sunshine and amnesia. My first movements dispelled the amnesia. I was stuck with the sunshine. A long, warm shower helped loosen the kinks in my stiff body and made the sunshine look better, too. I decided breakfast might make me feel almost human again, so I headed for the kitchen. I got sidetracked.

Tracey was asleep on my couch. I wandered over, sat on the edge of the coffee table, and watched her for a moment, curled up on her side, a blanket pulled up under her chin.

"Time to get up, Tyler."

At first there was no reaction, and then she stirred.

"Hmmmm?"

"I said, it's time to get up."

This time her eyes flew open, and there was momentary confusion in them until her memory woke up and filled her in. She stretched her arms above her head. "What time is it?"

I grabbed her left arm and looked at her watch. "Nearly ten. I thought I told you to go home?"

She sat up on the couch, and our knees nearly touched. "Don't let it go to your head, but I was worried about leaving you alone. You didn't look too well last night." She frowned as she studied the damage. "You don't look too well this morning, either."

"Thanks."

"For spending the night or telling you that you don't look so hot?"

I returned her grin. "Both."

"You're welcome."

I was working on my second cup of coffee and she was sipping her second glass of orange juice before the case came up.

"Easter Simmons didn't take the news of your discovery too well, did she?" Tracey asked.

"What makes you say that?"

She reached out with gentle fingers and touched my face. "Two cuts needing stitches, one puffy eye, one cut lip, and assorted bruises of varying colors."

"You left out the possible cracked ribs and the headache."

"I still think you should call the police."

"And tell them what? That two men I never saw clearly used my living room as a gym and me as a punching bag? Newman would love that."

"One man has been killed, Hunter. You could have been number two."

I leaned back and stretched out my legs. They ended up next to hers. I have a small kitchen table and long legs.

"But I wasn't. Doesn't that strike you as odd?"

"How many times *did* they hit you?"

"Think about it, Tracey. Brad Walters was killed because of what he knew. I know what he knew and all I got was a slap on the wrist. Easter Simmons hired those two to deliver their late-night message. I'd bet on that. But I'd also bet she had nothing to do with Brad Walters' death."

"Simply because all you got was a beating?"

"And a warning to mind my own business."

I watched her consider.

"If she didn't kill Brad Walters, who did?"

I shrugged. "I don't know."

"Some private investigator you are."

I grinned.

"As far as I can see, Easter Simmons is the only one with a motive," Tracey pointed out.

She was right. Because Charlie Whisk's little foray had turned up some interesting facts.

Fact number one: Brantley Simmons, age forty-five, was alive and prospering in L.A., impressing the pants off his father's colleagues with his brilliance in filling his father's shoes.

Fact number two: Brad Walters was Brad Walters. Had been since he was born, thirty years ago in Eagle Lake, Texas.

Fact number three: Easter Simmons knew Brad Walters. And vice versa. On her eighteenth birthday they were married.

Fact number four: Said marriage was never legally terminated.

And that had led me to a conversation and confrontation with Easter Simmons and fact number five: Someone had been blackmailing Easter with fact number four. She thought it was Brad Walters.

So Tracey was right. Easter Simmons had an excellent motive for killing Brad. At least most people would consider ten million plus dollars a good motive for murder, and ten million plus was what Easter stood to lose if certain people were to learn she wasn't Mrs. Simmons because she was still Mrs. Walters.

It's a big step from lying to murder," I said.

"Not for some people," Tracey said. "You're going to have to tell the police what you know sooner or later."

"I know. But not until I've talked to Charlie. He's checking something out for me."

"What else is there to check out about her?"

"Not her. Edgar, her chauffeur."

"His name is Edgar?"

I grinned. "I think it fits."

"You would. Why are you checking him out?"

I thought about the way Edgar had first tried to keep me from seeing Easter and then had hovered close by, answering some questions for her, attempting to block others, until Easter had told him to get lost. She had been nervous and then outraged and then resigned. All reactions that I had expected. I hadn't expected Edgar to be so antsy. Protective, yes. Antsy, no.

"Curiosity."

"You think Edgar took the bodyguard oath a little too seriously?"

"It's possible."

"Do you think he was guarding Easter's body privately as well as publicly?"

"Your mind is in the gutter again, Tyler." I got up from the table, taking my dirty dishes to the sink. "I'll meet you at the office in an hour. Charlie should be calling about then."

"Yes, sir, boss man, sir." She got up from the table. "Excuse me for forgetting my place, sir."

Forty-five minutes later I was in the office. I rewound the tape on my answering machine and settled into my chair to listen and go through the mail. The third message made me forget the mail.

"This is Easter Simmons, Mr. Hunter. I must talk to you as soon as possible. I will be flying out of Lexington at four thirty this afternoon. Please call me here at the hotel before three o'clock. I *must* talk to you."

I listened to the message again, the effect of her sultry voice dampened by obvious agitation.

I picked up the phone and began to dial.

"You can hang that up, Hunter. Mrs. Simmons has decided she has nothing to say to you."

Edgar watched me from the doorway. With my eyes on the gun in his hand, I replaced the receiver.

"How do you know that?"

He smiled. "She told me."

He moved into the office. The doorway was again blocked by an unsmiling gentleman of the same behemoth proportions as Edgar.

"Who's your friend?"

"Just someone I brought along."

Edgar's friend had a gun exactly like Edgar's, complete with silencer. I didn't like the looks of any of them—Edgar, his friend, or the guns.

"The message from Mrs. Simmons sounded urgent. What happened, Edgar? Did she figure out that you killed Brad Walters?"

"She's a lot smarter than most people give her credit for. I must say the same thing applies to you."

"People are always thinking of me as just another pretty face."

"How did you know that I killed Walters?"

I shrugged. "Who else could it be? Easter certainly didn't. All Walters really wanted was enough money for a small horse farm, and she was more than happy to give him that. In fact, she seemed surprised that Brad would even try blackmail."

"Ah, ah, ah. Put your hands back on the desk to where I can see them."

I smiled and obeyed. "I was surprised, too. For someone who was supposedly blackmailing a wealthy woman, Brad Walters had little to show for it. According to his bank account, he had nothing to show for it. But I guess that's because Brad Walters wasn't blackmailing Easter. You were. I don't know how you found out about her first marriage, but you did. I bet your bank account would have a lot to say."

He smiled again. I was beginning to hate that smile.

"To keep suspicion off yourself, you worked out an elaborate scheme for getting the money. What did you do? Have King Kong here mail the letters from Lexington?"

"Something like that."

"Funny. He doesn't look that bright."

There was no reaction that I could see from his door-filling friend. That could mean one of two things. Either he was too dumb to know he was being insulted, or he was a very disciplined man. Either way it didn't look too good for me.

"Why did you kill Brad Walters?"

"You're the man with all the answers. You tell me."

"You knew that once he talked to Easter your little charade would be in trouble. You couldn't let that happen, so you killed him. You, or maybe Godzilla here, followed me out to Willow Hill when I went to talk to him. Lucky for you he wanted to photograph that tree. It would have been hard to get into the farm undetected."

"His little hobby made it easy."

Now I knew I hated that smile.

"That left you with two other problems. Easter and me."

"Easter's no problem. She's too scared of losing all that money. And you weren't a problem until you started snooping where you had no business. Like I said, I underestimated you."

"It was your idea to hire me and not one of the larger agencies."

"I just pointed out to her that a larger agency would be more likely to find out about her past. She picked your name out of the phone book."

The Yellow Pages really do work. "So now what?" I asked.

"So now we take a little walk." Edgar motioned with his gun. "Get up nice and easy. Tony, you make sure he's not carrying a gun."

Tony patted me down professionally, never putting himself between me and Edgar's gun.

"He's clean," he grunted.

"Oh, it talks, too."

Tony shoved me in the direction of the door. He wasn't so insensitive after all.

"We're going to take a little walk across Vine Street," Edgar said. "I want you to behave yourself, Hunter. Got that?"

I nodded.

Edgar and Tony pocketed their guns and we left the office. No one passed us in the hall, and we met no one on the stairs. Outside, they positioned themselves on either side of me and herded me toward Vine. As we waited for the light to change, it occurred to me that we must look quite normal. I didn't feel normal.

The light changed and we crossed the street. Edgar smiled pleasantly and nodded at the young woman who passed us in the middle of the crosswalk. She smiled in return. Charming fellow, that Edgar.

I began to hope the light would change again. I preferred taking my chances in Lexington traffic, and one of them might get hit by some guy impatient to be wherever. No such luck. We reached the other side without incident, and Edgar steered me toward a gutted building. Tracey had told me it was being turned into a mini-mall with offices on the three upper floors.

Funny the things you remember in times of stress. I remembered the touch of her fingers on my face and the sight of her curled up on my couch. Damn!

Edgar removed a padlock and hustled me into the gloom of the building. I tried to drag my steps, but Tony shoved me on. I suspected he took pleasure in man-handling me.

I kept my eyes open for a break, any break, but breaks are hard to come by when you find yourself wedged between a rock and a hard place. And that's where I was. Literally.

Tony must have scouted the place out beforehand because it was he who guided me through the gloom and the dirt and the work-in-progress. I wondered where the work crew was. Didn't make much difference. They weren't there.

We ended up in a cluttered corner far from where we had entered. Suddenly, the walk from the office seemed all too short.

"End of the line for you, Hunter," Edgar said. That was certainly an original remark.

There was light streaming through windows in the wall behind me. It made it easier to see the guns and the smile on Edgar's face.

"What makes you so sure Easter will keep quiet?"

It was a stall and Edgar knew it and didn't seem to mind.

"Like I said. She's too afraid of losing all that money. Brantley Simmons would just love to throw her out on her pretty little tail. And who would believe that she didn't kill Walters herself just to keep him quiet?"

"What about me? Isn't my death going to look suspicious?"

"A private investigator is bound to make enemies. And since the work here has been put on hold for two months, Easter and I will be long gone before your body is even found. And there's nothing in particular to tie you to Walters."

"You took the business card."

"It pays to be thorough. Which is why Tony will pay a visit to your pretty secretary."

I stiffened.

"Now, now. Don't get upset. He won't kill her. Just scare her a little."

I knew Tracey didn't scare easily, but telling them would be the same as sign-ing her death warrant.

"Put your hands over your heads, gentlemen. Now!"

Edgar and Tony whirled.

Every time I thought I had Tracey all figured out—wham!—she'd do some-thing to blow it all away. Like the Colman party we'd gone to. She was waiting for me in the Colmans' foyer, looking terrific in a long-sleeved black dress that fell from the base of her throat to the floor, interrupted only by a red belt. Exactly what I would have expected. Fashionable, attractive, but conservative.

Until she turned and headed into the party ahead of me, and I was left to pick up my lower jaw from the floor and put my eyes back in my head. Her "conservative" dress left her back bare to the waist. Bare and beautiful.

Now here she was, surprising the hell out of me again. Feet firmly planted, .45 automatic aimed squarely and steadily at Edgar and Tony, her face, her eyes, even her body making it clear she meant business. I sidled out of the line of fire. I'm at least as smart as Tony.

"I said, hands over your heads!" she barked.

They obeyed.

"You, Edgar. Put your gun on the floor very slowly."

He obeyed.

"Take two steps back."

He did.

"You." She pointed to Tony. "Do the same thing."

He hesitated, and I saw him considering alternatives.

"Now!" Her voice echoed in the hollow building.

"You'd better do it, Tony," I said. "She's got a nasty temper."

He complied, reluctantly.

"Hunter, do you think you can get their guns without getting yourself killed?" Her eyes never left Edgar and Tony.

"I'll try." I scooped up the two guns and stood next to her.

"Now, I want you two down on the floor, spread-eagled," she said.

They didn't like the idea, but they did it anyway.

"Hunter, what did I tell you about undesirables?"

I grinned. "What brings you to this neighborhood, Tyler?"

"Charlie called me at home. He tried the office and evidently your home phone isn't working. He filled me in on Edgar. You're in the wrong profession, Hunter. According to Edgar's bank account, chauffeuring is where the money is.

"Anyway, when I got to the office, I heard voices, so I eavesdropped until Edgar started talking about taking a walk. I went downstairs to the pawn shop and watched until you disappeared into this building. Then I borrowed a gun from the showcase, told them to call the police, and followed you over here. Oh, by the way, you'd better point one of those guns at them. This one isn't loaded."

I chuckled and took aim. Poor Tony looked positively ill.

"You could have just called the police," I pointed out. "Coming over here was dangerous."

"I was afraid they might not get here in time."

"Why, Tyler, you really do care."

"Of course I care, Hunter. I still haven't been paid this week."

I love that smile.

LOUISIANA

MARJEVA'S BLACK CAT
by Edward Earl Sparling

As Marjeva, pleasant scoundrel, went down to the banana wharves through a breaking dawn he was confronted suddenly by a black cat. It was a great, round, fat, black devil of a cat with eyes that stared strangely.

Marjeva should have been agitated, but Marjeva was no Christian and laid no stock by the civilized superstitions. He was a pagan from the Summer Lands. His was some erotic Indian god of unpronounceable name from the fastnesses of his Honduras mountains.

Of the two, the cat and the Spaniard, the cat was the more surprised, and after blinking unsteadily for a moment turned and scampered precipitately down the nearest alleyway.

"Hah!" ejaculated Marjeva as he saw it go.

There was high approval in his tone. Under his pagan tenets the chance meeting could assure nothing but good fortune. And being an under-boss of the wharves, at the very moment on his way to work, he translated the omen in particular terms.

"Hah, I am promote'," he promised himself. "It means nothing rather I be promote'."

That put him in such an altogether congratulatory mood that he arrived at the wharves a full ten minutes ahead of the whistle.

The *Tchula* lay off the heading of the wharves. It was one of the last boats of the run, this being already late in the year. There was a sharpness to the air as the greasy tug puffed up to the landing with the banana boat, and there was a gray mist over the River that spoke of early rains. It was a dismal, disheartening day, but Marjeva hummed softly as the *Tchula* sidled into position under the fruit chutes. He, himself, superintended the opening of the hatches.

"Be care, *muchachos*," he warned his men as the square holes came open.

The warning was well. As he shot his flashlight down into the fruit he saw

192

exactly what he had expected. Under each of the hatches there was vicious life, tarantulas and scorpions.

Half paralyzed, they were lying as near the gray upper cheerlessness as possible. It had been a hard trip for these tropic lovers—cold, chilling, killing. They were numbed with it, and even at the sudden light and the voices, they did not scuttle away into the depths of the green fruit, but only moved uneasily in the square patches of light.

It was not unusual to find them thus at the top of the sea of bananas. On the cool days near the end of the banana run they always came to the top to avoid a blighting death. During the warm days they kept toward the bottom of the hold and were a dozen times more dangerous. What Angellico, the big Italian full-boss, did this morning *was* unusual, though.

Angellico came up while Marjeva was making preparations to clear the hatches. Angellico was beyond himself with lack of sleep. He was in haste to get the *Tchula* finished during the day. He would have to get some rest during the day, for there was fun awaiting him across the River, a round-eyed Sicilian girl, with a body of mandolin curves.

He came sidling down the deck as Marjeva finished inspecting the last hatchway. He squinted an eye down into the fruit.

"Hmmf," he observed. "Spider. Dump in that sack there."

Marjeva posted the men in the hold, taking the precaution to put an extra man under the chutes to shake each bunch of fruit free of any clinging life.

"Hey. No," ordered Angellico. "No need shake the bannan. The spider all come on top. Use'a the shovel."

"Veneno," protested Marjeva.

"It saves time."

"You hurry the taran'la too queek there be trouble, my frien'," said Marjeva.

"You hurry them quick or I make quick some trouble myself."

Marjeva shrugged inscrutably. "Oh-a well." What difference to him. Had he not met a black cat in the dawn? Certainly it would not be he who got a tarantula down his back. Certainly it would not be he. One did not meet black cats for nothing.

Angellico moved over to the rail where the ship physician, up early, was indolently enjoying his morning cigarette and watching the work. The Italian over-boss complained to him.

"How long I been handling bannan not to know the spider come all to the top of a cold day."

The doctor raised a velvet eyebrow and waxed his moustache thoughtfully.

"They are dangerous," he murmured. "One bite. It is not necessary twice. One poor wretch I had last. . . ."

Angellico did not wait for the finish. "Who should know much danger if not me!" He stamped off grumbling.

Typical of the wharves, Angellico was a man to have his own mind about things. He had begun on the wharves as a runner, unable to speak a word of

English, and had come to his place of eminence by bluster, bullying and even a little bravery. A man had to have some bravery to run a banana wharf. Angellico's chest was wide and hairy, like a great ape's, and sometimes he pounded it in an ape way. His face jutted out into a sharp visor where his eyebrows lashed across his oily forehead and into a mountain of a chin below his flat, grubby nose.

The big Italian hated Marjeva, the slight-figured under-boss, instinctively. Marjeva was everything he was not. The Spaniard had even cameo features, and hair like waves of dark water, and was, moreover, witty and intelligent. While Angellico blustered, the Spaniard moved thoughtfully. Angellico hated him as most blustering men do hate thoughtful ones.

A call from the hold now shook the over-boss out of his anger. The spiders found at the top of the fruit had been removed to a sack, Marjeva reported.

"Good," cried Angellico, and shrilled his whistle.

The line of fruit runners swung into position on the wharf. The big automatic carriers creaked and the chain carrying the canvas baskets, each large enough for one bunch of fruit, began dropping into the hold. The first load went over, and the second. A giant Jamaica Negro caught a bunch on his shoulders, settled it across his expansive neck, grinning and chattering in his machine-gun, unintelligible English. Old Pedro, the counter, clanged his counting table bell.

The runners caught their loads and hurried them back toward the waiting freight cars. Negroes, Spaniards, Italians, Chinese. Black backs, yellow backs, tan backs heaved under the odorous burden of the half-ripened fruit. But never was there a white back among them. Banana running is not for your white backs. It is the hardest work along the miles of waterfront. Even the self-respecting Negro roustabout goes wide of it if he can.

To Angellico, the Italian, it seemed that never had the toiling backs moved so slowly. They crawled, flagged. They dragged. They loitered and lagged. The hours went by with maddening monotony. Angellico's nerves fell into shreds. He went a dozen times to the hatches to measure the progress, each time returning to his post more disgusted. The fruit lay stacked in the hold inexhaustibly. And across the River a full-flavored Sicilian girl was waiting with lips like strawberry wines and kisses like sugar cane at the cutting—aaahg!

The big Italian grated the imprecation over his teeth and strode the deck of the ship in a tempest. He cursed his men, calling them women and white-blooded mongrels. He warned them that henceforth he would have real men for his fruit. He wished openly that regulations were such that he could go down among them and make them move fast with his big fists, flay them until they ran or the skins came off their backs.

Marjeva, the Spaniard, watched the growing tempest blandly, and yet crucially. For something would certainly happen before the day was out. Where or how or why it would happen, Marjeva did not know or care. He left that to the black cat.

The Spaniard's eyes suddenly flickered. Something was up. Angellico was coming over to the wharf from the ship gesticulating violently.

"Is this a hospital?" railed the over-boss when he reached Marjeva's side.

Marjeva shrugged. Angellico threw his big hands in the air. "Do they expect me to make work and send me cripples for men?" he wagged an angry thumb at one of the Negro runners. "Look. A man with just one foot. *Holy Mother.* Why should I be cursed with such as that?"

Marjeva regarded the Negro and frowned. Angellico was right, for once at least. Joe-Joe had no business on the wharves. He was not half a man. He came only to the shoulders of the others in the toiling line. And he was a cripple, with one foot bent under him until he walked only on two toes. And yet Joe-Joe had gotten his injuries on the wharves—the day that the lumber crane broke and two men were killed. Marjeva was in mind to offer a word in the fellow's defense.

Joe-Joe, moving up for the fresh load, took the words out of his mouth.

"How I'm gonna move faster," the Negro mumbled. And he cursed. He didn't curse the big boss. It was just a general oath, but it was the little something Angellico had been waiting for, the something that would allow him to use his heavy fists.

Angellico roared, leaped and struck all in the moment. Joe-Joe sprawled askew on the floor, the fruit falling and squashing about him.

The others in the line wavered and stopped, the Italians easing their loads to enjoy the fun, the Spaniards and Chinese standing impassively with the fruit balanced on their shoulders, the Negroes taking it variously, some shivering damply, others glowering but holding their tongues.

Marjeva's blood was colder in his veins. Perhaps this was where the black cat's prophecy would come true—if the Negro came up with a knife—if—but no; Joe-Joe came up like a whipped dog.

Angellico turned on the line. "Get along. Get along. What this is, hey? A show?"

He kicked Joe-Joe to help him to his feet.

"Don't never . . . again," he warned. "Never. Next time. . . ." Incoherent at fresh thought of the insolence he shook his arms savagely at the entire length of the wharves.

The little Negro shambled back into line. The groan of the automatic carriers became again audible. Old Pedro dropped back to his counting table, the bell clanging monotonously once more, marking time like a dull clock. The line moved on. Marjeva sighed. It was just one incident in the day's work, to be forgotten as quickly as ended.

But Joe-Joe was a shuffling fool, a black-skinned donkey. He forgot the blow and was whistling ten minutes later. What his simple brain could not forget was the litter of bananas scattered on the floor where he had fallen. They were a green temptation to him each time he passed the spot. The desire to gather them up to carry home with him that night began to itch him uncomfortably. As he passed the spot in his rounds he kicked them into a rough pile.

So then he stopped, dropping out of the line for a few moments, to bundle the fruit into his burlap apron. He was within his rights. The rule of the wharves is that the loose fruit on the floor belongs to the runners. And this purchased by his own skin was surely his. But he was a donkey to try it. Angellico was on him like a flash.

"You work, or get out. See. I have a-plenty troubl' by you. I find you once more, out you go."

The Negro dropped his fruit, his eyes showing white. He slipped back into his place. The line moved on.

"*Maria,*" grunted a swarthy Spaniard in the line. "Learn for once."

And up at the platform Marjeva sighed again and indicted his black cat for inefficiency.

The line moved on and it was almost dusk. Lights were already flickering on the far shore. The tugs were coming in from the River, tying up in their places, a row of grim, greasy River dwarfs. The night watchmen were appearing here and there in the darkening warehouses. The steel night doors were clanging.

And then it was that Marjeva lost patience with his black cat and took things into his own hands. He came to Angellico. The Italian boss, his patience at rough ends, waved him away. Marjeva insisted, finally managing to get his ear.

"Thees Negro fill his sack."

"What Negro?"

"Thees one giv' fight."

Angellico bristled to attention.

"You hav' tol' him no take more, hey?" explained the Spaniard. "But thees Negro fill up. You be grab heem, the boss? But I do eef you say."

Angellico grew bilious. "Don't for tell what I do. I know for what it shall be done."

He strode over to the weary line, taking in the wharf at one apoplectic glance. Marjeva was close to his arm to point out the particular sack. There it was, so full that it lolled over on one side.

"What this is?" bellowed the over-boss. "Who this belongs to?"

A shudder ran down the line.

"Who this is?" roared the over-boss.

Still there was no answer. Angellico grasped the sack by its closed neck, flung it open, plunged his free hand in to spill out the fruit. There would be terrible punishment for this. He would make it an object lesson they would remember as long as they lived. They must all understand the reason for it. They must. . . .

But something was wrong. Angellico did not spill out the accusing fruit. He straightened and even in the falling dusk they could see the pained surprise on his face, the dumb astonishment. Then he flung his arm wide with a great cry and shook his hand as though to loosen it from the wrist.

They all saw at the same time—a black shape huddling off along the floor, a black shape the size of a woman's hand, and a cry went through them.

"*Aranya.*"

"Spider. Banana Spider."

"*Mateo.*"

Angellico crumpled to the floor where he stood, overcome with shock and fear. His fall toppled the sack sideways, and those standing too close to it scattered, for half a dozen more evil shapes moved out along the floor.

Pandemonium broke on the wharf. Someone called loudly and vainly on a saint. Wharf watchmen came running. The Captain of the *Tchula* appeared on deck, giving orders, asking questions in the same breath. Another ship officer searched blatantly for the doctor. Someone with more wisdom called an ambulance. The mechanicians deserted the engine switches and the carriers groaned on piling up the fruit in confusion in the abandoned receiving basket.

Only Marjeva remained composed. Marjeva smiled upon himself in the dusk. He smiled also at the black cat, and his eyes were malicious even as the cat's had been in the gray dawn.

Marjeva did not need to investigate. He knew what had happened. The big boss had plunged his hand into the very sack to which had been given the tarantulas and scorpions that morning.

Marjeva knew. Marjeva had added bananas to the sack and had placed it there.

MAINE

COLT .24

by Rick Hautala

DIARY ENTRY ONE: approximately 10:00 A.M. on Valentine's Day—*hah!* What irony!

If you've ever spent any time in academic circles, you've no doubt heard the expression "Publish or perish." Simply put, it means that if you intend to keep your cushy teaching position, at least at any decent college or university, you've got to publish in academic journals. I suppose this is to prove you've been doing research, but it also contributes to the prestige of your school.

My experience, at least in the English department here at the University of Southern Maine, is that the more obscure and unread the periodical, the more prestige is involved. I mean, if you write novels or stories that don't pretend to art, you can kiss your tenure good-bye. A good friend of mine here did just that—wrote and sold dozens of stories and even one novel, but because it was seen as "commercial" fiction, he didn't keep his job. After he was denied tenure, a few years back, he and I used to joke about how he had published *and perished!*

I have reason to be cynical. The doctor who talked with me last night might have fancier, more clinical terms for it, but I might be tempted to translate his conclusions about me to something a little simpler: let's try "crazy as a shit-house rat."

That's crazy, all right; but just read on. I'm writing this all down as fast as I can because I know I don't have much time. I'm fighting the English teacher in me who wants to go back and revise and hone this all down until it's perfect, but if I'm right . . . Oh, Jesus! If I'm *right.* . . .

Look, I'll try to start at the start. Every story has a beginning, a middle, and an end, I've always told my students. Life, unfortunately, doesn't always play out that way. Sure, the beginning's at birth and the end's at death—it's filling up the middle part that's a bitch.

198

I don't know if this whole damned thing started when I first saw Rose McAllister . . . Rosie. She was sitting in the front row the first day of my 8:00 A.M. Introduction to English Literature class last fall. It might have been then that everything started, but I've gotta be honest. I mean, at this point, it doesn't matter. I think I'll be dead . . . and *really* in Hell within . . . maybe four hours.

So when I first saw Rosie, I didn't think right off the bat: God! I want to have an affair with her.

That sounds so delicate—"have an affair." I wanted to, sure; but that was after I got to know her. We started sleeping together whenever we could . . . which wasn't often, you see, because of Sally. My wife. My dear, departed wife!

I guess if I were really looking for the beginning of this whole damned mess, I'd have to say it was when we started our study of Marlowe's *Doctor Faustus.* Your basic "deal with the devil" story. I didn't mention too much of this to the police shrink because . . . well, if you tell someone like that that you struck a deal with the devil, sold him your soul—yes, I signed the agreement with my own blood—you expect him to send you up to the rubber room on P-6. If I'm wrong, I don't want to spend my time writing letters home with a Crayola, you know.

I'm getting ahead of myself, but as I said, I don't have much time . . . at least, I don't think so.

Okay, so Rosie and I, sometime around the middle of the fall semester, began to "sleep together." Another delicate term because we did very little "sleeping." We got whatever we could, whenever we could—in my office, usually, or—once or twice—in a motel room, once in my car in the faculty parking lot outside of Bailey Hall. Whenever and wherever.

The first mistake we made was being seen at the Roma, in Portland, by Hank and Mary Crenshaw. The Roma! As an English teacher, I can appreciate the irony of *that,* too. Sally and I celebrated our wedding anniversary there every year. Being seen there on a Friday night, with a college sophomore ("young enough to be your daughter!" Sally took no end of pleasure repeating), by your wife's close (not best, but close) friend is downright stupid. I still cringe when I imagine the glee in Mary's voice when she told Sally. Hell! I never liked Mary, and she never liked me. Hank—he was all right, but I always told Sally that Mary was *her* friend, not mine.

So, Sally found out. Okay, so plenty of married men (and women) get caught screwing around. Sometimes the couple can cope—work it out. Other times, they can't. We couldn't. I should say, Sally couldn't. She set her lawyer—Walter Altschuler—on me faster than a greyhound on a rabbit. That guy would have had my gonads if they hadn't been attached!

But I'm not the kind of guy who takes that kind of stuff—from *anyone!* And, in an ironic sort of way, I'm getting paid back for that, too. If someone sics a lawyer on me, I'm gonna fight back.

Now here's where it gets a little weird. If I told that police shrink all of this, he'd bounce me up to P-6 for sure. I said we were reading *Faustus,* and that's when I decided to do a bit of—let's call it research. I dug through the library and found what was supposedly a magician's handbook—you know, a grimoire. I decided to try a bit of necromancy.

Look, I'm not crazy! I went into it more than half-skeptical. And I want to state for the record here that I . . .

Diary entry two: two hours later. Times's running out for sure!

Sorry for the interruption. I'm back now after wasting two hours with the shrink again. He ran me over the story again, but—I think—I held up pretty well. I didn't tell him what I'm going to write here. I want this all recorded so if I'm right . . . If I'm right. . . .

Where was I? Oh yeah. Necromancy. A deal with the devil. Yes—yes—*yess!* Signed in *blood!*

The library on the Gorham campus had a grimoire. Well, actually a facsimile of one, published a few years ago by Indiana University Press. It's amazing what's published these days. I wonder if the person who edited that text—I can't remember his name—kept his job. I looked up a spell to summon the devil and— Now I *know* you're gonna think I'm crazy! I did it! I actually summoned up the devil!

Laugh! Go ahead! I'll be dead soon—in Hell!—and it won't matter to me!

I have a key to Bailey Hall, so I came back to my office late at night— sometime after eleven o'clock, so I could be ready by midnight. After making sure my door was locked, I started to work. Pushing back the cheap rug I had by my desk (to keep the rollers of my chair from squeaking), I drew a pentagram on the floor, using a black Magic Marker. I placed a black candle—boy, were they hard to find—at each of the five points and lighted them. Then, taking the black leather-bound book, I began to recite the Latin incantation backwards. Actually, I was surprised that it worked—my Latin was so rusty, I was afraid I'd mispronounce something and end up summoning a talking toadstool or something. But it worked—it *actually* worked! In a puff of sulfurous fumes Old Nick himself appeared.

Looking around, he said, "Well, at least you're not another damned politician! What do you want in return for your soul?"

With his golden, cat-slit eyes burning into me, I had the feeling he already knew—more clearly than I did at that moment. Anyway, I told him. I said that I wanted an absolutely foolproof way of killing my wife and not getting caught. I told him I was willing to sign my soul over to him—yes! Dear God! In *blood!* If I could somehow get rid of Sally and be absolutely *certain* I wouldn't get caught.

I'm writing this, you must know by now, in a jail cell. I'm the prime suspect, but I haven't been charged with anything. I have a perfect alibi, you see, and there are other problems, too; but if you read the *Evening Express,* you'll know soon enough that I didn't get away with it.

What the devil did was hand me a revolver; he called it a Colt .24—a specially "modified" Colt .45—and a box of nice, shiny, brass-jacketed bullets. He told me all I had to do, after I signed the agreement, of course, was point the gun at Sally—he suggested I sneak home sometime before lunch someday—pull the trigger, throw the gun away, and make *sure* I went to work as usual the next day. If I did what he said, he guaranteed I'd go free.

Sounded okay to me. At this point, I was well past rationally analyzing the situation. I was under a lot of pressure, you've got to understand. My wife's lawyer had stuck the end nozzle of his vacuum cleaner down into my wallet and was sucking up the bucks. I'd been without sleep for nearly two days and nights running—I was getting so worked up about Sally.

And the capper was Rosie. As soon as she found out that Sally knew about us, she cooled off. Maybe—I hate to think it!—it was just the chance of getting caught that added to her excitement—her sense of adventure. Once we got caught, the thrill was gone for her. Could she have been *that* shallow?

I wasn't completely convinced this whole business with the devil had really worked, because . . . well, I must've fallen asleep after he pricked my finger so I could sign the contract, gave me the gun, and disappeared. I woke up, stiff-necked and all, flat on my back on the floor of my office just before my eight o'clock class the next morning. The candles had burned out, but in the early morning light, I could see the pentagram still there, so I knew I hadn't dreamed *everything*. I also had the gun—a Colt .24.

I'd been asleep— I don't know how long. Not more than four hours, I figure. I had started the summoning at midnight, like you're supposed to. I have no idea how long it took, but—at least for me—old Satan didn't waste any time with visions of power and glory, or processions of spirits. Nothing, really. At times, thinking about it, I could just as easily have been talking to Old Man Olsen, the janitor in Bailey Hall!

But, as I said, I also had the gun, and—damned if I didn't decide then and there that I'd use it. I had my two classes first. But after that, I was going straight home and point it at Sally and pull the trigger—even if, then and there, it blew her out through the picture window. I'd reached my limit which, I'd like to think, was considerably beyond what most men can stand.

So I did. After the second class—between classes I had time to drag the rug back and gulp down some coffee and an Egg McMuffin—I took off for home. Sally, as luck would have it, was—Damn! Here they come again!

Diary entry three: more than an hour gone—mere minutes left!

This time the police came in again. Talk about being confused. I think they'd like to charge me. But my alibi is solid and they can't get my gun to fire. So they asked me to fill them in on my relationship with Sally. They said that maybe it could give them a lead on who else might have killed her. They said I'd probably be released shortly. *Hah!* As if that might make a difference.

Well, as I was saying—Sally was home and her lawyer, old Walter-baby— was there with her. I sort of wondered why he was there—at *my* house. Maybe nosing around gave him a better idea how to skin me to the bone. Or maybe getting into her pants was part of his fee. But I couldn't afford to leave a witness, so whatever he was doing, that was just his tough luck. One more lawyer in Hell wasn't going to matter.

I walked in from the kitchen and nodded a greeting to the two of them, sitting on the couch. I said something about having forgotten some test papers as I put the briefcase down on the telephone table, opened it, and slowly took out the gun. Keeping it shielded from them with the opened top of the briefcase, I brought the gun up, took aim at him and squeezed the trigger. Not once—not twice—*three* times! Good number, three. A literature teacher knows all about the significance of the number three.

Nothing happened! There was no sound—although I had been careful to slip a bullet into each chamber before I left the office. There was no kick in my hand. There wasn't even much of a *click*. The only thing I could think was that maybe the Colt wouldn't work for someone who wasn't part of the deal. So I pointed it at her and fired off three more shots—with the same result. I do remember smelling—or thinking I smelled—a faint aroma of spent gunpowder, but I chalked that up to wishful thinking.

Sally and Walter ignored me, just kept right on talking as I gawked at them . . . so I slipped the gun back into the briefcase, shut it, and went up to the bedroom and shuffled around a bit, sounding busy while I tried to figure things out. I'd been packing to move out, but Sally—against old Walter-baby's advice, I might add—had said it was all right for me to stay at the house until the apartment I'd rented in town opened up the first of the month. Thanks, Sally. As it turned out, that was the last favor you ever did for me—except a day later, when you dropped dead!

So I left the house for my next class—with Sally and Walter sitting on the couch just as alive as they could be—feeling as though I'd been ripped off—set up or something by the devil. His gun was a dud, as far as I was concerned.

Back in my office about two that afternoon, I checked the Colt and was surprised to see six empty shells in the chamber—no bullets. Could I have been dumb enough to load the gun with empty shells? I didn't think so, but I tossed the empties and slipped in six new bullets from the devil's box. I was getting a little bit scared that I *had* hallucinated the summoning, but that still didn't explain where I had gotten the Colt.

By then I wasn't thinking too clearly, so I decided to test the gun right there in my office. I sighted along the barrel at one of the pictures on my wall—one of my favorites, actually: a silkscreen advertisement for the Dartmouth Christmas Revels—and gently squeezed the trigger. Nothing happened. Quickly, I aimed at my doctoral dissertation—now *there* was something else to hate—on the top shelf of my bookcase and pulled the trigger.

Nothing.

Again, aiming at the pencil sharpener beside the door, I squeezed the trigger. *Nada!*

I pointed at the wall and snapped the trigger three more times, and still nothing happened. The tinge of gunpowder I thought I smelled couldn't have really been there, I thought . . . just my imagination, I guessed. But you shouldn't ever *guess* when the devil has your soul!

Again, though—and it struck me as really weird this time—when I opened the chamber all six bullets were spent. Maybe they were dummies or something—not really made of lead. Or maybe I was the dummy being led. I got the box, now minus a total of twelve bullets, and after inspecting them closely—they seemed real—reloaded, put the gun on the desk, and tilted back in my chair.

I'd been had, for sure, I thought, with rage and stark fear tossing me like a seesaw. I had signed my soul over to the devil for *what?* For a revolver that didn't even work!

Anyway, like I said, the next day at noon, Sally was dead. Our neighbor, Mrs. Benton, said she heard three gunshots from our house. Afraid that there was a robbery or something going on, she stayed home and, clutching her living room curtains to hide herself as she watched our house, called the Gorham police. They came shortly after that, and found Sally dead of three gunshot wounds to the head.

I, of course, didn't know this at the time. I was just coming back to my office, following a graduate seminar on Elizabethan Drama. I hadn't gone home the night before and had been forced to sleep—again—on my office floor, so I wasn't in the best of moods.

I spent the next couple of hours sitting at my desk, working through a stack of tests and pondering everything that had happened recently when there was a knock on the door. I scooped the Colt into the top desk drawer but, foolishly, didn't slide the drawer completely shut before I went to the door. Two uniformed policeman entered, politely shook hands, and then informed me that my wife had been murdered . . . shot to death by a Colt. 45.

I fell apart—wondering to myself which I felt more—shock or relief. I hadn't done it, but *someone* had! The policemen waited patiently for me to gain control of myself and explained that they wanted to know where I had been in the past three hours. Apparently Mrs. Benton had seen fit to fill them in on our domestic quarrels. They also wanted to know if I owned a Colt .45.

If this whole story has a tragic mistake—for me, at least—it was not following the devil's advice to the letter. That's how he gets you, you know. I should have *realized* that! He had said that if I aimed the gun at Sally, pulled the trigger, and then threw the gun away, I'd never be caught.

But I didn't throw the damned thing away.

If you had asked me then, I suppose I would have said the gun was worthless. What difference would it make if I kept it or tossed it? I hadn't summoned the devil that night. I'd fallen asleep and, beaten by exhaustion and the pressure I was under, I'd had a vivid nightmare. I hadn't *really* summoned the devil. Stuff like that didn't *really* happen!

I gave the cops my alibi, and it was solid. When the shots rang out, I was more than twenty miles from my house, on the university's Portland campus, lecturing on Shakespeare's use of horse imagery in his history plays. You can't go against the testimony of a roomfull of graduate students.

About then one of the policemen noticed the revolver in the desk drawer, and, eyeing me suspiciously, asked if they could take a look at it. Sure. There was no denying that I did own a Colt .45, but after they inspected it for a moment, I took it from them.

"Look," I said, hefting the Colt. "This sucker doesn't even work. It's a model or something." I opened the chamber, showed them that the gun was loaded, clicked it shut, and, with a flourish, pressed the barrel to my temple.

"See?" I said, as I snapped the trigger three times. "Nothing happens. It's a fake."

That seemed to satisfy them. They thanked me for my cooperation and left, saying they'd wait in the hallway until I felt ready to come with them to the hospital to identify the body.

But they had no more than swung the door shut behind them when shots rang out in my office! I was just turning to pick up my briefcase when the center of the Christmas Revels poster blew away. I turned and stared, horrified, as the top row of books on the bookcase suddenly jumped. I could see a large, black, smoking hole in the spine of my dissertation. Then the pencil sharpener by the door exploded into a twisted mess of metal. Three more shots removed pieces of plaster and wood from the office walls.

With the sound of the six shots still ringing in my ears, I heard the two policemen burst back into my office. They both had their revolvers drawn and poised.

"I thought that gun didn't work," one of them shouted, leaning cautiously against the door frame. He was looking at me suspiciously, but then his expression changed to confusion when he registered that the Colt wasn't in my hand. It was lying on the desk, where I had placed it as they left.

"Man, I don't know what's going on here," the other one said. "But you better come downtown until we can check the ballistics to make *sure* this wasn't the gun that killed her."

I was in a state of near shock—I'm sure my face had turned chalky white because I felt an icy numbness rush across my cheeks and down the back of my neck. A sudden realization was beginning to sink in. It had been almost—*no!*—*exactly* twenty-four hours ago that I had aimed and shot the revolver six times in my office. Six times! And nothing had happened—until *now!*

This bit about the ballistics test had cracked my nerve. I mean, at this point I was convinced that it hadn't been coincidence. The shots I had banged off twenty-four hours earlier must have done in Sally. And I knew that, if the cops checked it out, the ballistics would match.

What about sleazy Walter Altschuler? Was he dead, too? With a sudden sickening rush, I remembered what the devil had said to me the night I summoned him . . . he said the gun was a Colt *.24!* A special, *modified* Colt .45!

I tried to force myself to appear calm. *Damn my soul to Hell!* I had pointed the gun to my head as a *beau geste* and pulled the trigger—three times! I remembered—now—that when I had done that, I *had* smelled a trace of spent gunpowder . . . like I had that morning at the house, when I had targeted Walter and Sally.

Then Joan Oliver, the department secretary poked her head—cautiously, I might add—into my office to tell the policemen they had a phone call. I fell apart completely, knowing what it would be. Walter Altschuler had been found dead in his car in the Casco Bank parking lot in downtown Portland with three .45 caliber bullet wounds in his head.

I'd been *had!* I signed that damned contract . . . in *blood!* And I *had had* that damned gun. And it *had* worked! And the devil *had* cheated me, but good, in the bargain.

So while sitting here in the cell, after coming to my senses this morning, I asked for some paper and a pen. If I'm wrong, I don't want to tell my story and be committed. But if I'm right, I want to get all of this down to leave a permanent record before those bullets from Hell blow my hea

MARYLAND

WILL YOU ALWAYS BE HELPING ME?

by Thomas Walsh

IT TOOK ONLY two or three minutes for Donovan to discover that Miss 1449 had her stuff pretty well cleaned out. The fur coat was gone—hocked, of course, Donovan knew—and most of her other things had vanished with it; there was left one dress, a light fall coat, a pair of brown shoes well worn at the heels, some underwear, a couple of nightgowns, and two empty traveling bags. After giving a morose upward stare to the single pair of stockings hanging from the shower curtain rail in the bathroom Donovan growled and shook his head. It was one of the times he became overwhelmingly convinced that a hotel dick had the lousiest job in the world.

She was, he thought, no professional deadbeat; Miss 1449 had never used her head. For the fur coat had at least given her a front and when, in a cold November, she suddenly stopped wearing it you knew two things: Miss 1449 had hocked it, so Miss 1449 was broke.

Donovan sighed—of course he'd have to tell Kelleher how this looked—and rolled an unlit cigarette around between his lips. Before he could touch a match to it the door in back of him opened and Miss 1449 came in.

She didn't scream when she saw him standing by her bed, but for a breath, stiffening slightly, she remained perfectly still—a pause just long enough to let Donovan shut off whatever action she might have taken by growling at her in a gruff voice.

"I'm Donovan, lady—the house detective. You don't have to be scared."

She got some recognition into her eyes while he was silently cursing the fool at the desk who should have spotted her coming in and phoned up to let him know. Donovan adopted toughness by lowering his lids slightly and making his voice cold and sharp, while she put her hat on the dresser and placed a paper bag beside it.

He said, "You owe the Maryland House eighty-two dollars and sixty cents, lady. When you didn't pay up this morning like you said you would, Mr. Kelleher told me to come up here and look around. You know we got the right to hold whatever baggage there is if you can't settle your bill."

"I suppose you have," Miss 1449 said. She wasn't argumentative or indignant about it like some. Sitting down in the chair under the lamp she added, quietly enough, "I'm afraid there isn't very much of my stuff left to hold now."

"Not eighty-two dollars' worth," Donovan told her toughly.

She was a small dark girl with brown hair parted in the middle. The tailored suit she had on looked crisp on her slender body, severely businesslike, but not unattractive. Donovan had noticed that she had a level pair of eyes and an erect way of carrying her head; he was considerably relieved that those things didn't fail her even now. Apparently she wasn't the bawling type.

He sat down on the bed looking across at the paper bag she had set on the dresser by her hat. Buns, Donovan thought; buns were always cheap and filling. Lighting his cigarette and squinting at her through the match flame he asked in that hardboiled voice: "How did you get into this?"

She gave him a quick outline. Her name was Marjorie Thorne. She'd come from a small town in Indiana, had worked for two years for a lawyer in Philadelphia; had lost her job with the lawyer when the firm dissolved. Through a friend she had heard of a job down here but when she came down it had already been filled. Still she had a little money saved—four hundred dollars—and it had seemed that she might find a job here as well as anywhere else. So she had stayed on; and the first Saturday she'd gone to a bargain sale in one of the big stores. She felt no one touch her pocketbook; it must have been much later when she discovered it was hanging open on her arm. All the money was gone—all except some change.

"How about getting money from home?" Donovan asked. "Any chance of that?"

Hopelessly Miss 1449 answered, "I'm afraid there isn't."

He lectured her in a tone he tried to make stinging and scornful. That was the trouble with girls like her, he said; they never thought about the people they got in bad by acting the way they did. Kelleher, the manager, and he—they were the ones that would be left holding the bag.

Twisting her fingers together in her lap, Miss 1449 whispered she was sorry, never losing the desperately strained white smile that would not look directly into his face.

Over her, properly righteous, Donovan rubbed his red hair with the palm of one hand.

"I guess that fixes it all up," he said. "You haven't got any money and you can't pay your bill; but if you're sorry, why that takes care of everything."

The girl lowered her head still more from his eyes. Through the window behind her, in the ice-blue November dusk, Donovan saw lights winking on in the tall buildings all around—comfortable lights, looking warm and moneyed and assured. He stared down at her with his eyes uneasy. No family at all? Her head shook again. That was fine, Donovan said; coming to the Maryland House when she was in a spot like that was using her head all right. Walking up and down, he stopped by the dresser and hefted the paper bag. Buns of course. That all she had to eat?

"Oh—" Looking up there for the first time, Miss 1449 flushed a little. "I wasn't very hungry tonight. I didn't feel like—"

"Like roast turkey or duck," Donovan said. He looked very disgusted with her.

He stared down at the straight part in her hair and cleared his throat. He was aware that he should let Kelleher handle this, that he should just tell her to get her hat and come on downstairs with him, because there wasn't a thing in the world he could do for her.

But Donovan was shamefacedly conscious that he couldn't act on it. November, pretty cold, a little change in her purse, no place to go—what could he do? Turn her out—sure. But if he wanted to sleep tonight—

"Look," he said, making every third or fourth word louder than the others just to keep the appearance of toughness about him and not let her imagine he was getting soft. "I'll tell you what I'm going to do. I'll say downstairs I read a letter you left lying around—from an uncle. I'll tell Kelleher he says he's going to send you some money on the fifteenth—that's Saturday. Saturday you just walk out of here and don't come back. He'll take a chance on waiting till then because of the money you owe already. Understand that?"

When she started to speak Donovan growled, "Shut up." He didn't want to talk any more about it; he knew he was being silly the way it was. "I'll give you that time to look around and get settled someplace. Saturday, remember. After that you're on your own. Another thing—" His eyes had noticed the paper bag on the dresser again. Those buns! "I'm eating out at 6. You could come along if you wanted."

She got out of her chair—no higher than his shoulder, Donovan thought, her face pale from strain, or from living on buns all week.

"Oh, no," Miss 1449 said. Her voice was pretty shaky then. "I couldn't do that. I—"

Donovan glowered at her. "It's an invitation, understand—not a proposition. Six in the drugstore downstairs. You be there or I'll come up after you."

In his own tiny room under the roof he ran a comb through his hair and straightened his tie. He had a lean face, hot-looking blue eyes, a thin sharp nose, a wide mouth; all his life he had got sore easily and at a lot of things. Just now he was sore mostly at himself but he was sore at Miss 1449, too. Going down in the elevator he could feel his anger bubbling and fizzing like seltzer poured into a glass, so that at 6 when she appeared timidly in the drugstore entrance he took her arm without a word and led her off.

In a restaurant around the corner he ordered a planked steak for two. In the course of events he discovered that she did have one relative. An uncle. Very well off too, running an auto agency, back in Cohane, Indiana. Years ago, when her mother had been very ill and she was still in school, he would not help them. Now she would never ask again.

"You haven't any friends here at all?"

Well—she'd heard there was a boy here who had gone to school with her back in Cohane, Indiana. But she'd never thought of looking him up because she'd never liked him much. What could he do for her? It was Donovan who pointed out that it couldn't hurt to get in touch with him; he might be able to find her a job. And it was Donovan too who insisted that she phone this Arthur Ellison in the morning. Two days later that was the thing he could not forget. . . .

Back at the hotel her hand rested small and cool in his. If, she said, there were only some other word than thanks.

The next afternoon it developed that Arthur Ellison had been delighted to hear from her and was coming that night to take her to dinner. Fine, Donovan thought—a two-buck meal saved for him. But somehow that wasn't a complete satisfaction.

He managed to be around that evening when they got back to the Maryland House. An oily guy, Donovan thought. Arthur Ellison held on to her hand for quite a while before she got into the elevator. Then he remained where he was—a young man, tall, palely fat, with a heavy mouth and black eyes as lusterless as soot. For five minutes he stood there very still, very absorbed, the way a man would when he turned over something important in his mind.

Donovan put him down as a guy he didn't like. Later one thought came back to him: What had he been figuring out there?

Thursday—his day off—Donovan took Miss 1449 to lunch. They stopped on the way at an out-of-town newspaper stand because she wanted to get a copy of the *Cohane Inquirer,* but it was all sold out; a big guy had bought them all that morning. Marjorie Thorne asked to have one saved for her tomorrow. She hadn't, she explained to Donovan, seen one since she left Philadelphia three weeks ago. In the windy November sunshine the *Cohane Inquirer* had never been less important. In his old car Donovan took her to all the places he thought a girl like her would want to see: the museum and the art gallery, the big new library, city hall, the girls' college way out in the suburbs. There was nothing important about the day. It would have been hard to say just why Donovan knew he would never forget any of it.

She told him how very nice Arthur Ellison had been; that evening he had insisted that she dine with him again. Tomorrow morning he was calling for her at the hotel, because by then he'd have arranged an interview with his friend who worked in a law office and he was going to take her over there himself. He even—she flushed there and smiled in rather a troubled fashion at Donovan. Last night he had even proposed to her.

Donovan's jaws tightened, relaxing only when she said she took that as a joke. That was the only way she could take it—the first time she'd seen him, after seven or eight years! She supposed he was lonely in the city, and an old friend, someone from Cohane. . . . Of course she'd never dream of it.

Yeah, Donovan said. He hoped she wouldn't. But all night he rather worried about it.

The next day he spent around the entrance because he wanted to see her and discover how she had made out about that job. And that day she didn't come back to the Maryland House at all—not at 2, or at 4, or at 6. At 10 that night when he called her room, thinking somehow he had missed her, there wasn't any answer.

Then Donovan began to be anxious about her. Coming away from the switchboard, he met Kelleher at the cigar stand, talking to the girl behind the counter—Kelleher in a snapping, grouchy mood.

"What's this about 1449?" Kelleher asked, looking at him angrily from under his gray brows. "Aren't we paying you to keep us up on stuff like that, Donovan? Only for the girl here I'd never have known it. One thing I'll tell her—married or not she'll pay her bill before she moves out of here."

"What about her?"

Grunting at him sourly, Kelleher held out a copy of the morning paper, folded over to the last sheet. Halfway down there was a list of marriage licenses issued the day before: Ellison, Arthur, 26, 3132 Norega Avenue; Thorne, Marjorie, 24, Maryland House.

When he looked up Kelleher was gone. Broke, Donovan thought, a sickness settling in him, out of work, up against it; and this old town friend saying he loved her and wanted to take care of her. It wasn't too hard to understand.

And yet Donovan couldn't believe it. She wouldn't have laughed at Arthur Ellison yesterday if she had meant to marry him. Not a girl as nice as Miss 1449. She'd been gone all day. Not a word, not a call. Where, Donovan thought? With the old friend from Cohane she had already refused but who had taken out a license anyway?

He was uneasy at the thought. His fear was crystallized by a scene he had almost forgotten—the newspaper stand yesterday, the *Cohane Inquirers* all gone, the clerk telling them of the big guy who had bought them up—a big guy who might be Arthur Ellison. Why would Arthur Ellison buy them up? *Because there was something inside he did not want her to read?*

A soft, oppressive weight of dread hung dead on Donovan's heart. Without waiting to get his hat or coat he hurried to the newsstand they had visited the day before.

The clerk there, remembering him, pulled out the paper he'd saved for the lady. Only gave the big guy two that morning, he told Donovan; said two was all he had.

"Thanks," Donovan said. His voice was dry. What did this big guy look like?

Oh—the clerk considered. Fat. Kind of pale. Funny eyes. Donovan nodded. Going off a few steps, he opened the *Cohane Inquirer*. What was in here that Arthur Ellison had not wanted her to see? Nothing on the first page, the second, the third. On the fourth, in a three-column spread of small social items, he saw Miss 1449's name.

"Miss Marjorie Thorne, formerly of this town and until last month known to be employed in Philadelphia, is still being diligently sought as we go to press. Since the passing three weeks ago of her uncle, Mr. Fred Sibley, no information as to her whereabouts has been uncovered. Mr. Sibley's only living kin and the sole beneficiary under his will—"

Donovan had it then; as soon as he read those words everything dropped into place. Arthur Ellison knew about the will; Miss 1449 didn't. In Philadelphia she had left no forwarding address and since she had been here she had written to no friend back in Cohane; therefore, no one in Cohane knew where she was. No one but Arthur Ellison who bought the Cohane papers. When Miss 1449 would not marry him he had taken out a marriage license anyway. With another girl, someone he bribed. Under Marjorie Thorne's name he might have married her.

If he had, Donovan thought, cold sweat dampening his palms, Miss 1449 was going to die tonight, in some quiet way, accidental, well thought out. In an instant Donovan was as sure of that as he was of his name; Miss 1449 would have to die, since she said she wouldn't marry him—to leave a grieving widower. A widower with all the proper papers in his pocket, so that when the funeral was over back in Cohane the lawyers would come and tell him about the estate he would pretend he never knew existed. Her uncle had died? Left her money? No, he had not known it.

In one jagged flash it became that exact and detailed in Donovan's mind. Before he had figured out what to do he found himself running for a cab, one line of print, from the paper Kelleher had shown him, vivid in his mind. Ellison, Arthur, 26, 3132 Norega Avenue. . . .

He found out Arthur Ellison had left there, moved his things very early that morning. No, the landlady said, she had no idea where he could be found now.

Where? Donovan thought. In what shadowed room might Miss 1449's hands reach out for Donovan's, might her voice be crying his name? It seemed he could hear that now—thin with distance, remote and terrified. Donovan, Donovan—help me, Donovan. Help me!

The heavy-faced man riding south in his coupé on the Philadelphia Pike looked at the clock on the dashboard and saw that it was five past one. Getting on to two then, when he'd be in—a good time. Streets empty, houses dark. No one at all to see him. Even the girl asleep. Five minutes at the apartment and it would all be over.

He felt that he wasn't nervous at all, but instead very cool and collected. It all had turned out exactly as he had wanted it—the girl alone in the apartment, sleeping soundly, unaware of the marriage license listed that morning in the paper in her name and his. She hadn't seen that—he had indeed taken good care she shouldn't by keeping her with him all that day—and so she would suspect nothing. Why should she, when she did not even know her uncle was dead?

To get her to the apartment all he had had to say was that his sister Zelda was coming in from Cohane, due by car in the early morning at the furnished apartment he had taken for her. And he couldn't stay there to meet her, he must go to Philadelphia tonight on business. His sister then, who had known Marjorie Thorne back in Indiana, ringing the bell in the morning and no one there to greet her, to explain how he could not be there. He knew no tenants; the landlady would be away.

Of course Marjorie Thorne had offered, before he even asked her, to stay there tonight if he wanted her to. It would be a slight repayment for all the trouble he had gone to that day for her. She remembered Zelda well; she'd let her in, explain why Arthur was not there.

The apartment was all right, Mr. and Mrs. Arthur Ellison—that's how he had listed it with the landlady. She had never seen the girl. Rented the place himself last night; taken the girl there tonight, at 10:00, just enough time to spare to get his train to Philadelphia. The landlady's apartment had been dark then—an old woman, asleep early. She would have no chance to talk to the girl before the morning. And by then—

He pursed his heavy mouth. By then everything would be all right. Only the other girl, that Agnes Barclay. . . . Still, if she never found out what happened to Marjorie Thorne, how could she cause trouble? Sick of the city she was, sick of the dime-a-dance place where he'd met her some weeks ago; for a ticket back to Alabama and a hundred dollars she had not asked questions. Yesterday afternoon she had gone with him for the license; an hour later, as Marjorie Thorne, she had married him in a little suburban parsonage.

The minister had not questioned it, nor the minister's two friends whom he had called in as witnesses. Why should they? Why should anyone? The girl was old Sibley's only kin. So there'd be no disappointed relatives to grow ugly about her marriage and her sudden death. The lawyers might wonder a bit, but there would be nothing definite to lead them on. Agnes Barclay was dark and small, not very different in size from Marjorie Thorne; from a photograph, the minister, if he were ever asked, would hesitate to be too positive.

They never could prove anything against him except through Agnes Barclay. And he had bought her ticket for tonight's train and in the morning she'd be back in Alabama, not knowing what had happened here, never getting any Maryland papers. For at first the death would seem an accident—a line or two on an inside page. And if by some chance Agnew Barclay found out what had happened the night she started home, why then he would tell her she was in it as deep as he.

Everything, then, was in order. He had left for Philadelphia tonight on the 10:45. He could prove that; ask them how he could possibly get back the same night when no more trains ran until 6:00 the next morning?

They did not know about the car; he would put it in dead storage tomorrow, using the name he had bought it with. They would surmise that he might have used a car—Philadelphia and Maryland, not far apart. But they could not prove it. The men who rented cars could only shake their heads. No car to anyone like that. Nope!

So he thought he had been clever to buy the car and to register at that hotel in Philadelphia. He would get back there tomorrow in time to have breakfast and to muss the bed; who could swear that he had ever left it?

No, everything was fine; in all of it he could see no flaw. In the city now he parked the car two blocks away from the apartment, in a patch of shadow by the park.

How quiet the streets, how empty! His shadow, enormous, preceded him. In the deep silence a sudden feeling of tremendous pride surged up in him. Against the dark-windowed houses he saw himself a solitary figure of unconquerable power.

He threw out his arms in a grotesque and shadowy sweep, a giant in a world of dwarfs. Then he saw the apartment house before him with no lights showing in any of the windows. All asleep! His key, the street door opened, the halls inside quiet and empty. Two flights up; the carpet smothered all sound. Number seven. Careful now. If she heard—

He worked the lock back softly, with the greatest of patience, cunningly, a match breadth at a time. No rasp, no creak, no sound. Inside, the door closed quietly behind him. His eyes saw in the darkness the dim bulk of chair and table, the upright dark rectangle of the bedroom door.

And then the white shape of the bed, the darkness of her hair against the pillow. And somewhere below—a sound to smash the stillness—the ringing of a bell. A telephone; frozen against the wall, he recognized that at once. No sound after it, silence again. The call answered, whoever received it had gone back to sleep. No need for alarm.

Curtains fluttered by the window. Watching her, he forced the sash down. One faint rasp. She stirred. Quiet then, Arthur Ellison. The heater cord in his hand. How many apartments had he looked at before he found one that had a gas heater? Couldn't ask for one, of course—that would be remembered afterward. Couldn't even notice it when he saw one here. The rubber cord well worn, a tiny bit loose at the top—saw at once it was exactly what he wanted. Gone to sleep with it on, they'd think in the morning. Yanked it slightly perhaps, while arranging it. Too bad. A young girl just married.

His fingers touched the nozzle; a hiss came, not loud. She did not move again. Then the bedroom door closed after him quietly. A pause in the corridor—but no sound, no sound.

And inside, behind the closed bedroom door, a hiss, steady but never enough to rouse—just a thickening in the air, insensible in sleep. The coupé now, he thought, and the ride back to Philadelphia. Breakfast early in the hotel coffee room as if he'd just come down. Fine—everything fine!

The downstairs hall as empty as before. Still he moved quickly across the entry, down the stoop. A car racing in the silence, tires whining as it took this corner—drunks late from a party. Why should they notice him?

The car stopping at the curb by him. He walked faster, slightly breathless. Two men coming. One of them was stocky and red-haired. He grabbed Arthur Ellison's arm, punched him hard in the face. *Damn you—where have you got her?*

He took Arthur Ellison's keys and ran up the steps.

"Police," Arthur Ellison said to the second man who had remained with him, "I'm going to call the police. You can't attack—"

The other man looked at him with small hard eyes. "I'm police, brother—I'm all the police you're going to want."

"Police?" Arthur Ellison whispered. The words rustled like dry paper in his throat.

Tears began to glisten on his pale fat cheeks. He tried to recapture the feeling he had had walking here from the car. It was gone. The policeman's fingers hurt his arm—clamped in the flesh, tightly, firmly, as if they were never going to let him go.

"How did I find you?" Donovan repeated after her in Room 1449 at the Maryland House, with morning sunlight bright on the breakfast tray.

"I began by figuring—well, you wouldn't go to a hotel with him. If I was right I knew he had to have the setup perfect so that nobody was gonna suspect anything afterward, so that you were all set as Mr. and Mrs. Arthur Ellison. If he couldn't take you to a hotel, where could he take you?

"He was living at a boarding house; but he'd moved that morning early. So I knew he had some place to take you—some place private and quiet. What fits that? A furnished apartment was all I could think of. And where does anybody look for one? In the newspaper. So I got all the afternoon papers for day before yesterday—if he had the place to go to early in the morning he must have found it the night before—and began to call the numbers listed in the ads. After a couple of hours I hit the right one. Then I came out in a squad car with a cop from headquarters. I guess we got there only a minute or so after he turned on the gas."

"Will you always be helping me, Donovan?" Miss 1449 said. Her voice was soft and her eyes all dark and starry. "Why were you worried when I didn't come home yesterday? Why did you bother about me so much?"

Why, Donovan thought? He lit himself a cigarette and muttered that well, he just wondered where she was. Staying out like that. He couldn't think of anything else to add. Because she was rich now. If he said anything she'd think— There was one safe question: when was she going back to Cohane?

"When?" She took some coffee, dark eyes watching him over the cup brim. "Very soon, I'm afraid. When I left, Donovan, I said I'd never come back—not until I had a husband to show off. But now I suppose—"

Donovan got off a grin, slightly stiff. He said he guessed there'd be enough guys around now.

"Donovan," Miss 1449 said. Her voice was angry but her expression wasn't.

"Will I actually have to say it for you, Donovan? Will I? Because I could never, never, never do that!"

Donovan tried to show her how it was, that he didn't have much of a job, that he certainly wasn't any kind of guy to show off, that he couldn't ask her to marry him now she had money because then she'd think—

"What?" Miss 1449 asked softly. "That you loved me?"

So in the end it wasn't any use. What could he do? Donovan took her in his arms and Donovan kissed her; and she knew then, if Donovan didn't, that she wouldn't have to go back to Cohane, Indiana, alone.

MASSACHUSETTS

A CASE OF INNOCENT EAVESDROPPING

by Helen McCloy

THE GIRLS OF the Thursday Club were good bridge players. They never gossiped during play, only afterward.

"You're so brave, Maggie," said Heloise. "I don't see how you're going to put up with it."

"I don't either, but I must." Maggie Markel tried to look like Joan of Arc for a moment and failed. She was too plump and she put out too many erotic signals—plunging neckline, skin-tight jeans, hair rumpled to look as if she had just come from lovemaking.

"It's not as if there weren't homes for old people like her," said Doris.

"I know." Maggie's voice shook on the edge of righteous indignation. "But you see George has got this mother-fixation. He won't put his mother in a nursing home and he won't let her go on living alone after sixty-five, so I'm stuck with her."

"Anything we can do to help?"

"Guess not, Doris, unless you want to come over someday and shove arsenic in her soup."

Everybody laughed.

So many of Mrs. Markel's contemporaries had died that no one called her "Jessie" any more. Even she was beginning to think of herself as "Mrs. Markel" or even "Ms. Markel" when she was feeling modern.

When the moving men took her furniture away to the auctioneer's, her apartment looked as bare as it had when she first moved in after her husband's death.

"You do understand," George had said then. "Maggie and I would love to have you live with us, but—"

"Of course I understand. Your father's mother spent a whole summer with us the year you were born. Every time I put booties on your feet, she yanked them off."

216

But George changed when his mother had her first heart attack.

"You might die there all alone, Mom, before you could get to a telephone. You'll have to come and live with us now."

"Couldn't I share an apartment with someone else?"

"Who?"

"Aren't there nursing homes?"

"A foretaste of hell that costs the earth."

The Thursday Club did not meet again until after Christmas. Maggie was the first to reach Heloise's house.

"You're looking perky," said Heloise. "Mother-in-law die and leave you a million?"

"No, but I've solved my problem."

"Arsenic or strychnine?"

"Neither."

"You don't mean to say you're getting along with her?"

"Like a house afire." Maggie lit a cigarette and smiled through the drift of smoke.

"What did you do?"

"Put her to work. How glad I am I took that course in applied psychology. You see, work is therapy. I wasn't fair to her when she first came. I treated her like a guest and that deprived her of a sense of belonging to the family. You won't believe this, but she used to waste a lot of time reading. Why, I can't imagine. We've got television, as I kept pointing out to her."

"And she doesn't read now?"

"She hasn't time. I've got her scrubbing all the pots and pans that can't go into the dishwasher, running the vacuum cleaner, and polishing the silver. She even minds Greg when he gets home from kindergarten so I can go out. She sits up with him whenever George and I have an evening on the town. It's a symbiotic exchange."

"And a lot cheaper than hiring a maid."

"Of course. If I had a maid I'd have to pay her two-fifty a month at least."

"But don't you have to pay for Mrs. Markel's food?"

"No way! Her income is just a trickle—savings account and social security—but it's still an income, around three-fifty a month. I make her endorse all checks to me and I deposit them in my account. Then I let her have fifty a month, ten a week for little things and an extra ten for emergencies."

"So she's paying you three hundred a month."

"She'd have to pay a lot more in a nursing home and she wouldn't get the love and companionship she gets from me."

"How generous."

"Don't you think I am? She does. She's pathetically grateful. Even if I could afford a maid, I wouldn't get one now because she needs this work to recover her identity."

"Who does?" demanded Doris from the doorway.

"Her mother-in-law. You've got to hear this, but you won't believe it."

"Oh, yes, I will. I live next door to them."

Mrs. Markel went to bed early these days. She was too tired to do anything else in the evening now. Sometimes she even dozed off in her chair after dinner. Perhaps it was just as well because she was not happy in the room allotted to her.

Someone else had taken her apartment now, so she could never go back to it; but she still remembered her view from the tenth floor—roofs and sky and all the creatures of the upper air, a flock of starlings darting past her windows or a jet from Logan a few thousand feet up still laboring to climb.

Here, when she looked out of her one ground-floor window, she was looking straight across a narrow strip of grass into the window of the house next door. She could see a bed pulled up close to that window and a woman, even older than herself, lying on the bed with two angry eyes glaring back at her.

"It's Miss Joralemon," Maggie had explained the first time. "If you don't like being watched, keep your blind down."

"But that would be like having no window at all."

"Oh, you can raise it at night. A professional homemaker takes care of her, gives her a sleeping pill after supper, and draws a curtain across her window so she sleeps right through the night."

"What's the matter with her?"

"Arthritis. Very bad. She's paralyzed. Lucky you don't have anything like that."

It hardly seemed the moment for Mrs. Markel to mention that the arthritis in her right hip had begun to trouble her again.

"Look at those hands," went on Maggie. "Warped and overlapping like pretzels. Her left hand is the worse and that's too bad because she's left-handed. Something nasty about lefties. They're bad luck to themselves and others. I don't trust them."

Mrs. Markel had learned to avoid arguments with Maggie, so she did not protest. She did remember that "sinister" comes from a Latin word meaning both left-handed and unlucky and that Buddhists call the path of evil the "left-hand path." Once again she realized that prejudice is a kind of frozen cruelty.

The neighbors on the other side were quite different. Frank Leslie was a stockbroker with a future that Maggie described as "brilliant." His wife, Doris, had money of her own which showed in their neat hedges and lavish flowerbeds. Theirs was a corner house with a broad sweep of lawn on this side.

They came over for dinner and bridge several times a month and always tried to include Mrs. Markel in the conversation, but she could see it was an effort. She liked Doris, a placid, natural blonde, but she didn't feel quite at home with Frank. There was a little too much flashing of black eyes and white teeth.

Her happiest moments were with Greg, her five-year-old grandson. He had a throaty little chuckle all his own, the joy of life made audible, but as the days went on he seemed to laugh less often. Was it her imagination or was it fact that he rarely laughed when he was with his mother? It was plain he loved her, yet sometimes he was anxious in her presence as if he were afraid of losing her.

When school came to an end Greg was switched to a day camp, really an outdoor kindergarten which met only in the morning. As soon as Maggie discovered that Mrs. Markel was always there when the boy got home at noon, Maggie herself was there less often. Mrs. Markel did not mind this at all.

If the day was fair she and the boy went outdoors on the side of the house away from Miss Joralemon where there was more space and a sandbox had been installed. That was how Mrs. Markel got to know her neighbor on this side, Doris Leslie.

She could not help noticing a trace of hostility in most of the things Doris said about Maggie. *If I had a little boy I'd always be here myself when he got back from day camp . . . I wish she wouldn't wear such tight jeans. She's not exactly a teenager.*

Mrs. Markel had a great distaste for what she called cattiness and Maggie herself called bitchiness. She had to exercise a good bit of tact and ingenuity to turn the conversation away from Maggie whenever she was with Doris.

When July came, Mrs. Markel and Greg sat in the kitchen where it was cooler than outdoors.

"We were going to put in air conditioning this year," said Maggie. "But prices went up and George's paycheck didn't."

One sultry afternoon when Greg was painting a portrait of Mrs. Markel in water colors and she was shelling peas, Maggie burst into the kitchen, her arms full of groceries.

"Have you forgotten? This is the night the Leslies are coming to dinner and I'm going to make one of my Penang curries. You'll have to clear all this stuff away and pitch in."

So the peas went into the refrigerator and the water colors were put away in Greg's bedroom and he and Mrs. Markel were set to chopping condiments.

Mrs. Markel had learned to dread the days when Maggie made her one party dish. The condiments alone took hours. There were little green onions, hard-boiled eggs, dried herring, green peppers, and cashew nuts to chop; pineapple, coconut, and orange peel to grate; bacon to mince and raisins to seed if no seedless raisins were available. Thank God she didn't make her own chutney. It came out of a bottle at a caviar price.

And that was only the beginning. Into the curry itself went shrimp, tomatoes, celery, carrots, apples, more onions, more peppers, butter, and fifteen seasonings ranging from common herbs and white wine to cayenne pepper and imported curry powder.

When the mess was finally simmering in a huge kettle and the dining table was set with a dozen little condiment dishes for each person, every pot and pan in the kitchen had been used and they were all stacked in the kitchen sink waiting for Mrs. Markel to take over; but she couldn't do so just then because Greg must be given supper and a bath and put to bed while Maggie was dressing for dinner.

Greg was not a bit sleepy even after Mrs. Markel told him one installment of his favorite bedtime serial featuring two little mice named Lightfoot and Snow-foot. He wouldn't let her go until she left him with a nightlight which she knew Maggie would disapprove of. As it was, Mrs. Markel barely had time to change her dress before dinner.

When she came into the living room Maggie was already there resplendent in a new dress, a shapeless floating smock and loose wide slacks of silk chiffon; the colors, bluish lavender over pinkish mauve, blended with her amethyst necklace.

"You're making an occasion of this," said Mrs. Markel.

"I'd like to live this way all the time," snapped Maggie. "But, of course, as things are. . . ."

George was a little surprised when he came in late and tired from his office.

"Bridge night," said Maggie. "Did you forget?"

"I'm afraid I did." He forced a smile. "Hello, Mom, you're looking younger than I feel."

Mrs. Markel knew this was absurd, but she was grateful that he took the trouble to tell such a pretty lie. She looked at him as she often did, trying to convince herself that this independent, grownup man had once been a dreamy little boy like Greg, completely under her control.

He hardly had time to wash his hands before the Leslies crossed the lawn between the two houses and came up on the side porch to tap on a French window. Frank had brought champagne. Doris, sophisticated in black crêpe, with black pearls around her white throat, made Maggie look a little suburban, or so Mrs. Markel thought.

At the table they put her between the two men. Both worked hard to keep a conversation going but she slipped away as soon as dinner was over and shut the kitchen door so they wouldn't hear her scrubbing pots and pans.

By the time she got through she was so tired that she fell asleep the moment she got into bed, only to wake up again in the middle of the night.

The room was stifling. She threw off her bedclothes and opened the door into the hall, hoping for cross-ventilation, but not a breath stirred. A glass of cold water from the kitchen might help. Then she could sit up and wait for George, who was at a meeting of the Town Zoning Board.

She slipped into a cotton kimono and went down the hall into the living room. It looked cool in the moonlight, but it felt just as hot as her own room. Perhaps if she went out on the porch for a minute. . . .

Her bare feet were silent on the plushy carpet as she crossed the floor. One of the French windows was standing open. There were no outdoor lights, but she caught a murmur of voices.

She took a step nearer. Then she saw Maggie and Frank Leslie sitting close together on a swinging couch in shadow beyond the moonlight.

". . . money," he was saying. "I can't get any more out of Doris, but isn't your mother-in-law's savings account a joint account with George? If it is and if he could get hold of her passbook, he can draw all the money he wants. He doesn't have to tell her."

"He'd say that was stealing. She didn't make it a joint account so he could draw on it while she was alive. She just made it that way so he could inherit it without waiting for probate. Besides, even if you or I could make him do that, how could we make him hand the money over to you?"

"I'm a broker. Remember? I'd promise to double it by a smart investment."

"He'd never take a chance on losing her money. That really would be stealing, or so he'd say."

"He seems to have a lot of weirdo hangups."

"It's the way she brought him up."

"Then what are you and I going to use for money? We can't take off for Costa Rica without some capital. How much longer do you think his mother will live with her heart condition?"

The world was still for a moment as if everything was listening.

Even Maggie's voice was hushed when she spoke. "The doctor won't fix a date. He says it could happen in a year or so."

"Oh, great. I suppose that means she'll hang on for years until she's like Miss Joralemon."

Maggie's voice rose, shattering the stillness. "I can't bear it. Why do doctors prolong old age? Wasn't there an English doctor a few years ago who wanted a law to forbid all hospitals to treat any patients over sixty-five? She wouldn't be alive now if—"

"Watch it, kid. That's called murder."

"It isn't really. It's mercy killing. Does she want to be like Miss Joralemon?"

Frank laughed. "How does that rhyme go? *Thou shalt not kill; but needest not strive officiously to keep alive. . . .*"

"What's so funny?"

"Forget it, Maggie."

"Forget what?"

"This whole Costa Rica business, you, me, everything."

"Can't we go on as we are without Costa Rica?"

"You know we can't. Doris suspects already. So does your kid."

"Greg? He's only a baby."

"Oh, he doesn't know what's going on. He just knows there's something. Remember that day he nearly caught us? That mustn't happen again. It's Costa Rica or nothing, but I'm not going there broke and I'm not going to get myself hung up on a murder rap, so forget it."

"Oh, Frank. . . ."

Mrs. Markel had never heard such desolation in a human voice, but Frank was unmoved.

"Listen, Maggie. Don't you go and do anything foolish on your own. I won't stand by you if you do. Understand?"

Maggie reached for him.

With clinical detachment Mrs. Markel saw them kiss and writhe in each other's arms. At last she saw the man's figure slip silent as a shadow across the moonlit lawn to his own house. She stepped back behind the dining-room door as Maggie crossed the living room and went down the hall to her own bedroom.

What a chance they had taken! Didn't they realize that George might come home at any moment? Or had they realized and decided to savor the risk? Was there always an element of mischief in adultery?

Mrs. Markel didn't sit up for George after all. Shock had exhausted her. Now sleep brought her fearful dreams. She was screaming at a policeman, "You must do something!"

He answered calmly, "Don't you know that you dreamed the whole thing?"

Dr. Basil Willing had first come to Boston after the death of his wife. He had wanted to be near his only daughter while she was going to college there. Now his daughter was married and living abroad, but he was still in Boston.

Some lectures he gave at Harvard on forensic psychiatry had led the Boston police to consult him about the Case of the Pleasant Assassin. Before long they were asking for his counsel on any crime with a psychiatric twist, but it happened that it was from a news story in the *Boston Globe* that he first learned about the arrest of George Markel for the murder of his wife, Maggie.

Mr. Markel's mother, Jessie Markel, who lived with the couple and their son, had slept late. When she woke around eleven, she had found a note from George on the kitchen table: *Maggie's asleep. I'm taking Greg to camp on my way to the office.*

Mr. and Mrs. Markel had separate rooms because Mr. Markel was an insomniac who liked to work on sketches and plans for his advertising agency in his own room when he could not sleep.

This morning the elder Mrs. Markel had tiptoed every time she passed the closed door of her daughter-in-law's room until noon. Then, a little worried, she eased the door open and saw at once that Maggie was dead.

The police told a *Globe* reporter that Maggie Markel was killed by a blow from a blunt instrument just behind the right ear some time between eight P.M. and midnight. There was no sign of a weapon and no sign of anyone breaking into the house.

George Markel had once taken an Army course in unarmed combat. He would know where and how to strike. He claimed he had spent the entire time from eight P.M. to midnight at a meeting of his Town Zoning Board and did not get home until one A.M., but the few witnesses who saw him at the meeting had noticed him only sporadically. Rumor said that an eyewitness in his own neighborhood, Miss Cordelia Joralemon, had seen George shortly after eight P.M. in his wife's bedroom and—

Basil's telephone rang. Captain Grogan of District One, alias Beacon Hill, wanted to know if Dr. Willing would be able to see Mrs. Markel and Miss Joralemon today. The suburban police wanted their reliability as witnesses evaluated by a psychiatrist. Mrs. Markel was so anxious to clear her son that she had offered to come into Boston to see Dr. Willing this afternoon. . . .

He noticed that she had let her dark hair go gray, but she had kept a neat figure and had a firm voice. She looked at the expanse of roof and sky and river beyond Basil's twentieth-floor windows. "Nice to have a view."

"You have one, too?"

"I used to. It was a smaller apartment than this, on the tenth floor of an old building, but there was a view and I miss it now . . . Dr. Willing, Miss Joralemon is lying."

"What makes you think so?"

"She's unstable. We knew she was watching us all day from her bedside window. Now the police have discovered that she watched us most of the night as well. She never swallowed the sleeping pills she was supposed to take. She made a tiny hole in the curtain her homemaker drew across the window at night. We never suspected anything like that. On hot summer nights we left our windows open on that side and never pulled down our blinds."

"A compulsive voyeur?"

"Apparently. I suppose she was lonely. I would feel sorry for her if she wasn't now trying to get my son convicted of murder. She doesn't claim she saw him kill Maggie, but she does claim she saw him in Maggie's room during the time Maggie was killed."

"Had she any reason to hate your son?"

"I can't think of any. Couldn't it be unmotivated malice?"

"Or unconscious perjury," said Basil. "The act of seeing involves interpretation and that leaves room for self-deception. Eyewitnesses rarely invent, but they always edit whatever they see and whatever they remember. That's why science had to invent the experimental method."

"Can you prove self-deception?"

"Sometimes." Basil's eyes wandered to the golden dome of the State House just below his windows. "Could the distance between Miss Joralemon's window and your son's house possibly be as little as eight feet?"

"I have no idea, but the houses are close together on that side."

Basil rose. "Let's go out and measure it."

She picked up a small handbag with a smile. "I have plenty of quarters and dimes. I hoard them so I'll always have exact change for the MBTA."

"You won't need them this time. My car's in the basement garage."

They were on Storrow Drive before he spoke again. "I can't help your son unless you tell me everything. Did he have a motive?"

She hesitated only a moment, then told him about Maggie and Frank Leslie.

"The Leslies say now they were at home together all yesterday evening, but I saw Frank with Maggie part of that time. He didn't leave until around eleven."

"So Doris Leslie is lying for his sake?"

"And for her own. She had the obvious motive for killing Maggie—jealousy—but Frank's motive is almost as plain. If he was cooling towards Maggie and she wasn't cooling towards him, he would be afraid that Maggie might tell

Doris everything and ask her to divorce him. In that case he'd lose Doris *and* her money."

"Was Maggie capable of doing that?"

"She was capable of threatening to do it. I don't know if she would have done it or not."

The houses in the row were built in pairs, close together on one side, more separated on the other. Some contractor had saved money on excavation and plumbing that way, yet he could still advertise the places as one-family homes, each with an ample lot.

Basil measured the distance between the two houses, window to window. "A lot closer to eight feet than I would have believed possible."

"How did you know it would be close to eight feet?"

"I didn't know, Mrs. Markel. I just hoped."

Miss Joralemon was sitting up in bed. Her eyes were round and hard, the right one bright as a bird's, the left one cloudy with incipient cataract. Basil had never seen arthritic fingers more cruelly twisted.

"Why should I answer your questions?" she demanded.

"The police think it will help them, but I should warn you that anything you say may be used against you."

"The Miranda bit?" She cackled. "Nobody accuses you of murder when you're paralyzed."

"But you might be accused of perjury."

"Not me. I always tell the truth and shame the devil. What do you want to know?"

He pulled the cord that drew the curtain across the window. The material was an Indian cotton print, a busy pattern that distracted attention from a hole hardly an inch in diameter.

"I made that hole months ago so I could watch them," said Miss Joralemon. "That's how I saw George Markel night before last. He didn't know I was watching. How could he?"

"What time was it when you saw him?"

"Exactly twenty minutes after eight, a time when he says he was at the Zoning Board."

"How can you be sure of the exact time? I don't see a clock in this room."

"There isn't any."

"A watch perhaps?"

"My watch is at the jeweler's being repaired."

"I suppose you heard a time signal on the radio or television?"

"I don't hold with television and I threw my radio out when those mean commentators began saying horrible things about poor, dear, sweet Mr. Nixon. Night before last I got the time from Maggie Markel's own clock sitting right on her bedside table."

The small clock in Maggie's room was plainly in view. It was about three to three-and-a-half inches high, white plastic made to look like Dresden china, with gilt-edged scrolls and a scatter of rosebuds. Standing by the window, Basil had no trouble reading the time—five minutes to four.

"And you could see the clock looking through this little hole in the curtain?"

"Of course. Try it and you'll see for yourself."

He sat down on a chair beside her bed so that the level of his eyes and their distance from the curtain were the same as hers. Holding his head steady, he tried to look through the little hole with both eyes, but it was too small. He closed his left eye and looked with his right, then closed his right and looked with his left.

"Is that how you did it? Please show me."

She also found the hole too small to use both eyes with comfort. She closed her right eye and looked with her left, then reversed eyes as Basil had done.

"You can see that clock as plain as a pikestaff," she said.

"So you can . . . sometimes."

"What do you mean 'sometimes'?"

"You are left-handed, aren't you, Miss Joralemon?"

"What's that got to do with anything?"

"It suggests that your left eye is your dominant eye."

"I never heard of a dominant eye."

"It's just as important to seeing as a dominant hand is to handling. If you want to know which of your eyes is dominant, there are tests you can take."

"I don't care which eye is dominant."

"You should."

"Why?"

"If your left eye is dominant, you are lying when you say that you saw George Markel in his wife's room at twenty after eight the night before last."

"What do you mean?"

"There is no timepiece in this room. The curtain is at arm's length from your eyes. You have to hold your head steady to look through such a small hole. In focusing under that difficulty there is a natural tendency to look first with the dominant eye and then with the other eye as you did just now."

"What of it?"

"In your case, vision in your dominant left eye is too blurred with incipient cataract for you to see numerals on a clockface at this distance, but when you switch to your subdominant right eye, you cannot see the clock at all."

"How do you know?"

"This is one of the tests we use in medicine to discover which eye is dominant. We ask the patient to look through a hole as small as this, at eye level and arm's length, focusing on a small object about eight feet away, first with one eye and then with the other. When he looks with the dominant eye he sees the small object plainly; but when he switches to the subdominant eye it vanishes in a flash as if someone had snatched it away though he knows it is still there. It's an eerie experience. It teaches you what a slender hold we have on reality through our senses."

Miss Joralemon glowered at him. "Then, thanks to you, I won't be a witness and get my picture in the papers?"

So that was her motive for accusing George Markel.

Basil looked at her ravaged face and marveled at the tenacity of human vanity.

A month later Captain Grogan came to consult Basil Willing about another matter. When they were through, Grogan said, "Now you've wrecked our case against George Markel, isn't it time you found out who did kill his wife?"

"That sounds like the true word spoken in jest."

"More truth than jest. We like our consultants to build up our cases, not tear them down."

"You didn't want to convict an innocent man, did you?"

"No, but—you might as well talk now. She's dead."

"Mrs. Markel?"

"Who else?" Grogan took a sip of Scotch. "I had to let it ride. I couldn't find enough evidence against her, but you must have known something. Did you look for evidence?"

"Not very hard after I asked her doctor how long she had to live with that heart and he said two or three months. He hadn't told the family. He didn't want to upset them."

"How did you know it was she?"

"There was nobody else once you assumed that George Markel was at the Zoning Board when Maggie was killed, just as he said, and that Frank Leslie left Maggie and went home to Doris at the crucial time, just as Mrs. Markel said. The boy was only five and loved his mother. Why else would he be afraid of losing her? There was no sign of anyone breaking into the house. So it had to be Mrs. Markel."

"Weapon?"

"Mrs. Markel hoarded quarters and dimes for the transit. A double handful weighs a lot. Put it in a limp silk bag or a stocking and you've got a lethal weapon. Wash the stocking and put the coins back in a purse or a piggy bank and the police can search for days without finding any sign of a weapon anywhere."

"How did she know where to strike?"

"George Markel had had unarmed combat training. He'd tell her about that, showing off as young men do to their mothers."

"Motive?"

"I got this only a few days ago." Basil took a letter from a folder.

DEAR DR. WILLING,

Thank you for saving George. I've always felt you knew or suspected the truth, but I don't believe you know the real motive. So I'm leaving this letter to be mailed to you after my death. I wasn't half as much afraid of Maggie and Frank killing me for my money as I was of their being caught afterward. Think how newspaper and television *people would have wallowed in that. It would have destroyed George and little Greg. As it is, I'm hoping they'll never know who killed her.*

YOURS SINCERELY,
JESSIE MARKEL

Grogan shuddered. "These domestic crimes. . . ."

"I know," said Basil. "French astronomers talk about the *frisson* of infinity, the chilly shiver we all feel when we look out towards the space beyond stars; but sometimes I think that what we see when we look into ourselves is far more frightening."

MICHIGAN

DEATH MAKES A COMEBACK
by James O'Keefe

VIOLENT DEATH WAS no novelty to Sgt. James Peyton. He had seen far worse than a brunette with a bruise on her forehead and a slit throat.

He felt as if he had just touched a live wire.

He wide-eyed the older detective. "Dad—"

Lt. Lawrence Peyton raised a cautionary hand.

"Please, Jimmy." His voice dropped. "I wish I'd never told you about him."

"But the MO—"

"Sh. The husband hears you, spreads the rumor *he's* back. . . ." He glanced at the bedroom door as if he expected something to enter and devour them.

Lucy Welch's long hair spread out like a nun's veil on the gray carpet beneath her. Her brown eyes stared up at Jimmy.

She wore a red tube top and tight, black designer jeans. How perfectly, color-wise, her top and lipstick coordinated with her throat.

Jimmy hoped his necrophilic fantasies weren't too obvious. He must mention that to Dr. Larsen tomorrow.

Jimmy Peyton was a fat little boy in a blond, blue-eyed hunk disguise. He had fooled many women, since he always took off before the disguise slipped.

Lieutenant Peyton surveyed the huge, decadently ornate bedroom. He was a great, bloated version of his son with a cloud-gray crew cut. "Judging by that crap on the dressing table, she liked spending money."

"Or knew how to get some guy to spend it for her."

Lieutenant Peyton winked approvingly, which gave Jimmy a glow, then turned his attention to the bed. "Black silk sheets. Now, what does that tell you?"

"I don't think you should jump to conclusions, Dad."

"You want to get to my rank, you'd better."

The glow faded.

* * *

The Welch living room was expensively furnished, spotlessly clean, and coldly neat. Jimmy couldn't wait to leave it.

George Welch had a thin, vinegary face and rust-colored hair, parted down the middle.

"I understand," said Lieutenant Peyton, "you were divorced?"

"Separated," said Welch as if he were about to have the lieutenant beheaded. "We were happily married; but we were having difficulties, so we decided to spend some time apart."

"I see. So what happened tonight?"

"We were supposed to go to dinner and that play at the Birmingham Theater. I came by to get her; and I found her like that."

Jimmy noted Welch's granite formality. Indifference to his wife's death? Shock? Or something else?

"Did you," asked Lieutenant Peyton, "notice anything unusual as you pulled up?"

Welch hesitated. "No."

"Sure?"

"I'm sure."

"Okay. Now, did your wife have any enemies?"

"Yes." Like he was a cat and the question was a nice, juicy mouse. "She recently became friendly—just friendly—with a man named Eric Dimke. According to Lucy, he was used to getting his way with women; and when she turned him down, he didn't take it well."

"What did he do?"

"She wouldn't tell me. But I got the impression she was scared of him."

"You know where this guy lives?"

He gave them an address in Flat Rock.

"Think he's telling the truth?" asked Jimmy back in the car.

"Not completely. Maybe not at all. Not about that trial separation; that's for sure. Once she got her hands on his money and that house, that little bitch was through with him.

"And all you need to jump to conclusions about that is eyes."

The address was in a sparsely populated area.

They turned into a driveway, the headlights revealing a bedraggled Oldsmobile parked so close to the road they almost rear-ended it.

They crossed what felt to Jimmy's ankles like a balding, unmowed lawn.

Lieutenant Peyton sidestepped something. "Look out for this junk." A lone streetlamp and the light from the house dimly illuminating scattered auto innards.

"I don't believe it," said Jimmy.

"Believe what?"

"That a woman as well off as her would take up with anyone who lived here."

"Now who's jumping to conclusions?"

*　　*　　*

The big, black leather reclining chair was the only piece of furniture in that room that did not need reupholstering, distinctive in a room whose walls bore cheap prints of flowers, gleaming on an unshampooed rug; and as anyone who had known him ten minutes might have expected, Eric Dimke occupied it.

He was a great bronzed ape with a creamy white Elvis pompadour. As he leaned back, his unbuttoned shirt spread open, displaying his pectorals.

Only Jimmy seemed to notice the woman. She viewed the proceedings as she had greeted the Peytons at the door: with dumb animal indifference through which muted anger only occasionally flickered. Blotches marred otherwise satisfactory features.

Lieutenant Peyton repeated Welch's accusations.

"He's full of it."

"Did you know Mrs. Welch?" asked the lieutenant.

"Sure I knew her. Lotsa guys knew her. She was hangin' around the Flat Top Bar—I dunno, five, six weeks before I got talkin' to her."

"What would a woman from Indian Village be doing in a bar around here?"

Dimke shrugged. "I wouldn't go to no bars in Detroit after dark. I got the idea she went to bars all over the place. I mean, she was lookin' for action. Or maybe she just didn't want to go to no bars around where she lived 'cause she thought her old man might catch her."

"She was afraid of him?"

"I think she was. I got the idea he was this wimp she'd just married for his money; and I asked her why she didn't leave him; and she said, 'That's something I'd rather not go into'; and she got this funny look in her eyes. Know what I mean?"

"Yeah. You got to know Mrs. Welch quite well, didn't you?"

Dimke's face went cold. "Like what do you mean?"

"Well, she told you about her marriage. She told you about other bars she went to. Welch knew your name and address, which kind of suggests she did too. I mean, you can't blame us for—uh—jumping to conclusions."

Jimmy flinched.

Another shrug. "So I let her talk to me. So I let her think I was comin' on to her." He and Lieutenant Peyton studied each other. "So maybe I was. Hey, I been married—what?—twelve years? I used to be real big with the ladies. So I let some fine-lookin' chick make some moves on me, show me I still got it. Even the most happily married man's gotta do that or he gets stale. Right, hon?"

"I guess so."

They were precinct bound.

"What do you think of his story?" asked Jimmy.

"Story's fine. But did you notice Mrs. Dimke's wrists?"

Jimmy vaguely recalled bruises.

"And the way she acted?"

"She acted bored."

"She acted scared. She was scared to let us see how scared she was, so she held herself in. There's plenty she could tell us, but she knows what he'll do to her if she does."

"So it's between Welch and Dimke?"

"One thing's sure: it wasn't him."

"Him?"

Lieutenant Peyton grinned. "You know."

The lieutenant flipped on his office light. "The bloodstains show she was killed in the bedroom. And there was no sign of a struggle, so it was evidently someone she trusted." He started going through the mail on his desk. "I mean, can you see anyone letting *him* get that close—and in her bedroom yet?"

He glanced at one of the envelopes, started moving it to the bottom, then glanced at it again.

His face went blank.

"What's wrong, Dad?"

The old man struggled to smile. "Now, you got me doing it. Where's the letter opener?" He went through his top drawer, then the second drawers on each side, then the next, growing more frantic with each drawer. "Where the hell is the damn letter opener?"

"Dad." He grabbed the envelope and ripped off an edge.

Lieutenant Peyton snatched it back, clawed out the paper inside, shook it open, and read it.

He offered it to his son with a trembling hand, looking as if he were going to vomit.

The hand-printed words flew up like fists: "Lucy Welch was my return performance. Mephistopheles."

Jimmy foggily heard his father: "First good hunch you had since you got promoted out of uniform; and it had to be about him."

The bar was on the first level of the Renaissance Center. It was a slow night. The bartender and all but two of the patrons were engrossed in a televised Tigers game.

The Peytons sat, hunched over drinks, in the dim red glow, remembering seven years ago. . . .

Lieutenant Peyton recalled a young blonde, nude on a morgue slab. Her face was like the wholesome farm girls on the cover of his folks' *American Magazines,* except for the lump on her head and the gash across her throat.

An officer read from a notebook: "Her name was Helen Dunn. Twenty-three years old. She was a barmaid." He named a bar near Wayne State University. "Her boss was emptying out some trash, right after opening up, when he found her body behind some cans."

"Had there been any trouble recently?"

"Nothing in particular; but you know how barmaids are."

"Yeah." He replaced the sheet, wondering how to say what he had to say without revealing too much. He decided it was impossible. "I want this to have top priority. I want to know who works there, who drinks there—everything."

"Something special about this, sir?"

"Maybe I just don't like to see twenty-three-year-old girls die."

He was not fooling the officer. He did not care.

The "something special" was a printed note now in his desk drawer: "Helen Dunn begins her beauty sleep tonight. It's going to be a long one. Mephistopheles. . . ."

Anyone can write a note, blame a personal killing on a fictional psychopath. The police investigated the murder with more than usual diligence, but spread no alarms.

Peyton dismissed the note as a blind a week and a half later, but spent the next two months going through his mail on the brink of cardiac arrest.

He had just stopped fearing postal deliveries when the second note arrived: "I'm afraid Tracy Huggins won't have much time for studying from now on. But that doesn't matter. She's never going to graduate. Mephistopheles."

He shut off his feelings and scoured the day's reports, then called every Huggins in the phone book.

He went home with no idea who Tracy Huggins was. . . .

The next morning, during coffee, someone tapped him on the shoulder.

It was another detective. "Weren't you the one who was looking for Tracy Huggins?"

"Yes."

"Her folks just reported her missing. She hasn't been seen since leaving a late class at Wayne two nights ago."

Six days later, a deputy sheriff on horseback found her behind some bushes in Hines Park. . . .

Wayne State was on its guard. Patrols, curfews, inspection of credentials, hot lines to a special task force—there was no way this character could strike again.

As long as he confined himself to WSU.

One April night, Debra Meredith, twenty-tour, divorced, went to a singles bar in Farmington. She left, according to witnesses, about twelve-fifteen.

She was found the next morning in the driver's seat of her car in an Oak Park shopping center. This time, the note was on her lap: "Debra Meredith was looking for action. She found it. Mephistopheles."

The investigation was soon statewide; but there were few leads, all false, by that early morning in June when a priest at the University of Windsor found Julie McKinnon, of Toronto, in some bushes.

The Windsor police received a note the next day: "Julie McKinnon felt so safe on this side of the water. Now she feels so sorry. Mephistopheles. . . ."

That was the end of it.

Until now.

* * *

The whitewashed walls of Dr. Whitney Larsen's office were decorated with framed degrees, including a Ph.D.; professional-looking photographs, taken by the doctor himself, of breathtaking landscapes ("I won't shoot anything warm-blooded, even with a camera"); and numerous paintings, portraits and abstracts and everything in between, of dogs ("I like dogs. My dogs have lasted longer, and pleased me more, than all my marriages").

Dr. Larsen's build resulted from another hobby: fine food. He was not fat yet; but it was a distinct possibility. He was a tall man with black, curly, thinning hair. His hazel eyes studied Jimmy Peyton, who haltingly detailed his fantasies about Lucy Welch.

The doctor realized he was expected to say something profound. "Was she good-looking—uh, as corpses go, that is?"

"Mrs. Welch had been an attractive woman in her lifetime."

Larsen chuckled. "Could it be, if you'd jumped her bones, that really would've shown Daddy?"

"I don't know."

Conversation stopped. Jimmy studied the plaques and pictures while Dr. Larsen studied him.

"Jimmy," said the doctor finally, "I get the feeling you're not all here with me. Like there's something really bugging you; and all this stuff about having the hots for a corpse is just your way of sidestepping it."

He did not prod. He had learned the reluctant revelations were often the most significant, and that no patient was obliged to make them.

"When we got back to headquarters, there was this envelope on my father's desk. . . ."

"So now," said Dr. Larsen, "he's back; and you're going to deliver him to daddy as a Father's Day present—" he glanced at his 1984 calendar—"two months late."

"Not exactly."

"Then, what exactly?"

Jimmy laid a folded piece of paper on the desk. "This is the note."

Dr. Larsen's face soured. "Anyone ever tell you you watch too much television?" He read the note, his expression grim, then became haughty. "Ziss fellow iss obviously overzexed; but zen, aren't ve all? Ven he vas a kinder, hiss mama locked him in ze closet ven she caught him vearing her undervear—hoo-ha!—undt ven he vas in dere, he seen papa t'rough da keyhole makin' nice-nice mit a floozie." Jimmy's expression was granite. "Seriously, if you don't already know as much as I could tell you about this guy—maybe, if you don't know even more—I'd be worried about your future as a cop."

"Think he wants to get caught?"

"Hell, no. Anymore than you want to break your neck when you go on one of those super coasters at Cedar Point. I mean, besides hating women—which, I hope to God, you've already figured out—he likes excitement."

"But why did he stop for seven years, then go back to it?"

"One sure way to find out."

"What?"

"Have him make an appointment with me."

Judy Franklin was Lucy Welch's sister. Lieutenant Peyton could see a resemblance muddied by drink and fat. Her brown, boy-length hair was flecked with gray. Her face was cosmetically embalmed.

She had a Georgia accent. "That wimp she married didn't kill her, that boyfriend did."

"We have them under observation, ma'am."

"You should have their rear ends in jail."

"Why?" Her body tightened with rage. "I mean, what makes you suspect them?"

He took his notebook from a drawer, placed it open on the desk, and poised a pen over it.

She relaxed a little. "I only met Welch once, back in 1977, when Lucy brought him home for a Fourth of July picnic. They weren't married yet, think she just met him. Didn't like him then. Every time I turned around, he was hangin' around her; or he wasn't far away, watchin' her.

"And the way he watched her. I been in enough bars to know when a man watches you that way, you don't want no part of him.

"Couldn't understand what she seen in him till I found out he had money." Some of his feeling about that must have shown in his face. "Well, you didn't have to live on what was left of your daddy's paycheck from his ladies and his drinking."

"So you met him only once; and you're basing a murder accusation on that?"

"That and the letters she sent me. He was just like I thought he was—jealous and clingy and all-around weird."

"Do you have any of these letters?"

"Not now I don't. I threw 'em out a long time ago."

Aren't you the sentimental bitch? "So all you have against Welch is hearsay? What about Dimke?"

She tensed again. "I suppose you'd say that was hearsay too, specially since she never said nothin' right out. But a sister knows. You just go out there—he lives out in Flat Rock—and take a look at that wife of his. He coulda done that to her, he coulda done this to Lucy."

"Good point." He thought it best not to mention having already done so and coming to the same conclusion, or seeking someone much deadlier than Welch or Dimke.

Or that he was now drawing an unflattering caricature of the mayor of Detroit.

Lieutenant Peyton was obviously uneasy the next few days. He finally told Jimmy why over lunch. "Remember the last time I was after this guy; and I came in one night, real nervous, and glanced over my shoulder like I thought someone was following me; and you and your mother wanted to know why?"

Jimmy searched his memory, then shook his head. "But now that you mention it, was someone following you?"

"Maybe. I don't know. That was after Tracy Huggins disappeared. Her folks came to headquarters, raised hell. Said I should've told the papers about that first note. Then, they would've known. Then, they could've done something. Stuff like that.

"Heard they hung around the rest of the day, still pretty steamed up. Made me kind of paranoid."

"What did they do when her body was found?"

"I got a phone call the next day. They just said, 'Satisfied?' then hung up. I could tell it was Huggins."

"Dad?"

"Yes?"

"Did she bring it all back?" The old man's brows twitched. "I've seen her in the halls."

He was referring to Judy Franklin.

Jimmy brought Dr. Larsen up to date. From Judy Franklin's mouth to the doctor's ear, the story was naturally mangled. But one point survived. And finally someone saw its significance.

"She won't leave us alone," said Jimmy. "She won't let us do our job."

"Well," said Dr. Larsen, "she gave you information that, on the face of it, was worth checking out; and as far as she can see, you didn't; and you won't explain why."

"The commissioner wants to keep a lid on it. He thinks this guy might be a copycat. Says he never heard of a psychopath starting up again, years later, in the same area."

"Tell the commissioner for me that, if psychos obeyed rules, they wouldn't be psychos. Unless he had reasons he didn't want to talk about."

"What do you mean?"

"Nothing. The point is you don't seem to be satisfied with knowing you're doing the best you can. The victim's sister's got to see it. I mean, if you desperately need to have everybody approve of you, how the hell are you ever going to arrest anybody?" He glanced at his watch. "Which might be a good thing to think about until next week."

Jimmy counted out Dr. Larsen's fee. "I guess Mephistopheles has become kind of our obsession."

"Then, my bet's on him."

"Why?"

"Obsessed people can't think straight. Try some relaxation when you get to your desk in the morning."

Jimmy hesitated as he laid a five-dollar bill on the pile. "I noticed you became thoughtful when I told you what she said, like something'd occurred to you."

"You'll never give up trying to turn me into a consultant."

"Did something occur to you?"

"Okay. If I tell you, will you remember it was your idea?"

"Sure."

"And this is the last time you ask me for advice?"

"Agreed."

"Then here it is. . . ."

Jimmy went looking for a certain book of photographs, which he found after two difficult days.

That night, he took the book to a certain bar. Helen Dunn's boss scanned the page in which Jimmy was interested and, without prompting, singled out the right man. "This guy. I know I seen him hangin' around here, botherin' Helen, not long before it happened." He scanned the rest of the page. "I recognize some of these other people too; but if you're lookin' for someone who was botherin' her—this guy."

The rest were dead ends.

The Hugginses slammed the door at the mention of his name.

The owner of the singles bar stared at him. "Seven years ago! I can't even remember who the hell was here last night."

Julie McKinnon's acquaintances were far away by now.

He was wasting time.

Time enough for Patti Bukowski to leave her East Detroit home and her husband of three years, Gil, because things were getting too crazy. Time enough for her to move to a downtown Detroit apartment building to experience being answerable to no one.

She spent the first evening in Hart Plaza on the great, terraced stone structure that overlooked the darkness of the Detroit River.

She was too absorbed in the solitude and the glow of the Windsor skyline at sunset to notice him until he sat beside her.

Patti gave up two and a half weeks later, only partly because she missed Gil.

She was afraid of a man who had seemed so nice at Hart Plaza.

Gil had suggested she wait until tomorrow; but what could be the harm of going home tonight?

"Patti."

She turned, feeling as if she had just stepped off a thousand-foot cliff. "Oh. Hi."

"Where are you going?"

"I don't think that's any of your business."

"You're going back to him, aren't you?"

She looked for her car key. If she ignored him, he would most likely get the hint.

She did not see him reach into his pocket, take out a small chain, welded to a sinker and two slugs, and raise it over his head.

"Patti," he cooed.

"What!"

"Hold it right there." A figure emerged from the shadows, waving a gun at the man. "Up against the car and spread the feet."

Jimmy Peyton showed her his credentials, read the suspect his rights, and patted him down. He found a switchblade knife, on which flecks of blood were later discovered, and an envelope addressed to Lieutenant Peyton. (It contained a hand-printed note: "Gil Bukowski's waiting for his wife to come home. He'll have a long wait. Mephistopheles.")

"I know this guy," said Patti.

"So do we. George Welch."

"I decided," said Jimmy at his next session with Dr. Larsen, "I'd gotten as far as I could with Welch's yearbook; and if he was really killing them 'cause they rejected him, like you said, I'd better just shadow him till he made his next move." He shook his head. "Dad must've asked seven years ago about guys they were having trouble with."

"Pretty girls don't comment on every guy who gets too persistent; there's just too many of them. And I doubt Welch's victims realized how sick he was."

"But how did you know it was him?"

Dr. Larsen's face soured. "I didn't know diddly. I just made some good guesses.

"Like he lied about what he was doing at the scene of the crime, which I hear you cops have a way of considering suspicious. I mean, we're supposed to believe she was dressed the way you say she was because she expected the kind of guy you say Welch was? Come now.

"And it would answer your father's question—you know, why would Lucy Welch let Mephistopheles walk right up to her in her own bedroom?—if until recently it'd been his bedroom too.

"But the closest I came to a brilliant deduction like William Powell and Warner Oland and Basil Rathbone in all those old movies was: seven years ago in June, the Mephistopheles murders mysteriously stopped. One month later, Welch turns up at a Fourth of July party, engaged to Lucy. And no sooner does Lucy dump Welch than Mephistopheles comes out of retirement and makes her his next victim. I mean, I wouldn't hang anybody on that; but it does bear checking out.

"Now that I've answered your question, I've got one."

"Okay."

"Why were you so hung up on this guy?" Jimmy was still trying to formulate an answer when the doctor added, "In other words, how much of you do you see in him?"

He had a way of returning abruptly to the point.

MINNESOTA

THE STATE OF THE ART

by A. Heyst

THE VOICE WAS dark and smooth, like chocolate pudding.

"Hey, baby, stayin' secure?"

I switched the phone onto the squawk box and turned on the tape recorder. is was business.

"Last time I looked."

"Look again, baby. One of your workin' fold is spreading the green around. Like he's printin' it."

I swung around to switch on my terminal. That year I was more or less working for an outfit called IMM, a big financial house that lived on top of their own skyscraper. Normally I had a pretty good view from the window behind my terminal. Now it was all snow, flung straight at the glass by a moaning wind.

"Got a name?" I said, as I keyed up the personnel database.

"Nope. But he works nights. On the computer."

"Well, that's where the money is. Description?"

The voice turned pro, just like that.

"Male, caucasian, five-nine, hundred and fifty pounds, reddish blond hair, blue eyes. Could be as young as forty or as old as sixty. Can't tell with you Nordic types. Dresses like a Guindon cartoon."

"Yeah, here's a match. What's the beef?"

"No beef, baby. He's starting to attract the eye of some heavy people. Gonna start acquirin' unwanted partners. It could get messy for a lot of people."

"And you're worried. A narc with a heart of gold."

"Just returning a favor. Besides, there ain't enough of them funny little folk. Gotta protect our endangered species."

With that he hung up. I released the personnel database and started a couple of audit routines running. I took tips like this seriously. There's a law of conservation of money just like there's a law of conservation of energy, and they both say about the same thing: if it's going somewhere, it's coming from somewhere.

* * *

The snow had stopped and the wind hadn't started. The clouds hung low and distinct above the skyscrapers like a gray lid. Snow-smoothed outlines covered the litter and made it my kind of a morning. Perfect tracking weather.

I sat across the street from the IMM employee entrance and kept watch through a little hole in my iced-up car window. It was cold, but I had been cold before.

He came out twenty minutes before quitting time. Wool cap with earflaps that tied under his chin, a great big scarf, an overcoat that was a size too big, and hightop galoshes with his trousers neatly tucked inside. Just like a Guindon cartoon.

He got a snowbrush out of his car and went to work very carefully, beginning with the roof. When he had all the snow off, he scraped every square inch of glass. Then he broke the ice off the windshield wipers. He got inside and started the engine, letting it warm up the regulation three minutes. And then we were off.

He drove west a couple of blocks and stopped at an automatic teller machine. I knew the bank. Then it was south on Hennepin to a condo near Loring Park. He didn't live there, but plenty of fancy ladies did. Not too bad, as these things go. Twenty minutes early off work on account of the snow, twenty minutes late home to mama on account of the snow, time for a quickie in between. I left him to his fun and pointed myself toward a hippie restaurant where they made their own sausage, to stoke up and warm up and wait for banker's hours.

The bank where he did his business had been taken over by a California holding company, who had hired some image outfit to do something about all that Midwest stodge. The image outfit had redecorated all the banks to look like Marin County fern bars. This probably looked great in home-office presentations but lost something in a Minnesota winter, when you could practically see the ferns cringe when the door opened.

The word "security" had been too inorganic for the image outfit, so my opposite number had the title of Director of Accounts Integrity. He and I had played some very secret games together back when he and I and the world had been young.

I found him in his little office, staring at a computer terminal. The bank's inspirational message of the day was displayed as a banner across the top of the screen. It didn't seem to be inspiring him much.

"I need an account history," I said, by way of hello.

"A shocking request. Violation of personal privacy and abuse of corporate power. What's the name?"

"Johnson."

"Wonderful." There were eighteen pages of Johnsons in the Minneapolis phone book.

"Johnson, Ingemar Ingebretson," I said, following it with the social-security number.

"Hot on his trail," he said, making the keyboard sing. Someday they should stop calling us flatfeet and start calling us flatfingers.

"Ing-e-mar Ing-e-bretson Yon-son," he said in a pretty good Scandinavian singsong, "you're doing all right for a squareheaded Swede."

"Dane," I said as I watched the neat pattern of prosperity displayed in green columns on the screen. "His mother was a Rasmussen."

"Racist pig. Either way, his investments are turning out nicely."

Indeed they were. The account record showed automatic deposit after automatic deposit from some of IMM's most successful money-market funds. Funds that Ingemar Ingebretson Johnson was not a member of.

"All transactions properly authenticated," my buddy said, a question of accounts integrity in his eye, "or were they?"

"Of course they were."

IMM's authentication scheme was pure state of the art. Every officer with funds-transfer authority was issued a new password every day. The password was used by a cryptographic technique called Beelzebub to encode every transaction, just the way spies encode messages. If you didn't know the password, you couldn't decode the transaction, and if you couldn't decode a transaction, you couldn't forge one. I knew the scheme was close to perfect. I had installed it myself.

One way to react when you discover that somebody has punched a hole in your system is to assume that something small has happened and to go off on a search for tiny cracks. Anybody with half a crypto background knew there weren't any tiny cracks in Beelzebub. I had considerably more than half a crypto background, and I went off looking for the impossible.

The search took me up and down phone lines, through program and data files, and into a lot of binary back alleys. In the course of it I found plenty of impossible things, all lying around as sharp and clear as Johnson's tracks in the snow. They led me right up to his front door.

It opened off a tiny little porch at the end of a well shoveled walk in the old part of town. I stood there for a moment and listened to him get it for the way he had stacked the teacups. She had to be his wife to talk to him like that. Her voice cut right through the storm windows. On the other hand, maybe it was cutting through the brick. I blotted it out with the doorbell.

He opened the door. His hair was thinning but his eyes were bright and lively. He was wearing a patched sweater and a pair of old-fashioned carpet slippers and he looked as if he were expecting me.

"Come in," he said. She was still going on from the kitchen about the teacups. "Marybeth," he called back, "it's somebody from the Apple Club at work. Come to see my machine. We'll be downstairs."

We went through rooms and short corridors. The place had a kind of desperate tidiness about it, with things piled neatly in unlikely places. He talked over his shoulder as we went down the basement stairs.

"I said what I did to keep from upsetting Marybeth. She upsets easily."

"I heard."

"You have to understand Marybeth. She has a college degree."

I knew he didn't, and I said nothing. In college they would have taught him to think the way they thought, in neat categories. What he had done was neat, but it didn't have anything to do with a college professor's categories.

He opened a door at the bottom of the stairs and we stepped into a little room that had probably been the coal bunker in the old days. An Apple with a green-screen monitor and a hard disk sat on a table. Homemade bookshelves lined the walls. They held a very select library on cryptography—every issue of *Cryptologia* from the beginning, all of the papers by Diffie, Hellman, and Rivest, and some very hard to find things by Friedman. I was impressed.

"Nice hobby," I said, trying to get things started. I was better at a keyboard than I was at this business.

"Something to think about while the tapes spin," he said. "Being a computer operator gets duller every year. Drink?"

I tried not to sound surprised.

"Sure."

He pulled a copy of *The Codebreakers* off the shelf and fetched a pint bottle from behind it.

"Marybeth objects to drinking. Says it clouds your mind."

Not yours, brother, I thought as I let him pour me a shot of pretty decent brandy.

"Well," I said after a polite interval, "I guess you know why I'm here."

"Of course. You wanted to meet the man who broke Beelzebub."

It was his moment and I let him have it. He had earned it. I had only one question.

"On an Apple?"

"I have an M68000 board for it. Runs almost as fast as a VAX in machine language. I can break a transaction back to cleartext and extract a password in a little over twelve hours."

It took a moment and another sip of brandy to let that sink in. Beelzebub had been certified by the codebreaking agency that is so secret it doesn't have a name. Those boys had used machines a million times faster than Johnson's to try and crack Beelzebub, and failed. But then a talent for codebreaking is one of those things that pops up in unlikely places. A lot of people who have it treat it as a hobby. The rest, like the boys in the no-name agency, are deadly serious.

"Well, now, we're going to have to figure out what to do about this."

"Oh, you won't do anything about it. I only take what I need to make my life bearable, which isn't much. And if you prosecute, my defense will involve explaining how I did it. You know what that means."

I knew. Since Beelzebub had been certified it had become, with a little pushing, the standard code technique for commercial systems. It protected—or used to protect—a hell of a lot of sensitive and expensive information. I drained my drink, saluted him with my glass, and got out of there.

*   *   *

The big boss at IMM had his desk placed in the far back corner of a ballroom-sized office, so that you got to sweat plenty on the way to the hot seat beside it. It was a trick he had learned from Mussolini.

He had learned a lot of other tricks, including hiring independents to follow along in my footsteps. No way did I want some headhunting cowboy to stumble over this situation. So I had made various appointments, paid my respects to various flunkies, straightened my tie, and ridden up to the fortieth floor. Just to test the temperature of the water.

"There's a little leak," I said when I finally got to the highbacked chair beside his desk.

"How little?" he said, peering over the glasses that gave him the look of a scholarly reptile.

"Three, five grand a month."

"Plug it."

"I don't think we want to."

He looked at me, his face as cold as the air outside. He made a science of that sort of thing. It intimidated a lot of people who, unlike me, had never been seriously intimidated in their lives. I continued.

"This fellow is onto some basic flaw in the system. If we close in on him he may go for a big killing. In any case, it will cost a lot more than the lossage to fix the problem. Not to mention the publicity."

He dismissed my statement with a wave. It was a very expressive wave. I was just a tiresome underling unable to break out of my parochial mindset.

"Can you track it down?"

I became alert, trying not to show it.

"Sure."

"Then find whoever is doing this and make him disappear."

"I don't understand."

"Of course you understand. I know where you've come from. I heard it, very discreetly you understand, at an affair for supporters of the current Administration. And I want you to know that I approve. This country has just sat back and taken it for too long." He paused to let that sink in. It sank in.

"And so it's very simple. You know how these things are done. A threat arises, you deal with it. So find this person. And make him disappear."

I sat for a moment, trying to think.

"There's a bonus in it for you."

I stood up.

"I'll see what I can do," I said. And then I hurried out to set a contact marker.

It looked the way safe houses always do: reasonably clean, reasonably new, and not a human touch anywhere. Harry sat on the sofa, his feet up on a coffee table, flicking his cigar ash on the floor to give the sanitization team something to do. It was an old habit of his. I knew all his old habits. He had been my case officer for a long time.

"My cover's been blown. Somebody talked out of school at a political shindig."

"Sure. Last Administration it was left-wing dingbats blowing covers because intelligence work is immoral. Now it's right-wing dingbats playing James Bond at cocktail parties." He spat out a flake of tobacco. Harry wasn't exactly above politics, he was more to one side. "I was about to pull you out of that place anyway. That three-piece suit is starting to get on my nerves."

Harry shifted his cigar from one side of his mouth to the other without taking his eyes off me. It was his way of asking a question without asking it. This had been a shallow-cover mission from the start. I had been sent into IMM to install Beelzebub, as part of an operation to strengthen financial institutions from attack by the next generation of terrorists. The next generation will raise their war chests using keyboards in a place like IMM, not by robbing banks. A hole in my cover wasn't enough reason to pull a Marylander like Harry up into the snow country. I answered the unasked question.

"IMM has a genius working for it."

"What kind of a genius?"

"A cryptographic genius. Meek little computer operator. He broke Beelzebub. Using an M68000-equipped Apple, of all things."

This caused Harry to take the cigar out of his mouth—something that seldom happened. "Tell me more."

"Not much more to tell. He must have discovered a flaw in the basic principle, because he can break its back in twelve hours on that little machine. I didn't ask how he did it. The top-secret part of my brain is already full."

He was awed. "That was certified algorithm."

"Well, he just decertified it."

"Are you sure?"

"Absolutely. He left a trail a mile wide. He wanted to get caught—so he could have somebody to show it off to."

"This is serious."

"The big boss at IMM thinks so. He's ordered me to make Johnson disappear. In the interests of financial security."

Harry clamped his cigar back in his mouth, gave me his best Churchillian glower. "Who'll miss him?"

"Nobody much."

"Then you make him disappear. In the interests of national security."

Making people disappear takes a lot of staff work. Briefings have to be given, clearances obtained, supplemental budgets approved. Then you have to wait for the right kind of weather. And your immediate reward is a brief, ugly moment of staring down into a terrified face.

"I really hate to fly," he said.

"It'll be over before you know it."

I peered out the window of the operations shack of the little country airfield we had hired and plowed for the event. The owner clearly thought we were running drugs, and just as clearly didn't care. Nobody but our people was within five miles of the place.

The Learjet was painted pearl-gray and seemed to simply materialize out of the snowladen clouds. It flared over the perimeter fence and touched down in a little storm of its own making. It taxied over to us and wheeled in a half circle. We heard the near side engine spool down, and the little door in the side opened like a drawbridge.

Johnson clutched his shopping bag full of notes and working papers, now so highly classified that officially they didn't exist. I started wondering if we were going to have a hard time getting him on the airplane.

"Look," I said, "you'll love it. Six acres of supercomputers in the basement. Barbed wire and triple electric fence to keep out any distractions. People to talk to about your work. Plenty of problems to work on. A whole new life."

"I get airsick. It's terribly embarrassing."

"The steward will give you something. You can sleep all the way if you like."

Then he visibly screwed up his courage and marched out to the airplane. He turned and waved just before he stepped in. The door closed, the engine spooled up, and he was gone in a cloud of snow.

I was back at IMM the next morning, up on the fortieth floor with the big boss.

"Johnson's wife just reported him missing."

"Oh, really?"

"In a couple of days the cops'll find his car at the airport. Nobody will remember seeing him. It will be a very small mystery for a very short time."

"Very good. Very good indeed."

"State of the art," I replied.

MISSISSIPPI

CRIME WAVE IN PINHOLE
by Julie Smith

DOGGONEDEST THING COME in the mail yesterday—a letter of commendation from the Miami Police Department, thankin' me for solvin' a murder case. Me, Harry January, Pinhole, Mississippi's chief of police and sole officer of the law! I figured my brethren on the Bay of Biscayne had taken leave of their senses.

But I got to studyin' on the thing a while and I looked up the date I was supposed to've perpetrated this triumph and the whole thing come back to me. Blamed if I *didn't* solve a murder for them peckerwoods—it just wasn't no big thing at the time.

It happened the day Mrs. Flossie Chestnut come in, cryin' and takin' on cause her boy Johnny'd been kidnapped. Least that was her suspicion, but I knew that young'un pretty well and in my opinion there wasn't no kidnapper in Mississippi brave enough for such a undertakin'. Bein' as it was my duty, however, I took down a report of the incident, since he *could've* got hit by a car or fell down somebody's well or somethin'.

Mrs. Flossie said she hadn't seen a sign of him since three o'clock the day before when she caught him ridin' his pony standin' up. Naturally she told him he oughtn' to do it 'cause he could break his neck and it probably wasn't too easy on the pony neither. Then she emphasized her point by the administration of a sound hidin' and left him repentin' in the barn.

She wasn't hardly worried when he didn't show up for supper, on account of that was one of his favorite tricks when he was sulkin'. Seems his practice was to sneak in after ever'body else'd gone to sleep, raid the icebox, and go to bed without takin' a bath. Then he'd come down to breakfast just like nothin' ever happened. Only he didn't that mornin' and Mrs. Flossie had ascertained his bed hadn't been slept in.

I told Mrs. Flossie he would likely be home in time for lunch and sent her on back to her ranch-style home with heated swimmin' pool and green-house full of orchids. Come to think about it, her and her old man were 'bout the only folks in town had enough cash to warrant holdin' their offspring for ransom, but I still couldn't believe it. Some say Pinhole got its name cause it ain't no bigger'n one, and the fact is we just don't have much crime here in the country. I spend most of my mornin's playin' gin rummy with Joshua Clow, who is retired from the dry-goods business, and Mrs. Flossie had already played merry heck with my schedule.

But there wasn't no sense grumblin' about it. I broadcast a missin' juvenile report on the police radio and commenced to contemplatin' what to do next. Seemed like the best thing was to wait till after lunch, see if the little varmint turned up, and, if he didn't, get up a search party. It was goin' to ruin my day pretty thorough, but I didn't see no help for it.

'Long about that time, the blessed phone rang. It was young Judy Scarborough, down at the motel, claimin' she had gone and caught a live criminal without my assistance and feelin' mighty pleased with herself. Seems she had noticed that a Mr. Leroy Livingston, who had just checked in at her establishment, had a different handwritin' when he registered than was on the credit card he used to pay in advance. Young Judy called the credit company soon as her guest went off to his room and learned the Mr. Livingston who owned the car was in his sixties, whereas her Mr. Livingston wasn't a day over twenty-five.

It sounded like she had a genuine thief on her hands, so I went on over and took him into custody. Sure enough, his driver's license and other papers plainly indicated he was James Williamson of Little Rock, Arkansas. Among his possessions he had a employee identification card for Mr. Leroy Livingston of the same town from a department store where Mr. Livingston apparently carried out janitorial chores.

So I locked up Mr. Williamson and got on the telephone to tell Mr. Livingston we had found his missin' credit card. His boss said he was on vacation and give me the number of his sister, with whom he made his home. I called Miss Livingston to give her the glad tidin's, and she said her lovin' brother was in Surfside, Florida. Said he was visitin' with a friend of his youth, a Catholic priest whose name she couldn't quite recollect, 'cept she knew he was of Italian descent.

By this time I was runnin' up quite a little phone bill for the taxpayers of Pinhole, but I can't never stand not to finish what I start. So I called my brother police in Surfside, Florida, meanwhile motionin' for Mrs. Annie Johnson to please set down, as she was just come into the station. Surfside's finest tells me there is a Father Fugazi at Holy Name Church, and I jot down the number for future reference.

"What can I do for you, Annie?" I says then, and Mrs. Annie gets so agitated I thought I was goin' to have to round up some smellin' salts. Well, sir, soon's I got her calmed down, it was like a instant replay of that mornin's colloquy with Mrs. Flossie Chestnut. Seems her boy Jimmy has disappeared under much the same circumstances as young Johnny Chestnut. She punished him the day before for somethin' he was doin' and hadn't laid eyes on him since. Just to make some conversation and get her mind off what might'a happened I says, casual like, "Mind if I ax you what kind'a misbehavior you caught him at?" And she turns every color in a Mississippi sunset.

But she sees it's her duty to cooperate with the law and she does. "I caught him makin' up his face," she says.

"Beg pardon?"

"He was experimentin' with my cosmetics," she says this time, very tight-lipped and dignified, and I begin to see why she is upset. But I figure it's my duty to be reassurin'.

"Well, now," says I, "I reckon it was just a childish prank—not that it didn't bear a lickin' for wastin' perfectly good face paint—but I don't 'spect it's nothin' to be embarrassed about. Now you run along home and see if he don't come home to lunch."

Sweat has begun to pour off me by this time as I realize I got two honest-to-Pete missin' juveniles and a live credit-card thief on my hands. Spite of myself, my mind starts wanderin' to the kind of trouble these young'uns could've got theirselves into, and it ain't pretty.

I broadcast another missin' juvenile report and start thinkin' again. Bein' as it was a Saturday I knew it wouldn't do no good callin' up the school to see if they was in attendance. But what I could do, I could call up Liza Smith, who's been principal for two generations and knows ever'thing about every kid in Pinhole.

She tells me Jimmy and Johnny is best friends and gives me two examples of where they like to play. Lord knows how she knew 'em. One is a old abandoned culvert 'bout two miles out of town and the other is a giant oak tree on ol' man Fisher's land, big enough to climb in but no good for buildin' a treehouse, on account of the boys have to trespass just to play there. Which is enough in itself to make Fisher get out his shotgun.

It was time to go home for lunch and my wife Helen is the best cook in Mississippi. But I didn't have no appetite. I called her and told her so. Then I took me a ride out to the culvert and afterwards to ol' man Fisher's place. No Jimmy and no Johnny in neither location.

So's I wouldn't have to think too much about the problem I got, I called up Father Fugazi in Surfside. He says, yes indeed, he had lunch with his ol' friend Leroy Livingston three days ago and made a date with him to go on a auto trip to DeLand the very next day. But Livingston never showed up. Father Fugazi never suspected nothin', he just got his feelin's hurt. But in the frame of mind I was in, I commenced to suspect foul play.

Now I got somethin' else to worry about, and I don't need Frannie Mendenhall, the town busybody and resident old maid, bustlin' her ample frame through my door, which she does about then. Doggone if Frannie ain't been hearin' noises again in the vacant house next door. Since this happens reg'lar every six months, I'm inclined to pay it no mind, but Frannie says the noises was different this time—kinda like voices, only more shrill. I tell Frannie I'll investigate later, but nothin' will do but what I have to do it right then.

Me and Frannie go over to that vacant house and I climb in the window I always do, but this time it's different from before. Because right away I find somethin' hadn't oughta be there—a blue windbreaker 'bout the right size for a eight-year-old, which is what Jimmy and Johnny both are. I ask Frannie if those noises coulda been kids' voices and she says didn't sound like it but it could be. I ask her if he heard any grown-ups' voices as well. She says she ain't sure. So I deduce that either Jimmy or Johnny or both has spent the night in the vacant house, either in the company of a kidnapper or not.

I go back to the station and call the Chestnuts and the Johnsons. Ain't neither Jimmy nor Johnny been home to lunch, but ain't no ransom notes arrived either. Oh, yeah, and Johnny's favorite jacket's a blue windbreaker. And sure enough, it ain't in his closet.

No sooner have I hung up the phone than my office is a reg'lar behive of activity again. Three ladies from the Baptist church have arrived, in as big a huff as I have noticed anybody in all month. Turns out half the goods they was about to offer at a church bake sale that very afternoon have mysteriously disappeared and they are demandin' instant justice. There ain't no question crime has come to the country. I say I will launch an immediate investigation and I hustle those pillars of the community out of my office.

Course I had my suspicions 'bout who the thieves were—and I bet you can guess which young rascals I had in mind—but that still didn't get me no forrader with findin' 'em.

I made up my mind to take a walk around the block in search of inspiration, but first I called the Dade County, Florida, sheriff's office—which is in charge of Surfside, which is a suburb of Miami. I asked if they had any unidentified bodies turn up in the last few days and they acted like they thought I was touched, but said they'd check.

I walked the half block up to the square, said hello to the reg'lars sittin' on the benches there, and passed a telephone pole with some sorta advertisement illegally posted on it. I was halfway around the square without a idea in my head when all of a sudden it come to me—the meanin' of that poster on the telephone pole. It said the circus was comin' to town.

I doubled back and gave it a closer squint. It said there was gone to be a big time under the big top on October 19, which was that very Saturday. But the date had been pasted over, like on menus when they hike up the prices and paste the new ones over the old ones. I peeled the pasted-over date off and saw that the original one was October 18, which was the day before. Course I don't know when that date's been changed, but it gives me a idea. I figure long as them circus folks ain't changed their minds again, they oughta be pitchin' tents on the fairgrounds right about then.

It ain't but five minutes before I'm out there makin' inquiries, which prove fruitful in the extreme. Come to find out, two young gentlemen 'bout eight years of age have come 'round seekin' careers amid the sawdust and the greasepaint not half an hour before. They had been politely turned down and sent to pat the ponies, which is what I find 'em doin'.

In case you're wonderin', as were the Chestnuts and the Johnsons, it wasn't nothin' at all to study out once I seen that poster. I thought back to one young'un ridin' his pony standin' up and another one tryin' on his mama's pancake and I couldn't help concludin' that Johnny and Jimmy had aspirations to gainful employment, as a trick rider and a clown respectively.

Then I see that the date of the engagement has been changed and I figure the boys didn't catch onto that development till they had done run away from home and found nothin' at the fairgrounds 'cept a sign advisin' 'em accordingly. Course they could hardly go home, bein' as their pride had been sorely injured by the lickin's they had recently undergone, so they just hid out overnight in the vacant house, stole baked goods from the Baptist ladies to keep theirselves alive, and hared off to join the circus soon's it showed up.

That's all there was to it.

All's well that ends well, I says to the Chestnuts and the Johnsons, 'cept for one little detail—them kids, says I, is going to have to make restitution for them cakes and cookies they helped theirselves to. And I'm proud to say that come the next bake sale them two eight-year-olds got out in the kitchen and rattled them pots and pans till they had produced some merchandise them Baptist ladies was mighty tickled to offer for purchase.

Meanwhile, I went back to the station and found the phone ringin' dang near off the hook. It was none other than the Miami Police Department sayin' they had gotten a mighty interestin' call from the sheriff's office. Seems the body of a man in his sixties had floated up on the eighteenth hole of a golf course on the shore of Biscayne Bay three days previous and they was handlin' the case. So far's they knew, they said, it was John Doe with a crushed skull, and could I shed any further light?

I told 'em I reckoned Father Fugazi in Surfside most likely could tell 'em their John Doe was Leroy Livingston of Little Rock, Arkansas, and that I had a pretty good idea who robbed and murdered him.

Then I hung up and had me a heart-to-heart with Mr. James Williamson, credit-card thief and guest of the people of Pinhole. He crumbled like cold bacon in no time a-tall, and waxed pure eloquent on the subject of his own cold-blooded attack on a helpless senior citizen.

I called them Miami police back and said to send for him quick, 'cause Pinhole didn't have no use in the world for him. So I guess there ain't no doubt I solved a murder in Miami. I just didn't hardly notice it.

MISSOURI

THE VERY BEST
by John Lutz

I AM AT the national handball championships in Saint Louis when the contact is made. Handball isn't the most popular sport in the country, but these men I'm watching are the best. There is great pleasure for me in watching the best do anything, for the best have elevated their trade to an art. Usually they are paid well, and they deserve the money—just as I deserve to be paid well, for I'm the best at what I do.

I have a very unusual trade. My work brings me in contact with some of the most important figures in organized crime, and yet I never break the law, for in my trade being the best means above all being the most careful. Really, there's no reason I should ever have to operate illegally. My name is as well-known and respected among certain law officers as it is among their adversaries.

In the criminal world there are certain highly paid professional assassins. It is a job that requires many of the same skills my trade demands, though certainly the risks are much higher. That's one of the reasons I chose my line of work. Of course there are other reasons, my instinct being among them. Just as in professional football there are offensive and defensive players, so I concluded it could be in my business. Some men's instincts are to destroy; mine are to preserve. With infinite care and flawless professionalism, I save lives.

"Otto Bellom would like to talk to you about a job," the soft voice at my side says as the handball slams against the unyielding wall.

At first I pretend not to hear the voice as I consider Otto Bellom. He is a top man in the Midwest, a very rich man. He has been at or near the top for many years, and I know he will have the highest caliber enemies. If the job is protecting Bellom I know I'll have to earn my pay, but I also know that pay will be high.

"I'll talk to him," I say. "Where?"

"Fairview Motel, Cabin 33," the soft voice says. "You name the time."

I turn and take in the owner of the voice very carefully. A small, light-complexioned man in a conservative gray suit, he is frowning and studiously looking away from me.

"Is Bellom at the motel now?" I ask.

Gray Suit nods.

"Then the time is now," I say with a smile. He looks a little surprised as I turn to walk away. "Enjoy the rest of the match."

The Fairview Motel is a typical modern layout, one story, built in a squared U around a large swimming pool. There are several people in and around the pool, half a dozen running children, a pretty blonde girl poised on the diving board. I watch her dive. Fair.

Cabin 33 is one of the middle units. After parking my car I cut along a small walkway, count my way over, and knock on the back door.

"Who is it?" The voice is muffled through the door, but the apprehension isn't.

"Howard Deal," I say. "You sent a little man in a gray suit to tell me you wanted to talk."

After a moment's hesitation the door opens slowly and Otto Bellom motions me in with his hand. In his other hand he holds a small revolver.

"Put it away," I say calmly.

He does and I enter, closing the door behind me.

Bellom is a man of medium height, but very fat. He wears expensive clothes, tailor-cut white shirt, silk tie, expensive-looking shoulder holster. On his left ring finger a diamond manages to glint in the dim light.

Some glasses, an ice bucket, and a bottle of scotch sit on a tray near the night stand.

"Straight?" Bellom asks.

I nod and he pours out two drinks over ice and hands me one.

"It's about a job," he says. "I'm told you're the very best protector in the business."

"That's why I get three hundred dollars a day plus expenses, five thousand minimum."

The price doesn't sway Bellom, as I knew it wouldn't. The expression remains fixed on his padded, small-eyed features, but I see perspiration on his scalp near the roots of his thinning hair.

"I'll need your services for a month," he says, "until George Hogan takes the witness stand at the senate investigations."

"The government is protecting Hogan," I say. "They're almost as good as I am." I take my first sip of scotch, after Bellom has drunk half of his. It's the very best.

"I don't want you to protect Hogan," Bellom says, "I want you to protect me until he testifies. I know what he's going to say, and when he says it they'll place Frank Vero under immediate arrest."

Vero, I know, is a big vending machine man in the east. "And . . . ?"

"Vero knows the government might subpoena me for his trial. I know enough to put him in the chair, and he doesn't want me ever to reach a courtroom. He's hired somebody to scratch me—I got the true word—the one they call the Eskimo."

My interest perks up. I've heard about the Eskimo, a very ingenious assassin. Once he planted explosives in a victim's hearing aid, then telephoned and talked in a soft voice to get him to turn up the aid and activate the charge. With the new explosives, you can plant enough in a small item like a hearing aid to blow out the side of a room.

He didn't deal only in explosives. Sometimes he used an ice pick with a loosened handle so he could push it in, then pull, and leave only the thin shaft inside his victim. He got Mike Royce that way walking down crowded Fifth Avenue in New York. They say if it's done right there's not much pain at first and the victim doesn't even know he's been struck. The Eskimo does it right. Mike Royce walked fifty feet before he fell over dead. I guess the Eskimo might have been across the street by that time.

The ice pick game is how he got his nickname, though for all anybody knows he might be a real Eskimo. No one ever seems to know what he looks like. That's one reason he's the best.

"I'll take the job," I say. "Where's it going to be?"

Bellom downs his drink and looks relieved. "I think I can make it easy for you, Deal. I'm going to spend the next month working out of my place in the hills—nobody around for miles. If it's okay with you, we can go there tomorrow and I'll show you the layout on the way."

"Why not today?" I say. "The first thing you have to do is check out of this motel."

"No." Bellom shakes his head. "I wish we could make it now, but I've got some business that has to be done. We can leave tomorrow morning about nine."

"All right," I say, savoring the last of the excellent scotch, "but understand one thing: tomorrow at nine you become my responsibility, and you follow my orders or I don't work for you."

"Sure, sure," Bellom says, wiping the sweat from his forehead. "I understand, you got your reputation. . . ."

I unclip my initialed gold fountain pen from my shirt pocket and scribble a phone number on the inside of a matchbook. "Reach me there if you have to," I tell him. "And remember, at nine sharp tomorrow you're mine for a month."

At exactly nine the next morning we leave the Fairview Motel. Gray Suit, whom Bellom swears can be trusted and whose name is Maury Sims, drives Bellom's big sedan ahead of us. I drive my late model gray hardtop with Bellom beside me.

The plush hideaway is about forty miles outside the city limits, accessible only by a narrow gravel road with a locked gate across it. Around the redwood house the area is flat and clear, but beyond the clearing are high wooded hills. Bellom tells me the property is surrounded by an electrical fence running through the woods around us.

The inside of the house is surprisingly plush, and wide sliding doors open out onto a stone patio and a swimming pool. The pool is surrounded by a high wooden fence, and as I step out and look around I see that a swimmer would be a target only from a distant line of wooded hills.

"Only a few people know where I am," Bellom says, as Maury brings in the suitcases.

"If the Eskimo is after you," I say, "he'll find you." I watch him pale. The best thing I can have working for me is a properly frightened and cautious client.

While Bellom is unpacking, I survey everything carefully and make my plans. The house is completely isolated, well constructed, with specially installed, thick, bullet-resistant glass in all the windows. Our one big threat is from some-one coming at us through the woods, though the layout of the nearby highways makes approach from some quarters impractical, if not impossible. The nearest town is Grantville, fourteen miles away, population eight hundred. A stranger would be noticed instantly there.

I walk back from the patio to meet with Bellom and Maury to give them their instructions. Bellom is not to leave the house, not even for a swim, without informing me. Maury, armed with his revolver, is to sleep in the small outbuild-ing alongside the house, near the edge of the woods where they grow closest to us. I'll take up residence in the small wooden beach house near the gate to the pool, where I can watch the narrow road.

Maury is to answer all telephone calls and drive my car into Grantville every other day at different times to pick up the mail. I've already phoned the post office and asked them to stop deliveries. No one, I tell Maury emphatically, absolutely no one, is to enter these grounds for the next month. The Eskimo has been known to use the old telephone repairman ruse in order to plant a bomb.

I then send Maury back to the city to buy two German shepherds, which we will chain near the woods where approach is most likely. When they bark, Maury is to investigate.

After making sure Bellom and Maury understand, I take my suitcase into the beach house and settle in. It's not too uncomfortable a place, though small. It has a toilet, wash basin, and some lockers that will do for a closet. Bellom gives me a cot and pillow from inside the house. I unpack my equipment, including my seven-shot revolver, my semi-automatic rifle, and powerful binoculars. There is only one window in the tiny beach house, so that afternoon I drill through the other three redwood walls, then use a crowbar to widen the holes until they're large enough to see and shoot through. Bellom can deduct the damage from my pay. I imagine he'll be happy to.

By nightfall Maury is back with the dogs and we get everything set up. There is an extension phone in the beach house, and Bellom is to inform me when he goes to bed or anyplace else.

A week passes smoothly. Bellom relaxes through most of his days, more at ease now that he knows he has the best to protect him. Usually in the afternoons he swims, and afterward conducts some business by telephone. He gets a lot of mail, too, brought up by Maury from Grantville. In the early evening before supper Bellom and Maury sit and play gin rummy while I make my regular check of things. At night Maury and I sleep alternately, him in the outbuilding, me in the beach house, keeping our vigilance.

On Tuesday night of the second week, I awake to the frantic barking of the dogs. Everything has been thought out. Maury is to investigate the barking as I tuck my revolver into my belt, grab the rifle, and head in a low run for the house.

The living room lights are blazing as I crash open the door and hurl myself inside.

Bellom is standing in the middle of the living room wearing his robe and slippers. "What's going on?" he asks. "Why are the dogs barking?" His puffy face is pale with fright and his lower lip trembles.

I don't answer as I move to the opposite wall and turn out the lights. Then I go to a window and peer out into the moonless night. A figure is walking boldly up the walk to the house. As it comes nearer I see that it's Maury.

"Nothing," Maury says when he enters. "I checked and there was nothing there. It must have been some animal."

Only one of the dogs is barking now, and as we listen he barks less frequently, then is quiet.

"Maybe," I say. "You go and sit with Bellom while he sleeps. I'll stay on guard outside until morning."

I wait until they go into the bedroom before leaving, locking the door behind me.

Hot as it is, it's good to get out of the cool house; like many fat people, Bellom keeps the air conditioner on too high. Glancing at my watch, I see that it's three A.M., and I make a slow, careful circuit around the house. Then silently I scamper up on the roof to see in all directions, and I spend the rest of the night comfortably enjoying the summer breeze as I watch.

The next two nights pass peacefully, without a hint of trouble.

A little before eleven Friday morning Maury knocks on the beach house door and sticks his head in. "The post office in Grantville just called," he says. "The guy told me he was sorry he forgot to hold the delivery and the carrier's coming up here with a package."

I swing off the cot and stand up, tucking in my shirt. "Did you say a package?"

Maury nods and moves back to let me out the door.

"You stay with Bellom," I say. I watch him walk to the house, and before climbing into my car I duck back into the beach house and get my black bag.

Still some distance from the gate I pull the car to the side, then walk the rest of the way. I go through the gate, locking it again behind me, and I choose a spot about a hundred feet down the road to wait for the mail carrier with the package.

Fifteen minutes later I hear a motor, and a blue jeep with U. S. Mail printed in white letters on the door bounces into view. I step out and flag it down.

"You have a package for Mr. Bellom," I say, smiling.

The carrier is a scrawny old man with a worn delivery cap on his head, and he eyes me suspiciously.

"If you don't mind, I'll take it here," I tell him pleasantly.

"You ain't Mr. Bellom," he says. "I come this far, might as well drive up the rest of the way."

"That won't be necessary," I say. "I'm staying with Mr. Bellom and he sent me down here to get the package." I smile again and slip a ten dollar bill through the jeep window.

The old man smiles back at me with the few teeth he has and lets out a high little cackle as he accepts the money. "You'll have to sign for it," he says, "and I'll give you an acknowledgment slip, too." He's a born bureaucrat.

He hands me a pink slip of paper and I pull my fountain pen from my pocket and sign it. I hand it back to him with the pen and he fills out a yellow form and hands it out the window for me with the package.

"Thanks," I say, clipping the pen back in my pocket and standing casually with the brown package until he drives away.

Then I gently lower the package to the ground and run back to my car for the black bag. As I jog, I look at the yellow slip of paper. There is a space for point of origin, and the old carrier's shaky writing says Dallas, Texas. Who does Bellom know in Dallas?

I return with the bag and stare down at the package. It's about twelve inches square, tied with twine, the address printed in black ink. I pick it up and carry it to the side of the road in the shade. Then I open my bag and spread out my special tools.

After hastily examining the package with my stethoscope and detecting no clockwork, I feel much safer, and I begin the very delicate operation of opening it.

There is a plastic case inside with some newspaper wrapped around it for protection. I proceed with care, and twenty minutes later I have the case open and find it filled with small wine bottles. The printed matter says it's a wine-taster's kit, and there are samples of wine from all over the world.

With my needle-nosed pliers I break a small piece from the case. Ordinary plastic. Then I examine the corks of the bottles. Enough of the right explosive can be packed into a cork to destroy half of Bellom's fancy summer house. But the corks are solid. They are of ordinary cork.

I remove the cork from each bottle then and sniff the wine, sometimes testing the barest bit of it on the tip of my finger. For all I know it could be doctored with some tasteless poison, but I'm sure the bottles contain no explosives. After putting everything back in order I close the case, lift it by its handle, and take it, the paper, and my bag back to the car.

"What is it?" Bellom asks as I set the case, now loosely wrapped again, down on his desk.

"Open it," I tell him. "It's safe. It's a wine-taster's kit from a friend of yours in Dallas."

"I don't know anybody in Dallas."

"Somebody knows you. That's where the post office said it came from. Could it be a friend of yours who knows you enjoy wine and just happened to send it to you?"

Bellom sticks out his fat lips and nods. "It's possible."

"But not likely," I tell him sharply. "Don't lower your guard. I'll leave that wine here but I don't want you to take so much as a sip. Clear?"

"Clear," Bellom says. "If you want, I'll pour the stuff down the sink."

"That's not necessary. We'll leave it here as a reminder. Just don't touch it."

I walk back to the beach house. The sun is high now over the green spread of trees on the surrounding hills, and as I walk, tiny insects spring from the grass to avoid my footfalls. It's good to get back into the dim coolness of the beach house and lie on the cot, but I don't enjoy the shade for long. After about fifteen minutes I hear someone approaching outside. There's a knock on the door.

"Telephone for you, Mr. Deal." It's Maury's voice.

I sit up. "Okay." As I listen to him walk away I wonder. No one knows I'm up here; I've told no one.

I lift the receiver on the extension phone gently and press it to my ear. "Deal here."

"Mr. Deal, this is the Eskimo."

I stand up quickly, ready to act.

"If you'll check," the soft voice on the other end of the phone says, "you'll discover that Mr. Bellom is quite cold."

Click, buzz.

For only a second I stand still in disbelief, then I'm out the door and racing for the house. Maury is standing off to the side looking at me in surprise. "Stand guard out here!" I command him as I run past.

Without breaking stride I kick open the door to the living room and wind up crouching inside with gun drawn.

Bellom is sitting at his deck in the corner, staring at me with shocked eyes.

"Where's the wine?" I ask, slipping my gun back into my belt.

"Right there, where you left it." Bellom stands and we stare down at the loosely tied brown paper.

"You didn't drink any?"

Bellom shakes his head. "I swear I didn't."

The telephone rings. Once . . . twice. . . .

As Bellom reaches to answer it, I grab his wrist. He stands watching as I lift the receiver and hold it silently to my ear. No one breathes.

"Mr. Deal?"

Immediately I recognize the Eskimo's voice, and for the first time I sense something familiar in it.

"This is Deal."

"Is Mr. Bellom there?"

"He's here," I said calmly, "and he's alive."

"It's eleven fifty-nine and a half, Mr. Deal. That's very important. I also have some very important information to relate to you. Do you have a pen and paper?"

Again the voice gnaws at my memory. "Yes, go ahead," I say, sliding an envelope across the desk and reaching for my pen.

Even before I start to uncap the pen. I know. The weight, the balance! The newly engraved initials! It isn't my pen!

It isn't a pen at all!

As I drop the receiver I hear the high cackling laugh come over the wire. I hurl the gold pen at the window, but it merely strikes the thick glass and bounces back to the center of the room. I scramble on the carpet for it, grasping for it.

For just one horrible instant I see but do not hear the explosion.

MONTANA

WILD THINGS
by Clark Howard

TREE O'HARA LAY prone on the ground and peered down at a little crossroads settlement through twelve-power binoculars. He was in a stand of tall pines six hundred yards or so up the mountain. The settlement, which did not even have a name, consisted of a Conoco gas station, a general store, and a roadhouse restaurant, each occupying a corner where the two mountain highways intersected. The fourth corner was unimproved and stood vacant except for a roadsign which read BUTTE 112.

It was Sunday afternoon and both the Conoco station and the general store were closed. The roadhouse restaurant was open but there was only one car parked in front of it: a five-year-old Cadillac with California plates.

Tree lowered the binoculars and got to his feet. He was a tall, once lean man, now beginning to flesh out with his age approaching forty; but still muscular, still quick. His most striking feature was his eyes—they were cold, and so black and flat they could have passed as sightless. He wore denim jeans and a Levi jacket over a faded work shirt; on his feet were lace-up lumberjack boots.

Leaving the edge of the pines, Tree walked briskly another hundred yards into the forest where he had left his horse. It was an Appaloosa, the horse—its foreparts white as a perfect cloud, its loin and shank spotted with round black markings. A mare, she stood just under fifteen hands high. When Tree had caught her, wild, in the Nez Perce National Forest four years earlier she had been a fast and trim thousand or so pounds. Now he reckoned she weighed around twelve hundred. She had fattened out from their inactive life in the upper forest. Tree rode her on a regular basis only twice a month, when he came down to the settlement for supplies. But she was a happy animal—she loved the man who had captured her, and Tree guessed that if he ever had to do any hard riding, she would run her heart out for him.

The mare snorted and dug at the ground with one hoof as Tree approached.

258

"Easy, Elk," he said quietly. Elk City, west of the Bitterroot Range, was where he had roped her, so he had named her Elk. He rubbed her throat now to calm her, then stepped back to the saddle and put his binoculars in a case hanging from the horn. From a blanket roll behind the saddle he removed a pair of telephone-pole climbers and buckled them to the inside of his legs. From one saddlebag, he took a telephone lineman's intercept set—a receiver with a dial built into it and two magnesium clips for tapping into a wire—and hooked it onto his belt. "Keep still," he said to Elk, rubbing her throat again.

Walking fifty feet to a string of telephone poles that went up and over the mountain, Tree put on gloves and climbed one of them to its crossbeam. He hooked one arm around the beam to steady himself. With his free hand he laid the intercept set on the beam, attached the magnesium clips to one of the telephone wires, and got a dial tone in the receiver. He dialed the number of the restaurant at the crossroads. John Grey Sky, the Shoshone owner, answered.

"John," said Tree without preliminary, "who's the Caddy belong to?"

"Oh, Tree, it's you. The Caddy? Nobody, man. A couple of sharpies and some bimbo passing through. They're slopping down beer and arguing about which route to take to Chicago."

"What do they look like?" Tree asked. "The men, I mean."

"Losers," said John. "Small-timers. punks."

"You're sure? They're not just pulling an act?"

"Listen, brother, I know rabble when I see it," John assured him. "You're safe. Come on down. I got your supplies."

"Okay," Tree said. He had hesitated just a beat before answering. He hoped John Grey Sky had not noticed. He and John had been friends for twenty-five years, since attending Caribou Indian School together as young boys. It would never do to insult a friend of such long standing by doubting his judgment. If Grey Sky said he would be safe, Tree had to assume he would be. All the same, when he got back to Elk and put his equipment away, he took a loaded forty-five automatic from the saddlebag, jacked a round into the chamber, thumbed the safety on, and stuck it in his waistband under the Levi jacket where it could not be seen.

Tree led the Appaloosa to the edge of the pines and tied her reins to a buffalobur shrub. The bush had just enough prickly spines on it to discourage Elk from nibbling the reins untied and following him, as she liked to do. "Be a good girl," he said, scratching her ears. "I'll bring you an apple."

Tree made his way down the slope and came onto the highway around the bend from the roadhouse. He approached the crossroads from behind the closed Conoco station, aware with every step of the gun in his waistband. From the side of the station he studied the car with the California plates. The tires were fairly worn, there was some rust on the chrome, and a small dent in the right rear fender had been left unrepaired. It looked like a loser's car, all right, just as Grey Sky had said. All the same, Tree was glad he had the gun.

Hurrying across to the rear of the roadhouse, Tree slipped through the open back door into the kitchen. John Grey Sky was scraping down his fry grill. "Hey, bro," he said.

"Hey, John." Tree's eyes swept the room, looking for anything out of the ordinary. Through the service window he could hear the voices of Grey Sky's three customers.

"Your supplies are there on the meat table," Grey Sky said.

Tree stepped over to a butcher block and examined the contents of a burlap bag: cheese, coffee, tins of meat, dry cereal, powdered milk, beef jerky, magazines, a dozen fresh apples for Elk. "You get my animal food?" he asked the roadhouse owner.

"Under the table."

Tree pulled out a twenty-pound sack of processed dry animal food pellets. Similar to the food sold commercially to feed dogs and cats, it differed in that it contained flavors attractive to wild as opposed to domestic animals.

"You must be feeding half the wild things on that mountain," Grey Sky commented. "They're going to have to learn to scavenge all over again after you're gone."

Tree felt himself tense. "After I'm gone where?"

John Grey Sky shrugged. "Wherever."

Tree stared at his friend's back. Grey Sky could get a lot of money for betraying Tree O'Hara. Tree wondered if his friend was ever tempted.

The voices from the front of the restaurant grew louder. "You're getting a free lift to Chicago," a man's voice said. "Least you could do is be a little more friendly."

"Drop dead," a woman's throaty voice replied. There was a loud cracking noise then—the unmistakable sound of a face being slapped.

Frowning at each other, Tree and Grey Sky walked out from the kitchen. One of the men was standing, half bent over the table. The woman, seated, was staring up at him defiantly, one side of her face turning an angry red.

"You kick dogs, too?" she asked.

He hit her again, backhanded, on the other side of her face.

"Hey, man, no rough stuff in here!" Grey Sky said.

The man raised his hand again.

"Don't do it," Tree said. His voice, like his eyes, was flat and hard. It was clearly an order.

The man at the table turned around, one hand reaching for an empty beer bottle. "Who the hell are you?"

"Don't matter who I am," Tree said. He pulled back one side of his Levi jacket to expose the gun. "Don't hit her again."

"You gonna kill me if I do?" the man challenged with a sneer.

"Not, just cripple you," Tree replied matter-of-factly. "I'll put one in your left instep. Blow your foot all to pieces."

The other man at the table intervened. "Hold it, chief," he said with a forced smile. "We don't want no hassle." He took the bottle from his friend's hand and put it down. "Come on, Lou, forget it. It's their patch." Picking up the check Grey Sky had given them, he looked at it and put some money on the table. "You coming?" he asked the woman.

"Not on your life," she said. Both sides of her face were now violently red.

"Please yourself. Come on, Lou."

The two men started to leave.

"Wait a minute, I've got a suitcase in that car!" the woman said urgently.

"Come on," Tree said. He went outside and stood with her while Lou opened the trunk and set her suitcase on the ground. Then the two men got in the Caddy and drove off.

The woman picked up her suitcase and followed Tree back inside. "Thanks," she said.

"Forget it," Tree told her. He studied her for a moment. She was, he guessed, an old twenty-five. There was no telling what her true hair color was—bottle blonde with black roots was what he could see. Too much makeup. A well used but still good body. A bimbo, he thought. Like Grey Sky had said. The kind who'd take a free ride with two losers in a five-year-old Caddy.

"What time's the next bus through here?" she asked uncomfortable under Tree's scrutiny.

"Friday," said Grey Sky.

"Friday! This is only Sunday. Are you kidding me?"

"I never kid about anything as serious as bus service. Just once a week the bus comes over the mountain. Rest of the time it follows the Interstate around the mountain." Grey Sky looked over at his friend. Tree was staring at him, the realization having just dawned on him that the roadhouse owner was right. "Didn't think about that, did you, Galahad?" asked Grey Sky.

"Where the hell am I going to stay until Friday?" the woman asked in a half whine. "I don't have money for a motel."

"That works out just fine," Grey Sky said, "cause there's no motel any- way."

"Well, what am I gonna do!" she shrieked.

Tree looked at his friend. Grey Sky held both hands up, palms out.

"Not me, bro. I got my wife, four kids, my wife's mother, my unemployed brother-in-law and *his* wife and two kids—all in a two-bedroom, one-bath house. Sorry."

"Could you let her sleep here, put a cot in the kitchen—?"

Grey Sky shook his head. "My insurance don't allow overnight occupation of the premises. If she accidentally burned the place down, I couldn't collect a nickel. You're going to have to handle this good deed yourself, Galahad."

Tree glared at his friend. Grey Sky was obviously enjoying himself.

He could hear the woman panting as she trudged along behind him, lugging her suitcase with both hands. "How—much farther—is it?" she gasped.

"Not far." Carrying the burlap bag of supplies on one shoulder, the sack of animal food on the other, Tree deliberately kept his pace slow to allow her to keep up with him. But when he saw that she was falling too far behind anyway, he stopped to let her rest.

"How come you live up in the mountains anyway?" she demanded. "You antisocial? Don't you like people?"

"As a matter of fact, I don't," he said, "very much."

Now it was her turn to study him. She was not sure whether she liked what she saw. Those eyes of his didn't seem to have even a degree of warmth in them. "What'd that fellow down there say your name was? Galahad?"

"He was just trying to be funny. My name's Tree O'Hara."

"Tree? How'd you get a name like that?"

"My mother's family name. She was Indian. I'm one-quarter Minnetonka."

"Oh. Well, my name's Violet. I was named after a flower. You can call me Vi."

He nodded. "Come on," he said, "let's go on."

After one more rest stop, they came to the edge of the pines where Elk waited. As they approached, the mare snorted and pawed the ground edgily. "She smells you," Tree said. "She knows you're a woman. She's jealous.—Come on—easy, baby," he said to Elk, putting an arm under her neck.

"Sure is a funny-looking horse," Vi said. "Looks like the front of one and the back of another, stuck together."

Tree threw her an irritated glance. "This happens to be an Appaloosa. It's one of the most intelligent breeds of horse in the world, as well as one of the fastest. This horse has more stamina and endurance than any other breed you can name. It is the best stock horse, the best show horse—"

"All's I said was it was funny-looking," she interrupted. "I'm sorry, but that's my opinion. Personally, I like Palaminos. Like Trigger, you know?"

Tree turned away in disgust. *Trigger!* A Hollywood horse. Great spirits!

Tree lashed the two sacks one on top of each other just behind the blanket roll, then helped Vi into the saddle. She had to hike her skirt far up on her thighs in order to straddle the horse's back, but it didn't seem to bother her. Tree noticed that her legs were well rounded, fleshy—in fact, all of her was well rounded and fleshy; she wasn't skinny anywhere, a fact that Tree approved of. He didn't care for overly slim women—they always looked too fragile, like stickwood. Elk was of a different mind, however; the mare did not like the woman at all, and showed it by shuffling around skittishly and snorting loudly through flared nostrils. Tree finally had to cut up an apple and feed it to her so they could be on their way.

The trip to the cabin took another two hours, Tree leading the horse and rider while carrying Vi's suitcase in his free hand. He didn't mind the walk—in fact, he was glad to get the exercise because he knew he was about ten pounds overweight. For the first couple of years after he had gone into hiding he had made a point of exercising five days a week—calisthenics, weight-lifting, jogging through the woods. That, along with chopping wood and pumping water out of his cistern, had kept him nicely in shape. But for the past three or four years he had grown lazy: sleeping late, not watching his diet, lying around like a much older man. He had become complacent in his mountain hideaway. He felt safe there; only rarely did he feel threatened any more. After six years, he figured they had stopped looking for him.

Probably.

Maybe.

Tree and the woman arrived at the cabin just at twilight. It sat on a small clearing at the six-thousand-foot level in the Beaverhead Forest, just east of the Continental Divide. When the clouds were high, Chief Joseph Pass could be seen from the porch. If they were very high, one could regularly see the moon and the sun at the same time, in different parts of the sky. The natural beauty of the place was indelible. The woman didn't notice the scenery, however—she was too acutely aware of how isolated it was.

"Look, before we go in," Vi said, "I think we ought to get something straight. I had a falling-out with those other two guys because they had some weird ideas about how I should pay for my ride. I hope you're not thinking along those same lines as far as room-and-board goes."

"I'm not," Tree told her.

He said it a little too quickly to suit her. With a little too much determination. She hesitated on the porch, not following him into the cabin.

"Listen, no offense, you understand," she said, "but you're not—well, *peculiar* or anything, are you? I mean, living up here all alone—"

Tree returned to the doorway and faced her. "Why don't you lighten up?" he said. "You'll be safe here. But if you don't believe me, hike on back down the mountain and make other arrangements."

"A girl can't be too careful, is all I mean. I have this problem in that men usually find me very attractive—"

"I don't," Tree assured her. "My taste runs to darker women. When I get lonely, I ride down to the Salmon River Reservation. Lots of nice Nez Perce and Shoshone women down there. They like me because my skin's light. I stay for a few days and then come back home. I was just down to the reservation last week, so I'm settled for about a month now. Like I said, you're safe."

Turning, he walked away. When she finally came into the cabin several minutes later, she found her suitcase on the bed in the tiny bedroom. Tree had decided, he told her, to sleep on the couch. Not because he was such a gentleman—he just didn't like the idea of leaving her out in the main room alone all night. The main room—which was a kitchen-living room—was where he had the television, shortwave receiver, his books, magazines, guns, ammunition: things he didn't want her fooling with. Sleeping on the couch, he could keep an eye on everything.

After Tree took care of Elk, rubbing her down briskly and putting her in the one-horse lean-to stable he had built onto the rear of the cabin, he came back into the cabin just in time to hear Vi, in the bedroom, say, "Damn!"

"What's the trouble?" he asked.

"My cosmetics bag! It was in the back seat of the car! I don't have any makeup!"

"Tough break," he said indifferently.

He went into the kitchen, unpacked his supplies, and began preparing supper. Presently Vi came in.

"Listen, I can cook," she said. "Why don't you let me fix supper?"

"I'll do it," he replied. "I know how I like things."

Vi shrugged. Strolling, she looked the place over. "You've got enough books," she commented. "All the comforts of home, too—radio, TV, everything. How do you manage it way up here?"

"I manage," Tree said. He was not about to share any confidences with her. For electrical power he had illegally tapped into a main power line running across the mountain. For water he had a cistern next to the cabin. For television, a microwave dish he had assembled on the roof, which stole signals from the sky. For shortwave, a simple antenna wire strung up a high tree. For backup, a battery-operated generator, constantly charging off the tapped electricity.

"Okay if I look at these old magazines?" she asked, standing in front of the bookcase where he kept them.

"Sure. But do me a favor first. Step around back and make sure I closed the lean-to door, will you? I don't want Elk to be in a draft."

While she was out of the cabin, he went quickly to the bookcase, took a small scrapbook from one of the shelves, and put it on top of the bookcase out of her sight and reach. Then he returned to the kitchen.

They shared an uneasy supper, both telling whatever lies they felt necessary to project or protect their respective images. Tree told Vi he had originally come to live in the mountains to avoid the Vietnam draft, and had not gone back because he didn't relish the idea of steady employment. He said he worked down at the roadhouse restaurant during tourist season to earn enough to live on the rest of the year. Vi told Tree that she was a model on her way to Chicago for a job at Marshall Field's. Because she wasn't due there for another week, she had accepted a ride with the two guys in the Cadillac. She had thought, she said, that they were legitimate businessmen, traveling salesmen or something, and had been very surprised to learn they were just a couple of petty hustlers.

Because each of them was lying, neither Tree or the woman asked any questions of the other. They kept conversation to a minimum. After supper, Vi found that she was extremely tired. It was the climb and the altitude, Tree told her. "Your blood's thinned out. Better go to bed." She did, and fell into an immediate deep sleep.

When he was sure she was sleeping soundly, Tree slipped into the bedroom and got her purse. He brought it into the main room and searched it. There was an expired Illinois driver's license, a faded Social Security card, an address book containing no names that Tree recognized, a blank, unmailed postcard with a photo on it of Harold's Club in Reno, and twelve dollars.

A loser's purse for sure, Tree thought. He put it back in the bedroom.

Later, Tree fed Elk, opened his nightly bottle of beer, chewed a little peyote, and watched an old John Garfield movie on some channel he was pulling in from a satellite. When the movie was over, he spread his sleeping bag on the couch, stripped, climbed in, and went to sleep, the forty-five lying loaded and cocked on the floor just inches away.

The next morning, Vi found him out back of the cabin with his wild things. She stood out of sight around a corner of the cabin and watched him feed them from the sack of pellet food he had brought back. She was amazed at the number and variety of the animals. Some of them she couldn't even identify—others, like the rabbits, squirrels, and small deer she knew. Tree knelt right in their midst and fed them from his open hand. The sight of it was a wonder to her.

"You can come around and watch it you want to," he told her without looking around. "Just don't make any sudden moves."

Vi eased around the corner but stayed well back from the menagerie. "How'd you know I was there?" she asked curiously.

"This little mule deer told me," he said, scratching the middle forehead of a somewhat scroungy, unattractive deer. "I saw its nostrils flare—that meant a new scent was close by. Mule deer have very poor eyesight; they have to depend on their sense of smell for survival." He looked at her over his shoulder and grinned. "Plus which, I saw your shadow."

"Oh, you!" She moved a little closer. "What in the world are all of them? What's that reddish one with the yellow belly?"

"Ermine weasel. Turns pure white in the winter. That's when the trappers go after them."

"And that one, by the deer?"

"Pronghorn. It's a kind of bastard antelope." He stood up and started pointing. "That's a wolverine over there: baby wolf. This big guy with the white mark on his forehead is a badger. My mother's people named him. They called the white mark a badge.' I bet you didn't know 'badge' was an Indian word."

She shook her head. "No."

Tree smiled. "Most cops don't, either."

"What's that one, with the partly webbed feet?"

"That's the one the ladies like: she's a mink. Next to her there—that big shiny grey animal—that's a marten."

From a nearby limb came a clipped, scolding bird call. Tree looked over at a long-tailed black-and-white bird chattering noisily.

"All right," he said. He stepped out of the center of the wild things, closing the bag, and came over to where Vi stood. From a wooden storage box, he removed another bag and scooped out a handful of its contents. "Bird seed," he said. He took her hand. It felt good. "Come on."

She let him lead her over to a low aspen and watched him hold out his open hand to feed the bird. "It's a magpie," he told her. "Biggest nag in the woods. Never gives you a minute's peace if he's hungry." After a couple of minutes, he closed his hand. "That's enough, Porky. I named him Porky 'cause he's such a pig."

He bobbed his chin toward another tree, a spruce. "Want to see an owl?" They walked over to a low, heavily leafed limb where a small, unpleasant-looking owl was hunched. Its oversized head seemed to comprise half of its body, and its big direct eyes and hooked beak gave it a definite aura of hostility.

"Is it mad?" Vi asked, holding back tentatively.

"No," said Tree, "just sleepy. He'll burrow down into the leaves and go to sleep in a bit." Tree fed the owl, as he had the magpie, from his palm. "Mostly he eats forest mice, but he likes these seeds, too." With the last of the seed, he led Vi to a small flat boulder jutting up from the ground like a fist. He sprinkled the rest of the seed on the flat of the rock and drew Vi a few feet away from it. "Now you'll see my favorite wild thing," he said quietly.

As they watched, a glossy black bird with wild yellow eyes swooped gracefully onto the rock and, after a cautious look around, began eating. As it ate, it honed its already razor-sharp talons on the rock.

"That's Midnight," Tree told her. "A raven."

"Won't it eat out of your hand like the others?"

"Not yet. He doesn't trust me enough yet. Someday he will. In another few years."

They walked back to the rear of the cabin. A few of the wild things were still there. Vi shook her head in wonder. "I didn't know animals were that friendly."

"They aren't, as a rule," Tree said. "That wolverine there, she's a natural enemy to the mink, the rabbit, and the marten. They're usually her prey. And the badger generally goes after the ermine weasel when he sees one. But they know I don't allow any fighting here in the clearing. I chase them off if they start fighting. It doesn't take long for them to learn that not fighting is best. Animals are a lot smarter than people."

"You really love them, don't you? These animals?"

"Yeah, I guess I do," Tree admitted. "It makes me feel good when I bring two natural enemies together and get them both to eat out of my hand at the same time."

"Too bad that can't be done with people," Vi remarked. "It would stop all the war and killing in the world."

"No, it wouldn't," Tree said quietly. "People would still kill, for sport. Man is the only animal that kills for sport. You'd never stop that. Man will always have to kill. It's his nature."

Vi stared at him. As he spoke, his eyes seemed to grow colder.

The next morning when Vi came out of the bedroom, Tree was at his short-wave set listening to an English-language broadcast from Moscow. "Don't look at me," she said. "I'm totally out of makeup and I look *awful*."

Tree did look at her, and liked what he saw. "You look fine to me," he said. "Nice and scrubbed." He switched off the radio. "Want to go fishing with me?" he asked. He didn't want to leave her alone in the cabin.

"I don't know how to fish."

"I'll teach you. Or you can just watch. We can take some food and have a picnic."

Vi consented and together they packed a knapsack with lunch. Tree got his lines and bait, and they trudged up-mountain several hundred yards toward a narrow stream of cold snow-water coming from high up.

"How come everything's always *up*hill?" Vi complained, taking his hand so he could help her. "Isn't anything ever downhill?"

"Nothing worthwhile," Tree replied matter-of-factly.

They walked along the stream and Tree showed her how to set fish lines without poles or other apparatus. "Poles scare fish off," he explained. "They cast a shadow over the water."

When he had the lines set, they walked on to a point where the stream bed dropped six feet, creating a low waterfall. There the water rushed and formed whitecaps, and occasionally they could see a mountain trout swimming upstream, actually jumping up the falling water. They found a place to open the knapsack and eat. While they were there, Vi told him about herself.

"I was one of those young girls with stars in her eyes who went out to California to get into the movies. Or TV. Or modeling—*anything*, you know, except the nine-to-five office bit. It took me a while to realize I wasn't the only one with big ideas. There were hundreds of others just like me. We were all pilgrims who made it to Mecca—only Mecca turned out to be Hustle City. I was lucky—I ended up waiting tables at a Hamburger Hamlet. A lot of others weren't lucky. They ended up on drugs or selling themselves on Hollywood Boulevard for some pimp, or even worse. That's why when the two sports in the Cadillac asked if I wanted a ride east, I took it."

"No modeling job at Marshall Field's?"

Vi shook her head. "The most I've got to look forward to is a monotonous job in some dull office."

"That's more than some people have got," Tree commented darkly.

That night, her third night at the cabin, Tree let her cook for him. She made breaded pork/chops from his freezer and managed to whip up some decent mashed potatoes from his dehydrated food stock.

"Not bad," he said. "Where'd you learn to cook?"

"Marshall High School, on the west side of Chicago. Home Ec was required. Where'd you go to school?"

"A reservation in Idaho."

"What was it like living on a reservation?"

"Poor," he said quietly. "Cold poor. Hungry poor. Hard-knock poor."

"How'd you get away from it?"

"I joined the Army." He realized the slip at once.

"You told me you came up here to evade the draft," she reminded him.

Tree looked down at the table for a long, silent moment. Finally he met her eyes. "That was a lie. But I can't tell you the truth. Let's just leave it alone for the rest of the time you're here, okay?"

They resumed eating, with no further conversation for several minutes. Finally Vi put her fork down and rose.

"I told you the truth about me," she said. It was clearly an accusation. She left the table and went outside.

Tree finished his supper, cleared off the table, and washed the dishes. Then he got an apple out of the food locker for Elk and went outside. Vi was sitting on the porch looking up at a sky full of stars that looked close enough to touch.

"Want to feed this apple to Elk?" Tree asked.

"Elk doesn't like me," Vi said.

"She's just not used to you. Come, you can feed her." Vi did not move. Tree coaxed her. "Come on. I'll show you how. It's easy. Come on."

Finally Vi got up and went with him around to the lean-to. Tree cut the apple into sixths and showed Vi how to hold her hand out straight, palm up, so that the horse could take the food with its lips and not hurt Vi's hand with its powerful teeth. Vi was nervous, but Elk, whose affections could always be bought with fresh apples, played the perfect lady and ate properly.

"Go ahead, scratch her neck," Tree said. "She likes that."

"Don't we all," Vi replied mostly to herself.

Vi petted the Appaloosa for awhile, then Tree closed the stall and they returned to the porch.

"I'll let you help me feed the wild things in the morning if you like," he offered.

"You don't have to."

"I don't want you to be mad."

"I'm not. I don't blame you for not trusting me."

"It's not that I don't trust you. It's just something I don't talk about. Not to anybody."

She was sitting in a shaft of light from the window and Tree saw her shrug. "Okay,"she said.

"I'm sorry."

Another shrug. "Sure."

They sat without speaking for ten minutes, listening to the night sounds of the cool, high-mountain evening. Finally Vi stood up. "I think I'll go to bed. Goodnight."

"Goodnight."

Tree remained on the porch for a long time, thinking about things—the vivid dangerous past, the nebulous, unsure future, and the clear, demanding present. He admitted to himself that he wanted the woman, then told himself in definite, forceful language that he could not have her. Alone is safest, he reminded himself. Alone is smartest. Alone is best.

He grunted softly. Alone was also loneliest.

It was midnight when he finally went inside, stripped down, and slid into his sleeping bag. But he couldn't sleep. It was as if he was waiting for something.

He was still awake when she came to him in the darkness.

At first they were skittish about her, made nervous by the sight and scent of her so close. But because they trusted Tree so completely, they gradually eased their way up to her. Soon she was kneeling in their midst just as Tree did, and they were nuzzling her hands, putting front paws up on her legs, making their individual little noises to get her attention. She learned that the mule deer and the pronghorn would nibble at her ears with their lips if she paid too much attention to the ground animals and not enough to them. Feeding the wild things was a decided thrill for Vi—she couldn't wait for the next day to feed them again.

"I want to feed them every morning!" she said with delight. Tree looked curiously at her and Vi's smile faded. "I forgot," she said. "I've only got two more mornings, haven't I? The bus comes over the mountain on Friday."

Tree nodded. "Yes. On Friday."

They went swimming that afternoon, in the same stream in which they'd fished the previous day. Vi thought she was going to freeze.

"It's like ice water!" she shrieked.

"It *is* ice water," Tree said, laughing. "It's melted snow from way up. Move around—you'll get warm."

She did move around, but she did not warm up. After five minutes she had to get out. Tree wrapped her in a blanket and left her on the bank while he swam for another quarter hour. When he came out, his tan body shone like the coats of the wild things who were his friends.

After their swim, they walked arm-in-arm back to the cabin and Tree built a fire. They stretched out on a Najavo blanket in front of the fireplace, chewed some peyote, slept, woke up and made love, and slept again.

That night, Tree said, "You don't want to leave, do you?"

Vi shrugged. "I don't want to mess with your life, Tree. You've got everything you want up here. The one thing you haven't got—well, it's available down on the Salmon River Reservation when you want it, and you don't have to bring it home with you." She looked away from him. "I think it would be bad for both of us if I stayed."

They didn't discuss it any further that night, each retreating into silence.

On Thursday morning, Tree was sick.

"My cooking," Vi said lightly. "Now you know why I've never married."

"Probably the peyote," he told her. "It gives you a great feeling but sometimes it raises hell with the digestive system. How's your stomach?"

"Fine. Let me mix you some cold powdered milk—that'll probably settle it."

The milk helped some, but later in the day he had severe nausea and a bad headache.

"Do you have any medicine up here at all?" Vi asked He directed her to a cabinet in the kitchen where he had aspirin, codeine, and Valium tablets. She gave him two of each and made him take a nap in the bedroom.

While he was sleeping, she went to the bookcase and took down the scrapbook he had hidden on top of it. She had watched through the window the night he had put it there. Opening it on the table, she read the newspaper clippings he had saved. The stories they told were different, but they all had common headlines: LABOR LEADER SLAIN, one read.

GANGLAND BOSS FOUND DEAD, read another.
WITNESS MURDERED IN HOTEL.
RACKETS INFORMER EXECUTED.
GAMBLER KILLED IN MIAMI.
The clippings had datelines covering a five-year period. The last one was dated six years earlier.

Tree came out of the bedroom while she still had the scrapbook open in front of her. He was very pale, but his eyes were still dark and dangerous. He was fully dressed and Vi couldn't tell whether he had his gun or not.

He sat down heavily across from her.

"You enjoy my press notices?" he asked.

Vi closed the scrapbook. "They ended six years ago. That was when you came to live up here. What happened?"

"They wanted me to hit a woman," he said. "A young woman with a brace on one leg, who was going into a convent of handicapped nuns who taught handicapped children. She was heir to a lot of money, but she was going to take a vow of poverty and give it all to the order she was joining. A cousin who was her only living relative bought the hit. Prior to then, I had never hit anybody but gangsters and punks—a stoolie now and then, a gambler who welshed on somebody. Now they wanted me to do a crippled young woman who never hurt nobody. They wanted me to run her down in the street so it'd look like a hit-and-run, an accident." Tree shook his head. "I couldn't do it. So I took off."

"And now there's a contract on *you*," Vi concluded.

"A big one," Tree confirmed. "And it keeps getting bigger every year." Suddenly he buried his face in his hands. "I'm sick, Vi—" he said weakly.

She helped him back to bed, mixed him some more powdered milk and made him eat a few soda crackers to see if that would help calm his stomach.

Sitting on the bed beside him, she felt his forehead. "No fever," she reported.

"Maybe it's the flu," he said. "My muscles and joints ache like hell."

After he ate, she massaged him where he hurt and gave him more aspirin and Valium. Then she tucked him in and stroked his cheek.

"How'd you get to be a—you know," she asked curiously.

"A paid killer?" Tree smiled wanly. "In the Army. I was a P.O.W. I did time with a Ranger captain who had mob connections. When we were exchanged and went home, he asked me to work for him. It sounded better than going back to the reservation." He reached up and touched her hand. "You won't go tomorrow, will you?"

"No. I won't leave you while you're sick."

He had a miserable night. Between bouts of diarrhea and vomiting, he was left weak and shaky. She helped him to and from bed, gave him more medication, more milk, more crackers. His muscle and joint aches agonized him all through the night—even codeine tablets failed to curb the pain.

Toward morning he still had no fever, but his pulse had become very weak and his eyes no longer looked threatening. When Vi took his gun from under his pillow where she had noticed it, he didn't complain—he knew he did not have the strength to fire it, anyway. Still, he was relieved to see her merely lay it on the nearby bureau and leave it there.

Two hours after sunup, he was breathing very lightly and was extremely pale. She was holding his head up, feeding him a little warm oatmeal.

"Feed them," he said feebly.

"I will," she assured him. "After I feed you. You're sick, they're not."

When he had eaten as much as she thought he could, she let his head back down and wiped his face with a damp cloth. She opened a window for him to get some fresh air and cleaned up the dishes they had used during the night. When she came back in to check on him he was barely awake. Just enough to say faintly, "The wild things—"

"All right," she said. "I'll do it right now."

He gave her a faint smile. She bent and kissed him lightly on the lips.

Out back, Vi got a bucket of pellet food from the storage locker and went over to where the animals waited. She held out her hand to them, but they would not come. They merely stared at her. She tossed a handful of food to them, but they didn't touch it. Maybe they smell the arsenic on my hands, she thought.

She shrugged, poured the bucket of food on the ground, and went back inside to see if Tree was in a coma yet.

NEBRASKA

I ALWAYS GET THE CUTIES
by John D. MacDonald

KEEGAN CAME INTO my apartment, frosted with winter, topcoat open, hat jammed on the back of his hard skull, bringing a noisy smell of the dark city night. He stood in front of my birch fire, his great legs planted, clapping and rubbing hard palms in the heat.

He grinned at me and winked one narrow gray eye. "I'm off duty, Doc. I wrapped up a package. A pretty package."

"Will bourbon do, Keegan?"

"If you haven't got any of that brandy left. This is a brandy night."

When I came back with the bottle and the glasses, he had stripped off his topcoat and tossed it on the couch. The crumpled hat was on the floor, near the discarded coat. Keegan had yanked a chair closer to the fire. He sprawled on the end of his spine, thick ankles crossed, the soles of his shoes steaming.

I poured his brandy and mine, and moved my chair and the long coffee table so we could share either end of it. It was bursting in him. I knew that. I've only had the vaguest hints about his home life. A house crowded with teen-age daughters, cluttered with their swains. Obviously no place to talk of his dark victories. And Keegan is not the sort of man to regale his co-workers with talk of his prowess. So I am, among other things, his sounding board. He bounces successes off the politeness of my listening, growing big in the echo of them.

"Ever try to haggle with a car dealer, Doc?" he asked.

"In a mild way."

"You are a mild guy. I tried once. Know what he told me? He said, 'Lieutenant, you try to make a car deal maybe once every two years. Me, I make ten a day. So what chance have you got?'"

This was a more oblique approach than Keegan generally used. I became attentive.

"It's the same with the cuties, Doc—the amateurs who think they can bring

272

off one nice clean safe murder. Give me a cutie every time. I eat 'em alive. The pros are trouble. The cuties leave holes you can drive diesels through. This one was that woman back in October. At that cabin at Bear Paw Lake. What do you remember about it, Doc?"

I am always forced to summarize. It has got me into the habit of reading the crime news. I never used to.

"As I remember, Keegan, they thought she had been killed by a prowler. Her husband returned from a business trip and found the body. She had been dead approximately two weeks. Because it was the off season, the neighboring camps weren't occupied, and the people in the village thought she had gone back to the city. She had been strangled, I believe."

"Okay. So I'll fill you in on it. Then you'll see the problem I had. The name is Grosswalk. Cynthia and Harold. He met her ten years ago when he was in med. school. He was twenty-four and she was thirty. She was loaded. He married her and he never went back to med. school. He didn't do anything for maybe five, six years. Then he gets a job selling medical supplies, surgical instruments, that kind of stuff. Whenever a wife is dead, Doc, the first thing I do is check on how they were getting along. I guess you know that."

"Your standard procedure," I said.

"Sure. So I check. They got a nice house here in the city. Not many friends. But they got neighbors with ears. There are lots of brawls. I get the idea it is about money. The money is hers—was hers, I should say. I put it up to this Grosswalk. He says okay, so they weren't getting along so good, so what? I'm supposed to be finding out who killed her, sort of coordinating with the State Police, not digging into his home life. I tell him he is a nice suspect. He already knows that. He says he didn't kill her. Then he adds one thing too many. He says he *couldn't* have killed her. That's all he will say. Playing it cute. You understand. I eat those cuties alive."

He waved his empty glass. I went over and refilled it.

"You see what he's doing to me, Doc. He's leaving it up to me to prove how it was he couldn't have killed her. A reverse twist. That isn't too tough. I get in touch with the sales manager of the company. Like I thought, the salesmen have to make reports. He was making a western swing. It would be no big trick to fly back and sneak into the camp and kill her, take some money and junk to make it look good, and then fly back out there and pick up where he left off. She was killed on maybe the tenth of October, the medical examiner says. Then he finds her on the twenty-fourth. But the sales manager tells me something that needs a lot of checking. He says that this Grosswalk took sick out west on the eighth and went into a hospital, and he was in that hospital from the eighth to the fifteenth, a full seven days. He gave me the name of the hospital. Now you see how the cutie made his mistake. He could have told me that easy enough. No, he has to be cute. I figure that if he's innocent he would have told me. But he's so proud of whatever gimmick he rigged for me that he's got to let me find out the hard way."

"I suppose you went out there," I said.

"It took a lot of talk. They don't like spending money for things like that. They kept telling me I should ask the L.A. cops to check because that's a good force out there. Finally I have to go by bus, or pay the difference. So I go by bus. I found the doctor. Plural—doctors. It is a clinic deal, sort of, that this Grosswalk went to. He gives them his symptoms. They say it looks to them like the edge of a nervous breakdown just beginning to show. With maybe some organic complications. So they run him through the course. Seven days of tests and checks and observations. They tell me he was there, that he didn't leave, that he *couldn't* have left. But naturally I check the hospital. They reserve part of one floor for patients from the clinic. I talked to the head nurse on that floor, and to the nurse that had the most to do with Grosswalk. She showed me the schedule and charts. Every day, every night, they were fooling around with the guy, giving him injections of this and that. He couldn't have got out. The people at the clinic told me the results. He was okay. The rest had helped him a lot. They told him to slow down. They gave him a prescription for a mild sedative. Nothing organically wrong, even though the symptoms seemed to point that way."

"So the trip was wasted?"

"Not entirely. Because on a hunch I ask if he had visitors. They keep a register. A girl came to see him as often as the rules permitted. They said she was pretty. Her name was Mary MacCarney. The address is there. So I go and see her. She lives with her folks. A real tasty kid. Nineteen. Her folks think this Grosswalk is too old for her. She is tall Irish, all black and white and blue. It was warm and we sat on the porch. I soon find out this Grosswalk has been feeding her a line, telling her that his wife is an incurable invalid not long for this world, that he can't stand hurting her by asking for a divorce, that it is better to wait, and anyway, she says, her parents might approve of a widower, but never a guy who has been divorced. She has heard from Grosswalk that his wife has been murdered by a prowler and he will be out to see her as soon as he can. He has known her for a year. But of course I have told him not to leave town. I tell her not to get her hopes too high because it begins to look to me like this Grosswalk has knocked off his wife. Things get pretty hysterical, and her old lady gets in on it, and even driving away in the cab I can hear her old lady yelling at her.

"The first thing I do on getting back is check with the doctor who took care of Mrs. Grosswalk, and he says, as I thought he would, that she was as healthy as a horse. So I go back up to that camp and unlock it again. It is a snug place, Doc. Built so you could spend the winter there if you wanted to. Insulated and sealed, with a big fuel-oil furnace, and modern kitchen equipment, and so on. It was aired out a lot better than the first time I was in it. Grosswalk stated that he hadn't touched a thing. He said it was unlocked. He saw her and backed right out and went to report it. And the only thing touched had been the body.

"I poked around. This time I took my time. She was a tidy woman. There are twin beds. One is turned down. There is a very fancy nightgown laid out. That is a thing which bothered me. I looked at her other stuff. She has pajamas which are the right thing for October at the lake. They are made from that flannel stuff. There is only one other fancy nightgown, way in the back of a drawer. I have found out here in the city that she is not the type to fool around. So how come a woman who is alone wants to sleep so pretty? Because the husband is coming back from a trip. But he couldn't have come back from the trip. I find another thing. I find deep ruts off in the brush beside the camp. The first time I went there, her car was parked in back. Now it is gone. If the car was run off where those ruts were, anybody coming to the door wouldn't see it. If the door was locked they wouldn't even knock maybe, knowing she wouldn't be home. That puzzles me. She might do it if she didn't want company. I prowl some more. I look in the deep freeze. It is well stocked. No need to buy stuff for a hell of a while. The refrigerator is the same way. And the electric is still on."

He leaned back and looked at me expectantly.

"Is that all you had to go on?" I asked.

"A murder happens here and the murderer is in Los Angeles at the time. I got him because he tried to be a cutie. Want to take a try, Doc?"

I knew I had to make an attempt. "Some sort of device?"

"To strangle a woman? Mechanical hands? You're getting too fancy, Doc."

"Then he hired somebody to do it?"

"There are guys you can hire, but they like guns. Or a piece of pipe in an alley. I don't know where you'd go to hire a strangler. He did it himself, Doc."

"Frankly, Keegan, I don't see how he could have."

"Well, I'll tell you how I went after it. I went to the medical examiner and we had a little talk. Cop logic, Doc. If the geography is wrong, then maybe you got the wrong idea on timing. But the medico checks it out. He says definitely the woman has been dead twelve days to two weeks when he makes the examination. I ask him how he knows. He says because of the extent of decomposition of the body. I ask him if that is a constant. He says no—you use a formula. A sort of rule-of-thumb formula. I ask him the factors. He says cause of death, temperature, humidity, physical characteristics of the body, how it was clothed, whether or not insects could have gotten to it, and so on.

"By then I had it, Doc. It was cute. I went back to the camp and looked around. It took me some time to find them. You never find a camp without them. Candles. They were in a drawer in the kitchen. Funny looking candles, Doc. Melted down, sort of. A flat side against the bottom of the drawer, and all hardened again. Then I had another idea. I checked the stove burners. I found some pieces of burned flaked metal down under the heating elements.

"Then it was easy. I had this Grosswalk brought in again. I let him sit in a cell for four hours and get nervous before I took the rookie cop in. I'd coached that rookie for an hour, so he did it right. I had him dressed in a leather jacket and work pants. I make him repeat his story in front of Grosswalk. 'I bought a chain saw last year,' he says, acting sort of confused, 'and I was going around to the camps where there are any people and I was trying to get some work cutting up fireplace wood. So I called on Mrs. Grosswalk. She didn't want any wood, but she was nice about it.' I ask the rookie when that was. He scratches his head and says, 'Sometime around the seventeenth I think it was.' That's where I had to be careful. I couldn't let him be positive about the date. I say she was supposed to be dead a week by then and was he sure it was her. 'She wasn't dead then. I know her. I'd seen her in the village. A kind of heavy-set woman with blonde hair. It was her all right, Lieutenant.' I asked him was he sure of the date and he said yes, around the seventeenth like he said, but he could check his records and find the exact day.

"I told him to take off. I just watched that cutie and saw him come apart. Then he gave it to me. He killed her on the sixteenth, the day he got out of the hospital. He flew into Omaha. By then I've got the stenographer taking it down. Grosswalk talks, staring at the floor, like he was talking to himself. It was going to be a dry run. He wasn't going to do it if she'd been here in the city or into the village in the previous seven days. But once she got in the camp she seldom went out, and the odds were all against any callers. On his previous trip to Omaha he had bought a jalopy that would run. It would make the fifty miles to the lake all right. He took the car off the lot where he'd left it and drove to the lake. She was surprised to see him back ahead of schedule. He explained the company car was being fixed. He questioned her. Finally she said she hadn't seen or talked to a living soul in ten days. Then he knew he was set to take the risk.

"He grabbed her neck and hung on until she was dead. He had his shoulders hunched right up and around his ears when he said that. It was evening when he killed her, nearly bedtime. First he closed every window. Then he turned on the furnace as high as it would go. There was plenty of oil in the tank. He left the oven door open and the oven turned as high as it would go. He even built a fire in the fireplace, knowing it would be burned out by morning and there wouldn't be any smoke. He filled the biggest pans of water he could find and left them on the top of the stove. He took money and some of her jewelry, turned out the lights and locked the doors. He ran her car off in the brush where nobody would be likely to see it. He said by the time he left the house it was like an oven in there.

"He drove the jalopy back to Omaha, parked it back in the lot, and caught an 11:15 flight to Los Angeles. The next morning he was making calls. And keeping his fingers crossed. He worked his way east. He got to the camp on the twenty-fourth—about 10 in the morning. He said he went in and turned things off and opened up every window, and then went out and was sick. He waited nearly an hour before going back in. It was nearly down to normal temperature. He checked the house. He noticed she had turned down both beds before he killed her. He remade his. The water had boiled out of the pans and the bottoms had burned through. He scaled the pans out into the lake. He said he tried not to look at her, but he couldn't help it. He had enough medical background to know that it had worked, and also to fake his own illness in L. A. He went out and was sick again, and then he got her car back where it belonged. He closed most of the windows. He made another inspection trip and then drove into the village. He's a cutie, Doc, and I ate him alive."

There was a long silence. I knew what was expected of me. But I had my usual curious reluctance to please him. He held the glass cradled in his hand, gazing with a half smile into the dying fire. His face looked like stone.

"That was very intelligent, Keegan," I said.

"The pros give you real trouble, Doc. The cuties always leave holes. I couldn't bust geography, so I had to bust time." He yawned massively and stood up. "Read all about it in the morning paper, Doc."

"I'll certainly do that."

I held his coat for him. He's a big man. I had to reach up to get it properly onto his shoulders. He mashed the hat onto his head as I walked to the door with him. He put his big hand on the knob, turned, and smiled down at me without mirth.

"I always get the cuties, Doc. Always."

"You certainly seem to," I said.

"They are my favorite meat."

"So I understand."

He balled one big fist and bumped it lightly against my chin, still grinning at me. "And I'm going to get you too, Doc. You know that. You were cute. You're just taking longer than most. But you know how it's going to come out, don't you?"

I don't answer that any more. There's nothing to say. There hasn't been anything to say for a long time now.

He left, walking hard into the wild night. I sat and looked into my fire. I could hear the wind. I reached for the bottle. The wind raged over the city, as monstrous and inevitable as Keegan. It seemed as though it was looking for food—the way Keegan is always doing.

But I no longer permit myself the luxury of imagination.

NEVADA

PAYOFF ON DOUBLE ZERO
by Warner Law

ALTHOUGH SHE WAS typing from her shorthand notes, the middle-aged secretary kept sneaking glances at Sam Miller across the outer office. He was waiting to see her boss, Mr. Collins, who was the owner and manager of the casino in the Starlight Hotel. This is a relatively old establishment, not far out of town on the Las Vegas Strip.

To women in general, and to middle-aged secretaries in particular, Sam was almost surrealistically handsome, too all-American to believe in one look. He was in his early 20s, well over six feet tall, broad in the shoulders and lithe below. His blond hair was cut short, his face was tanned, his nose perfectly straight, his teeth white, his smile a gift of pleasure. His eyes were true blue and his gaze was of such clear and steady honesty that it made even a secretary with a pure conscience and a fine Methodist background feel somewhat shifty and sinful when she met it. She knew that Mr. Collins would be eager to hire Sam—though he'd pretend he wasn't and he'd give the boy a little hard time first. The Starlight needed dealers and rarely did they find one who was such a poster picture of integrity. More than that, Sam's looks would draw most of the women gamblers in Vegas, the younger ones with an urge to bed him and the older ones with an impulse to mother him. Then the intercom buzzed and Mr. Collins said that he was ready to see Mr. Miller.

Sam went in and carefully shut the door behind him. Mr. Collins posed behind his massive desk, right hand extended, a smile of limited cordiality on his face. Sam had heard that Mr. Collins was Balkan by birth, with a name of many jagged syllables that had been carefully naturalized and neutralized. He was a man in his 60s, olive in coloring, wearing a light-gray silk suit exactly shaded to match his hair.

Sam shook his hand and smiled and said, "How do you do, sir?"

"It's a pleasure to meet you, Sam Miller. Sit down. Tell me the story of your life." Mr. Collins had only a trace of a foreign accent.

278

Sam sat. "All of it?"

"Well, it can scarcely have been a very long life. How old are you?"

"Twenty-two, sir."

"Might I see your driver's license?"

"Sure." Sam took it from his wallet and handed it over the desk and Mr. Collins gave it a quick glance and passed it back.

"Have you ever been arrested?"

"No, sir."

"Be certain, now. The rules of the Nevada Gaming Commission require me to check."

"No, sir. I've never been arrested for anything."

"Why do you wish to be a dealer?"

"To make some money and save it, so I can go to college full time."

"Where do you come from originally?"

"I was born in Los Angeles and I went to Hollywood High, and then I enlisted in the Marine Corps, rather than be drafted."

"What did you do in the Marine Corps?"

"I got sent to Vietnam."

"Did anything happen to you?"

"Yes. I got shot three times."

"You have my profound sympathy. Were they serious wounds?"

"One was. It was in the stomach. The others were just flesh wounds. Anyway, I finally got discharged last summer."

"Do you happen to have your discharge papers on your person?"

Sam produced them and Mr. Collins looked them over and handed them back.

"And after your discharge?"

"My uncle had a liquor store in Hollywood and I went to work for him. But we were held up four times. Twice I got clobbered with revolver butts and once I was shot in the foot, and finally my uncle was pistol-whipped and he said the hell with it and sold the store and I was out of a job."

"You've crowded a good deal of action into your short life."

Sam smiled. "Not intentionally. And then somebody suggested I might get a job dealing up here in Las Vegas, and my math was always pretty good, and so I came up and took a course at Mr. Ferguson's Dealers' School and, as you've seen from the diploma your secretary brought in, I graduated yesterday."

Mr. Collins picked up the diploma and handed it to Sam. "Why did you come here—that is, instead of to some other casino?"

"Mr. Ferguson said he thought you might be hiring dealers and that you were a good man to work for. He also said that you were the smartest man in Vegas."

"Did he, now? It's the first I've heard of it. As it happens, however, I've been talking to Ferguson on the phone about you. He says you were one of the best students he's had in a long time. How is your roulette?"

"Pretty fair, I think."

"We shall see. A little test. Thirty-two has come up," Mr. Collins began, and then rattled on with, "and a player has two chips straight up on it, one split, two chips on corners, four chips on three across and three chips on the first column. How many chips do you pay this player?"

It took Sam four seconds to answer, "A hundred and forty-seven."

"You forgot the column bet."

"No, sir. I didn't. You said the first column. Thirty-two is in the second column." Sam smiled a little. "Which you very well know."

Mr. Collins did not smile. "These are quarter chips. How much has the player won?"

"Seven stacks plus seven. Thirty-six seventy-five."

Now Mr. Collins smiled. "Can you start work this afternoon at four? That's the middle shift—four till midnight."

"Yes, sir."

"You'll get forty dollars per shift, plus your share of the dealers' tips. Like most casinos, we pool them and whack them up evenly. You'll average around two-fifty, two-seventy-five for a forty-hour week. Is that satisfactory?"

"Yes, sir." Sam rose as if to leave.

"Sit down. I have something to tell you. I and I alone own the gaming license here. I am not answerable to anyone. I have no connection with the Mafia nor any other bunch of criminals. We do not cheat our players, we do not cheat the Nevada Gaming Commission and we do not cheat the Internal Revenue Service. Furthermore, if any dealer tries to cheat the house in favor of himself or a player, he gets no mercy from me."

"Mr. Ferguson told me you ran an honest game."

"It is *more* than an honest game. A little test. Number seven has come up. Having made sure that the number is not covered, you clear the board of chips. But then a player says, 'Just a minute, here! I had a chip on seven, but you took it away!' You know for certain that this player is lying through his teeth. What do you do?"

"Well . . . I'd send for my pit boss."

"No. You apologize to the player and you pay him. Only if the player does this more than once do you call for your pit boss—who will have been at your side by that time, anyway. The point I am making is that as far as *you* are concerned, every player is honest, and he is always right. You are not a policeman and you are not a detective. That is the job of your pit boss and it is also my job. *It is not yours.*"

"Yes, sir."

Mr. Collins rose and extended his hand. "Nice to have you with us. Keep your hands off our cocktail waitresses. There are plenty of other pretty girls in this town."

At 3:45 that afternoon, Sam walked again into the Starlight Hotel. Being one of the older Strip hotels, it was not a large one. The casino itself was a separate wing. People came to play there because it was neither noisy nor garish, like the newer and much larger Strip casinos. The slots were in a separate room, so their clatter did not disturb the serious gamblers. On the depressed oval that was the casino floor, there were two crap tables, three 21 tables and three roulette tables. There was no wheel of fortune and no bingo and no race-track betting. This was a casino for players who appreciated quiet. Even the stickmen at the crap tables kept their continuous chatter down.

Sam didn't know where to report for work, but he found a small bar through an archway on the upper level of the room and went in and inquired of the barman, whose name turned out to be Chuck. He told Sam how to find the dealers' room.

Sam followed a corridor to the rear of the building, where he found a room with some wall lockers and a few easy chairs and tables. Other dealers were there, hanging up their jackets and putting on their green aprons. A scrawny little man in a dark suit came up to Sam. He looked 50 and had a sour, sallow face.

"Sam Miller?"

"Yes, sir."

"I'm Pete and I'm your pit boss on this shift." He turned to the other dealers. "Boys, this is Sam Miller." They grunted friendly greetings. "You'll get to know 'em all," Pete told Sam. "But this is Harry." He took Sam over to meet a tall man of 70 with weary eyes. "You'll be working together. You can begin by stacking for Harry tonight."

"Pleased to meet you, sonny boy," Harry said and shook Sam's hand and looked at him and reacted. "My God—you look fifteen years old."

In the casino, Sam found that his roulette-table setup was almost identical with the one in Ferguson's school. There were six stools along the players' side of the table. By the wheel on the dealer's right were stacks of chips in different colors—white, red, green, blue, brown and yellow. They were all marked STAR-LIGHT but had no stated value. Since the minimum bet was a quarter, their value was so presumed.

Past the colors were stacks of dollar tokens. These were of base metal, minted for the casino. To the right of the tokens were stacks of house checks, with marked denominations of five dollars ranging upward to $50. The casino also had house checks worth $100 and $500 and $1,000, but these were seldom seen in any quantity at a roulette table.

In front of the dealer was a slot in which rested a plastic shingle, and when players bought chips with currency, the bills were shoved down through the slot and into the locked cashbox under the table.

Since this was now the end of a shift, Mr. Collins came up with his keys and an empty cashbox. He exchanged one box for the other and walked off with the full one toward the cashier's office, followed by an armed and uniformed security guard.

For the first hour, Sam merely stacked the chips and the occasional checks that Harry shoved over to him. It was a quiet game, without plungers or cheaters or arguments. Then Harry went off for a break and Sam took over the dealing.

Not long after, a woman came up to Sam's table. She was in her 50s, tall and scrawny, and her mouth held more than her share of the world's teeth. She was wearing a gold-lamé blouse over orange slacks. She sounded rather drunk as she said, "Gimme a coupla stacksa quarters." She handed Sam a ten-dollar bill. He slotted the money and passed her two stacks of red chips. "I don' like red," she said. "It doesn't go with my slacks. You got another color?"

"How about green?" Sam asked her, smiling.

"Green is jus' fine," she said and soon picked up the two stacks Sam put in front of her.

Sam started the ball whirring.

"I been playin' this roulette for years and years," the woman announced to the table at large, "an' there's no such thing as a system. No such thing as a system! You just gotta let the chips fall where they may, as the fella said!"

She then turned her back to the table, with 20 chips in each hand, and tossed them all over her shoulders onto the board. They clattered down every which way and knocked other bets out of position, and a great many of the chips rolled off the table and onto the floor. The other players cried out in annoyance. Sam removed the ball from the wheel. Pete started over, pausing to push one of several buttons on a small table in the center of the enclosure.

"I'm sorry, ma'am," Sam told the woman, "but we can't bet that way."

She giggled. "I'm jus' lettin' the chips fall where they may!"

"Even so," Sam said with an engaging smile, "if your bets aren't in correct positions, I won't know how to pay you when you win."

The other players had been patiently bending over and retrieving green chips from the floor. Sam gathered them and stacked them for her and made sure they were all there.

"I'm real sorry to make all this trouble," the woman said, smiling at Sam. "Let's see, now, most of 'em fell around twenny, so that's where I'll kinda put 'em. Around twenny." With drunken carefulness, she began to slather her chips around number 20.

In the distance, Sam saw Mr. Collins approaching from his office—where he had just heard the warning buzz from Pete. He walked up and stood at the head of the table, but said nothing.

Sam put the ball in motion. The woman watched it spin. "It's just got to be twenny," she said. "Or else I am bankrupt!"

The ball fell into number 20. "Ooooooh!" She jumped up and down and clapped her hands. "I won! I won!"

Sam counted the green chips on the board. "Six straight up on twenty, nine splits, ten on corners. That's four hundred and forty-three chips, plus these twenty-five left on the board."

"How much is that in money?" the woman asked.

"One hundred and seventeen dollars," Sam said.

Mr. Collins had come up behind her. "My congratulations, Mrs. Burke," he said.

She turned. "Oh, dear Mr. Collins. How are you?"

"It's always such a pleasure to see you here," Mr. Collins said. "As a matter of fact, I've been meaning to call you. Before you break the bank, why don't you cash in and come and have a drink with me? I need your advice about a piece of real estate."

In moments, Mrs. Burke had been paid her winnings and was walking off happily on Mr. Collins' arm. Under the chatter of the players, Pete murmured to Sam, "Very nicely handled, son. What Howard Hughes and Kerkorian don't own in Vegas, Mrs. Burke does."

On Sam's second night of dealing, nothing whatever happened. But on his third night, there was trouble.

A fat-faced young man with a sullen mouth and pimples had been betting regularly on 14 and losing. He was playing with ten-dollar house checks, but he didn't look as if he could afford them, and he kept increasing his bets until he was up to $50 a spin, straight up on 14. Despair came into his eyes.

This time, 15 came up. There was no bet on it. Sam cleared the board.

"Hold on, there!" the young man said."What about my fifty on fifteen?"

Sam smiled politely. "I think it was on fourteen, sir."

Pete had already pushed a button and was at Sam's side.

"Not this time it wasn't!" the young man said. "I finally got tired of fourteen and bet on fifteen. You were just so used to seeing me bet on fourteen that you made a mistake, that's all."

Eighteen hundred dollars was involved. Sam glanced over at Pete, but before the pit boss could speak, a distinguished-looking white-haired man at the very end of the table called to Sam. "I'm afraid the young man up there is right." His manner was reluctant and apologetic. "I'm sorry to be difficult, but I did see him bet on fifteen. I wondered at the time if he'd made a mistake or was changing his number after all this time."

The smartest man in Vegas had by now come up behind the bettor. "Pay the bet, Sam," he said. "I want no arguments here."

"Yes, sir," Sam said and reached for some checks.

Pete stopped him with a hand and said, "We don't have that much here at the table, Mr. Collins."

This was not true.

"Oh?" said Mr. Collins. "Well, let's go to my office, then. If you and your friend would come with me, I'll see that—"

"My *friend?*" the young man asked. "Why, I've never—"

The older man said from the foot of the table, "I've never seen that young fellow before in my life!"

"Oh?" Mr. Collins looked surprised. "I'm sorry. I'd presumed you two were friends."

"I never laid eyes on that gentleman before in my life!" the young man said.

"I understand," said Mr. Collins. "However, sir," he said to the older man, "I'll need a brief statement from you affirming that you saw the bet being placed. It's required by the Nevada Gaming Commission in these instances."

This was rubbish.

The older man sighed and picked up his chips and came round the table and offered his hand and a smile to the young man and said, "My name is John Wood."

"I'm George Wilkins and I'm real sorry to put you to all this trouble, but thank you for sticking up for me. What I mean"—he nodded toward Sam—"young fellows like this are obviously so new they make normal mistakes."

Sam wished he could knock this young man down and kick his teeth out. The two walked away with Mr. Collins. They did not return to the casino floor. When midnight came and Sam went off duty, he passed Mr. Collins on the upper level and asked him, "What happened to those two cheaters?"

Mr. Collins smiled. "Why do you so presume, Sam?"

"Because there was no bet on fifteen and anybody who said otherwise is a liar."

Laughing, Mr. Collins said, "Sam, you wouldn't believe how stupid some people can be. I asked to see their driver's licenses, as a matter of form. Without thinking, they showed them to me. What do you think I learned?"

"Don't tell me they have the same name?!"

"No, no. But their addresses showed that they live two houses apart. In Van Nuys, California."

"My God! What did you do to them?"

"Nothing. I left them alone in my office for a minute and when I came back, they were gone. I presume they're well back in California by now." The smartest man in Vegas patted Sam on the shoulder and said, "Good night, Sam," and walked off.

It was around 11 on Sam's fourth night that things really began to happen. Sam was dealing and Harry was stacking for him. The table was crowded and all the colors were in use. Behind the seated players, others stood, betting with coins and house checks. As the ball began to slow, Sam said. "No more bets, please."

A man started shouting, "Let me through! Here, now—let me through! Get out of the way, damn it!"

He was a tall man in his 70s and he wore a white Stetson. He had a white mustache under a long red nose. He shouldered his way through the standers. He held two packages of bank-strapped currency above his head and when he reached the table, he threw them both in the general area of number 23 and announced, "That's two thousand dollars right smack on twenty-three! Straight up!"

Sam quickly picked up the packs and tossed them off the betting area. "I'm sorry, sir." The ball fell into number 11.

The old man's reedy voice rose above the murmur at the table. "What's the matter, young fella? Something the matter with my money?" He was wearing a white-silk Western shirt and an apache tie with a gold tie slide in the shape of a nugget, and over all he had on a spotless white-buckskin suit with long fringes and with stitched patch pockets high and low. Sam had seen a similar suit in a Las Vegas store window for $295.

"This is perfectly good money!" the old man said, showing off the two packs.

They contained $100 bills, which, as Sam knew, usually come from a bank strapped in units of ten. These looked to be fresh from the Bureau of Engraving and Printing.

Sam smiled at the old man. "Of course it is, sir. But, for one thing, you were too late for this roll; and for another, there's a two-hundred-dollar maximum bet on the numbers; and for still another, we don't use paper money on this table."

"Well, sell me some chips, damn it!"

"I will sir, but we're out of colors and—"

Pete had come to the table and he now asked, "What denomination would you like to play with, sir?"

"Hundreds! Hundred-dollar chips, if you've got 'em." Everyone at the table was now listening and the old man turned and smiled and said, "My name's Premberton! Bert Premberton! From up Elko way! Pleased to make your acquaintance!" He shook hands with those whom he could reach.

"I'll have to get some hundred-dollar checks from the cashier, Mr. Premberton," Pete said. "How many would you like?"

"Well, now. . . ." The old man pondered and brought out package after package of strapped $100s from his various pockets and stacked them on the table in front of him. Twenty thousand dollars was visible. There was a stunned silence around the table. "Sold a ranch today." Premberton told everyone simply. "Or it finally got through escrow, I should say." To Pete, he said, "Oh, hell. Let's just start with two thousand. But get plenty, while you're at it." He handed Sam two packages of $100s and stuffed the others back into his pockets.

Sam handed them to Pete, who broke the paper straps and fanned the bills and nodded and said, "Two thousand. I'll be right back."

"Here, now!" the old man bellowed. "What if twenty-three comes up while you're gone, hey? I want two hundred on it, every time. Twenty-three is gonna be a hot one tonight, I can tell you for true!"

"You'll be covered on every roll, Mr. Premberton," Pete said, starting off.

"Take over for me," Sam told Harry and walked after Pete, catching up with him outside the roulette enclosure. "Pete?" The pit boss stopped and turned. "I don't like this old man," Sam said. "I've got a kind of feeling about him."

"Why?"

"Well, for one thing, he's been drinking, and I didn't like the way he butted his way to the table, and—well, I just don't trust him is all."

"It is not your job to trust people. As long as his money's good, I don't care if—"

But maybe it isn't. Maybe it's—"

Mr. Collins had walked up to them. "Troubles?"

"Maybe it's counterfeit," Sam finished.

Pete smiled. "You have got to be kidding."

Mr. Collins took the bills from Pete and ruffled through them and handed them back and motioned the pit boss toward the cashier's window. Then he sighed.

"Sam, you still have a good deal to learn. For all practical purposes—as far as we are concerned—there is no such thing as a hundred-dollar bill that is counter-feit. Oh, they do exist, but they're extremely rare, for the reason that printers don't bother with them because they're so difficult to pass. We get fives and tens and twenties and now and then a fifty. But I don't think I've seen a funny hundred in twenty years. In any case, there are two places in which no one but an idiot would deliberately pass even *one* phony hundred-dollar bill, and one is a bank and the other is a casino. Both places have smart cashiers and men with guns."

"I'm sorry," Sam said. "I didn't know that. I was only trying to protect the house."

"It is not your job to protect the house. I thought I'd made that perfectly clear when we first met. Would you get back to your table now, please?"

"Yes, sir."

Pete came up to them, carrying a plastic rack nearly full of $100 house checks. "I got quite a few, just in case," he said. "And to make our boy detective here happy, I asked both Ruth and Hazel to check out those bills; they're both experts in the currency department, and they assure me that the twenty hundreds are the genuine article, with the serial numbers in sequence, just as they left the Bureau of Engraving and Printing."

"I'm sorry to be so stupid," Sam said and followed Pete back to the table, where he and the pit boss piled the checks neatly in stacks of 20. Harry reached for one stack, knocked off four checks and handed the remaining 16 to Prember-ton, saying "Two thousand, sir, less four hundred for the last two rolls."

The old man grunted his understanding and placed two checks on 23. He then began looking around the casino as if for someone, finally saw her, put two fingers into his mouth and produced a shrill whistle. He waved a hand and shouted, "Over here, honey!"

A girl came toward the table and tried to get through the crowd. "Let her through, there!" the old man cried. "That's my little bride, there! Let her through, damn it!"

People gave way and the girl soon joined Premberton, who hugged and kissed her. The girl blushed and said, "Oh, Bert! Not here!"

The girl was spectacularly lovely. She was in her early 20s and had golden hair and large young breasts. Her mouth was full and sensuous, but her wide blue eyes gave her an expression of innocence.

"Folks! I want you to meet my sweet little honey bunch, Vikki!" He kissed her again and hugged her and then ran his hand up and around her buttocks. "We got hitched this very mornin'!" There was a silence around the table, partly of incredulity and partly of disapproval. "And the reason twenty-three is goin' to be a hot number tonight is that today is February the twenty-third and it's also my own little hot number here's birthday, and she's twenty-three this very day! What do you think of that?" Premberton turned to Harry and asked, "You're sure, now, that two hundred is all I can bet at a time?"

"Yes, sir," Harry said as the ball slowed. "That's our limit." The ball dropped once and bounced about and finally fell into 23 and remained there. "Twenty-three," Harry announced and smiled at Vikki. "Happy birthday, young lady."

"Hey, now!" the old man shouted and clapped everyone he could reach on the back. "What'd I tell you? Twenty-three's goin' to be a hot number tonight!"

Harry pushed three and a half stacks over to the old man. "Seventy checks, sir. Seven thousand dollars."

The other players started exclaiming in excitement and people who heard the commotion began to crowd around the table to watch. Premberton told Vikki to open her shoulder bag and he dumped the 70 checks into it. "You'll get that Rolls-Royce automobile for a weddin' present yet, honey bunch!" Then, to Harry, "Say, now! My little bride here can play, too, can't she?'

"Surely, sir," Harry said.

"Well, you jest do that, Vikki honey! You put two hundred on twenty-three along with me, you hear?"

After the old man had bet his two checks, Vikki added two more from her purse. Harry turned to Sam. "Take over for a couple of minutes, would you?" Harry walked off and Sam stepped into his place and Pete came up to stack for Sam. Other players began piling chips onto 23. Sam set the ball spinning. It eventually fell into number five.

"You got to do better'n that, young fella!" the old man shouted.

Sam smiled at him. "I'm trying, sir, I really am."

"I sure wish we could bet more than four hundred," the old man said. "Twenty-three is sure goin' to be a hot one tonight!"

A man standing next to Premberton volunteered: "You can also play splits if you want to, sir, and corners and three across."

"How's that?"

Using his finger as a pointer, the man showed him what he meant.

"Well, I'm jest goin' to bet that way, then!" He started to cover the board all around 23 and then said, "I'm goin' to need some more chips, young fella." He brought out three more packs of $100s and handed them to Sam, who broke the straps and counted the bills.

"Three thousand," Sam announced and slotted the money. Then he reached for the stack and a half Pete had ready for him and passed the checks to the old man, who finished covering 23 and its surrounding numbers. As the ball whirred, Sam figured that if 23 came up, the Prembertons would win $20,200. The number turned out to be 22, but the old man had $5000 coming to him because of his bets on splits and corners and three across. When Sam passed his winnings to him, the old man dumped them into Vikki's purse and bet again as before. The next three numbers were losers for Premberton, who was then almost out of visible checks.

"Better give me five thousand this time, young fella," he said, bringing five packages of money from his pocket. It was slotted and Sam gave him two and a half stacks. Harry returned and took over the stacking from Pete. The ball fell into 24. Sam paid the old man another 50 checks, and these, too, went into Vikki's purse.

"Start thinkin' what color you want that Rolls-Royce automobile painted, honey bunch."

The next two numbers were zero and 36 and Premberton was down again in checks. "Five thousand more, young fella." The money came out and was counted and sent down into the cashbox and the old man got his two and a half stacks.

"Take over for me?" Sam asked Harry. To Pete as he passed, Sam said. "Got to take a leak." He crossed the casino floor and went up to the upper level, where Mr. Collins was standing, his eyes in constant motion as he surveyed and studied the activity below.

"How is it going, Sam?"

"Mr. Collins, I don't like what's going on at my table."

"Oh? Troubles?"

"Well, whenever that old man wins, he dumps his checks into his wife's bag, but when he loses, he cashes some more of his hundred-dollar bills."

"So?"

"She has close to seventeen thousand in there right now."

"So?" Mr. Collins shrugged. "Sam, some players feel luckier when they're playing with house money and others prefer to pocket our money and play with their own. It's their business. It is not yours."

"I know. But I keep getting the feeling there's something phony about the old man. I mean, as if he were Walter Brennan, playing a rich old rancher. Except that Walter Brennan would convince me and this Mr. Premberton doesn't. It's like he's overacting his part. And the way he fondles that pretty little girl who's young enough to be his granddaughter—well, it makes you kind of sick."

Mr. Collins smiled. "I see. It's not just a roulette dealer I've hired. I have in addition a drama critic and an arbiter of morals." His smile faded. "Has this old gentleman tried any funny business with his bets?"

"Well, no. Not yet, anyway."

"Nor will he. Sam. I'll tell you how to spot a potential cheater on sight. When an ordinary player comes into this casino, he will glance around casually and then decide where he wants to go and go there. But when a cheater comes in— and by this I mean someone who has cheated before elsewhere and may well do so here—he will stop and look carefully at the face of every dealer and pit boss on the floor, for fear he'll be recognized from the past. When I see this, I make sure that this player is watched every minute he's here."

"That's very interesting," Sam said. "I'd never thought of that."

"I saw this old man walk down from the bar. He looked around for the nearest roulette table and hurried to it. In addition, it happens that Chuck the bartender knows him. He's from up near Elko and he recently sold one of his ranches, which is why he has all this bank cash on him. Also, he got married this morning and he's celebrating."

"He told us, at the table."

"All right. Sam, I will tell you one more time and only one more time: The overall problems involved in running this casino are mine. They are not yours. Please don't make me lose my patience with you."

"No, sir. I'm sorry." Sam walked off and into the men's room and in a couple of minutes came out. As he passed the archway leading to the bar he paused and then went in. There were few customers and Chuck was drying glasses.

"Hi, Sammy boy."

Sam said, "Chuck—this old man—this Mr. Premberton. Mr. Collins says you know him."

Chuck nodded. "He's a rancher from up near Elko. He got married this—"

Sam cut in with, "But do you know him? From before, I mean?"

"Well, no, but—"

"So how do you know so much about him?"

"He was in here earlier, talking to people, buying everybody drinks, showing off his new little wife—you know."

"Thanks, Chuck." Sam walked out of the bar and down to his table. Pete moved away, so that Sam could take over the stacking. From the stacks of $100 checks, it was apparent that Premberton had lost a few thousand while Sam had been away. Now the old man handed Harry another five packages of $100s, which went down the slot.

Sam passed two and half stacks to Harry, who said, "You mind rolling? I'm really beat."

"Sure." As Sam took Harry's place, he glanced at his watch and saw that it was 11:45. In 15 minutes the shift would end.

Number 34 came up, and then six. One of the players had given up his seat to Vikki, who now sat directly across from Sam. "Whatever happened to number twenty three?" she asked with a smile. It began as a casual smile, but then she glanced up and saw that the old man was engrossed in betting and she looked at Sam and smiled, but directly now. With this smile, all innocence left her eyes.

Sam indicated 23. "I'm afraid it's hidden under all those chips."

"Well, see if you can find it for us."

Sam sent the ball spinning. "I'll do my very best, Mrs. Premberton." The number turned out to be 26. Sam gave the old man 33 checks, which Vikki dumped into her bag. There had to be over $20,000 in that bag by now, but then, almost as much had come out of Premberton's pockets.

The next two numbers were two and 12. The old man was out of checks again. "Gimme some of them chips, Vikki, honey."

"Oh, Bert. Don't you think we should stop? It's been a long day and it's almost midnight, and—"

"Jest one more roll. I got a hunch it'll be twenty-three."

Vikki passed a handful of checks to Premberton, who leaned over the table to bet and then silently collapsed and fell onto the table and lay still. When it was plain that he wasn't going to move, Vikki cried out and reached over and touched him.

Others at the table were saying, "Is he dead?" "He's had a heart attack!" "Get a doctor, somebody!"

Pete had already pushed buttons. Two security guards hurried up, herded people aside and got to the old man, who now groaned and opened his eyes and managed to push himself erect. The guards held him up.

"What happened?" Premberton asked.

Mr. Collins hurried up. "Help him to my office," he told the guards. "The hotel doctor is on his way."

"I'm all right,' Premberton said. "Jest had a little dizzy spell."

"I insist," said Mr. Collins.

The guards started off with the old man. Vikki followed, but Sam called, "Don't forget your husband's checks, Mrs. Premberton." Sam hadn't started the ball rolling. He picked up the old man's bets and handed them to her.

"Thank you. You're very kind." She hurried off toward Mr. Collins's office.

The table quieted down as Sam started the ball rolling. "How did they do, all told?" Sam asked Harry.

He studied the stacks of checks by the wheel and said, "They're up a hundred. It's getting close to midnight, thank the saints. I'm really beat."

In a few minutes, after the graveyard shift had come onto the floor, Sam and Harry walked up to the higher level, where they met Mr. Collins coming out of his office.

"How's the old man?" Harry asked.

"All right, the doctor says. It was just a faint. His wife tells me he had no dinner and a lot of drinks, and I gathered that they'd spent the afternoon in bed."

"It kind of turns your stomach," Sam said. "That old man and that little girl."

"It may turn yours, sonny boy," Harry said sourly. "But I ain't quite dead yet and it don't turn mine." He walked off.

"They ended a hundred to the good," Sam told Mr. Collins.

"I'm just relieved it was nothing more serious than a faint."

"Do you suppose he can get back to their motel all right?" Sam asked.

"That's for *me* to worry about, Sam," Mr. Collins said in a warning tone.

"Sorry," Sam said and walked away.

In the dealers' room, Sam hung up his apron and chatted with some of the dealers and combed his hair and put on his jacket and then went into the bar and ordered a beer. He enjoyed it, and ordered another, and was starting on that when Mr. Collins came into the bar and up to him.

"Sam, the old man wants to see you."

"Me? Why? How is he?"

"All right. They're about to leave."

Sam followed Mr. Collins into his office, where Premberton was striding around, a highball in hand. Vikki was sitting, also with a drink.

"Hello there, young fella!" the old man said.

"How do you feel sir?" Sam asked.

"Fit as a fiddle. I'm terribly sorry about causin' all that commotion at your table. And I meant to leave you a little tip. Gimme a hundred, Vikki." She did and the old man handed a check to Sam.

"Thanks very much, sir. And I hope that you and Mrs. Premberton will have a very happy marriage."

Mr. Collins said, "You'll have to excuse me. It's the end of a shift and I have to go and collect the cash from the tables."

"We're jest leavin' ourselves, sir," Premberton said. "Let's go cash in, Vikki honey, and see if we've won anything."

The four left the office together and Sam said good night to the Prembertons, who went off toward the cashier. Mr. Collins said to Sam, "The tip goes in the box."

Sam nodded and smiled and walked down to the floor and dropped the check into the dealers' tip box. Mr. Collins watched this and nodded approval and walked into the cashier's office.

Sam went back to the bar to finish his beer. Through the archway he saw the Prembertons cashing in. Mr. Collins came out with some empty cashboxes and gave the couple a smile and started off for the tables. Soon Sam saw the old man and the girl walk out of the casino, arm in arm. In a few minutes, Sam finished his beer, left the casino and drove off up the Strip.

After about two miles, he came to the Slumbertime Motel and parked. He got out and walked along a ground-level porch to room 17. A light was on inside. Sam knocked. A man opened the door.

"Yes?" he asked.

Sam frowned. "I'm looking for Mr. Haskins."

"He must be in another room."

"No. He lives here, in seventeen. Or did."

"Well, I checked in here at ten tonight and he wasn't here then."

"I'm sorry to have bothered you," Sam said and hurried down the porch to the office, where he pinged the desk bell. In a moment, a man in a bathrobe came from a rear room. "I'm looking for Mr. Haskins and his granddaughter," Sam said. "They were in seventeen and sixteen."

"They checked out."

"They *did?*"

"About nine tonight."

"Oh. Did—did they leave anything for me? For Sam Miller?"

"Yes, they did." The manager found an envelope and looked at it. " 'For Sam Miller.' " Sam took the envelope, thanked him and hurried out to his car. Getting in, he tore open the envelope and found a sheet of paper with writing on it. In order to read it, he flicked on his overhead light. The note read:

Dear Sammy darling honey. By the time you get this, Grandpa and I will be on our way to somewhere else. I mean, if everything goes OK at your casino tonight. I'm crossing my legs for good luck! Grandpa has decided not to leave you your share, for two reasons.

For one thing, he needs the $6000 more than you, because he's an old man and isn't young anymore, like you. Also, he thinks you're a wonderful person and should be straight, and he says he's afraid that if you get your first taste of what he calls ill-gotten gains, it will turn you into a crook like himself for the rest of your life and this he wouldn't like to see. Good-bye. I'll really miss you. You sure are good in bed, Sammy honey.

Love, Vikki.

Sam turned off the light and sat in the darkness for a moment. Then fury overcame him and he slammed both hands against his steering wheel again and again, and tears of frustration blurred his eyes.

And then the passenger door opened and the interior light went on and Sam turned to see Mr. Collins standing there.

"Troubles, Sam?" He slid onto the seat and shut the door.

Sam's eyes widened and his mouth fell open. "How? . . . How? . . ."

"I followed you here. I've been sitting in my car over there, and I saw you get turned away from that room, and I saw you get that letter from the manager, and I saw the look on your face when you read it." He brought out a cigarette. "So your friends ran out on you, did they—without giving you your cut?"

"I . . . I . . . don't know what you mean."

"Oh, knock it off, Sam." He lit his cigarette. "You're in serious trouble. Your only hope is to level with me. Where in the name of God did you three manage to *get* a hundred and eighty phony hundred-dollar bills? And what are the old man and his wife to you?"

Sam considered for a moment and then shrugged. "She's his granddaughter. Their name is Haskins." He turned on his overhead light. "Oh, hell." He handed Mr. Collins Vikki's note. "You might as well read this."

Mr. Collins did. "The old man may be selfish, but he's right, you know. That six thousand would have meant the end of you as an honest person." Sam turned off the light. "Where did you meet these two?"

"They were customers of my uncle's liquor store. I got to know Vikki and pretty soon we had a real thing going. Then, when my uncle sold the store, I was out of a job, and one day old Bert asked me how honest I was and I said that depended, and he told me about all these hundreds he had."

"Where did he get them?"

"He'd bought them a long time ago, very cheaply. But he'd never passed any. He had an idea about how they could all be changed in one place at one time—in a casino. He didn't care if he won, you see—he just wanted to change his counterfeits for good money. So he offered me a third if I'd help him and he paid my way through Mr. Ferguson's school. I had to get a job as a dealer up here, so I could find out exactly how things worked in a particular casino."

"Sam, you are a crook. You are a criminal."

"All I did tonight was to keep warning you about the old man and his money."

"You were just setting me up."

"I guess so." Sam sighed. "For all the good it did me."

"Was the old man's faint staged?"

"Yes. He knew he had to stop before midnight, when you'd open the cashboxes and spot his bills. But he figured that if he just stopped right then, you might be suspicious, so he faked a faint."

"And whose idea was it that you should try to *make* me suspicious of them?"

Sam smiled modestly. "Well, it was mostly mine—after I'd met you. I figured that if I questioned the first two thousand and you made sure they were genuine—then you wouldn't have any doubts about the next eighteen thousand. And also, I wanted to be sure you wouldn't connect me with it when it was all over."

Mr. Collins smiled a little. "It was a slick operation, Sam. And it almost worked. But your gamble paid off on the house number—which is double zero for you."

"Where did I go wrong?"

"Well, for one thing, you objected too much and I began to wonder why. And at the end, you wondered if the old man could get back to his *motel*. But meanwhile, the girl had told me they were staying at the Flamingo *Hotel*. I figured something was wrong somewhere. And when I opened your cashbox and found the funny money, it all fell into place."

"What . . . are you going to . . . do about me?"

Mr. Collins shrugged. "Nothing. I expect you back at work tomorrow." Sam looked at him in disbelief. "Sam, unless you're crazy, you'll never try anything funny on me again. And it's my solemn duty to the Nevada gaming industry to make sure you never work for anybody else."

"But . . . but what about the eighteen thousand in phony hundreds you're stuck with?"

"What makes you think so, Sam?"

"Because I saw Vikki cash in before you'd opened the cashboxes. That was good money she walked out with!"

"What makes you think so?"

"I . . . don't understand you."

"Because you'd finally made me suspicious, I'd opened *your* cashbox ten minutes earlier. It was while you were in the dealers' room and the bar. I saw to it that among the twenty thousand your friends walked out with were the same identical one hundred and eighty counterfeit hundreds they'd walked in with." Mr. Collins opened the car door and slid out. "Good night, Sam. See you tomorrow."

So saying, the smartest man in Vegas shut the car door and walked off into the darkness.

NEW HAMPSHIRE

A SECRET PLACE
by Don Gilbert

WHEN DELL HICKMAN awakened, the sun was well up and a white-coated young man was standing at the foot of his bed. After a moment he remembered where he was—the Gabriel Nursing Home.

Gabriel come blow your horn, Dell thought.

"Good morning, Gramp," the white-coated man said, "how come you're not up yet? You're usually the first one dressed around here. And today is your birthday."

"I had dreams, Harry. I don't remember what they were but they made me wakeful."

That was not exactly truthful—Dell remembered hazily what those dreams had been. They came often of late, very private dreams that he saw no reason to tell even his son, Aron, let alone Harry. They had to do with a trip he'd taken to New Hampshire when he was around thirty. What had started out as a proxy visit for his ailing father—a settlement of some family property—had ended up as the most important event in his life. He had met his sweet Fran and married her after a whirlwind week. What a time of revelation that had been for both of them!

He slid his pajamaed legs out of bed, thinking what a cheerful cuss Harry was, so gentle with old people, even if he was getting paid for it. "I've laid out fresh clothes for you," Harry said. "Your son is coming for you at eleven. How old did you say you'd be today?"

"Ninety since five o'clock this morning," Dell said, hoping he was right but not too sure. Yesterday, today, tomorrow were becoming increasingly jumbled in his mind. But he had found that a bold front usually carried the day. And what lay far back in the mystery of his mind was no one else's affair.

"I hope I'm as sound as you when I reach your age."

People were always saying things like that, but Dell chose to believe Harry meant it. In his prime Dell had been five foot eight, a muscular hundred and sixty-five pounds. He'd never wanted to be a big man, just big enough to face the world and protect the ones he loved. Big men sort of collapsed as time went by. Dell was still erect. He wore glasses and had store teeth, but his shock of white hair was vigorous. The doctor said his heart murmur was nature's way of telling him to be careful—very careful. No sudden or unusual physical exertion. No undue mental excitement.

Just the same, his mind was no longer what it had been. Dell figured it was something like a hibernating animal who slumbers, comes awake, shifts about, then sleeps again. He was careful not to say things that might lead to questions: old secrets must be kept forever buried. Fran was dead for fifteen years now. She had never kept a secret from him, but he had from her. She had never once doubted his integrity, but he had only deceived to shield her.

After Fran died, he sold the two farms—his folks' homestead and the new farm across the creek Fran and he had purchased. Aron, now past fifty and a successful lawyer at the county seat, had had no desire to become a farmer. Nor had he desired to complicate his life by becoming a landlord. So Dell had sold the farms, keeping only the homestead cabin and the white pines along the creek. He gave the new owners an option on that property, too, if Aron decided to sell it later on.

Aron and his wife Sue had wanted him to come and live with them. They had a ranch-type house just outside of town with plenty of room, and his grandchildren loved him, but Dell could not agree to such an arrangement. He cared for his family with an encompassing devotion, but he was afraid of what might happen if he became too close an accessory to their lives. It was lonely at the cabin without Fran, but it would be lonely anywhere without her. And he had found a surprising peace there, a privacy that barricaded his secret self.

It wasn't until he was eighty-eight that he decided to move into the Gabriel Nursing Home.

Harry said, "I'll bring your breakfast tray in here, Gramp. An egg, fruit, toast, and coffee. Enough to keep you going 'til your birthday feast. O.K.?"

"O.K.," Dell said, the past receding into a mist.

It was a beautiful summer day as Aron tooled his sportscar off the freeway onto country macadam. Dell felt a possessive fulfillment sitting beside his son.

"Well, Dad," Aron asked, "what would you like to do? Your favorite daughter-in-law packed us a snack for noon: sandwiches, fruit, and coffee—not enough to spoil your birthday dinner. I think the kids have something special planned, by the way. There's been a lot of whispering going on the last few days."

Dell relaxed. "You know what I'd like to do today, son? Just see the farms. See how the crops are coming along. Maybe stop at our old place if the Petersons are home. Go down to the cabin—" He stopped, then added hesitantly, "I hope you and Sue and the kids will keep the cabin after I'm gone."

He glanced obliquely at his son—a handsome man with clear hazel eyes, a frosting of gray in his curly auburn hair, a cameo profile like his mother's. A strong man, a thoughtful son, and a good father.

"Don't worry, Dad. The way things are going, no-trespass signs on all the farms, a man will have to have a place of his own if he hunts."

'I'm not trying to back you into a corner, Aron. Whatever you decide about the cabin and the old pines will be O.K. with me."

"The kids would raise the roof if anyone mentioned selling the cabin."

They had gone over this a dozen times before but now Dell settled back with a sense of relief. They passed a horse and carriage neatly clipping along. It was odd to see such an anachronism, although it was becoming a more common sight in the district. Amish people were buying many of the old farms and their religion forbade modern conveniences such as cars. Dell had owned one of the first cars in the neighborhood but he still liked the sight of a horse and buggy.

Fran and he had once had a neat little outfit—a single buggy with a sorrel driving mare. Annie was her name. Smarter than many a human. Everyone had horse rigs in those days. A man got to know every outfit in the district. Dell could still remember many of them and the names of their owners. Or could he? Certainly some of the past seemed sharper than the present, yet he knew the accuracy of his memory could not be trusted.

Now, just for the fun of it, he tried to recall some of the rigs that had traveled this road when it was still plain dirt. Ah, there was one, all alone, as if the others shunned it. A shiny black carriage with red wheel-spokes, its buttoned side-curtains seldom pulled back.

Whose? What did it really matter? But it did. In memory he could see the outfit boldly silhouetted against the sky. People said, and Dell believed it to be true, you could take that rig anywhere in the neighborhood, turn it around, set the gray gelding that pulled it on the right road to home, and he would arrive safe at his barn with never a twitch of the guiding reins.

But *whose rig?* Irritated, Dell could not remember. Yet there was something about the driver—he had vanished, completely, mysteriously. A mystery that had never been solved. Dell turned toward his son with a question on his lips even as a warning sounded far back in his brain. Careful. Never talk about that rig. Why? Someday he might remember.

"We're getting on home ground," Aron said. "Want to stop and say hello to the Petersons?"

"How about when we come back? It's most noon now, and they'd want us to eat with them. I'm anxious to get to the cabin."

And it was so. Excitement tingled through him like a magnetic force.

Around a concealing band of trees, past the Petersons, Aron left the macadam for a narrow dirt road. Waist-high cornfields lay beyond hedges of hazel brush and, over a knoll, Dell could see the stand of white pine and tamarack on the land he still owned along the creek.

Suddenly Dell thought: I never really owned that land or those trees. I was only their caretaker. You can never really own the Lord's land, but if you care for it it will care for you and guard your secrets.

The car rumbled over a plank bridge, below which peat-brown water flowed silently over pale sand. The road ran straight between poplar and birch, ending on umber needles before the cabin door.

"How about a cup of coffee now?" Aron asked.

"Later," Dell said. "First I want to take a walk to the creek. Just me if you don't mind, son. There's something I want to remember down there, something important I can't put my finger on."

Aron hesitated. "O.K., Dad, but don't hurry. And don't stay long. I'll take a look around to see that everything's shipshape, then I'll come down the trail to meet you."

"When we get back it will be time for my medication," Dell said, wanting Aron to know he remembered about things.

He got out of the car and stood leaning against it for a moment, his feet testing familiar turf. Then he moved slowly down the sandy trail and into the pine shadows. The strange urgency that had nagged him ever since they had passed the Amish buggy possessed him wholly now, quickening his steps until he had to command himself to be more controlled, to remember the doctor's orders. Aron could no longer see him, but still he felt the need to dissemble. That was hard to do because a breeze in the pines was a hurrying sound. And suddenly he felt young, strong, the man he had been fifty years before.

From behind him he heard the scurry of ghostly buggy wheels in a patch of sand. A voice from the dead past shouted: Dell Hickman, stop where you are!

In an illusion of reality Dell swung about. What do you want with me, Amos Devlin? It was the carriage of his memory pulled by the gray gelding. He knew the man and the outfit now.

You know what I want well enough. I stopped at your cabin but there was no one home.

My wife and son are away for a few days. She's caring for a sick friend in town.

Good. I want to talk to you alone. I hope you've seen the light by now.

My wife being away makes no difference. She agrees with me. The answer to your proposition is still no.

I want that creek timber, Dell, and I'll have it! Why else would I take a mortgage on this sandpatch so you could buy a decent farm? Even a fool should have surmised that, and you're no fool. You've got nothing to lose and much to gain. I'm offering you easy payments on your mortgage and you can have the creek land back when I'm through logging it. All your neighbors with stands of pine have sold to me!

The others didn't sell willingly, you forced them to. There's hardly a man in the district who isn't in debt to you. I'm one man you can't bully, Amos Devlin. I'll lose my farm before I sell those trees! And my wife goes along with me—we think as one!

I wonder about that, but we shall see. You know me well enough to realize that when I want something I always have two strings to my bow.

I know there's little you'd hesitate at.

Amos Devlin leaned past the carriage curtains, the seams of his gaunt face hard as flint. *Now there is something you don't know that I do. I'm no angel, but I don't intend to use this knowledge if you're reasonable. I made a trip to the New Hampshire town your wife came from. It was just a shot in the dark, a spooky sort of feeling I had about her. Shall I go on?*

Dell stood quiet, completely stunned. He had never believed anything like this could happen in a million years. His own beloved Fran. And he had promised to honor and protect her! To guard her secret!

I see by your face you know what I'm talking about, that your wife has told you. But to make sure you understand I'll go on.

NO!

Perhaps we should talk this over with your wife.

NO!

Don't be a damned fool. I know what I'm talking about. Your wife was never married before she met you, but I happened in the country cemetery where her stillborn daughter is buried.

A red mist swirled before Dell's eyes. It seemed his head, his heart, his whole body was bursting with blood. There was no fear in Devlin's face. He reached out and lifted the buggywhip from its socket.

We could talk this over with your wife but look at things my way and the affair can be settled right now. See things my way and your wife need never know of my visit.

Rage possessed Dell. Fran had told him everything before they were married and he believed her implicitly. It was the old talk of young love, false promises, and ultimate betrayal. Dell had offered her a new life, protection, and deliverance. And she had given him much more in return. Now what they had constructed so secretly, day by day, was about to be demolished! His hand clamped on Devlin's bony wrist. He wrenched him from the carriage and sent him crashing into the sweet fern.

The gray gelding snorted but stood still. Abruptly, the insane rage that had possessed Dell burned away, replaced by chill reason. Devlin lay very still, face down on the ground. His heart beating wildly, Dell dropped to his knees and turned him face up. Blood was oozing and starting to clot around a hole in his temple where a jagged rock had penetrated the skull. Dell felt for a pulse. There was no heartbeat.

Without reasoning he decided what he must do. He must dispose of the body and destroy all signs of Devlin's visit. He felt he dared not face the law with a true account of what had happened. Even if his story was believed—and few who knew him would doubt it—he had killed a man. And he couldn't tell what had happened without revealing Fran's secret. He would land in prison, and what would become of his wife and son then? There was only one course for him to follow as he saw it.

Dell knew that Devlin's horse would not move until commanded, so he was *taken care of for the moment. With the strength of desperation, he heaved Devlin over his shoulder and moved down the woodsy trail. The place he sought was deep in the pines and tamaracks, close to the creek. There was an opening some twenty foot across, a green-scummed morass with gaseous bubbles popping on its surface. Noisome in late summer and shunned except for snakes and frogs. There was no breeze and in the sticky stillness Dell could hear the far muttering of thunder. Sweat coursed down his ribs as he staggered down the trail with his burden. Reinforcing the quaking bog with a short log to stand on, he inserted the corpse feet first into the mire, working it gradually downward. This required patience and by the time the deed was accomplished, Dell was half mad and it was full dusk.*

Thunder from scattered storms was a constant rumbling by the time Dell got Devlin's rig back to the main road. Buttoning down the loose side-curtains, he started the willing horse toward town and slipped into the woods for home. When he drove into town for Fran and Aron two days later, the place was buzzing with Amos Devlin's disappearance. The gray gelding had brought the carriage safe home and was found the next morning still patiently waiting outside his barn. But Devlin had disappeared. The sheriff and his deputies searched, questioned, called in law officers far from the state capital—all to no avail. Stories circulated but each one petered out. The series of thunderstorms that had passed through the area the afternoon and night of the disappearance seemed to have obliterated any clues that might have existed.

Truth to tell, no one really mourned the man who, people whispered, had made a fortune from others' misfortunes.

Sweat-drenched and dizzy from the noon heat, the laboring of his old heart, and the physical exertion he had momentarily recalled, Dell still followed down the woodsy trail. He was now more confused than ever, and the momentary total recall of long-past events was entirely gone. When he came to the secret place where some forty years ago he had forced Amos Devlin's stiffening corpse beneath the surface of the quagmire, he had no idea why he had come there. The springs, far beneath the surface, had long since dried up or found other outlets, leaving behind only a swampy opening bordered by cattails and haunted by dragonflies.

Dell moved slowly back up the trail, not knowing why but only that he must. He was very dizzy now and the pain in his chest was like a knife thrust. He stumbled, righted himself, and went staggering on.

"Dad—" A voice was calling from long ago and far away. "Yes? Yes—" he quavered and tears stung his eyes.

His feet caught in a trailing bramble vine, his heart seemed to explode in his chest, and the world before him swirled into blackness.

He pitched forward on the trail. He no longer heard the calling voice, or the pad of running feet, or the knowing whisper of the pines.

NEW JERSEY

SCARED IN NEW JERSEY
by Ronnie Klaskin

DEAR MILLIE:

I never thought I would be writing to you for advice. I love reading your column in the paper, but the thought that *I* would actually be writing to you one day was the furthest thing from my mind.

You see, I've been close to idyllically happy, just like the heroines in the romance novels I love to read. I've got an almost perfect husband. Gregory—that's not his real name, of course—is very handsome and successful. He doesn't smoke or drink or go out with other women. He's an attorney. We have a beautiful home in the suburbs and I go to the health spa and the beauty parlor and wear fashionable clothes. What more could a woman ask for?

Now for the problem, Millie. Gregory bought a new car, a dark-blue Mercedes. Gregory loves that car. He keeps it polished and clean. There isn't a scratch on it. When Gregory drives his car—his pride and joy, he calls it (we don't have any children)—he gets absolutely infuriated with the other drivers on the road. Murderous. He's made some of the most dire threats—he'd like to pull this one from his car and beat him to a pulp; he'd like to scrunch that car to waste metal, with the driver in it. I think he really means it and that the only thing that's stopped him so far is that he wouldn't risk scratching the Mercedes. But if anyone should do so much as dent a fender of that Mercedes, there's no telling what Gregory would do. I'm,

SCARED IN NEW JERSEY

DEAR SCARED IN NEW JERSEY:

I can understand your feelings. I can also understand Gregory's. There is something about a brand new car that brings out the worst in people.

I remember when my Cadillac was new. I was so proud of it. When people cut me off I would use language, I regret to admit, that I would never print in this paper. Finally I scratched it myself, back-parking a little too close to a tree.

Cars are alter-egos. Especially to men. Gregory's behavior, I'm sorry to say, sounds rather normal. The likelihood that he will actually commit violence seems very remote.

DEAR MILLIE:

Well, it finally happened. I don't want to say you were wrong, but, you see, you don't know Gregory. I do.

We were driving along on a fairly deserted road the other night on the way home from a dinner-dance. It looked like Gregory was up for a judgeship. He was in a very good mood. Then these kids in an old tan Ford came speeding past and cut ahead of us. Gregory became livid. He raced after them, totally ignoring the speed limit. When he caught up with them he forced their car off the road into a ditch. "Probably drunk drivers," he said. "This way they can't cause an accident." Luckily no one was hurt. But I'm still,

SCARED IN NEW JERSEY

DEAR SCARED IN NEW JERSEY:

Sorry about the bad advice last time. I didn't realize it was so serious. As you say, I don't know Gregory and you do. It sounds to me as though he needs professional help. You should have him see a psychotherapist or have him speak to his clergyman.

DEAR MILLIE:

We no longer have a clergyman. Gregory got into a fight with our minister some years back, and as a result we stopped going to church. Gregory says we might start attending again now that he is about to become a judge.

I did suggest to Gregory that he see a psychiatrist and he belted me across the mouth. "How can you be so dumb?" he shouted. "Don't you realize what that would do to my career?"

My lower lip bled a lot when Gregory hit me, and now it's all blue and swollen. Gregory is very upset. He usually tries not to leave any marks. He squeezes my shoulder until I cry out in pain or twists my arm all the way back. Anyway, he won't be seeing a therapist.

BRUISED IN NEW JERSEY

DEAR BRUISED IN NEW JERSEY:

I was horrified when I read your letter. If Gregory won't go for therapy, then you must go by yourself.

DEAR MILLIE:

How could I possibly go for therapy? If Gregory knew, he'd kill me. He controls all the money in the house. Oh, he's very generous—I have charge accounts at all the best stores—but he'd know it if I tried to pay a therapist.

Gregory isn't really a cruel husband. He only hits me when I deserve it. I try to be a good wife, but sometimes I get lazy. Once in a while I don't have Gregory's dinner waiting when he gets home. He's hungry and has worked hard all day in order to provide me with our lovely home and all our lovely things. He's entitled.

Once Gregory almost broke my arm, he twisted it back so hard. It was when I said I wanted to return to college. I wouldn't have time, he said, to be a proper wife. My arm hurt for weeks. I couldn't have done class papers anyway.

My father used to keep me in line by punishing me also. It worked. I did well in school and helped my mother with the housework. I met Gregory in my first year of college, right after my father died of a heart attack. It was very romantic. Gregory was a lot older—he was already practicing law—and he took me to the finest restaurants and brought me red roses. When we got married I quit school to keep house for him. I wish I could be a perfect wife. After all, Gregory is an almost perfect husband.

TRYING HARD IN NEW JERSEY

DEAR TRYING HARD IN NEW JERSEY:

If you won't go to therapy, please call the nearest women's center. Perhaps they can put you in touch with a support group for battered wives. That will not cost anything and Gregory needn't find out.

DEAR MILLIE:

I did call the women's center and they do have a group for abused wives. I went down there twice and I think they might have been able to help me if I'd stayed, but the most awful coincidence happened.

There is a woman reporter who was writing a series of articles on Gregory, now that he was going to be a judge. She was also doing an article on battered women and she recognized me when she came to the center. We had met before when she wrote about Gregory's perfect home and domestic life for our newspaper's Sunday supplement.

Anyway, she called Gregory and asked if I was doing volunteer work for the women's center. It never occurred to her that I might be a battered wife. It was in the evening, after a very tough day, that Gregory got her call. He had his jacket off and his shirt sleeves rolled up. His keys and wallet were on the buffet in the dining room. We had just finished dinner and I was clearing the table.

Gregory was furious. He looked as he had in the car when he forced those boys off the road that day. His face was purple. The veins in his neck and forehead bulged. He knocked the dishes out of my hand and I really thought he would kill me, he was so mad.

One thing I learned in the women's center was not to just stay around and take it. I grabbed Gregory's car keys from the buffet and ran out and got into the Mercedes. I locked the doors. Gregory ran out after me, shouting. He tried the doors of the car and when he realized they were locked he stood in front of the car and blocked my way.

Oh, you were so right, Millie, when you said that being in a new car can encourage feelings of violence in the driver. They should put warnings in all new cars: "Driving this vehicle can be dangerous to your mental health." I never understood what it was that Gregory had been feeling until that moment.

AWAITING TRIAL IN NEW JERSEY

NEW MEXICO

LINE OF FIRE
by Helen Nielsen

THE MAN DROVE down from the White Mountains in a four-year-old king-cab pickup. He was tall enough to fill that cab with barely enough clearance for his gray cattleman's hat and lean enough to make his weathered face appear older than forty-six years. He wore a sheepskin coat, but changed to a brown corduroy jacket at a gas and coffee shop at Florence Junction. Even then the jacket was uncomfortable by the time he reached the city. It was just eleven o'clock in the morning, so he drove directly to the downtown police headquarters. He was on a mission he never wanted to undertake, in order to do a thing he had never expected to do in his lifetime.

A swarm of activity inside the building precluded inquiry, so he made his way unescorted to the open door of Lieutenant Vernon Pauley's office. The two men inside took no notice of his arrival. One, barrel-chested and with a shock of graying hair, was seated at the desk. Facing him stood a younger officer whose uniform appeared to have been slept in on a regular basis.

"Sergeant Deaver, are you still here?" the seated man queried. "You're off duty in the daytime, aren't you?"

The sergeant nodded. "I stayed on to write up this report on Officer Torres's death," he explained. "After the ambulance arrived, I joined the search for the killer's gray sedan. When I came in, the place was so full of reporters and TV cameras I couldn't so much as write my own name."

"And twenty-four hours later they're still hanging around," Pauley agreed. "Tell me, Deaver, do you think the killer was a drug dealer?"

"Probably. A lone car in that bank parking lot at two A.M. looked suspicious. He could have been waiting for a contact. One thing's sure, he wasn't about to be searched. Lieutenant, I told Torres to stay in the car while I investigated, but he walked right into that gun. I guess a rookie always wants to make waves. I'd like to go back to working alone."

Pauley scanned the report as the sergeant spoke. "So you did knock the gun

304

out of the killer's hand and fire it as he sped away. At least we have the weapon."

"It's at ballistics. I doubt it can be traced."

"I'm afraid you're right," Pauley agreed. "It looks like a professional job.— And you look exhausted. Nothing worse can happen to an officer than to see his partner killed. Get out of here now. Take off a few days and try to let go of it."

Pauley looked up from the report as he spoke. When his gaze came in line with the doorway, he reacted with surprise and shock. The man in the doorway had removed his hat, loosening a cascade of red, wavy hair. He stood well over six feet in heeled boots, and spoke in a quiet voice. "I'm supposed to see Lieutenant Pauley. My name is Raymond Wagner, Senior."

"Senior," the lieutenant repeated and the tension level plummeted. "Come in, Mr. Wagner. You gave me a start. The resemblance to your son is remarkable!"

"It sure is!" the sergeant echoed.

"Deaver—go home."

The sergeant didn't delay. He sidled through the doorway, still eyeing Wagner, and passed from view. "I'm sorry you were kept waiting," Pauley apologized. "We had a personal tragedy here night before last. We're all pretty preoccupied."

Wagner didn't comment. He had trouble of his own. "I came about my son," he said. "May I see him now?"

Pauley removed a suede jacket from the back of his chair. It covered the service revolver on his hip when he put it on. "I'll take you over myself," he said. "You made good time getting here. Did you drive all night?"

"All morning," Wagner corrected. "I was on a hunting trip with my younger son when your office called the ranch. It was early this morning before I got the message."

"Then you really did make good time. I heard it was snowing in the mountains." The weather was of no importance, but what else was there to talk about on the way to the morgue?

A part of Wagner's mind still insisted it was only a bad dream, but he followed like a sleepwalker as the lieutenant led the way to a large white room with a white-tile floor where an attendant pulled out a drawer from the wall and shattered the fantasy. This was reality: the body of a red-haired boy whose blue eyes would never again open, whose generous mouth would never again smile— because an ugly wound in his chest had ended a life used only nineteen years.

Wagner choked out the required words. "Yes, that's Rusty. That's my son." It seemed a betrayal. He wanted to cry out that it wasn't Rusty—it was an impostor. "Who did this to him?" he demanded.

"A Smith and Wesson .38 was found beside the body," Pauley answered. "It fired the shot that killed your son. His are the only prints on it."

"Wait a minute," Wagner protested. "Are you trying to say that Rusty committed suicide? He had no reason!"

"No suicide has a reason that's valid to anyone but himself—especially a teenager. Of course, it might have been accidental."

"I can't buy that. Rusty hunted with me for meat on the table since he was twelve. That boy had respect for a weapon."

"Unless he had been drinking or using a controlled substance."

"Drugs, you mean? Not Rusty! I won't let you write off my son as a drunk or an addict. If I took your gun from you right now and shot you dead, I could wipe off my fingerprints and substitute yours. You know that."

If Wagner hadn't looked so capable of carrying out the suggestion, the lieutenant might not have backed down so quickly. "Don't get so upset, Mr. Wagner," he protested. "We won't know anything definite until after the autopsy."

"There's a bruise on my son's left cheek," Wagner said. "He could have been in a fight."

It was a small bruise, hardly more than a scratch, but the lieutenant didn't try to explain it away. "The autopsy will cover everything," he promised, "and I have a detective on campus today checking out your son's relationships for possible bad blood. I questioned the young lady who discovered his body yesterday. Pamela Foster. Do you know her?"

"Rusty mentioned her a few dozen times. We've never met."

Lieutenant Pauley took a notebook and pen from his pocket and began to write. "I'll give you her telephone number. She seems to be a nice girl. I know you'll want to see her. Now, when the autopsy is complete, the body will be released to the undertaker of your choice. Where are you staying, Mr. Wagner?"

It was all so efficient—like communicating with an answering machine. "I haven't made any plans," Wagner said. "But you can reach me at The Gathering. It's a restaurant."

"Best steakhouse in the city," Pauley remarked. "That's Sally Turner's place. Do you know her?"

"We go back a ways."

"Good! That's what you need right now—to be with a friend."

A friend. Sally was that for sure, and it was strictly here's-your-hat-what's-your-hurry time at police headquarters.

When Wagner entered The Gathering, he ignored the busy dining room and went directly to his usual booth in the bar. The walls were covered with old photographs of Sally Turner in her rodeo days, and Wagner was with her in more than a few of them. They were from the "before Martha" era. Martha was the surprise bride he brought back from Ruidoso, where he had gone shopping for another kind of filly. Two weeks later, Sally married Tim Turner on the rebound, but that was ancient history. Tim drank too much, drove too fast, and died in his mangled Cadillac within a year. And it was five years since Martha was laid to rest in the churchyard near the ranch.

A pretty waitress in a cowgirl costume brought a menu Wagner had no chance to open before Sally slid into the booth beside him. "Red Wagner will have the best steak in the house—blood rare," she ordered. "But first bring a sour mash on the rocks and a Dos Equis. No, make that two beers, honey. I can't stand to see a man drink alone."

Sally might touch up her hair to maintain that golden color, but her figure hadn't changed since the rodeo photos. She placed a warm hand over one of Wagner's and squeezed hard. "Your foreman called to tell me what happened. Oh, Red, I'm so *damned* sorry."

Wagner didn't know how much he needed the whiskey until after the first swallow. The warmth that spread through his body began to ease the tension and loosen his tongue. "That Lieutenant Pauley doesn't care what happened to Rusty," he complained. "All any of the police are concerned about is some officer who was killed."

"You sure got that right, Red. The boys in blue do take care of their own."

The words came from a handsome Indian of indeterminate age as he deposited the steaming steak platter on the table. He wore a white starched shirt and a black bowtie. His name was Joseph, but he had been billed as "Injun Joe" in his rodeo days.

"What's this savage doing wearing a bowtie?" Wagner demanded.

Joseph grinned. "Sally made me *maitre d'*. Pay's good but I don't like the fringe benefits."

"And you don't like those 'damned badges,' " Sally added. "Pay no attention to him, Red. Pauley's okay. He's under a lot of fire over this cop killing. There's talk a drug dealer is involved."

"In that case, the police should question some of those professors out on campus," Joseph said, "or maybe some of their own."

"Joe, shut up. I haven't made you janitor yet, but I should. You pick up more dirt than a vacuum cleaner. Red isn't interested in our local scandals."

The steak was disappearing fast, and the waitress brought another whiskey as soon as a glass was empty. "I sure am interested," Wagner said, "but I haven't slept since I can't remember when. I've got to get moving and find a motel."

"I'm going to pretend I didn't hear that," Sally remarked. She took a house key from her purse and slid it across the table. "I'll be late tonight. A wedding party's coming in and I won't leave until it's over. But you know where my house is. Take any bed you want."

"You'll never get a better offer," Joseph said. "And if you come up empty on this so-called police investigation, Red, let me know. I've got a cousin who's into tribal rituals. He might conjure up a vision of what happened to Rusty."

"If I chewed as much peyote as that cousin of Joseph's," Sally scoffed, "I'd have visions, too."

Wagner knew he wouldn't be allowed to pay for the food and drink, but he wanted to leave a tip for the waitress. When he dropped some bills on the table, Pauley's note fell open beside them. "Pamela Foster," Sally read.

"Do you know her?"

Sally fell into a momentary silence, as if trying to decide how much she wanted to say. "I've met her. Rusty brought her in a few times."

"I've got to call her. She found Rusty's body." He started to dig in his pocket for coins.

Sally smiled. "Maybe you don't remember, Red, but my house has all the modern conveniences—even a telephone."

Sally's house was a few miles from the restaurant. Traffic thinned as the street wound upward, leaving the city spread out in a hollow bowl while an impending sunset lengthened shadows on foothills ahead. But no exterior spectacle could compare to the sight of the welcoming beds inside the house. Wagner glanced in on the master bedroom—pink and feminine as Sally in her non-professional hours. It was Sally's room, but this wasn't Sally's grief. This grief belonged to Red Wagner and his memories of Martha. He moved on to a guest room with a white-tile bath and shower. He began peeling off his clothing at the sight of it.

The needle spray brought him back from a stupor of exhaustion. He increased the pressure and let the water massage strength back into his body. He luxuriated in the warmth until his eyes focused on the tile walls that enclosed him, and his stomach began to churn even before his mind remembered the white-tile room where Rusty waited. An emotional dam that had held for twenty-four hours began to crumble. It burst, finally, in a moan—a cry so deep and outraged it might have come from a forest animal trying to free itself from a cruel trap. *Big boys don't cry, Rusty. Big boys pick themselves up and go on*. But big men sob out their hearts when there's nothing else left to do.

After a long time, Wagner realized he was sitting on the floor of the shower while the spray beat down on his head. He struggled to his feet and turned off the water. Wrapping himself in a bath sheet, he stumbled into the bedroom. He was asleep by the time his head touched the pillow. . . .

A telephone was ringing. Wagner stirred awake and extricated one arm from the bath sheet. The house was dark except for a shaft of light coming from the bathroom and a digital clock on the night table blinked 8:05 as he picked up the instrument. It was Pamela Foster. She had talked with Sally and learned where to locate him. Could he come to her apartment? He certainly could. He scratched the address on the telephone pad and started looking for his clothes.

She lived in an area near the university where students could almost afford the rent on old stucco apartments and duplexes. She opened the door at Wagner's first knock.

"Hi," she said. "Come in. You look just like Rusty."

She was shoulder high to Wagner, with hazel eyes and short auburn hair. She wore canvas shoes, tight bluejeans, and an oversized sweater that had belonged to Rusty. She beckoned him into a small living room cluttered with newspapers and lighted only by a small color TV with the audio turned off.

"I made fresh coffee," she announced. "Do you mind drinking it in the kitchen? It's not so messy there."

"The kitchen's the best room in the house," Wagner said.

She smiled briefly. "That's what Rusty used to say. I baked a chocolate cake, too. It's from a mix, but it's pretty good. I just couldn't go back to class today, and I got tired of TV and all those newspapers. They don't even mention Rusty."

The cake was surprisingly good and so was the coffee. But Pamela ignored them both and began her story of the previous afternoon. Rusty was to have met her in the campus library at 2:00 P.M. When he hadn't appeared by 2:30, she tried to reach him by telephone and failed to get an answer. Fearing that he might be ill, she had driven to his residence. His car was in the driveway, but there was no response to the doorbell. It was then that she called the landlord from the front unit and they entered the apartment. Rusty, dressed only in Jockey shorts, was sprawled on the floor near his bed.

"Mr. Lopez tried to turn him over," she added, "and saw all the blood. He yelled, 'Don't touch anything!' so I ran back to his house and called the police."

The story was recited in a monotone that suggested much retelling. The police had come, followed shortly by a medical examiner who pronounced that rigor mortis was complete. Rusty had been dead for at least twelve hours.

Pamela pushed a lock of hair from her forehead and replenished Wagner's cup. "The lieutenant asked me a lot of questions. Was Rusty troubled about anything? Was he depressed when he left me Sunday night?"

"You were with Rusty Sunday night?"

She smiled in recollection. "Rusty bought tickets to a concert I wanted to hear. He must have paid a lot for them, because when he stopped to buy a pizza on the way home I had to loan him five dollars. We came back here to eat the pizza. I had only one can of beer in the fridge, so I gave it to Rusty. I drank apple juice."

"And that's all Rusty drank—one can of beer?"

"Right. He turned on TV and started to watch an old horror movie, but I had an early class on Monday and asked him to leave. It was after one-thirty then. He left a little later."

"Did he have a bruise on his cheek?" Wagner asked.

Pamela shook her head. "He might have had lipstick on his cheek—and he sure wasn't depressed. Is it important?"

"It might be. He has one now. The police are checking the campus for any possible enemies."

For the first time during the conversation Pamela appeared frightened. "I don't think they'll find anything," she reflected, "but I'll tell you before you hear it all wrong from somebody else."

It wasn't an easy story to relate. Pamela was a first-year student from a small town and a protective family, and her naiveté had cost her dearly. Flattered by the attentions of a senior letterman, she accepted his invitation to a date which, it developed, included dinner, dancing, and rape.

"It's called 'date rape,'" she explained, "and it happens to more coeds than ever admit it. I learned that too late."

"Did you go to the police?" Wagner asked.

"What good would that do? The guys say it was a part of a regular relationship, and the police buy it. I couldn't even tell my parents. They would have taken me out of school, and I want an education! I bore down on the books and stopped dating."

"What about Rusty?"

"Well, one day my old VW wouldn't start in a campus parking lot, and Rusty came along and started it. He even followed me home in case my car conked out again. Later, when he kept asking for dates, I told him what had happened. He was furious."

"What did he do?"

"Nothing—I asked him not to. But one day a few months later we were walking on campus when Sid Kelsey—the senior—passed us, and Rusty remarked that sanitation should be more careful about keeping trash off the sidewalk. Kelsey yelled back, 'You should thank me, cowboy, for warming her up for you!' Rusty decked him. Knocked him out cold. Rusty said, 'He'll live,' and we walked on. That was the end of it."

"Are you sure?" Wagner persisted.

"It had to be. Kelsey graduated at mid-term. He moved to Albuquerque and probably doesn't even remember my name. I sure can't see him coming back to sneak in Rusty's back door and shoot him."

"Why the back door?"

"Because it was standing open when we found Rusty's body."

It was two cups of coffee later before Wagner could break away from the girl. She wanted to talk about Rusty, about the ranch, about anything that would ward off another lonely night, but he had his mind on an open back door that Pauley had neglected to mention. Mr. Lopez, Pamela had explained, said that sometimes the lock didn't catch. Possibly it hadn't caught tonight.

He remembered a short cut to Rusty's place through a small shopping center that was all but deserted at night, and approached down an alleyway to the carport. He parked beside Rusty's red Camaro that was ancient in years but pampered to perfection.

The unit was a small cottage secluded by shrubbery that would have muffled even a gunshot, and Wagner was eerily aware that he walked where a killer might have walked and reached for a doorknob a killer might have turned. But he hadn't touched the knob before he was suddenly impaled in the glare of a flashlight. Instinctively, he swung at whoever was behind the light and hit solid flesh. The light fell to the ground and focused on Sergeant Deaver sprawled on the grass. He wasn't in uniform, but one hand was reaching for a gun.

Since the gun wasn't yet in the sergeant's hand, Wagner grasped it and helped the policeman to his feet.

"What are you doing here?" Deaver demanded.

"I could ask you the same question."

"I followed you. I was in the shopping center when you drove through. Don't you know this place is officially sealed?" Deaver retrieved his flashlight from the ground and focused it on the door. It was padlocked and posted with a police-department warning. "When Lieutenant Pauley gives the word, you can get inside. Right now, Mr. Wagner, you can get off this property or face arrest."

"My son died in this building," Wagner protested.

It was a waste of breath. The sergeant wasn't going to leave until he did. So Wagner returned to his truck and headed back toward Sally's house. Deaver's headlights in the rearview mirror kept him company for several blocks. It was almost like being run out of town.

Sally was entitled to sleep late in the morning, but Wagner had business downtown. He located a mortician and arranged for a simple casket and no chapel service. Rusty would be buried in the mountains in a grave next to Martha's. Because the body could not be picked up until the medical examiner and the district attorney signed a release, Wagner returned to the morgue with instructions of where he could be reached when ready.

The morgue attendant remembered him. "About that bruise on your son's left cheek," he advised, "minute particles of red dust or sand were embedded in the flesh. He might have fallen or scraped against a brick wall."

"Could it have been caused by a blow?"

"Oh, no. It was a slight abrasion no way connected to the cause of death. Tests for drugs and alcohol were negative, too."

Wagner had one more question. "Has anyone other than Pauley and myself come to view the body?" he asked.

The attendant shook his head. "They don't, Mr. Wagner. People just don't come to a morgue unless it's required."

Pauley wasn't in his office. One of the staff directed Wagner to a pistol range, where he found the lieutenant observing qualifying tests. "Glad to see you!" Pauley shouted above the noise. "You can probably take your son home tomorrow!"

"And will that be the end of it?" Wagner asked.

They moved back a few feet to a quieter spot. "As long as there's any doubt, our files remain open on a case," Pauley answered. "We haven't been sitting on our hands, Mr. Wagner. I can tell you, to begin with, that your son had no academic problems."

"I know that," Wagner said.

"His medical record shows no illness that could cause a suicidal depression—"

"I know that, too."

"—and the only campus trouble we found concerns a former student who had insulted Pamela Foster. That individual has since married the daughter of a New Mexico state senator and is honeymooning in Hawaii."

"So you can scratch Kelsey."

"Right. There's still the landlord, Lopez, who had access to the apartment, but he was in bed with his wife and has no motivation for murder. That leaves only Pamela Foster.—You look shocked, Mr. Wagner. But she could have had motivation. A lovers' quarrel. Insecurity. A bad experience with one man could have made her overly dependent on your son. He might not have wanted a commitment and she was afraid of losing him."

"That's pretty farfetched," Wagner protested.

Pauley shook his head. "Nothing is too farfetched in my profession. If I haven't seen it all already, I probably will tomorrow. Miss Foster says she didn't have a key to your son's apartment, but I'm sure he would have let her in at any hour. But, putting aside speculation, if it is a murder then it's more than likely that some crazed addict was trying to get money for another fix. The danger in a citizen having a gun for protection is that the criminal is on the offensive and gets to it first."

The lieutenant turned his attention back to the firing range and let Wagner absorb what he had said. "Why didn't you tell me the back door was open when Rusty's body was found?" Wagner challenged.

Without turning around, Pauley answered, "Didn't I? I have a lot of things on my mind. This morning I had to send Deaver on a trip to the desert to ID an abandoned sedan found by the Highway Patrol. The inside was clean, but there's a clear handprint on the left front fender where Officer Torres tried to catch himself and enough cocaine traces in the trunk to make it clear why he was shot. The sedan was stolen and the gun we have is untraceable. Frustrating, isn't it?" He looked back at Wagner appraisingly. "You come on strong," he reflected, "and I know why. After you left my office yesterday, I remembered Red Wagner. You were big time on the rodeo circuit for years."

"Anything wrong with that?"

"Temperament. Anyone with star quality usually has a low boiling point. Come with me, Wagner."

They walked together to a vacated pistol range. The lieutenant took his service revolver from the holster and checked the chambers. He handed the gun to Wagner.

"Go ahead," he said. "Give it a try."

Wagner weighed the weapon in his hands. He took careful aim and fired once. The shot was far off center.

"Red Wagner can do better than that," Pauley chided. "Think of that target as a murderer—a murderer who killed your son."

Wagner tensed as all his faculties came to bear on the target. He aimed and fired in rapid succession—each shot a bull's-eye. He kept on pressing the trigger on an empty gun until the lieutenant wrested it from his grip. "That's better," he said. "Take out your frustration on the target. Don't play private eye and knock my officers around."

Wagner started to protest that he hadn't meant to strike the sergeant, but now Pauley was smiling. "Come upstairs to my office," he said, "and I'll see if the lab work is finished so you can get inside that unit legally."

When Pauley relinquished the key to Rusty's lodging, he brought two plastic bags to his desk. One held a revolver that Wagner quickly identified. "I can't give you the gun," Pauley said, "it's evidence. I can give you these other items found on the body or taken from the premises, but you'll have to sign for them."

The gold ring was a high-school class ring, the gold watch a graduation gift.

The leather wallet was opened to check the contents: a driver's license, social security card, bank card, two twenty-dollar bills, and two photos that caught Wagner by surprise. One, a faded snapshot, was of Martha and himself. The other was a recent school photo of fourteen-year-old Scotty.

"Nice-looking family," Pauley remarked.

It was that, but now young Scotty was all Wagner had left.

It was necessary to pick up a suit of clothes for delivery to the mortician. Wagner telephoned Sally to explain his whereabouts and she insisted on meeting him at the cottage. "You need moral support," she said.

"Joe's peyote-chewing cousin might come in handy, too," he told her.

He was glad to have company. All of the shades were drawn when they entered the cottage, and turning on the lights made visible the dark stain on the carpet where Rusty's life had bled away. It was a spartan environment: one large room containing a bed, a dresser, an overcrowded bookcase, a chair, and the essential stereo and TV. A narrow hall dividing kitchen and bath led to the rear door. Wagner walked back to test the lock. He opened the door and stared out toward the carport.

"What are you looking for?" Sally asked.

"Something that has to be here but I don't see it," he said.

"Well, that's better than something that isn't here and you can see it."

"There's no brick out here," Wagner concluded and closed the door. Sally had found the closet and removed a cloth suitcase. She asked why he was interested in brick and he explained.

"There are brick buildings on campus," she remarked, "but don't ask me what Rusty would be doing there after one-thirty in the morning.—Didn't he own anything but jeans? Oh, here's a white shirt with lipstick on it."

They both knew whose lipstick it was. "How well do you know Pamela Foster?" Wagner asked.

"Well enough to know she was terrified when Rusty brought her to me. She was afraid that campus coyote had made her pregnant. I took her to my gynecologist. Luckily, it wasn't so."

"Drugs, rape, suicide—it's so damned unfair," Wagner said. "We send our kids to a university so they can have a better life, and we send them into a jungle. I know Pauley thinks Rusty shot himself, and I can't live with that! I can't believe my son could be so troubled he couldn't turn to his own father—"

When his voice broke, Sally touched his arm. "You worry me, Red. I'm coming up to the ranch to stay a while later on."

It was a question more than a statement, and Wagner answered. "I'd like that—later on."

"Good. Now let's try to find a suit to go with this shirt."

Rusty owned one suit—navy-blue, coat, vest, and trousers. Sally searched the trouser pockets before folding it and found seventeen cents. The coat pockets yielded two ticket stubs for a rock concert and a statement from an automatic bank-teller transaction. "At the price of those tickets," she remarked, "it's no wonder Rusty needed a forty-dollar withdrawal."

It took a few seconds for the import of her words to register. "Let me see that statement," Wagner demanded.

He had been given a billfold containing two twenty-dollar bills, and it had taken all this time to recall that Rusty had had no cash for a pizza after the concert. The statement was specific as to the amount, the location of the bank, the date, and the exact time of withdrawal. When Wagner had absorbed all of this information, he asked Sally to take the clothing to the mortician because something else demanded his immediate attention.

The bank was where it had to be—in the shopping center Rusty used as a short cut. In the daytime it was crowded, but the bank stood apart from the other structures and its parking lot was reached by a one-way lane with tire shredders to insure the traffic flow.

Wagner parked and walked to the automatic-teller window where Rusty had made his last transaction on Monday at 1:59 A.M. The window was shaded from the desert sun by a low overhanging roof. By night it would have been lighted, but there would be no other lights anywhere except from widely spaced streetlamps. It was unlikely that Rusty would have noticed a sedan and a police car parked thirty feet away, but he would have reacted to the shooting.

Wagner examined the wall of the bank: white stucco. The walk was cement, the paving asphalt. There was no brick to fall against in fright. He looked up at the roof. Above a wooden supporting beam, the construction was red tile, and one of the tiles was chipped. Stretching as far as he could, he managed to pick off a fragment of the tile and wrap it in his handkerchief. He then ran an exploratory hand along the beam until he touched metal. A pocket knife removed the bullet.

The bullet bounced on Pauley's desk and spun to a stop. "Send this to ballistics," Wagner said. "I'll bet my ranch it came from the same gun that killed Torres." Then, carefully, he unfolded the handkerchief to display the fragment of tile. "This can go to the medical examiner for a match with the particles found in my son's cheek."

"Where did you get these?" Pauley demanded.

"Playing private eye at this address." Wagner placed the bank statement in the lieutenant's hand. He was a smart man: he could read the place and the date and the time. He could follow the logic laid out to him.

"My son was standing at this automatic-teller window when a shot was fired that hit the roof above and sprayed shattered tile into his cheek. What would you do if you were caught in the line of fire?"

"Run for cover," Pauley answered.

"Right. For Rusty, the nearest cover was his car, but the only way home was to drive through the scene of the shooting. He saw the killer and the killer saw him—that's why my son was murdered. Lieutenant, we're looking for the same man."

For a man who had seen everything, the lieutenant still looked surprised. "Do you think a drug dealer fleeing for his life would take the time to follow your son and kill him?" he challenged.

"It's possible," Wagner conceded, "but that's not exactly what I said."

When Sergeant Deaver reported back from his trip to the desert, he found Wagner still in the lieutenant's office and Pauley frowning over some paperwork. "Sergeant," he said, "something's missing from your report on Torres' death. There's no description of the killer."

"With all the fast action," Deaver explained, "I didn't notice much. And he's long gone, Lieutenant."

"Not necessarily. A car abandoned out of the city doesn't mean the man is gone. He could be anywhere—even in that shopping center where you spotted Wagner last night. What were you doing there at that hour? Meeting someone?"

The sergeant tensed. He reminded Wagner of a wild deer catching the scent of danger.

"No, sir," he said tightly, "I needed cigarettes. Look, about the killer—I can look through the mug shots."

Pauley shook his head. "I doubt that would be productive. Another thing omitted from your report is any mention of a third car parked outside the bank."

"I pulled into the lot from the street," Deaver explained. "If another car was parked farther back, I couldn't have seen it."

"But you must have seen the man at the lighted teller window."

"I didn't look in that direction."

"Not even when you took a shot at him?"

That wild deer would have been long gone, but Deaver seemed rooted to the floor. "I didn't shoot—" he began.

"You didn't shoot at the fleeing sedan, obviously," Pauley interrupted. "Only two shots were fired from the gun you sent to ballistics. The first killed Officer Torres and the other landed in a beam of the bank roof a few inches from the teller window. The man at that window was Mr. Wagner's son."

"No!" Deaver shouted. "I saw no one at that bank!"

Wagner moved closer to the desk. "I sure hate to call a man a liar," he said, "but you weren't with the officers who found my son's body, Sergeant, and you never saw him at the morgue—so how could you agree with the lieutenant yesterday morning on the strong family resemblance if you hadn't seen my son?"

The ringing telephone on the desk silenced any answer. Pauley took the call, listened, thanked the caller, and put down the phone. He seemed older when he looked at Deaver again.

"You shot Torres, didn't you?" he said quietly. "It doesn't make sense any other way. Rusty Wagner had to be silenced because what he witnessed wasn't a drug dealer shooting a police officer—it was one police officer shooting another. When did you learn Torres was an investigator for internal affairs? And when did he learn that you were the contact the dealer was waiting to meet?"

"You can't prove a thing!" Deaver shouted.

"I won't have to. You'll be so busy plea bargaining with the D.A. we won't have to do anything but turn on the recorder. That telephone call confirmed that an inquiry was made at two-ten on Monday morning for an ID on the license plates on Rusty Wagner's car. You had all the time you needed to eliminate the only witness to the shooting and feel confident it would pass for just another teenage suicide. As for Torres, he was the victim of an unidentified drug dealer who supplied you with an unidentifiable gun."

Pauley shoved back his chair and stood up. "Sergeant Deaver," he ordered, "place your badge and your gun on my desk."

The lieutenant was looking into Deaver's eyes, but Wagner watched his hand. The gun came out of the holster but not butt-end first. Wagner smashed the sergeant's wrist against the desktop and caught the weapon as Deaver fled the office. "Don't shoot!" Pauley roared, but Wagner was already racing off in pursuit.

Deaver had a head start but needed wheels for a getaway. Wagner caught up with him in the parking lot. Shoving the gun under his belt, he dove onto the hood of the moving vehicle Deaver had commandeered and grabbed the wiper well with both hands. It wasn't all that different from bulldogging a steer. They sped toward the street just as a mortician's van nosed into the driveway. Deaver spun the wheel and executed a turn wide enough for Wagner to leap clear seconds before the vacated hood pleated itself into a cement wall.

Deaver crawled from the car and twisted about to face a man who now held a gun in his hand. "I didn't want to kill your son," he cried. "I went to see if he recognized me. He reached for his gun—"

From a distance, Pauley still shouted, "Don't shoot!" but something he'd said earlier rang in Wagner's mind: "*—a murderer who killed your son.*"

When he pulled the trigger, a shower of broken glass spewed out from a window above Deaver's head. By that time, Pauley had panted his way to the scene, and stared in disbelief. "*You* couldn't miss!" he gasped.

Wagner handed the gun to the lieutenant butt-end first. "Only if I try," he said. "Take your prisoner. I'm sick of the sight of him."

On the following morning, Wagner drove to the mortuary and helped load Rusty's casket in the back of the pickup. The sky was overcast and the weather would worsen along the way, but a waterproof tarp protected the precious cargo.

When all was secure, he got into the truck and headed north. He had come down from the mountains seeking vengeance, but vengeance could bring no peace. The only comfort to be had was the knowledge that Rusty was clean. No drugs, no senseless suicide. He had come to the jungle and remained a man, and that was how he was going home.

NEW YORK

THE ADVENTURE OF THE ONE-PENNY BLACK

by Ellery Queen

"Ah!" said old Uneker. "It iss a terrible t'ing, Mr. Quveen, a terrible t'ing, like I vass saying. Vat iss New York coming to? Dey come into my store—*polizei*, undt bleedings, undt whackings on de headt. . . . Diss iss vunuff my oldest customers, Mr. Quveen. He too hass hadt exberiences. . . . Mr. Hazlitt, Mr. Quveen. . . . Mr. Quveen iss dot famous detectiff feller you read aboudt in de papers, Mr. Hazlitt. Inspector Richardt Quveen's son."

Ellery Queen laughed, uncoiled his length from old Uneker's counter, and shook the man's hand. "Another victim of our crime wave, Mr. Hazlitt? Unky's been regaling me with a feast of a whopping bloody tale."

"So you're Ellery Queen," said the frail little fellow; he wore a pair of thick-lensed goggles and there was a smell of suburbs about him. "This *is* luck! Yes, I've been robbed."

Ellery looked incredulously about old Uneker's bookshop. "Not *here?*" Uneker was tucked away on a side street in mid-Manhattan, squeezed between the British Bootery and Mme. Carolyne's, and it was just about the last place in the world you would have expected thieves to choose as the scene of a crime.

"Nah," said Hazlitt. "Might have saved the price of a book if it had. No, it happened last night about ten o'clock. I'd just left my office on Forty-fifth Street—I'd worked late—and I was walking crosstown. Chap stopped me on the street and asked for a light. The street was pretty dark and deserted, and I didn't like the fellow's manner, but I saw no harm in lending him a packet of matches. While I was digging it out, though, I noticed he was eyeing the book under my arm. Sort of trying to read the title."

"What book was it?" asked Ellery eagerly. Books were his private passion.

Hazlitt shrugged. "Nothing remarkable. That best-selling nonfiction thing, *Europe in Chaos;* I'm in the export line and I like to keep up to date on international conditions. Anyway, this chap lit his cigarette, returned the matches,

317

mumbled his thanks, and I began to walk on. Next thing I knew something walloped me on the back of my head and everything went black. I seem to remember falling. When I came to, I was lying in the gutter, my hat and glasses were on the stones, and my head felt like a baked potato. Naturally thought I'd been robbed; I had a lot of cash about me, and I was wearing a pair of diamond cuff links. But—"

"But, of course," said Ellery with a grin, "the only thing that was taken was *Europe in Chaos*. Perfect, Mr. Hazlitt! A fascinating little problem. Can you describe your assailant?"

"He had a heavy mustache and dark-tinted glasses of some kind. That's all. I—"

"He? He can describe not'ing," said old Uneker sourly. "He iss like all you Americans—blindt, a *dummkopf*. But de book, Mr. Quveen—de book! Vhy should any von vant to steal a book like dot?"

"And that isn't all," said Hazlitt. "When I got home last night—I live in East Orange, New Jersey—I found my house broken into! And what do you think had been stolen, Mr. Queen?"

Ellery's lean face beamed. "I'm no crystal-gazer, but if there's any consistency in crime, I should imagine another book had been stolen."

"Right! And it was my second copy of *Europe in Chaos!*"

"Now you do interest me," said Ellery, in quite a different tone. "How did you come to have two, Mr. Hazlitt?"

"I bought another copy from Uneker two days ago to give to a friend of mine. I'd left it on top of my bookcase. It was gone. Window was open—it had been forced; and there were smudges of hands on the sill. Plain case of housebreaking. And although there's plenty of valuable stuff in my place—silver and things—nothing else had been taken. I reported it at once to the East Orange police, but they just tramped about the place, gave me funny looks, and finally went away. I suppose they thought I was crazy."

"Were any other books missing?"

"No, just that one."

"I really don't see. . . ." Ellery took off his *pince-nez* eyeglasses and began to polish the lenses thoughtfully. "Could it have been the same man? Would he have had time to get out to East Orange and burglarize your house before you got there last night?"

"Yes. When I picked myself out of the gutter I reported the assault to a cop, and he took me down to a nearby stationhouse, and they asked me a lot of questions. He would have had plenty of time—I didn't get home until one o'clock in the morning."

"I think, Unky," said Ellery, "that the story *you* told me begins to have point. If you'll excuse me, Mr. Hazlitt, I'll be on my way. *Auf wiedersehen!*"

Ellery left old Uneker's little shop and went downtown to Center Street. He climbed the steps of Police Headquarters, nodded amiably to a desk lieutenant, and made for his father's office. The Inspector was out. Ellery twiddled with an ebony figurine of Bertillon on his father's desk, mused deeply, then went out and began to hunt for Sergeant Velie, the Inspector's chief of operations. He found the mammoth in the Press Room, bawling curses at a reporter.

"Velie," said Ellery, "stop playing bad man and get me some information. Two days ago there was an unsuccessful manhunt on Forty-ninth Street, between Fifth and Sixth Avenues. The chase ended in a little bookshop owned by a friend of mine named Uneker. Local officer was in on it. Uneker told me the story, but I want less colored details. Get me the precinct report like a good fellow, will you?"

Sergeant Velie waggled his big black jaws, glared at the reporter, and thundered off. Ten minutes later he came back with a sheet of paper, and Ellery read it with absorption.

The facts seemed bald enough. Two days before, at the noon hour, a hatless, coatless man with a bloody face had rushed out of the office building three doors from old Uneker's bookshop, shouting: "Help! Police!" Patrolman McCallum had run up, and the man yelled that he had been robbed of a valuable postage stamp—"My one-penny black!" he kept shouting. "My one-penny black!"— and that the thief, black-mustached and wearing heavy blue-tinted spectacles, had just escaped. McCallum had noticed a man of this description a few minutes before, acting peculiarly, enter the nearby bookshop. Followed by the screaming stamp dealer, he dashed into old Uneker's place with drawn revolver. Had a man with black mustache and blue-tinted spectacles come into the shop within the past few minutes? "*Ja*—he?" said old Uneker. "Sure, he iss still here." Where? In the back room looking at some books. McCallum and the bleeding man rushed into Uneker's back room; it was empty. A door leading to the alley from the back room was open; the man had escaped, apparently having been scared off by the noisy entrance of the policeman and the victim a moment before. McCallum had immediately searched the neighborhood; the thief had vanished.

The officer then took the complainant's statement. He was, he said, Friederich Ulm, dealer in rare postage stamps. His office was in a tenth-floor room in the building three doors away—the office of his brother Albert, his partner, and himself. He had been exhibiting some valuable items to an invited group of three stamp collectors. Two of them had gone away. Ulm happened to turn his back; and the third, the man with the black mustache and blue-tinted glasses, who had introduced himself as Avery Beninson, had swooped on him swiftly from behind and struck at his head with a short iron bar as Ulm twisted back. The blow had cut open Ulm's cheekbone and felled him, half-stunned; and then with the utmost coolness the thief had used the same iron bar (which, said the report, from its description was probably a "jimmy") to pry open the lid of a glass-topped cabinet in which a choice collection of stamps was kept. He had snatched from a leather box in the cabinet an extremely high-priced item—"the Queen Victoria one-penny-black"—and had then dashed out, locking the door behind him. It had taken the assaulted dealer several minutes to open the door and follow. McCallum went with Ulm to the office, examined the rifled cabinet, took the

names and addresses of the three collectors who had been present that morning—
with particular note of "Avery Beninson"—scribbled his report, and departed.

The names of the other two collectors were John Hinchman and J. S. Peters. A
detective attached to the precinct had visited each in turn, and had then gone to
the address of Beninson. Beninson, who presumably had been the man with
black mustaches and blue-tinted spectacles, was ignorant of the entire affair; and
his physical appearance did not tally with the description of Ulm's assailant. He
had received no invitation from the Ulm brothers, he said, to attend the private
sale. Yes, he had had an employee, a man with black mustaches and tinted
glasses, for two weeks—this man answered Beninson's advertisement for an
assistant to take charge of the collector's private stamp albums, had proved satisfactory, and had suddenly, without explanation or notice, disappeared after two
weeks' service. He had disappeared, the detective noted, on the morning of the
Ulms' sale.

All attempts to trace this mysterious assistant, who had called himself William
Planck, were unsuccessful. The man had vanished among New York City's
millions.

Nor was this the end of the story. For the day after the theft old Uneker himself
had reported to the precinct detective a queer tale. The previous night—the night
of the Ulm theft—said Uneker, he had left his shop for a late dinner; his night
clerk had remained on duty. A man had entered the shop, had asked to see
Europe in Chaos, and had then to the night clerk's astonishment purchased all
copies of the book in stock—seven. The man who had made this extraordinary
purchase wore black mustaches and blue-tinted spectacles!

"Sort of nuts, ain't it?" growled Sergeant Velie.

"Not at all," smiled Ellery. "In fact, I believe it has a very simple
explanation."

"And that ain't the half of it. One of the boys told me just now of a new angle
on the case. Two minor robberies were reported from local precincts last night.
One was uptown in the Bronx; a man named Hornell said his apartment was
broken into during the night, and what do you think? Copy of *Europe in Chaos*
which Hornell had bought in this guy Uneker's store was stolen! Nothing else.
Bought it two days ago. Then a dame named Janet Meakins from Greenwich
Village had *her* flat robbed the same night. Thief had taken her copy of *Europe in
Chaos*—she'd bought it from Uneker the afternoon before. Screwy, hey?"

"Not at all, Velie. Use your wits." Ellery clapped his hat on his head. "Come
along, you Colossus; I want to speak to old Unky again."

They left Headquarters and went uptown.

"Unky," said Ellery, patting the little old bookseller's bald pate affectionately,
"how many copies of *Europe in Chaos* did you have in stock at the time the thief
escaped from your back room?"

"Eleffen."

"Yet only seven were in stock that same evening when the thief returned to
buy them," murmured Ellery. Therefore, four copies had been sold between the

noon hour two days ago and the dinner hour. So! Unky, do you keep a record of your customers?"

"*Ach,* yes! De few who buy," said old Uneker sadly. "I addt to my mailing lisdt. You vant to see?"

"There is nothing I crave more ardently at the moment."

Uneker led them to the rear of the shop and through a door into the musty back room from whose alley door the thief had escaped two days before. Off this room there was a partitioned cubicle littered with papers, files, and old books. The old bookseller opened a ponderous ledger and, wetting his ancient forefinger, began to slap pages over. "You vant to know de four who boughdt *Europe in Chaos* dot afternoon?"

"*Ja.*"

Uneker hooked a pair of greenish-silver spectacles over his ears and began to read in a singsong voice. "Mr. Hazlitt—dot's the gentleman you met, Mr. Quveen. *He* bought his second copy, de vun dot vass robbed from his house. . . . Den dere vass Mr. Hornell, an oldt customer. Den a Miss Janet Meakins—*ach!* dese Anglo-Saxon names. *Schrecklich!* Undt de fourt' vun vass Mr. Chester Singermann, uff t'ree-tvelf East Siggsty-fift' Street. Und dot's all."

"Bless your orderly old Teutonic soul," said Ellery. "Velie, cast those Cyclopean peepers of yours this way." There was a door from the cubicle which, from its location, led out into the alley at the rear, like the door in the back room. Ellery bent over the lock; it was splintered away from the wood. He opened the door; the outer piece was scratched and mutilated. Velie nodded. "Forced," he growled. "This guy's a regular Houdini."

Old Uneker was goggle-eyed. "Broken!" he shrilled. "Budt dot door is neffer used! I didn't notice not'ing, undt de detectiff—"

"Shocking work, Velie, on the part of the local man," said Ellery. "Unky, has anything been stolen?" Old Uneker flew to an antiquated bookcase; it was neatly tiered with volumes. He unlocked the case with anguished fingers, rummaging like an aged terrier. Then he heaved a vast sigh. "*Nein,*" he said. "Dose rare vons . . . Not'ing stole."

"I congratulate you. One thing more," said Ellery briskly. "Your mailing list—does it have the business as well as private addresses of your customers?" Uneker nodded. "Better and better. Ta-ta, Unky. You may have a finished story to relate to your other customers after all. Come along, Velie; we're going to visit Mr. Chester Singermann."

They left the bookshop, walked over to Fifth Avenue, and turned north, heading uptown. "Plain as the nose on your face," said Ellery, stretching his long stride to match Velie's. "And that's pretty plain, Sergeant."

"Still looks nutty to me, Mr. Queen."

"On the contrary, we are faced with a strictly logical set of facts. Our thief stole a valuable stamp. He dodged into Uneker's bookshop, contrived to get into the back room. He heard the officer and Friederich Ulm enter, and got busy thinking. If he were caught with the stamp on his person. . . . You see, Velie, the only explanation that will make consistent the business of the subsequent thefts of the same book—a book not valuable in itself—is that the thief, Planck, slipped the stamp between the pages of one of the volumes on a shelf while he was in the back room—it happened by accident to be a copy of *Europe in Chaos,* one of a number kept in stock on the shelf—and made his escape immediately thereafter. But he still had the problem of regaining possession of the stamp—what did Ulm call it?—the 'one-penny black,' whatever *that* may be. So that night he came back, watched for old Uneker to leave the shop, then went in and bought from the clerk all copies of *Europe in Chaos* in the place. He got seven. The stamp was not in any one of the seven he purchased, otherwise why did he later steal others which had been bought that afternoon? So far, so good. Not finding the stamp in any of the seven, then, he returned, broke into Unky's little office during the night—witness the shattered lock—from the alley, and looked up in Unky's Dickensian ledger the names and addresses of those who had bought copies of the book during that afternoon. The next night he robbed Hazlitt; Planck evidently followed him from his office. Planck saw at once that he had made a mistake; the condition of the weeks-old book would have told him that this wasn't a book purchased only the day before. So he hurried out to East Orange, knowing Hazlitt's private as well as business address, and stole Hazlitt's recently purchased copy. No luck there either, so he feloniously visited Hornell and Janet Meakins, stealing their copies. Now, there is still one purchaser unaccounted for, which is why we are calling upon Singermann. For if Planck was unsuccessful in his theft of Hornell's and Miss Meakins's books, he will inevitably visit Singermann, and we want to beat our wily thief to it if possible."

Chester Singermann, they found, was a young student living with his parents in a battered old apartment-house flat. Yes, he still had his copy of *Europe in Chaos*—needed it for supplementary reading in political economy—and he produced it. Ellery went through it carefully, page for page; there was no trace of the missing stamp.

"Mr. Singermann, did you find an old postage stamp between the leaves of this volume?" asked Ellery.

The student shook his head. "I haven't even opened it, sir. Stamp? What issue? I've got a little collection of my own, you know."

"It doesn't matter," said Ellery hastily, who had heard of the maniacal enthusiasm of stamp collectors, and he and Velie beat a precipitate retreat.

"It's quite evident," explained Ellery to the Sergeant, "that our slippery Planck found the stamp in either Hornell's copy or Miss Meakins's. Which robbery was first in point of time, Velie?"

Seem to remember that this Meakins woman was robbed second."

"Then the one-penny black was in her copy. . . . Here's that office building. Let's pay a little visit to Mr. Friederich Ulm."

Number 1026 on the tenth floor of the building bore a black legend on its frosted-glass door:

ULM
Dealers in
Old & Rare Stamps

Ellery and Sergeant Velie went in and found themselves in a large office. The walls were covered with glass cases in which, separately mounted, could be seen hundreds of canceled and uncanceled postage stamps, Several special cabinets on tables contained, evidently, more valuable items. The place was cluttered; it had a musty air astonishingly like that of Uneker's bookshop.

Three men looked up. One, from a crisscrossed plaster on his cheekbone, was apparently Friederich Ulm himself, a tall gaunt old German with sparse hair and the fanatic look of the confirmed collector. The second man was just as tall and gaunt and old; he wore a green eyeshade and bore a striking resemblance to Ulm, although from his nervous movements and shaky hands he must have been much older. The third man was a little fellow, quite stout, with an expressionless face.

Ellery introduced himself and Sergeant Velie; and the third man picked up his ears. "Not *the* Ellery Queen?" he said, waddling forward. "I'm Heffley, investigator for the insurance people. Glad to meet you." He pumped Ellery's hand with vigor. "These gentlemen are the Ulm brothers, who own this place. Friederich and Albert. Mr. Albert Ulm was out of the office at the time of the sale and robbery. Too bad; might have nabbed the thief."

Friederich Ulm broke into an excited gabble of German. Ellery listened with a smile, nodding at every fourth word. "I see, Mr. Ulm. The situation, then, was this: you sent invitations by mail to three well-known collectors to attend a special exhibition of rare stamps—object, sale. Three men called on you two mornings ago, purporting to be Messrs. Hinchman, Peters, and Beninson. Hinchman and Peters you knew by sight, but Beninson you did not. Very well. Several items were purchased by the first two collectors. The man you thought was Beninson lingered behind, struck you—yes, yes, I know all that. Let me see the rifled cabinet, please." The brothers led him to a table in the center of the office. On it there was a flat cabinet, with a lid of ordinary thin glass framed by a narrow rectangle of wood. Under the glass reposed a number of mounted stamps, lying nakedly on a field of black satin. In the center of the satin lay a leather case, open; its white lining had been denuded of its stamp. Where the lid of the cabinet had been wrenched open there were the unmistakable marks of a "jimmy," four in number. The catch was snapped and broken.

"Amatchoor," said Sergeant Velie with a snort. "You could damn' near force that locked lid up with your fingers."

Ellery's sharp eyes were absorbed in what lay before him. "Mr. Ulm," he said, turning to the wounded dealer, "the stamp you call 'the one-penny black' was in this open leather box?"

"Yes, Mr. Queen. But the leather box was closed when the thief forced open the cabinet."

"Then how did he know so unerringly what to steal?" Friederich Ulm touched his cheek tenderly. "The stamps in this cabinet were not for sale; they're the cream of our collection; every stamp in this case is worth hundreds. But when the three men were here we naturally talked about the rarer items, and I opened this cabinet to show them our very valuable stamps. So the thief saw the one-penny black. He was a collector, Mr. Queen, or he wouldn't have chosen that particular stamp to steal. It has a funny history."

"Heavens!" said Ellery. "Do these things have histories?"

Heffley, the man from the insurance company, laughed. "And how! Mr. Friederich and Mr. Albert Ulm are well known to the trade for owning two of the most unique stamps ever issued, both identical. The one-penny black, as it is called by collectors, is a British stamp first issued in 1840; there are lots of them around, and even an uncanceled one is worth only seventeen and a half dollars in American money. But the two in the possession of these gentlemen are worth thirty thousand dollars a piece. Mr. Queen—that's what makes the theft so dog-gone serious. In fact, my company is heavily involved, since the stamps are both insured for their full value."

"Thirty thousand dollars!" groaned Ellery. "That's a lot of money for a little piece of dirty paper. Why are they so valuable?"

Albert Ulm nervously pulled his green shade lower over his eyes. "Because both of ours were actually initialed by Queen Victoria, that's why. Sir Rowland Hill, the man who created and founded the standard penny-postage system in England in 1839, was responsible for the issue of the one-penny black. Her majesty was so delighted—England, like other countries, had had a great deal of trouble working out a successful postage system—that she autographed the first two stamps off the press and gave them to the designer—I don't recall his name. Her autograph made them immensely valuable. My brother and I were lucky to get our hands on the only two in existence."

"Where's the twin? I'd like to take a peep at a stamp worth a queen's ransom."

The brothers bustled to a large safe looming in a corner of the office. They came back, Albert carrying a leather case as if it were a consignment of golden bullion, and Friederich anxiously holding his elbow, as if he were a squad of armed guards detailed to protect the consignment. Ellery turned the thing over in his fingers; it felt thick and stiff. It was an average-sized stamp rectangle, imper-forate, bordered with a black design, and containing an engraving in profile view of Queen Victoria's head—all done in tones of black. On the lighter portion of the face appeared two tiny initials in faded black ink—V.R.

"They're both exactly alike," said Friederich Ulm. "Even to the initials."

"Very interesting," said Ellery, returning the case. The brothers scurried back, placed the stamp in a drawer of the safe, and locked the safe with painful care. "You closed the cabinet, of course, after your three visitors looked over the stamps inside?"

"Oh, yes," said Friederich Ulm. "I closed the case of the one-penny black itself, and then I locked the cabinet."

"And did you send the three invitations yourself? I noticed you have no type-writer here."

"We use a public stenographer in Room 1102 for all our correspondence, Mr. Queen."

Ellery thanked the dealers gravely, waved to the insurance man, nudged Sergeant Velie's meaty ribs, and the two men left the office. In Room 1102 they found a sharp-featured young woman. Sergeant Velie flashed his badge, and Ellery was soon reading carbon copies of the three Ulm invitations. He took note of the names and addresses, and the two men left.

They visited the collector named John Hinchman first. Hinchman was a thick-set old man with white hair and gimlet eyes. He was brusque and uncom-municative. Yes, he had been present in the Ulms' office two mornings before. Yes, he knew Peters. No, he'd never met Beninson before. The one-penny black? Of course. Every collector knew of the valuable twin stamps owned by the Ulm brothers; those little scraps of paper bearing the initials of a queen were famous in stampdom. The theft? Bosh! He, Hinchman, knew nothing of Benin-son, or whoever it was that impersonated Beninson. He, Hinchman, had left before the thief. He, Hinchman, furthermore didn't care two raps in Hades who stole the stamp; all he wanted was to be let strictly alone.

Sergeant Velie exhibited certain animal signs of hostility; but Ellery grinned, sank his strong fingers into the muscle of the Sergeant's arm, and herded him out of Hinchman's house. They took the subway uptown.

J. S. Peters, they found, was a middle-aged man, tall and thin and yellow as Chinese sealing wax. He seemed anxious to be of assistance. Yes, he and Hinchman had left the Ulms' office together, before the third man. He had never seen the third man before, although he had heard of Beninson from other col-lectors. Yes, he knew all about the one-penny blacks, had even tried to buy one of them from Friederich Ulm two years before; but the Ulms had refused to sell.

"Philately," said Ellery outside to Sergeant Velie, whose honest face looked pained at the word, "is a curious hobby. It seems to afflict its victims with a species of mania. I don't doubt these stamp-collecting fellows would murder each other for one of the things."

The Sergeant was wrinkling his nose. "How's she look now?" he asked rather anxiously.

"Velie," replied Ellery, "she looks swell—and different."

They found Avery Beninson in an old brownstone house near the River; he was a mild-mannered and courteous host.

"No, I never did see that invitation," Beninson said. "You see, I hired this man who called himself William Planck, and he took care of my collection and the bulky mail all serious collectors have. The man knew stamps, all right. For two weeks he was invaluable to me. He must have intercepted the Ulms' invita-tion. He saw his chance to get into their office, went there, said he was Avery

Beninson. . . ." The collector shrugged. "It was quite simple, I suppose, for an unscrupulous man."

"Of course, you haven't had word from him since the morning of the theft?"

"Naturally not. He made his haul and lit out."

"Just what did he do for you, Mr. Beninson?"

"The ordinary routine of the philatelic assistant—assorting, cataloguing, mounting, answering correspondence. He lived here with me for the two weeks he was in my employ." Beninson grinned deprecatingly. "You see, I'm a bachelor—live in this big shack all alone. I was really glad of his company, although he *was* a queer one."

"A queer one?"

"Well," said Beninson, "he was a retiring sort of creature. Had very few personal belongings, and I found those gone two days ago. He didn't seem to like people, either. He always went to his own room when friends of mine or collectors called, as if he didn't want to mix with company."

"Then there isn't anyone else who might be able to supplement your description of him?"

"Unfortunately, no. He was a fairly tall man, well advanced in age, I should say. But then his dark glasses and heavy black mustache would make him stand out anywhere."

Ellery sprawled his long figure over the chair, slumping on his spine. "I'm most interested in the man's habits, Mr. Beninson. Individual idiosyncrasies are often the innocent means by which criminals are apprehended, as the good Sergeant here will tell you. Please think hard. Didn't the man exhibit any oddities of habit?"

Beninson pursed his lips with anxious concentration. His face brightened. "By George, yes! He was a snuff taker."

Ellery and Sergeant Velie looked at each other. "That's interesting," said Ellery with a smile. "So is my father—Inspector Queen, you know—and I've had the dubious pleasure of watching a snuff taker's gyrations every since my childhood. Planck inhaled snuff regularly?"

"I shouldn't say that exactly, Mr. Queen," replied Beninson with a frown. "In fact, in the two weeks he was with me I saw him take snuff only once, and I invariably spent all day with him working in this room. It was last week; I happened to go out for a few moments, and when I returned I saw him holding a carved little box, sniffing from a pinch of something between his fingers. He put the box away quickly, as if he didn't want me to see it—although I didn't care, lord knows, so long as he didn't smoke in here. I've had one fire from a careless assistant's cigarette, and I don't want another."

Ellery's face had come alive. He sat up straight and began to finger his *pince-nez* eyeglasses studiously. "You didn't know the man's address, I suppose?" he asked slowly.

"No, I did not. I'm afraid I took him on without the proper precautions." The collector sighed. "I'm fortunate that he didn't steal anything from me. My collection is worth a lot of money."

"No doubt," said Ellery in a pleasant voice. He rose. "May I use your telephone, Mr. Beninson?"

"Surely.

Ellery consulted a telephone directory and made several calls, speaking in tones so low that neither Beninson nor Sergeant Velie could hear what he was saying. When he put down the instrument he said: "If you can spare a half-hour, Mr. Beninson, I'd like to have you take a little jaunt with us downtown."

Beninson seemed astonished; but he smiled, said: "I'd be delighted," and reached for his coat.

Ellery commandeered a taxicab outside, and the three men were driven to Forty-ninth Street. He excused himself when they got out before the little bookshop, hurried inside, and came out after a moment with old Uneker, who locked his door with shaking fingers.

In the Ulm brothers' office they found Heffley, the insurance man, and Hazlitt, Uneker's customer, waiting for them. "Glad you could come," said Ellery cheerfully to both men. "Good afternoon, Mr. Ulm. A little conference, and I think we'll have this business cleared up to the Queen's taste. Ha, ha!"

Friederich Ulm scratched his head; Albert Ulm, sitting in a corner with his hatchet knees jackknifed, his green shades over his eyes, nodded.

"We'll have to wait," said Ellery. "I've asked Mr. Peters and Mr. Hinchman to come, too. Suppose we sit down?"

They were silent for the most part, and not a little uneasy. No one spoke as Ellery strolled about the office, examining the rare stamps in their wall cases with open curiosity, whistling softly to himself. Sergeant Velie eyed him doubtfully. Then the door opened, and Hinchman and Peters appeared together. They stopped short at the threshold, looked at each other, shrugged, and walked in. Hinchman was scowling.

"What's the idea, Mr. Queen?" he said. "I'm a busy man."

"A not unique condition," smiled Ellery. "Ah, Mr. Peters, good day. Introductions, I think, are not entirely called for . . . Sit down, gentlemen!" he said in a sharper voice, and they sat down.

The door opened and a small, gray, birdlike little man peered in at them. Sergeant Velie looked astounded, and Ellery nodded gaily. "Come in, Dad, come in! You're just in time for the first act."

Inspector Richard Queen cocked his little squirrel's head, looked at the assembled company shrewdly, and closed the door behind him. "What the devil is the idea of the call, son?"

"Nothing very exciting. Not a murder, or anything in your line. But it may interest you. Gentlemen, Inspector Queen."

The Inspector grunted, sat down, took out his old brown snuff box; and inhaled with the voluptuous gasp of long practice.

Ellery stood serenely in the hub of the circle of chairs, looking down at curious faces. "The theft of the one-penny black, as you inveterate stamp fiends call it," he began, "presented a not uninteresting problem. I say 'presented' advisedly. For the case is solved."

"Is this that business of the stamp robbery I was hearing about down at Head-quarters?" asked the Inspector.

"Yes."

"Solved?" asked Beninson. "I don't think I understand, Mr. Queen. Have you found Planck?"

Ellery waved his arm negligently. "I was never too sanguine of catching Mr. William Planck, as such. You see, he wore tinted spectacles and black mustachios. Now, anyone familiar with the science of crime detection will tell you that the average person identifies faces by superficial details. A black mustache catches the eye. Tinted glasses impress the memory. In fact, Mr. Hazlitt here, who from Uneker's description is a man of poor observational powers, recalled even after seeing his assailant in dim street light that the man wore a black mustache and tinted glasses. But this is all fundamental and not even particularly smart. It was reasonable to assume that Planck wanted these special facial characteristics to be remembered. I was convinced that he had disguised himself, that the mustache was probably a false one, and that ordinarily he does not wear tinted glasses."

They all nodded.

"This was the first and simplest of the three psychological sign posts to the culprit." Ellery smiled and turned suddenly to the Inspector. "Dad, you're an old snuff addict. How many times a day do you stuff that unholy brown dust up your nostrils?"

The Inspector blinked. "Oh, every half-hour or so. Sometimes as often as you smoke cigarettes."

"Precisely. Now, Mr. Beninson told me that in the two weeks during which Planck stayed at his house, and despite the fact that Mr. Beninson worked side by side with the man every day, he saw Planck take snuff only *once*. Please observe that here we have a most enlightening and suggestive fact."

From the blankness of their faces it was apparent that, far from seeing light, their minds on this point were in total darkness. There was one exception—the Inspector; he nodded, shifted in his chair, and coolly began to study the faces about him.

Ellery lit a cigarette. "Very well," he said, expelling little puffs of smoke, "there you have the second psychological factor. The third was this: Planck, in a fairly public place, bashes Mr. Friederich Ulm over the face with the robust intention of stealing a valuable stamp. Any thief under the circumstances would desire speed above all things. Mr. Ulm was only half-stunned—he might come to and make an outcry; a customer might walk in; Mr. Albert Ulm might return unexpectedly—"

"Just a moment, son," said the Inspector. "I understand there are two of the stamp thingamajigs in existence. I'd like to see the one that's still here."

Ellery nodded. "Would one of you gentlemen please get the stamp?"

Friederich Ulm rose, pottered over to the safe, tinkered with the dials, opened the steel door, fussed about the interior a moment, and came back with the leather case containing the second one-penny black. The Inspector examined the thick little scrap curiously; a thirty-thousand-dollar bit of old paper was as awesome to him as to Ellery.

He almost dropped it when he heard Ellery say to Sergeant Velie: "Sergeant, may I borrow your revolver?"

Velie's massive jaw seesawed as he fumbled in his hip pocket and produced a long-barreled police revolver. Ellery took it and hefted it thoughtfully. Then his fingers closed about the butt and he walked over to the rifled cabinet in the middle of the room.

"Please observe, gentlemen—to expand my third point—that in order to open this cabinet Planck used an iron bar; and that in prying up the lid he found it necessary to insert the bar between the lid and the front wall four times, as the four marks under the lid indicate.

"Now, as you can see, the cabinet is covered with thin glass. Moreover, it was locked, and the one-penny black was in this closed leather case inside. Planck stood about here, I should judge, and mark that the iron bar was in his hand. What would you gentlemen expect a thief, working against time, to do under these circumstances?"

They stared. The Inspector's mouth tightened, and a grin began to spread over the expanse of Sergeant Velie's face.

"But it's so clear," said Ellery. "Visualize it. I'm Planck. The revolver in my hand is an iron 'jimmy.' I'm standing over the cabinet. . . ." His eyes gleamed behind the *pince-nez,* and he raised the revolver high over his head. And then, deliberately, he began to bring the steel barrel down on the thin sheeting of glass atop the cabinet. There was a scream form Albert Ulm, and Friederich Ulm half-rose, glaring. Ellery's hand stopped a half-inch from the glass.

"Don't break that glass, you fool!" shouted the green-shaded dealer. "You'll only—"

He leaped forward and stood before the cabinet, trembling arms outspread as if to protect the case and its contents. Ellery grinned and prodded the man's palpitating belly with the muzzle of the revolver. "I'm glad you stopped me, Mr. Ulm. Put your hands up. Quickly!"

"Why—why, what do you mean?' gasped Albert Ulm, raising his arms with frantic rapidity.

"I mean," said Ellery gently, "that you're William Planck, and that brother Friederich is your accomplice!"

The brothers Ulm sat trembling in their chairs, and Sergeant Velie stood over them with a nasty smile. Albert Ulm had gone to pieces; he was quivering like an aspen leaf in high wind.

"A very simple, almost an elementary, series of deductions," Ellery was saying. "Point three first. Why did the thief, instead of taking the most logical course of smashing the glass with the iron bar, choose to waste precious minutes using a 'jimmy' four times to force open the lid? *Obviously to protect the other stamps in the cabinet which lay open to possible injury,* as Mr. Albert Ulm has just graphically pointed out. And who had the greatest concern in protecting these other stamps—Hinchman, Peter, Beninson, even the mythical Planck himself? Of course not. Only the Ulm brothers, owners of the stamps."

Old Uneker began to chuckle; he nudged the Inspector. "See? Didn't I say he vass smardt? Now me—me, I'd neffer t'ink of dot."

"And why didn't Planck steal these other stamps in the cabinet? You would expect a thief to do that? Planck did not. But if the *Herren* Ulm were the thieves, the theft of the other stamps became pointless."

"How about that snuff business, Mr. Queen?" asked Peters.

"Yes. The conclusion is plain from the fact that Planck apparently indulged only once during the days he worked with Mr. Beninson. Since snuff addicts partake freely and often, Planck wasn't a snuff addict. Then it wasn't snuff he inhaled that day. What else is sniffed in a similar manner? Well—drugs in powder form—heroin! What are the characteristics of a heroin addict? Nervous, drawn appearance; gauntness, almost emaciation; and most important, telltale eyes, the pupils of which contract under influence of the drug. Then here was another explanation for the tinted glasses Planck wore. They served a double purpose—as an easily recognizable disguise, and also to conceal his eyes, which would give his vice addiction away! But when I observed that Mr. Albert Ulm"—Ellery went over to the cowering man and ripped the green eyeshade away, revealing two stark, pinpoint pupils—"wore this shade, it was a psychological confirmation of his identity as Planck."

"Yes, but that business of stealing all those books," said Hazlitt.

"Part of a very pretty and rather farfetched plot," said Ellery. "With Albert Ulm the disguised thief, Friederich Ulm, who exhibited the wound on his cheek, must have been an accomplice. Then with the Ulm brothers the thieves, the entire business of the books was a blind. The attack on Friederich, the ruse of the bookstore escape, the trail of the minor robberies of copies of *Europe in Chaos*— a cleverly planned series of incidents to authenticate the fact that there was an outside thief, to convince the police and the insurance company that the stamp actually was stolen when it was not. Object, of course, to collect the insurance without parting with the stamp. These men are fanatical collectors."

Heffley wriggled his fat little body uncomfortably. "That's all very nice, Mr. Queen, but where the deuce is that stamp they stole from themselves? Where'd they hide it?"

"I thought long and earnestly about that, Heffley. For while my trio of deductions were psychological indications of guilt, the discovery of the stolen stamp in the Ulms' possession would be evidential proof." The Inspector was turning the second stamp over mechanically. "I said to myself," Ellery went on, "in a reconsideration of the problem: What would be the most likely hiding place for the stamp? And then I remembered that the two stamps were identical, even the initials of the good Queen being in the same place. So I said to myself: if I were Messrs Ulm, I should hide that stamp—like the character in Edgar Allan Poe's famous tale—in the most obvious place. And what is the most obvious place?"

Ellery sighed and returned the unused revolver to Sergeant Velie. "Dad," he remarked to the Inspector, who started guiltily, "I think that if you allow one of the philatelists in our company to examine the second one-penny black in your fingers, you'll find that the *first* has been pasted with noninjurious rubber cement precisely over the second!"

NORTH CAROLINA

BROTHERS ON THE BEACH

by Edward D. Hoch

THE TEMPERATURE WAS in the mid-forties on the December day when Ben Snow stepped off the train at Elizabeth City and went about the business of renting a horse and buggy for the remainder of his journey to the shores of the Atlantic.

He often felt there was something contrary about his gradual journey east at a time when the nation had just about completed its western expansion. There were forty-five states now, stretching from coast to coast, and already there was talk that the territories of Oklahoma, New Mexico, and Arizona would soon be admitted to the Union. He'd fought Indians in the West in his younger days, and even journeyed to Mexico on occasion, but now it was the East that drew him. Cities like Buffalo and Savannah and New Orleans.

Rivers like the Mississippi and the Delaware had only been names on a rarely studied map when he was young. Now that he was past forty and the nation had entered the Twentieth Century, things were different. The West didn't need Indian fighters any more, or hired guns whose draw was as fast as Billy the Kid's.

Ben Snow had never been a man to settle down as a ranch hand. He'd considered working for Pinkerton's, putting his crime-solving abilities to some use, but the detective agency's deep involvement in strikebreaking wasn't to his liking. So he drifted, taking jobs where he found them, helping out old friends when he could.

He'd never been as far east as North Carolina before, and he quickly noted that back here men didn't wear gunbelts on the street in 1903. He left his in his suitcase while he dickered for the horse and buggy. "Kitty Hawk," he said to the man at the stable. "How far is it?"

"About thirty-five miles," the man answered. "You take the road east to Barco and then turn south along the coast. It's on a narrow cape that runs all the way down to Hatteras and beyond, but you can get a ferry to take you across. Why'd anyone want to go to Kitty Hawk in December, though? There's nothing there

332

but a beach, and it's too damn cold for swimming. The wind beats across there like a gale most of the time."

"I have to see a man," Ben answered. "How much for the horse and buggy?"

They dickered a bit before Ben finally drove off in the buggy. He'd noticed a few automobiles—as people were starting to call them—on the streets of the city, but he hadn't felt brave enough to try one. Besides, he didn't know what sort of roads awaited him along the coastal sand spit.

It was shortly after he'd passed through Barco and headed south along the coast, getting his first view of the turbulent Atlantic, when a lone horseman overtook him. The man was young and handsome, with curly blond hair, and he sat well in the saddle. "Would you be Ben Snow?" he asked, drawing abreast of the buggy.

"That's me."

He leaned over to offer his hand. "Roderick Claymore. My brother Rudolph hired you, but he had to go to the state capital on business and he asked that I meet you."

They pulled up and Ben swung down from the buggy. "I'm a lot more comfortable on a horse," he admitted, "but with my suitcase, the buggy seemed best."

Claymore took out a cigar and offered Ben one. "How much did my brother tell you?"

"Only that he was hiring me to guard a section of beach at Kitty Hawk for the next week or so. He wanted someone from far away, and that's what he got. He hired me last week in St. Louis."

Roderick Claymore nodded, puffing on the thin cigar. "About three years ago, a pair of brothers from Dayton, the Wrights, started coming here and flying gliders off the dunes at Kitty Hawk. Seems they wrote the Weather Bureau and were told this was the best testing area for gliders because the winds off the ocean blow at a fairly constant twenty miles an hour or better."

"Does this glidertesting bother you?"

"It didn't at first. No one paid much attention to them. But now things are changing. We own some land nearby and it's important that we don't have a lot of trespassers. They're planning something for Monday that could bring the whole country to our door."

"What would that be?"

"Last summer they started shipping in parts for a powered craft they've been constructing there on the beach. They built their own lightweight gasoline engine—four cylinders, watercooled."

"I don't know much about engines," Ben admitted.

"It's to drive two eight-foot wooden propellers mounted to the rear of the wings. This craft won't be a glider. It'll take off and fly by itself, with one of the Wrights aboard. That's why we need you."

Ben Snow smiled slightly. "To shoot it down?"

"Hardly."

"Back in '96, out West, there was a fellow billed himself as The Flying Man. He strapped wings to his arms and tried to glide off hilltops. Somebody killed him one day during an exhibition, and I helped solve the murder. I'm just telling you so you'll know which side of the fence I'm on. I've killed plenty of men in my day, but never one who didn't deserve it. I'm not a hired gun, despite what you and your brother might have heard."

"Look here, Snow, we don't want any hired guns. But if those crazy Wrights bring a thousand people to that beach to see their flight on Monday, we want them kept off our property any way that's necessary."

"All right," Ben agreed. "Where am I staying?"

"There's a lady teacher has a house in Kill Devil Hills, just a few miles from Kitty Hawk. We rented a room there for you."

"That'll be just fine."

It seemed ironic to Ben that he'd had to travel east to North Carolina to find the legendary pretty schoolmarm who was supposed to inhabit every western town. Elizabeth Boyers was a dark-haired beauty, probably past thirty but with a fine girlish figure and a smile that could melt the coldest heart. She lived alone in the house across the street from the one-room school building where she taught.

"There aren't many children here," she admitted. "They're mostly from older families who've lived here all their lives. But someone has to teach them. If I left, they'd have to take the ferry to the mainland."

It was Sunday and they were strolling on the beach together, looking over the site where the Wrights would attempt their flight the following day.

"Do you think they'll make it?" he asked.

"Frankly, no. Not after what happened to Langley last Wednesday."

"Who's Langley?"

She laughed. "You don't keep up with the newspapers, Mr. Snow. Samuel Langley, the inventor, had a $50,000 grant from the War Department to develop a flying machine. He spent five years on it, and last Wednesday he tried to launch it from the roof of a houseboat in the Potomac River with boatloads of Washington reporters and government officials looking on. But a wing tip caught on its catapult and the craft broke apart in the air. Langley is secretary of the Smithsonian Institution. If he can't build a proper flying machine, these brothers from a bicycle shop in Dayton can hardly be expected to do it."

"Will there be reporters here tomorrow?"

"Not if the Wrights can help it. They're trying to keep it secret until the flight is successful. Then they'll send a telegram to their father asking that the press be notified."

"Then why is Claymore so worried?"

She hesitated before answering. "Who hired you—Roderick or Rudolph?"

"Rudolph. He's the older one, isn't he? He came to me in St. Louis and offered to pay my expenses and a week's salary if I'd come here to guard his beach. It seemed to me he could have hired someone from here in town for half the money."

"They do own some land down the beach. I've seen them digging there. I kidded them about looking for pirate treasure. These islands along the Atlantic coast have always had pirate legends connected with them."

"Why did you ask which one hired me?"

"Oh," she answered casually, "I've had a little trouble with the younger one, Roderick—the one who brought you here yesterday. I went out with him a few times last year and he asked me to marry him. I said no, but he won't accept that. Now I'm engaged to someone else and he's bothering me. I wouldn't have taken their money for the room if I didn't need it."

"What do they do for a living when they're not digging for buried treasure?"

"They have an ice business. They deliver blocks of ice to homes and businesses in all the towns around here."

"Never had anything like that out where I come from."

She smiled at him. "This is civilization. This is the Twentieth Century."

When they returned to the house after inspecting—at a distance—the Wright brothers' flying machine, Ben found Rudolph Claymore waiting for him. Rudolph was larger and tougher than his younger brother, and while Roderick sat well on a horse Ben couldn't imagine this man ever riding one. In St. Louis, where he'd hired Ben, Rudolph had seemed like a successful businessman. Here, in his home territory, there was something vaguely sinister about him.

"You saw that flying contraption of theirs?" he asked Ben.

Ben nodded. "Looks backwards to me. The tail seems to be in the front. But flying isn't my line."

"If we're in luck, they'll crash tomorrow like that fellow Langley did. But if it's successful and people start pouring in here, I'll need you to guard our beach property for the next week or so."

"Couldn't you have hired someone from one of the towns around here for that purpose?" Elizabeth said. "Why bring Mr. Snow all the way from St. Louis?"

"I want someone who'll be here today and gone tomorrow, not one of the town boys who'll have a few drinks at the bar and get to talking too much. Mr. Snow's got a good reputation out West. When I asked around for someone to hire, he was the one everyone mentioned."

Claymore took Ben aside and gave him a down payment on his fee, along with the travel expenses. "You brought your gun, didn't you?"

"I have it," Ben assured him.

"Wear it tomorrow, but keep it under your coat."

When he'd gone, Ben asked Elizabeth, "What do you think is so valuable about that strip of sand?"

"Besides the pirate treasure?" she answered with a smile. "I have no idea."

Ben slept restlessly that night, wondering what the morning would bring.

What it brought was more of the same as far as the weather was concerned. A cool breeze was blowing off the ocean and he found he needed the wool jacket he'd brought with him from the Midwest. He buckled his gunbelt under it, making certain all chambers of the Colt six-shooter were loaded. He wondered vaguely if there were laws back East against carrying concealed weapons. Maybe that's why the Claymore brothers had wanted someone from far away.

"Are you up, Mr. Snow?" Elizabeth called to him through the bedroom door.

"Sure am. I'll be right down."

"Breakfast is ready. My fiancé, Mark Freen, is joining us."

Freen was an agreeable chap with brown hair and a ready smile. Like Elizabeth, he was a teacher, though his school was on the mainland. "I'm playing hooky today," he explained. "We both are. This might be an historic occasion—right here at Kitty Hawk."

Ben was surprised to see that a fair crowd of local residents had gathered along the beach. "Those are the Wright brothers," Elizabeth said, pointing out two men in caps and jackets. They seemed to be in their thirties. "Orville and Wilbur."

"Do you know them personally?"

"I've spoken with them. They've been here since September assembling the *Flyer*. That's the name of it. And last year they made over a thousand controlled glider flights here. Everyone knows them by now."

They were interrupted by the arrival of an older man with thick glasses and a beard. "Oh, Professor—I want you to meet Ben Snow." Elizabeth Boyers performed the introductions as if they were both her oldest friends. "Ben, this is Professor Minder from the university at Raleigh."

Ben shook hands and asked, "Did you come all this distance for today's flight?"

"Not exactly," the professor replied. "I'm doing research just south of here, on Roanoke Island. You may remember it was the site of Sir Walter Raleigh's lost colony."

Ben nodded and turned up his collar against the chill wind. "I hope they get started soon. It's cold out here."

The *Flyer* had been pulled from its storage shed by the Wrights and five assistants. Ben heard someone in the crowd comment that it weighed over six hundred pounds. They positioned it on a level stretch of sand at the base of a hundred-foot-high dune named Kill Devil Hill. Then the brothers flipped a coin and Wilbur won the toss. After the *Flyer* had been placed aboard a low trolley on the single sixty-foot rail of a greased launching track, he climbed aboard and lay face down in a cradlelike harness across the lower wing, working the wing and rudder controls with his body in a final check before takeoff.

The crowd tensed and Ben glanced around for some sign of the Claymores. There were figures farther down the beach, but he couldn't tell who they were. His attention returned to the *Flyer* as the gasoline engine sputtered into life. The twin propellers started to turn and the machine glided down its greased track. There was the beginning of a roar from the crowd and cameras poised to capture the moment of flight.

Then, unaccountably, the engine stalled at takeoff. The *Flyer* dropped to the sand with a soft thud.

As the crowd groaned, Orville rushed forward to pull his brother from the craft. "It's over," Elizabeth said sadly. "It'll never fly."

"Another Langley," Mark Freen said, summing it all up.

Wilbur stood up, free of the craft, and the brothers began inspecting the damage. Ben turned and noticed Professor Minder sitting on the sand. "Excitement too much for you?" he asked in fun, bending down to offer his hand.

That was when he saw the knife protruding from Minder's back and realized the man he'd just met had been murdered.

The investigation of a murder case was far different in the East than anything Ben had known out West. There, a sheriff bothered little with clues or suspects. There he looked for eyewitnesses or the person with the likeliest motive, and if justice came at all it was usually swift and deadly. On that windswept beach in North Carolina, while the Wrights worked to repair their damaged aircraft, justice was slow and plodding. Justice was a pair of State Police officers with notebooks, taking down names and addresses and setting up a camera to take a photograph of the murder scene.

There was a general agreement among all witnesses that the brothers Wright couldn't have had a hand in the killing, since all eyes were on them during the entire period. But that did little to narrow the field of suspects. Any one of the dozens of spectators could have been the guilty party, and in the eyes of the State Police that included Ben Snow.

"Private citizens don't wear gunbelts in North Carolina," one of them told him pointedly. "This isn't the wild West."

"Tell that to the dead man," Ben replied.

The officer's name was Rellens, and he eyed Ben as if he'd like to lock him away in a cell. "What are you doing here, anyway?"

"I was hired by the Claymore brothers to guard their strip of beach land. They feared some of the crowd might wander down that way."

"So you're guarding it from up here?"

"I can see it from here. I can see no one's on it."

"Were the Claymores here today?"

"I didn't see them."

"Pretty strange if they missed something like this," Rellens said.

Ben had been thinking the same thing as his eyes traveled over the spectators. Some had started to drift away, but the majority had stayed after giving their names, drawn by the twin spectacles of the murder investigation and the Wrights' efforts to repair their flying machine.

Then he saw Rudolph Claymore striding over the dunes in their direction. He left Rellens and went to meet his employer. "What happened here?" Rudolph demanded. "I just got word there's been a killing—"

"That's right," Ben said. "A professor named Minder."

"Minder! I know the man! He's been working on an island nearby!"

"Someone stabbed him."

"Is my brother here?"

"I haven't seen him all morning."

"He didn't come to work today and I assumed he was down here. I had to cover the entire ice route myself." Rudolph Clamore glanced along the windswept beach. "What about our property?"

"No one's gone near it," Ben assured him.

"Not Minder, before he was killed?"

"Not unless it was early this morning before I got here. You didn't say anything about guarding it day and night."

"No, no. I just thought you might have noticed him wandering down that way."

"I think it's about time you tell me what this is all about," Ben said. "I might be able to help the investigation if I knew all the facts."

"All right," Claymore agreed. "Come to my house tonight. I'll have my brother there, too, if I can find him. Here's the address. It's in the village of Kitty Hawk."

Elizabeth and Freen had been over by the damaged aircraft and were hurrying back. "Orville says the repairs will take a few days, but they hope to try again on Thursday," she said. "Will you be staying that long, Mr. Snow?"

"I expect so. The Claymores hired me for the week."

"I saw that policeman, Rellens, talking to you. Did he ask for your help?"

"Not exactly."

"Does he have any suspects?"

"Right now I may be his prime suspect. He noticed I was wearing a gunbelt."

"That's absurd! We were all standing together."

"But Professor Minder was right behind us. With all eyes on the Wrights and their machine, I suppose I could have reached around and stabbed him. Someone did."

"But why? He was a sweet old man. Why would anyone kill him?"

"What do you know about him? What was he doing here?"

"Mark knows more about him than I do. He went over to see him on Roanoke Island a few weeks ago."

"He was studying evidence of the so-called Lost Colony," Freen explained. "You know, the colony founded by Sir Walter Raleigh that vanished from that island between 1587 and 1590."

Ben's knowledge of early colonial history was vague at best, but he nodded and urged Freen to continue.

"Well, a colony of some eighty-five men and women remained on the island in

1587 while a ship returned to England for supplies. The war between England and Spain prevented the supplies from reaching Roanoke until 1590, and by that time all that could be found was a deserted, ransacked fortress. None of the settlers was ever found. The name *Croatoan* was carved into a post—apparently the name of an island to the south. They may have gone there, or they may have been killed by Indians. It's one of the mysteries of history."

"And Professor Minder thought he'd found new evidence of what happened," Elizabeth Boyers interjected. "He was over here a few times pursuing his studies."

"Interesting," Ben admitted. "But why should anyone kill him? Why would something that happened over three hundred years ago cost a man his life?"

They returned to the house without an answer. Later that afternoon, while Elizabeth and Freen were alone, Ben walked back up the beach alone. From a distance he watched the Wright brothers and their helpers working on the flying machine. He saw that Rellens was still there, too, pacing back and forth as he examined the trampled sand.

That evening Ben Snow rode over to the address Claymore had given him. It was one of a handful of houses in the tiny village of Kitty Hawk, and Rudolph came out on the porch to greet him as he parked his buggy. "Come in, Snow. My brother's already here."

Ben entered and took a chair in the sparsely furnished parlor. A woman's touch was obviously lacking and it occurred to him for the first time that the elder Claymore was probably not married. He shook hands with Roderick and said, "I didn't see you this morning."

"I had business," Roderick answered. "I hear the flying machine never got off the ground."

"They're repairing it. They plan to try again on Thursday."

Rudolph came in and sat down. "Some of the folks around here are helping them. We got more important things on our minds."

"Tell me about it," Ben suggested. "Tell me why that property of yours is so valuable. Is there really pirate treasure buried there?"

The older brother smiled slightly. "Next best thing, according to Professor Minder. You know about the Lost Colony and that business on Roanoke Island?"

"A little."

"Well, historians have always speculated that the colonists went south to another island, if they weren't killed by Indians. Minder went there and nosed around. He decided they came north instead, right here to the beach at Kitty Hawk. Look at this here map. You can see that the abandoned Fort Raleigh was at the very northern tip of Roanoke, not ten miles across the water from where we are now."

"Minder told you this?"

"Damned right!" Roderick said. "He did a little digging by our property there and came up with evidence of settlement!"

Rudolph showed Ben a bowl with a piece missing from it. "See this? It's not Indian. It's the sort the colonists brought with them from England."

"But you were keeping this a secret?" Ben asked."

"Had to! Other people own some of that beach land, especially near the village here. We started buying it up. An old settlement like that could mean a spot people would pay to see. It could make us rich."

"Who knew about this?" Ben asked.

"Only the two of us and Minder. That's why I went so far away to hire a guard. I didn't want any of the locals getting wind of what we were trying to hide."

"How much land have you bought?"

"Around twenty thousand dollars' worth so far. Minder agreed to act as a middleman so the people wouldn't know we were the buyers."

"And that's what you've been digging for?" Ben asked.

Rudolph nodded. "We uncovered some more things on our own, too—a few trinkets and a sword."

Roderick scratched at his cheek. "We'd better check on those land deeds in the morning. With Minder dead, we could be out twenty grand."

"I've already thought of that," his brother answered sourly.

Ben left them going over their records, trying to establish the extent of their possible losses.

On Tuesday afternoon, the State Police officer, Rellens, showed up at the Boyers house to see Ben. He sat down heavily and flipped open his notebook. "This case has taken a couple of surprising turns," he said. "I need to interview witnesses again, especially those who were standing closest to the victim."

"Miss Boyers is teaching today," Ben told him.

"You'll do for a beginning. It seems one of the men in that crowd of spectators gave a false name and address. Dick Roer, of Kill Devil Hills. No such person."

"You think you let the murderer walk away?"

"Looks like it," he said glumly. "I seem to remember him vaguely. Had a Teddy Roosevelt mustache and was wearing a wool cap. Of course, the mustache could have been a fake. Do you remember anyone looking like that near you?"

"No," Ben answered honestly. "But I wasn't concentrating on the crowd."

"All right." Rollens closed his notebook, preparing to leave.

"You said the case had taken a couple of surprising turns. What else?"

"The dead man—Minder. It turns out he was a fake, too. There's no Professor Minder connected with any of the universities in Raleigh."

"Interesting," Ben admitted. "Two men with false identities on the beach yesterday—one a murderer and one a victim."

"It looks that way." Rellens nodded.

"But why was Minder using a false name? Who was he?"

"We'll find out," Rellens promised. "You'll be here for the next few days, Mr. Snow?"

"At least till after Thursday's flight."

"That's good," Rellens said and was gone.

On Wednesday Ben Snow sought out Rudolph Claymore on his ice route. He found him lugging fifty-pound blocks into a little café in Kill Devil Hills. "I wanted to ask you about your brother," he said.

"He's back at the ice house. You can find him there."

"He was in love with Elizabeth Boyers, wasn't he?"

"Still is, far as I know. But she's sappy over that teacher, Mark Freen. It hit my brother hard."

"Ever hear of someone named Dick Roer around here?"

"Can't say that I have."

"Rellens thinks that was the name the killer used on Monday."

"Never heard of him." Claymore climbed into the back of his wagon and used an ice pick to loosen another fifty-pound block.

"That looks like hard work."

Rudolph shrugged. "It's a living." He flipped the pick into the next block in line. "It pays the bills till something big like that Lost Colony comes along."

"What if the Lost Colony never happens? What if Professor Minder was a fraud?"

Rudolph Claymore blinked and stared at Ben. "What are you saying?"

"Have you and your brother checked on that property yet?"

"He's doing it today."

"I wish you luck," Ben said and started to walk away.

"Wait a minute!" Claymore said, hurrying after him. "What are you trying to tell me?"

"That Minder was a fraud. That wasn't his real name, and chances are those trinkets in the sand were put there by him so you'd find them. Out West we call it salting a mine—putting a few gold nuggets near the surface for the suckers to find."

"But the property—"

"If he was trying to swindle someone, it must have been you. He probably took your twenty thousand and faked some papers, without ever buying the land."

"That—"

Ben left him standing by his ice wagon, still swearing.

The younger Claymore was a bit more difficult to track down. He was gone from the ice house by the time Ben reached it and he had to stop at a couple of nearby bars before he spotted Roderick's horse tethered outside the village stable. He found the young man inside, seeing to the repair of one of his saddle stirrups.

"I had a talk with your brother this morning," Ben told him. "Could I have a few words with you outside?"

Roderick shrugged. "I suppose so. You going to be on guard at the beach again tomorrow?"

"I'll be there. But when you hear what I have to say, you may decide you don't need me." Ben told him quickly what he'd told his brother, about Professor Minder's false identity and the probable swindle. Roderick's reaction wasn't quite as violent as his brother's, but it was obvious he was upset.

"I always wondered about that guy. He didn't seem right for a professor."

"Have you checked on the deeds yet?"

"I was on my way there now."

"There's something else," Ben said.

"What's that?"

"The police think Minder's killer is a man named Dick Roer."

The color drained from Roderick's face.

"That's you, isn't it? Dick Roer is a simple anagram for Roderick."

"I don't know what you mean."

"You were on the beach Monday morning, wearing a wool cap and a false mustache. You killed Professor Minder."

"I didn't! That's not true!"

"Why else would you be there in disguise?"

"That's none of your business. We hired you to guard our property, not to snoop around."

"If you don't answer me, you'll have to answer to the police."

He glowered and started to walk away, then thought better of it. "All right—if you must know. I wanted to see Elizabeth!"

"See her?"

"With him. With that Freen fellow. I wanted to hear what they were talking about."

"You disguised yourself to spy on Elizabeth Boyers?"

"Yes." His voice had dropped and he wouldn't meet Ben's eyes. "I love her."

"You can't accept the fact that she might find pleasure with another man?"

"I just wanted to hear what they talked about, to see for myself if she really cared for him. That's all. I barely realized Minder was there."

"All right," Ben said, not knowing whether he believed him or not. "Will you be there in the morning?"

"Yes," Roderick answered.

"In disguise?"

"There's no point in it now, is there?"

Thursday morning dawned clear but freezing cold. When Ben reached the beach at Kitty Hawk in the company of Mark Freen and Elizabeth, they were saying the wind off the ocean was blowing at twenty-seven miles an hour. The few spectators were bundled against the cold and some were doubting the Wright brothers would attempt the flight.

But shortly after nine A.M., Wilbur and Orville gathered up their five assistants and once more hauled the machine from its shed. It was lifted onto the trolley at the base of Kill Devil Hill.

In addition to Elizabeth and Freen, who'd taken off another day from their teaching, both Claymore brothers were in attendance. And Ben saw Rellens pacing nearby. The cast was assembled.

Rudolph came up to stand next to Ben. "What did you say to my brother yesterday? Whatever it was, he's been pretty upset by it. He didn't even want to come out here today."

"I notice he's staying clear of Elizabeth Boyers."

"Well, they used to go together. I suppose he's jealous of her friend."

It seemed to take the Wrights forever to make their adjustments to the *Flyer* and the cold wind drove a few of the less hardy souls away. Orville was busy setting up the tripod for his camera, then aiming it at the end of the launching track. If the plane became airborne, he wanted a picture for the ages.

Finally, at 10:30, they were ready.

It was young Orville's turn to be at the controls this time and he glanced around for someone to snap the shutter of his camera. He called to one of the townspeople who'd been helping out and asked him to take the picture if the plane became airborne. Then he climbed aboard the *Flyer* and strapped himself down. Wilbur pulled the cap down more snugly on his head and gripped the lower right wingtip of the biplane.

The engine started and the propellers began to turn. The *Flyer* moved on its track. Wilbur began trotting alongside, holding the wingtip steady.

"He didn't do that on Monday," Rudolph Claymore remarked.

And then Orville opened the throttle more, bringing the engine to full power. The time was 10:35.

"No, he didn't," Ben Snow agreed. "But how did you know if you weren't here?"

The *Flyer* lifted from its track, airborne. Wilbur released the wing as the camera shutter clicked. A cheer went up from the small group of spectators.

The machine wobbled and swooped down, its runner hitting the sand. The flight had lasted only twelve seconds, never more than ten feet off the ground, but it had covered 120 feet.

People were running forward. Rudolph Claymore started to move but Ben restrained him. "You knew what happened on Monday because you were here. Because you came to murder the man who'd swindled you."

"You think I was this Dick Roer?"

"No, that was your brother, spying on Elizabeth."

"But everyone else in the crowd was accounted for!"

"You never joined the crowd, Rudolph. You hid behind a sand dune, and while all eyes were on the Wrights at the crucial moment, you sneaked up just close enough to *throw* that knife into Minder's back, just like you flipped that ice pick into the cake of ice yesterday. You never came closer than fifteen or twenty feet, and the sand was too trampled to show footprints. No one saw you because we were all looking in the opposite direction."

"But I didn't know he was a swindler until you told me yesterday!" Rudolph argued.

"You put on a very good act, but I think you knew. When your brother met me, he said you'd gone to the state capital on business. That's Raleigh, where Minder claimed to teach. You checked on him while you were there and discovered he was a fake. You came back here and killed him the first chance you had."

Rellens had been overhearing the conversation and now he stepped forward. "Do you have anything to say, Mr. Claymore?"

The fight had gone out of Rudolph. "Only that he deserved to die for swindling us. No jury will convict me."

Ben Snow left town the following morning. The Claymores' land didn't need protection any longer and he never heard what the jury decided. For that matter, it was a few years before he heard the Wright brothers mentioned again. They made four successful flights that December 17th at Kitty Hawk, and their father spread the news, but only two newspapers in the country carried a report the following day.

No crowds came to Kitty Hawk. The Claymores hadn't needed Ben Snow after all.

NORTH DAKOTA

FIRST STAND
by Barry N. Malzberg

DEAR EDITOR:

A mystery set in North Dakota you request, this for a book containing mysteries set in each and every one of the fifty states plus Washington, D.C. This is a problem. I could write a run-of-the-mill mystery, a Brooklyn or Gowanus, Pasadena or Ventura type of work with the venue changed to "North Dakota," of course, an old and honored kind of freelancer's cheating, but this doesn't seem quite right to me, *indigenous* is the word with which I grew up, something like the struggle in Vietnam in all the decades of this century was indigenous, not imposed, not that McNamara's Band ever noticed. So the idea was to write a real North Dakota mystery but that, for this Easterner, is a toughie: "Black Hills" I thought right away, or "Wounded Knee," but they're in *South* Dakota, as is Mount Rushmore. (How about someone who looks like Cary Grant scampering amidst those great carvings? But that's for the South Dakota writer.) Custer's Last Stand would be great (who killed Custer *before* the encounter with the Sioux and then assumed his command?; that's my theory anyway) but it occurred in what became Montana. And the events from which *Psycho,* film and novel, were taken occurred in Minnesota if I am not mistaken.

So it's a tough one, a tough assignment to be sure, but then it occurred to me that John Jacob Astor set up the fur-trading exchanges in the northern Dakota territory in the early 1800s and for most of that century there was little in that state but exchange personnel and Indians (and the bearers of the furs, of course) and this gave me an idea of sorts, suppose that at one of these exchanges, in the late 1880s, one of the trappers, an old guy, venerable as they come, let's call him Dan McGrew in honor of the apocryphal folklore, is murdered, knifed and scalped and left dead on the counter of a bar at the outpost, discovered the next morning by the bartender lurching in to clean up the glasses and the other accrued whiskey damages of the night, the bartender sees McGrew and panics, cries for help and soon the bar is flooded, not only the trappers and the traders but one of Astor's emissaries himself who had been on one of his semi-annual visits to check on receipts and procedures poured into the bar. There is much consternation, much yelling and screaming; McGrew had been well enough liked to the degree that men in these surroundings can admit to affection, and there is obviously a murderer somewhere on the premises, perhaps one of the trappers has gone berserk and is now concealing himself. But all hands are present and accounted for in quick count and this somehow is even worse, the murderer is amongst them, donning a sane face. It is not only the issue of the corpse which concerns, it is the fact that McGrew had been in his last week at the outpost, he has had enough of this life, he and the emissary were going to leave together when the emissary's duties were done. "This is a dead trade, boys," McGrew had said at the bar in conversations now grimly recalled, "the times are turning, everything is turning, the Indians are our only entertainment and they are on their way to the happy hunting grounds, statehood beckons and an honest hooker has the Oklahoma territory instead, we'll be off the circuit soon. The Forty-Niners got the gold, but how much company is a mink in winter?" And so on and so forth, McGrew being of a thoughtful as well as ominous cast of mind.

Well, there is much more that could be said and some descriptive material could be inserted about the look of the Badlands in the dusk, the perpetual dusk that falls on the twilit Dakota territory in this sullen March, but description is of only passing mention in the short story and the pathetic fallacy is not quite successful in the 1890s, outside the work of Thomas Hardy or Henry James, so to speak. Let us say too that this is not a standard deductive mystery; this is not a matter, tea-and-cozy style, of examining the personalities of the trappers to determine through cunning planting of evidence who hated McGrew or had lost his love to McGrew years before; the emissary didn't do it either. No, this is a different kind of mystery, one of motive rather than identity because in due course the murderer is found to be an Indian, a sullen and articulate brave known (in this camp) as "Jack" for no reason other than that his Indian name is unpronounceable. Jack is a liaison, he is one of the many Indians who are used by the trappers to negotiate with the remnants of the Sioux, the Sioux do much of the actual trapping and conveyance of the animals, and Jack, who speaks a passable English and a ferocious

Sioux, is an intermediary. Jack is the only one without a satisfactory alibi and suspicion has already settled upon him *before* the Indian comes into the bar, some hours after the murder, McGrew's body having been removed to a cold and distant locker on the fringes, and confesses to the crime. "Of course I did it," Jack says, even before the question can be asked, "I did it and I did it and I would do it again." And even as the trappers lunge toward him, even as the emissary removes the Colt caliber forty-five that he feels he must carry in these rough parts at all times, Jack says, "He was going to kill *me,* it was self-defense, I did it to protect my own life" and he removes the knife, the very weapon of murder, tosses it, handle first, on the bar, thrusts out his palms in the timeless gesture of harmlessness, of surrender. "Murderer, murderer, *he's* the murderer!" Jack shouts.

The Indian then proceeds to tell a strange and wondrous tale; Jack was one of the attacking band at Custer's last, terrible, already mythic battle; crippled through honorable injury some weeks earlier he had ridden at the rear of the band but had been one of the first to enter the shattered Little Big Horn after the massacre. Standing there next to Sitting Bull, looking at the carnage, the reeking corpses, the twisted and terrible features of Custer himself, Custer not at all poised or heroic in death but quite a brutalized figure slain in the act of trying to scale a wall, Jack felt that he had seen then as if for the first time the utter futility not of combat itself but the very assumptions of combat, of contest. "We die so that we may live, that's what they tell us," Jack said to the trappers, "but I understood that Custer did not believe that then, all that Custer believed was in getting over the wall. My leg hurt, my hands hurt, my heart hurt but all of me much less than that band who had died.

"I could not tell any of this to Sitting Bull, to Rain-in-the-Face," Jack said, "I could see that they would not understand, that they would have thought me cowardly, no fit bearer of the prize. So I left Little Big Horn, clutching my staff, went back to the camp and later away. In the years following I learned how to speak English, I learned how to work within the world of the white man, I learned the ways and means of exchange, I made myself useful to all in the small ways that I could, holding to myself the knowledge of Little Big Horn that to die was to die and there was nothing else, no other truth. Until your man McGrew last night in the bar recognized me as one who had been at Little Big Horn. How did he know? Because one of the braves had told him, he said. Because he had known for a long time. Because he had known for a *very* long time and had kept that knowledge to himself but now he was leaving, he was leaving at last and he did not have to conceal this. 'You killed Custer,' he said. He was very drunk. Drink fell easily and heavily within Dan McGrew, as you called him, plummeted to his heart. 'You killed Custer,' he said again and laughed. 'But you really didn't, because I am going to kill *you*.'

"Do you want me to tell you that he attacked me? I will not tell you that; he was a belligerent, stupid, harmless old drunk, he could kill no one, nothing except himself, but looking at the face, looking at the benign and killing stupidity drifting over his features it was not him I saw but Custer, the dead Custer crouched, slammed against the wall, the terror of his features hardened into cunning and I realized then what I should have realized those many years ago, that your Dan McGrew was right, I didn't kill Custer, but I *could* have. I could have killed him. It was only a matter of opportunity. *Any* of us could have killed him. He wanted so badly to die. It was only a matter of who was fortunate enough to deliver that thrust.

"And seeing this, knowing this, I went with my knife to the Custer at the bar, seeing in his face that wishfulness that had been in Custer's and I did the necessary and the splendid. Did it as any brave would have done his duty in or out of that terrible time. And stand now exposed but unashamed before you. And that is all."

There is more to this story—the reaction of the trappers, the emissary's cry of fury, the emissary's struggle to reach the gun, the way in which the men restrained him, the way in which Jack threw himself to the ground and waited then, waited as he always would for the white man's judgment, but that, properly speaking, is not part of this story. It is part of a much larger story which does not take place only in North Dakota but in many other places. And has not, has not stopped yet. *Indigenous,* that is the word I am seeking. Indigenous, to those badlands—

                                        Sincerely,

New Jersey
1988

OHIO

THE TOMATO MAN'S DAUGHTER

by Joyce Harrington

THE RIVER MAN sat on the deck of his houseboat sipping a cold beer. While he sipped, he watched the Tomato Man's daughter.

Elva Mildrum moved up and down the long green lanes of the tomato vines, sometimes stooping, sometimes stretching, always filling her bushel basket with bright red fruit. She was a tiny one, the Tomato Man's daughter, but golden pretty and a hard worker to boot.

The River Man licked his lips and popped the top off another beer from the cooler at his side. The river lapped tiredly against the sides of the houseboat and the high white ball of the sun sucked the juice out of all the earth. Nothing moved, except Elva steadfastly picking tomatoes, and the endless hordes of mosquitoes that had to move or die.

"Hey, Elva! Come on down!" The River Man called across the grass slope that lay between the houseboat and the tomato fields.

Elva parted the dark green leaves of the tomato vines, saw him, and waved. The River Man pulled his sticky T-shirt away from his broad freckled chest. The shirt was stained gray with sweat, and sweat ran out of the gray stubble of his crew cut and down the creases of his square red face.

"Come on down, honey," he called again and waved a beer can temptingly in her direction.

Elva shimmered through the fence of staked-up tomato vines. On small bare feet she floated down the slope toward the houseboat. She carried a ripe tomato in each hand.

Like a fairy princess, thought the River Man. Just like a damn fairy princess. Sweet dear Jesus! He wiped sweat from his forehead with the back of his hairy freckled arm.

Elva climbed the narrow board that served as a gangplank. She stood before him and held out a tomato.

349

"Eat it. It's good," she said.

"Thank you kindly, Elva. I will." He took the tomato from her hand. "Will you set yourself down?"

"Pa sees me here he'll whip me," she stated sadly.

"Where is your mean old Daddy?"

"Gone to Columbus. Told me to don't do anything but pick tomatoes."

"Well, he can't see you if he's in Columbus. Set down and take a rest from picking. Ain't healthy to pick all day in this heat."

"I dunno." The girl shifted restlessly around the cluttered deck and the River Man's eyes followed her hungrily. She wore faded blue shorts and a pink cotton blouse with the sleeves cut out. For all her work in the tomato fields only her arms were stained with sunburn. Her legs gleamed pale and dewy, and the downy golden fuzz on her calves seemed to the River Man like the pelt of a small defenseless animal. Her face was shaded by a wide straw hat.

"Come on, Elva honey. Set down and relax." He patted the aluminum folding chair beside his own invitingly. "Will you have a beer?"

Elva sighed and sat down. "Don't mind if I do. Thank you, Mr. Heskill."

"How many times I got to tell you. Don't call me Mister. I'm Woody to my friends. You *are* my friend, ain't you, Elva?"

"Yessir."

"Good. And I'm your friend. Now drink up."

Side by side they sat on the deck of the houseboat, Elva guiltily watching the tomato fields and Woody Heskill, the River Man, watching Elva. He watched her as she took a bite out of the ripe tomato in one hand and noisily sucked the juice. He watched as she sipped from the frosty wet beer can in her other hand and belched softly after each sip.

He breathed in the sharp green tang that flowed from her body. All summer she carried the bitter pungent odor of tomato vines heated in the sun. It was in her hair and on her hands and in the shallow bony place between her small white breasts. The River Man stirred uneasily and marveled at how he'd never noticed Elva until this summer and now he couldn't seem to stop wanting more of her.

"Gettin' pretty warm out here, ain't it?"

"M-m-m." Pale juice and a few tomato seeds ran down Elva's chin. She wiped it away with the back of her hand.

"Might be a tad cooler inside. Would you like to go inside, Elva honey?"

"Don't mind if I do."

Elva ripened out of season. It was almost Christmas before the Tomato Man noticed that some stray seedling had taken root in his daughter's body.

"Who done it to you, Elva?"

"Who done what, Pa?"

"Judas Priest, girl! If you're old enough to swell up like a prize pumpkin, you're old enough to know what's been done to you. Who you been sleeping with?"

"Nobody, Pa. I always sleep alone. You know that." Elva was mystified.

Earl Mildrum, tomato grower and lay preacher, accustomed to tidy platitude and comfortable euphemism in public and private utterance, was forced to be explicit. At the end of his embarrassed monologue Elva was enlightened.

"Oh, that," she said. "That was Mr. Heskill."

"Anybody else?" demanded her father.

"No, I don't think so," said Elva, trying to look thoughtful.

"You don't think so! Don't you know?"

Earl Mildrum launched into a jaw-breaking sermon, dwelling at length on the fiery torments reserved for wayward daughters, and the shame they brought on the heads of their hardworking, respectable fathers striving only to raise them up clean and pure without the guiding hand of a mother who'd had the temerity to die of a ruptured appendix when Elva was a baby.

Elva, as always, listened rapt and uncomprehending to the words which tumbled from her father's mouth. They were fine words, words of biblical certainty: damnation and abomination, fornication and harlotry. Elva loved the strong ringing sound of the words, and thought that when her father spoke them he must be like the prophets of old telling the people how bad they were.

But she didn't really understand the words or their connection with events in the River Man's houseboat way last August. Hellfire couldn't be hotter than the tomato fields in August, and surely if she had to burn, as her father said she must, surely there would be a river nearby with a houseboat and a cooler full of beer. Elva waited, open-mouthed and vacant-eyed for him to finish.

". . . so he'll have to marry you, girl. That's all there is to it."

Elva smiled, much taken with the notion of getting married, and said, "Can I have a puppy for a wedding present?"

After bashing Elva a few satisfying whacks with a handy tomato stake, Earl Mildrum left her howling in her room and marched across his winter-stiffened fields to the River Man's domain.

In addition to the houseboat Woody Heskill's armada included several rowboats and canoes, a perpetually deflated rubber raft, a fiberglass fishing skiff, and the flagship of his fleet, an ancient PT-boat said to have seen action in the South Pacific. This relic perched on the slope overlooking the river, well out of reach of high water.

The River Man had grandiose plans for scraping its rust and recaulking its seams, with the objective of a voyage downriver to Cincinnati. But year after year the old Navy veteran sat high and dry, manned by snakes and spiders and occasional children playing war games.

Earl Mildrum scowled as he left his own neat fields and stepped into alien country. Behind him his acres stretched brown and clean waiting only for spring and the burgeoning of the queenly tomato. Four-foot tomato stakes lay bundled in military ranks and covered with plastic sheeting at precise intervals along the edges of the fields. Order prevailed in the Tomato Man's territory.

Before him sprawled chaos. Long yellow grass flattened by winter rains and shriveled by frost was studded with bits and pieces of broken-down machinery. Lengths of rusty chain lay in wait to trip him. The PT-boat loomed gray and menacing to his left, a haven for hibernating rattlesnakes. Across the fallow cluttered field to his right the River Man's house strewed itself along a short rise overlooking the river.

Whenever Woody Heskill felt the need for more room in his house, he simply tacked on an addition and cut a doorway through to the adjacent room. The basic house was a square green shingled affair, but fore and aft, port and starboard, the house sailed off in all directions in a maze of salvaged brick and aluminum siding, fiberglass awnings and the gray rotting timbers of an unfinished addition.

The River Man was not content with water transport as a way of life. His dooryard was littered with cannibalized cars, crippled motorcycles, disabled tractors, and a large shiny new camper, wheelless and foundered on four cinder blocks. It was the River Man's dream to construct for himself an amphibious craft in which he could swoop down the highways of southern Ohio, dipping into the river when it pleased him, emerging on the West Virginia or the Kentucky side, astounding both sides of the river with his marvelous machine. He tinkered on his dream in a weatherbeaten shack to one side of the house.

Earl Mildrum had difficulty finding the front door. There were doors aplenty, but none revealed a doorbell. He couldn't tell which door was intended to receive guests, especially a guest on such a diplomatic mission as his. In all the years that the Tomato Man and the River Man had lived side by side in the valley, they had never been on visiting terms.

The Tomato Man rapped loudly on a door that had three small rectangular windows set diagonally into peeling veneer. There was no answer. He squinted off into the pale lemony winter sunlight that defined the River Man's property.

Acres of junk, he thought. It's a crying shame. Acres of junk and not a single thing growing on it ever. Except only weeds. He envisioned the field cleared of debris, tilled and tamed into fruitfulness. He could grow a lot of tomatoes on that idle field. He rapped again.

"You lookin' for me?"

The voice came from behind. Earl Mildrum turned slowly, searching the cluttered yard for a sign of the speaker.

"Over here," came the voice again. "In the camper. Hurry up, man. It's cold outside."

The Tomato Man spotted the close-cropped gray head protruding from the half-opened door of the camper. He trotted over, picking his way carefully through scattered wheel rims and dead batteries. He stopped at the narrow steps of the camper and called through the door.

"Woody Heskill. Come on out of there. I got to talk to you."

"Can't talk outside," the voice replied. "It's too cold. Come on in, Earl. I seen you coming across the field. Says to myself, 'I ain't seen old Earl Mildrum since the Lion's club carnival last summer. Wonder what he's comin' here for.' Come on in, man. Don't stand there with the door open."

The Tomato Man hoisted himself reluctantly onto the narrow steps and entered the camper. He would have preferred to conduct this discussion outdoors in the neutral air, or at the very least in a large room where he could pace judiciously, gesture and declaim and maintain the advantage by weight of oratory. Inside the cramped space of the camper he would be at a disadvantage both by being well within enemy territory and by having his words and motions confined to fit the boxlike interior.

The inside of the camper was hot and fuggy with the smell of coal oil and stale food. A small heater spewed warmth and fumes into the atmosphere. The tiny sink was stacked full of used TV dinner trays and a grocery sack on the floor bulged with empty beer cans. At the rear of the camper both bunks were a tumble of heaped bedding and musty pillows. Earl Mildrum eyed them speculatively.

Woody Heskill buttoned a plaid shirt over his thermal underwear and tucked the tails into his green workpants.

"Costs too much to heat that big old house," he said. "I been wintering out here. Set you down, Earl. Bet I know what you come for. Time you got a new truck, ain't it? I got just the thing for you. It's down at Bud Wither's garage. Ain't exactly new, but it's only got six thousand miles on her. Clean as a whistle and—"

"Hold on, Woody. I didn't come here to talk about no truck."

The Tomato Man slid onto the vinyl-covered bench behind the small pedestal table. Although he was short and compact, his bulky mackinaw jacket made it a tight squeeze. He was hot and uncomfortable, but felt that removing his jacket would lend the proceedings an unwelcome air of informality. Bad enough that Woody Heskill was perched on the rim of the sink with his feet swinging inches above the floor.

"You and me, we got to come to a little understanding."

"Yeah? What about? Care for a beer?" Woody reached down and unlatched the tiny refrigerator. Earl could see that there was nothing in it but rows of pop-top cans. Woody gathered up two cans, but put one back when Earl said stiffly, "No, thanks. No beer."

"What do we got to understand? You got some gripe about my property being an eyesore? 'Member what happened last time?"

"No, it ain't that. I still think it's a shameful waste of good land. But that ain't what I come to talk about."

The River Man threw back his head and laughed. "I do believe you had your way, you'd plant the whole world in tomatoes."

"What's wrong with tomatoes?"

"Nothin'. Nothin' atall." Woody emptied half his beer can at one pull. "Well, what *is* on your mind? You got a face on you like a hanging judge, and I can't wait to hear the bad news."

"Well. It's about Elva."

"Oh, it is."

"Ah . . . Elva is . . . Um, Elva's going to . . . well, she says you're the daddy."

"Oh, she does."

"Well? Is that all you got to say?"

"Where's your shotgun, Earl?" The River Man chuckled. "Suppose I say I never laid a finger on that girl?"

"Elva don't tell lies."

"No. Elva don't. Would you say she's just a tad too dumb to go telling lies?"

"Now, look here, Woody," Earl blustered. "She maybe ain't the brightest thing in creation, but you got no call to insult her. If she was smart she never would of took up with you. She's a good cook and does what you tell her to do. She'll give you no trouble. And besides, she's kinda pretty, even if I say so myself."

"She got all her teeth?"

"'Course she does. Wisdom teeth and all. And she don't smoke."

Woody shook his head and finished off his beer. "Anybody ever tell you you're a filthy mean old horse-trader? Suppose I say I already got a wife?"

"Now you're the one telling lies. Everybody knows you got no wife. Never had. Never would have if I don't make you do the right thing by Elva."

"Suppose I say I just won't do it." Woody aimed his empty can at the grocery sack and missed. "I'm too old a dog to get housebroke at this stage of the game. Why, Earl, I'd just make her miserable."

Earl Mildrum reared back and planted his forearms squarely on the little table. His chin jutted forward and his eyes narrowed craftily.

"Suppose I tell you that Elva's only seventeen. And suppose I tell you that unless you're prepared to walk nice and gentlemanly into church next Sunday afternoon, I am prepared to march that little lady right down to the police station where she will tell the whole story. Everybody knows that Elva don't tell lies."

"Like that, is it?" The River Man snaked another beer out of the refrigerator. "Well, well. I hear that old man Lutz wants to sell his houseboat. It's a lot bigger than mine, more suited to a family man, if you know what I mean. Elva sure does like living on a houseboat in the summer."

"I'll go see him about it."

"Why, thank you kindly. That's a fine wedding present you're offering."

"If you'll agree to clear all that junk off of your big field and let me plant tomatoes."

"Share the profit? Half and half?"

"Sixty forty. Unless you're willing to pitch in on the work."

"Sixty forty." The River Man laughed. "I'm a lover, not a field hand."

"It's a deal, then?"

"It's a deal. Care for a beer?"

"Don't mind if I do."

The Tomato Man's daughter became the River Man's wife with scarcely any change in the quality of her life. There was just more of it. She still kept house in her father's neat white cottage and cooked his meals for him. Then she would scurry across the fields to the sprawling heap on the river bank where she would chip away at the years' accumulation of rubbish and dirt, and cook meals for her husband and herself. Neither her father nor her husband suggested that they take meals together and thus ease Elva's chores, and Elva didn't think of it herself.

Once in a while Woody Heskill would look up from his tinkering and say, "Hey, Elva honey, don't bother cleaning up. Place gets too messy, I'll just bull-doze the whole thing into the river and let it float away. Come sit beside me and have a beer."

And Elva would say, "Just a minute. Soon's I finish scrubbing this wall"—or hauling this trash or washing this window or whatever she happened to be doing.

If there was one thing in this world that Elva understood, it was work. When her hands were busy she felt good. There was only one thing that made her feel better, and she yearned for summer when the new houseboat would float on the river and she and Woody could sit on the deck with the beer cooler between them, and then go inside when the heat got too much for them. Drinking beer in the house and then going off to the cold dark bedroom wasn't the same. It didn't have the same delicious feeling of playing hooky, of running off to sea and spitting in the eye of all the rules.

In late April, Elva bore fruit, a red-faced wrinkled girl-baby with a thatch of red-gold fuzz on its head.

"Looks like a little old shriveled-up tomato," said her father. "Elva, you gonna be able to help with setting out the seedlings? It's getting close to time."

"Sure, Pa. I'll be there."

Her husband said, "Now, you just take it easy, Elva honey. Your daddy can afford to get himself a hired hand to help out this year. You're gonna have plenty to do taking care of this little monkey. What you want to call her?"

Earl Mildrum spoke up first. "I think you should call her Amelia, after your mother."

"I think you should call her Earleen, after your mean old daddy," said the River Man.

The two men glared at each other across Elva's hospital bed.

"I'm gonna call her Dandy, 'cause that's what she is. Just plain Dandy." Elva felt important with the baby cradled in the crook of her arm, and both her hus-band and her father waiting on her decision. "Dandy June Heskill, that's her name."

Dandy June lived in a laundry basket on the deck of the new houseboat. Woody brought an old rocking chair down from the house and placed it beside the laundry basket. For a week Elva did nothing but rock Dandy June and feed her, while Woody beamed proudly and poked at the baby's tiny clenched fists.

"Ain't she something else?" he said. "You done real good, Elva."

The weather was mild and clear for May, promising a long hot summer. Good tomato weather.

Each evening the Tomato Man would trot across his fields and down to the houseboat.

"How you doin' there, Elva? Gotta get those tomatoes in next week."

"Doin' fine, Pa. Just fine. Me and Dandy June'll get those seedlings in. Don't you worry."

And Woody Heskill would mutter, "Don't have to do it if you don't want to, Elva honey."

On the Saturday evening, in addition to his reminder about planting time, Earl Mildrum said wistfully, "Elva, I ain't had a clean shirt to put on my back for three days. You gonna do some washing pretty soon?"

Elva stirred in her rocking chair. "Guess I will, Pa. Guess I'll do that right now." She put Dandy June in her basket and took the basket by its two handles and drifted off up the fields behind her sternly marching father. Woody Heskill glowered after them and opened another beer.

By Monday when the truck arrived bearing the seedlings in long wooden flats, Elva was back on course cooking and cleaning, washing and polishing, swinging like a pendulum between the houseboat and her father's cottage. Wherever she went, Dandy June and the laundry basket went too. While Elva set out tomato seedlings in neat rows, Dandy June slept in the basket in the shade of a tall old elm.

When Dandy June cried, Elva sat under the tree with her, fed her and played with her, and dearly loved her fat red baby. Elva worked harder than she ever had in her seventeen years, and was happier than she could ever remember being. She felt she could go on tending tomatoes and Dandy June and the chores of two households forever. She felt important.

One morning, when the tomato vines were knee-high and the yellow blossoms and the green horny worms had both put in their appearances, her father said to her, "Elva, I seen some mole holes round and about. There's some mole bait down in the cellar. You put it out today."

Dutifully Elva went to the cellar and got the can of mole bait. She spelled out the label to herself. *Chopped Poison Peanut Pellets*. And tried to read the instructions. CAUTION, it said. LEAD ARSENATE. But the fine print defeated her, and she decided that the best thing would be to put a handful or so into each mole hole that she could find.

She deposited Dandy June under her tree and spent the morning searching out mole holes and dropping the poison in. The mole bait was a funny color for peanuts, sort of a pinkish gray, but it smelled like peanuts and Elva guessed that moles couldn't see very well anyway. Once in a while she thought of the little furry star-nosed creatures deep in the earth coming up to nibble at the poisoned peanuts. She didn't like to think of what would happen to them after they nibbled. But Pa said to put out the mole bait, so she had to do it. And anyway, they ate the roots of the tomato plants.

When Dandy June cried her lunch cry, Elva put the lid on the can of mole bait and put it back in the cellar. She picked up the laundry basket and carried it across the fields toward the houseboat. She was thirsty and thought a beer would taste awful good. She would sit in the rocking chair and sip a beer and feed Dandy June. Woody was out on the river somewhere trying out a new second-hand outboard motor.

As Elva crossed the fields, knee-deep in tomato vines, she saw someone sitting on the porch of the River Man's house. It wasn't Woody. Even at this distance she could see it was a woman. The woman just sat there on the top step with her elbows on her knees and her head in her hands. She looked tired. Elva decided to see who it was.

"Hi," she called out. "Hey, hi. You waitin' for somebody?"

The woman looked up, shading her eyes against the noon sun, but said nothing. As Elva drew closer, she saw that there was a small battered suitcase beside the woman on the porch.

"Hi, there," Elva said as she came up to the porch. She set the laundry basket down and Dandy June, who had been soothed by the motion, began crying again. "Nice day, ain't it?"

The woman looked at her with tired, aching eyes. "Woodrow Heskill live here?"

"Uh-huh. But he ain't here now. He mostly lives down on the houseboat." Elva pointed. "But he ain't there neither."

"Where is he?" The woman sighed.

"Oh, I dunno. Out on the river someplace. He comes and goes."

"Same old Woody." The woman sighed again. "Well, I guess I'll have to wait for him. Got noplace else left to go."

Elva picked up Dandy June to stop her crying and looked closely at the woman. She looked to be about forty years old, but it was hard to tell because of the dark circles under her eyes and the heavy makeup that couldn't conceal the tired lines of her face. The dark roots of her hair turned suddenly to dry brassy yellow about two inches from her scalp. She wore a sagging orange jersey dress meant for a bigger woman and high-heeled pointy-toed black patent-leather shoes. The leather was cracked and bulged over large bunions.

"Well," said Elva. "I got to go feed the baby. Are you hungry, Ma'am?"

"That your baby?"

"Uh-huh. Her name's Dandy June. Mine's Elva."

"You're pretty young to be mother of a baby. I never had a kid. If I had he might be looking after me now, instead of me having to look up old Woody."

"Is Woody your brother?"

"No."

"Cousin?"

"No."

"Any kind of kin?"

"For what it's worth, he's my husband. Though I ain't set eyes on him for fifteen, sixteen years. Did you say something about food?"

"Well, yes. Would you care for some lunch?"

"You're a good kid. Yeah, I could use some lunch. I ain't had anything to eat since yesterday afternoon. Used my last money for a bus ticket to get here. What did you say your name was? Mine's Lauretta."

"Elva. My daddy grows all those tomatoes over there."

"Yeah? And I bet you got a handsome young hubby who works in the fields and takes you to the drive-in movies on Saturday nights."

"No."

The woman looked sharply at Elva.

"You got a husband?"

"Oh, yes." Elva grinned proudly.

"Woody's not *your* brother?"

"No, Ma'am."

"And he's not your cousin?"

"No, Ma'am."

"Oh, my God. This is too good." The woman hooted. "Don't tell me. Let me guess."

Elva giggled. It was kind of funny, come to think of it.

"You mean to tell me that sweet little lump you're holding was fathered by that shiftless old river rat?"

Elva giggled and nodded.

"And you actually married him?"

"Pa made me. But it's okay. I don't mind."

"You don't mind!" The woman shook with laughter. "Oh, this is too much." She gasped and shuddered and her laughter turned suddenly to a fit of coughing that racked her frail body.

"Oh, Ma'am. Lauretta. Mrs. Heskill. Can I get you something?"

The woman choked and put her head down onto her knees. Her answer was muffled in the skirt of her orange jersey dress.

"Got any whiskey?"

"Oh, yes, Ma'am. I believe Woody has some down on the houseboat. Can you make it that far?"

The woman raised her head and smiled. "Little girl, for a glass of sipping whiskey, I could make it to the moon."

When the River Man came in off the river, he found a party in progress on the deck of the houseboat.

"Hey, now. It's Woody himself," cried Lauretta, limp and feverishly animated in the rocking chair. She held the whiskey bottle straight-armed toward him. "Have a drink, Woody. Have a drink with Number One wife. And with wifey Number Two." She nodded and bowed elaborately to Elva.

Elva sat giggling on the deck, Dandy June in her laundry basket on one side, a neat pile of hard-boiled eggshells and empty beer cans on the other. "Havanegg, havanegg," she chanted. "Eatanegg, you old river rat. Whoops! Guess I ate 'em all."

Woody Heskill mopped sweat off the back of his neck with a blue bandanna handkerchief. "Sweet dear Jesus! Never thought to see you again, Lauretta. What brings you here?"

Lauretta shrieked with high shrill laughter. "Smelled your whiskey clear in Dayton. Said to myself, 'The old river rat won't let you down, Lauretta. Might's well go see if he's still alive and kicking.' " She widened her heavily mascaraed eyes in a maudlin parody of sentiment. "Remember those good old days in Dayton, Woody? Me waiting table all day, and you sleeping? You never did like Dayton much. Dayton made you mean and sleepy." Lauretta subsided into sullen memories.

The River Man turned to his young wife. "You okay, Elva honey?"

"Havanegg. Havabeer. Havababy. Don't cry." Elva giggled.

"Is there any beer left?" Woody asked.

"Don't mind if I do." Elva sighed and fell asleep on the deck.

Woody Heskill reached into the cooler and pulled out the last can of beer.

"I'm sending Elva away. Should of done that in the first place. It's bigamy. That's what it is. You should of told me you already had a wife."

"I did, Earl. I told you. You didn't believe me."

"You didn't say it so's I could believe you. I thought you was just trying to squirm out of your duty to Elva."

"Look here, Earl. Lauretta'll go away. She hates it here. She never did like the country life. That's why we split up in the first place. I'll give her a little money and she'll go away. Elva don't have to leave. It's only that Lauretta's sick and tired and had a dust-up with her present boy friend. Just give her a few days to pull herself together and I'll give her the bus fare back to Dayton. And she'll go. She don't want to stay with me. She don't even like me. She just needs a little vacation."

The two men stood in the dim cool camper, the Tomato Man short and square and angry, the River Man bemused by his need to hang onto Elva. Lauretta was in the River Man's house sleeping off the effects of the previous afternoon and evening, while a white-faced and repentant Elva, under instructions from her father, was removing all her belongings from the houseboat.

"Where are you gonna send her, Earl?"

"Where you can't find her. You ain't ever gonna see her again, Woody. And you ain't ever gonna see Dandy June neither. My daughter and my grand-baby are too proud to live sinfully with another woman's husband."

"Oh, stop spouting, Earl. That's my baby as much as it is your grand-baby. And Elva don't mind about Lauretta."

"No. Elva don't mind. Elva never minds. That's why I got to mind for her. And I mind a lot. She's going. Today."

Earl Mildrum stomped out of the camper and marched away across the deep green tomato fields. Woody Heskill stood in the doorway and thought about how Elva had come to him. He hadn't really wanted her except as a pretty playtoy through the hot summer days. He hadn't courted her or paid much attention to her. He'd let old Earl bulldoze him into marrying her, and she fitted easily into his ways.

That was the thing about Elva. She was an easy person to have around. He'd grown used to the green tomato smell of her, to the warmth of her kitten-soft body in his bed. And then there was Dandy June. Woody tried to puzzle out how he felt about them, about losing both of them. He never thought or spoke of love, but it pained him to think of sitting on the deck of the houseboat with only the beer cooler for company.

Elva cried in the kitchen. Her clothes were all packed and ready for the trip. She was going to her mother's sister's place in Indiana. She didn't want to go. She rubbed the welts on her legs where the peach-tree switch had stung and burned. They only itched now, but Elva still cried.

The real hard pain was inside her. When Earl Mildrum had told her that morning that he wanted her to leave, that she must clear all her things out of the houseboat and that she and Dandy June would have to go and live with Aunt Millie, she had defied him.

"No," she said. "I ain't going."

"You're going," he said. "Nobody will know you there. You can keep your shame to yourself. Anybody asks, you can tell them your husband died in a car wreck."

"I ain't ashamed and I ain't going. I got a husband. You made me get married. It's all your doing."

That was when he'd cut the peach-tree switch and whipped her just as if she was a little kid and not a married woman with a baby. She had cried at first from the cutting pain of the switch on her bare legs, but she kept on crying long after that pain had turned numb.

Even as she wept, Elva's idle hands caused her misgivings. The kitchen was swept and clean; Dandy June was taking her afternoon nap. There would be no more meals to cook in this house. Or on the houseboat. Elva was waiting for her father to finish irrigating the long tomato rows. Then they would be off in the car on the long drive to Indiana. At the thought of the drive a new freshet of tears fell down Elva's cheeks.

"Got to find something to do," she muttered.

She got out the big old kettle and a jug of syrup.

"I'll make something for his sweet tooth," she said to herself. "I'll make something sweet and leave it for him and he'll find it when he comes back from taking me to Aunt Millie's. I'll be in Indiana and he'll be here and he'll have something sweet to eat to remember me by."

She poured syrup and sugar into the kettle and added a tad of water. She put the kettle on the stove and stirred it a bit. While it was heating, she ran down to the cellar. When she came back the syrup was bubbling. She stirred and stirred and when the syrup was sticky and thick she poured in the contents of the can she'd brought from the cellar. It was a funny color, but after the sugar syrup turned brown no one would be able to tell the difference.

Elva stirred the mixture in the big iron kettle and her tears stopped flowing. What was it Pa always said? "The Devil makes work for idle hands." Yes. Well, it was true.

She smiled as she thought of coming back from Indiana after Pa ate the peanut brittle. Would they call her on the phone? Or send a telegram? Either way would be just as good. "Your Pa's dead," they would say. "Come home." And she would come back home and live on the houseboat and work in the tomato fields. Woody would still be there, but she didn't mind about that.

The syrup bubbled and thickened. When it was brown and so thick she could hardly stir it any more, she slicked it down with a gob of butter and threw in a spoonful of soda. The syrup formed up and turned butterscotch yellow. She poured the sticky yellow mess onto a cookie sheet and smoothed it out. All the lumps and bumps were covered with yellow candy. It looked real good. And it smelled real good. She set the cookie sheet on the window sill to cool.

Elva put the kettle in the sink to soak the sticky candy off. While she was scrubbing the stove clean, she heard a sound at the window.

"Psst. Elva. Elva honey."

"Oh, Woody. You better go away. Pa sees you here, he'll whip me again."

"Elva. Come away with me. We'll get on the houseboat and float downriver. We'll go as far as we want to and then we'll stop a while. Just you and me. And Dandy June."

"Pa told me not to set foot out of the house until he's ready to go."

"You always gonna do what he tells you to do?"

"I guess so. I guess I just don't know what else to do." Elva felt the tears starting up again, and scrubbed hard at the sticky kettle.

"What's this here?" Woody was poking at the hardened sheet of candy on the window sill. "It sure smells good.

"Oh, it's just some peanut brittle. I made it for Pa."

"Elva, I just don't understand you. He treats you like a dumb little puppy dog and you go making peanut brittle for him." Woody poked at the candy again. "It's hard enough to crack. Elva, break me off a little piece of peanut brittle. I just love homemade peanut brittle."

"Woody, get your hands off of that. That's for Pa. Nobody else."

"If you want it, come and get it." Woody snatched up the tray of candy and backed off from the window. "This looks too good for your mean old Daddy. If you don't come and get it, Elva, I'm gonna eat it all up."

Elva stood at the window. "Woody, put it back. Please, Woody. I can't come out there. Pa said not."

"Elva, you got to make up your mind. Either you're gonna go all your life doing what he tells you or you're gonna come with me on the houseboat. I'm gonna set right here and eat this peanut brittle till you make up your mind which one it is."

Woody sat down on a stump in the yard and picked up a rock to crack the hard sheet of candy. Elva stood in the window and watched him.

"Please don't break it," she cried. "Please don't eat it. It's for Pa."

"Make up your mind, little lady. It's either him or me."

"Woody, I can't. I just plain can't. I don't know what to do." Her voice trailed off in a plaintive moan. She stood in the window and watched him raise the heavy rock and bring it down on the shiny surface of the peanut brittle.

"No! Oh, no!" she cried. "It was for Pa. I only meant it for Pa."

"Well, Devil take your mean old Daddy. He ain't getting none of this."

Elva watched as Woody lifted a jagged chunk of candy and put it into his mouth. His hard square teeth chomped up and down and he licked his lips.

"This is real good, Elva. You ought to come on out and have some." Woody ate another piece of candy.

Elva, in the window, shivered. Woody was right. It was either him or Pa. One or the other. Dimly she realized that if Woody wasn't there, she wouldn't have to make up her mind. She wouldn't have to go away. Pa would always be there to tell her what to do, and she could just go on tending to Dandy June, tending tomatoes, cooking and cleaning. She could be happy and busy and work hard without all this having to make up her mind between them. It would be better that way. Without Woody.

"Come on out, Elva honey. Come out and have a bit of this peanut brittle. It's real good. Come on down to the houseboat and we'll eat it all up and have a beer."

"I'm sorry, Woody. I really meant it for Pa. But you can have it if you want it. It's all the same to me. I don't mind."

Elva closed the window. She put the lid back on the empty can of mole bait and threw it in the trash. The kitchen was neat and clean. She sat down to wait for her father to come in from irrigating the tomato fields. He would tell her what to do next.

OKLAHOMA

MISSING PERSONS CASE
by Gary W. Campbell

IT WAS A warm summer's day with the puffy white clouds and bright blue sky found only in the plains states. Parking the tan squad car with the gold six-pointed star on the door, Sheriff Hoagy Hogan climbed laboriously out. He adjusted his gun belt under the belly it had taken him 45 years to achieve and sauntered toward the deputy's car. He didn't turn on his flashing lights; the deputy's seemed enough.

Bart Miller, the twenty-year-old, tall, gawky deputy, ran toward him, relief on his freckled face. Hoag noticed red dust on the deputy's gray-uniformed knees. Not far behind Bart, the squat, heavily jowled construction foreman and one of the burly hard-hatted workers followed.

"I'm sure glad to see you, Hoag," Bart said.

"What've you got?" the sheriff asked in a slightly bored voice.

"One of the bulldozers dug somebody up."

Hoag raised a hand to stop the deputy. "Who found it?"

"I did, sir," the construction worker said. "I'm Bill Matthews."

Taking a kitchen match from his shirt pocket, Hoag stuck it in his mouth and nodded to Matthews. "Tell me just like it happened."

Matthews rubbed a weatherbeaten face. "I was leveling that bump by the river," he said, pointing. "The new bridge will cross there. I backed the dozer off because it was lunchtime, and as I climbed off, I saw something white. It was a skull."

"You leave it where you found it?"

"Sure, Sheriff—didn't touch it. But I can't tell you exactly where the dozer picked it up. I cut about a twenty-yard swath."

Hoag turned to McClary, the foreman. "I'm afraid I'm going to have to hold up the project. Don't know how long yet." McClary scowled and nodded. Turning back to his deputy, Hoag said, "Call Doc Hudson?"

"Yes, sir. He's on the way."

"How many people know about this?" the sheriff asked.

McClary answered. "I told everyone to take a long lunch. Just the four of us here know."

A ten-year-old black Cadillac stopped behind the sheriff's car, and a man with a fringe of white hair climbed out. "What you got here, Hoag?" he called.

"I ain't seen it yet, Doc. Come on."

They all followed Matthews to the dozer, and Doc Hudson knelt by the skull. "What do you think?" Hoag asked, squatting next to him and sucking on the match.

"Female," the doctor told him. "About twenty give or take a couple of years."

Hoag felt a tightness in his gut. He couldn't decide whether to grimace or smile. He did a little of both. "Think you can make an I.D.?"

Hudson shrugged. "Frankly, I don't know. Find me the rest of her."

"How long's she been there?" Hoag asked, almost holding his breath.

The doctor shook his head. "No way to tell here. Want me to take her with me?"

Standing, Hoag stretched with his fist in his back and considered for a moment. "I think I know who it is, Doc. I think I'm going to close a case twenty years old. You take the skull with you, though, and see if you can make anything of it."

Hoag turned back to his deputy. "Round up the rest of our so-called police force. I want this kept hushed up, and I want you and the rest to find the skeleton." He shifted his gaze to the construction foreman. "McClary, tell your people they got today and tomorrow off. Maybe the day after, we'll see. If I don't have all I need by then, there won't be enough." His eyes half closed, and a gleam peeked out of them. "I've got to talk to some people."

Hoag stopped at his office and dug a folder out of the Unsolved File. He read it over, then tucked it under his arm and went back to the car.

Nancy Carswell had disappeared almost 20 years before. She'd been 19. A deputy sheriff at the time, Hoagy Hogan was convinced that Nancy had been killed by Ray Fielding, her stepfather. He could never prove it because he couldn't find a body. Now, certain the skull was Nancy's, he intended to double-check with the surviving witnesses and then have a chat with Fielding.

He couldn't talk to one of the witnesses. Frannie Amos had died eight years before at 93. Frannie had told young deputy Hogan that she'd seen Nancy running down the road toward the Washita River. Nancy hadn't been carrying luggage, and about ten minutes later, Fielding's car had gone down that same road at high speed. She said Fielding passed her place back and forth ten times before night finally fell, but he didn't seem to really be looking for anything.

Hoag's first stop was at the local feed and grain store. Juan Hernandez, who owned it, had been a ranch hand at the Fielding place. His memory of what he'd seen that night was just as clear as on the day Hoag first started that file twenty years before.

Nancy had run from the house to her car. Her blouse had been torn. After trying unsuccessfully to start her car, she ran down the road. About ten minutes later, Fielding came out of the house, visibly angry. He got into his car and followed Nancy. He came back just after dark, and to Hernandez he no longer seemed angry.

Sarah Arbetter lived in a shack on the east side of town where the river touched the city limits. When Hoag arrived, she had her fishing pole stuck out the back window, dangling the line into the river. Chewing on the now-soggy match, Hoag leaned against the window.

"How's your memory?" he asked.

Sarah pushed her coarse silver hair from her eyes with a gnarled hand. "I ain't but sixty-one years old, Hoagy Hogan. I can still remember being birthed."

Hoag spat out a piece of match. "About Nancy Carswell."

Before speaking, Sarah reeled in her fishing line and put the pole away. She leaned against the window sill to get a better look at the sheriff. "That was a long time ago, Hoag, but I remember it like yesterday. What brings it up now?"

"I think we found her body," he said unemotionally. His gaze remained on the churning water.

Sarah sighed heavily. "Buried by the river like we thought?"

"Yep. I'd like you to remember back and tell me like I didn't know anything about it."

"Okay, Hoag," she said, nodding. "I stayed on as cook after Mrs. Fielding died, mainly to take care of Nancy. She was supposed to go to college that year, but her mother's death just took all the steam out of her. Well, she was beginning to get over it. Then after living in the same house with her for three years, Ray Fielding finally noticed she was a woman. Boy, did he notice!"

"Ray make advances?"

"You bet he did," Sarah growled, "but Nancy did her best to ignore him. After all, he had been her mother's husband. Anyways, I don't think she liked Ray very much."

Hoag still leaned against the building, his only movement in the jerking match. "What happened that night?" he asked.

Sarah pulled a thin black cigar from her shirt pocket and took her time lighting it. Hoag's nose winced. "Well, it all came to a head that night," she said. "Ray finally got so direct that she couldn't pretend she didn't understand any more. Of course, she turned him down flat. I was in the kitchen, and they were in the dining room. I could hear real good. Ray, he got mad and started calling her names and said how she owed him.

"Well, Nancy ran up to her room, and I guess started to pack. He followed, and I kept my distance, but I went up there, too. They had a big fight in her room. I heard him rip her blouse, then there was a scuffle, and she came running out. She wasn't bothering with no luggage either." Sarah chuckled. "After she was gone, since Ray didn't come out, I went in. She'd knocked him cold with a lamp."

"How long was he unconscious, Sarah?"

"Oh, about ten minutes, I guess. I didn't help him, you see, because I was afraid he'd wake up sooner. I wanted Nancy to have all the lead she could get. 'Course, I didn't realize then that she hadn't taken her car."

"Then he went after her?" Hoag prompted.

"Yeah, burning up the road with that fancy convertible of his. I figured she was safe by then. Ray would cool down when he couldn't find her, and he'd at least let her come back for her things. Didn't figure she'd want to live at the ranch any more."

"Probably wouldn't have," Hoag said, flipping the remains of his match into the river. None of this was new, but maybe with the skull, it would now be enough. "What then?" he asked.

"Well, he came in about dark. He was calmer, and he said he was worried. Told me she hadn't taken her car and that he'd looked all over for her and couldn't find her. He was very apologetic and sorry for the way he'd acted."

That covered everything she'd told him 20 years ago. He sighed heavily. "Anything else you can add, Sarah?"

"No, Sheriff. That's about all there was to it. 'Cept, of course, that nobody ever saw Nancy again."

Nodding, Hoag frowned. "Thanks a lot, Sarah." He started to leave.

"Now, wait a minute, Hoag." He turned back. Sarah was scratching her chin. "He had a button missing from that fancy suitcoat he was wearing. At the time I thought he lost it during that scuffle in Nancy's room, but I never did find it."

Hogan almost smiled. "You'd know that button if you saw it again?"

Her face screwed up angrily. "Sure would. It was made of bone, and he told me it was Indian's bones. Said it was probably some of my ancestors killed by his ancestors."

Hoag drove across the cattle guard under the old timber archway leading to the Fielding ranch. The last word of the *Trespassers Will Be Shot* sign had been painted over to read *Prosecuted*, and the cars and equipment were newer, but other than that the ranch looked much the same as it had 20 years before.

Hoag passed acres of pasture land and finally stopped in the oval drive near the double front doors. As he walked up, he counted seven marble steps. He knocked on one of the carved oak doors and waited till a young Mexican in a white jacket opened it.

"Sheriff Hogan," he said. "I've come to see Mr. Fielding."

The young man stepped aside. "In the study," he said with the slightest trace of accent.

"I know the way," Hoag told him.

The door to the study was open, and the sheriff paused there for a moment, watching Fielding go over some paperwork. The wood paneling was dark and rich, the carpet plush and expensive. It was the same, but Fielding had changed. His hair was white, though still thick, and his face badly wrinkled. Burst veins colored his nose. Too much booze, Hoag thought.

"Ray," the sheriff finally said.

Fielding glanced up. "Oh, Sheriff. Come in. Take a seat. What can I do for you?"

Hoag didn't sit. He leaned against the door facing and watched his man carefully. "It's about a missing-person report you filed twenty years ago. We've found Nancy."

A white eyebrow arched, and Fielding clenched an empty cigarette holder in his teeth. "Really?" he said.

"Yeah," Hoag said a bit more coldly than he intended, "really I've wondered about one thing ever since I read that first report, Ray. Why didn't she take her car when she ran away?"

Fielding shrugged. "Beats me. The deputy who came here at the time tried the car, and it started."

"Nancy didn't know anything about cars, did she?"

"I suppose not. That young deputy was you, wasn't it, Hoag?"

The sheriff nodded. "I've always wondered about that spot on her coil wire where the grease was wiped off. It looked like someone had taken it off and put it back on. That's premeditation, Ray."

"Where did you find her?" Fielding asked.

"Near the bank of the Washita, Ray," Hogan said disinterestedly. "Right where you buried her."

"I didn't kill her," Fielding said as if bored of repeating the line. "I never could find her that night."

"I can't believe that, Ray," Hoag said, finally stepping into the room. "I didn't then, and I don't now. But now I've got proof. Her skeleton was found this morning. There was a bone button in what used to be her fist, and Sarah Arbetter identified it as the one missing from the coat you wore that night."

Fielding shrank in his chair as if all the air had gone out of him. "I searched and searched for that damn button." He glanced up at Hogan. "I'm sixty-seven years old, Hoag. I'm tired of Nancy wrecking my sleep. I'm glad it's over."

Taking his handcuffs from his pocket, Hoag approached him. "Shall we?" . . .

Hoag sat at his desk, writing his report. He'd had to tell Fielding a couple of lies, but there was no law against that. Now, while the rest of the force was still searching for a skeleton, a deputy was typing up Fielding's confession. Though Hogan was closing a twenty-year-old murder case, he didn't feel any satisfaction. It never brought them back.

Doc Hudson entered the office and sat in the chair next to the sheriff's desk. "Got some word on your skull, Hoag." The sheriff didn't brighten much. "It's Indian," Hudson went on, "probably Kiowa. At least a hundred and fifty years old. I'm going to call State University. There must be a burial mound somewhere around there, and they'll want to know about it."

Hoag settled back in his chair and thought, his face impassive. "No way it could be more recent?"

"No way."

The sheriff punched his intercom button. "Bart, listen to what I tell the doctor. It goes for you too."

"Yes, sir."

Leaving the intercom open, Hogan nodded to himself and wandered to the file cabinet. "Remember Rena Adams? She married Wesley Herman. About a year after they married, she turned up missing. Wes said they had a fight, and she went home, but she never got to her mother's. She was last seen strolling with Wes near the river bank." He pulled the file and turned to the doctor. "Before anyone finds out how old that skull is, I've got some people I want to talk to— about the Rena Adams case."

OREGON

COYOTE AND QUARTER-MOON

by Bill Pronzini & Jeffrey Wallmann

WITH THE LAUREL County deputy sheriff beside her, Jill Quarter-Moon waited for the locksmith to finish unlatching the garage door. Inside, the dog—a good-sized Doberman; she had identified it through the window—continued its frantic barking.

The house to which the garage belonged was only a few years old, a big ranch-style set at the end of a cul-de-sac and somewhat removed from its neighbors in the expensive Oregon Estates development. Since it was a fair Friday morning in June, several of the neighbors were out and mingling in a wide crescent around the property; some of them Jill recognized from her previous visit here. Two little boys were chasing each other around her Animal Regulation Agency truck, stirring up a pair of other barking dogs nearby. It added to the din being raised by the Doberman.

At length the locksmith finished and stepped back. "It's all yours," he said.

"You'd better let me go in with you," the deputy said to Jill.

There was a taint of chauvinism in his offer, but she didn't let it upset her. She was a mature twenty-six, and a full-blooded Umatilla Indian, and she was comfortable with both her womanhood and her role in society. She was also strikingly attractive, in the light-skinned way of Pacific Northwest Indians, with hip-length brown hair and a long willowy body. Some men, the deputy being one of them, seemed to feel protective, if not downright chivalric, toward her. Nothing made her like a man less than being considered a pretty-and-helpless female.

She shook her head at him and said, "No thanks. I've got my tranquilizer dart gun."

"Suit yourself, then." The deputy gave her a disapproving frown and stepped back out of her way. "It's your throat."

Jill drew a heavy padded glove over her left hand, gripped the dart gun with her right. Then she caught hold of the door latch and depressed it. The Doberman stopped barking; all she could hear from inside were low growls. The dog sensed that someone was coming in, and when she opened the door it would do one of two things; back off and watch her, or attack. She had no way of telling beforehand which it would be.

The Doberman had been locked up inside the garage for at least thirty-six hours. That was how long ago it had first started howling and barking and upsetting the neighbors enough so that one of them had complained to the Agency. The owner of the house, Jill had learned in her capacity as field agent, was named Edward Benham; none of the neighbors knew him—he'd kept to himself during the six months he had lived here—and none of them knew anything at all about his dog. Benham hadn't answered his door, nor had she been able to reach him by telephone or track down any local relatives. Finally she had requested through the Agency offices, a court order to enter the premises. A judge had granted it, and along with the deputy and the locksmith, here she was to release the animal.

She hesitated a moment longer with her hand on the door latch. If the Doberman backed off, she stood a good chance of gentling it enough to lead it out to the truck; she had a way with animals, dogs in particular—something else she could attribute to her Indian heritage. But if it attacked she would have no choice except to shoot it with the tranquilizer gun. An attack-trained, or even an untrained but high-strung, Doberman could tear your throat out in a matter of seconds.

Taking a breath, she opened the door and stepped just inside the entrance. She was careful to act natural, confident; too much caution could be as provoking to a nervous animal as movements too bold or too sudden. Black and short-haired, the Doberman was over near one of the walls—yellowish eyes staring at her, fangs bared and gleaming in the light from the open doorway and the single dusty window. But it stood its ground, forelegs spread, rear end flattened into a crouch.

"Easy," Jill said soothingly. "I'm not going to hurt you."

She started forward, extending her hand, murmuring the words of a lullabye in Shahaptian dialect. The dog cocked its head, ears perked, still growling, still tensed—but it continued to stay where it was and its snub of a tail began to quiver. That was a good sign, Jill knew. No dog wagged its tail before it attacked.

As her eyes became more accustomed to the half light, she could see that there were three small plastic bowls near the Doberman; each of them had been gnawed and deeply scratched. The condition of the bowls told her that the dog had not been fed or watered during the past thirty-six hours. She could also see that in one corner was a wicker sleeping basket about a foot and a half in diameter, and that on a nearby shelf lay a curry comb. These things told her something else, but just what it meant she had no way of knowing yet.

"Easy, boy . . . calm," she said. She was within a few paces of the dog now and it still showed no inclination to jump at her. Carefully she removed the thick glove, stretched her hand out so that the Doberman could better take her scent. "That's it, just stay easy, stay easy. . . ."

The dog stopped growling. The tail stub began to quiver faster, the massive head came forward and she felt the dryness of its nose as it investigated her hands. The yellow eyes looked up at her with what she sensed was a wary acceptance.

Slowly she put away the tranquilizer gun and knelt beside the animal, murmuring the lullabye again, stroking her hand around its neck and ears. When she felt it was ready to trust her she straightened and patted the dog, took a step toward the entrance. The Doberman followed. And kept on following as she retraced her path toward the door.

They were halfway there when the deputy appeared in the doorway. "You all right in there, lady?" he called.

The Doberman bristled, snarled again low in its throat. Jill stopped and stood still. "Get away, will you?" she said to the deputy, using her normal voice, masking her annoyance so the dog wouldn't sense it. "Get out of sight. And find a hose or a faucet, get some water puddled close by. This animal is dehydrated."

The deputy retreated. Jill reached down to stroke the Doberman another time, then led it slowly out into the sunlight. When they emerged she saw that the deputy had turned on a faucet built into the garage wall; he was backed off to one side now, one hand on the weapon holstered at his side, like an actor in a B movie. The dog paid no attention to him or to anyone else. It went straight for the water and began to lap at it greedily. Jill went with it, again bent down to soothe it with her hands and voice.

While she was doing that she also checked the license and rabies tags attached to its collar, making a mental note of the numbers stamped into the thin aluminum. Now that the tenseness of the situation had eased, anger was building within her again at the way the dog had been abused. Edward Benham, whoever he was, would pay for that, she thought. She'd make certain of it.

The moment the Doberman finished drinking, Jill stood and faced the bystanders. "All of you move away from the truck," she told them. "And keep those other dogs quiet."

"You want me to get the back open for you?" the deputy asked.

"No. He goes up front with me."

"Up front? Are you crazy, lady?"

"This dog has been cooped up for a long time," Jill said. "If I put him back in the cage, he's liable to have a fit. And he might never trust me again. Up front I can open the window, talk to him, keep him calmed down."

The deputy pursed his lips reprovingly. But as he had earlier, he said, "It's your throat," and backed off with the others.

When the other dogs were still Jill caught hold of the Doberman's collar and led it down the driveway to the truck. She opened the passenger door, patted the seat. The Doberman didn't want to go in at first, but she talked to it, coaxing, and finally it obeyed. She shut the door and went around and slid in under the wheel.

"Good boy," she told the dog, smiling. "We showed them, eh?"

Jill put the truck in gear, turned it around, and waved at the scowling deputy as she passed him by.

At the Agency—a massive old brick building not far from the university—she turned the Doberman over to Sam Wyatt, the resident veterinarian, for examination and treatment. Then she went to her desk in the office area reserved for field agents and sat down with the Benham case file.

The initial report form had been filled out by the dispatcher who had logged the complaint from one of Benham's neighbors. The report listed the breed of Benham's dog as an Alaskan husky, female—not a Doberman, male. Jill had been mildly surprised when she went out to the house and discovered that the trapped dog was a Doberman. But then, the Agency was a bureaucratic organization, and like all bureaucratic organizations it made mistakes in paperwork more often than it ought to. It was likely that the dispatcher, in checking the registry files for the Benham name, had either pulled the wrong card or miscopied the information from the right one.

But Jill kept thinking about the sleeping basket and the curry comb inside the garage. The basket had been too small for the Doberman but about the right size for a female husky. And curry combs were made for long-haired, not short-haired dogs.

The situation puzzled as well as angered her. And made her more than a little curious. One of the primary character traits of the Umatilla was inquisitiveness, and Jill had inherited it along with her self-reliance and her way with animals. She had her grandmother to thank for honing her curiosity, though, for teaching her never to accept any half-truth or partial answer. She could also thank her grandmother, who had been born in the days when the tribe lived not on the reservation in northeastern Oregon but along the Umatilla River—the name itself meant "many rocks" or "water rippling over sand"—for nurturing her love for animals and leading her into her present job with the Agency. As far back as Jill could remember, the old woman had told and retold the ancient legends about "the people"—the giant creatures, Salmon and Eagle and Fox and the greatest of all, Coyote, the battler of monsters, who ruled the earth before human beings were created, before all animals shrank to their present size.

But she was not just curious about Benham for her own satisfaction; she had to have the proper data for her report. If the Agency pressed charges for animal abuse, which was what she wanted to see happen, and a heavy fine was to be levied against Benham, all pertinent information had to be correct.

She went to the registry files and pulled the card on Edward Benham. The dispatcher, it turned out, *hadn't* made a mistake after all: the breed of dog listed as being owned by Benham was an Alaskan husky, female. Also the license and rabies tag numbers on the card were different from those she had copied down from the Doberman's collar.

One good thing about bureaucratic organizations, she thought, was that they had their filing systems cross-referenced. So she went to the files arranged according to tag numbers and looked up the listed owner of the Doberman.

The card said: *Fox Hollow Kennels, 1423 Canyon Road, Laurel County, Oregon.*

Jill had heard of Fox Hollow Kennels; it was a fairly large place some distance outside the city, operated by a man named Largo or Fargo, which specialized in raising a variety of pure-bred dogs. She had been there once on a field investigation that had only peripherally concerned the kennel. She was going to make her second visit, she decided, within the next hour.

The only problem with that decision was that her supervisor, Lloyd Mortisse, vetoed it when she went in to tell him where she was going. Mortisse was a lean, mournful-looking man in his late forties, with wild gray hair that reminded Jill of the dried reeds her grandmother had strung into ornamental baskets. He was also a confirmed bureaucrat, which meant that he loved paperwork, hated anything that upset the routine, and was suspicious of the agents' motives every time they went out into the field.

"Call up Fox Hollow," he told her. "You don't need to go out there; the matter doesn't warrant it."

"I think it does."

"You have other work to do, Ms. Quarter-Moon."

"Not as important as this, Mr. Mortisse."

She and Mortisse were constantly at odds. There was a mutual animosity, albeit low-key, based on his part by a certain condescension—either because she was a woman or an Indian, or maybe both—and on her part by a lack of respect. It made for less than ideal working conditions.

He said, "And I say it's not important enough for you to neglect your other duties."

"Ask that poor Doberman how important it is."

"I repeat, you're not to pursue the matter beyond a routine telephone call," Mortisse told her sententiously. "Now is that understood?"

"Yes. It's understood."

Jill pivoted, stalked out of the office, and kept right on stalking through the rear entrance and out to her truck. Twenty minutes later she was turning onto the long gravel drive, bordered by pine and Douglas fir, that led to the Fox Hollow Kennels.

She was still so annoyed at Mortisse, and preoccupied with Edward Benham, that she almost didn't see the large truck that came barreling toward her along the drive until it was too late. As it was, she managed to swerve off onto the soft shoulder just in time, and to answer the truck's horn blast with one of her own. It was an old Ford stakebed, she saw as it passed her and braked for the turn onto Canyon Road, with the words *Fox Hollow Kennels* on the driver's door. Three slat-and-wire crates were tied together on the bed, each of which contained what appeared to be a mongrel dog. The dogs had begun barking at the sound of the horns and she could see two of them pawing at the wire mesh.

Again she felt both her curiosity and her anger aroused. Transporting dogs in bunches via truck wasn't exactly inhuman treatment, but it was still a damned poor way to handle animals. And what was an American Kennel Club-registered outfit which specialized in purebreds doing with mongrels?

Jill drove up the access drive and emerged into a wide gravel parking area. The long whitewashed building that housed Fox Hollow's office was on her right, with a horseshoe arrangement of some thirty kennels and an exercise yard behind it. Pine woods surrounded the complex, giving it a rustic atmosphere.

When she parked and got out, the sound of more barking came to her from the vicinity of the exercise yard. She glanced inside the office, saw that it was empty, and went through a swing-gate that led to the back. There, beside a low fence, a man stood tossing dog biscuits into the concrete run on the other side, where half a dozen dogs—all of these purebred setters—crowded and barked together. He was in his late thirties, average-sized, with bald head and nondescript features, wearing Levi's and a University of Oregon sweatshirt. Jill recognized him as the owner, Largo or Fargo.

"Mr. Largo?" she said.

He turned, saying, "The name is Fargo." Then he set the food sack down and wiped his hands on his Levi's. His eyes were speculative as he studied both her and her tan Agency uniform. "Something I can do for you, miss?"

Jill identified herself. "I'm here about a dog," she said, "a male Doberman, about three years old. It was abandoned inside a house in Oregon Estates at least two days ago; we went in and released it this morning. The house belongs to a man named Benham, Edward Benham, but the Doberman is registered to Fox Hollow."

Fargo's brows pulled down. "Benham, did you say?"

"That's right. Edward Benham. Do you know him?"

"Well, I don't recognize the name."

"Is it possible you sold him the Doberman?"

"I suppose it is," Fargo said. "Some people don't bother to change the registration. Makes a lot of trouble for all of us when they don't."

"Yes, it does. Would you mind checking your records?"

"Not at all."

He led her around and inside the kennel office. It was a cluttered room that smelled peculiarly of dog, dust, and cheap men's cologne. An open door on the far side led to an attached work room; Jill could see a bench littered with tools, stacks of lumber, and several slat-and-wire crates of the kind she had noticed on the truck, some finished and some under construction.

Along one wall was a filing cabinet and Fargo crossed to it, began to rummage inside. After a time he came out with a folder, opened it, consulted the papers it held, and put it away again. He turned to face Jill.

"Yep," he said. "Edward Benham. He bought the Doberman about three weeks ago. I didn't handle the sale myself; one of my assistants took care of it. That's why I didn't recognize the name."

"Is your assistant here now?"

"No, I gave him a three-day weekend to go fishing."

"Is the Doberman the only animal Benham has bought from you?"

"As far as the records show, it is."

"Benham is the registered owner of a female Alaskan husky," Jill said. "Do you know anyone who specializes in that breed?"

"Not offhand. Check with the American Kennel Club; they might be able to help you."

"I'll do that." Jill paused. "I passed your truck on the way in, Mr. Fargo. Do you do a lot of shipping of dogs?"

"Some, yes. Why?"

"Just curious. Where are those three today bound?"

"Portland." Fargo made a deliberate point of looking at his watch. "If you'll excuse me, I've got work to do. . . ."

"Just one more thing. I'd like to see your American Kennel Club registration on the Doberman you sold Benham."

"Can't help you there, I'm afraid," Fargo said. "There wasn't any AKC registration on that Doberman."

"No? Why not? He's certainly a purebred."

"Maybe so, but the animal wasn't bred here. We bought it from a private party who didn't even know the AKC existed."

"What was this private party's name?"

"Adams. Charles Adams. From out of state—California. That's why Fox Hollow was the first to register the dog with you people."

Jill decided not to press the matter, at least not with Fargo personally. She had other ways of finding out information about him, about Fox Hollow, and about Edward Benham. She thanked Fargo for his time, left the office, and headed her truck back to the Agency.

When she got there she went first to see Sam Wyatt, to check on the Doberman's health. There was nothing wrong with the animal, Wyatt told her, except for minor malnutrition and dehydration. It had been fed, exercised, and put into one of the larger cages.

She looked in on it. The dog seemed glad to see her; the stub of a tail began to wag when she approached the cage. She played her fingers through the mesh grille, let the Doberman nuzzle them.

While she was doing that the kennel attendant, a young redhead named Lena Stark, came out of the dispensary. "Hi, Jill," she said. "The patient looks pretty good, doesn't he?"

"He'll look a lot better when we find him a decent owner."

"That's for sure."

"Funny thing—he's registered to the Fox Hollow Kennels, but they say he was sold to one Edward Benham. It was Benham's garage he was locked up in."

"Why is that funny?"

"Well, purebred Dobermans don't come cheap. Why would anybody who'd pay for one suddenly go off and desert him?"

"I guess that is kind of odd," Lena admitted. "Unless Benham was called out of town on an urgent matter or something. That would explain it."

"Maybe," Jill said.

"Some people should never own pets, you know? Benham should have left the dog at Fox Hollow; at least they care about the welfare of animals."

"Why do you say that?"

"Because every now and then one of their guys comes in and takes most of our strays."

"Oh? For what reason?"

"They train them and then find homes for them in other parts of the state. A pretty nice gesture, don't you think?"

"Yes," Jill said thoughtfully. "A pretty nice gesture."

She went inside and straight to the filing room, where she pulled the Fox Hollow folder. At her desk she spread out the kennel's animal licensing applications and studied them. It stood to reason that there would be a large number and there were; but as she sifted through them Jill was struck by a peculiarity. Not counting the strays Fox Hollow had "adopted" from the Agency, which by law had to be vaccinated and licensed before being released, there were less than a dozen dogs brought in and registered over the past twelve months. For a kennel which claimed to specialize in purebreds, this was suspiciously odd. Yet no one else had noticed it in the normal bureaucratic shuffle, just as no one had paid much attention to Fox Hollow's gathering of Agency strays.

And why *was* Fox Hollow in the market for so many stray dogs? Having met Fargo, she doubted that he was the humanitarian type motivated by a desire to save mongrels from euthanasia, a dog's fate if kept unclaimed at the Agency for more than four days. No, it sounded as if he were in some sort of strange wholesale pet business—as if the rest of the state, not to mention the rest of the country, didn't have their own animal overpopulation problems.

But where did Edward Benham, and the Doberman, fit in? Jill reviewed the Benham file again, but it had nothing new to tell her. She wished she knew where he'd gone, or of some way to get in touch with him. The obvious way, of course, was through his place of employment; unfortunately, however, pet license applications did not list employment of owners, only home address and telephone number. Nor had any of his neighbors known where he worked.

Briefly she considered trying to bluff information out of one of the credit-reporting companies in the city. Benham had bought rather than rented or leased his house, which meant that he probably carried a mortgage, which meant credit, which meant an application listing his employment. The problem was that legitimate members of such credit companies used special secret numbers to identify themselves when requesting information, so any ruse she might attempt would no doubt fail, and might even backfire and land her in trouble with Mortisse.

Then she thought of Pete Olafson, the office manager for Mid-Valley Adjustment Bureau, a local bad-debt collection service. Mid-Valley could certainly belong to a credit-reporting company. And she knew Pete pretty well, had dated him a few times in recent months. There wasn't any torrid romance brewing between her and the sandy-haired bachelor, but she knew he liked her a good deal—maybe enough to bend the rules a little and check Benham's credit as a favor.

She looked up Mid-Valley's number, dialed it, and was talking to Pete fifteen seconds later. "You must be a mind-reader, Jill," he said after she identified herself. "I was going to call you later. The University Theater is putting on *Our Town* tomorrow night and I've wangled a couple of free passes. Would you like to go?"

"Sure. If you'll do me a favor in return."

Pete sighed dramatically. "Nothing is free these days, it seems. Okay, what is it?"

"I want to know where a man named Edward Benham is employed. Could you track down his credit applications and find out from them?"

"I can if he's got credit somewhere."

"Well, he owns his own home, out in Oregon Estates. The name is Benham. B-e-n-h-a-m, Edward. How fast can you find out for me?"

"It shouldn't take long. Sit tight; I'll get back to you."

Jill replaced the handset and sat with her chin propped in one palm brooding. If the lead to Edward Benham through Pete didn't pan out, then what? Talk to his neighbors again? Through them she could find out the name of the real estate agent who had sold Benham his home . . . but it was unlikely that they would divulge personal information about him, since she had no official capacity. Talk to Fargo again? That probably wouldn't do her any good either. . . .

The door to Lloyd Mortisse's private office opened; Jill saw him thrust his wild-maned head out and look in her direction. It was not a look of pleasure. "Ms. Quarter-Moon," he said. "Come into my office, please."

Jill complied. Mortisse shut the door behind her, sat down at his desk, and glared at her. "I thought," he said stiffly, "that I told you not to go out to Fox Hollow Kennels."

Surprised, Jill asked, "How did you know about that?"

"Mr. Fargo called me. He wanted to know why you were out there asking all sorts of questions. He wasn't pleased by your visit; neither am I. Why did you disobey me?"

"I felt the trip was necessary."

"Oh, you felt it was necessary. I see. That makes it all right, I suppose."

"Look, Mr. Mortisse—"

"I do not like disobedience," Mortisse said. "I won't stand for it again, is that clear? Nor will I stand for your harassing private facilities like Fox Hollow. This Agency's sole concern in the Benham matter is to house the Doberman for ninety-six hours or until it is claimed. And I'll be the one, not you, to decide if any misdemeanor animal-abuse charges are to be filed against Mr. Benham."

Jill thought that it was too bad these weren't the old days, when one of the Umatilla customs in tribal disputes was to hold a potlatch—a fierce social competition at which rival chiefs gave away or destroyed large numbers of blankets, coppers, and slaves in an effort to outdo and therefore vanquish each other. She would have liked nothing better than to challenge Mortisse in this sort of duel, using bureaucratic attitudes and red tape as the throwaway material. She also decided there was no point in trying to explain her suspicions to him; he would only have said in his supercilious way that none of it was Agency business. If she was going to get to the bottom of what was going on at Fox Hollow, she would have to do it on her own.

"Do you understand?" Mortisse was saying. "You're to drop this matter and attend to your assigned duties. And you're not to disobey a direct order again, under any circumstances."

"I understand," Jill said thinly. "Is that all?"

"That's all."

She stood and left the office, resisting an impulse to slam the door. The wall clock said that it was 4:10—less than an hour until quitting time for the weekend. All right, she thought as she crossed to her desk. I'll drop the matter while I'm on Agency time. But what I do and where I go on my own time is *my* business. Mortisse or no Mortisse.

It was another ten minutes, during which time she typed up a pair of two-day-old reports, before Pete Olafson called her back. "Got what you asked for, Jill," he said. "Edward Benham has a pretty fair credit rating, considering he's modestly employed."

"What does he do?"

"He's a deliveryman, it says here. For a kennel."

Jill sat up straight. "Kennel?"

"That's right," Pete said. "Place called Fox Hollow outside the city. Is that what you're after?"

"It's a lot more than I expected," Jill told him. Quickly she arranged tomorrow night's date with him, then replaced the receiver and sat mulling over this latest bit of news.

If she had needed anything more to convince her that something was amiss at Fox Hollow, this was it. Fargo had claimed he didn't know Edward Benham; now it turned out that Benham worked for Fargo. Why had he lied? What was he trying to cover up? And where was Benham? And where did the Doberman fit in?

She spent another half hour at her desk, keeping one eye on the clock and pretending to work while she sorted through questions, facts, and options in her mind. At ten minutes of five, when she couldn't take any more of the inactivity, she went out into the kennel area to see Lena Stark.

"Release the Doberman to me, will you, Lena?" she asked. "I'll bring him back later tonight and check him in with the night attendant."

"Why do you want him?"

"I like his looks and I want to get better acquainted. If it turns out neither Fox Hollow nor Benham decides to claim him, I may just adopt him myself."

"I don't know, Jill . . . ."

"He's all right, isn't he? Sam Wyatt said he was."

"Sure, he's fine. But the rules—"

"Oh, hang the rules. Nobody has to know except you and me and the night attendant. I'll take full responsibility."

"Well . . . okay, I guess you know what you're doing."

Lena opened the cage and the Doberman came out, stubby tail quivering, and nuzzled Jill's hand. She led it out through the rear door, into the parking lot to where her compact was parked. Obediently, as if delighted to be free and in her company, the dog jumped onto the front seat and sat down with an expectant look.

Jill stroked its ears as she drove out of the lot. "I don't want to keep calling you 'boy,'" she said. "I think I'll give you a name, even if it's only temporary. How about Tyee?" In the old Chinook jargon, the mixed trade language of Indians and whites in frontier days, *tyee* was the word for chief. "You like that? Tyee?"

The dog cocked its head and made a rumbly sound in its throat.

"Good," Jill said. "Tyee it is."

She drove across the city and into Oregon Estates. Edward Benham's house, she saw when she braked at the end of the cul-de-sac, looked as deserted as it had this morning. This was confirmed when she went up and rang the doorbell several times without getting a response.

She took Tyee with her and let him sniff around both front and back. The Doberman showed none of the easy familiarity of a dog on its own turf; rather, she sensed a wary tenseness in the way he moved and keened the air. And when she led him near the garage he bristled, made low growling noises. He was as much a stranger here as she was, Jill thought. But then why had he been locked in Benham's garage?

She would have liked to go inside for a better look around, but the locksmith had relocked the doors, as dictated by law, before leaving the premises that morning. The house was securely locked too, as were each of the windows. And drawn drapes and blinds made it impossible to see into any of the rooms from outside.

Jill took Tyee back to her compact. She sat for a time, considering. Then she started the engine and pointed the car in an easterly direction.

It was just seven o'clock when she came up the access drive to Fox Hollow Kennels and coasted to a stop on the gravel parking area near the main building. There were no other vehicles around, a *Closed* sign was propped in one dusty pane of the front door, and the complex had a deserted aura; even the dogs in the near kennels were quiet.

She got out, motioning for Tyee to stay where he was on the front seat. The setting sun hung above the tops of the pines straight ahead, bathing everything in a dark-orange radiance. Jill judged that there was about an hour of daylight left, which meant that an hour was all she would have to look around. Prowling in daylight was risky enough, though if she were seen she might be able to bluff her way out of trouble by claiming she had brought Tyee back to his registered owner. If she were caught here after dark, no kind of bluff would be worth much.

The office door was locked, but when she shook it, it rattled loosely in its frame. Jill bent for a closer look at the latch. It was a spring-type lock, rather than a deadbolt. She straightened again, gnawing at her lower lip. Detectives in movies and on TV were forever opening spring locks with credit cards or pieces of celluloid; there was no reason why she couldn't do the same thing. No reason, that was, except that it was illegal and would cost her her job, if not a prison term, were she to be caught. She could imagine Lloyd Mortisse smiling like the Cheshire Cat at news of her arrest.

But she was already here, and the need to sate her curiosity was overpowering. The debate with her better judgment lasted all of ten seconds. Then she thought: Well, fools rush in—and she went back to the car to get a credit card from her purse.

Less than a minute of maneuvering with the card rewarded her with a sharp click as the lock snapped free. The door opened under her hand. Enough of the waning orange sunlight penetrated through the windows, she saw when she stepped inside, so that she didn't need any other kind of light. She went straight to the filing cabinets, began to shuffle through the folders inside.

The kennel records were in something of a shambles; Jill realized quickly that it would take hours, maybe even days, to sort through all the receipts, partial entries, and scraps of paper. But one file was complete enough to hold her attention and to prove interesting. It consisted of truck expenses—repair bills, oil company credit card receipts, and the like—and what intrigued her was that, taken together, they showed that the Fox Hollow delivery truck consistently traveled to certain towns in Oregon, northern California, and southern Washington. Forest Grove, Corvallis, Portland, McMinnville, Ashland, La Grande, Arcata, Kirkland. . . . These, and a few others, comprised a regular route.

Which might explain why Edward Benham was nowhere to be found at the moment; some of the towns were at least an overnight's drive away, and it was Benham's signature that was on most of the receipts. But the evident truck route also raised more questions. Why such long hauls for a small kennel? Why to some points out of state? And why to these particular towns, when there were numerous others of similar size along the way?

"Curiouser and curiouser," Jill murmured to herself.

She shut the file drawers and turned to the desk. Two of the drawers were locked; she decided it would be best not to try forcing them. None of the other drawers, nor any of the clutter spread across the top, told her anything incriminating or enlightening.

The door to the adjacent workroom was closed, but when she tried the knob it opened right up. That room was dimmer but there was still enough daylight filtering in to let her see the tools, workbench, stacks of lumber, finished and unfinished crates. She picked through the farrago of items on the bench; caught up slats and corner posts of an unassembled cage, started to put them down again. Then, frowning, she studied one of the wooden posts more carefully.

The post was hollow. So were the others; the inner lengths of all four had been bored out by a large drill bit. When fitted into the frame of a fully constructed cage the posts would appear solid, their holes concealed by the top and bottom sections. Only when the cage was apart, like now, would the secret compartments be exposed, to be filled or emptied.

Of what?

Jill renewed her search. In a back corner were three rolls of cage wire—and caught on a snag of mesh on one roll was a small cellophane bag. The bag was out of easy sight and difficult to reach, but she managed to retrieve it. It looked new, unopened, and it was maybe 3 x 5 inches in size. The kind of bag—

And then she knew. What the bag was for, why the corner posts were hollowed out, what Fox Hollow was involved in. And it was ugly enough and frightening enough to make her feel a chill of apprehension, make her want to get away from there in a hurry. It was more than she had bargained for—considerably more.

She ran out of the workroom, still clutching the cellophane bag in her left hand. At the office door she peered through the glass before letting herself out, to make sure the parking area remained deserted. Then she set the button-lock on the knob, stepped outside, pulled the door shut, and started across to her compact.

Tyee was gone.

She stopped, staring in at the empty front seat. She had left the driver's window all the way down and he must have jumped out. Turning, she peered through gathering shadows toward the kennels. But the dogs were still quiet back there, and they wouldn't be if the Doberman had gone prowling in that direction. Where, then? Back down the drive? The pine woods somewhere?

Jill hesitated. The sense of urgency and apprehension demanded that she climb into the car, Tyee or no Tyee, and drive away pronto. But she couldn't just leave him here while she went to tell her suspicions to the county sheriff. The law would not come out here tonight no matter what she told them; they'd wait until tomorrow, when the kennel was open for business and when they could obtain a search warrant. And once she left here herself she had no intention of coming back again after dark.

She moved away from the car, toward the dark line of evergreens beyond. It was quiet here, with dust settling, and sounds carried some distance; the scratching noises reached her ears when she was still twenty paces from the woods. She'd heard enough dogs digging into soft earth to recognize the sound and she quickened her pace. Off to one side was a beaten-down area, not quite a path, and she went into the trees at that point. The digging sounds grew louder. Then she saw Tyee, over behind a decayed moss-festooned log, making earth and dry needles fly out behind him with his forepaws.

"What are you doing?" she called to him. "Come here, Tyee."

The Doberman kept on digging, paying no attention to her. She hurried over to him, around the bulky shape of the log. And then she stopped abruptly, made a startled gasping sound.

A man's arm and clenched hand lay partially uncovered in the soft ground.

Tyee was still digging, still scattering dirt and pine needles. Jill stood frozen, watching part of a broad back encased in a khaki shirt appear.

Now she knew what had happened to Edward Benham.

She made herself move, step forward and catch hold of the Doberman's collar. He resisted at first when she tried to tug him away from the shallow grave and what was in it; but she got a firmer grip and pulled harder, and finally he quit struggling. She dragged him around the log, back out of the trees.

Most of the daylight was gone now; the sky was grayish, streaked with red, like bloody fingermarks on faded cloth. A light wind had come up and she felt herself shiver as she took the Doberman toward her compact. She was anything but a shrinking violet, but what she had found at Fox Hollow tonight was enough to frighten Old Chief Joseph or any of the other venerable Shahaptian warriors. The sooner she was sitting in the safety of the Laurel County Sheriff's office, the better she—

And the figure of a man came out from behind her car.

She was ten feet from the driver's door, her right hand on Tyee's collar, when the man rose up into view like Nashlah, the legendary monster of the Columbia River. Jill made an involuntary cry, stiffened into a standstill. The Doberman seemed to go as tense as she did; a low rumble sounded in his throat as the man came toward them.

Fargo. With a gun in his hand.

"You just keep on holding that dog," he said. He stopped fifteen feet away, holding the gun out at arm's length. "You're both dead if you let go his collar."

She was incapable of speech for five or six seconds. Then she made herself say, "There's no need for that gun, Mr. Fargo. I'm only here to return the Doberman . . . ."

"Sure you are. Let's not play games. You're here because you're a damned snoop. And I'm here because you tripped a silent alarm connected to my house when you broke into the office."

It was not in Jill's nature to panic in a crisis; she got a grip on her fear and held it down, smothered it. "The office door was unlocked," she said. "Maybe you think you locked it when you left but you didn't. I just glanced inside."

"I don't buy that either," Fargo said. "I saw you come out of the office; I left my car down the road and walked up here through the trees. I saw you go into the woods over there, too."

"I went to find the dog, that's all."

"But that's not what you found, right? He's got dirt all over his forepaws— he's been doing some digging. You found Benham. And now you know too much about everything."

"I don't know what you're talking about."

"I say you do. So does that cellophane bag you're carrying."

Jill looked down at her left hand; she had forgotten all about the bag. And she had never considered the possibility of a silent alarm system. She had a lot to learn about being a detective—if she survived to profit by her mistakes.

"All right," she said. "It's drugs, isn't it? That's the filthy business you're in."

"You got it."

"Selling drugs to college kids all over the Pacific Northwest," she said. That was the significance of the towns on the Fox Hollow shipping route: they were all college or university towns. Humboldt State in Arcata, Lewis & Clark in Portland, Linfield College in McMinnville, Eastern Oregon College in La Grande. And the state university right here in this city. That was also why Fox Hollow had taken so many stray dogs from the Agency; they needed a constant supply to cover their shipment of drugs—cocaine and heroin, probably, the kind usually packaged and shipped in small cellophane bags—to the various suppliers along their network. "Where does it come from? Canada?"

"Mexico," Fargo said. "They bring it up by ship, we cut and package and distribute it."

"To kennels in those other cities, I suppose."

"That's right. They make a nice cover."

"What happens to the dogs you ship?"

"What do you think happens to them? Dogs don't matter when you're running a multimillion-dollar operation. Neither do snoops like you. Nobody fouls up this kind of operation and gets away with it."

Tyee growled again, shifted his weight; Jill tightened her grip on his collar. "Did Benham foul it up? Is that why he's dead?"

"He tried to. His percentage wasn't enough for him and he got greedy; he decided to hijack a shipment for himself—substitute milk sugar and then make off with the real stuff. When he left here on Wednesday for Corvallis he detoured over to his house and made the switch. Only one of the crates had the drugs in it, like always; he had to let the dog out of that one to get at the shipment and it turned on him, tried to bite him."

"This dog, the Doberman."

"Yeah. He managed to lock it up inside his garage, but that left him with an empty crate and he couldn't deliver an empty, not without making the Corvallis contact suspicious. So he loaded his own dog, the husky, inside the crate and delivered it instead. But our man checked the dope anyway, discovered the switch, and called me. I was waiting for Benham when he got back here."

"And you killed him."

Fargo shrugged. "I had no choice."

"Like you've got no choice with me?"

He shrugged again. "I forgot all about the Doberman, that was my mistake. If I hadn't, I wouldn't have you on my hands. But it just didn't occur to me the dog would raise a ruckus and a nosy Agency worker would decide to investigate."

"Why did you lie to me before about knowing Benham?"

"I didn't want you doing any more snooping. I figured if I gave you that story about selling him the Doberman, you'd come up against a dead-end and drop the whole thing. Same reason I called your supervisor: I thought he'd make you drop it. Besides, you had no official capacity. It was your word against mine."

"Lying to me was your second mistake," Jill said. "If you kill me, it'll be your third."

"How do you figure that?"

"I told somebody I came out here tonight. He'll go to the county sheriff if I disappear, and they'll come straight to you."

"That's a bluff," Fargo said. "And I don't bluff. You didn't tell anybody about coming here; nobody knows but you and me. And pretty soon it'll just be me." He made a gesture with the gun. "Look at it this way. You're only one person, but I got a lot of people depending on me: others in the operation, all those kids we supply."

All those kids, Jill thought, and there was a good hot rage inside her now. College kids, some of them still in their teens. White kids, black kids—Indian kids. She had seen too many Indian youths with drug habits; she had talked to the parents of a sixteen-year-old boy who had died from an overdose of heroin on the Umatilla reservation, of a seventeen-year-old girl, an honor student, killed in a drug raid at Trout Lake near the Warm Springs development. Any minority, especially its restless and sometimes disenchanted youth, was susceptible to drug exploitation; and Indians were a minority long oppressed in their own country. That was why she hated drugs, and hated these new oppressors, the drug dealers like Fargo, even more.

Fargo said, "Okay, we've done enough talking—no use in prolonging things. Turn around, walk into the woods."

"So you can bury me next to Benham?"

"Never mind that. Just move."

"No," she said, and she let her body go limp, sank onto her knees. She dropped the cellophane bag as she did so and then put that hand flat on the gravel beside her, keeping her other hand on Tyee's collar. The Doberman, sensing the increase of tension between her and Fargo, had his fangs bared now, growling steadily.

"What the hell?" Fargo said. "Get up."

Jill lowered her chin to her chest and began to chant in a soft voice—a Shahaptian prayer.

"I said get up!"

She kept on chanting.

Fargo took two steps toward her, a third, a fourth. That put less than five feet of ground between them. "I'll shoot you right where you are, I mean it—"

She swept up a handful of gravel, hurled it at his face, let go of Tyee's collar, and flung herself to one side.

The gun went off and she heard the bullet strike the ground near her head, felt the sting of a pebble kicked up against her cheek. Then Fargo screamed, and when Jill rolled over she saw that Tyee had done what she'd prayed he would— attacked Fargo the instant he was released. He had driven the man backward and knocked him down and was shaking his captured wrist as if it were a stick; the gun had popped loose and sailed off to one side. Fargo cried out again, tried to club the Doberman with his free hand. Blood from where Tyee's teeth had bitten into his wrist flowed down along his right arm.

Jill scrambled to her feet, ran to where the gun lay and scooped it up. But before she could level it at Fargo, he jacknifed his body backwards, trying to escape from the Doberman, and cracked his head against the front bumper of her compact; she heard the thunking sound it made in the stillness, saw him go limp. Tyee still straddled the inert form, growling, shaking the bloody wrist.

She went over there, caught the dog's collar again, talked to him until he let go of Fargo and backed off with her. But he stood close, alert, alternately looking at the unconscious man and up at her. She knelt and hugged him, and there were tears in her eyes. She disliked women who cried, particularly self-sufficient Indian women, but sometimes . . . sometimes it was a necessary release.

"You know who you are?" she said to him. "You're not Tyee, you're Coyote. You do battle with monsters and evil beings and you save Indians from harm."

The Doberman licked her hand.

"The Great One isn't supposed to return until the year 2000, when the world changes again and all darkness is gone; but you're here already and I won't let you go away. You're mine and I'm yours from now on—Coyote and Quarter-Moon."

Then she stood, shaky but smiling, and went to re-pick the lock on the office door so she could call the Laurel County sheriff.

PENNSYLVANIA

THE GETTYSBURG BUGLE
by Ellery Queen

THIS IS A very old story as Queen stories go. It happened in Ellery's salad days, when he was tossing his talents about like a Sunday chef and a redheaded girl named Nikki Porter had just attached herself to his typewriter. But it has not staled, this story; it has an unwithering flavor which those who partook of it relish to this day.

There are gourmets in America whose taste buds leap at any concoction dated 1861–1865. To such, the mere recitation of ingredients like Bloody Angle, Minié balls, Little Mac, "Tenting Tonight," the brand of Ulysses Grant's whisky, not to mention Father Abraham, is sufficient to start the passionate flow of juices. These are the misty-hearted to whom the Civil War is "the War" and the blue-gray armies rather more than men. Romantics, if you will; garnishers of history. But it is they who pace the lonely sentrypost by the night Potomac, they who hear the creaking of the ammunition wagons, the snap of campfires, the scream of the thin gray line, and the long groan of the battlefield. They personally flee the burning hell of the Wilderness as the dead rise and twist in the flames; under lanterns, in the flickering mud, they stoop compassionately with the surgeons over quivering heaps. It is they who keep the little flags flying and the ivy ever green on the graves of the old men.

Ellery is of this company, and that is why he regards the case of the old men of Jacksburg, Pennsylvania, with particular affection.

Ellery and Nikki came upon the village of Jacksburg as people often come upon the best things, unpropitiously. They had been driving back to New York from Washington, where Ellery had had some sleuthing to do among the stacks of the Library of Congress. Perhaps the Potomac, Arlington's eternal geometry, giant Lincoln frozen in sadness brought their weight to bear upon Ellery's decision to veer towards Gettysburg, where murder had been national. And Nikki

386

had never been there, and May was coming to its end. There was a climate of sentiment.

They crossed the Maryland-Pennsylvania line and spent timeless hours wandering over Culp's Hill and Seminary Ridge and Little Round Top and Spangler's Spring among the watchful monuments. It is a place of everlasting life, where Pickett and Jeb Stuart keep charging to the sight of those with eyes to see, where the blood spills fresh if colorlessly, and the high-pitched tones of a tall and ugly man still ring out over the graves. When they left, Ellery and Nikki were in a mood of wonder, unconscious of time or place, oblivious to the darkening sky and the direction in which the nose of the Duesenberg pointed. So in time they were disagreeably awakened by the alarm clock of nature. The sky had opened on their heads, drenching them to the skin instantly. From the horizon behind them Gettysburg was a battlefield again, sending great flashes of fire through the darkness to the din of celestial cannon. Ellery stopped the car and put the top up, but the mood was drowned when he discovered that something ultimate had happened to the ignition system. They were marooned in a faraway land, Nikki moaned; making Ellery angry, for it was true.

"We can't go on in these wet clothes, Ellery!"

"Do you suggest that we stay here in them? I'll get this crackerbox started if . . ." But at that moment the watery lights of a house wavered on somewhere ahead, and Ellery became cheerful again.

"At least we'll find out where we are and how far it is to where we ought to be. Who knows? There may even be a garage."

It was a little white house on a little swampy road marked off by a little stone fence covered with rambler rose vines, and the man who opened the door to the dripping wayfarers was little, too, little and weatherskinned and gallused, with eyes that seemed to have roots in the stones and springs of the Pennsylvania countryside. He smiled hospitably, but the smile became concern when he saw how wet they were.

"Won't take no for an answer," he said in a remarkably deep voice, and he chuckled. "That's doctor's orders, though I expect you didn't see my shingle— mostly overgrown with ivy. Got a change of clothing in your car?"

"Oh, yes!" said Nikki abjectly.

Ellery being a man, hesitated. The house looked neat and clean, there was an enticing fire, and the rain at their backs was coming down with a roar. "Well, thank you . . . but if I might use your phone to call a garage—"

"You just give me the keys to your car trunk."

"But we can't turn your home into a tourist house—"

"It's that, too, when the good Lord sends a wanderer my way. Now see here, this storm's going to keep up most of the night and the roads hereabout get mighty soupy." The little man was bustling into waterproof and overshoes. "I'll get Lew Bagley over at the garage to pick up your car, but for now let's have those keys."

So an hour later, while the elements warred outside, they were toasting safely in a pleasant little parlor, full of Dr. Martin Strong's homemade poppy-seed twists, scrapple, and coffee. The doctor, who lived alone, was his own cook. He was also, he said with a chuckle, mayor of the village of Jacksburg and its chief of police.

"Lot of us in the village run double harness. Bill Yoder of the hardware store's our undertaker. Lew Bagley's also the fire chief. Ed MacShane—"

"Jacksburger-of-all-trades you may be, Dr. Strong," said Ellery, "but to me you'll always be primarily the Good Samaritan."

"Hallelujah," said Nikki, piously wiggling her toes.

"And make it Doc," said their host. "Why, it's just selfishness on my part, Mr. Queen. We're off the beaten track here, and you do get a hankering for a new face. I guess I know every dimple and wen on the five hundred and thirty-four in Jacksburg."

"I don't suppose your police chiefship keeps you very busy."

Doc Strong laughed. "Not any. Though last year—" His eyes puckered and he got up to poke the fire. "Did you say, Miss Porter, that Mr. Queen is sort of a detective?"

"Sort of a!" began Nikki. "Why, Dr. Strong, he's solved some simply unbeliev—"

"My father is an inspector in the New York police department," interrupted Ellery, curbing his new secretary's enthusiasm with a glance. "I stick my nose into a case once in a while. What about last year, Doc?"

"What put me in mind of it," said Jacksburg's mayor thoughtfully, "was your saying you'd been to Gettysburg today. And also you being interested in crimes . . . ." Dr. Strong said abruptly, "I'm a fool, but I'm worried."

"Worried about what?"

"Well . . . Memorial Day's tomorrow, and for the first time in my life I'm not looking forward to it. Jacksburg makes quite a fuss about Memorial Day. It's not every village can brag about three living veterans of the Civil War."

"Three?" exclaimed Nikki. "How thrilling."

"Gives you an idea what the Jacksburg doctoring business is like," grinned Doc Strong. "We run to pioneer-type women and longevity . . . I ought to have said we *had* three Civil War veterans—Caleb Atwell, ninety-seven, of the Atwell family, there are dozens of 'em in the county; Zach Bigelow, ninety-five, who lives with his grandson Andy and Andy's wife and seven kids; and Abner Chase, ninety-four, Cissy Chase's great-grandpa. This year we're down to two. Caleb Atwell died last Memorial Day."

"A, B, C," murmured Ellery.

"What's that?"

"I have a bookkeeper's mind, Doc. Atwell, Bigelow, and Chase. Call it a spur-of-the-moment mnemonic system. A died last Memorial Day. Is that why you're not looking forward to this one? B following A sort of thing?"

"Didn't it always?" said Doc Strong with defiance. "Though I'm afraid it ain't—isn't as simple as all that. Maybe I better tell you how Caleb Atwell died.

"Every year, Caleb, Zach, and Abner have been the star performers of our Memorial Day exercises, which are held at the old burying ground on the Hookerstown road. The oldest of the three—"

"That would be A. Caleb Atwell."

"That's right. As the oldest, Caleb always blew taps on a cracked old bugle that's 'most as old as he was. Caleb, Zach, and Abner were in the Pennsylvania Seventy-second of Hancock's Second Corps, Brigadier General Alexander S. Webb commanding. They covered themselves with immortal glory—the Seventy-second, I mean—at Gettysburg when they fought back Pickett's charge, and that bugle played a big part in their fighting. Ever since it's been known as the Gettysburg bugle—in Jacksburg, anyway."

The little mayor of Jacksburg looked softly down the years. "It's been a tradition, the oldest living vet tootling that bugle, far back as I remember. I recollect as a boy standing around with my mouth open watching the G.A.R.s—there were lots more then—take turns in front of Maroney Offcutt's general store . . . been dead thirty-eight years, old Offcutt . . . practicing on the bugle, so any one of 'em would be ready when his turn came." Doc Strong sighed. "And Zach Bigelow, as the next oldest to Caleb Atwell, he'd be the standard bearer, and Ab Chase, as the next-next oldest, he'd lay the wreath on the memorial monument in the burying ground.

"Well, last Memorial Day, while Zach was holding the regimental colors and Ab the wreath, Caleb blew taps the way he'd done nigh onto twenty times before. All of a sudden, in the middle of a high note, Caleb keeled over. Dropped in his tracks deader than church on Monday."

"Strained himself," said Nikki sympathetically. "But what a poetic way for a Civil War veteran to die."

Doc Strong regarded her oddly. "Maybe," he said. "If you like that kind of poetry." He kicked a log, sending sparks flying up his chimney.

"But surely, Doc," said Ellery with a smile, for he was young in those days, "surely you can't have been suspicious about the death of a man of ninety-seven?"

"Maybe I was," muttered their host. "Maybe I was because it so happened I'd given old Caleb a thorough physical checkup only the day before he died. I'd have staked my medical license he'd live to break a hundred and then some. Healthiest old copperhead I ever knew. Copperhead! I'm blaspheming the dead. Caleb lost an eye on Cemetery Ridge . . . I know—I'm senile. That's what I've been telling myself for the past year."

"Just what was it you suspected, Doc?" Ellery forbore to smile now, but only because of Dr. Strong's evident distress.

"Didn't know what to suspect," said the country doctor shortly. "Fooled around with the notion of an autopsy, but the Atwells wouldn't hear of it. Said I was a blame jackass to think a man of ninety-seven would die of anything but old age. I found myself agreeing with 'em. The upshot was we buried Caleb whole."

"But Doc, at that age the human economy can go to pieces without warning like the one-hoss shay. You must have had another reason for uneasiness. A motive you knew about?"

"Well . . . maybe."

"He was a rich man," said Nikki sagely.

"He didn't have a pot he could call his own," said Doc Strong. "But somebody stood to gain by his death just the same. That is, if the old yarn's true.

"You see, there's been kind of a legend in Jacksburg about those three old fellows, Mr. Queen. I first heard it when I was running around barefoot with my tail hanging out. Folks said then, and they're still saying it, that back in '65 Caleb and Zach and Ab, who were in the same company, found some sort of treasure."

"Treasure . . . ." Nikki began to cough.

"Treasure," repeated Doc Strong doggedly. "Fetched it home to Jacksburg with them, the story goes, hid it, and swore they'd never tell a living soul where it was buried. Now there's lots of tales like that came out of the War"—he fixed Nikki with a stern and glittering eye—"and most folks either cough or go into hysterics, but there's something about this one I've always half-believed. So I'm senile on two counts. Just the same, I'll breathe a lot easier when tomorrow's ceremonies are over and Zach Bigelow lays Caleb Atwell's bugle away till next year. As the older survivor Zach does the tootling tomorrow."

"They hid the treasure and kept it hidden for considerably over half a century?" Ellery was smiling again. "Doesn't strike me as a very sensible thing to do with a treasure, Doc. It's only sensible if the treasure is imaginary. Then you don't have to produce it."

"The story goes," mumbled Jacksburg's mayor, "that they'd sworn an oath—"

"Not to touch any of it until they all died but one," said Ellery, laughing outright now. "Last-survivor-takes-all department. Doc, that's the way most of these fairy tales go." Ellery rose, yawning. "I think I hear the featherbed in that other guest room calling. Nikki, your eyeballs are hanging out. Take my advice, Doc, and follow suit. You haven't a thing to worry about but keeping the kids quiet tomorrow while you read the Gettysburg Address!"

As it turned out, the night shared prominently in Doc Martin Strong's Memorial Day responsibilities. Ellery and Nikki awakened to a splendid world, risen from its night's ablutions with a shining eye and a scrubbed look; and they went downstairs within seconds of each other to find the mayor of Jacksburg, galluses dangling on his pants bottom, pottering about the kitchen.

"Morning, morning," said Doc Strong, welcoming but abstracted. "Just fixing things for your breakfast before catching an hour's nap."

"You lamb," said Nikki. "But what a shame, Doctor. Didn't you sleep well last night?"

"Didn't sleep at all. Tossed around a bit and just as I was dropping off my phone rings and it's Cissy Chase. Emergency sick call. Hope it didn't disturb you."

"Cissy Chase," Ellery looked at their host. "Wasn't that the name you mentioned last night of—?"

"Of old Abner Chase's great-granddaughter. That's right, Mr. Queen. Cissy's an orphan and Ab's only kin. She's kept house for the old fellow and taken care of him since she was ten." Doc Strong's shoulders sloped.

Ellery said peculiarly: "It was old Abner . . . ?"

"I was up with Ab all night. This morning, at six-thirty, he passed away."

"On Memorial Day!" Nikki sounded like a little girl in her first experience with a fact of life.

There was a silence, fretted by the sizzling of Doc Strong's bacon.

Ellery said at last, "What did Abner Chase die of?"

Doc Strong looked at him. He seemed angry. But then he shook his head. "I'm no Mayo brother, Mr. Queen, and I suppose there's a lot about the practice of medicine I'll never get to learn, but I do know a cerebral hemorrhage when I see one, and that's what Ab Chase died of. In a man of ninety-four, that's as close to natural death as you can come . . . No, there wasn't any funny business in this one."

"Except," mumbled Ellery, "that—again—it happened on Memorial Day."

"Man's a contrary animal. Tell him lies and he swallows 'em whole. Give him the truth and he gags on it. Maybe the Almighty gets tired of His thankless job every once in an eon and cuts loose with a little joke." But Doc Strong said it as if he were addressing, not them, but himself. "Any special way you like your eggs?"

"Leave the eggs to me, Doctor," Nikki said firmly. "You go on up those stairs and get some sleep."

"Reckon I better if I'm to do my usual dignified job today," said the mayor of Jacksburg with a sigh. "Though Abner Chase's death is going to make the proceedings solemner than ordinary. Bill Yoder says he's not going to be false to an ancient and honorable profession by doing a hurry-up job undertaking Ab, and maybe that's just as well. If we added the Chase funeral to today's program, even old Abe's immortal words would find it hard to compete! By the way, Mr. Queen, I talked to Lew Bagley this morning and he'll have your car ready in an hour. Special service, seeing you're guest of the mayor." Doc Strong chuckled. "When you planning to leave?"

"I *was* intending . . . ." Ellery stopped with a frown. Nikki regarded him with a sniffy look. She had already learned to detect the significance of certain signs peculiar to the Queen physiognomy. "I wonder," murmured Ellery, "how Zach Bigelow's going to take the news."

"He's already taken it, Mr. Queen. Stopped in at Andy Bigelow's place on my way home. Kind of a detour, but I figured I'd better break the news to Zach early as possible."

"Poor thing," said Nikki. "I wonder how it feels to learn you're the only one left." She broke an egg viciously.

"Can't say Zach carried on about it," said Doc Strong dryly. "About all he said, as I recall, was: 'Doggone it, now who's goin' to lay the wreath after I toot the Gettysburg bugle!' I guess when you reach the age of ninety-five, death don't mean what it does to young squirts of sixty-three like me. What time'd you say you were leaving, Mr. Queen?"

"Nikki," muttered Ellery, "are we in any particular hurry?"

"I don't know. Are we?"

"Besides, it wouldn't be patriotic. Doc, do you suppose Jacksburg would mind if a couple of New York Yanks invited themselves to your Memorial Day exercises?"

The business district of Jacksburg consisted of a single paved street bounded at one end by the sightless eye of a broken traffic signal and at the other by the twin gas pumps before Lew Bagley's garage. In between, some stores in need of paint sunned themselves, enjoying the holiday. Red, white, and blue streamers crisscrossed the thoroughfare overhead. A few seedy frame houses, each decorated with an American flag, flanked the main street at both ends.

Ellery and Nikki found the Chase house exactly where Doc Strong had said it would be—just around the corner from Bagley's garage, between the ivy-hidden church and the firehouse of the Jacksburg Volunteer Pump and Hose Company No. 1. But the mayor's directions were a superfluity; it was the only house with a crowded porch.

A heavy-shouldered young girl in a black Sunday dress sat in a rocker, the center of the crowd. Her nose was as red as her big hands, but she was trying to smile at the cheerful words of sympathy winged at her from all sides.

"Thanks, Mis' Plum . . . That's right, Mr. Schmidt, I know . . . But he was such a spry old soul, Emerson, I can't believe . . . ."

"Miss Cissy Chase?"

Had the voice been that of a Confederate spy, a deeper silence could not have drowned the noise. Jacksburg eyes examined Ellery and Nikki with cold curiosity, and feet shuffled.

"My name is Queen and this is Miss Porter. We're attending the Jacksburg Memorial Day exercises as guests of Mayor Strong"—a warming murmur, like a zephyr, passed over the porch—"and he asked us to wait here for him. I'm sorry about your great-grandfather, Miss Chase."

"You must have been very proud of him," said Nikki.

"Thank you, I was. It was so sudden— Won't you set? I mean— Do come into the house. Great-grandpa's not here . . . he's over at Bill Yoder's, on some ice. . . ."

The girl was flustered and began to cry, and Nikki took her arm and led her into the house. Ellery lingered a moment to exchange appropriate remarks with the neighbors, who, while no longer cold, were still curious; and then he followed. It was a dreary little house with a dark and damp parlor.

"Now, now, this is no time for fussing—may I call you Cissy?" Nikki was saying soothingly. "Besides, you're better off away from all those folks. Why, Ellery, she's only a child!"

And a very plain child, Ellery thought, with a pinched face and empty eyes; and he almost wished he had gone on past the broken traffic light and turned north.

"I understand the parade to the burying ground is going to form outside your house, Cissy," he said. "By the way, have Andrew Bigelow and his grandfather Zach arrived yet?"

"Oh, I don't know," said Cissy Chase dully. "It's all such a dream, seems like."

"Of course. And you're left alone. Haven't you any family at all, Cissy?"

"No."

"Isn't there some young man—?"

Cissy shook her head bitterly. "Who'd marry me? This is the only decent dress I got, and it's four years old. We lived on Great-grandpa's pension and what I could earn hiring out by the day. Which ain't much, nor often. Now. . . ."

"I'm sure you'll find something to do," said Nikki, very heartily.

"In Jacksburg?"

Nikki was silent.

"Cissy." Ellery spoke casually, and she did not even look up. "Doc Strong mentioned something about a treasure. Do you know anything about it?"

"Oh, that." Cissy shrugged. "Just what Great-grandpa told me, and he hardly ever told the same story twice. But near as I was ever able to make out, one time during the War him and Caleb Atwell and Zach Bigelow got separated from the army—scouting, or foraging, or something. It was down South somewhere, and they spent the night in an old empty mansion that was half-burned down. Next morning they went through the ruins to see what they could pick up, and buried in the cellar they found the treasure. A big fortune in money, Great-grandpa said. They were afraid to take it with them, so they buried it in the same place in the cellar and made a map of the location and after the War they went back, the three of 'em, and dug it up again. Then they made the pact."

"Oh, yes," said Ellery. "The pact."

"Swore they'd hold onto the treasure till only one of them remained alive, I don't know why, then the last one was to get it all. Leastways, that's how Great-grandpa told it. That part he always told the same."

"Did he ever say how much of a fortune it was?"

Cissy laughed. "Couple of hundred thousand dollars. I ain't saying Great-grandpa was cracked, but you know how an old man gets."

"Did he ever give you a hint as to where he and Caleb and Zach hid the money after they got it back North?"

"No, he'd just slap his knee and wink at me."

"Maybe," said Ellery suddenly, "maybe there's something to that yarn after all."

Nikki stared. "But Ellery, you said—! Cissy, did you hear that?"

But Cissy only drooped. "If there is, it's all Zach Bigelow's now."

Then Doc Strong came in, fresh as a daisy in a pressed blue suit and a stiff collar and a bow tie, and a great many other people came in, too. Ellery and Nikki surrendered Cissy Chase to Jacksburg.

"If there's anything to the story," Nikki whispered to Ellery, "and if Mayor Strong is right, then that old scoundrel Bigelow's been murdering his friends to get the money!"

"After all these years, Nikki? At the age of ninety-five?" Ellery shook his head.

"But then what—?"

"I don't know." But when the little mayor happened to look their way, Ellery caught his eye and took him aside and whispered in his ear.

The procession—near every car in Jacksburg, Doc Strong announced proudly, over a hundred of them—got under way at exactly two o'clock.

Nikki had been embarrassed but not surprised to find herself being handed into the leading car, an old but brightly polished touring job contributed for the occasion by Lew Bagley; for the moment Nikki spied the ancient, doddering head under the Union Army hat in the front seat she detected the fine Italian whisper of her employer. Zach Bigelow held his papery frame fiercely if shakily erect between the driver and a powerful red-necked man with a brutal face who, Nikki surmised, was the old man's grandson, Andy Bigelow. Nikki looked back, peering around the flapping folds of the flag stuck in the corner of the car. Cissy Chase was in the second car in a black veil, weeping on a stout woman's shoulder. So the female Yankee from New York sat back between Ellery and Mayor Strong, against the bank of flowers in which the flag was set, and glared at the necks of the two Bigelows, having long since taken sides in this matter. And when Doc Strong made the introductions, Nikki barely nodded to Jacksburg's sole survivor of the Grand Army of the Republic, and then only in acknowledgment of his historic importance.

Ellery, however, was all deference and cordiality, even to the brute grandson. He leaned forward, talking into the hairy ear.

"How do I address your grandfather, Mr. Bigelow? I don't want to make a mistake about his rank."

"Gramp's a general," said Andy Bigelow loudly. "Ain't you, Gramp?" He beamed at the ancient, but Zach Bigelow was staring proudly ahead, holding fast to something in a rotted musette bag on his lap. "Went through the War a private," the grandson confided, "but he don't like to talk about that."

"General Bigelow—" began Ellery.

"That's his deef ear," said the grandson. "Try the other one."

"General Bigelow!"

"Hey?" The old man turned his trembling head, glaring. "Speak up, bub. Ye're mumblin'."

"General Bigelow," shouted Ellery, "now that all the money is yours, what are you going to do with it?"

"Hey? Money?"

"The treasure, Gramp," roared Andy Bigelow. "They've even heard about it in New York. What are you goin' to do with it, he wants to know?"

"Does, does he?" Old Zach sounded grimly amused. "Can't talk, Andy. Hurts m' neck."

"How much does it amount to, General?" cried Ellery.

Old Zach eyed him. "Mighty nosy, ain't ye?" Then he cackled. "Last time we counted it—Caleb, Ab, and me—came to nigh on a million dollars. Yes, sir, one million dollars." The old man's left eye, startlingly, drooped. "Goin' to be a big surprise to the smart-alecks and the doubtin' Thomases. You wait an' see."

Andy Bigelow grinned, and Nikki could have strangled him.

"According to Cissy," Nikki murmured to Doc Strong, "Abner Chase said it was only two hundred thousand."

"Zach makes it more every time he talks about it," said the mayor unhappily.

"I heard ye, Martin Strong!" yelled Zach Bigelow, swiveling his twig of a neck so suddenly that Nikki winced, expecting it to snap. "You wait! I'll show ye, ye durn whippersnapper, who's a lot o' wind!"

"Now, Zach," said Doc Strong pacifyingly. "Save your wind for that bugle."

Zach Bigelow cackled and clutched the musette bag in his lap, glaring ahead in triumph, as if he had scored a great victory.

Ellery said no more. Oddly, he kept staring not at old Zach but at Andy Bigelow, who sat beside his grandfather grinning at invisible audiences along the empty countryside as if he, too, had won—or was on his way to winning—a triumph.

The sun was hot. Men shucked their coats and women fanned themselves with handkerchiefs and pocketbooks.

"It is for us the living, rather, to be dedicated . . ."

Children dodged among the graves, pursued by shushing mothers. On most of the graves there were fresh flowers.

"—that from these honored dead . . ."

Little American flags protruded from the graves, too.

". . . gave the last full measure of devotion . . ."

Doc Martin Strong's voice was deep and sure, not at all like the voice of that tall ugly man, who had spoken the same words apologetically.

". . . that these dead shall not have died in vain . . ."

Doc was standing on the pedestal of the Civil War Monument, which was decorated with flags and bunting and faced the weathered stone ranks like a commander in full-dress uniform.

"—that this nation, under God . . ."

A color guard of the American Legion, Jacksburg Post, stood at attention between the mayor and the people. A file of Legionnaires carrying old Sharps rifles faced the graves.

"—and that government of the people . . ."

Beside the mayor, disdaining the simian shoulder of his grandson, stood General Zach Bigelow. Straight as the barrel of a Sharps, musette bag held tightly to his blue tunic.

". . . *shall not perish from the earth.*"

The old man nodded impatiently. He began to fumble with the bag.

"*Comp-'ny! Present—arms!*"

"Go ahead, Gramp!" Andy Bigelow bellowed.

The old man muttered. He was having difficulty extricating the bugle from the bag.

"Here, lemme give ye a hand!"

"Let the old man alone, Andy," said the mayor of Jacksburg quietly. "We're in no hurry."

Finally the bugle was free. It was an old army bugle, as old as Zach Bigelow, dented and scarred in a hundred places.

The old man raised it to his earth-colored lips.

Now his hands were not shaking.

Now even the children were quiet.

Now the Legionnaires stood more rigidly.

And the old man began to play taps.

It could hardly have been called playing. He blew, and out of the bugle's bell came cracked sounds. And sometimes he blew and no sounds came out at all. Then the veins of his neck swelled and his face turned to burning bark. Or he sucked at the mouthpiece, in and out, to clear it of his spittle. But still he blew, and the trees in the burying ground nodded in the warm breeze, and the people stood at attention listening as if the butchery of sound were sweet music.

And then, suddenly, the butchery faltered. Old Zach Bigelow stood with bulging eyes. The Gettysburg bugle fell to the pedestal with a tiny clatter.

For an instant everything seemed to stop—the slight movements of the children, the breathing of the people, even the rustling of the leaves.

Then into the vacuum rushed a murmur of horror, and Nikki unbelievingly opened the eyes which she had shut to glimpse the last of Jacksburg's G.A.R. veterans crumpling to the feet of Doc Strong and Andy Bigelow.

"You were right the first time, Doc," Ellery said.

They were in Andy Bigelow's house, where old Zach's body had been taken from the cemetery. The house was full of chittering women and scampering children, but in this room there were only a few, and they talked in low tones. The old man was laid out on a settee with a patchwork quilt over him. Doc Strong sat in a rocker beside the body, looking very old.

"It's my fault," he mumbled. "I didn't examine Caleb's mouth last year. I didn't examine the mouthpiece of that bugle. It's my fault, Mr. Queen."

Ellery soothed him. "It's not an easy poison to spot, Doc, as you know. And after all, the whole thing was so ludicrous. You'd have caught it in autopsy, but the Atwells laughed you out of it."

"They're all gone. All three." Doc Strong looked up fiercely. "Who poisoned their bugle?"

"God Almighty, don't look at me," said Andy Bigelow. "Anybody could of, Doc."

"Anybody, Andy?" the mayor cried. "When Caleb Atwell died, Zach took the bugle and it's been in this house for a year!"

"Anybody could of," said Bigelow stubbornly. "The bugle was hangin' over the fireplace and anybody could of snuck in durin' the night . . . . Anyway, it wasn't here before old Caleb died; *he* had it up to last Memorial Day. Who poisoned it in *his* house?"

"We won't get anywhere on this tack, Doc," Ellery murmured. "Bigelow. Did your grandfather ever let on where that Civil War treasure is hidden?"

"Suppose he did." The man licked his lips, blinking, as if he had been surprised into the half-admission. "What's it to you?"

"That money is behind the murders, Bigelow."

"Don't know nothin' about that. Anyway, nobody's got no right to that money but me." Andy Bigelow spread his thick chest. "When Ab Chase died, Gramp was the last survivor. That money was Zach Bigelow's. I'm his next o' kin, so now it's mine!"

"You know where it's hid, Andy." Doc was on his feet, eyes glittering. "Where?"

"I ain't talkin'. Git outen my house!"

"I'm the law in Jacksburg, too, Andy," Doc said softly. "This is a murder case. Where's that money?"

Bigelow laughed.

"You didn't know, Bigelow, did you?" said Ellery.

"Course not." He laughed again. "See, Doc? He's on your side, and he says I don't know, too."

"That is," said Ellery, "until a few minutes ago."

Bigelow's grin faded. "What are ye talkin' about?"

"Zach Bigelow wrote a message this morning, immediately after Doc Strong told him about Abner Chase's death."

Bigelow's face went ashen.

"And your grandfather sealed the message in an envelope—"

"Who told ye that?" yelled Bigelow.

"One of your children. And the first thing you did when we got home from the burying ground with your grandfather's corpse was to sneak up to the old man's bedroom. Hand it over."

Bigelow made two fists. Then he laughed again. "All right, I'll let ye see it. Hell, I'll let ye dig the money up for me! Why not? It's mine by law. Here, read it. See? He wrote my name on the envelope!"

And so he had. And the message in the envelope was also written in ink, in the same wavering hand:

Dere Andy now that Ab Chase is ded to—if sumthin happins to me

you wil find the money we been keepin all these long yeres in a iron
box in the coffin *wich we beried Caleb Atwell in*. I leave it all to you
my beluved grandson cuz you been sech a good grandson to me.
Yours truly Zach Bigelow.

"In Caleb's coffin," choked Doc Strong.

Ellery's face was impassive. "How soon can we get an exhumation order,
Doc?"

"Right now," exclaimed Doc. "I'm also deputy coroner of this district!"

And they took some men and they went back to the old burying ground, and in
the darkening day they dug up the remains of Caleb Atwell and they opened the
casket and found, on the corpse's knees, a flattish box of iron with a hasp but no
lock. And, while two strong men held Andy Bigelow to keep him from hurling
himself at the crumbling coffin, Doctor-Mayor-Chief of Police-Deputy Coroner
Martin Strong held his breath and raised the lid of the iron box.

And it was crammed to the brim with moldy bills of large denominations.

In Confederate money.

No one said anything for some time, not even Andy Bigelow.

Then Ellery said, "It stood to reason. They found it buried in the cellar of an
old Southern mansion—would it be Northern greenbacks? When they dug it up
again after the War and brought it up to Jacksburg they probably had some faint
hope that it might have some value. When they realized it was worthless, they
decided to have some fun with it. This had been a private joke of those three
old rascals since, roughly, 1865. When Caleb died last Memorial Day, Abner
and Zach probably decided that, as the first of the trio to go, Caleb ought to have
the honor of being custodian of their Confederate treasure in perpetuity. So
one of them managed to slip the iron box into the coffin before the lid was
screwed on. Zach's note bequeathing his 'fortune' to his 'beloved grandson'—in
view of what I've seen of his beloved grandson today—was the old fellow's final
joke."

Everybody chuckled; but the corpse stared mirthlessly and the silence fell
again, to be broken by a weak curse from Andy Bigelow and Doc Strong's
puzzled: "But Mr. Queen, that doesn't explain the murders."

"Well, now, Doc, it does," said Ellery; and then he said in a very different
tone: "Suppose we put old Caleb back the way we found him, for your re-
exhumation later for autopsy, Doc—and then we'll close the book on your Memorial Day murders."

Ellery closed the book in town, in the dusk, on the porch of Cissy Chase's
house, which was central and convenient for everybody. Ellery and Nikki and
Doc Strong and Cissy and Andy Bigelow—still clutching the iron box dazedly—
were on the porch, and Lew Bagley and Bill Yoder and everyone else in Jacksburg, it seemed, stood about on the lawn and sidewalk, listening. And there was
a touch of sadness to the soft twilight air, for something vital and exciting in the
life of the village had come to an end.

"There's no trick to this," began Ellery, "and no joke, either, even though the men who were murdered were so old that death had grown tired waiting for them. The answer is as simple as the initials of their last names. Who knew that the supposed fortune was in Confederate money and therefore worthless? Only the three old men. One or another of the three would hardly have planned the deaths of the other two for possession of some scraps of valueless paper. So the murderer has to be someone who believed the fortune was legitimate and who— since until today there was no clue to the money's hiding place—knew he could claim it legally.

"Now of course that last-survivor-take-all business was pure moonshine, invented by Caleb, Zach, and Abner for their own amusement and the mystification of the community. But the would-be murderer didn't know that. The would-be murderer went on the assumption that the *whole* story was true, or he wouldn't have planned murder in the first place.

"Who would be able to claim the fortune legally if the last of the three old men—the survivor who presumably came into possession of the fortune on the deaths of the other two—died in his turn?"

"Last survivor's heir," said Doc Strong, and he rose.

"And who is the last survivor's heir?"

"Zach Bigelow's grandson, Andy." And the little mayor of Jacksburg stared hard at Bigelow, and a grumbling sound came from the people below, and Bigelow shrank against the wall behind Cissy, as if to seek her protection. But Cissy only looked at him and moved away.

"You thought the fortune was real," Cissy said scornfully, "so you killed Caleb Atwell and my great-grandpa so your grandfather'd be the last survivor so you could kill him the way you did today and get the fortune."

"That's it, Ellery," cried Nikki.

"Unfortunately, Nikki, that's not it at all. You all refer to Zach Bigelow as the last survivor—"

"Well, he was," said Nikki in amazement.

"How could he not be?" said Doc Strong. "Caleb and Abner died first—"

"Literally, that's true," said Ellery, "but what you've all forgotten is that Zach Bigelow was the last survivor *only by accident.* When Abner Chase died early this morning, was it through poisoning, or some other violent means? No, Doc, you were absolutely positive he'd died of a simple cerebral hemorrhage—not by violence, but a natural death. Don't you see that if Abner Chase hadn't died a natural death early this morning, *he'd still be alive this evening?* Zach Bigelow would have put the bugle to his lips this afternoon, just as he did, just as Caleb Atwell did a year ago . . . *and at this moment Abner Chase would have been the last survivor.*

"And who was Abner Chase's only living heir, the girl who would have fallen heir to Abner's 'fortune' when, in time, or through her assistance, he joined his cronies in the great bivouac on the other side?

"You lied to me, Cissy," said Ellery to the shrinking girl in his grip, as a horror very like the horror of the burying ground in the afternoon came over the crowd of mesmerized Jacksburgers. "You pretended you didn't believe the story of the fortune. But that was only after your great-grandfather had inconsiderately died of a stroke just a few hours before old Zach would have died of poisoning, and you couldn't inherit that great, great fortune, anyway!"

Nikki did not speak until they were twenty-five miles from Jacksburg. Then all she said was, "And now there's nobody left to blow the Gettysburg bugle," and she continued to stare into the darkness toward the south.

RHODE ISLAND

THE RHODE ISLAND LIGHTS
by S. S. Rafferty

THE AUTUMN OF 1736 was kind indeed to the coast of the northern colonies. Normally expected foul winds and fouler weather turned out to be a cool, clear sky and a placid sea lapping gently like a puppy against the eddyrock from Boston to New York. For the first time in 18 months, Captain Jeremy Cork and I were once again ensconced in our natural surroundings at the Oar and Eagle at Sea Bluff on the Connecticut littoral.

"Well, by jing," I said, opening the letters that had come by the post rider early that evening, "it appears that your social puzzles have produced some coin at last."

He was sitting at what he euphemistically calls his "work" table, absorbed in a newly arrived book from England. He looked up and grunted a slight note of interest.

"You remember Squire Delaney of the Rhode Island colony?"

"Of course, Oaks. We helped him in the Narragansett Pacer affair."

"Yes, well, he has seen fit to give your spermacite candle factory in Warwick a substantial contract. It's rather astounding, though. What could he possibly do with two-pound candles? My God, it says here, 'For delivery to the Pharos at Point Judith.' Could Delaney have fallen in with some pagan ritual?"

Cork closed the book and looked up at me with that smirk-a-mouth he uses when he is about to jape me. "Perhaps we ought to refuse the contract. We wouldn't want to be party to the Dark Arts, hey?"

Now there you have it. As Cork's financial yeoman, I am patiently building him an empire of holdings that may some day make him the richest man in the Americas. However, it is part of his sport to ignore my efforts and waste his time in the solution of crimes, which he calls "social puzzles." He has other unprofitable pastimes which are not mentionable in Christian company. This present piece of sarcasm about refusing the Delaney contract was a backhanded reminder that I once proposed the importation of shrunken heads from Spanish America. I said, give the public what it wants, but he was against it.

"I didn't say 'Dark Arts,' sir, you did. I was merely curious about the use of so large a candle, and in such quantity."

"Actually, Oaks, I am guilty of bad imagery. White Arts would have been a better choice."

I looked at him querulously, and he went on, "Even in the absence of all the information, we have the thread of the tapestry. Where does the good Squire live?"

"In the Rhode Island colony."

"More specifically, at Point Judith, does he not?"

"Yes, he owns his horse ranch, as he calls it, and everything in sight."

"And does not Point Judith's recent notoriety bring anything to mind?"

"Of course, the shipwrecks! Four, over the summer, I believe. Shifting sand-bars and tricky shoals, the *Gazette* reported."

"And here we have a wealthy, public-spirited man ordering immense can-dles—"

"A lighthouse! He's building a lighthouse."

"Or Pharos, as mariners term it. But if he is now ordering his light source, I would guess that the Pharos is already built. Now that is something I want to see."

With *The Hawkers*, the ship he owns but never sails in, away to the Indies, we were forced to make the trip overland, and arrived at the Delaney ranch three days later.

I must point out here that our party also included Tunxis, a tame Quinnipiac, who serves as Cork's shadow and as my vexation. Although he speaks passable English, the Indian always talks to Cork in Injun jabber, and a three-day trip spent with two men laughing over incomprehensible jokes is not my recommen-dation for pleasant travel.

I once heard a back-stair rumor that Cork was related to the Quinnipiac by blood. I would have no truck with that notion. However, when observing Cork's demeanor once he entered the woods and wild, I admit to some doubts. He and Tunxis possess uncanny hearing, and I swear their sense of smell is even better than their eyesight. Perhaps it is these underlying animal instincts that give Cork his reputation as a detector.

In any case, I spent three days ahorse with two boys on a frolic with Nature.

In a previous visit to the Delaneys, I marveled at the luxury of their center-hall mansion. It had changed only for the better, now sprouting another wing. This annex, I assumed, was to accommodate the issue of the ever-fruitful Madame Delaney. As we were to learn later, the Delaneys, having produced seven brawny sons, were now one shy of matching that mark with females.

We arrived at dinnertime, but were not in peril of taking pot-luck. At the Delaney table it is always pot-wealth. There was the normal complement of cod chowder, steamed lobster and clams, and, of course, great hot bowls of succotash and pork. But, good wife that she was, Madame Delaney also served one of the original dishes for which she is justly famous. On this evening it was a platter of succulent squabs, which were as curious as they were delicious. Under Cork's prodding, she told us that they were spit-roasted and basted with a pungent, salty liquor used in China, called sauce of soy. I know little of the Chinese, but their bellies must be content. Since Tunxis refuses to eat or sleep under a roof, he took his repast outdoors.

Later we were sitting in the drawing room with clay bowls and mugs of Delaney's usquebaugh, a potent corn liquor of dark Scotch-Irish reputation, when I brought up a point that had bothered me since we arrived.

"When we turned into your property, Squire, I could see two towers far off the Point. Yet your order said a Pharos."

"Technical terminology, Oaks," Cork cut in. "One or several lights in one place are considered a unit, and referred to in the singular. I assume, Squire, that you have gone to the expense of two towers to give sailors a seamark that is clearly different from others along the coast."

"That and more," the Irishman said.

"Is it worth doubling the investment, just to be different?" I asked.

Cork refilled his bowl and said, "You'll have to forgive Oaks, Squire. He is a businessman, not a navigator."

"Nor am I, Captain, but mariners tell me it is worth the investment. Perhaps if you will explain it to Oaks, it will further clarify my own mind."

"Surely. Well, Oaks, you have certainly been at sea at night. It is something like waking up in a pitch-black room."

"I leave that to the helmsman," I said.

"And whom does he leave it to? Like an awakened man in a dark room, he can bump into things, not having a bearing on a fixed point. However, when our man at sea bumps into something, it is not a chair or a footstool, producing but a stubbed toe. No, my friend, his obstacle can be a reef or shoal, which can tear the bottom from his craft and send her under."

"What about stars?"

"Helpful in deep water, but when near a landfall, you require well defined objects ashore. Most charts are not well defined. The sextant is only valuable in skilled hands, and then, of course, there are starless nights. But we are digressing into science. The Squire has put up two lights to tell all at sea who might be off course that the two lights are Point Judith and nowhere else, and I compliment him on his public spirit."

"Oh, that I could accept, it, Captain," said the Squire, with a moan. "But I cannot. The Pharos was built to protect my own good name, as well as the men at sea."

"Go on, man," the Captain said, squinting his eyes in interest.

"You might have read of the shipwrecks off these shores over the past year."

"Yes," I said, "the *Boston Weekly Gazette* mentioned them."

"But what they didn't mention was the ugly rumor that spread in these parts and which implied that I had somehow contrived to cause these wrecks for salvage rights."

"Did you salvage them?"

"Yes, Captain, the first one. But after the rumors I stopped. God help me, my eldest son is at this moment apprenticed to the master of a coaster. Would I be so callous?"

"Indeed not. But tell me, why do you carry the financial load alone? Other townships have raised Pharos with lotteries. Why not here?"

"The townspeople, like those everywhere, resent the wealthy, and feel they can't afford it. Those lottery-built lighthouses are near ports where a lighthouse tax is collectible. Such is not the case here. I bear the load, but alas, not out of public spirit."

"Tell me, Squire," Cork asked, "is there any suspicion that the wrecks might have been caused by foul play?"

"It's a perplexing question. The shoals off our shore are treacherous, and the sandbars seem to have shifted, so accident is highly possible. I have personally surveyed the surrounding waters at low tide, and I had a young fellow from Yale draw up some charts. When word got out that I was going to erect a lighthouse, a single one, all hell broke loose from here to Narragansett."

"But why?" I asked. "You would be protecting shipping by warning them away from underwater hazards."

"And away from Narragansett Bay, or so the dockmen up there claim. As Cork said, night navigation is tricky at best, and if my lone light was a beacon of danger, there was fear that a ship's master would steer a northerly parallel course to the light and end up in Buzzard's Bay, which would enrich New Bedford."

"That's nonsense," Cork growled, "and can be proved so."

"Captain, did you ever try to explain logic and reason to a group of more than three or four men? Especially on a technical subject?"

"Touché," Cork said, with a smile.

"Well, how do two lighthouses solve the problem?" I asked.

"The Yale student suggested it. Our charts show that a deep channel cuts through the shoals. If a means could be found to guide a ship through it at night, a master could safely change from a northerly course to a westerly line, go through the channel, and then swing northeast towards Narragansett."

"Aha." Cork slapped his knee and tossed his head back. "I should have seen it at once when I noticed that the two towers are not in parallel line. The second tower is set back, is it not?"

"Twenty-five feet."

"So you have not only a distinctive seamark, but a unique navigation aid. You present the sailor with a simple light-in-one sighting."

"That's precisely the term John Knox, the student, used."

Following this discussion was becoming as difficult as listening to Cork and Tunxis talk Injun. "Forgive me, gentlemen," I said, "but this is all beyond me."

"Shall I explain, Squire?"

"Pray do. I barely understand it myself."

"Probably because the academician likes to cloak his knowledge in long words. Actually, a light-in-one sighting is simple, but it is more easily demonstrated than explained. May I conduct an experiment for Oaks here so that he might understand?"

The Squire seemed delighted with the entertainment, and Cork set to it. "First, Oaks, you will go into that closet on the far wall. When you emerge, the room will be in darkness except for these two candles, which will be burning on the table to represent the two towers on the Point.

"Now, when you emerge from the closet, you will be facing north, and the floor area in front of you will be cleared of all furniture. This will represent the safety of deep water. Now, as you walk due north, keep your eye on the candles. At a certain point, you will see the two lights start to merge into one. It is no illusion, Oaks. The lights really aren't moving, *you* are. Now the trick is to get you to change to a westerly course. That would be to your left, and bring you forward without breaking your neck on the stools I will have scattered there to represent the shoals."

"Captain," I said suspiciously, "I don't mind barked shins, but a broken neck?"

"Have faith in the system, Oaks, as must the mariner. When the lights merge into one, you will turn to your left and proceed so through the aisle I will have made between the stools, to represent the deep channel. Now I have a question, Squire. Are the lanterns designed to emit light on a 180-degree radius?"

"Yes, that's the reason for the immense candles."

"To be sure. So when Oaks is safely through the aisle, he will again see two lights."

"Correct."

"Then you have nothing to fear, Oaks. Now into the closet while I scale the mathematics to fit our simplified situation in this room. Well, come, my boy, you will be just as safe as in your own bed."

On Cork's guarantee I left my dark closet and entered the room. The candles burned brightly on the table to my left, and I gingerly walked forward. I was amazed to see the candles appear to move, and when they merged into one, I turned left with some trepidation. To my surprise all went well, and when the candles were two again, I turned north again.

"Amazing," I said after the other tapers were lit and the furniture put back to rights.

"Well, you must appreciate that this was a crude example of how a light-in-one works," Cork said, taking some more usquebaugh. "This student, this Knox fellow, has obviously made precise calculations, to place the lights in their proper positions."

"He was at it for weeks, spending nights out in a skiff while my son Secundus and I lit fires from rude poles placed ashore at different angles and heights. Once we had the proper mathematics, we started construction. In the last three weeks of operation we personally have traversed the channel at least fifty times. Three ships' masters have also taken their crafts through successfully.

"Copies of the charts were sent to all the major ports to the south and the harbormasters have written back that they have made the information known to north-bound ships."

"And what of fog or heavy rain?" I asked.

"I am sorry to say that the lights are useless in foul weather, but we have tried to overcome that weakness by firing a star rocket every hour on the hour. At least it will be some warning, and will keep the taint of malicious rumor from my good name. Being accused of placing false lights to lure ships upon the rocks is a heinous charge."

"And punishable by death under Admiralty Law," Cork added with a note of grimness. "But it seems your troubles are over. Is John Knox still with you? I should like to meet him."

"To be sure. He is manning Tower One, while Secundus is in Tower Two. We have decided to hire keepers, but not for a while."

I smiled to myself at the Squire's penchant for naming things by number. A less precise man would have called the first tower the forward tower, and the second the aft, or rear, tower. But what could you expect from a man who had named his seven sons, Primus, Secundus, Tertius, and so on? He once told me that he originally had planned to use the names of the Apostles, but was fore-warned by his wife that he was overreaching himself. The female Delaneys were being named for the nine Muses. The Squire is clearly a man of stern de-termination.

"So, my lads," he said, raising his mug, "I give you the Point Judith Pharos, long may it shine." As he said it, Delaney walked to a large bow window and threw back the drapes. "There are my beauties," he said and raised his glass anew.

Out in the distance, through a starless night, were the dark landsides of the towers, eerie halos of light radiating above their silhouettes as their fiery faces shone out to sea. As we watched the halos glistening, Cork explained that the halo was called a corona, and the rears of the lanterns were much like a view from the dark side of the moon. Then suddenly a toll of bells and the wail of handhorns sounded off in the distance.

"Why, it's like New Year's Eve," I said jokingly. Cork touched my arm and cocked his head into the sounds. He turned and looked at the Squire, who was white with fear.

"Oh, God," Delaney said, lips trembling, "a shipwreck!"

The ensuing hours of that horror-filled night will never be erased from my memory. Out in the darkness lay a sinking ship, its timbers grinding chillingly like the broken spine of a wounded and thrashing beast. Small boats with sur-vivors bobbled in the surf as citizens from the surrounding countryside rushed to aid them. It was near dawn when the last of the longboats dispatched from shore returned from a sweep of the wreck area.

THE RHODE ISLAND LIGHTS

As the longboat was hauled onto the beach, the last survivors tumbled out. One was a young sailor of no more than 20. His hand was bleeding, and one of the countrymen came forward to help him. As he lifted the lad to carry him, he cried out in anger, "It's Primus Delaney, it is. The old devil Squire is at it again!"

By noon the Squire and Primus had been placed under arrest and locked in the brig of a Royal Frigate in Narragansett harbor. The charges were barratry, collusion to shipwreck, and murder, since three hands were lost in the tragedy. The towers were closed by Royal Navy order, and the Delaney household was in chaos.

Before the two Delaneys were clapped in irons, however, Cork was able to piece together the gist of what had happened at sea.

The doomed ship was the *Queen of Tortuga*, out of New York, bound for Narragansett. Her master, who was injured but alive, was Captain Amos Whittleby. At the time of the wreck he had been below deck, having left Primus as the watch officer, and helmsman Fergus Kirk at the wheel.

According to Primus, he had been given charts of his father's new enterprise and was anxious to use the navigation aid. On sighting the two beacons, he sounded the ship's bell and ordered Kirk into the channel-crossing maneuver.

"The lights were joined beautifully," he told us earlier that morning, while being fed hot broth by his mother. All the survivors had been taken to the Delaney home for care, but it was obvious that most of the crew were suspicious and angry. "I kept the lights in sight until they were one, and then told the helmsman to bring her into the west. All went well, and when the lights started to part again, I thought we were through the channel. In fact, I could see the fore and aft lights of a smaller craft still further west. I was about to order us back north, when the crunch of the bottom came, and—well, after that it was hell."

"And now, in broad daylight," Cork said at the time, "we can see that the wreck lies hundreds of feet from the entrance of the channel. So you were on a dead heading for the shoal all the time."

"Yet I couldn't have mistaken the lights' merge, Captain Cork. Fergus Kirk can tell you the same thing."

But it seemed the helmsman couldn't.

"Aye, the boy may be telling the truth," the Scotsman told us later. "I kept my eyes peeled to the compass, and could nae say what the lights done. This I do ken, sirs. No wee laddie should have say on the course of a bark under sail."

Cork interrogated the rest of the crew, but at the time of the wreck all were at meal or asleep in the fo'c'sle. A second hand on the night watch admitted to being asleep on the forward hatch. The others on the watch were lost in the disaster.

Captain Whittleby refused to answer any questions, and replaced cooperation with threats and castigation.

"You have one of two choices, Captain Cork," he snarled as his battered head was being bandaged by a crewman. "Either the light scheme is faulty, or the boy

was derelict in his duty. In either case, one of the Delaneys will swing for it, and
I want to be there to see the execution."

"We are assured the lights were operating properly, and the system has been
tested time and again, Captain Whittleby," Cork had said with some annoyance.
"But while we are speaking of dereliction, may I ask why the youngest mate in
your crew was given command of the ship in a difficult passage? Surely you
should have been on deck, or at the least your first mate."

"The setting of watches is my own business, Captain Cork, and I resent the
accusation of dereliction. Why wouldn't I trust young Delaney? He was in home
waters and following his father's charts. And I'm sure, if you are a mariner, you
well know the youngest eyes and ears in the crew are called on when needed in a
rough crossing."

"Then you admit to a rough crossing."

"He admits to nothing, sir." The speaker was the local man who had helped
young Primus from the boat. His name was Myles Swaith, and he was truly no
friend of the Delaneys. "I have heard of your reputation, Captain Cork—how
you are able to twist and contort things to fit your own ends. But not this time.
Delaney has lorded it over this vicinity for years, but now he's for it, and there's
no help for him."

"There really isn't you know," I said to Cork when we left the room. "We
ourselves are witness to the lighthouses working, and if Knox's calculations are
correct, then it's error on Primus' part. But if the calculations are wrong, it's the
Squire's neck."

"Yes," Cork said, stroking his barba in thought, "but when you have spent
time at sea, Oaks, you learn not to trust the surface of the waves. It's what's
below that counts. Let's talk to Knox and Secundus."

The lighthouse keepers were in a bedroom on the second floor. John Knox was
in his mid-twenties, with flaxen blond hair and an aquiline nose. Secundus Delaney needed no description once you have seen the Squire or any of his offspring. The same red hair and round pixie face. It was as if they had all come
from the same mold, which, when you thought about it, was precisely the case.

Knox sat in a chair with his head in his hands. Secundus, a lad of 18, lay
despondently on the bed.

"I can't believe it, Captain," Knox said after we had introduced ourselves. "I
am positive of my calculations. We tested them over and over again. If anyone
should be blamed, it should be me."

"That's not true," Secundus said, getting up and patting his friend's shoulder.
"My father and I have also used the system, and we know it works. And several
ships' masters have done the same."

"All it proves is that your brother made an error," Knox said. "So what does
that solve?"

"Mr. Knox," Cork broke in, "self-pity is a poor companion in dire straits.
The Squire tells me that copies of the charts were sent to harbormasters of all
major ports to the south. Did you draw those charts?"

"Why, yes, I did. Oh, I see what you mean. I must have made an error on one of them, and somehow it got to New York and on to the *Queen of Tortuga*. Then I *am* to blame!"

"Possibly. But there is another aspect. The New York chart could have been changed. How were they sent?"

"By coaster, sir," Secundus explained, "out of 'Gansett. It was the quickest way."

"And Primus' copy of the chart went down with the *Queen of Tortuga*. How fortunate." Cork smiled.

"Fortunate?" Knox looked perplexed.

"Fortunate for Primus' neck. I believe there will be a trial, and I plan to defend him. I have that right, as a ship's master and owner. Now we have a point of doubt in our favor. If the Court will accept the argument that the chart could have been changed—ever so slightly, for a jot on a chart is hundreds of yards at sea—then we introduce the possibility of collusion from a third party."

Knox's face took on brightness for the first time. "Why, I never thought of that. But wait, Captain, the harbormaster at New York—wouldn't he know?"

"I doubt that he would remember. Most seamen do not memorize charts they will never use."

Secundus smacked his hands together and let out a howl of glee. "Captain, sir, you're a marvel," he cried.

There was a commotion downstairs, and we all went down to find Primus and his father chained together and guarded by six towering Royal Marines. An English Captain named Cricker read formal charges and led the men away over the shrieks and wails of the Delaney women.

The rest of the day was spent within the legal machinery in preparation for a naval inquiry. Once in the town of Narragansett, we called on a local lawyer of some reputation. Giles Pomfret was an old eagle, trained in the Inns of Court, and regarded as a sound scholar. His offices were on the second floor of the Blue Whale, and after an explanation of the situation he sat back slowly touching the fingers of one hand to the other.

"I bow to you, Captain, in marine law, but this doubt-casting element about a chart being mysteriously changed—well, it is a thin line, sir. A very thin line, indeed, since the chart itself is fathoms down."

"That is only my first line, Mr. Pomfret, and I think you will agree that a good defense is the sum of many ramparts."

The old man nodded and then smiled. "To show you how ill equipped I am for the case, when you first said 'barratry,' my mind immediately went to the civil-law interpretation—the habitual maintenance of lawsuits or quarrels. Now in marine law, it means to sink a ship, does it not?"

"Technically, it is the use of fraud or gross or criminal negligence on the part of the master or mariners of a ship to the owner's prejudice."

"Yes. Yes, of course. And the Delaney boy being on the deck watch is the mariner in this case. But what of the charge of wrecking and murder?"

"The changed-chart theory, if proved, will obliterate all charges."

"Well, Captain"—Pomfret shook his head—"I wish you good fortune, but I'll also pray for the Delaneys at the same time. I will, however, prepare the necessary papers to allow you to represent them at the inquiry. If, however, this goes to a full Court, I suggest that you hire the finest marine lawyer money can buy."

We bid him goodbye on that sour note, and, when we were on the street, Cork walked in silence.

Finally he stopped for a moment and said, more to himself than to me, "Strange, a lawyer in a busy port, and he knows nothing of marine law."

"It could be his age. He seems in his dotage."

"That may be," he said, and then stopped a young boy. "Hey, my lad, who is the harbormaster in these waters?"

"That be old Peg and Patch, sir," the boy replied with a shudder.

"Old Peg and Patch, hey? And I suppose you address him so when you bid him good day?"

The lad lowered his head and then shot it up again. "When I sees him I brings myself about, sir. Beware churned waters, my old man says," he told us through a toothless grin.

"A fearsome fellow, then?"

"Like the devil himself, sir. Some says he was a pirate and lived with wild natives on a far-off isle where he was a cannyball."

"And where would his headquarters be, lad?"

"At the foot of Tillford's dock, sir, but you won't find 'im there. Best look in Sadie's, by the Front Street." Then he said, wide-eyed, "If ye have the heart, for you 'pear to be of quality."

"Mere clothes, my lad," Cork said, tossing a coin to him.

One of the outstanding aspects of New England life is the righteous piety of the population. Yet, in its port towns, there is usually one low place where evil flourishes and slakes the appetites of men home from long voyages. Sadie's was buried deep in the cellar of an old warehouse. Through the thick and acrid smoke I could see a stairway that led to the upper part of the building, and dared not think of the evil doings that must occur up there. A crone with tousled hair paid court to our obvious means, and directed us to the harbormaster at a table in a far corner.

From the boy's description I expected to see a demonic sot, racked with depravity. However, Captain Robert Tinker (for that was his true name) was a well kept man of 60. The appellation of Peg and Patch sprang from the spotless patch over his left eye and the ivory stump that served as his left leg from the knee down. To my further surprise he was a reasonably well-spoken Englishman of some education.

After we had taken seats, he must have noticed my own amazement, or sensed it.

"From the look on your face, Mr. Oaks, I take it you have been talking to the townspeople. I am no ogre, sirs. The eye and the limb were lost to gunfire in the service of King and Country. I guess I am resented because I was granted my post by Royal Appointment. Let me assure you, it is no sinecure."

An unbelievably buxom wench came to the table, and Captain Tinker ordered a bottle of madeira. *His* madeira.

"I take it you are here on the Delaney business, gentlemen. What service can I do for you?"

"I am told," Cork began, "that copies of the Point Judith charts were put aboard coasters and taken to southern ports."

"Aye. Four in all. Put them aboard myself, explaining in each case the Pharos to the ship's master."

"Do you recall the ships?"

"Ah, let me see, the *Tarrymae* was one."

"Excuse me, Captain," Cork interrupted, "to simplify it, which ship was New York bound?"

"The *Ice Cloud*, under Master Swaith."

"Miles Swaith?"

"Nay, his brother, Ishmael."

"Interesting. There were four wrecks in this area over the summer months, I gather."

"Aye. The Judith shoals were becoming a graveyard, until the Squire came along with this Pharos idea."

"Now I'm told that Delaney took salvage rights on the first bottom, but who took rights in the other wrecks?"

"The 'Gansett Corporation. After the rumors started when the *Bristol Girl* went down, Delaney wouldn't put an oar in the water. So Miles Swaith and a few local businessmen formed a group and took the jobs. Damned shame about young Delaney, though. Shouldn't put the deck under a youngster, I always say."

"Then you believe it to have been an accident?"

"What else, sir? I myself put the Pharos plan to the test and went through the channel like it was the Thames. Say now, don't go taking on this bilge that the Squire was a wrecker. He's as true as magnetic north."

"To be sure. You will be called as a witness if there is a trial, and I trust you will hold that position."

"You have my bond, sir."

When Cork offered to pay for the madeira, which was excellent, Tinker refused. "First one's free, Captain," he said. "It's good for business. You see, I own this place."

That evening, on our return to the Delaney ranch, we took a meager supper in our rooms. The hearty familial spirit that had been drawn from the home had left only bleakness in its aftertide.

"It appears that the name Swaith abounds in this affair," I said, over the cold turkey and corn bread.

"Yes, the brother could have changed the charts, but we are on slanderous grounds. I want something with more meat to it."

"Your second rampart?"

"And a third, if we can find one."

With this, there was a tap at the window, which at first I thought was rain. Getting up, Cork opened the casement to admit Tunxis. Despite the fact that we were on the second floor, the Indian's sudden appearance was not in the least jarring to me. To come to the second floor like a normal person he would have to enter under a roof, so it was natural that he would scale the trellis to converse with Cork. The climb up must have winded him slightly, or set his mind a-bubble, for he spoke in English. Thrusting a sack through the window, he said, "Here, like you say, lower beach."

"Good fellow, Chawcua, and who was with you?"

"White man named Clint."

"Good. Wait below."

When Cork had closed the window again, he returned to the table with the sack and sat down.

"What's in that thing?" I asked, sniffing the air. "A skunk?"

"No. My second line of defense, Oaks."

I reached across, opened the sack, and quickly closed it. "Animal droppings. Dung is your second rampart?"

"Evidence is often as repulsive as the crime, Oaks. Now I'm off for the third."

"Not without me," I said, getting to my feet.

"You're a stout fellow, my lad, but not this time."

"And why not? Am I some slip of a girl, some piece of frippery? I may not have the woodsy wiles of that redskin, but I'm man enough to a given task."

There were few times in my long relationship with him that I experienced true camaraderie. He reached out, clapped my shoulder, looked at me with those cold blue eyes, and smiled. "I never doubted that, my friend. Come, we have some climbing of our own to do."

My moment of gallantry stuck in my throat as we approached the base of the forward tower on the Point. With the ground-level hatches of both structures sealed tight with Royal lead, Cork proposed to scale the side of the thirty-foot edifice fronting the sea.

"Not only is it dangerous, but pointless," I said, as Tunxis uncurled roping lines.

"Wrong on both counts, Oaks. The facing is of fine hammered sandstone with a wide bond, so, despite the mist, the footing is sure. As for examining the light room, it is crucial to the case. I will go first, Tunxis to follow. Once up, we will haul you up by rope."

"If you climb, I climb."

He looked at the Indian, and Tunxis nodded. A savage was giving his accord to my own valor. Perhaps, at last, I was accepted by him.

I will not embarrass myself by describing the toil and fear of the ascent. From one slippery stone to the next, never looking down into the blackness, I inched my way up into more blackness. Above me I heard the shatter of glass, as Cork broke one of the panes in the tower windows, and a sharp tug on the guy line around my waist alerted me that the end of the climb was near.

"Take care of the broken pane, Oaks," Cork whispered. "Reach above your head and you will find a rod running around the ceiling on the inside."

I swung into the window frame and got to my feet. Cork was examining the apparatus with a shielded candle. The now dark light was a wondrous machine. Twelve large candles were imbedded in a holding plate before a concave plate of polished brass. The candles, when lit, must have reflected a most powerful light out to sea.

"What are you doing, Captain?" I asked, as he tugged at the base of the holding plate.

"Solid as Gibraltar," he said. "Let's take the ladder below."

One by one we descended into a round room directly below the light chamber. It had been fitted out as living quarters for a permanent keeper, when he was eventually hired. A chair and a writing table were at one side of the room. Tunxis lit the lamp with his candle while Cork rummaged around. He found nothing in the table drawer, and obviously nothing of interest in the few books on the shelf.

"Looks like a wild goose," I said, sitting on the chair, still winded from the climb and the excitement.

"Perhaps," Cork muttered as he pulled back a curtain hanging on ring hoops to expose a bed.

"Are lighthouse keepers allowed to sleep?"

"We all must, eventually, Oaks. With the coal-fired beacons along the English coast, there is little chance of the light going out, so the keepers sleep. I'm sure that when Delaney hires a regular keeper, he will keep a night watch."

"Keepers, you mean," I corrected him. An opportunity I rarely have.

He looked at me from the shadows cast by the lamp and gave me that smirk-a-mouth again. "You! A man of ledgers and coin! My word, Oaks, that is astounding. One man can handle both towers. Stationed in this forward tower, he could see if the rear tower was lit at all times. What's below there, Tunxis?"

The Indian's head poked up the ladderway hatch from the deck below.

"Supplies, candles."

"Well," I said, "what next? I hope we are not going to climb the other tower."

"No need. Come, lads, there is nothing more here." Cork snuffed the lamp.

When we arrived back at the house, Tunxis went wherever he goes, and we entered to find a note from Lawyer Pomfret. Cork did not read it in front of Madame Delaney, but waited till we were in our rooms. He then tore open the sealed envelope and read quickly.

"They move with great haste in this matter." He tossed the paper to me and I read it with a sinking heart. Disregarding all the niceties and legal terms, its essence was that a Naval Court of Inquiry would convene two days hence to take advantage of the fact that Admiral Fenley-Blore, of his Majesty's fleet, was in the area, and had agreed to preside over the panel.

"My, my, a flag officer, no less. Is that good or bad, Captain?"

He shrugged. "All bad pennies have an obverse. If we lose, there is little chance for appeal in London. A Fleet Admiral's stamp will settle it forever."

"And if we win, that also ends it forever. But two days is so short a time to prepare."

"For us, yes. I feel other forces have been planning for weeks. But no use wailing over it. We must set some things to our advantage. Fetch me Secundus, will you, while I pen a note."

A note indeed. It was a missive of polite flattery and obeisance to Admiral Fenley-Blore. Cork expressed concern over the meager accommodations available in Narragansett to a naval hero of the Admiral's stature. He went on to describe the luxury of the Delaney home and extended its hospitality to further add to the Admiral's comfort, and suggested that the Court be convened in the main hall of the Delaney mansion in order that the Admiral's august presence have the proper dignified surroundings. The most amusing part was his signing it, "Your obedient servant." Cork has bowed to no man, and I am sure he has never been obedient.

Secundus was dressed for the night ride, and took the letter. "Mind, lad, for the Admiral's hands, and no other's. By the bye, before you go. Was anyone aware that your brother's ship was making for these waters?"

"Surely. It was posted in the harbormaster's office. Not the exact day, but on or about, you know."

"Estimated date of return, yes. Well, off you go."

The Admiral arrived the next afternoon with two aides. Fenley-Blore was an English sailor of the old line. In the days of Queen Bess he would surely have been one of the Sea Dogs. A shortish man, he tended toward portliness in his twilight years. But the weight of girth and age had not slowed his step or his agile mind. Cork, the sly fox, fawned over him like a lass to a fiddler.

It wasn't until the next morning that I saw through the reason for Cork's uncommon actions. We were at breakfast, and Fenley-Blore was saying, "Wild turkey, you say? Now that should be good sport, hunting from horseback. But I'm afraid we will have to get on with this inquiry business. I enjoy these sojourns ashore, but I must get back to sea."

"I understand, Admiral," Cork soothed him, "but why not have the best of all possible worlds? We can hunt today and hold the inquiry tonight. You have the power to convene at any hour, so why not at your leisure?"

"Well put. Tonight it is. Feel a bit sheepish at trying a man in his own home, though."

"Command is not always easy, Admiral."

He had hooked him. The inquest was to be held that night.

Before I describe that evening of surprises, dejections, and finally, of an uncanny solution, I must explain that I have simplified the text to avoid all the technical terms that fog understanding for the layman. I myself kept copious notes, and it took Cork three days to explain them to me. The air in the main hall that night was thick with such phrases as "points to the larboard," "keel lines," "true and magnetic course," and "lines of divination," as well as an hour's worth of talks and arguments about sails and winds and crosswinds.

The main point is that a ship was wrecked due either to negligence or to a faulty system—or so the Court claimed.

Cork went immediately to work on the changed-chart theory. He carefully laid the groundwork by describing how the copies of the chart sent to New York *could* have been changed. He was about to strengthen his question of doubt when one of the Admiral's aides leaned over and whispered into his superior's ear.

"Excuse me, Captain Cork," Fenley-Blore said, "but this line that the chart used aboard the *Queen of Tortuga* by young Delaney being missing is not correct."

I looked up at Cork, who was standing at our table facing the Court. His face showed surprise, and a chart was handed down the line of nine officers on the panel to the Admiral.

"Captain Cork," the Admiral continued, picking up the chart, "this was found with the flotsam of the *Tortuga*. It bears the inscription: *Delaney, Point Judith Pharos*. Would you kindly verify that it is the same as the original chart?"

Cork called John Knox, who was sworn in. The student looked at the chart carefully and said, "I'm afraid it's accurate, Captain," causing a murmur from the small group of townsmen who sat at the back of the long room. It appeared that Cork's first line of defense was breached, and I could see no rampart to fall back upon.

The Captain now went into skirmish maneuvers. He called the Delaneys, and Primus and his father both took an oath to their stories. He also put on the stand a Captain Jeggs, one of the mariners who had tested the system, and he too swore to Heaven that it was a genuine chart.

Next came Fergus Kirk, who would swear to nothing except that he was Fergus Kirk. He stuck to his story that he had been watching the compass. As Kirk stepped down, a voice from the back of the room said, "If it pleases the Admiral and the panel, sir, may I be recognized?"

I turned to see Lawyer Pomfret walking slowly forward. The Admiral recognized Pomfret, who stood facing Cork.

"Gentlemen, I am Giles Pomfret, counselor-at-law, representing the Virron Shipping concern of Maiden Lane, New York, owners of the *Queen of Tortuga*."

He shifted on his feet like a nervous bird, and faced the panel.

"We, of course, have an interest in this matter and its outcome, and it seems to me that the good Captain here has everyone in sight taking an oath. We can't believe both Delaneys and still have a logical explanation of the matter. Now I'm a local man and would like to see fairness tendered, but my clients demand justice."

"And, from justice, restitution?" Cork asked.

"Captain, you're a fine fellow and a superior host," the Admiral smiled, "but we will have to get more answers than we have so far."

Cork was about to resume, when Captain Jeggs motioned to him, and both men talked in low whispers for a few moments. "Admiral, I have no further need of Captain Jeggs. We have his testimony, and he has a tide to catch."

"Excused, and good weather, Captain," the Admiral said, tossing him a half salute.

"Now, gentlemen." Cork walked forward as a chair was brought up for Pomfret, who sat and crossed his spindly legs. "The crux of the matter is the Pharos system itself, and to fully understand it, the panel should see it in operation."

The Admiral pointed his finger at Cork. "Now see here, Captain, I have no intention of setting sail to watch lights."

"No need, Admiral. We can exhibit it right here, with your permission. It's very simple. All we will need is two candles and total darkness. I would use my friend Oaks to demonstrate, but that could be viewed as prejudice, so I will call on a man who has asked for Justice, Lawyer Pomfret."

The lawyer gladly accepted, and the room was set up much as we had it when I played the part of the ship. One major exception was that Cork had the panel table moved forward. That put us all facing the wall along which Pomfret would walk in darkness.

"Now, to truly imitate the conditions of the night in question," Cork said, before the tapers were extinguished, "I have fashioned a shield for the back of the candle holders. In that way, only Mr. Pomfret will be able to tell us what he sees. Now remember, Pomfret, when the lights are one, make your turn, not before or after, for those chairs could give you a nasty knock."

The lawyer left the room, and we waited, adjusting our eyes to the darkness. Cork lit the candles, for we could all see the halos above the shields. "Come ahead," he shouted, and a door opened and I could hear Pomfret slowly shuffling across the room ahead. Four, five seconds, and then he said, "I'm turning now," and then the crash of old bones and heavy mahogany chairs followed instantly.

It would have been a comic sight to see the old man lying on the floor rubbing his painful leg, had it not sunk the Squire once and for all. But then it occurred to me that Pomfret had deliberately turned too soon, in order to create a negative impression. I went forward in the low-lighted room and informed Cork in a low tone.

"Excuse me, gentlemen," Cork said to the Court, while he helped the snarling man to his feet. "It has been suggested to me that our legal friend here may have resorted to deceit to prejudice the case."

"That's a lie," Pomfret shouted, dusting himself off.

"You are correct, sir. I believe you did turn when the lights became one. Just as young Delaney did."

"Then you have proved the case against the Squire," the Admiral said.

"I have proved a case. Let us see who fits the mold."

He walked over to the window and drew back the drapes to the oh's and ah's of everyone. The Admiral came to his feet and hurried to the window. "What are those lights doing on?" he roared. The two towers had glowing halos above their tops. "They were ordered sealed, and by the gods, I'll hang any man who has broken them open."

"There are ways around seals, just as there are ways around systems, Admiral. Say, isn't that a ship out there? See the fore-and-aft running lights riding the waves?"

"You're right, Cork." The Admiral spoke with sudden anxiety.

An aide who had come to the Admiral's side muttered, "He'll have her on the beach in a moment."

The Admiral was now purple with rage. "Cork, I hold you responsible for the safety of that ship. It was lured into the area by those blasted lights."

"I take the responsibility, sir. May I produce the master of that 'ship'?"

"How? By magic?"

"No, by voice." Cork opened the window and called, "Ahoy!"

It *seemed* like magic, for the ship turned its prow into the beach and headed straight for the window. Then, as it got closer, we could see the trick.

"It's a donkey!" the Admiral cried. "A beast with lanterns hung over its head and tail."

"And the movement of a donkey walking on the beach would give an observer at sea the illusion that he was looking at a distant ship riding the waves."

"That's an old wrecker's trick, a damnable one," Fenley-Blore swore. "But what has this demonstration to do with the Pharos being faulty?"

"If we will all take our seats again, I will explain," Cork replied.

When the room was back to order, Cork addressed us. He now knew he was in safe water, and he played like a dolphin.

"Actually, I am presenting the evidence for acquittal in reverse. You will recall that Primus felt he was on a safe course when the beacons were joined, because he saw the running lights of a ship ahead. That disturbed me, because the over-all plot was so well conceived, so wondrously scientific, that I couldn't believe such a shoddy element would be allowed to mar it. It was just too much sugar in the bun.

"The man out there with the animal is named Clint. On the morning after the wreck he and my Indian friend searched the beach area and found what my yeoman calls 'filthy evidence' that a beast of burden had traversed the ground. Now, Admiral, you are correct that this has nothing to do with the performance of the Pharos. I say it worked perfectly that night, and will continue to work perfectly."

"My shin seems to give that a sound argument," Pomfret put in.

"I am sorry about that, Mr. Pomfret. It was not done in malice, but perhaps with a touch—only a touch, mind you—of indignation at your performance in your office two days ago. I am sure you are skilled in marine law, and I do not like to be lied to. But leave it, sir. This conspiracy required a genius and a fool, and you are neither."

"Cork, get to the point," the Admiral admonished, irritably.

"I beg pardon. Would you be kind enough to walk the same course which was so painful to Mr. Pomfret? Oh, no, I will not have the lights out this time. Please, sir."

The Admiral got to his feet with a look of simmering anger and took a place at the far wall. Cork re-lit the candles and nodded for the old sailor to start. Fenley-Blore was a quarter of the way across when he stopped.

"What the devil are you doing, Cork? You're passing a screen over the forward candle."

"Yes, exactly as I did when Pomfret was our ship. Only in the lit room you can see the trick. Just as Primus Delaney could not see the trick out over the blackness of the sea. Seize him, Oaks."

John Knox was a slippery fellow, but I held him fast.

"You can't prove a thing, Cork," Knox said. "How could I hold a screen in front of the candles up there? It's too big for one man to do."

"When I said this conspiracy needed a genius and a fool, I should have added a dupe, but I didn't want to forewarn you, Mr. Knox. You have told us that you went to Yale College. Did you graduate?"

"No, I went only two years."

"That's strange. Yale is a fine school, but more regarded for its humanities and theology than for its science."

"My father was a master builder, and taught me his trade."

"Builder, yes. The construction of the towers is sound. But what of seamanship, navigation?"

"I've read books."

"Good sailors learn their trade before the mast, as soldiers learn their craft in battle." This last drew smiles from the entire panel.

"I suggest you are a dupe, Mr. Knox. To devise this plan would require years at sea, years of experience with difficult passages. And, I might add, an accurate mathematical ability.

"As for holding a screen in front of the lamp, I agree that it would be impossible for one man to do it alone, and if you blew out the candles, there would be no corona, or halo, to be seen from the back of the tower to gull us all into thinking that the light was in proper working order.

"Also, if you were simply to hold up a screen in front of the light, no purpose would be served. A ship running on a parallel line would see it one second and not the next. The abruptness of the change would make a mere cabin boy suspicious. No, Knox, the screen would have to move slowly between the lights from left to right to give the illusion that the lights were joining, long before that would really happen."

"That would be some trick," Knox said contemptuously. "What would I use? I took nothing from the tower that night, and it has been sealed since."

"You had no need to take anything away. The tools are still there in all their innocence. One thing I noted about your tower when I broke in the other night is that it is efficient. Yet the only purpose of a rod that runs around the ceiling of the front wall seems to be to give intruders a handhold. Another inefficiency is a bed that gives the sleeper privacy, when a lone keeper needs no privacy. Thus we have your screen, or curtain, which could be attached to the rod in the light chamber and used to slowly eclipse the light source from the front, while still providing a halo at the back."

"That's fanciful conjecture, Cork."

"No, I think the two gentlemen entering the room will back it up. Did it work, Captain Jeggs?"

Jeggs and a naval officer came forward and told of sailing out off the Point while Tunxis worked the curtain in Tower One.

"You are the dupe, Knox, and you have the privilege of going to the hanging string alone if you choose. Shall I produce the fool and the genius, or would you care to throw yourself on the Admiral's mercy?"

Knox looked at Fenley-Blore and back at Cork. He was frightened now, like an animal in a trap.

"Swaith! Miles Swaith is the culprit!" he screamed. "When I came here to build only one tower, he offered me money to advise the Squire against it, because he had been wrecking the ships with that donkey trick and spreading rumors about the Delaneys. When the Squire insisted on going ahead, Miles Swaith brought me the Pharos scheme, plans, charts, and all. Believe me, Squire, I didn't know Primus was aboard that ship. When I saw the running lights through the long glass, I didn't know it was the *Queen of Tortuga*."

Miles Swaith was on his feet frothing at the mouth. "He can't bring me into this, he can't! I deny everything he says, and it's his word against mine."

"And your donkey against whose, Swaith? When I sent Tunxis to scour the neighborhood with Mr. Clint, he learned that you are the only one in the immediate vicinity who keeps such a beast. Oxen are used hereabouts, which, as any wrecker knows, are too slow and too even-footed to give the illusion of a cruising ship. Admiral, I give you Miles Swaith, the fool in the plot. If he had followed his master's plan, and trusted the light system alone, without using the donkey trick, we would have never uncovered the plot."

"By the Duke's guns!" The Admiral thumped the table. "When I first laid eyes on you I said, 'There is a remarkable fellow.' Now I double it, sir. You are a genius."

"I thank you, sir, but there is only one genius abounding, and we must pin him before we have the lot."

"If you can do that, my boy, I'll give you a man-of-war for a toy. I don't know when I've enjoyed myself more. Well, go on, go on." The Admiral was as gleeful as a small lad on Christmas morning.

"I have given profound thought to his identity. Swaith is discounted, for he is merely a rude and greedy bumpkin. Our student is too limited in skill. So who have we? Let me see. We need a master mariner, to be sure, and a scientist of some prowess. Forgive me, Admiral, if this description seems to fit you."

For a moment the old boy looked concerned, and then he broke into laughter. "Very remarkable fellow," he said to the aide at his side.

"But, combined with these laudable attributes, we need also a man with a smidgen of evil, with an attraction to the low life. The criminal mind operates that way. A cut-purse or a highwayman will risk his life for a bag of gold, and then squander it on wine and whores. Another forgiveness, Admiral, but when I asked your naval lieutenant to accompany Captain Jeggs on tonight's cruise, I also requested that he have your Captain of Marines arrest a suspect—the only one who qualifies as a master mariner and a scientist with a touch of evil. May I produce him?"

The commotion at the back of the room turned all our heads. There, between two Marines, was Captain Robert Tinker, the harbormaster, old Peg and Patch, as the street urchin had so aptly named him. . . .

Well, nothing is more jubilant than an Irishman who has just escaped the noose, and since both Delaneys were free, it was merriment in double time at the ranch. Fiddlers were called, punch-bowls filled, and great sides of meat were put to the spits. The celebration lasted until past dawn, when the Admiral and his party took their leave.

"Technically, he owes you a ship of the line," I said as we repaired to our rooms. "He made you that promise before witnesses."

"What would we do with it, Oaks? Start a navy? You know, this idea of closing off the Pharos light with a screen is intriguing when properly done. If a clock mechanism could be devised to shield the beacon for a specific amount of time—say, seconds or minutes—ships could recognize the seamark by the frequency of the light flashes."

"Excellent idea, and possibly profitable. Put it to paper tomorrow."

"It *is* tomorrow, and I'm for sleep."

So, I fear, it is to be with all his tomorrows. Sleep. Drink. Carouse. And, of course, solve. I shall persevere in spite of him.

SOUTH CAROLINA

THE GOLD-BUG

by Edgar Allan Poe

MANY YEARS AGO I contracted an intimacy with a Mr. William Legrand. He was of an ancient Huguenot family, and had once been wealthy; but a series of misfortunes had reduced him to want. To avoid the mortification consequent upon his disasters, he left New Orleans, the city of his forefathers, and took up his residence at Sullivan's Island, near Charleston, South Carolina.

This island is a very singular one. It consists of little else than the sea sand, and is about three miles long. Its breadth at no point exceeds a quarter of a mile. It is separated from the mainland by a scarcely perceptible creek, oozing its way through a wilderness of reeds and slime, a favorite resort of the marsh hen. The vegetation, as might be supposed, is scant, or at least dwarfish. No trees of any magnitude are to be seen. Near the western extremity, where Fort Moultrie stands, and where are some miserable frame buildings, tenanted, during summer, by the fugitives from Charleston dust and fever, may be found, indeed, the bristly palmetto; but the whole island, with the exception of this western point, and a line of hard, white beach on the seacoast, is covered with a dense undergrowth of the sweet myrtle, so much prized by the horticulturists of England. The shrub here often attains the height of fifteen or twenty feet, and forms an almost impenetrable coppice, burdening the air with its fragrance.

In the inmost recesses of this coppice, not far from the eastern or more remote end of the island, Legrand had built himself a small hut, which he occupied when I first, by mere accident, made his acquaintance. This soon ripened into friendship—for there was much in the recluse to excite interest and esteem. I found him well-educated, with unusual powers of mind, but infected with misanthropy, and subject to perverse moods of alternate enthusiasm and melancholy. He had with him many books, but rarely employed them. His chief amusements were gunning and fishing, or sauntering along the beach and through the myrtles, in quest of shells or entomological specimens:—his collection of the latter might

421

have been envied by a Swammerdamm. In these excursions he was usually accompanied by an old Negro, called Jupiter, who had been manumitted before the reverses of the family, but who could be induced neither by threats nor by promises to abandon what he considered his right of attendance upon the footsteps of his young "Massa Will." It is not improbable that the relatives of Legrand, conceiving him to be somewhat unsettled in intellect, had contrived to instill this obstinacy into Jupiter, with a view to the supervision and guardianship of the wanderer.

The winters in the latitude of Sullivan's Island are seldom very severe, and in the fall of the year it is a rare event indeed when a fire is considered necessary. About the middle of October, 18—, there occurred, however, a day of remarkable chilliness. Just before sunset I scrambled my way through the evergreens to the hut of my friend, whom I had not visited for several weeks—my residence being at that time in Charleston, a distance of nine miles from the island, while the facilities of passage and re-passage were very far behind those of the present day. Upon reaching the hut I rapped, as was my custom, and getting no reply, sought for the key where I knew it was secreted, unlocked the door, and went in. A fine fire was blazing upon the hearth. It was a novelty, and by no means an ungrateful one. I threw off an overcoat, took an armchair by the crackling logs, and awaited patiently the arrival of my hosts.

Soon after dark they arrived and gave me a most cordial welcome. Jupiter, grinning from ear to ear, bustled about to prepare some marsh hens for supper. Legrand was in one of his fits—how else shall I term them?—of enthusiasm. He had found an unknown bivalve, forming a new genus, and, more than this, he had hunted down and secured, with Jupiter's assistance, a *scarabaeus* which he believed to be totally new, but in respect to which he wished to have my opinion on the morrow.

"And why not tonight?" I asked, rubbing my hands over the blaze, and wishing the whole tribe of *scarabaei* at the devil.

"Ah, if I had only known you were here!" said Legrand, "but it's so long since I saw you; and how could I foresee that you would pay me a visit this very night of all others? As I was coming home I met Lieutenant G——, from the fort, and, very foolishly, I lent him the bug; so it will be impossible for you to see it until the morning. Stay here tonight, and I will send Jup down for it at sunrise. It is the loveliest thing in creation!"

"What! Sunrise?"

"Nonsense! No! The bug. It is of a brilliant gold color—about the size of a large hickory nut—with two jet black spots near one extremity of the back, and another, somewhat longer, at the other. The *antennae* are—"

"Dey ain't no tin in him, Massa Will, I keep a-tellin' on you," here interrupted Jupiter; "de bug is a goole-bug: solid, ebery bit of him, inside and all, sep him wing—neber feel half so hebby a bug in my life."

"Well, suppose it is, Jup," replied Legrand, somewhat more earnestly, it seemed to me, than the case demanded, "is that any reason for your letting the birds burn? The color"—here he turned to me—"is really almost enough to warrant Jupiter's idea. You never saw a more brilliant metallic luster than the scales emit—but of this you cannot judge till tomorrow. In the meantime I can give you some idea of the shape." Saying this, he seated himself at a small table, on which were a pen and ink, but no paper. He looked for some in a drawer, but found none.

"Never mind," said he at length, "this will answer," and he drew from his waistcoat pocket a scrap of what I took to be very dirty foolscap and made upon it a rough drawing with the pen. While he did this, I retained my seat by the fire, for I was still chilly. When the design was complete, he handed it to me without rising. As I received it, a loud growl was heard, succeeded by a scratching at the door. Jupiter opened it, and a large Newfoundland, belonging to Legrand, rushed in, leaped upon my shoulders, and loaded me with caresses; for I had shown him much attention during previous visits. When his gambols were over, I looked at the paper, and, to speak the truth, found myself not a little puzzled at what my friend had depicted.

"Well!" I said, after contemplating it for some minutes, "this *is* a strange *scarabaeus,* I must confess; new to me; never saw anything like it before— unless it was a skull, or a death's-head—which it more nearly resembles than anything else that has come under my observation."

"A death's-head!" echoed Legrand. "Oh—yes—well, it has something of that appearance upon paper, no doubt. The two upper black spots look like eyes, eh? And the longer one at the bottom like a mouth—and then the shape of the whole is oval."

"Perhaps so," said I; "but, Legrand, I fear you are no artist. I must wait until I see the beetle itself, if I am to form any idea of its personal appearance."

"Well, I don't know," said he, a little nettled. "I draw tolerably—*should* do it, at least—have had good masters, and flatter myself that I am not quite a blockhead."

"But my dear fellow, you are joking then," said I; "this is a very passable *skull*—indeed, I may say that it is a very *excellent* skull, according to the vulgar notions about such specimens of physiology—and your *scarabaeus* must be the queerest *scarabaeus* in the world if it resembles it. Why, we may get up a very thrilling bit of superstition upon this hint. I presume you will call the bug *scarabaeus caput hominis,* or something of that kind—. There are many similar titles in the natural histories. But where are the antennae you spoke of?"

"The *antennae!*" said Legrand, who seemed to be getting unaccountably warm upon the subject; "I am sure you must see the *antennae.* I made them as distinct as they are in the original insect, and I presume that is sufficient."

"Well, well," I said, "perhaps you have—still I don't see them"; and I handed him the paper without additional remark, not wishing to ruffle his temper; but I was much surprised at the turn affairs had taken; his ill humor puzzled me— and, as for the drawing of the beetle, there were positively *no antennae* visible, and the whole *did* bear a very close resemblance to the ordinary cuts of a death's-head.

He received the paper very peevishly and was about to crumple it, apparently to throw it in the fire, when a casual glance at the design seemed suddenly to rivet his attention. In an instant his face grew violently red—in another as excessively pale. For some minutes he continued to scrutinize the drawing minutely where he sat. At length he arose, took a candle from the table, and proceeded to seat himself upon a sea chest in the farthest corner of the room. Here again he made an anxious examination of the paper, turning it in all directions. He said nothing, however, and his conduct greatly astonished me; yet I thought it prudent not to exacerbate the growing moodiness of his temper by any comment. Presently he took from his coat pocket a wallet, placed the paper carefully in it, and deposited both in a writing desk, which he locked. He now grew more composed in his demeanor; but his original air of enthusiasm had quite disappeared. Yet he seemed not so much sulky as abstracted. As the evening wore away he became more and more absorbed in reverie, from which no sallies of mine could arouse him. It had been my intention to pass the night at the hut, as I had frequently done before, but, seeing my host in this mood, I deemed it proper to take leave. He did not press me to remain, but, as I departed, he shook my hand with even more than his usual cordiality.

It was about a month after this (and during the interval I had seen nothing of Legrand) when I received a visit, at Charleston, from his man, Jupiter. I had never seen the good old Negro look so dispirited, and I feared that some serious disaster had befallen my friend.

"Well, Jup," said I, "what is the matter now? How is your master?"

"Why, to speak de troof, massa, him not so berry well as mought be."

"Not well! I am truly sorry to hear it. What does he complain of?"

"Dar! Dat's it! Him nebber plain of notin—but him berry sick for all dat."

"*Very* sick, Jupiter! Why didn't you say so at once? Is he confined to bed?"

"No, dat he ain't! He ain't find nowhar—dat's just whar de shoe pinch—my mind is got to be berry hebby bout poor Massa Will."

"Jupiter, I should like to understand what it is you are talking about. You say your master is sick. Hasn't he told you what ails him?"

"Why, massa, tain't worf while for to git mad about de matter. Massa Will say nuffin at all ain't de matter wid him—but den what make him go about looking dis here way, wid he head down and he soldiers up, and as white as a gose? And den he keeps a syphon all de time—"

"Keeps a what, Jupiter?"

"Keeps a syphon wid de figgurs on de slate—de queerest figgurs I ebber did see. Ise gitten to be skeered, I tell you. Hab for to keep mighty tight eye pon him noovers. Todder day he gib me slip fore de sun up, and was gone de whole ob de blessed day. I had a big stick ready cut for to gib him deuced good beating when he did come—but Ise sich a fool dat I hadn't de heart arter all—he look so berry poorly."

"Eh—what?—ah, yes!—upon the whole I think you had better not to be too severe with the poor fellow—don't flog him, Jupiter—he can't very well stand it—but can you form no idea of what has occasioned this illness, or rather this change of conduct? Has anything unpleasant happened since I saw you?"

"No, massa, dey ain't bin noffin onpleasant *since* den—'twas *fore* den, I'm feared—'twas de berry day you was dare."

"How? What do you mean?"

"Why, massa, I mean de bug—dare now."

"The what?"

"De bug—I'm berry sartain dat Massa Will bin bit somewhere bout de head by dat goole-bug."

"And what cause have you, Jupiter, for such a supposition?"

"Claws enuff, massa, and mouff, too. I nebber did see sich a deuced bug—he kick and he bite ebery ting what cum near him. Massa Will cotch him fuss, but had for to let him go gin mighty quick, I tell you—den was de time he must ha' got de bite. I didn't like de look ob de bug mouff, myself, no how, so I wouldn't take hold ob him wid my finger, but I cotch him wid a piece ob paper dat I found. I rap him up in de paper and stuff piece ob it in he mouff—dat was de way."

"And you think, then, that your master was really bitten by the beetle, and that the bite made him sick?"

"I don't tink noffin about it—I nose it. What make him dream bout de goole so much, if taint cause he bit by de goole-bug? Ise heerd bout dem goole-bugs fore dis."

"But how do you know he dreams about gold?"

"How I know? Why, cause he talk about it in he sleep—dat's how I nose."

"Well, Jup, perhaps you are right; but to what fortunate circumstance am I to attribute the honor of a visit from you today?"

"What de matter, massa?"

"Did you bring any message from Mr. Legrand?"

"No, massa, I bring dis here pissel," and here Jupiter handed me a note which ran thus:

My Dear——

Why have I not seen you for so long a time? I hope you have not been so foolish as to take offense at any little *brusquerie* of mine; but no, that is improbable.

Since I saw you I have had great cause for anxiety. I have something to tell you, yet scarcely know how to tell it, or whether I should tell it at all.

I have not been quite well for some days past, and poor old Jup annoys me, almost beyond endurance, by his well-meant attentions. Would you believe it?—he had prepared a huge stick the other day, with which to chastise me for giving him the slip, and spending the day, *solus,* among the hills on the mainland. I verily believe that my ill looks alone saved me a flogging.

I have made no addition to my cabinet since we met.

If you can in any way make it convenient, come over with Jupiter. *Do* come. I wish to see you *tonight,* upon business of importance. I assure you that it is of the *highest* importance. Ever yours,

William Legrand

There was something in the tone of this note which gave me great uneasiness. Its whole style differed materially from that of Legrand. What could he be dreaming of? What new crotchet possessed his excitable brain? What "business of the highest importance" could *he* possibly have to transact? Jupiter's account of him boded no good. I dreaded lest the continued pressure of misfortune had, at length, fairly unsettled the reason of my friend. Without a moment's hesitation, therefore, I prepared to accompany the Negro.

Upon reaching the wharf, I noticed a scythe and three spades, all apparently new, lying in the bottom of the boat in which we were to embark.

"What is the meaning of all this, Jup?" I inquired.

"Him syfe, massa, and spade."

"Very true; but what are they doing here?"

"Him de syfe and de spade what Massa Will sis pon my buying for him in de town, and de debbil's own lot of money I had to gib for em."

"But what, in the name of all that is mysterious, is your 'Massa Will' going to do with scythes and spades?"

"Dat's more dan *I* know, and debbil take me if I don't blieve 'tis more dan he know, too. But it's all cum ob de bug."

Finding that no satisfaction was to be obtained of Jupiter, whose whole intellect seemed to be absorbed by "de bug," I now stepped into the boat and made sail. With a fair and strong breeze we soon ran into the little cove to the northward of Fort Moultrie, and a walk of some two miles brought us to the hut. It was about three in the afternoon when we arrived. Legrand had been awaiting us in eager expectation. He grasped my hand with a nervous *empressement* which alarmed me and strengthened the suspicions already entertained. His countenance was pale even to ghastliness, and his deep-set eyes glared with unnatural luster. After some inquiries respecting his health, I asked him, not knowing what better to say, if he had yet obtained the *scarabaeus* from Lieutenant G——.

"Oh, yes," he replied, coloring violently, "I got it from him the next morning. Nothing should tempt me to part with that *scarabaeus*. Do you know that Jupiter is quite right about it!"

"In what way?" I asked, with a sad foreboding at heart.

"In supposing it to be a bug of *real gold*." He said this with an air of profound seriousness, and I felt inexpressibly shocked.

"This bug is to make my fortune," he continued, with a triumphant smile, "to reinstate me in my family possessions. Is it any wonder, then, that I prize it? Since Fortune has thought fit to bestow it upon me, I have only to use it properly and I shall arrive at the gold of which it is the index. Jupiter, bring me that *scarabaeus!*"

"What! De bug, massa? I'd rudder not go fer trubble dat bug—you mus git him for your own self." Hereupon Legrand arose, with a grave and stately air, and brought me the beetle from a glass case in which it was enclosed. It was a beautiful *scarabaeus,* and, at that time, unknown to naturalists—of course a great prize in a scientific point of view. There were two round black spots near one extremity of the back, and a long one near the other. The scales were exceedingly hard and glossy, with all the appearance of burnished gold. The weight of the insect was very remarkable, and, taking all things into consideration, I could hardly blame Jupiter for his opinion respecting it; but what to make of Legrand's concordance with that opinion, I could not, for the life of me, tell.

"I sent for you," said he, in a grandiloquent tone, when I had completed my examination of the beetle, "I sent for you, that I might have your counsel and assistance in furthering the views of Fate and of the bug—"

"My dear Legrand," I cried, interrupting him, "you are certainly unwell and had better use some little precautions. You shall go to bed, and I will remain with you a few days, until you get over this. You are feverish and—"

"Feel my pulse," said he.

I felt it, and, to say the truth, found not the slightest indication of fever.

"But you may be ill and yet have no fever. Allow me this once to prescribe for you. In the first place, go to bed. In the next—"

"You are mistaken," he interposed; "I am as well as I can expect to be under the excitement which I suffer. If you really wish me well, you will relieve this excitement."

"And how is this to be done?"

"Very easily. Jupiter and myself are going upon an expedition into the hills, upon the mainland. In this expedition, we shall need the aid of some person in whom we can confide. You are the only one we can trust. Whether we succeed or fail, the excitement which you now perceive in me will be equally allayed."

"I am anxious to oblige you in any way," I replied; "but do you mean to say that this infernal beetle has any connection with your expedition into the hills?"

"It has."

"Then, Legrand, I can become a party to no such absurd proceeding."

"I am sorry—very sorry—for we shall have to try it by ourselves."

"Try it by yourselves! The man is surely mad!—But stay! How long do you propose to be absent?"

"Probably all night. We shall start immediately, and be back, at all events, by sunrise."

"And will you promise me upon your honor, that when this freak of your is over, and the bug business (good God!) settled to your satisfaction, you will then return home and follow my advice implicitly, as that of your physician?"

"Yes; I promise; and now let us be off, for we have no time to lose."

With a heavy heart I accompanied my friend. We started about four o'clock—Legrand, Jupiter, the dog, and myself. Jupiter had with him the scythe and spades—the whole of which he insisted upon carrying—more through fear, it seemed to me, of trusting either of the implements within reach of his master, than from any excess of industry or complaisance. His demeanor was dogged in the extreme, and "dat deuced bug" were the sole words which escaped his lips during the journey. For my own part, I had charge of a couple of dark lanterns, while Legrand contented himself with the *scarabaeus,* which he carried attached to the end of a bit of whipcord, twirling it to and fro, with the air of a conjuror, as he went. When I observed this last plain evidence of my friend's aberration of mind I could scarcely refrain from tears. I thought it best, however, to humor his fancy, at least for the present, or until I could adopt some more energetic measures with a chance of success. In the meantime I endeavored, but all in vain, to sound him in regard to the object of the expedition. Having succeeded in inducing me to accompany him, he seemed unwilling to hold conversation upon any topic of minor importance, and to all my questions vouchsafed no other reply than "We shall see!"

We crossed the creek at the head of the island by means of a skiff, and, ascending the high grounds on the shore of the mainland, proceeded in a north-westerly direction, through a tract of country excessively wild and desolate, where no trace of a human footstep was to be seen. Legrand led the way with decision, pausing only for an instant, here and there, to consult what appeared to be certain landmarks of his own contrivance upon a former occasion.

In this manner we journeyed for about two hours, and the sun was just setting when we entered a region infinitely more dreary than any yet seen. It was a species of tableland, near the summit of an almost inaccessible hill, densely wooded from base to pinnacle, and interspersed with huge crags that appeared to lie loosely upon the soil, and in many cases were prevented from precipitating themselves into valleys below, merely by the support of the trees against which they reclined. Deep ravines, in various directions, gave an air of still sterner solemnity to the scene.

The natural platform to which we had clambered was thickly overgrown with brambles, through which we soon discovered that it would have been impossible to force our way but for the scythe; and Jupiter, by direction of his master, proceeded to clear for us a path to the foot of an enormously tall tulip tree, which stood, with some eight or ten oaks, upon the level, and far surpassed them all, and all other trees which I had then ever seen, in the beauty of its foliage and form, in the wide spread of its branches, and in the general majesty of its appearance. When we reached this tree, Legrand turned to Jupiter, and asked him if he thought he could climb it. The old man seemed a little staggered by the question, and for some moments made no reply. At length he approached the huge trunk, walked slowly around it, and examined it with minute attention. When he had completed his scrutiny, he merely said, "Yes, massa, Jup climb any tree he ebber see in he life."

"Then up with you as soon as possible, for it will soon be too dark to see what we are about."

"How far mus go up, massa?" inquired Jupiter.

"Get up the main trunk first, and then I will tell you which way to go—and here—stop! Take this beetle with you."

"De bug, Massa Will!—De goole-bug!" cried the Negro, drawing back in dismay. "What for mus tote de bug way up de tree? D—n if I do!"

"If you are afraid, Jup, a great big Negro like you, to take hold of a harmless little dead beetle, why you can carry it up by this string—but if you do not take it up with you in some way, I shall be under the necessity of breaking your head with this shovel."

"What de matter now, massa?" said Jup, evidently shamed into compliance; "always want for to raise fuss wid old nigger. Was only funnin' anyhow. *Me* feered de bug! What I keer for de bug?" Here he took cautiously hold of the extreme end of the string, and, maintaining the insect as far from his person as circumstances would permit, prepared to ascend the tree.

In youth, the tulip tree, or *Liriodendron tulipiferum,* the most magnificent of American foresters, has a trunk peculiarly smooth, and often rises to a great height without lateral branches; but, in its riper age, the bark becomes gnarled and uneven, while many short limbs make their appearance on the stem. Thus the difficulty of ascension, in the present case, lay more in semblance than in reality. Embracing the huge cylinder, as closely as possible, with his arms and knees, seizing with his hands some projections, and resting his naked toes upon others, Jupiter, after one or two narrow escapes from falling, at length wriggled himself into the first great fork, and seemed to consider the whole business as virtually accomplished. The *risk* of the achievement was, in fact, now over, although the climber was some sixty or seventy feet from the ground.

"Which way mus go now, Massa Will?" he asked.

"Keep up the largest branch—the one on this side," said Legrand. The Negro obeyed him promptly, and apparently with but little trouble, ascending higher and higher, until no glimpse of his squat figure could be obtained through the dense foliage which enveloped it. Presently his voice was heard in a sort of halloo.

"How much fudder is got for go?"

"How high up are you?" asked Legrand.

"Ebber so fur," replied the Negro; "can see de sky fru de top ob de tree."

"Never mind the sky, but attend to what I say. Look down the trunk and count the limbs below you on this side. How many limbs have you passed?"

"One, two, three, four, fibe—I done pass fibe big limb, massa, pon dis side."

"Then go one limb higher."

In a few minutes the voice was heard again, announcing that the seventh limb was attained.

"Now, Jup," cried Legrand, evidently much excited, "I want you to work your way out upon that limb as far as you can. If you see anything strange, let me know."

By this time what little doubt I might have entertained of my poor friend's insanity was put finally at rest. I had no alternative but to conclude him stricken with lunacy, and I became seriously anxious about getting him home. While I was pondering upon what was best to be done, Jupiter's voice was again heard.

"Mos feered for to ventur pon dis limb berry far—tis dead limb putty much all de way."

"Did you say it was a *dead* limb, Jupiter?" cried Legrand in a quavering voice.

"Yes, massa, him dead as de doornail—done up for sartain—done departed dis here life."

"What in the name of heaven shall I do?" asked Legrand, seemingly in the greatest distress.

"Do!" said I, glad of an opportunity to interpose a word. "Why come home and go to bed. Come now!—That's a fine fellow. It's getting late, and, besides, you remember your promise."

"Jupiter," cried he, without heeding me in the least, "do you hear me?"

"Yes, Massa Will, hear you ebber so plain."

"Try the wood well, then, with your knife, and see if you think it *very* rotten."

"Him rotten, massa, sure nuff," replied the Negro in a few moments, "but not so berry rotten as mought be. Mought ventur out leetle way pon de limb by myself, dat's true."

"By yourself! What do you mean?"

"Why, I mean de bug. 'Tis *berry* hebby bug. Spose I drop him down fuss, and den de limb won't break wid just de weight ob one nigger."

"You infernal scoundrel!" cried Legrand, apparently much relieved, "what do you mean by telling me such nonsense as that? As sure as you drop that beetle I'll break your neck. Look here, Jupiter, do you hear me?"

"Yes, massa, needn't hollo at poor nigger dat style."

"Well! Now listen! If you will venture out on the limb as far as you think safe, and not let go the beetle, I'll make you a present of a silver dollar as soon as you get down."

"I'm gwine, Massa Will—deed I is," replied the Negro very promptly. "Mos out to the eend now."

"*Out to the end!*" here fairly screamed Legrand. "Do you say you are out to the end of that limb?"

"Soon be to de eend, massa,—o-o-o-o-oh! Lorgol-a-marcy! What *is* dis here pon de tree?"

"Well," cried Legrand, highly delighted, "what is it?"

"Why, taint noffin but a skull—somebody bin lef him head up de tree, and de crows done gobble ebery bit ob de meat off."

"A skull, you say! Very well! How is it fastened to the limb? What holds it on?"

"Sure nuff, massa; mus look. Why dis berry curous sarcumstance, pon my word—dare's a great big nail in de skull, what fastens ob it on to de tree."

"Well now, Jupiter, do exactly as I tell you—do you hear?"

"Yes, massa."

"Pay attention, then! Find the left eye of the skull."

"Hum! Hoo! Dat's good! Why dare ain't no eye lef at all."

"Curse your stupidity! Do you know your right hand from your left?"

"Yes, I nose dat—nose all bout dat—'tis my lef hand what I chops de wood wid."

"To be sure! You are left-handed; and your left eye is on the same side as your left hand. Now, I suppose, you can find the left eye of the skull, or the place where the left eye has been. Have you found it?"

Here was a long pause. At length the Negro asked: "Is de lef eye of de skull pon de same side as de lef hand of de skull, too? Cause de skull ain't got not a bit ob a hand at all—nebber mind! I got de lef eye now—here de lef eye! What mus do wid it?"

"Let the beetle drop through it, as far as the string will reach—but be careful and not let go your hold of the string."

"All dat done, Mass Will; mightly easy ting for to put de bug fru de hole— look out for him dare below!"

During this colloquy no portion of Jupiter's person could be seen; but the beetle, which he had suffered to descend, was now visible at the end of the string, and glistened, like a globe of burnished gold, in the last rays of the setting sun, some of which still faintly illumined the eminence upon which we stood. The *scarabaeus* hung quite clear of any branches, and, if allowed to fall, would have fallen at our feet. Legrand immediately took the scythe, and cleared with it a circular space, three or four yards in diameter, just beneath the insect, and, having accomplished this, ordered Jupiter to let go the string and come down from the tree.

Driving a peg, with great nicety, into the ground, at the precise spot where the beetle fell, my friend now produced from his pocket a tape measure. Fastening one end of this at that point of the trunk of the tree which was nearest the peg, he unrolled it till it reached the peg, and thence farther unrolled it, in the direction already established by the two points of the tree and the peg, for the distance of fifty feet—Jupiter clearing away the brambles with the scythe. At the spot thus attained a second peg was driven, and about this, as a center, a rude circle, about four feet in diameter, described. Taking now a spade himself, and giving one to Jupiter and one to me, Legrand begged us to set about digging as quickly as possible.

To speak the truth, I had no especial relish for such amusement at any time, and, at that particular moment, would most willingly have declined it; for the night was coming on, and I felt much fatigued with the exercise already taken; but I saw no mode of escape, and was fearful of disturbing my poor friend's equanimity by a refusal. Could I have depended, indeed, upon Jupiter's aid, I would have had no hesitation in attempting to get the lunatic home by force; but I was too well assured of the old Negro's disposition, to hope that he would assist me, under any circumstances, in a personal contest with his master. I made no doubt that the latter had been infected with some of the innumerable Southern superstitions about money buried, and that his fantasy had received confirmation by the finding of the *scarabaeus,* or, perhaps, by Jupiter's obstinacy in maintaining it to be "a bug of real gold." A mind disposed to lunacy would readily be led away by such suggestions—especially if chiming in with favorite preconceived ideas—and then I called to mind the poor fellow's speech about the beetle's being "the index of his fortune." Upon the whole, I was sadly vexed and puzzled, but, at length, I concluded to make a virtue of necessity—to dig with a good will, and thus the sooner to convince the visionary, by ocular demonstration, of the fallacy of the opinions he entertained.

The lanterns having been lit, we all fell to work with a zeal worthy a more rational cause; and, as the glare fell upon our persons and implements, I could not help thinking how picturesque a group we composed and how strange and suspicious our labors must have appeared to any interloper who, by chance, might have stumbled upon our whereabouts.

We dug very steadily for two hours. Little was said; and our chief embarrassment lay in the yelpings of the dog, who took exceeding interest in our proceedings. He at length became so obstreperous, that we grew fearful of his giving the alarm to some stragglers in the vicinity; or, rather, this was the apprehension of Legrand; for myself, I should have rejoiced at any interruption which might have enabled me to get the wanderer home. The noise was, at length, very effectually silenced by Jupiter, who, getting out of the hole with a dogged air of deliberation, tied the brute's mouth up with one of his suspenders, and then returned, with a grave chuckle, to his task.

When the time mentioned had expired, we had reached a depth of five feet, and yet no signs of any treasure became manifest. A general pause ensued and I began to hope that the farce was at an end. Legrand, however, although evidently much disconcerted, wiped his brow thoughtfully and recommenced. We had excavated the entire circle of four feet diameter, and now we slightly enlarged the limit, and went to the farther depth of two feet. Still nothing appeared. The gold-seeker, whom I sincerely pitied, at length clambered from the pit, with the bitterest disappointment imprinted upon every feature, and proceeded, slowly and reluctantly, to put on his coat, which he had thrown off at the beginning of his labor. In the meantime I made no remark. Jupiter, at a signal from his master, began to gather up his tools. This done, and the dog having been unmuzzled, we turned in profound silence towards home.

We had taken, perhaps, a dozen steps in this direction, when, with a loud oath, Legrand strode up to Jupiter, and seized him by the collar. The astonished Negro opened his eyes and mouth to the fullest extent, let fall the spades, and fell upon his knees.

"You scoundrel," said Legrand, hissing out the syllables from between his clenched teeth, "you infernal black villain! Speak, I tell you! Answer me this instant, without prevarication! Which—which is your left eye?"

"Oh, my golly, Massa Will! Ain't dis here my lef eye for sartain?" roared the terrified Jupiter, placing his hand upon his *right* organ of vision, and holding it there with a desperate pertinacity, as if in immediate dread of his master's attempt at a gouge.

"I thought so! I knew it! Hurrah!" vociferated Legrand letting the Negro go, and executing a series of curvets and caracols, much to the astonishment of his valet, who, arising from his knees, looked mutely from his master to myself, and then from myself to his master.

"Come! We must go back," said the latter; "the game's not up yet," and he again led the way to the tulip tree.

"Jupiter," said he, when he reached its foot, "come here! Was the skull nailed to the limb with the face outwards, or with the face to the limb?"

"De face was out, massa, so dat de crows could get at de eyes good, widout any trouble."

"Well, then, was it this eye or that through which you dropped the beetle?" Here Legrand touched each of Jupiter's eyes.

"'Twas dis eye, massa—de lef eye—jis as you tell me," and here it was his right eye that the Negro indicated.

"That will do—we must try it again."

Here my friend, about whose madness I now saw, or fancied that I saw, certain indications of method, removed the peg which marked the spot where the beetle fell, to a spot about three inches to the westward of its former position. Taking, now, the tape measure from the nearest point of the trunk to the peg, as before, and continuing the extension in a straight line to the distance of fifty feet, a spot was indicated, removed by several yards from the point at which we had been digging.

Around the new position a circle, somewhat larger than in the former instance, was now described, and we again set to work with the spades. I was dreadfully weary, but scarcely understanding what had occasioned the change in my thoughts, I felt no longer any great aversion from the labor imposed. I had become most unaccountably interested—nay, even excited. Perhaps there was something, amid all the extravagant demeanor of Legrand—some air of forethought, or of deliberation, which impressed me. I dug eagerly, and now and then caught myself actually looking, with something that very much resembled expectation, for the fancied treasure, the vision of which had demented my unfortunate companion. At a period when such vagaries of thought most fully possessed me, and when we had been at work perhaps an hour and a half, we were again interrupted by the violent howlings of the dog. His uneasiness, in the first instance, had been, evidently, but the result of playfulness or caprice, but he now assumed a bitter and serious tone. Upon Jupiter's again attempting to muzzle him, he made furious resistance, and, leaping into the hole, tore up the mold frantically with his claws. In a few seconds he had uncovered a mass of human bones, forming two complete skeletons, intermingled with several buttons of metal, and what appeared to be the dust of decayed woolen. One or two strokes of a spade upturned the blade of a large Spanish knife, and, as we dug farther, three or four loose pieces of gold and silver coin came to light.

At the sight of these the joy of Jupiter could scarcely be restrained, but the countenance of his master wore an air of extreme disappointment. He urged us, however, to continue our exertions, and the words were hardly uttered when I stumbled and fell forward, having caught the toe of my boot in a large ring of iron that lay half-buried in the loose earth.

We now worked in earnest, and never did I pass ten minutes of more intense excitement. During this interval we had fairly unearthed an oblong chest of wood which, from its perfect preservation and wonderful hardness, had plainly been subjected to some mineralizing process—perhaps that of the bichloride of mercury. This box was three feet and a half long, three feet broad, and two and a half feet deep. It was firmly secured by bands of wrought iron, riveted, and forming a kind of open trelliswork over the whole. On each side of the chest, near the top, were three rings of iron—six in all—by means of which a firm hold could be obtained by six persons. Our utmost united endeavors served only to disturb the coffer very slightly in its bed. We at once saw the impossibility of removing so great a weight. Luckily, the sole fastenings of the lid consisted of two sliding bolts. These we drew back—trembling and panting with anxiety. In an instant, a treasure of incalculable value lay gleaming before us. As the rays of the lanterns fell within the pit, there flashed upwards a glow and a glare, from a confused heap of gold and of jewels, that absolutely dazzled our eyes.

I shall not pretend to describe the feelings with which I gazed. Amazement was, of course, predominant. Legrand appeared exhausted with excitement, and spoke very few words. Jupiter's countenance wore, for some minutes, as deadly a pallor as it is possible, in the nature of things, for any Negro's visage to assume. He seemed stupefied—thunderstricken. Presently he fell upon his knees in the pit, and, burying his naked arms up to the elbows in gold, let them there remain, as if enjoying the luxury of a bath. At length, with a deep sigh, he exclaimed, as if in a soliloquy:

"And dis all cum ob de goole-bug? De putty goole-bug! De poor little goole-bug what I boosed in dat sabage kind ob style! Ain't you ashamed ob yourself, nigger? Answer me dat!"

It became necessary, at last, that I should arouse both master and valet to the expediency of removing the treasure. It was growing late, and it behooved us to make exertion, that we might get everything housed before daylight. It was difficult to say what should be done, and much time was spent in deliberation—so confused were the ideas of all. We, finally, lightened the box by removing two-thirds of its contents, when we were enabled, with some trouble, to raise it from the hole. The articles taken out were deposited among the brambles, and the dog left to guard them, with strict orders from Jupiter neither, upon any pretense, to stir from the spot, nor to open his mouth until our return. We then hurriedly made for home with the chest; reaching the hut in safety, but after excessive toil, at one o'clock in the morning. Worn out as we were, it was not in human nature to do more immediately. We rested until two, and had supper, starting for the hills immediately afterwards, armed with three stout sacks, which, by good luck, were upon the premises. A little before four we arrived at the pit, divided the remainder of the booty, as equally as might be, among us, and, leaving the holes unfilled, again set out for the hut, at which, for the second time, we deposited our golden burdens, just as the first faint streaks of the dawn gleamed from over the treetops in the east.

We were now thoroughly broken down; but the intense excitement of the time denied us repose. After an unquiet slumber of some three or four hours' duration, we arose, as if by preconcert, to make examination of our treasure.

The chest had been full to the brim, and we spent the whole day, and the greater part of the next night, in a scrutiny of its contents. There had been nothing like order or arrangement. Everything had been heaped in promiscuously. Having assorted all with care, we found ourselves possessed of even vaster wealth than we had at first supposed. In coin there was rather more than four hundred and fifty thousand dollars—estimating the value of the pieces, as accurately as we could, by the tables of the period. There was not a particle of silver. All was gold of antique date and of great variety—French, Spanish, and German money, with a few English guineas, and some counters, of which we had never seen specimens before. There were several very large and heavy coins, so worn that we could make nothing of their inscriptions. There was no American money. The value of the jewels we found more difficulty in estimating. There were diamonds—some of them exceedingly large and fine—a hundred and ten in all, and not one of them small; eighteen rubies of remarkable brilliancy; three hundred and ten emeralds, all very beautiful; and twenty-one sapphires, with an opal. These stones had all been broken from their settings and thrown loose in the chest. The settings themselves, which we picked out from among the other gold, appeared to have been beaten up with hammers, as if to prevent identification. Besides all this, there was a vast quantity of solid gold ornaments; nearly two hundred massive finger and earrings; rich chains—thirty of these, if I remember; eighty-three very large and heavy crucifixes; five gold censers of great value; a prodigious golden punch bowl, ornamented with richly chased vine leaves and Bacchanalian figures; with two sword handles exquisitely embossed, and many other smaller articles which I cannot recollect. The weight of these valuables exceeded three hundred and fifty pounds avoirdupois; and in this estimate I have not included one hundred and ninety-seven superb gold watches, three of the number being worth each five hundred dollars, if one. Many of them were very old, and as timekeepers valueless—the works having suffered, more or less, from corrosion—but all were richly jeweled, and in cases of great worth. We estimated the entire contents of the chest, that night, at a million and a half of dollars; and, upon the subsequent disposal of the trinkets and jewels (a few being retained for our own use), it was found that we had greatly undervalued the treasure.

When, at length, we had concluded our examination, and the intense excitement of the time had in some measure subsided, Legrand, who saw that I was dying with impatience for a solution of this most extraordinary riddle, entered into a full detail of all the circumstances connected with it.

"You remember," said he, "the night when I handed you the rough sketch I had made of the *scarabaeus*. You recollect also, that I became quite vexed at you for insisting that my drawing resembled a death's-head. When you first made this assertion I thought you were jesting; but afterwards I called to mind the peculiar spots on the back of the insect, and admitted to myself that your remark had some little foundation in fact. Still, the sneer at my graphic powers irritated me—for I am considered a good artist—and, therefore, when you handed me the scrap of parchment, I was about to crumple it up and throw it angrily into the fire."

"The scrap of paper, you mean," said I.

"No; it had much of the appearance of paper, and at first I supposed it to be such, but when I came to draw upon it, I discovered it, at once, to be a piece of very thin parchment. It was quite dirty, you remember. Well, as I was in the very act of crumpling it up, my glance fell upon the sketch at which you had been looking, and you may imagine my astonishment when I perceived, in fact, the figure of a death's-head just where, it seemed to me, I had made the drawing of the beetle. For a moment I was too much amazed to think with accuracy. I knew that my design was very different in detail from this—although there was a certain similarity in general outline. Presently I took a candle, and seating myself at the other end of the room, proceeded to scrutinize the parchment more closely. Upon turning it over, I saw my own sketch upon the reverse, just as I had made it. My first idea, now, was mere surprise at the really remarkable similarity of outline—at the singular coincidence involved in the fact, that unknown to me, there should have been a skull upon the other side of the parchment, immediately beneath my figure of the *scarabaeus,* and that this skull, not only in outline, but in size, should so closely resemble my drawing. I say the singularity of this coincidence absolutely stupefied me for a time. This is the usual effect of such coincidences. The mind struggles to establish a connection—a sequence of cause and effect—and, being unable to do so, suffers a species of temporary paralysis. But when I recovered from this stupor, there dawned upon me gradually a conviction which startled me even far more than the coincidence. I began distinctly, positively, to remember that there had been *no* drawing upon the parchment when I made my sketch of the *scarabaeus.* I became perfectly certain of this; for I recollected turning up first one side and then the other, in search of the cleanest spot. Had the skull been then there, of course I could not have failed to notice it. Here was indeed a mystery which I felt it impossible to explain; but, even at that early moment, there seemed to glimmer, faintly, within the most remote and secret chambers of my intellect, a glow-worm-like conception of that truth which last night's adventure brought to so magnificent a demonstration. I arose at once and, putting the parchment securely away, dismissed all further reflection until I should be alone.

"When you had gone, and when Jupiter was fast asleep, I betook myself to a more methodical investigation of the affair. In the first place I considered the manner in which the parchment had come into my possession. The spot where we discovered the *scarabaeus* was on the coast of the mainland, about a mile eastward of the island, and but a short distance above high-water mark. Upon my taking hold of it, it gave me a sharp bite, which caused me to let it drop. Jupiter, with his accustomed caution, before seizing the insect, which had flown towards him, looked about him for a leaf, or something of that nature, by which to take hold of it. It was at this moment that his eyes, and mine also, fell upon the scrap of parchment, which I then supposed to be paper. It was lying half-buried in the sand, a corner sticking up. Near the spot where we found it, I observed the remnants of the hull of what appeared to have been a ship's longboat. The wreck seemed to have been there for a very great while; for the resemblance to boat timbers could scarcely be traced.

"Well, Jupiter picked up the parchment, wrapped the beetle in it, and gave it to me. Soon afterwards we turned to go home, and on the way met Lieutenant G——. I showed him the insect, and he begged me to let him take it to the fort. Upon my consenting, he thrust it forthwith into his waistcoat pocket, without the parchment in which it had been wrapped, and which I had continued to hold in my hand during his inspection. Perhaps he dreaded my changing my mind, and thought it best to make sure of the prize at once. You know how enthusiastic he is on all subjects connected with natural history. At the same time, without being conscious of it, I must have deposited the parchment in my own pocket.

"You remember that when I went to the table, for the purpose of making a sketch of the beetle, I found no paper where it was usually kept. I looked in the drawer, and found none there. I searched my pockets, hoping to find an old letter, when my hand fell upon the parchment. I thus detail the precise mode in which it came into my possession; for the circumstances impressed me with peculiar force.

"No doubt you will think me fanciful—but I had already established a kind of *connection*. I had put together two links of a great chain. There was a boat lying upon a seacoast, and not far from the boat was a parchment—*not a paper*—with a skull depicted upon it. You will, of course, ask, 'Where is the connection?' I reply that the skull, or death's-head, is the well-known emblem of the pirate. The flag of the death's-head is hoisted in all engagements.

"I have said that the scrap was parchment, and not paper. Parchment is durable—almost imperishable. Matters of little moment are rarely consigned to parchment; since, for the mere ordinary purposes of drawing or writing, it is not nearly so well adapted as paper. This reflection suggested some meaning—some relevancy—in the death's-head. I did not fail to observe, also, the *form* of the parchment. Although one of its corners had been, by some accident, destroyed, it could be seen that the original form was oblong. It was just such a slip, indeed, as might have been chosen for a memorandum—for a record of something to be long remembered and carefully preserved."

"But," I interposed, "you say that the skull was *not* upon the parchment when you made the drawing of the beetle. How then do you trace any connection between the boat and the skull—since this latter, according to your own admission, must have been designed (God only knows how or by whom) at some period subsequent to your sketching the *scarabaeus?*"

"Ah, hereupon turns the whole mystery; although the secret, at this point, I had comparatively little difficulty in solving. My steps were sure, and could afford but a single result. I reasoned, for example, thus: When I drew the *scarabaeus,* there was no skull apparent upon the parchment. When I had completed the drawing I gave it to you, and observed you narrowly until you returned it. *You,* therefore, did not design the skull, and no one else was present to do it. Then it was not done by human agency. And nevertheless it was done.

"At this stage of my reflections I endeavored to remember, and *did* remember, with entire distinctness, every incident which occurred about the period in question. The weather was chilly (oh, rare and happy accident!), and a fire was blazing upon the hearth. I was heated with exercise and sat near the table. You, however, had drawn a chair close to the chimney. Just as I placed the parchment in your hand, and as you were in the act of inspecting it, Wolf, the Newfoundland, entered, and leaped upon your shoulders. With your left hand you caressed him and kept him off, while your right, holding the parchment, was permitted to fall listlessly between your knees, and in close proximity to the fire. At one moment I thought the blaze had caught it, and was about to caution you, but, before I could speak, you had withdrawn it, and were engaged in its examination. When I considered all these particulars, I doubted not for a moment that *heat* had been the agent in bringing to light, upon the parchment, the skull which I saw designed upon it. You are well aware that chemical preparations exist, and have existed time out of mind, by means of which it is possible to write upon either paper or vellum, so that the characters shall become visible only when subjected to the action of fire. Zaffre, digested in *aqua regia,* and diluted with four times its weight of water, is sometimes employed; a green tint results. The regulus of cobalt, dissolved in spirit of niter, gives a red. These colors disappear at longer or shorter intervals after the material written upon cools, but again become apparent upon the re-application of heat.

"I now scrutinized the death's-head with care. Its outer edges—the edges of the drawing nearest the edge of the vellum—were far more *distinct* than the others. It was clear that the action of the caloric had been imperfect, or unequal. I immediately kindled a fire, and subjected every portion of the parchment to a glowing heat. At first, the only effect was the strengthening of the faint lines in the skull; but upon persevering in the experiment, there became visible at the corner of the slip, diagonally opposite to the spot in which the death's-head was delineated, the figure of what I at first supposed to be a goat. A closer scrutiny, however, satisfied me that it was intended for a kid."

"Ha! Ha!" said I. "To be sure I have no right to laugh at you—a million and a half of money is too serious a matter for mirth—but you are not about to establish a third link in your chain—you will not find any especial connection between your pirates and a goat—pirates, you know, have nothing to do with goats; they appertain to the farming interest."

"But I have said that the figure was *not* that of a goat."

"Well, a kid then—pretty much the same thing."

"Pretty much, but not altogether," said Legrand. "You may have heard of one

Captain Kidd. I at once looked upon the figure of the animal as a kind of punning or hieroglyphical signature. I say signature, because its position upon the vellum suggested this idea. The death's-head at the corner diagonally opposite, had, in the same manner, the air of a stamp, or seal. But I was sorely put out by the absence of all else—of the body to my imagined instrument—of the text for my context."

"I presume you expected to find a letter between the stamp and the signature."

"Something of that kind. The fact is, I felt irresistibly impressed with a presentiment of some vast good fortune impending. I can scarcely say why. Perhaps, after all, it was rather a desire than an actual belief; but do you know that Jupiter's silly words, about the bug being of solid gold, had a remarkable effect upon my fancy? And then the series of accidents and coincidences—these were so *very* extraordinary. Do you observe how mere an accident it was that these events should have occurred upon the *sole* day of all the year in which it has been, or may be, sufficiently cool for fire, and that without the fire, or without the intervention of the dog at the precise moment in which he appeared, I should never have become aware of the death's-head, and so never the possessor of the treasure?"

"But proceed—I am all impatience."

"Well; you have heard, of course, the many stories current—the thousand vague rumors afloat about money buried, somewhere upon the Atlantic coast, by Kidd and his associates. These rumors must have had some foundation in fact. And that the rumors have existed so long and so continuous, could have resulted, it appeared to me, only from the circumstance of the buried treasure still *remaining* entombed. Had Kidd concealed his plunder for a time, and afterwards reclaimed it, the rumors would scarcely have reached us in their present unvarying form. You will observe that the stories told are all about money-seekers, not about money-finders. Had the pirate recovered his money, there the affair would have dropped. It seemed to me that some accident—say the loss of a memorandum indicating its locality—had deprived him of the means of recovering it, and that this accident had become known to his followers, who otherwise might never have heard that treasure had been concealed at all, and who, busying themselves in vain, because unguided, attempts to regain it, had given first birth, and then universal currency, to the reports which are now so common. Have you ever heard of any important treasure being unearthed along the coast?"

"Never."

"But that Kidd's accumulations were immense is well known. I took it for granted, therefore, that the earth still held them; you will scarcely be surprised when I tell you that I felt a hope, nearly amounting to certainty, that the parchment so strangely found, involved a lost record of the place of deposit."

"But how did you proceed?"

"I held the vellum again to the fire, after increasing the heat; but nothing appeared. I now thought it possible that the coating of dirt might have something to do with the failure; so I carefully rinsed the parchment by pouring warm water over it, and, having done this, I placed it in a tin pan, with the skull downwards, and put the pan upon a furnace of lighted charcoal. In a few minutes, the pan having become thoroughly heated, I removed the slip and to my inexpressible joy, found it spotted, in several places, with what appeared to be figures arranged in lines. Again I placed it in the pan, and suffered it to remain another minute. Upon taking it off, the whole was just as you see it now."

Here Legrand, having reheated the parchment, submitted it to my inspection. The following characters were rudely traced, in a red tint, between the death's-head and the goat:

        53‡‡†305))6*;4826)4‡.)4‡);806*;48†8¶60))85;1‡(;:‡*8†83 (88)5
        *†;46 (;88*96*?;8)*‡ (;485);5*†2:*‡(;4956*2 (5*—4)8¶8*;4069285);
)6†8)4‡‡;1(‡9;48081;8:8‡1;48†85;4) 485†528806*81 (‡9;48;(88;4(‡
        ?34;48)4‡;161;:188;‡?;

"But, said I, returning him the slip, "I am as much in the dark as ever. Were all the jewels of Golconda awaiting me upon my solution of this enigma, I am quite sure that I should be unable to earn them."

"And yet," said Legrand, "the solution is by no means so difficult as you might be led to imagine from the hasty inspection of the characters. These characters, as anyone might readily guess, form a cipher—that is to say, they convey a meaning: but then, from what is known of Kidd, I could not suppose him capable of constructing any of the more abstruse cryptographs. I made up my mind, at once, that this was of a simple species—such, however, as would appear, to the crude intellect of the sailor, absolutely insoluble without the key."

"And you really solved it?"

"Readily; I have solved others of an abstruseness ten thousand times greater. Circumstances, and a certain bias of mind, have led me to take interest in such riddles, and it may well be doubted whether human ingenuity can construct an enigma of the kind which human ingenuity may not, by proper application, resolve. In fact, having once established connected and legible characters, I scarcely gave a thought to the mere difficulty of developing their import.

"In the present case—indeed in all cases of secret writing—the first question regards the *language* of the cipher; for the principles of solution, so far, especially, as the more simple ciphers are concerned, depend upon, and are varied by, the genius of the particular idiom. In general, there is no alternative but experiment (directed by probabilities) of every tongue known to him who attempts the solution, until the true one be attained. But, with the cipher now before us, all difficulty was removed by the signature. The pun upon the word 'Kidd' is appreciable in no other language than the English. But for this consideration I should have begun my attempts with the Spanish and French, as the tongues in which a secret of this kind would most naturally have been written by a pirate of the Spanish main. As it was, I assumed the cryptograph to be English.

"You observe there are no divisions between the words. Had there been divisions, the task would have been comparatively easy. In such case I should have commenced with a collation and analysis of the shorter words, and had a word of a single letter occurred, as is most likely, (*a* or *I,* for example), I should have considered the solution as assured. But, there being no division, my first step was to ascertain the predominant letters, as well as the least frequent. Counting all, I constructed a table thus:

Of the character 8 there are 33.
; " 26.
4 " 19.
‡) " 16.
* " 13.
5 " 12.
6 " 11.
†1 " 8.
0 " 6.
92 " 5.
:3 " 4.
? " 3.
¶ " 2.
—. " 1.

"Now, in English the letter which most frequently occurs is *e.* Afterwards, the succession runs thus: *a o i d h n r s t u y c f g l m w b k p q x z. E* predominates so remarkably that an individual sentence of any length is rarely seen in which it is not the prevailing character.

"Here, then, we have, in the very beginning, the groundwork for something more than a mere guess. The general use which may be made of the table is obvious—but in this particular cipher we shall only very partially require its aid. As our predominant character is 8, we will commence by assuming it as the *e* of the natural alphabet. To verify the supposition, let us observe if the 8 be seen often in couples—for *e* is doubled with great frequency in English—in such words, for example as *meet, fleet, speed, seen, been, agree, etc.* In the present instance we see it doubled no less than five times, although the cryptograph is brief.

"Let us assume 8 then, as *e.* Now, of all *words* in the language *the* is most usual; let us see, therefore, whether there are not repetitions of any three characters, in the same order of collocation, the last of them being 8. If we discover repetitions of such letters, so arranged, they will most probably represent the word *the.* Upon inspection, we find no less then seven such arrangements, the characters being ;48. We may, therefore, assume that ; represents *t,* 4 represents *h,* and 8 represents *e*—the last being now well confirmed. Thus a great step has been taken.

"But, having established a single word, we are enabled to establish a vastly important point; that is to say, several commencements and terminations of other words. Let us refer, for example, to the last instance but one, in which the combination ;48 occurs—not far from the end of the cipher. We know that the ; immediately ensuing is the commencement of a word, and of the six characters succeeding this *the,* we are cognizant of no less than five. Let us set these characters down, thus, by the letters we know them to represent, leaving a space for the unknown—

t eeth

"Here we are enabled, at once, to discard the *th,* as forming no portion of the word commencing with the first *t;* since, by experiment of the entire alphabet for a letter adapted to the vacancy, we perceive that no word can be formed of which this *th* can be a part. We are thus narrowed into

t ee,

and, going through the alphabet, if necessary, as before, we arrive at the word *tree,* as the sole possible reading. We thus gain another letter, *r,* represented by (with the words *the tree,* in juxtaposition.

"Looking beyond these words, for a short distance, we again see the combination ;48, and employ it by way of *termination* to what immediately precedes. We have thus:

the tree ;4 (‡?34 the,

or, substituting the natural letters, where known, it reads thus:

the tree thr‡?3h the.

"Now, if in place of the unknown characters, we leave blank spaces, or substitute dots, we read thus:

the tree thr...h the,

when the word *through* makes itself evident at once. But this discovery gives us three new letters, *o, u* and *g,* represented by ‡ ? and 3.

"Looking now, narrowly, through the cipher for combinations of known characters, we find, not very far from the beginning, this arrangement:

83(88, or egree,

which, plainly, is the conclusion of the word *degree,* and gives us another letter, *d,* represented by †.

"Four letters beyond the word *degree,* we perceive the combinations:

;46 (;88

"Translating the known characters, and representing the unknown by dots, as before, we read thus:

th.rtee.

an arrangement immediately suggestive of the word *thirteen,* and again furnishing us with two new characters *i* and *n,* represented by 6 and *.

"Referring, now, to the beginning of the cryptograph, we find the combination,

53‡‡†.

"Translating, as before, we obtain

good.

which assures us that the first letter is *A,* and that the first two words are *A good.*

"It is now time that we arrange our key, as far as discovered, in a tabular form, to avoid confusion. It will stand thus:

5	represents	a
†	"	d
8	"	e
3	"	g
4	"	h
6	"	i
*	"	n
‡	"	o
(	"	r
;	"	t

"We have, therefore, no less than ten of the most important letters represented, and it will be unnecessary to proceed with the details of the solution. I have said enough to convince you that ciphers of this nature are readily soluble, and to give you some insight into the *rationale* of their development. But be assured that the specimen before us appertains to the very simplest species of cryptograph. It now only remains to give you the full translation of the characters upon the parchment as unriddled. Here is it:

"A good glass in the bishop's hostel in the devil's seat forty-one degrees and thirteen minutes northeast and by north main branch seventh limb east side shoot from the left eye of the death's-head a beeline from the tree through the shot fifty feet out."

"But," said I, "the enigma seems still in as bad a condition as ever. How is it possible to extort a meaning from all this jargon about 'devil's seats,' 'death's-heads,' and 'bishop's hotels'?"

"I confess, replied Legrand, "that the matter still wears a serious aspect, when regarded with a casual glance. My first endeavor was to divide the sentence into the natural division intended by the cryptographist."

"You mean to punctuate it?"

"Something of that kind."

"But how was it possible to effect this?"

"I reflected that it had been a *point* with the writer to run his words together without division, so as to increase the difficulty of solution. Now, a not over-acute man, in pursuing such an object, would be nearly certain to overdo the matter. When, in the course of his composition, he arrived at a break in his subject which would naturally require a pause, or a point, he would be exceedingly apt to run his characters, at this place, more than usually close together. If you will observe the MS. in the present instance you will easily detect five such cases of unusual crowding. Acting upon this hint, I made the division thus:

"A good glass in the bishop's hostel in the devil's seat—forty-one degrees and thirteen minutes—northeast and by north—main branch seventh limb east side—shoot from the left eye of the death's-head—a beeline from the tree through the shot fifty feet out."

"Even this division," said I, "leaves me still in the dark."

"It left me also in the dark," replied Legrand, "for a few days; during which I made diligent inquiry, in the neighborhood of Sullivan's Island, for any building which went by the name of the 'Bishop's Hotel'; for, of course, I dropped the obsolete word 'hostel.' Gaining no information on the subject, I was on the point of extending my sphere of search, and proceeding in a more systematic manner, when, one morning, it entered into my head, quite suddenly, that this 'Bishop's Hostel' might have some reference to an old family, of the name of Bessop, which, time out of mind, had held possession of an ancient manor house, about four miles to the northward of the Island. I accordingly went over to the plantation, and re-instituted my inquiries among the older Negroes of the place. At length one of the most aged of the women said that she had heard of such a place as *Bessop's Castle,* and thought that she could guide me to it, but that it was not a castle, nor a tavern, but a high rock.

"I offered to pay her well for her trouble, and, after some demur, she consented to accompany me to the spot. We found it without much difficulty, when, dismissing her I proceeded to examine the place. The 'castle' consisted of an irregular assemblage of cliffs and rocks—one of the latter being quite remarkable for its height as well as for its insulated and artificial appearance. I clambered to its apex, and then felt much at a loss as to what should be next done.

"While I was busied in reflection, my eyes fell upon a narrow ledge in the eastern face of the rock, perhaps a yard below the summit upon which I stood. This ledge projected about eighteen inches, and was not more than a foot wide, while a niche in the cliff just above it gave it a rude resemblance to one of the hollow-backed chairs used by our ancestors. I made no doubt that here was the 'devil's seat' alluded to in the MS., and now I seemed to grasp the full secret of the riddle.

"The 'good glass,' I knew, could have reference to nothing but a telescope, for the word 'glass' is rarely employed in any other sense by seamen. Now here, I at once saw, was a telescope to be used, and a definite point of view, *admitting no variation,* from which to use it. Nor did I hesitate to believe that the phrases, 'forty-one degrees and thirteen minutes,' and 'northeast and by north,' were intended as directions for the leveling of the glass. Greatly excited by these discoveries, I hurried home, procured a telescope, and returned to the rock.

"I let myself down to the ledge, and found that it was impossible to retain a seat upon it except in one particular position. This fact confirmed my preconceived idea. I proceeded to use the glass.

"Of course, the 'forty-one degrees and thirteen minutes' could allude to nothing but elevation above the visible horizon, since the horizontal direction was clearly indicated by the words, 'northeast and by north.' This latter direction I at once established by means of a pocket-compass; then, pointing the glass as nearly at an angle of forty-one degrees of elevation as I could do it by guess, I moved it cautiously up or down, until my attention was arrested by a circular rift or opening in the foliage of a large tree that overtopped its fellows in the distance. In the center of this rift I perceived a white spot, but could not at first distinguish what it was. Adjusting the focus of the telescope, I again looked, and now made it out to be a human skull.

"Upon this discovery I was so sanguine as to consider the enigma solved; for the phrase 'main branch, seventh limb, east side,' could refer only to the position of the skull upon the tree, while 'shoot from the left eye of the death's-head,' admitted also of but one interpretation, in regard to a search for buried treasure. I perceived that the design was to drop a bullet from the left eye of the skull, and that a beeline, or, in other words, a straight line, drawn from the nearest point of the trunk through 'the shot,' (or the spot where the bullet fell), and thence extended to a distance of fifty feet, would indicate a definite point—and beneath this point I thought it at least *possible* that a deposit of value lay concealed."

"All this," I said, "is exceedingly clear, and, although ingenious, still simple and explicit. When you left the Bishop's Hotel, what then?"

"Why, having carefully taken the bearings of the tree, I turned homewards. The instant that I left the 'devil's seat,' however, the circular rift vanished. Nor could I get a glimpse of it afterwards, turn as I would. What seems to me the chief ingenuity in this whole business is the fact (for repeated experiment has convinced me it *is* a fact) that the circular opening in question is visible from no other attainable point of view than that afforded by the narrow ledge upon the face of the rock.

"In this expedition to the 'Bishop's Hotel,' I had been attended by Jupiter, who had no doubt observed for some weeks past the abstraction of my demeanor, and took especial care not to leave me alone. But, on the next day, getting up very early I contrived to give him the slip, and went into the hills in search of the tree. After much toil I found it. When I came home at night my valet proposed to give me a flogging. With the rest of the adventure I believe you are as well acquainted as myself."

"I suppose," said I, "you missed the spot, in the first attempt at digging, through Jupiter's stupidity in letting the bug fall through the right instead of through the left eye of the skull."

"Precisely. This mistake made a difference of about two inches and a half in the 'shot'—that is to say, in the position of the peg nearest the tree; and had the treasure been *beneath* the 'shot,' the error would have been of little moment; but the 'shot,' together with the nearest point of the tree, were merely two points for the establishment of a line of direction; of course the error, however trivial in the beginning, increased as we proceeded with the line, and by the time we had gone fifty feet, threw us quite off the scent. But for my deep-seated impressions that treasure was here somewhere actually buried, we might have had all our labor in vain."

"But your grandiloquence, and your conduct in swinging the beetle—how excessively odd! I was sure you were mad. And why did you insist upon letting fall the bug, instead of a bullet, from the skull?"

"Why, to be frank, I felt somewhat annoyed by your evident suspicions touching my sanity, and so resolved to punish you quietly, in my own way, by a little bit of sober mystification. For this reason I swung the beetle, and for this reason I let it fall from the tree. An observation of yours about its great weight suggested the latter idea."

"Yes, I perceive; and now there is only one point which puzzles me. What are we to make of the skeletons found in the hole?"

"That is a question I am no more able to answer than yourself. There seems, however, only one plausible way of accounting for them—and yet it is dreadful to believe in such atrocity as my suggestion would imply. It is clear that Kidd—if Kidd indeed secreted this treasure, which I doubt not—it is clear that he must have had assistance in the labor. But this labor concluded, he may have thought it expedient to remove all participants in his secret. Perhaps a couple of blows with a mattock were sufficient, while his coadjutors were busy in the pit; perhaps it required a dozen—who shall tell?"

SOUTH DAKOTA

MOURNER
by Joseph Hansen

A FEW WEEKS after Briggs Nelson's mother was bolted inside a shiny metal coffin and buried in the dry, dust-bowl earth of the cemetery at Stander, South Dakota, a parade straggled up Main Street, trying to be gay. Rodeo horses reared and shied between the flat, sun-bleached faces of the buildings. The old tomato-red fire engine coughed. The Legion drum and bugle corps marched in powder-blue uniforms and nickel-plated helmets. Sweating aldermen waved from open Packards on which bunting flapped.

But all Briggs noticed were the Indians.

They wore beaded jackets, fringed leather pants, paint, feather bonnets, and bear-claw necklaces. The men straddled spotted ponies. Their squaws walked behind, round-faced, stoical, with eyes black and glassy as basalt, braids down their backs, and, one or two of the young ones, with papooses in slings. Briggs had seen Indians before. There were big reservations near Stander. He had watched Indians in many parades and remained reasonable.

But not this time.

This time he broke away from his father and ran along beside them. He ran block after block—not fast, of course, but at a steady trot—until his legs ached and his mouth was dry. He didn't yell out loud, but inside his chest, where his heart beat like a tom-tom, he was yelling all the time. And when the parade broke up, and the Indians disappeared into the armory, he sat down on the hot tin fender of a parked Model T and almost bawled. Which was unreasonable too, and unsettling, because he was eleven years old and never cried any more. He hadn't even cried when his mother died.

But he couldn't get the Indians off his mind.

The next morning he went to the public library and lugged home all the books about Indians he was allowed. And all afternoon, and after supper, and then late into the night in his hot, slope-ceilinged little room—while his father on the other side of the wall walked forlornly up and down in his stocking feet, creaking the floor-boards—Briggs read of how the noble savages were tricked and sold out, decimated by the rifle bullet and the white man's diseases, and finally herded onto reservations in bitter and inhospitable lands, where they shivered, starved, and died.

What he read disturbed him. He wanted to do something, to get to the reservations somehow and to rouse the chiefs and braves, to set them on the warpath again, to avenge what had been done to them, to right their wrongs. But all he did in fact was to start a neighborhood enthusiasm for playing Indian. Along the alleys frequented by youngsters he knew, or in the scrubby clump of wind-bent oaks dying near the high school on the fringe of town, or farther out, in the abandoned gravel pit, bows and arrows displaced cap pistols. Pheasant feathers were rummaged out of cellar corners where they had blown the previous fall, when dads had brought home gunny sacks bulging with the big, limp birds, rainbow bright and full of buckshot. Headbands to hold the feathers were stitched by harassed mothers.

Mrs. Horst, the lady downstairs, sewed Briggs's. Realism was what he mainly sought in the games he contrived, pictorial realism. The farther off from home the games were played, the more nearly naked everybody got. But no one was burned at the stake or pinioned to the earth to be devoured by ants. Briggs didn't see the Indian that way.

Two other sad things had happened around the time Briggs's mother died. His father's shoe store had failed. And their new house had to be given back to the bank. After the funeral, the Nelson furniture had been moved into these four stuffy rooms on the top floor at Horst's, and Briggs's father had taken work—it was the Depression and jobs were scarce—traveling as a shirt salesman through the Dakotas, Montana, and Wyoming. He was able to return home nights when his trips didn't take him too far. When they did, he arranged for Briggs to stay with friends.

Twice he stayed with the Eameses, who had three kids, and twice with the Melgards who had two. But he wanted to stay with the Meisners because Mr. Lou Meisner was Sheriff of Stander County, and the Meisner house was over the jail. It was a big red-brick place that stood high on a mound of brown lawn that was like an enormous grave. And in the basement, in the grave, were the cells. Briggs knew they were there but his mother had never permitted him to see them. He'd had to imagine them, as in the Buck Jones and Tim McCoy movies— grimy, black-barred, crowded with sulky gunslingers. And the sight of Sheriff Meisner, large and heavy-bellied, a big brown revolver strapped to his thick thigh, lent conviction to these imaginings.

So Briggs was pleased when, six or eight weeks after the parade, by which time he had exhausted the library's stock of Indian lore, and had been sunburned so brown that he doubted, hopefully, that he would ever bleach back to his normal Scandinavian pallor, his father sent him to spend a week at the Meisners'. At night he shared the bed of Johnny, who was his own age and whose principal merit, so far as Briggs was concerned, was that he talked very little. Briggs liked to talk, and since it was too hot to sleep, he lay in the dry darkness beside Johnny and lectured him about Indians. He talked fast and indignantly, so that it was some time before Johnny could interrupt. When he did, it was very quietly.

"Dad's got an Indian in jail," he said.

Briggs sat up. "Right now? You mean downstairs? Locked up?"

"Sure. Name's Charlie Two Horses." Johnny yawned and turned on his side. "I'll take you to see him tomorrow."

"But what's he in jail for?" Briggs was shocked that the genial Sheriff would treat one of his red brothers that way. "What did he do?"

"I don't know. But he's a good guy." Johnny's voice faded sleepily. "Knows a lot of great cowboy songs."

The jail surprised Briggs by being bright and clean. The pale-gray paint was fresh, the cell bars naked, gleaming steel. Except for Charlie Two Horses the place was empty. And, being below ground, it was a lot cooler and more comfortable than the house upstairs. Briggs leaned his face against the cold, shiny bars and stared worriedly and with pity at the prisoner in the cell.

He was a brown, underfed young man in dirty work clothes. His stiff hair needed combing and there was grime under his fingernails. Briggs supposed the narrow eyes and hawk nose looked savage, all right, but because of his grin, which showed teeth white as the porcelain toilet at the back of his cell, it was easy to forget that his father had likely scalped some soldier of Custer's. Seated on the bunk, Charlie hunched his shoulders and made his guitar jangle and twang as if it were alive with mice. He tilted his head back and shut his eyes, trying to think of a song to sing.

" 'Whuppy Ti Yi Yay,' Charlie," Johnny said.

Charlie kept his eyes shut for a second longer, hunting up the words and tune. Then he let out an experimental yup-yup, and began:

" 'As I was out walkin' one mornin' for pleasure—' "

Briggs had always agreed with his mother when she called this kind of music trashy. They had both preferred the Walter Damrosch symphony broadcasts and records like "The Two Grenadiers." But, listening to Charlie's easy, drawling voice, watching his hands on the strings, his foot tapping in its ragged tennis shoe, Briggs guessed there was something to be said for it, even for "Pretty Redwing."

Charlie slid the guitar under a bunk. "Okay, that's all the songs today, kids. Now, you do me a favor. I'm out of makin's." He pulled a greasy calfskin pouch out of his shirt and took a dime from it. "Can you catch, Briggs?"

"I can," Johnny said.

"He asked me," Briggs said. "Sure, Charlie."

"Right." Charlie flipped the coin, spinning, in a high arc. It cleared the bars neatly, but when Briggs grabbed for it he missed and knocked it rolling. It tinkled across the cement floor into the cell opposite and flattened out under the bunk inside.

"Some catcher," Johnny said.

"I'll get it." Briggs ran to the door of the empty cell and tugged. He felt his face turn red. "It's locked."

"That's all right," Charlie said. "Johnny knows where the keys are." He winked at the Sheriff's son.

"Sure." Beside the door to the upstairs stood a big rolltop desk. Johnny pulled open its central drawer and brought out a shiny key ring. "Keys are all numbered," he told Briggs, "to match the cell doors they fit. See, here's six." He fitted the large key into the large keyhole, turned it, and swung the door open on its oiled hinges.

"Let me get it." Briggs felt urgent about this. He dodged in and slid on his knees to reach the dime under the cot, then stood up with his heart beating hard and walked back to the door. "There's the dime," he said to Johnny. "Now lock it."

Johnny turned his freckled face half away and looked at Briggs out of the corners of his eyes. "What?"

Across from them, Charlie said, "Get out of there, Briggs. If Johnny's dad come and found you in there, he'd be sore."

"You don't have to really lock it," Briggs pleaded. "Just shut the door. Only for a minute. I just want to see what it's like to be—locked up underground. Please."

"You're crazy," Johnny said. "Come on, I've got to put the keys back."

Briggs felt like yelling at him, but his father had told him to be polite because the Meisners were doing him a kindness, having him stay, so he came out. But, standing, staring into the empty cell, while Johnny locked the door and put the keys away, Briggs ached in his chest. Behind him, Johnny's voice had a lost, sad sound, echoing off the bare walls, asking Charlie:

"Bull Durham?"

"Yeah, and get it back here, will you? I'm clean out. Musta smoked all night." He flapped an empty sack at them, a scrap of soiled cloth with a black paper label. "So don't horse around, huh?"

"We won't." Johnny ran to the barred door that shut the jail off from the upstairs. He halted. "Come on, Briggs. What the heck's wrong with you?"

Briggs sighed. "Let's go."

When they came back, Charlie was asleep, sprawled face down on his bunk, the back of his shirt dark with sweat.

"Watch me wake him up," Johnny said, and raised the pudgy new tobacco sack to throw it.

Briggs caught his arm. "Don't. What do you want to wake him up for? He was awake all night. He was suffering. It's wrong to lock Indians up. They get sick and die, longing for the sky and the prairie."

Johnny looked at him sideways again. But he didn't throw the bag of Bull Durham. He laid it quietly on the crossbar of Charlie's cell door. Then they went upstairs and hung the key to the jail door on the hook at the top.

Briggs took the key down again in the middle of the night. Barefoot, pajamaed, he groped after it in the dark. It was pretty high up and his fingers trembled and were slippery with sweat, so the key refused to unhook itself at first. But finally he got it. His knees acted wobbly and he kept hold of the railing going down the cold stairs to the jail. The stairway jogged. He halted. Below, a light showed. He stood for a long time, heart banging, and wondered about that light. But he seemed to recall from some movie that prisoners were often kept lighted at night. So he went on down the rest of the steps, but very cautiously, as if there were broken glass on each one.

At the bottom, he squinted between the bars of the door. The jail looked grim at night. The light fell bleakly from a caged bulb in the ceiling. He couldn't see Charlie Two Horses but he could hear him breathe. He pushed the key into the lock. It turned noisily and the hard walls rattled back its noise. He flinched, but no one seemed to have heard. He swung the door out, went quickly to the desk for the key ring, ran with it to Charlie's cell, fumbled for the number five key, and opened the door.

Charlie ought to have been sitting miserable on his bunk, smoking, and yearning with vacant, haunted eyes for the great outdoors, or maybe pacing restlessly, like a caged coyote. Instead, he was asleep, on his back this time, arms flung out, mouth slack. He slept as if there were an arrow through him, as if he were dead.

"Charlie." The name came out weakly because Briggs felt small and scared suddenly, which shamed him. "Charlie," he said again, louder, but still from the doorway. The Indian only sighed. It wouldn't work. Briggs would have to move. He forced himself to cross the cell to the bunk. "Wake up, Charlie. Come on, wake up." Briggs was suddenly annoyed. He grabbed the Indian's shoulder and shook it. "Come on. You can get out now. You can get out."

"Huh?" Charlie opened his eyes and stared. Then he sat up so fast he nearly knocked Briggs over. "What the hell are you doing here?"

"I came to let you out. Look, the door's open. Both doors. You can leave, Charlie. You have to go quiet through the house, but you can leave. Everybody's asleep."

"You crazy kid," Charlie said, "you'll get in bad trouble." But just the same, he got off the bunk and walked, in his sleep-twisted shirt and pants, to the door. He swung it a little, maybe just to show himself it was really open. "Bad trouble," he repeated, only this time he was absent-minded about the meaning and he grinned to himself. "Jeez." He wiped his hand down over his face, walked into the open area between the cells, turned around twice, came back and looked at Briggs. He shook his head and laughed. "You're a crazy kid, but you're all right. All right." He squeezed Briggs's shoulder, then pulled his shoes and guitar from under the bunk. "Come on, let's go."

"No, I'm staying here." Briggs held out the key ring to the Indian. "Here. Lock me in."

"What? Listen, kid, forget that." Sweat shone on Charlie's forehead. "Come on. We've got to get out of here before the Sheriff comes down." He moved to the door.

"No," Briggs said. "I'm staying. Lock it up, Charlie. And here's the key to the door down there. It hangs on a hook at the top of the stairs. Put it back."

"Look, come on, Briggs," Charlie pleaded. "This ain't no game." He kept moving out of the cell and coming back while he talked. "No time for horsin' around. You're going to do this kind of thing, you can't play games."

"I'm not," Briggs said. "I want to stay here. I'm breaking the law anyway. Besides, Charlie, a white man doesn't mind. Red men mind jail. But a white man doesn't. Anyway, not so much."

"Oh?" Charlie stopped moving and blinked thoughtfully at Briggs for a moment. Then he shrugged. "Okay, okay, kid. Thanks." And he locked the door while Briggs stood inside.

"Goodbye, Charlie," Briggs said.

"So long, kid." The Indian dropped the key ring on top of the desk and he didn't bother to lock the stairway door. But that didn't matter a lot. Briggs went to the bunk that was still warm from Charlie's sleep. He lay down. The light glared in his eyes, and his heart was pounding so from excitement that he thought he never would, but after a long time he did fall asleep.

Mrs. Meisner found him there at six the next morning when she came down with the prisoner's breakfast on a tray. "Briggs Nelson!" she gasped. "Briggs Nelson!" Her bony face got red as a chicken's. She squawked like a chicken. She flapped to the stair door. "Lou, you better get on down here, right now!"

The Sheriff came, buckling on his gunbelt around his nightshirt. He was still nine-tenths asleep, and when his spindly wife pointed at the cell where Briggs stood in his pajamas, all he could manage at first was a grunt. The rest of the Meisners came down behind him, wide-eyed girls in pale flannel bathrobes and with curl-papers in their hair, and last of all Johnny, looking white under his freckles.

"What the hell?" the Sheriff finally managed to choke out. He clattered the key ring and scraped four or five keys around on the steel plate of the lock until he got the right one at last and could pull the door open and yank Briggs out. "What in all consolidated hell you done? Where's the Indian?"

"Gone," Briggs said loudly. "Back to the wide prairies and the open skies."

It wasn't a hard speech to make. He had practiced it. But he hadn't practiced any other speeches, so that when the Sheriff and his wife sat him down upstairs in the rollershade-darkened parlor and asked him questions about why he had set Charlie Two Horses free, and what kind of a way was this to act in somebody else's house, and what would his father say—he couldn't answer.

Somehow, they got his father back. He looked pale to Briggs, and strange, standing beside the big, sunburned Sheriff, apologizing in his thin, quiet voice. The Sheriff seemed ready to laugh about what had happened now. But Briggs's father never laughed any more. The best he could manage was a wan, crooked little smile.

"All right, Lou, if you say so, we'll forget it. You understand—it's just that he's—well, losing his mother, her being gone, he—"

"Sure, Henry, I know," the Sheriff said. "But I have to answer to the County.

Oh, hell, I can get Charlie Two Horses back easy enough. That's not it. He'll be drunk someplace by sundown. Just pick him up and dump him in the car. But supposing it'd been some killer, for instance."

"I understand, Lou." Briggs's father nodded tiredly. "Anyway, thanks." The two men shook hands and then stared at Briggs. His father sighed and tried the smile again that didn't work. "All right, son. Got your suitcase?"

And they went.

"What we'll do," his father said that night, "is go to Minneapolis. To your Aunt Christine's. All right with you? Nothing left for us here—not even the car now. When I got back today, after Lou called me, Reardon's had a man waiting. See, it wasn't quite paid for. God knows what good it will do them. Can't sell anybody a car today. Anyway, I sure can't travel for Hi-Style without it. There'll be a better job for me in Minneapolis. Well, some kind of job. Anyway, there'll be a home for you, with a woman in it. You like your Aunt Christine."

"Sure," Briggs said.

"If we sell the furniture," his father said, "we'll have enough for train fare to Minneapolis, and some left over to keep us till I get work."

After the furniture was gone, they didn't linger in the blank, brown-papered rooms above Horst's. They carried their suitcases through the rusty iron gates of the cemetery and up the long, curving cinder drive inside. They stood side by side staring down at the dry-grass-covered mound that was his mother's grave, and then his father cleared his throat and said:

"We can come back to her, come back to Stander sometime. Things won't always be this bad. Minneapolis isn't so far away. We can come to visit."

Briggs had never ridden on a train before. But it wasn't exciting. There was nothing to look at except flat land that the sun was burning up and from which the wind was all the time raking the topsoil. Dead cows lay in the fields, bloated sometimes, sometimes only skeletons. Farmhouses stood vacant, windows and doors boarded up, paint peeling. Barns leaned with the wind. Silos had fallen over.

The wheels of the train made sounds as if they were biting off sections of rail in even lengths and spitting them out. But all they were really doing, of course, was rolling, carrying him farther and farther from the dead grass on the mound in the cemetery, the shiny metal coffin down under it, away down, his mother lying prim and strange on her back inside. Briggs looked at his father.

"Some Indians," he said, "bury their dead at the tops of trees."

Then, for some reason, he cried.

TENNESSEE

THE COBBLESTONES OF SARATOGA STREET

by Avram Davidson

COBBLESTONES TO GO, said the headline. Miss Louisa lifted her eyebrows, lifted her quizzing-glass (probably the last one in actual use anywhere in the world), read the article, passed it to her sister. Miss Augusta read it without eyeglass or change of countenance, and handed it back.

"They shan't," she said.

They glanced at a faded photograph in a silver frame on the mantelpiece, then at each other. Miss Louisa placed the newspaper next to the pewter chocolate-pot, tinkled a tiny bell. After a moment a white-haired colored man entered the room.

"Carruthers," said Miss Augusta, "you may clear away breakfast."

"Well, *I* think it is outrageous," Betty Linkhorn snapped.

"My dear," her grandfather said mildly, "you can't stop progress." He sipped his tea.

"Progress my eye! This is the only decently paved street in the whole town—you know that, don't you, Papa? Just because it's cobblestone and not concrete—or macadam—or—"

"My dear," said Edward Linkhorn, "*I* remember when several of the streets were still paved with wood. I remember it quite particularly because, in defiance of my father's orders, I went barefoot one fine summer's day and got a splinter in my heel. My mother took it out with a needle and my father thrashed me . . . Besides, don't you find the cobblestones difficult to manage in high-heeled shoes?"

Betty smiled—not sweetly. "I don't find them difficult at all. Mrs. Harris does—but, then, if *she'd* been thrashed for going barefoot . . . Come on, Papa," she said, while her grandfather maintained a diplomatic silence, "admit it—if Mrs. Harris hadn't sprained her ankle, if her husband wasn't a paving contractor,

454

if his partner wasn't C. B. Smith, the state chairman of the party that's had the city, county *and* state sewn up for twenty years—"

Mr. Linkhorn spread honey on a small piece of toast. " 'If wishes were horses, beggars would ride—' "

"Well, what's wrong with that?"

" '—and all mankind be consumed with pride.' My dear, I will see what I can do."

His Honor was interviewing the press. "Awright, what's next? New terlets in the jail, right? Awright, if them bums and smokies wouldn't of committed no crimes they wouldn't be in no jail, right? Awright, what's next? Cobblestones? *Cob*blestones? Damn it, *again* this business with the cobblestones! You'd think they were diamonds or sumphin'. Aw*right*. Well, om, look, except for Saratoga Street, the last cobblestones inna city were tore up when I was a *boy,* for Pete's sake. Allathem people there, they're living inna past, yaknowwhatimean? All-athem gas lamps in frunna the houses, huh? Hitching posts and carriage blocks, for Pete's sake! Whadda they think we're living inna horse-and-buggy age? *Awright,* they got that park with a fence around it, private property, okay. But the streets belong to the City, see? Somebody breaks a leg on wunna them cob-blestones, they can *sue* the City, right? So—*cobblestones?* Up they come, anats all there is to it. Awright, what's next?"

His comments appeared in the newspaper (the publisher of which knew what side his Legal Advertisements were buttered on) in highly polished form. *I yield to no one in my respect for tradition and history, but the cobblestoned paving of Saratoga Street is simply too dangerous to be endured. The cobblestones will be replaced by a smooth, efficient surface more in keeping with the needs of the times.*

As the Mayor put it, "What's next?"

Next was a series of protests by the local, county, and state historical societies, all of which protests were buried in two-or-three-line items in the back of the newspaper. But (as the publisher put it, "After all, C.B., business is business. And, besides, it won't make any difference in the long run, anyway.") the Saratoga Street Association reprinted them in a full-page advertisement headed PROTECT OUR HERITAGE, and public interest began to pick up.

It was stimulated by the interest shown in the metropolitan papers, all of which circulated locally. BLUEBLOODS MAN THE BARRICADES, said one. 20TH CENTURY CATCHES UP WITH SARATOGA STREET, said another. BE-LOVED COBBLESTONES DOOMED, HISTORICAL SARATOGA STREET PREPARES TO SAY FAREWELL, lamented a third. And so it went.

And it also went like this: *To The Editor, Sir, I wish to point out an error in the letter which claimed that the cobblestones were laid down in 1836. True, the houses in Saratoga Street were mostly built in that year, but like many local streets it was not paved at all until late in the '90s. So the cobblestones are not as old as some people think.*

And it went like this, too:

Mr. Edward Linkhorn: Would you gentlemen care for anything else to drink?

Reporter: Very good whiskey.

Photographer: Very good.

Linkhorn: We are very gratified that a national picture magazine is giving us so much attention.

Reporter: Well, *you* know—human interest story. Not so much soda, Sam.

Photographer: Say Mr. Linkhorn, can I ask you a question?

Linkhorn: Certainly.

Photographer: Well, I notice that on all the houses—in all the windows, I mean—they got these signs, *Save Saratoga Street Cobblestones.* All but one house. How come? They *against* the stones?

Reporter: Say, that's right, Mr. Linkhorn. How come—?

Linkhorn: Well, gentlemen, that house, number 25, belongs to the Misses de Gray.

Reporter: de Gray? de Gray?

Linkhorn: Their father was General de Gray of Civil War fame. His statue is in de Gray Square. We also have a de Gray Avenue.

Reporter: His *daughters* are still living? What are they like?

Linkhorn: I have never had the privilege of meeting them.

Miss Adelaide Tallman's family was every bit as good as any of those who lived on Saratoga Street; the Tallmans had simply never *cared* to live on Saratoga Street, that was all. The Tallman estate had been one of the sights of the city, but nothing remained of it now except the name *Jabez Tallman* on real estate maps used in searching land titles, and the old mansion itself—much modified now, and converted into a funeral parlor. Miss Tallman herself lived in a nursing home. Excitement was rare in her life, and she had no intention of passing up any bit of attention which came her way.

"I knew the de Gray girls well," she told the lady from the news syndicate. This was a big fib; she had never laid eyes on them in her life—but who was to know? She had *heard* enough about them to talk as if she had, and if the de Gray girls didn't like it, let them come and tell her so. Snobby people, the de Grays, always were. What if her father, Mr. Tallman, *had* hired a substitute during the Rebellion? *Hmph.*

"Oh, they were the most beautiful things! Louisa was the older, she was blonde. Augusta's hair was brown. They always had plenty of beaux—not that I didn't have my share of them too, mind you," she added, looking sharply at the newspaper lady, as if daring her to deny it. "But nobody was ever good enough for *them.* There was one young man, his name was Horace White, and—oh, he was the *hand*somest thing! I danced with him myself," she said complacently, "at the Victory Ball after the Spanish War. He had gone away to be an officer in the Navy, and he was just the most handsome thing in his uniform that you ever saw. But *he* wasn't good enough for them, either. He went away after that— went out west to Chicago or some such place—and no one ever heard from him

again. Jimmy Taylor courted Augusta, and William Snow and Rupert Roberts—
no, Rupert was sweet on Louisa, yes, but—"

The newspaper lady asked when Miss Tallman had last seen the de Gray
sisters.

Oh, said Miss Tallman vaguely, many years ago. *Many* years ago . . . (Had she
really danced with anybody at the Victory Ball? Was she still wearing her hair
down then? Perhaps she was thinking of the Junior Cotillion. Oh, well, who was
to know?)

"About 1905," she said firmly, crossing her fingers under her blanket. "But,
you see, nobody was *good* enough for them. And so, by and by, they stopped
seeing *anybody*. And that's the way it was."

That was not quite the way it was. They saw Carruthers.

Carruthers left the house on Sunday mornings only—to attend at the A.M.E.
Zion Church. Sunday evenings he played the harmonium while Miss Louisa and
Miss Augusta sang hymns. All food was delivered and Carruthers received it
either at the basement door or the rear door. The Saratoga Street Association took
care of the maintenance of the outside of the house, of course; all Carruthers had
to do there was sweep the walk and polish the brass.

It must not be thought that because his employers were recluses, Carruthers
was one, too; or because they did not choose to communicate with the outside
world, he did not choose to do so, either. If, while engaged in his chores, he saw
people he knew, he would greet them. He was, in fact, the first person to greet
Mrs. Henry Harris when she moved into Saratoga Street.

"Why, hel-lo, Henrietta," he said. "What in the world are *you* doing here?"

Mrs. Harris did not seem to appreciate this attention.

Carruthers read the papers, too.

"What do they want to bother them old stones for?" he asked himself. "They
been here long as I can remember."

The question continued to pose itself. One morning he went so far as to tap the
Cobblestones story in the newspaper with his finger and raise his eyebrows
inquiringly.

Miss Augusta answered him. "They won't," she said.

Miss Louisa frowned. "Is all this conversation necessary?"

Carruthers went back downstairs. "That sure relieves my mind," he said to
himself.

"The newspapers seem to be paying more attention to the de Gray sisters than
to the cobblestones," Betty Linkhorn said.

"Well," her grandfather observed, "People *are* more important than cobblestones. Still," he went on, *"House of Mystery* seems to be pitching it a little
stronger than is necessary. They just want to be left alone, that's all. And I rather
incline to doubt that General M. M. de Gray won the Civil War all by himself, as
these articles imply."

Betty, reading further, said *Hmmm.* "Papa, except for that poor old Miss Tallman, there doesn't seem to be anyone alive—outside of their butler—who has ever *seen* them, even." She giggled. "Do you suppose that maybe they could be *dead? For years and years?* And old Carruthers has them covered with wax and just dusts them every day with a feather mop?"

Mr. Linkhorn said he doubted it.

Comparisons with the Collier brothers were inevitable, and newsreel and television cameras were standing by in readiness for—well, no one knew just what. And the time for the repaving of Saratoga Street grew steadily nearer. An injunction was obtained; it expired. And then there seemed nothing more that could be done.

"It is claimed that removal would greatly upset and disturb the residents of Saratoga Street, many of whom are said to be elderly," observed the judge, denying an order of further stay; "but it is significant that the two oldest inhabitants, the daughters of General M. M. de Gray, the Hero of Chickasaw Bend, have expressed no objection whatsoever."

Betty wept. "Well, why *haven't* they?" she demanded. "Don't they realize that this is the beginning of the end for Saratoga Street? First the cobblestones, then the flagstone sidewalks, then the hitching posts and carriage blocks—then they'll tear up the common for a parking lot and knock down the three houses at the end to make it a through street. Can't you *ask* them—?"

Her grandfather spread his hands. "They never had a telephone," he said. "And to the best of my knowledge—although I've written—they haven't answered a letter for more than forty years. No, my dear, I'm afraid it's hopeless."

Said His Honor: "Nope, no change in plans. T'morra morning at eight A.M. sharp, the cobblestones *go*. Awright, what's next?"

At eight that morning a light snow was falling. At eight that morning a crowd had gathered. Saratoga Street was only one block long. At its closed end it was only the width of three houses set in their little gardens; then it widened so as to embrace the small park—"common"—then narrowed again.

The newsreel and television cameras were at work, and several announcers described, into their microphones, the arrival of the Department of Public Works trucks at the corner of Saratoga and Trenton Streets, loaded with workmen and air hammers and pickaxes, at exactly eight o'clock.

At exactly one minute after eight the front door of number 25 Saratoga Street, at the northwest corner, swung open. The interviewers and cameramen were, for a moment, intent on the rather embarrassed crew foreman, and did not at first observe the opening of the door. Then someone shouted, *"Look!"* And then everyone noticed.

First came Carruthers, very erect, carrying a number of items which were at first not identifiable. The crowd parted for him as if he had been Moses, and the crowd, the Red Sea. First he unrolled an old, but still noticeably red, carpet. Next he unfolded and set up two campstools. Then he waited.

Out the door came Miss Louisa de Gray, followed by Miss Augusta. They moved into the now absolutely silent crowd without a word; and without a word they seated themselves on the campstools—Miss Louisa facing south, Miss Augusta facing north.

Carruthers proceeded to unfurl two banners and stood—at parade rest, so to speak—with one in each hand. The snowy wind blew out their folds, revealing them to be a United States flag with thirty-six stars and the banner of the Army of the Tennessee.

And while at least fifty million people watched raptly at their television sets, Miss Louisa drew her father's saber from its scabbard and placed it across her knees; and Miss Augusta, taking up her father's musket, proceeded to load it with powder and ball and drove the charge down with a ramrod.

After a while the workmen debated what they ought do. Failing to have specific instructions suitable to the new situation, they built a fire in an ashcan, and stood around it, warming their hands.

The first telegram came from the Ladies of the G.A.R.; the second, from the United Daughters of the Confederacy. Both, curiously enough, without mutual consultation, threatened a protest march on the City Hall. In short and rapid succession followed indignant messages from the Senior Citizens' Congress, the Sons of Union Veterans, the American Legion, the B'nai Brith, the Ancient Order of Hibernians, the D.A.R., the N.A.A.C.P., the Society of the War of 1812, the V.F.W., the Ancient and Accepted Scottish Rite, and the Blue Star Mothers. After that it became difficult to keep track.

The snow drifted down upon them, but neither lady, nor Carruthers, moved a thirty-second of an inch.

At twenty-seven minutes after nine the Mayor's personal representative arrived on the scene—his ability to speak publicly without a script had long been regarded by the Mayor himself as something akin to sorcery.

"I have here," the personal representative declared loudly, holding up a paper, "a statement from His Honor announcing his intention to summon a special meeting of the Council for the sole purpose of turning Saratoga Street into a private street, title to be vested in the Saratoga Street Association. *Then—*" The crowd cheered, and the personal representative held up his hands for silence. *"Then,* in the event of anyone sustaining injuries because of cobblestones, the City won't be responsible."

There were scattered boos and hisses. The representative smiled broadly, expressed the Municipality's respect for Tradition, and urged the Misses de Gray to get back into their house, please, before they both caught cold.

Neither moved. The Mayor's personal representative had not reached his position of eminence for nothing. He turned to the D.P.W. crew. "Okay, boys—no work for you here. Back to the garage. In fact," he added, "take the day off!"

The crew cheered, the crowd cheered, the trucks rolled away. Miss Louisa sheathed her sword, Miss Augusta unloaded her musket by the simple expedient of firing it into the air, the Mayor's representative ducked (and was immortalized in that act by twenty cameras). The Misses de Gray then stood up. Reporters crowded in, and were ignored as if they had never been born.

Miss Louisa, carrying her sword like an admiral as the two sisters made their way back to the house, observed Betty and her grandfather in the throng. "Your features look familiar," she said. "Do they not, Augusta?"

"Indeed," said Miss Augusta. "I think he must be Willie Linkhorn's little boy—are you?" Mr. Linkhorn, who was seventy, nodded; for the moment he could think of nothing to say. "Then you had better come inside. The girl may come, too. Go home, good people," she said, pausing at the door and addressing the crowd, "and be sure to drink a quantity of hot rum and tea with nutmeg on it."

The door closed on ringing cheers from the populace.

"Carruthers, please mull us all some port," Miss Louisa directed. "I would have advised the same outside, but I am not sure the common people would *care* to drink port. Boy," she said, to the gray-haired Mr. Linkhorn, "would you care to know why we have broken a seclusion of sixty years and engaged in a public demonstration so foreign to our natures?"

He blinked. "Why . . . I suppose it was your attachment to the traditions of Saratoga Street, exemplified by the cobble—"

"Stuff!" said Miss Augusta. "We don't give a hoot for the traditions of Saratoga Street. And as for the cobblestones, those dreadful noisy things, I could wish them all at the bottom of the sea!"

"Then—"

The sisters waved to a faded photograph in a silver frame on the mantelpiece. It showed a young man with a curling mustache, clad in an old-fashioned uniform. "Horace White," they said, in unison.

"He courted us," the elder said. "He never would say which he preferred. I refused Rupert Roberts for him, I gave up Morey Stone. My sister sent Jimmy Taylor away, and William Snow as well. When Horace went off to the Spanish War he gave us that picture. He said he would make his choice when he returned. We waited."

Carruthers returned with the hot wine, and withdrew.

The younger sister took up the tale. "When he returned," she said, "we asked him whom his choice had fallen on. He smiled and said he'd changed his mind. He no longer wished to wed either of us, he said. The street had been prepared for cobblestone paving, the earth was still tolerably soft. We buried him there, ten paces from the gas lamp and fifteen from the water hydrant. And there he lies to this day, underneath those dreadful noisy cobblestones. I could forgive, perhaps, on my deathbed, his insult to myself—but his insult to my dear sister, that I can *never* forgive."

Miss Louisa echoed, "His insult to *me* I could perhaps forgive, on my deathbed, but his insult to my dear sister—that I could *never* forgive."

She poured four glasses of the steaming wine.

"Then—" said Mr. Linkhorn, "you mean—"

"I do. I pinioned him by the arms and my sister Louisa shot him through his black and faithless heart with Father's musket. Father was a heavy sleeper, and never heard a thing."

Betty swallowed. "Gol-*ly*."

"I trust no word of this will ever reach other ears. The embarrassment would be severe . . . A scoundrel, yes, was Horace White," said Miss Augusta, "but— and I confess it to you—I fear I love him still."

Miss Louisa said, "And I. And I."

They raised their glasses. "To Horace White!"

Mr. Linkhorn, much as he felt the need, barely touched his drink; but the ladies drained theirs to the stem, all three of them.

TEXAS

THE CONQUEROR

by Richard Matheson

THAT AFTERNOON IN 1871, the stage to Grantville had only the two of us as passengers, rocking and swaying in its dusty, hot confines under the fiery Texas sun. The young man sat across from me, one palm braced against the hard, dry leather of the seat, the other holding on his lap a small black bag.

He was somewhere near 19 or 20. His build was almost delicate. He was dressed in checkered flannel and wore a dark tie with a stickpin in its center. You could tell he was a city boy.

From the time we'd left Austin two hours before, I had been wondering about the bag he carried so carefully in his lap. I noticed that his light-blue eyes kept gazing down at it. Every time they did, his thin-lipped mouth would twitch— whether toward a smile or a grimace I couldn't tell. Another black bag, slightly larger, was on the seat beside him, but to this he paid little attention.

I'm an old man, and while not usually garrulous, I guess I do like to seek out conversation. Just the same, I hadn't offered to speak in the time we'd been fellow passengers, and neither had he. For about an hour and a half I'd been trying to read the Austin paper, but now I laid it down beside me on the dusty seat. I glanced down again at the small bag and noted how tightly his slender fingers were clenched around the bone handle.

Frankly, I was curious. And maybe there was something in the young man's face that reminded me of Lew or Tylan—my sons. Anyhow, I picked up the newspaper and held it out to him.

"Care to read it?" I asked him above the din of the 24 pounding hoofs and the rattle and creak of the stage.

There was no smile on his face as he shook his head once. If anything, his mouth grew tighter until it was a line of almost bitter resolve. It is not often you see such an expression in the face of so young a man. It is too hard at that age to hold on to either bitterness or resolution, too easy to smile and laugh and soon forget the worst of evils. Maybe that was why the young man seemed so unusual to me.

"I'm through with it if you'd like," I said.

"No, thank you," he answered curtly.

"Interesting story here," I went on, unable to rein in a runaway tongue. "Some Mexican claims to have shot young Wesley Hardin."

The young man's eyes raised up a moment from his bag and looked at me intently. Then they lowered to the bag again.

" 'Course I don't believe a word of it," I said. "The man's not born yet who'll put John Wesley away."

The young man did not choose to talk, I saw. I leaned back against the jolting seat and watched him as he studiously avoided my eyes.

Still I would not stop. What is this strange compulsion of old men to share themselves? Perhaps they fear to lose their last years in emptiness. "You must have gold in that bag," I said to him, "to guard it so zealously."

It was a smile he gave me now, though a mirthless one.

"No, not gold," the young man said, and as he finished saying so, I saw his lean throat move once nervously.

I smiled and struck in deeper the wedge of conversation.

"Going to Grantville?" I asked.

"Yes, I am," he said—and I suddenly knew from his voice that he was no Southern man.

I did not speak then. I turned my head away and looked out stiffly across the endless flat, watching through the choking haze of alkali dust, the bleached scrub which dotted the barren stretches. For a moment, I felt myself tightened with that rigidity we Southerners contracted in the presence of our conquerors.

But there is something stronger than pride, and that is loneliness. It was what made me look back to the young man and once more see in him something of my own two boys who gave their lives at Shiloh. I could not, deep in myself, hate the young man for being from a different part of our nation. Even then, imbued as I was with the stiff pride of the Confederate, I was not good at hating.

"Planning to live in Grantville?" I asked.

The young man's eyes glittered. "Just for a while," he said. His fingers grew yet tighter on the bag he held so firmly in his lap. Then he suddenly blurted, "You want to see what I have in—"

He stopped, his mouth tightening as if he were angry to have spoken.

I didn't know what to say to his impulsive, half-finished offer.

The young man very obviously clutched at my indecision and said, "Well, never mind—you wouldn't be interested."

And though I suppose I could have protested that I would, somehow I felt it would do no good.

The young man leaned back and braced himself again as the coach yawed up a rock-strewn incline. Hot, blunt waves of dust-laden wind poured through the open windows at my side. The young man had rolled down the curtains on his side shortly after we'd left Austin.

"Got business in our town?" I asked, after blowing dust from my nose and wiping it from around my eyes and mouth.

He leaned forward slightly. "You live in Grantville?" he asked loudly as overhead the driver, Jeb Knowles, shouted commands to his three teams and snapped the leather popper of his whip over their straining bodies.

I nodded. "Run a grocery there," I said, smiling at him. "Been visiting up North with my oldest—with my son."

He didn't seem to hear what I had said. Across his face a look as intent as any I have ever seen moved suddenly.

"Can you tell me something?" he began. "Who's the quickest pistolman in your town?"

The question startled me, because it seemed born of no idle curiosity. I could see that the young man was far more than ordinarily interested in my reply. His hands were clutching, bloodless, the handle of his small black bag.

"Pistolman?" I asked him.

"Yes. Who's the quickest in Grantville? Is it Hardin? Does he come there often? Or Longley? Do they come there?"

That was the moment I knew something was not quite right in that young man. For, when he spoke those words, his face was strained and eager beyond a natural eagerness.

"I'm afraid I don't know much about such things," I told him. "The town is rough enough; I'll be the first man to admit to that. But I go my own way and folks like me go theirs and we stay out of trouble."

"But what about Hardin?"

"I'm afraid I don't know about that either, young man," I said. "Though I do believe someone said he was in Kansas now."

The young man's face showed a keen and heartfelt disappointment.

"Oh," he said and sank back a little.

He looked up suddenly. "But there are pistolmen there," he said, *"dangerous* men?"

I looked at him for a moment, wishing, somehow, that I had kept to my paper and not let the garrulity of age get the better of me. "There are such men," I said stiffly, "wherever you look in our ravaged South."

"Is there a sheriff in Grantville?" the young man asked me then.

"There is," I said—but for some reason did not add that Sheriff Cleat was hardly more than a figurehead, a man who feared his own shadow and kept his appointment only because the county fathers were too far away to come and see for themselves what a futile job their appointee was doing.

I didn't tell the young man that. Vaguely uneasy, I told him nothing more at all and we were separated by silence again, me to my thoughts, he to his—whatever strange, twisted thoughts they were. He looked at his bag and fingered at the handle, and his narrow chest rose and fell with sudden lurches.

A creaking, a rattling, a blurred spinning of thick spokes. A shouting, a deafening clatter of hoofs in the dust. Over the far rise, the buildings of Grantville were clustered and waiting.

A young man was coming to town.

Grantville in the postwar period was typical of those Texas towns that struggled in the limbo between lawlessness and settlement. Into its dusty streets rode men tense with the anger of defeat. The very air seemed charged with their bitter resentments—resentments toward the occupying forces, toward the rabble-rousing carpetbaggers and, with that warped evaluation of the angry man, toward themselves and their own kind. Threatening death was everywhere, and the dust was often red with blood. In such a town I sold food to men who often died before their stomachs could digest it.

I did not see the young man for hours after Jeb braked up the stage before the Blue Buck Hotel. I saw him move across the ground and up the hotel porch steps, holding tightly to his two bags.

Then some old friends greeted me and I forgot him.

I chatted for a while and then I walked by the store. Things there were in good order. I commended Merton Winthrop, the young man I had entrusted the store to in my three weeks' absence, and then I went home, cleaned up, and put on fresh clothes.

I judge it was near four that afternoon when I pushed through the batwings of the Nellie Gold Saloon. I am not nor ever was a heavy drinking man, but I'd had for several years the pleasurable habit of sitting in the cool shadows of a corner table with a whiskey drink to sip. It was a way that I'd found for lingering over minutes.

That particular afternoon I had chatted for a while with George P. Shaughnessy, the afternoon bartender, then retired to my usual table to dream a few presupper dreams and listen to the idle buzz of conversations and the click of chips in the back-room poker game.

That was where I was when the young man entered.

In truth, when he first came in, I didn't recognize him. For what a strange, incredible altering in his dress and carriage! The city clothes were gone; instead of a flannel coat he wore a broadcloth shirt, pearl-buttoned; in place of flannel trousers there were dark, tight-fitting trousers whose calves plunged into glossy, high-heeled boots. On his head a broad-brimmed hat cast a shadow across his grimly set features.

His boot heels had clumped him almost to the bar before I recognized him, before I grew suddenly aware of what he had been keeping so guardedly in that small black bag.

Crossed on his narrow waist, riding low, a brace of gunbelts hung, sagging with the weight of two Colt .44s in their holsters.

I confess to staring at the transformation. Few men in Grantville wore two pistols, much less slender young city men just arrived in town.

In my mind, I heard again the questions he had put to me. I had to set my glass down for the sudden, unaccountable shaking of my hand.

The other customers of the Nellie Gold looked only briefly at the young man, then returned to their several attentions. George P. Shaughnessy looked up, smiling, gave the customary unnecessary wipe across the immaculate mahogany of the bar top, and asked the young man's pleasure.

"Whiskey," the young man said.

"Any special kind, now?" George asked.

"Any kind," the young man said, thumbing back his hat with studied carelessness.

It was when the amber fluid was almost to the glass top that the young man asked the question I had somehow known he would ask from the moment I had recognized him.

"Tell me, who's the quickest pistolman in town?"

George looked up. "I beg your pardon, mister?"

The young man repeated the question, his face emotionless.

"Now, what does a fine young fellow like you want to know that for?" George asked him in a fatherly way.

It was like the tightening of hide across a drum top the way the skin grew taut across the young man's cheeks.

"I asked you a question," he said with unpleasant flatness. "Answer it."

The two closest customers cut off their talking to observe. I felt my hands grow cold upon the table top. There was ruthlessness in the young man's voice.

But George's face still retained the bantering cast it almost always had.

"Are you going to answer my question?" the young man said, drawing back his hands and tensing them with light suggestiveness along the bar edge.

"What's your name, son?" George asked.

The young man's mouth grew hard and his eyes went cold beneath the shadowing brim of his hat. Then a calculating smile played thinly on his lips. "My name is Riker," he said as if somehow he expected this unknown name to strike terror into all our hearts.

"Well, young Mr. Riker, may I ask you why you want to know about the quickest pistolman in town?"

"Who *is* it?" There was no smile on Riker's lips now; it had faded quickly into that grim, unyielding line again. In back I noticed one of the three poker players peering across the top of half-doors into the main saloon.

"Well, now," George said, smiling, "there's Sheriff Cleat. I'd say that he's about—"

His face went slack. A pistol was pointing at his chest.

"Don't tell me lies," young Riker said in tightly restrained anger. "I know your sheriff is a yellow dog; a man at the hotel told me so. I want the *truth.*"

He emphasized the word again with a sudden thumbing back of hammer. George's face went white.

"Mr. Riker, you're making a very bad mistake," he said, then twitched back as the long pistol barrel jabbed into his chest.

Riker's mouth was twisted with fury. "Are you going to *tell* me?" he raged. His young voice cracked in the middle of the sentence like an adolescent's.

"Selkirk," George said quickly.

The young man drew back his pistol, another smile trembling for a moment on his lips. He threw across a nervous glance at where I sat but did not recognize me. Then his cold blue eyes were on George again.

"Selkirk," he repeated. "What's the first name?"

"Barth," George told him, his voice having neither anger nor fear.

"Barth Selkirk." The young man spoke the name as though to fix it in his mind. Then he leaned forward quickly, his nostrils flaring, the thin line of his mouth once more grown rigid.

"You tell him I want to kill him," he said. "Tell him I—" He swallowed hastily and jammed his lips together. "Tonight," he said then. "Right here. At eight o'clock." He shoved out the pistol barrel again. "You *tell* him," he commanded.

George said nothing and Riker backed away from the bar, glancing over his shoulder once to see where the doors were. As he retreated, the high heel of his right boot gave a little inward and he almost fell. As he staggered for balance, his pistol barrel pointed restlessly around the room, and in the rising color of his face, his eyes looked with nervous apprehension into every dark corner.

Then he was at the doors again, his chest rising and falling rapidly. Before our blinking eyes, the pistol seemed to leap back into its holster. Young Riker smiled uncertainly, obviously desperate to convey the impression that he was in full command of the moment.

"Tell him I don't like him," he said as if he were tossing out a casual reason for his intention to kill Selkirk. He swallowed again, lowering his chin a trifle to hide the movement of his throat.

"Tell him he's a dirty rebel," he said in a breathless-sounding voice. "Tell him—tell him I'm a Yankee and I *hate* all rebels!"

For another moment he stood before us in wavering defiance. Then suddenly he was gone.

George broke the spell. We heard the clink of glass on glass as he poured himself a drink. We watched him swallow it in a single gulp. "Young fool," he muttered.

I got up and went over to him.

"How do you like *that?*" he asked me, gesturing one big hand in the general direction of the doors.

"What are you going to do?" I asked him, conscious of the two men now sauntering with affected carelessness for the doors.

"What am I *supposed* to do?" George asked me. "Tell Selkirk, I guess."

I told George about my talk with young Riker and of his strange transformation from city boy to, apparently, self-appointed pistol killer.

"Well," George said when I was finished talking, "where does that leave me? I can't have a young idiot like that angry with me. Do you know his triggers were filed to a hair? Did you see the way he slung that Colt?" He shook his head. "He's a fool," he said. "But a dangerous fool—one that a man can't let himself take chances with."

"Don't tell Selkirk," I said. "I'll go to the sheriff and—"

George waved an open palm at me. "Don't joke now, John," he said. "You know Cleat hides his head under the pillow when there's a shooting in the air."

"But this would be a slaughter, George," I said. "Selkirk is a hardened killer, you know that for a fact."

George eyed me curiously. "Why are you concerned about it?" he asked me.

"Because he's a boy," I said. "Because he doesn't know what he's doing."

George shrugged. "The boy came in and asked for it himself, didn't he?" he said. "Besides, even if I say nothing, Selkirk will hear about it, you can be sure of that. Those two who just went out—don't you think *they'll* spread the word?"

A grim smile raised Shaughnessy's lips. "The boy will get his fight," he said. "And may the Lord have mercy on his soul."

George was right. Word of the young stranger's challenge flew about the town as if the wind had blown it. And with the word, the threadbare symbol of our justice, Sheriff Cleat, sought the sanctuary of his house, having either scoffed at all storm warnings or ignored them in his practiced way.

But the storm *was* coming; everyone knew it. The people who had found some reason to bring them to the square—they knew it. The men thronging the Nellie Gold who seemed to have developed a thirst quite out of keeping with their normal desires—they knew it. Death is a fascinating lure to men who can stand aside and watch it operate on someone else.

I stationed myself near the entrance of the Nellie Gold, hoping that I might speak to young Riker, who had been in his hotel room all afternoon, alone.

At seven-thirty, Selkirk and his ruffian friends galloped to the hitching rack, tied up their snorting mounts, and went into the saloon. I heard the greetings offered them and their returning laughs and shouts. They were elated, all of them; that was not hard to see. Things had been dull for them in the past few months. Cleat had offered no resistance, only smiling fatuously to their bullying insults. And, in the absence of any other man willing to draw his pistol on Barth Selkirk, the days had dragged for him and for his gang, who thrived on violence. Gambling and drinking and the company of Grantville's lost women was not enough for these men. It was why they were all bubbling with excited anticipation that night.

While I stood waiting on the wooden sidewalk, endlessly drawing out my pocket watch, I heard the men shouting back and forth among themselves inside the saloon. But the deep, measured voice of Barth Selkirk I did not hear. He did not shout or laugh then or ever. It was why he hovered like a menacing wraith across our town. For he spoke his frightening logic with the thunder of his pistols and all men knew it.

Time was passing. It was the first time in my life that impending death had taken on such immediacy to me. My boys had died a thousand miles from me, falling while, oblivious, I sold flour to the blacksmith's wife. My wife had died slowly, passing in the peace of slumber, without a cry or a sob.

Yet now I was deeply in this fearful moment. Because I had spoken to young Riker, because—yes, I knew it now—he had reminded me of Lew, I now stood shivering in the darkness, my hands clammy in my coat pockets, in my stomach a hardening knot of dread.

And then my watch read eight. I looked up—and I heard his boots clumping on the wood in even, unhurried strides.

I stepped out from the shadows and moved toward him. The people in the square had grown suddenly quiet. I sensed men's eyes on me as I walked toward Riker's approaching form. It was, I knew, the distortion of nerves and darkness, but he seemed taller than before as he walked along with measured steps, his small hands swinging tensely at his sides.

I stopped before him. For a moment, he looked irritably confused. Then that smile that showed no humor flickered on his tightly drawn face.

"It's the grocery man," he said, his voice dry and brittle.

I swallowed the cold tightness in my throat. "Son, you're making a mistake," I said, "a very bad mistake."

"Get out of my way," he told me curtly, his eyes glancing over my shoulder at the saloon.

"Son, *believe* me. Barth Selkirk is too much for you to—"

In the dull glowing of saloon light, the eyes he turned on me were the blue of frozen, lifeless things. My voice broke off, and without another word, I stepped aside to let him pass. When a man sees in another man's eyes the insensible determination that I saw in Riker's, it is best to step aside. There are no words that will affect such men.

A moment more he looked at me and then, squaring his shoulders, he started walking again. He did not stop until he stood before the batwings of the Nellie Gold.

I moved closer, staring at the light and shadows of his face illuminated by the inside lamps. And it seemed as though, for a moment, the mask of relentless cruelty fell from his features to reveal stark terror.

But it was only a moment, and I could not be certain I had really seen it. Abruptly, the eyes caught fire again, the thin mouth tightened, and Riker shoved through the doors with one long stride.

There was silence, utter ringing silence in that room. Even the scuffing of my bootheels sounded very loud as I edged cautiously to the doors.

Then, as I reached them, there was that sudden rustling, thumping, jingling combination of sounds that indicated general withdrawal from the two opposing men.

I looked in carefully.

Riker stood erect, his back to me, looking toward the bar. It now stood deserted save for one man.

Barth Selkirk was a tall man who looked even taller because of the black he wore. His hair was long and blond; it hung in thick ringlets beneath his wide-brimmed hat. He wore his pistol low on his right hip, the butt reversed, the holster thonged tightly to his thigh. His face was long and tanned, his eyes as sky-blue as Riker's, his mouth a motionless line beneath the well-trimmed length of his mustaches.

I had never seen Abilene's Hickock, but the word had always been that Selkirk might have been his twin.

As the two eyed each other, it was as though every watching man in that room had ceased to function, their breaths, frozen, their bodies petrified—only their eyes alive, shifting back and forth from man to man. It might have been a room of statues, so silently did each man stand.

Then I saw Selkirk's broad chest slowly expanding as it filled with air. And as it slowly sank, his deep voice broke the silence with the impact of a hammer blow on glass.

"Well?" he said and let his boot slide off the brass rail and thump down onto the floor.

An instant pause. Then suddenly, a gasping in that room as if one man had gasped instead of all.

For Selkirk's fingers, barely to the butt of his pistol, had turned to stone as he gaped dumbly at the brace of Colts in Riker's hands.

"Why you dirty—" he began—and then his voice was lost in the deafening roar of pistol fire. His body was flung back against the bar edge as if a club had struck him in the chest. He held there for a moment, his face blank with astonishment. Then the second pistol kicked thundering in Riker's hand and Selkirk went down in a twisted heap.

I looked dazedly at Selkirk's still body, staring at the great gush of blood from his torn chest. Then, my eyes were on Riker again as he stood veiled in acrid smoke before the staring men.

I heard him swallow convulsively. "My name is Riker," he said, his voice trembling in spite of efforts to control it. "Remember that. *Riker.*"

He backed off nervously, his left pistol holstered in a blur of movement, his right still pointed toward the crowd of men.

Then he was out of the saloon again, his face contorted with a mixture of fear and exultation as he turned and saw me standing there.

"Did you see it?" he asked me in a shaking voice. "Did you *see* it?"

I looked at him without a word as his head jerked to the side and he looked into the saloon again, his hands plummeting down like shot birds to his pistol butts.

Apparently he saw no menace, for instantly his eyes were back on me again—excited, swollen-pupiled eyes.

"They won't forget me now, will they?" he said and swallowed. "They'll remember my name. They'll be afraid of it."

He started to walk past me, then twitched to the side and leaned, with a sudden weakness, against the saloon wall, his chest heaving with breath, his blue eyes jumping around feverishly. He kept gasping at the air as if he were choking.

He swallowed with difficulty. "Did you *see* it?" he asked me again, as if he were desperate to share his murderous triumph. "He didn't even get to pull his pistols—didn't even get to *pull* them." His lean chest shuddered with turbulent breath. *"That's* how," he gasped, *"that's* how to do it." Another gasp. "I showed them. I showed them all how to do it. I came from the city and I showed them how. I got the best one they had, the *best one.*" His throat moved so quickly it made a dry, clicking sound. "I showed them," he muttered.

He looked around blinking. "Now I'll—"

He looked around with frightened eyes, as if an army of silent killers were encircling him. His face went slack and he forced together his shaking lips.

"Get out of my way," he suddenly ordered and pushed me aside. I turned and watched him walking rapidly toward the hotel, looking at the sides and over his shoulder with quick jerks of his head, his hands half poised at his sides.

I tried to understand young Riker, but I couldn't. He was from the city; that I knew. Some city in the mass of cities had borne him. He had come to Grantville with the deliberate intention of singling out the fastest pistolman and killing him face to face. That made no sense to me. That seemed a purposeless desire.

Now what would he do? He had told me he was only going to be in Grantville for a while. Now that Selkirk was dead, that while was over.

Where would young Riker go next? And would the same scenes repeat themselves in the next town, and the next, and the next after that? The young city man arriving, changing outfits, asking for the most dangerous pistolman, meeting him—was that how it was going to be in every town? How long could such insanity last? How long before he met a man who would not lose the draw?

My mind was filled with these questions. But, over all, the single question—*Why?* Why was he doing this thing? What calculating madness had driven him from the city to seek out death in this strange land?

While I stood there wondering, Barth Selkirk's men carried out the blood-soaked body of their slain god and laid him carefully across his horse. I was so close to them that I could see his blond hair ruffling slowly in the night wind and hear his life's blood spattering on the darkness of the street.

Then I saw the six men looking toward the Blue Buck Hotel, their eyes glinting vengefully in the light, from the Nellie Gold, and I heard their voices talking low. No words came clear to me as they murmured among themselves, but from the way they kept looking toward the hotel I knew of what they spoke.

I drew back into the shadows again, thinking they might see me and carry their conversation elsewhere. I stood in the blackness watching. Somehow I knew exactly what they intended even before one of their shadowy group slapped a palm against his pistol butt and said distinctly, *"Come on."*

I saw them move away slowly, the six of them, their voices suddenly stilled, their eyes directed at the hotel they were walking toward.

Foolishness again; it is an old man's trademark. For, suddenly, I found myself stepping from the shadows and turning the corner of the saloon, then running down the alley between the Nellie Gold and Pike's Saddlery; rushing through the squares of light made by the saloon windows, then into darkness again. I had no idea why I was running. I seemed driven by an unseen force which clutched all reason from my mind but one thought—*warn him*.

My breath was quickly lost. I felt my coattails flapping like furious bird wings against my legs. Each thudding bootfall drove a mail-gloved fist against my heart.

I don't know how I beat them there, except that they were walking cautiously while I ran headlong along St. Vera Street and hurried in the backway of the hotel. I rushed down the silent hallway, my bootheels thumping along the frayed rug.

Maxwell Tarrant was at the desk that night. He looked up with a start as I came running up to him.

"Why, Mr. Callaway," he said, "what are—?"

"Which room is Riker in?" I gasped.

"Riker?" young Tarrant asked me.

"Quickly, boy!" I cried and cast a frightened glance toward the entranceway as the jar of bootheels sounded on the porch steps.

"Room 27," young Tarrant said. I begged him to stall the men who were coming in for Riker, and rushed for the stairs.

I was barely to the second floor when I heard them in the lobby. I ran down the dimlit hall, and reaching Room 27, I rapped urgently on its thin door.

Inside, I heard a rustling sound, the sound of stockinged feet padding on the floor, then Riker's frail, trembling voice asking who it was.

"It's Callaway," I said, "the grocery man. Let me in, quickly. You're in danger."

"Get out of here," he ordered me, his voice sounding thinner yet.

"God help you, boy, prepare yourself," I told him breathlessly. "Selkirk's men are coming for you."

I heard his sharp, involuntary gasp. *"No,"* he said. "That isn't—" He drew in a rasping breath. "How *many?"* he asked me hollowly.

"Six," I said, and on the other side of the door I thought I heard a sob.

"That isn't fair!" he burst out then in angry fright. "It's not fair, six against one. It isn't *fair!"*

I stood there for another moment, staring at the door, imagining that twisted young man on the other side, sick with terror, his heart jolting like club beats in his chest, able to think of nothing but a moral quality those six men never knew.

"What am I going to *do?"* he suddenly implored me.

I had no answer. For, suddenly, I heard the thumping of their boots as they started up the stairs, and helpless in my age, I backed quickly from the door and scuttled, like the frightened thing I was, down the hall into the shadows there.

Like a dream it was, seeing those six grim-faced men come moving down the hall with a heavy trudging of boots, a thin jingling of spur rowels, in each of their hands a long Colt pistol. No, like a nightmare, not a dream. Knowing that these living creatures were headed for the room in which young Riker waited, I felt something sinking in my stomach, something cold and wrenching at my insides. Helpless I was; I never knew such helplessness. For no seeming reason, I suddenly saw my Lew inside that room, waiting to be killed. It made me tremble without the strength to stop.

Their boots halted. The six men ringed the door, three on one side, three on the other. Six young men, their faces tight with unyielding intention, their hands bloodless, so tightly did they hold their pistols.

The silence broke. "Come out of that room, you Yankee bastard!" one of them said loudly. He was Thomas Ashwood, a boy I'd once seen playing children's games in the streets of Grantville, a boy who had grown into the twisted man who now stood, gun in hand, all thoughts driven from his mind but thoughts of killing and revenge.

Silence for a moment.

"I said, *come out!*" Ashwood cried again, then jerked his body to the side as the hotel seemed to tremble with a deafening blast and one of the door panels exploded into jagged splinters.

As the slug gouged into papered plaster across the hall, Ashwood fired his pistol twice into the door lock, the double flash of light splashing up his cheeks like lightning. My ears rang with the explosions as they echoed up and down the hall.

Another pistol shot roared inside the room. Ashwood kicked in the lock-splintered door and leaped out of my sight. The ear-shattering exchange of shots seemed to pin me to the wall.

Then, in a sudden silence, I heard young Riker cry out in a pitiful voice, "Don't shoot me any more!"

The next explosion hit me like a man's boot kicking at my stomach. I twisted back against the wall, my breath silenced, as I watched the other men run into the room and heard the crashing of their pistol fire.

It was over—all of it—in less than a minute. While I leaned weakly against the wall, hardly able to stand, my throat dry and tight, I saw two of Selkirk's men help the wounded Ashwood down the hall, the other three walking behind, murmuring excitedly among themselves. One of them said, "We got him good."

In a moment, the sound of their boots was gone and I stood alone in the empty hallway, staring blankly at the mist of powder smoke that drifted slowly from the open room.

I do not remember how long I stood there, my stomach a grinding twist of sickness, my hands trembling and cold at my sides.

Only when young Tarrant appeared, white-faced and frightened at the head of the steps, did I find the strength to shuffle down the hall to Riker's room.

We found him lying in his blood, his pain-shocked eyes staring sightlessly at the ceiling, the two pistols still smoking in his rigid hands.

He was dressed in checkered flannel again, in white shirt and dark stockings. It was grotesque to see him lying there that way, his city clothes covered with blood, those long pistols in his still, white hands.

"Oh, God," young Tarrant said in a shocked whisper. "Why did they kill him?"

I shook my head and said nothing. I told young Tarrant to get the undertaker and said I would pay the costs. He was glad to leave.

I sat down on the bed, feeling very tired. I looked into young Riker's open bag and saw, inside, the shirts and underclothes, the ties and stockings.

It was in the bag I found the clippings and the diary.

The clippings were from Northern magazines and newspapers. They were about Hickok and Longley and Hardin and other famous pistol fighters of our territory. There were pencil marks drawn beneath certain sentences—such as *Wild Bill usually carries two derringers beneath his coat* and *Many a man has lost his life because of Hardin's so-called "border roll" trick.*

The diary completed the picture. It told of a twisted mind holding up as idols those men whose only talent was to kill. It told of a young city boy who bought himself pistols and practiced drawing them from their holsters until he was incredibly quick, until his drawing speed became coupled with an ability to strike any target instantly.

It told of a projected odyssey in which a city boy would make himself the most famous pistol fighter in the Southwest. It listed towns that this young man had meant to conquer.

Grantville was the first town on the list.

UTAH

MEEK-AS-A-MOUSE McCABE
by Thomas Walsh

IT WAS ABOUT half-past two that afternoon when McCabe—Detective Franklin Delano McCabe, the night law student—got off the plane at the Salt Lake City Airport. An inexpensive rented sedan was waiting for him, as arranged by Inspector Malachi Hanrahan back in New York, and by a quarter to three Detective McCabe—wrinkled seersucker suit, thin serious face, hornrimmed reading glasses—closed Wiegmore on Torts, returned to his battered old suitcases his copy of Prosser on Evidence, and drove to the big interstate highway, heading west and south out of the city. Three hours later, and a hundred and fifty miles farther on, he entered the small town of Jenkins Grove, and turned off the highway at a sign that read: *Mountainview Crest—Reasonable Rates—Free Continental Breakfast—Mrs. Herbert R. Palmer, Prop.*

There was just the highway in front and a dozen or so neat-looking but rather old cabins. But the parking area was marked off trimly in white paint, and scattered about were attractive paintings of undersized cacti; and the young lady behind the desk appeared crisply businesslike in a simple white dress, a narrow black belt, and a glittering Navaho necklace.

"Sounds pretty good to me," Detective McCabe assured her, after being informed as to the rates in effect, the continental breakfast, and the available cabins—and, of course, after taking for himself a covert but sharp-eyed professional scrutiny. Very white teeth, the scrutiny informed him, complexion a rich ruddy gold from the desert sun, and manner as friendly and comfortable as Policewoman Gloria Fanning's was queenly, elegant, and altogether untouchable. "Now I might be around here for a week or two, because I'm trying to open up some territory for Johnson and Jones, the candy people. You ever try one of their Happy Holesome Nut Bars? It's our newest item and I can tell you it's the best."

But an inner door was jerked open then and a young girl of fifteen or so stamped out of it with an expression of fury on her face, and addressed the older girl in a hating and sullen manner, even with Detective McCabe present.

"Well, I don't care," she said as if continuing an argument that had been going on for some time. "I'm still going, Peggy Palmer, because I promised I would, so there. And why can't I? I simply defy you to give me one sensible reason, just one! Why can't I?"

So it's Peggy Palmer, Detective McCabe told himself. Fine, that settled one point anyway. The young lady in the white dress was second oldest in the Palmer family, the one left in charge here and the one next in line to her older sister back east—Mrs. John A. Knowlton, the well-known photographer's model of two years ago, but now the beautiful and bereaved widow. Knockouts, all the girls, even the kid. No wonder Malachi Hanrahan had called on Detective McCabe to handle this thing. Who else could he trust?

"Now I've told you before," Peggy Palmer said, while Detective McCabe stood unobtrusively to one side with his free gift box of Happy Holesome Nut Bars. "Mother left me in full charge here, and I'll have you over my knee in two seconds, big as you are, if you keep defying me like this. You just march straight back to your room, Miss Pert, because I happen to know all about this hayride you're talking about, and before I—"

Her eyes filled, her voice wobbled. But of course, Detective McCabe told himself, she was feeling the strain. She was old enough to understand the predicament her sister was in back East, if the kid did not. So—

She came around to him from the reservation desk.

"This way." She made an obvious effort to regain control over herself. "Just follow me, Mr. McCabe. I'll show you the cabins we have."

And Detective McCabe did as requested, feeling that he had been given a rather illuminating introduction to the discipline in effect around here, the taboos and the restrictions. An hour later, safely installed as the newest resident of Cabin 7 at Mountainview Crest, he reported from a drugstore telephone to Malachi Hanrahan back in New York.

"Can't help feeling that maybe you got the wrong slant on this family," Franklin Delano told him. "The kid was only about fifteen, I'd say, so this Peggy sure put her foot down good and hard. Really used her head, I'd say."

"And apparently turned yours," Malachi growled at him. "Now you know I have the mother here with me defending and protecting her darling oldest, which gave us the chance, all on the Q.T., to find out just what kind of an establishment they're running out there. So keep your wits about you, Franklin. I don't doubt they're all fetching hussies, the lot of them—which is why I picked you for the job. You see the point, I suppose. Who else could I trust around them?"

"Yeah," Detective McCabe said, with quiet bitterness. "Right, Inspector. Steady and reliable McCabe, wasn't it? I'm not cut out for the great lover, am I? I make people laugh sometimes. I ought to feel complimented if a decent and respectable girl even looks at me."

"Ah, not at all, not at all, laddie," Malachi comforted him, much too offhand and casual about it. "Talk sense. You've got to understand that we're up against a pretty tough proposition here. Maybe this Mrs. Knowlton killed her husband by knocking him down that flight of steps in their house out on Long Island last week or maybe she didn't. We don't know yet, which is why we're only questioning her so far. But we do know that they hadn't been getting on together for some time, or even living together. And so far we haven't been able to prove that she even visited him at the house that night.

"So the way it appears now, Franklin, or else was made to appear, is that some prowler broke in and assaulted him. But if there is something else back of it—well, I've got to know about the wife, don't you see? She met up with a good piece of hard cash when she met up with Knowlton two years ago. And then she married him just three days later, which to my mind is always a damned suspicious thing. Do you wonder why I want to find out a little more about the woman, and what kind of a family she comes from?

"So the way it appears now, Franklin, is that some prowler broke into the place and assaulted him. But the truth is something else, laddie. Well, how about the beautiful and bereaved widow having something to do with it? Now we find out that she has two sisters, and a just too-sweet-to-be-true old mother, all of whom make a living for themselves by renting out rooms for the night to all comers. Well, maybe I'm just a bit old-fashioned about some matters. Very probably I am. But what I was expecting you to find out for me, and damned quick, was the character of the family, their standing in the community, and their general background.

"So don't trust to your own impression of them, because I don't doubt that they've all got the same delicate ways as the old lady, the same slim and appealing figure, and the same Jezebel cunning. Now tell me the truth, Franklin, own up and admit the thing. Did you get even the least hint today that the pretty Peggy was deliberately setting herself out to beguile and bewitch you?"

Something happened at that moment in Detective McCabe, the night law student. Sudden and uncontrollable venom flashed out of him in half an instant.

"Well, I can tell you this much," he announced breathlessly. "Everybody knows I'm meek-as-a-mouse Detective McCabe, the kind of man who's afraid even to look at a girl. But when I walked in there tonight and found this one looking up at me from the desk, I didn't feel exactly eighty-five years old, for some reason. All she had to do was to give me that one look, and ever since I've been—"

"Eh?" Inspector Hanrahan put in, his voice rising excitedly. "What are you talking about? I thought everything has been settled for three years between you and the Fanning woman. It's well known. You never look at another girl. You never even had one. You're steady, level-headed, devoted, hard-working, and ambitious. Now is that the fact, Franklin, or isn't it?"

But Detective McCabe could not say just then. In fact, ever since the preceding night when a kind of midsummer madness had come over him on Gloria's living-room couch, nothing had made very much sense to him. He had begun nuzzling her gently and tenderly around the fringes of an expensive new hairdo, and even after three years had got his face smacked.

"Say, you just listen here," Gloria had told him angrily. "You better watch yourself. Look at what you've done to my new blouse, and my sixty-five-dollar hairdo. I like the nerve. Are you crazy or something?"

Detective McCabe, at that moment, had to grin crookedly. Yup, he told himself, after three years of going steady.

"Now don't play any of your games with the old man," Malachi ordered him. "Get hold of yourself now, brace up. Put that young hussy out of your thoughts and keep her out. You brought your law books along, didn't you?"

"Oh, yes," Detective McCabe admitted grimly. "You know I did. I suppose you were even counting on it, with a dumbhead like me."

"Ah, not at all, not at all," Malachi soothed him, "and remember this, laddie. You have the old man depending on you. So don't let him down, remember. You wouldn't, would you?"

Obviously not, Detective McCabe decided reluctantly. Unthinkable! He couldn't let Gloria Fanning down either, because three years ago, when plighting his troth, certain promises had been made by him. First, he would secure his law degree. Second, he would save up the sum of $10,000 in hard cash, for a down payment on a new house he would buy her out on the island. And then, but only then, the possibility of marriage. And meanwhile, not even the thought of any— well, silliness between them.

She knew how to control herself, and he'd better learn, instead of complaining about a little honest affection from her. He would have to admit that she never went on in that whining and immature way, so why should he? But Detective McCabe hadn't known the answer to that either—not unless he wanted something from Gloria Fanning that she didn't want from him, and had never even considered, apparently.

Those were the thoughts that kept nagging at him all that evening in Cabin 7 at Mountainview Crest, despite another of his long, doggedly intense sessions with Wiegmore on Torts, and Prosser on Evidence. But in the end the only conclusion he came to was that Gloria Fanning didn't mind much waiting for him until the year 2596, if conditions required it. But what did that mean? That the true spark wasn't there for him, and never had been? Suddenly he got up, slung Prosser across the room, hit it with Wiegmore, and then opened the front door.

Light splashed a foreshortened yellow triangle on the paved driveway, and a full moon gazed down placidly from the heavens. He made one step out from his tiny porch, inhaling deeply.

"Mr. McCabe," he heard someone entreating him the next instant, and in what seemed like blind panic. "Oh, please! Mr. McCabe."

He turned his head quickly and saw a big convertible, lights off, parked in front of the business office, with Peggy Palmer and a young man standing beside it and apparently wrestling. Everybody but him, Detective McCabe thought suddenly and passionately; everybody in the whole world. His fists clenched.

"Now you people break that up," he commanded, that order coming out of him with his still remembered curtness, authority, and decision. "What's going on here, anyway? What's the problem?"

The girl tore herself free and ran toward him, the owner of the convertible following. Detective McCabe moved straight for him, crazy elation flooding over him. Now, at long last, he felt that someone was going to pay for what he'd had to accept and endure for three long years with Policewoman Fanning; that perhaps now, if the Gods had any justice at all, someone might just be stupid enough to walk right up to Franklin in his present mood, threaten physical force, and practically ask for it.

And someone did. The other man rushed head-on at him, swung viciously with his right arm, and swung again. But Detective McCabe, who had mastered many arts in his precise and methodical manner, stepped into him with a left hook, bent him in half with a short vicious right cross, then heaved him, heels over teakettle back up the steering wheel. It took no more than the proper physical fitness, the right emotional attitude, and some three and a half seconds.

"Oh, sweet mercy of heaven," the girl whispered. "Stop this, stop this at once, Mr. McCabe. Someone will hear us."

She was perfectly correct in making that statement. The lights came on over in Cabin 5, and a short middle-aged man in baggy yellow pajamas glared out at them. The man in the convertible, still trying to catch his breath, nodded savagely but just once at Detective McCabe—another time, buddy, this ain't finished between us yet—and spun the convertible so fast that gravel splattered.

Miss Peggy Palmer, meantime, backed off toward the business office, and Detective McCabe noticed, for the first time, that she wore nothing at all but white slippers, Chinese pajamas, and a night robe. The robe was torn.

"But what happened?" she demanded, holding her robe together, and looking in a bewildered way after the convertible. "Why, that was Bud Grant, Mr. McCabe. He's always getting into fights with people. But he's always winning them. He's one of those small-town toughs who just—oh, Mr. McCabe, you were just wonderful. Did he hurt you?"

But Detective McCabe was hurriedly locating and donning the hornrimmed eyeglasses. He was appalled at himself, and even more appalled at what Malachi would have had to say about a dead giveaway of this nature.

"Why, I don't think so," he said. "It all happened too fast. You know that fellow?"

She adjusted the robe and her brown hair. It was all tousled.

"I've laughed at that man," she declared angrily. "I've insulted him. I've ordered him never even to talk to me on the street. Oh, I know what you think, Mr. McCabe, what you'd have to think at this hour. He rang the night bell five minutes ago, and I threw my robe on naturally and came out, thinking it was a late customer, and it was that man pestering me again, the way he does time after time. That's how it was, and that's all it was, Mr. McCabe."

"No need to explain," Detective McCabe said. "No need at all, Miss Palmer."

"And you still don't believe me," she said, throwing out one arm in a helplessly distracted gesture. "Oh, what can I do? I'm at the end of my rope, Mr. McCabe. Mama not here and my older sister Loretta in all that trouble back East, and that darned kid fighting with me every day in the week. Then that creature to come out here tonight, and give you the idea—"

She broke down. She started to make a blind headlong rush back to the business office, but tripped over a crack in the walk, and there was nothing for Franklin to do but pick her up. Then the brown hair brushed his lips; he felt the warmth of her slim golden arms under his fingers; and he sensed just one instant of accidental but almost overpowering closeness between himself and the Chinese pajamas. It was a closeness he had never been permitted to feel, or even to dream about, with Gloria Fanning. It seemed the promise, under the pale wisp of Utah moon high in the heavens, of a fabulous and enchanting secret in this girl, a secret preserved until this moment for no one but McCabe. The breeze whispered about it; the desert murmured even more softly back in the shadows; and he got the absurd notion that any second now the whole sky full of dim, heavy-looking Utah stars, was going to explode crazily away from him, to all quarters.

"Sometimes you don't even know why you're alive," she faltered, her breath touching him. "Oh, what's the point of it all, Mr. McCabe? What's the sense?"

But that was it, Detective McCabe thought. What was? If all you meant to a girl was $10,000 in cash, and a law degree, and if she could turn on you like an outraged and indignant Amazon because you dared touch that sixty-five-dollar hairdo—

"But you were just splendid," she said, pausing for one last moment in the office doorway. "Just splendid, Mr. McCabe. You handled him like a small boy. I couldn't believe my own eyes. Are you sure he didn't hurt you at all? Let me look."

She drew away, scrutinizing him anxiously—his hair, the line of his jaw, his blue eyes. She stopped on them, perhaps feeling what Detective McCabe felt. For that sudden and miraculous moment her lips widened. They kept looking at each other. That lasted for only about three and a half seconds, also. And yet, even in that brief interim, something having to do with Gloria Fanning ended once and for all in Detective McCabe, and something else began.

"Miss Palmer," he babbled, finally recovering himself. "Don't go in yet, Miss Palmer, please don't. I want to talk to you about something important. Listen."

She flushed, wrapping the robe even more tightly around herself.

"No," she said. "Not—"

"Well, I never," the man in Cabin 5 said. He slammed his door, and a moment after, Miss Palmer, still blushing, slammed hers.

"But I've told you," Detective McCabe declared, and declared angrily—in the same phone booth as the night before, in the same drugstore, and to the same Malachi Hanrahan talking to him. "Everybody respects them out here. They go to service every Sunday morning. They cook for all the church suppers. They're as upright and decent a family—"

"Now is that so?" Inspector Hanrahan demanded even more sharply. "Then how does it happen that we've got hold of a new witness back here, and he's almost ready to identify the Knowlton woman as the one he saw riding with him on the night train out of Southampton the night of the murder? Church suppers, is it? Well, I'll church-supper you. Keep on defending those people the way you are, and I'll have you back pounding a beat the minute you get off the plane back here at LaGuardia. So pay attention to that now, and get me the information I need. Just do as you're told!"

And after that there wasn't any possible help for it. But all the way down the line Peggy Palmer and family checked out one hundred percent, and later on in the day, when he got back to Mountainview Crest, the kid Mary Alice hovered excitedly around him, wanting to hear the whole story about Bud Grant last night, and running to fetch Franklin Delano a cold drink, a package of cigarettes, and the evening paper.

"Peggy likes you a lot, Mr. McCabe, and so do I. Are you married?"

Then Peggy herself appeared, and they sat out on the bench in front waiting for customers. And that evening there was a cookout supper of frankfurters and baked beans—homemade baked beans, the best Franklin Delano every remembered. Mary Alice was sent back to look after the office at eight o'clock. There was a yellow dress that time, with a yoked collar and white cuffs, and never could Franklin Delano remember anything half so fetching as a jade bracelet on a slim wrist, or as brown eyes meeting his every now and again with a shy, oddly helpless expression in them. It made his heart ache. But also, finally, it made him open the conversation with all the cunning duplicity of one of Malachi Hanrahan's brightest and most promising young men.

"Knew a fellow," he announced, while Miss Palmer poured another cup of coffee for him and passed the sugar. "Fellow that goes to night law school, old buddy of mine. Wants to get married, though, only this girl he has wouldn't even think of it. What she claims is that if they got married now it would only give him a lot of family responsibilities; set him back. Some girl, eh? What would you think?"

"Well," Miss Palmer said, now occupied with piling dishes together, and scraping them off, "I suppose the only question is whether she's the right girl for him, really. Do you think she is?"

"Not in my personal opinion," Detective McCabe said. "Nope, not any more. Only you know how long they've been going around together? Three years now."

"And now he's afraid to break it off with her," Miss Palmer said, scraping the last plate. "Then I'd say they're welcome to what they get, the two of them. Why, any normal girl ought to be able to tell the first minute, actually. She'd just know."

"Would she?" Detective McCabe said. "Right away, you mean? Like the very first time, maybe?"

"Oh, I think so," Miss Palmer said. "With of course the right man, that is."

Dusk shaded the valley below them. They could see the lights to Mountainview Crest and way beyond, on the other side of the valley, the toy cars of a transcontinental express whizzing past for Los Angeles. Every day Detective McCabe had watched it whiz by, and had even noted, with his methodical schoolmaster's habit, that it required exactly thirty-five minutes, even at sixty miles an hour, to pass from one end of the valley to the other. But what was he watching the lights of that train for? Here was the perfect opening for him, and she had offered it.

So—

"Miss Palmer," Detective McCabe said, bracing himself. "Listen I'd like to ask you something. I mean something about the other night. Remember how you looked at me then, and how I looked at you? It was like—like I never saw a girl before in my whole life. And if you felt anything at all like that, I want to know. I think it would be kind of important to me."

"Oh, of course," Miss Palmer said, and laughed softly. "And knew then and there—" She turned her head from him, winking her eyes desperately. "Now you stop this," she said. "Stop it, Mr. McCabe, stop it, stop it, stop it! You've got the idea that I'm pretty cheap and easy, haven't you? That I invited Bud Grant out here the other night, and that if you rush me right off my feet now, and play your cards real smoothly, and carefully—"

"Maybe you didn't have to invite him," another voice broke in from the shadows just behind Detective McCabe, a low hating voice, whisper-soft. "He's here, though, and he's here to take care of Little Miss High Hat personally. No, don't turn, fellow. Just stay right where you are, and watch those hands!"

But Detective McCabe turned, anyway. He saw Bud Grant framed dimly on the other side of the small charcoal grill, all set there. And then he saw Bud Grant fire twice at him through the heavy beach towel wrapped around his right arm. There was not very much noise, but still Detective McCabe staggered sideways, thrust out both hands, and pitched headlong into a panful of dully glowing red embers. He lay motionless there, breathing in low, rapid gasps. His eyes had become fixed, rigid-looking, and wide-open. So had his mouth.

"And you," Bud Grant said, moving around the fire to her. "I'm just a small-town tough, ain't I? I'm not in your class, or your bigshot brother-in-law. I was good enough to drive him down to New York. But when we got there it was another story. Get lost, boy. You're small-town, Bud. Don't bother people, he said. I guess I showed him just how small-time I was, and now I'm going to show you, too. Come here to me! You hear what I'm saying?"

It was pretty difficult, with the right side of your chest caved in, and with the remains of a charcoal fire under you, to wait for the right moment of furious inattention, to get out your service revolver with your left hand, and with no noise, and to bring down Mr. Bud Grant with just one clear and agonizing shot through the left kneecap. Detective McCabe managed it, however. It was necessary. Miss Palmer was depending on him. Then he hobbled to his knees, smashed the other man under the left ear with his service revolver, and then collapsed forward, not caring about anything else at that moment, into blackness, emptiness, and serene peace. . . .

"Well, here's the way I figure the thing," Detective McCabe explained afterward, and again over long distance, from the emergency room of the Cottonwood Grove General Hospital. "This Bud character, just because he drove Knowlton down to Las Vegas a couple of times this summer, and had a pretty high old time with him there, figured they were old drinking buddies. So he drove East with a pal of his, Ted Nolan, and bragged all the way what great friends he and Knowlton were, and how Knowlton would offer him the best in the house. But when they got there, it was not that way at all. Knowlton just brushed him off, or tried to, like a bit of dirt from the street. So Grant socked him, knocked him down that flight of stairs, and cracked his skull open.

"But he was lucky in that part—for the time being, anyway. Knowlton had got into a drunken rage that day and had fired all the servants. So there was no one to tell the police about who had paid a house call the night before. Out here tonight Grant had this fellow Nolan waiting in the car for him, and he admitted the whole thing.

"Then the other night Grant went over to the motel and got fresh with Miss Palmer. Only I walked in on it, and we had a fight, and because I got the better of it he decided to get even with me. I guess he figured to get rid of us by burying us in the woods out here. Oh, he had the whole thing figured all right, and maybe I would have too, if only you let me talk to Miss Palmer about it like I wanted to. But no, I had to work behind her back. I had to get myself nearly killed out here because you—"

"Now, now," Malachi Hanrahan said, not fazed in any way. "Who was it who insisted to you all along that the answer to the whole business had to be right out there in the state of Utah? Just think it over, laddie. You seem to be a little excited, and so is Policewoman Fanning, for that matter. They had to put her on a couch in Charley Molloy's office, because when the first news came in about you, somebody ran out of here shouting that you'd had the whole top of your head blown off. She went off into the whooping hysterics, and she's still yipping and yowling your name like a lost soul. Now will you talk to the woman, or give me a message?"

Detective McCabe was no longer alone, however; he had someone with him. She was adjusting his brand-new white sling gently. He spoke to her, without bothering to put his hand over the mouthpiece.

"I'm still asking you that same question I tried to ask you before," Detective McCabe said, with his heart thumping, and yet tolerably sure that he ought to be just about to home plate by this time, what with the older sister all cleared now, and with Franklin Delano himself the indomitable conquering hero. "Because I want to know the answer to it, and I'm not fooling. What happened the other night outside your office, after I hit that fellow, and you looked at me, and I looked at you? Did you feel something that—well, kind of turned over in you, and turned you all funny? Tell me the truth, Miss Palmer, I got to know. Did you?"

She looked down. She looked up helplessly. She looked away. Then she nodded at him in a rosy and shamefaced manner, tightened her fingers in his, and straightened his collar.

"What?" Malachi Hanrahan said. "You've got to speak up, Franklin, I don't hear you."

"That's all right," Detective McCabe said. "I wasn't talking to you, and there's no message. Just look out for that sixty-five-dollar hairdo, will you? That's really important."

"The what?" Malachi said, sputtering a moment. "Oh, now hold on there, the woman is your responsibility, laddie. What do you expect me or Charley Molloy to do about her?"

"No, she isn't," Detective McCabe said. "Not now. I tried a little shopping around out here, and I think I've done better. So—" An extraordinary elation and buoyancy came over him as his hand tightened. "So I guess there's only one possible suggestion for you. Do nothing about Miss Fanning. Do nothing at all, Inspector. You just let her yip."

Vermont

THE JABBERWOCKY MURDERS
by Fredric Brown

CHAPTER 1
Looking-Glass Shadow

'Twas brillig, and the slithy toves
Did gyre and gimble in the wabe:
All mimsy were the borogoves,
And the mome raths outgrabe.

I TOOK ANOTHER drink out of the bottle on my desk and then typed the last take and handed it to Jerry Klosterman to take over to his linotype. He looked it over.

"About one sentence strong, Doc," he said. "There were fourteen lines to fill."

"Then cut out the part about sullying the fair name of Carmel City," I told him.

He nodded and went over to the machine. I took the last drink and dropped the bottle into the wastebasket. Then I walked over to the window and looked out into the dusk while the mats clicked down the channels of the linotype. Smoothly and evenly. Jerry rarely poked a wrong key.

The lights of Oak Street flashed on while I stood there. Across on the other sidewalk Miles Harrison hesitated in front of Smiley's Inn, as though the thought of a cool glass of beer tempted him. I could almost see his mind work.

"No, I'm a deputy sheriff of Carmel County and I have a job to do yet tonight. The beer can wait."

His conscience won. He walked on. I wonder now whether, if he had known he'd be dead before midnight, he wouldn't have taken that beer. I think he would have. I'd have done it, but that doesn't prove anything, because I'd have taken it anyway. I never had a New England conscience like Miles Harrison.

But of course I wasn't thinking that then, because I didn't know any more than Miles did what was going to happen. I found mild amusement in his hesitation, and that was all.

Jerry called to me from the stone, where he had just dropped in the newly set lines at the bottom of the column.

"She's a line short now, Doc. But I can card it out."

"Lock it up and pull a stone proof," I said. "I'll be in Smiley's. I'll buy you a drink when you bring it over."

I put on my hat and went out.

That's the way it always was on Thursday evenings. The Carmel City Courier is a weekly, and we put it to bed all ready to run on Thursday night. Friday morning the presses roll—or to be more accurate the press, singular, which is a Miehle Vertical, shuttles up and down. And about Friday noon we start to distribute.

Big Smiley Wessen grinned when I came in.

"How's the editing business, Doc?" he said, and laughed as though he'd said something excruciating. Smiley has as much sense of humor as a horse.

"Smiley, you give me a pain," I said. It's safe to tell Smiley the truth. He always thinks you're joking anyway.

He grinned appreciatively. "Old Henderson?"

"Old Henderson it is," I said, and he poured it and I drank it.

He went down to the other end of the bar and I stood there, not thinking about anything. This time Thursday evening always was a letdown. So I just stood there and tried not to see myself in the mirror and didn't succeed.

I could see myself, Doc Bagden, a small man getting gray around the temples and thin on top. Editor of a small-town weekly and, thank goodness, not much chance of ever getting any higher than that. Another twenty—thirty years of that is bleak to look forward to, but anything else is bleaker. Nor a harp at the end of it. I envy some of my fellow townsmen their confidence in harps, for it might be something to wait around for.

I heard a car swing in to the curb out front and, for no reason, blow its klaxon.

"Al Carey," I told myself.

He came in, which was a treat for Smiley's Inn, for Alvin Carey usually went to swankier places in the nearby larger towns. Not that I blamed him for that. He had a spot to fill as the nephew of the town's richest man and naturally he spent as much of his uncle's money as he could get his hands on. Which was pretty much for Carmel City, although it wouldn't have made a splash in New York.

Of course I'd called him a wastrel—not by name—in editorials, because people expected me to. But I liked him, and had a hunch I'd make a worse scion of wealth than Alvin did.

Besides, he read a lot of the right things and had more of an idea of what it was all about than the rest of town.

"Hi, Doc," he said. "Have a drink, and when are we going to have another game of chess?"

"Old Henderson," I told Smiley. "Alvin, my son, I am playing chess now, and so are you. The White Knight is sliding down the poker. He balances very badly."

He grinned. "Then you're still in the second square. Have another drink."

"And there," I said, "it takes all the drinking I can do to stay in the same place. But that won't be for long. From the second square to the fourth, I travel by train, remember?"

"Then don't keep it waiting, Doc. The smoke alone is worth a thousand pounds a puff."

"Old Henderson," I said to Smiley.

Then Al left—he'd just come in for a short snort.

"What the devil were you guys talking about?" asked Smiley.

There wasn't any use trying to explain. "Crawling at your feet you may observe a bread-and-butter-fly," I said. "Its wings are thin slices of bread-and-butter, its body a crust, and its head is a lump of sugar."

"Where?" said Smiley. I don't think he was kidding.

Then Jerry Klosterman appeared with the rolled-up stone proof of the final page. I don't think I ever did get around to telling Smiley what Al and I had been talking about.

It was getting too much trouble to keep track of individual drinks, so I bought the rest of the bottle from Smiley, and got another glass for Jerry.

Then we took the page proof over to a table and spread it out, and I gave it a rapid reading. I marked a few minor errors and one major one—a line in an ad upside down. The ads, if you don't know, are the most important part of a newspaper. And I circled, for my own convenience, all the filler items that could be pulled out in case anything worth mentioning happened in Carmel City during the night. Not that it ever did or that it would tonight. Or so I thought.

"We can catch these in the morning," I told Jerry. "Won't have to go back tonight. Did you lock up?"

He nodded and poured himself another drink.

"There was a phone call for you just after you left," he said.

"Who?"

"Wouldn't give a name. Said it wasn't important."

"That," I said firmly, "is the fallacy of civilized life, so-called, Jerry. Why should things be arbitrarily divided into things that are important and that aren't? How can anyone tell? What is important and what is unimportant?"

Jerry is a printer. "Well, Doc, it's important that we get the paper up, isn't it?" he said. "And unimportant what we do afterward."

"Not at all," I told him. "Just the opposite, in fact. We get the blamed paper out of the way solely so we can do what we please afterward. That's what's important—if anything is."

* * *

Jerry shook his head slowly. "You're really not sure anything is, are you, Doc?" He picked up his drink and stared at it. "How's about death? Isn't that?"

"Somebody you like," I said. "His death can be important to you. But not your own. Jerry, there's one thing sure. If you were to die right now, you'd never live to regret it."

"Poor Doc," he said, downed his drink and stood up. "Well, I'm going home. I suppose you'll get tight, as usual."

"Unless I think of a better idea," I agreed. "And I haven't yet. So long, Jerry."

"So long, Doc."

I stared for a while at the calendar over the bar. It had the kind of picture on it that you usually see on calendars over bars. It was just a bit of bother to keep my eyes focused properly, although I hadn't had enough to drink to affect my mind at all.

One corner of my mind persisted in wondering if I could get Beal Brothers Store to continue running a half-column ad instead of going back to six inches. I tried to squelch the thought by telling myself I didn't care whether anybody advertised in the Courier or not. Or whether the Courier kept on being published. I didn't, much.

The picture on the calendar got on my nerves. "Smiley, there aren't any women like that," I said. "It's a lie. You ought to take it down."

"Women like what? Take what down?"

"Never mind, Smiley," I said. After all, the picture was a dream. Somebody's dream of what something ought to be like.

The air was hot and close, and Smiley was rattling glasses, washing them, back of the bar.

I turned around and looked out the window, and a car with two dead men in it went by. But I didn't know that, although I had a feeling of wide-awareness that should have told me, if there's anything in prescience.

"There goes Barnaby Jones to the bank," I told Smiley. That was all it meant to me.

"The bank?" Smiley answered. "Ain't it closed?"

I looked at him to see whether he was kidding, and then remembered he hadn't any sense of humor. But I thought everyone in town knew about the Barnaby Jones Company payroll. Old man Barnaby's shoe factory was in the next town, but he banked in Carmel City, where he lived, and every first and fifteenth he took the payroll over himself. Two trips, one for the day shift and one for the night shift. Miles Harrison had to strap on a gun and go with Barnaby over to the bank for the money and then guard him on the way.

"The bank opens up any time Barnaby Jones wants it to, Smiley," I explained. "Tonight's payroll."

"Oh," Smiley said, and laughed. I wanted to choke him.

Maybe there was something important, after all, I decided—a sense of humor. That was why I never stayed at Smiley's on Thursday evenings. I always bought a bottle and went home where my bookcase gives me the best company there is.

I bought a bottle and started home with it. It was still fairly early evening, but the streets were dark.

Darker than I thought.

CHAPTER 2
Smell of Blood

Beware the Jabberwock, my son!
The jaws that bite, the claws that catch!
Beware the Jubjub bird, and shun
The frumious Bandersnatch!

Maybe I weaved just a little along the sidewalk, for at this stage I'm never quite as sober as I am later on. But the mind—ah, it was a combination of crystal clarity with fuzziness around the edges. It's hard to explain or define, but that's a state of mind which makes even Carmel City tolerable.

Down Oak Street past the corner drugstore, Pop Hinkle's place, where I used to drink Cokes as a youngster, past Gorham's Feed Store, where I'd worked summers while I was going to college, past the bank, with Barnaby Jones' Packard still standing in front of it, past the Bijou, past Hank Greeber's undertaking parlor—beg pardon—H. Greeber, Mortician, past Bing Crosby-Dorothy Lamour at the Alhambra, with a lot of cars parked in front, and I recognized Alvin Carey's even with the klaxon silent—a big contrast from the sedate black Packard his uncle used, back at the bank—past Deek's music store, where I'd once bought a violin, past the courthouse, with a light still burning in the room I knew was the office of Pete Lane, the sheriff.

I almost turned in there, from force of habit, to see if there was any news. Then I remembered it was Thursday night, and kept on walking.

Out of the store district now, past the house Elsie had lived in and died in, while we were engaged, past the house Elmer Conlin had lived in when I bought the Courier from him—past my whole blasted life, on the way home.

But with a bottle in my pocket and good company waiting for me there, my old tried-and-true friends in the bookcase. Reading a book is almost like listening to the man who wrote it talk. Except that you don't have to be polite. You can take your shoes off and put your feet up on the table and drink and forget who you are.

And forget the newspaper that hung around your neck like a millstone every day and night of the week except this one.

So to the corner of Campbell Street and my turning.

My house ahead, with no lights waiting. But on the porch a shadow moved.

And came forward as I mounted the steps. The dim light from the street lamp back on the corner showed me a strange, pudgy little man. My own height, perhaps, but seeming shorter because of his girth. Light, insufficient to show his features clearly, nevertheless reflected glowing pin-points in his eyes, a cat-like gleam. Yet there was nothing sinister about him. A small, pudgy man is never sinister, no matter where nor when, nor how his eyes look.

"You are Doctor Bagden?" he inquired.

"Doc Bagden," I corrected him. "But not a doctor—of medicine. If you are looking for a doctor, you've got the wrong place."

"No I am aware that you are not a medico, Doctor. Ph.D., Harvard, 1913, I believe. Author of 'Lewis Carroll Through the Looking-Glass,' and 'Red Queen and White Queen.'"

It almost sobered me. Not that he had the right year of my magna cum laude, but the rest of it. The Lewis Carroll thing had been a brochure of a dozen pages, printed eighteen years ago, and not over five hundred copies run off. If one existed anywhere outside my own library, it was a surprise to me. And the "Red Queen and White Queen" article had appeared at least ten years ago in an obscure magazine long discontinued and forgotten.

"Why, yes," I said. "What can I do for you, Mr.—?"

"Smith," he said gravely, and then chuckled. "And the first name is Yehudi."

"No!" I said.

"Yes. You see, Doctor Bagden, I was named forty years ago when the name Yehudi, although uncommon, did not connote what it connotes today. My parents were not psychic, you see. Had they guessed the difficulty I might have in convincing people that I am not spoofing them when I tell them my given name—" He laughed ruefully. "I always carry cards."

He handed me one. It read:

YEHUDI SMITH

There was no address. Absently, I stuck it in my pocket.

"There's Yehudi Menuhin, the violinist, you know," he said. "And there's—"

"Stop, please," I said, "you're making it plausible. I liked it better the other way."

He smiled. "I have not misjudged you then. Have you ever heard of the Vorpal Blades?"

"Plural? No. Of course in Jabberwocky—in 'Alice Through the Looking-Glass,' there's a line about a—Great Scott! Why are we talking about vorpal blades on my front porch? Come on in. I have a bottle, and I presume it would be superfluous to ask a man who talks about vorpal blades whether he drinks."

I unlocked the front door and stepped in first to light the hall light. Then I ushered him back to my den. I swept the litter off the table—it's the one room my housekeeper, who comes in for a few hours every day—is forbidden to clean, and I brought glasses and filled them.

"Take that chair," I said. "This is the one I drink in. And now, Mr. Smith—to Lewis Carroll."

He raised his glass.

"To Charles Lutwidge Dodgson, known as Lewis Carroll when in Wonderland," he said.

We put down our glasses empty, and I filled them. I was more than glad I'd brought home a quart. There was a warm glow in my body—the glow I'd lost on the long walk home.

"And now," I said, "what of vorpal blades?"

"It's an organization, Doctor. A very small one, but just possibly a very important one. The Vorpal Blades."

"Admirers of Lewis Carroll, I take it?"

"Well, yes, but—" His voice became cautious. "—much more than that. I feel that I should tell you something. It's dangerous. I mean, really dangerous."

"That," I said, "is marvelous. Wonderful. Go on."

He didn't. He sat there and toyed with his glass a while and didn't look at me. I studied his face. It was an interesting face, and there were deep laughter-lines around his eyes and his mouth. He wasn't quite as young as I thought he was. One would have to laugh a long time to etch lines like those.

But he wasn't laughing now. He looked dead serious, and if he was faking, he was good. He looked serious, and he didn't look crazy. But he said something strange.

"You've studied Dodgson's fantasies thoroughly, Doctor. I've read your articles on them. Has it ever occurred to you that—that maybe they aren't fantasies?"

I nodded. "You mean symbolically, of course. Yes, fantasy is often closer to fundamental truth than fact."

"I don't mean that, Doctor. I mean—we think that Charles Dodgson had knowledge of another world and creatures of that world, and had entry into it, somehow. We think—"

The phone rang. Impatiently, I went out into the hall and answered it.

"Bagden speaking," I said.

"This is Evers, Doc. You sober?"

"Why?" I asked.

"You offered to sell me the Courier last week. I've been thinking it over. Seriously."

"I'll talk it over with you tomorrow, Evers," I told him. "Tonight I'm busy. I have a guest, and anyway if I talked to you tonight, I'd be tempted to sell the Courier for fifteen cents."

"And tomorrow?"

"At least twenty cents. Providing you take over the debts. But I can't talk now, honestly. I got to see a man about a Jabberwock."

"You are drunk, Doc."

"Not yet, and you're keeping me from it. 'Night."

I put the receiver back on the hook and went back to the den. I poured two more drinks before I sat down.

"Let's get one thing straight," I said. "Is this a roundabout way of selling me an insurance policy or something?"

"I assure you I have nothing to sell. Nor am I crazy, I hope. If I am, I have company. There are several of us, and we have checked our findings very thoroughly. One of us—" He paused with dramatic effect. "—checked them too thoroughly, without taking proper precautions. That is why there is a vacancy in our small group."

"You mean—what?"

He pulled a wallet from his pocket and from an inner compartment took a newspaper clipping, a short one of about four paragraphs. He handed it to me. I read it, and I recognized the type and the set-up, a clipping from the Bridgeport Argus. And I remembered now having read it, a few days ago. I'd considered clipping it as an exchange item, and then decided not to. The heading read as follows:

MAN SLAIN BY UNKNOWN BEAST

It had caught my eye and interest. The rest of the article brought matters down to prosaic facts.

A man named Colin Hawks, a recluse, had been found dead along a path through the woods. The man's throat had been torn, and police opinion was that a large and vicious dog had attacked him. But the reporter who wrote the article suggested the possibility that only a wolf or possibly even a lion or panther, escaped from a circus, could have caused the wounds.

I folded the article up again and handed it back to Smith. It didn't mean or prove anything, of course. Anybody could have clipped that article from a newspaper and used it to help substantiate a wild yarn. Undoubtedly somebody's vicious police dog, on the loose, had done the killing.

But something prickled at the back of my neck.

Funny what that word "unknown" and the thought back of it can do to you. If that story had told of a man killed by a dog or by a lion, either one, there's nothing more than ordinarily frightening about it. But if the man who writes the article doesn't know what it was did the killing and calls it an "unknown beast"—well, if you've got imagination, you'll see what I mean.

"You mean this man who was killed was one of your members?" I said.

"Yes. Are you willing to take his place?"

Silly, but there was that darned chill down my spine again. Was I alone here in the house with a madman?

He didn't look mad.

Funny, I thought, here I don't like life particularly. But now suddenly pops up danger, and I'm afraid. Afraid of what? A madman—or a Jabberwock?

And the absurdity of that brought me back to sanity and I wanted to laugh. I didn't, of course. I was host and even if fear of his slitting my throat wouldn't keep me from laughing at a possible madman, then politeness would.

Besides, hadn't I been bored stiff for years? With Carmel City and with myself and with everything in it? Now something screwball was happening and was I going to funk out before I got to first base?

I picked up my glass.

"If I say yes?" I asked.

"There is a meeting tonight, later. We will go to it. There you will learn what we are doing. The results, thus far, of our research."

"Where is the meeting to be held?"

"Near here. I came up from New York to attend it. I have directions to guide me to a house on a road called the Dartown Pike. About six miles out from Carmel City. My car will get us there, or get me there alone, if you do not care to come."

The Dartown Pike, I thought, about six miles out from here.

"You wouldn't by any chance be referring to the Wentworth Place?"

"That's the name. Wentworth. You know it?"

Right then and there, if it hadn't been for the drinks I'd taken, I should have seen that this was all too good to be true. I should have smelled blood.

"We'll have to take candles," I said. "Or flashlights. That house has been empty since I was a kid. We used to call it a haunted house. Would that be why you chose it?"

"Of course, Doctor. You are not afraid to go?"

Afraid to go? Gosh, yes, I was afraid to go.

"Gosh, no," I said.

CHAPTER 3

Appointment with Death

He took his vorpal sword in hand:
Long time the manxome foe he sought—
So rested he by the Tumtum tree,
And stood awhile in thought.

Perhaps I was a bit more drunk than I thought. I remember how utterly crystal clear my mind was, and that's always a sign. There's nothing more crystal clear than a prism that makes you see around corners.

It was three drinks later. I was interested particularly in the way Smith took those drinks. A little tilt to the glass and it was gone. Like a conjuring trick. He could take a drink of whisky neat with hardly a pause in his talking.

I can't do that, myself. Maybe because I don't really like the taste of whisky.

"Look at the dates," he was saying. "Charles Dodgson published 'Alice in Wonderland' in eighteen sixty-three and 'Through the Looking-Glass' in Seventy-one, eleven years later. He was only thirty-two or thereabouts when he wrote the Wonderland book, but he was already on the trail of something. You know what he had published previously?"

"I'm afraid I don't remember," I told him.

"In Eighteen Sixty, five years before, he'd written and published 'A Syllabus of Plane Algebraic Geometry' and only a year later his 'Formulae of Plane Trigonometry.' I don't suppose you have ever read them?"

I shook my head. "Math has always been beyond me."

"Then you haven't read his 'Elementary Treatise on Determinants,' either, I suppose. Nor his 'Curiosa Mathematica'? Well, you shall read the latter. It's nontechnical, and most of the clues to the fantasies are contained in it. There are further references in his Symbolic Logic,' published in Eighteen Ninety-six, just two years before his death, but they are less direct."

"Now, wait a minute," I said, "if I understand you correctly, your thesis is that Lewis Carroll—I can't seem to think of him as Dodgson—worked out through mathematics and symbolic logic the fact that there is another—uh—plane of existence. A through-the-looking-glass plane of fantasy, a dream plane—is that it?"

"Exactly, Doctor. A dream plane. That is about as near as it can be expressed in our language. Consider dreams. Aren't they the almost-perfect parallel of the Alice adventures? The wool-and-water sequence where everything Alice looks at changes. Remember in the shop, with the sheep knitting, how whenever Alice looked hard at any shelf to make sure what was on it, that shelf was always empty although the others around it were crowded full?"

" 'Things flow about so here,' was her comment," I said. "And the sheep asks if she can row and hands her a pair of knitting needles, and they turn into oars in her hands, and she's in a boat."

"Exactly, Doctor. A perfect dream sequence. And the poem Jabberwocky, the high point of the second book in my estimation, is in the very language of dreams. 'Frumious,' 'manxome,' 'tulgey'—words that give you a vague picture, in context, but that you can't put your finger on. Like something you hear in a dream, and understand, but which is meaningless when you awaken."

Between "manxome" and "tulgey" he'd downed his latest drink. I replenished his glass and mine.

"But why postulate the reality of such a world?" I asked him. "I see the parallel, of course. The Jabberwock itself is the epitome of dream-creatures, of nightmare. With eyes of flame, jaws that bite and claws that catch, it whiffles and burbles—Freud and James Joyce, in tandem, couldn't do any better than that. But why isn't a dream a dream? Why talk of getting through to it, except in the sense that we invade that world nightly in our dreams? Why assume it's more real than that?"

"You'll hear evidence of that tonight, Doctor. Mathematical evidence—and, I hope, further actual proof. The calculations are there, the methods, in Curiosa Mathematica. Dodgson was a century ahead of his time, Dr. Bagden. Have you read of the recent experiments with the subconscious of Liebnitz and Winton? They're putting forth feelers in the right direction—the mathematical approach.

"You see, only recently, aside from a rare exception like Dodgson, has science realized the possibility of parallel planes of existence, existences like nested Chinese boxes, one inside the other. With gaps between that consciousness, the mind can bridge in sleep under the influence of drugs. Why do the Chinese use opium except to bridge that gap? If the mind can bridge it, why not the body?"

"Down a rabbit-hole," I suggested. "Or through a looking-glass."

He waved a pudgy hand. "Both symbolic. But both suggestive of formulae you'll find in his Syllabus, formulae that have puzzled mathematicians."

I won't try to repeat the rest of what he told me. Partly, if not mainly, because I don't remember it. It was over my head and sounded like Einstein on a binge.

This must have been partly because I was getting drunker. At times there was a mistiness about the room and the man across the table from me seemed to come closer and then recede, his face to become clear and then to blur. And at times his voice was a blur of sines and cosines.

I gave up trying to follow.

He was a screwball, and so was I, and we were going to a haunted house to meet other screwballs and to try something crazy. I'm not certain whether we were going to try to fish a Bandersnatch out of limbo or to break through a looking-glass veil ourselves and go hunting one in its native element. Among the slithy toves in the wabe.

I didn't care which. It was crazy, of course, but I was having the best time I'd had since the Halloween almost forty years ago when we—but never mind that. It's a sign of old age to reminisce about one's youth, and I'm not old yet.

But part of the mistiness in the room was smoke. I hadn't opened the window and I looked across at it now and wondered if I wanted it opened badly enough to get up and cross the room.

A black square, that window, in the wall of this lighted room. A square of glass against which pressed murder and the monstrous night. As I watched it, I heard the town clock strike ten times. I reached for my glass and then pulled back my hand. I'd had enough, or too much, already for ten o'clock in the evening.

The window. A black square!

We are not clairvoyant.

Out there in the night a man, a man I knew, lay dead with his skull bashed in and blood and brains mixing with his matted hair. The pistol butt was raised to strike the other man's head.

A third murder was planned, already committed in a warped brain.

Ten o'clock, the hour they would ask an alibi.

"I was with Yehudi," I would say.

Who's Yehudi?

Oh, if murder was ever funny, this set-up was funny. Some day when I'm as drunk again as I was at ten o'clock that evening, I'll be able to laugh at it.

Murder and the monstrous night.

But I merely decided that the smoke was too thick after all, and I got up and opened the window. I could still walk straight.

Men were being murdered, and Smith spoke. "We'll have to leave soon," he said.

"Have another drink," I asked him. "I'm ahead of you. I drank at Smiley's." He shook his head. "I've got to drive."

I stood at the window and the cool air made me feel a bit less fuzzy. I took in deep draughts of it. Then, because if I left it wide open the room would be too cool when I returned, I pushed it down again to within an inch or two of the sill.

And there was my reflection again. An insignificant little man with graying hair, and glasses, and a necktie badly askew.

I grinned at my reflection. "You blasted fool, you," I thought to myself. "Going out with a madman to hunt Jabberwocks. At your age."

The reflection straightened its necktie, and grinned back. It was probably thinking:

> *"You are old, Father William," the young*
> *man said.*
> *"And your hair has become very white.*
> *And yet you incessantly stand on your head.*
> *Do you think, at your age, it is right?"*

Well, maybe it wasn't, but I hadn't stood on my head for a long time and maybe this was the last chance I'd ever have.

Over my shoulder, in the mirror of the window glass, I could see Smith getting to his feet. "Ready to go?" he asked.

I turned around and looked at him, at his bland, round face, at the laughter tracks in the corners of his eyes, at the rotund absurdity of his body.

And an impulse made me walk over and hold out my hand to him and shake his hand when he put it in mine rather wonderingly. We hadn't shaken hands when we'd introduced ourselves on the porch, and something made me do it now.

Just an impulse, but one I'm very glad I followed.

"Mr. Smith, frankly I don't follow or swallow your theory about Lewis Carroll," I said. "I'm going with you, although I don't expect any Jabberwocks. But even so, you've given me the most enjoyable evening I've had in a good many years. I want to thank you for it, in case I forget later. I'm taking the bottle along."

Yes, I'm glad I said that. Often after people are dead, you think of things you'd like to have said to them while you had the chance. For once, I said it in time.

He looked pleased as could be.

"Thanks, Doc," he said, shortening the title into a nickname for the first time. But also, for the first time, his eyes didn't quite meet mine.

We went out to his car, and got in.

It's odd how clearly you remember some things and how vague other things are. I remember that there was a green bulb on the speedometer on the dashboard of that car, and that the gear-shift lever knob was brightly polished onyx. But I don't remember what make of car it was, nor even whether it was a coupe or a sedan.

I remember directing him across town to the Dartown Pike, but I can't for the life of me recall which of several possible routes we took.

But then we were out of town on the pike, purring along through the night with the yellow headlight beams cutting long spreading swaths through the black dark.

"We've clocked five and a half miles from the town limits," Smith said. "You know the place? Must be almost there."

"Next driveway on your right," I told him.

Gosh, but the place must be old, I thought. It was an old house forty years ago when I was a boy of twelve. It had been empty then. My dad's farm had been a mile closer to town, and Johnny Haskins, who lived on the next farm, and I had explored it several times. In daylight. Johnny had been killed in France in 1917. In daytime, I hope, because he'd always been afraid of the dark. I'd picked up a little of that fear from him, and had kept it for a quite a few years after I grew up.

But not any more. Older people never stay afraid. By the time you pass the fifty mark, you've known so many people who are now dead that ghosts, if there were such things, aren't such strangers. You'd find too many friends among them.

"This it?" Smith asked.

"Yes," I said.

CHAPTER 4
Bottle from Wonderland

And as in uffish thought he stood,
The Jabberwock, with eyes of flame,
Came whiffling through the tulgey wood
And burbled as it came!

We stood in front of the house that had been the bugaboo of my childhood, and it looked just about as it had looked then.

I ran the beam of my flashlight up on the porch, and it seemed that not a board had changed.

Just imagination, of course. It had been lived in for twenty years since then. Colonel Wentworth had bought it in about 1915 and had lived there until he died eight years ago. But during those eight years it had stood empty and again it had gone to rack and ruin.

"The others aren't here yet," Smith said. "But let's go in."

We went up on the creaking porch and found the door was not locked. The beams of our flashlights danced ahead of us down the long dimness of the hallway.

Was someone else really coming here tonight? I wondered. Again that prickle of danger roughed the hair on the back of my neck. Undoubtedly I was a fool to have come here with a man I didn't know. But there was nothing dangerous about Smith, I felt sure. Crackpot he might be, but not a homicidal one.

We turned into a huge living room on the left of the hallway. There was furniture there, white-sheeted. But the sheets were not too dirty nor was there much dust anywhere. Apparently the inside of the place, at least, was being cared for.

Furniture under white muslin has a ghostly look.

I took the bottle out of my pocket and held it out to Smith, but he shook his head silently.

But I took a drink from it. The warm feeling began to drive the cold one from the pit of my stomach.

I didn't dare get sober now, I told myself, or I'd start wondering what I was doing there.

I heard the sound of a car turning in the driveway.

Or so it seemed. For we stood quiet a long time and nothing happened. No footsteps on the porch, no more car-sound. I began to wonder if I'd been mistaken.

Maybe a minute passed, maybe an hour. I took another drink.

Smith had laid his flashlight on top of the bureau, with the switch turned on, pointed diagonally across the room. The furniture made huge black shadows on the wall. He stood in the middle of the room and when he turned to face me the flashlight was full in his face.

He looked a bit scared himself, until he smiled.

"They'll be here soon, I'm sure," he said.

"How many are coming?" For some reason we were both talking softly, almost in whispers.

I was finding it hard, deucedly hard, to keep my eyes in focus on his face. It was an effort to stand up straight, and I took a step backward so I could lean against the wall. Somehow, I didn't want to sit down in one of those sheeted chairs.

I didn't feel any too good, now. I wished I was back home, so I could lie down for a while and let the bed go around in soothing circles.

Smith didn't seem to hear my question about how many were coming. Again I thought the engine of a car was running, but Smith turned and walked to the window, and the sound of his footsteps drowned the noise, if there was any noise.

When he reached the window, he stopped and I heard it again, distinctly. A car, if my ears told me aright, was driving away from the house. Had someone come, and gone? Finally the sound died away.

It didn't make sense, but then what did?

I was tired of listening to nothing and looking at Smith's back. He kept staring at the blank, black pane of window as though he could see out of it. I was sure he couldn't.

For no particular reason, I took another look around the room.

In the shadows of one corner there was a single article of furniture that was not covered by a dust sheet. It was a glass-topped table. A small, round three-legged affair, like a magician's table. There was something on it that I couldn't make out.

I looked away, and then, because something about it haunted me, I looked back. Where had I seen a table like that before? Somewhere.

No, a picture of one. I remembered now.

In the John Tenniel illustrations of Alice in Wonderland, of course. The glass-topped table Alice had found in the hall at the bottom of the rabbit hole. The table on which stood a little bottle with a label tied around the neck.

I walked over and, yes, there were two things on the table, as there should have been. A bottle and a key. The key was a small Yale key, and the bottle was really a vial, about two inches high, just as in the Tenniel picture.

The label, of course, said "DRINK ME." I picked the bottle up and looked at it unbelievingly, and I became aware that Smith was standing at my elbow. He must have heard me walking across the room and left the window.

He reached out, took the bottle from my hand and looked at it. He nodded.

"They've been here, then," he said.

"Who? You mean this—the table and the key and all—is part of—uh—what we came here for?"

He nodded again. "They brought this, and left it."

He loosened the cork in the bottle as he spoke.

"I'm sorry, Doc," he said. "I can't let you have the honor. But you're not really a member yet and—well—I am!"

He put the bottle to his lips and drank it off with the same quick motion he'd used in polishing off the whiskys I'd given him back in my room.

Don't ask me what I expected to happen. Whether I expected him to shut up like a telescope and shrink to about ten inches high, just the right height to go through the little door into the garden, I can't say. Only, like Alice, he'd neglected to take the key off the table first.

I don't know what I expected to happen. But nothing happened. He put the bottle back down on the table and went right on with what he'd been saying.

"When you have met the others and have been accepted, you may, if you wish, try out our—"

And then he died.

What the poison was, I don't know, but its action was sudden despite the fact that it had not paralyzed his lips or mouth. He died before he even started to fall. I could tell it by the sudden utter blankness of his face.

The thud of his fall actually shook the floor.

I bent over and shoved my hand inside his coat and shirt and his heart wasn't beating. I waited a while to be sure.

I stood up again, and my knees were wobbly.

If he'd tried to poison me! But he hadn't. He drunk it himself, and his death had been murder and not suicide. Nobody, no matter how mad he might be, would ever commit suicide in the offhand manner in which he'd tossed off the contents of that bottle.

The empty bottle had jarred off the table and was lying on the floor beside him and my eyes went from it back to the glass table and the key. I picked the key up and looked at it.

It was a false note, that key. It should have been a gold key, and small as it was, it should have been smaller. And not a Yale key. But maybe it opened something. What good is a key without a lock? I stuck it absently into my pocket and looked down again at Smith.

He was still dead.

And it was then that I got scared and ran. I'd seen dead men before, plenty of them, and it wasn't Smith I was afraid of.

It was the utter complete screwiness of everything that had been happening this mad night.

That, and the fact that I was alone. In a haunted house, too! Like all cynics who don't believe in haunted houses, I have a good deal of respect for them.

I stumbled and fell in the darkness of the hallway, and then remembered the flashlight in my hip pocket, and put it into action. I got out the door and off the porch before I even wondered where I was going, or why.

The police, of course. I'd have to get word to Sheriff Pete Lane as soon as I possibly could. I considered knocking someone awake in a nearby farmhouse and telephoning, but it would be quicker, in the long run, to take Smith's car and drive the six miles back to town. I could do that in fifteen minutes and it might take twice that long to find a telephone.

Beyond this, beyond notifying the sheriff, I wasn't thinking yet.

I had a hunch that if I thought about what had happened and tried to figure out what it all meant and why that "DRINK ME" bottle had been poison, I'd have gone off my rocker.

The less thinking I did before I talked to Pete Lane, the better off I'd be.

So I flashlighted my way around the corner of the house to where we'd left the car, and I got another jolt.

The car was there, or a car was there. But it was my own car, not the one Smith had driven me out in. My own Plymouth coupe, which up to that afternoon, had been out in my garage on blocks, with the air let out of the tires.

There'd been only a few miles left in those tires anyway and I'd decided to save those few miles for something important, if anything important ever came up.

Well, something important had come up, and here was my car. There was air in the tires, too. And gas in the tank, probably, unless somebody had towed it there.

I walked around it warily, almost expecting to see it vanish in a puff of smoke or to find the March Hare or the Mock Turtle seated behind the steering wheel. Those drinks were still with me.

But there wasn't anyone behind the steering wheel, and I got in. I flicked on the dashboard lights and looked at the gas gauge, and there were three gallons in the tank.

Could I have been driven here in my own car without realizing it? No, I remembered that onyx gear-shift knob, and the green light on the dashboard of the other car. And the instrument panel had been different. I was sure of that.

I took a deep breath and started the engine. It purred smoothly, and I eased the coupe out to the road and aimed it south for town.

I think I might have driven wide open if it hadn't been my own car. But the familiar feel of it sobered me a little more and that was just enough to realize how drunk I still was. The road ahead seemed like a weaving ribbon at times. And one of those tires might give way any minute.

I parked in front of the courthouse, and there was still a light on in the sheriff's office.

I started in, but stopped in the doorway long enough to take another drink. This wasn't going to be easy.

Pete Lane was talking on the telephone when I went into his office.

"You're blamed right, we're trying," he said into the mouth-piece. "I got two of my own men on it, and I've just notified the state police. Huh? No, we ain't told anybody else yet. No use doing that till we find 'em."

He hung up the receiver and looked at me. He looked angry and harassed. "What the devil do you want, Doc?" he said.

"I got to report a murder," I said. I closed the door and leaned against it. Then I was catapulted nearly off my feet and onto the sheriff's desk as the door opened violently from the outside. Harry Bates came in. He had his clothes on over his pajamas, for the bottoms of them showed below his trouser cuffs. His shoes weren't tied.

"Walter just phoned from Burlington," Bates said. "Your line was busy so I took it on the switchboard. He didn't find much."

Pete interrupted him. "Just a minute, Harry. What's this about a murder, Doc?"

"Out at the old Wentworth place on the road to Burlington. There's a man dead there."

"Is it Jones?"

"Jones?" The name didn't register with me. "No. His name was Smith, not Jones. Or that's what he told me. His first name was a funny one."

I didn't quite dare. There was the card Smith had given me, in my pocket. I handed it to Pete.

He looked at it and let out a howl.

"Yehudi?" he yelled. "Doc, if this is a rib, I'm going to smack you."

I sat down on the corner of the desk because I felt safer sitting down.

"It's no rib, darn it," I told him. "He got me out there with him, and then he took poison out of a bottle that we found."

Pete wasn't even listening to me. He was staring at the card I'd handed him. Suddenly he looked up.

"Doc, what's your bug number?" he asked me.

"My bug number?" For an awful instant I thought he was crazy too. Then I remembered that some people call the union label—that tiny device which, with the number of the shop, must appear on every job printed in a union print shop—the "bug."

"Seventeen," I told him, and he cursed.

"Doc, you printed this yourself," he said. He cursed again. "Yehudi! Doc, if you weren't drunk, I'd ram your teeth down your throat for barging in here like this. We got trouble, and I mean trouble. Barnaby Jones started for Burlington with his payroll, taking Miles Harrison along, three hours ago, and didn't show up there. Three hours, and it's only twenty miles. Get the devil out of here."

I didn't move.

"Pete, sure I'm drunk," I said. "But blast your hide, you've known me all your life, and would I pull a gag about something like this? I tell you there's a dead man at the Wentworth place. I went there with him. I'd never seen him before tonight."

"What'd you go there for?"

Although the incredulity had left his voice, I knew it wasn't the time to say why we went there. I could imagine his face if I told him a tenth of it.

"That's not important, now," I said. "Man, this is a murder. Come out there with me and I'll show you the body."

"Just a minute, Doc. Harry, is Walter still on the line?"

"He's waiting for us to call him back with instructions. Here's the number." He put a slip of paper on Pete's desk.

"Walter's got to drive past the Wentworth house anyway. I'll have him look in. What room?"

"Living room," I said. "Middle room on the north side, downstairs. He'll find a body on the floor, and he'll find a glass table, and a bottle lying by the body, with a label."

But I stopped just in time. Whew! Pete Lane picked up the phone and asked for Burlington.

CHAPTER 5
Head on a Platter

One, two! One, two! And through and through
The vorpal blade went snicker-snack!
He left it dead, and with its head
He went galumphing back.

No, I didn't feel good. In fact, I felt goofy.

But I sat in a chair back in the corner of Pete's office, with Pete barking orders to half a dozen people, in person and over the phone, and I felt glad that he was paying no attention to me.

He was holding my case in abeyance as being less important than the disappearance of Barnaby Jones and Miles Harrison. Maybe he had it down as a figment of my drunken imagination.

I kept wishing that he was right, but I knew better.

As soon as he got the report from Walter that the body was really there, he'd swarm all over me with questions. But I was only too glad to wait because then—with a body in hand, so to speak—the answers I'd have to give him would sound a lot more plausible.

The office was taking on a fuzzy look, and my tongue was starting to feel like an angora kitten. It was easier to keep my eyes shut than try to make them see straight. All I really wanted was to get this over with, go home and slide into bed.

But I heard Pete walking out of the office and opened my eyes and stood up. There was one thing I felt curious about and now was the time to find out. I walked over to his desk and picked up the Yehudi Smith calling card. I held it close to my eyes, and—yes, there was the little union label in the corner and the number seventeen under it. Either it had been printed in my own shop, or someone had gone to a little trouble to make it seem that it had. The type was ten-point Garamond. I had Garamond in stock.

I was putting the card down thoughtfully when Pete came back and saw me. "What's the idea of that card?" he asked.

"I was just wondering," I told him."I didn't print it, and Jerry Klosterman didn't either, or I'd have seen the order for it. I'd remember a name like that."

He laughed without humor. "Who wouldn't. Listen, Doc. I've done everything I can do at the moment about the Jones and Harrison business. The search is organized, and we'll find them. But until then—well, let's get back to this Wentworth place business. You say a man you don't know took you out there?"

I nodded.

"Anyone see him with you? What I mean is—can you prove it?"

"No, Pete. You'll have to take my word for it. That and the fact that he's still out there, dead."

"We'll skip that till I get the report. This card?" He looked at it and scowled. "Any other souvenirs?"

I shook my head, and then remembered.

"This," I said, and took the key from my pocket and handed it to him. Again, somehow, it looked familiar. But all Yale keys look alike. Still, the minute I'd given it to him, I wished I hadn't. It would probably turn out to open something at the Courier office. It might be as phony as that calling card.

"He gave you this key?" Pete asked.

"No, not exactly. I found it at the Wentworth house, but it may not be important."

Walter Hanswert came in without knocking. Walter is the man who does most of the work for the sheriff's office, but Pete Lane has the job and draws the pay. You'll find some hardworking horse like Walter back of every politically-elected sheriff, or else the mechanism of law and order goes to pot.

"Anything?" Pete said.

"Not a lead, Pete. I drove slow all the way back from Burlington, looking for any place a car might have skidded off the road or any sign of something to help us. No dice."

"How about the Wentworth house, Walter?"

"I stopped there. Not a thing. I went through it fast, from attic to cellar."

Maybe you stop being surprised after a while. This didn't really jar me.

"Walter, were you in the living room?" I said. "Didn't you find a glass table and a bottle on the floor?"

"Nope. That's the room Pete said to search. I even looked under all the dust covers. Couple of tables there, cloth-covered, but neither of them glass, and no bottle. Front door of the house was open."

"I left it open, I guess," I said.

My knees were getting that way again. I didn't want to argue, but I had to.

"Cuss it, Pete!" I cried. "There was a body there. Somebody took it away. Heaven knows why. Heaven knows what any of this is all about, but I didn't imagine they'd clean up things so quick."

He put a gentle hand on my shoulder. "Doc, Walter will drive you home. Sleep it off."

The word "sleep" got me. Oh, I knew quite well that I wasn't going to sleep off what had happened. But I could, and wanted to, sleep off this fuzziness. Tomorrow, in the clear light of day, maybe I could add things up and make sense out of them.

A few hours' sleep, I told myself, just two or three hours, and everything might look different.

"Okay, Pete," I said. "Perhaps you're right."

"Got your car here?"

"In front." I should have left it go at that, but my tongue was loose. "We took Smith's car out to the Wentworth's place, but mine was out there after he was killed. I don't know how that happened."

"Just a minute," said Pete. His face looked different. "Your car's really downstairs? I thought you had it blocked up? You had it out tonight?"

"Yes and no, Pete. I didn't take it out of the garage but it's out just the same."

"It's in front," Walter said. "I saw it."

Pete Lane looked at his assistant, and then back at me. "And you had it out on the Dartown Pike tonight, Doc?"

"I told you that," I said impatiently. I didn't know what he was getting at, but I didn't like the way he was doing it.

"Doc, you never liked Barnaby Jones, did you?"

"Barnaby?" I was surprised. "He's a stuffed shirt and a miser and a prig. No, I don't like him. Why?"

He didn't answer. He leaned back against the desk and stared into the far corner of the room, with his lips pursed as though he was whistling, but no sound coming out of them.

When he spoke, he didn't look at me this time. And his voice was soft. Almost soothing.

"Doc, we're going to take a look at that car of yours," he said. "You can wait up. No, you come along with us, and then I'll drive you home."

I didn't get the idea, but I didn't care particularly. Just so I got home, and the sooner the better.

We went outside, Pete, Walter and I, and I noticed that they worked it so I walked between them.

My car was parked right outside the door, and the sheriff's car, which Walter had used to drive to Burlington and back, was in front of it. An open roadster with the top down.

Pete opened the door of my coupe and looked in. He pulled a flashlight out of his pocket and flashed it around inside, and looked carefully at the seat cushions and the floorboards. He looked carefully, but didn't seem to find anything.

He fished through an assortment of junk in the glove compartment, and then reached into the door pocket. His face changed and he pulled his hand out slowly with a revolver in it. He held it by the cylinder, between his thumb and forefinger, just the way he'd first got hold of it.

"This yours, Doc?"

"No," I said.

He looked at me, hard, for a second or two and then sniffed at the end of the muzzle.

"Either hasn't been fired," he said, "or it's been cleaned." He was talking to Walter, not to me. "Let's look further."

He turned the gun over and held the lens of his flashlight close to the end of the butt. Even from where I stood back on the sidewalk I could see there was a smear there. A smear that might have been blood.

Pete Lane took a clean handkerchief from his pocket. It was folded and he shook it open and put it down on the running board of the coupe and laid the pistol gently on top of it.

"Where's the key to the rumble, Doc?" Pete asked me. "I'm afraid we'll have to look in there."

I shook my head. "Haven't got it. With me, I mean. When I blocked up the car, I took the keys off my ring and left them in the drawer of my desk. The one at home."

He turned and looked back in the car, aiming his flashlight at the instrument panel. The ignition key was in the lock there, but there were no other keys with it.

"That one isn't in your desk at home," said Pete. He walked around to the back of the car and stared at the lock in the handle of the rumble seat.

He looked at it a minute, then reached into his pocket and took out a key. The key I'd handed him. The key that had been on the glass table beside the "DRINK ME" bottle. The key that should have been the key to the little door into the garden where Alice had found the Two, Seven and Five of Hearts painting white roses red so the Queen wouldn't order their heads chopped off.

Pete put the key into the lock of the rumble seat and it fitted, and turned. He lifted the lid.

From where I stood, all I could see was a small brown leather grip, but I recognized it. It was the grip that Barnaby Jones used to carry the payroll money in, from Carmel City to Burlington.

But the grip wasn't resting on the seat. It was resting on something that was lying on the seat or it wouldn't have stuck up that way. I heard the hissing sound of Pete Lane sucking in his breath, and Walter Hanswert took a quick step to look down into the rumble seat, too.

I didn't. I didn't have to be sober to guess what was in there, and I'd already seen one murdered man tonight.

Somebody had done a beautiful job of something. I'd come galumphing back from my date with a Jabberwock carrying, not its head, but my own, on a silver platter to the police.

And shades of Old Henderson, what a story I had to go with the bodies of Barnaby Jones and Miles Harrison! A story based on a little man named Yehudi—the little man who wasn't there! Yehudi whom no one but myself had ever seen. I'd given the sheriff my two souvenirs of the evening and one had been printed in my own shop and the other was the key to my own car and the incriminating evidence in it.

I don't know whether I was suddenly very drunk or very sober to do what I did. But like a flash of lightning I had a picture of myself in court or an alienist's office telling him about a glass-topped table and a bottle labeled "DRINK ME" and the death of Yehudi the vanishing corpse.

I lunged for the running board of my coupe and got the pistol Pete had left there and forgotten for the moment in the excitement of his find in the rumble seat.

Pete yelled at Walter and Walter dived for me, but too late. I had straightened up with the pistol in my hand before he got within grabbing distance and he stepped back.

"Now, Doc," said Pete, in a wheedling voice, as one would use to a child. But there was fear in his eyes, plenty of it, although Walter's a brave man. He thought he was facing a homicidal maniac.

I didn't try to disillusion him. I didn't even have my finger inside the trigger guard. If he'd reached out and grasped the gun, I'd have let him take it.

"Step out from behind there, Pete," I said. "Both of you back into the courthouse."

I groped behind me and took the ignition key out of my own car and pocketed it. I wasn't going to take that car, with its ghastly burden. But I didn't want them to use it either.

I moved toward the sheriff's car while they sidled cautiously across the sidewalk toward the courthouse. I was gambling that Walter hadn't bothered to take the keys out when he'd come upstairs to report. And I was right.

They stepped through the doorway and the instant they were out of sight I heard running footsteps. Pete was sprinting for his office for his own gun, if I guessed correctly, and Walter would be taking the switchboard to block all the roads out of town.

That was all right by me. I wasn't going out of town. I put the murder gun down on the curb—I didn't want it any more than I wanted my own car—and got in Pete's car and drove off.

CHAPTER 6
Hidden Foe

"And hast thou slain the Jabberwock?
Come to my arms, my beamish boy!
O frabjous day! Callooh! Callay!"
He chortled in his joy.

Swinging around the corner, I gunned the engine to get up speed, and then shut it off. On momentum, I swung it into the alley back of the courthouse and let it coast to a stop.

Looking up, I could see the lighted window of Pete's room, and could imagine the frantic telephoning going on right now to stop and hold a car that would stand, probably unnoticed, for the rest of the night, right under his window.

I got out quietly by stepping over the door instead of opening it, and walked up the alley, going on tiptoe until I was out of earshot of the courthouse.

They'd be looking for me, I knew, at the outskirts of town, not in the middle of it. The place I had in mind ought to be safe for a couple of hours, at least. And I didn't care, beyond that. I wasn't making a getaway. I just wanted a chance to do a few chores and think out a few things before I gave myself up. Gave myself up, that is, unless I could work out my plans.

I went along the alley two blocks and turned in at the back door of Smiley's. Pete and his men, I felt sure, would be too busy to do any drinking for a while.

"Hi, Doc," Smiley said. "Thought you'd be asleep long ago." He laughed his meaningless laugh.

"Old Henderson, double," I said. "I've been asleep ever since I left here, Smiley. Maybe I can wake up. Leave that bottle on the bar."

There was a pinochle game in the back corner. Outside of that I had the place to myself.

I downed the double Henderson and felt a little better. I gave it time to get home and took another. There's a second-wind stage of inebriation, and hitting that was my only chance to get my mind hitting on six cylinders. Sobriety's good for thinking, too, but I hadn't a chance of getting sober for hours yet. The other way was quicker.

I looked at the calendar a while, but that didn't help. Things went in dizzying circles inside my head. Who's Yehudi? Where is what's left of him? Why did he drink the "DRINK ME"? Was he really expecting other members of some nitwit organization to show up there?

Had he been kidding me, or was he being kidded?

Jabberwocks. Glass tables with "DRINK ME" bottles and keys that should have been gold and led into a garden, but which were Yale and led into the nuthouse by way of a rumble seat. And of all names, Yehudi Smith!

Oh, it would have been funny, it would have been a wow of a practical joke, if there hadn't been three corpses cluttering up the scenery, and the fact that this meant the end of my freedom, whether I ended up in a bughouse or a hoosegow. Or at the end of a rope.

No, looking at the calendar didn't help.

"Give me a deck, Smiley," I said.

I took another drink while he got it, and deliberately I didn't think at all while I counted out the stacks for solitaire. Then, as I started the game, I let go. I mean, I didn't try to think, but I didn't try not to. I just relaxed.

Red queen on a black king. Wasn't the Red Queen the one who met Alice in the second square, and told her about the six squares she'd have to go through before she could be a queen herself?

And a black jack for the red queen.

But that was a red chess queen, not a card queen. The one who ran so fast. "A slow sort of country," she'd told Alice. "Now here, you see, it takes all the running you can do to keep in the same place."

An ace up on top, and then I took another drink before I put the red six on the black seven. The cards looked different now—sharp of outline, crystal clear.

Like my mind felt. Ten on the jack.

Yehudi had been a pawn. A sucker, like me. Somebody had moved him. Somebody had hired him to come there and pull a razzle-dazzle on me. To give me a story that nobody'd believe in ten lifetimes, a story whose only proof was a card some friend of mine had printed in my own shop. Yehudi had been made as incredible as possible, from Christian name to "DRINK ME."

There was only one answer to Yehudi. A character actor at liberty, probably hired in New York and brought here for the purpose of framing me. And he framed himself. Given a set of instructions for the evening that included the planted drink-me bottle, and went beyond it, because he hadn't been told what was in that bottle.

So Yehudi wasn't in on the real play. Somebody had hired Yehudi to play what he thought was an elaborate practical joke.

Nine on the ten, and bring up a deuce for my ace on top.

Somebody who knew me intimately, and who knew how I felt Thursday evenings and my predilection for Lewis Carroll and nonsense in general, and that I'd be sure to fall for a gag like Yehudi's. Someone who came to see me at the print shop and at home, once in a while, at least. Maybe to play chess with me?

Anyway, there was the other red queen.

"How you coming?" Smiley asked.

"I'm in the fifth square," I told him. "I crossed the third by railroad, with the Gnat. And I think I just crossed the brook into the fifth."

"Squares? There ain't any squares in solitare."

"Cards are rectangles," I said. "And what's a square but a rectangle somebody sat on? You're a swell guy, Smiley, but shut up."

He laughed and moved off down the bar.

I took another drink, but just a short one. The edges of the cards and the outlines of the pips on them were very sharp and clear now. No fuzziness, no mussiness.

Another ace for the top row.

Because, if the money was still in that bag that was planted in my car, there was only one person who benefited by what had happened tonight. The man who'd inherit Barnaby Jones' factory and his fortune. The one man who'd need a scapegoat, because of his a priori motive.

That was the sixth brook. I had a hunch I was entering the seventh square now. But I took a look back to be sure.

Alvin Carey would inherit his uncle's fortune. Al knew me pretty well. We played chess, and somebody who played chess had engineered the set-up tonight. Al Carey knew my screwy literary tastes, and my Thursday night habits. He'd dropped in here, in Smiley's, early. And that would have been to check up that I was running true to form.

Al Carey had enough money to have hired a character actor to lead me to the slaughter. Al Carey was smart enough to have made a dupe of the actor instead of an accomplice who could blackmail him afterwards.

Al Carey had everything.

Al Carey had me in a cleft stick. He'd finagled me into a situation so utterly preposterous that the more of the truth I told, the crazier I'd look. Nuttier than peanut brittle I'd look.

"Smiley," I said. "Come here. I want to ask you something."

He moved along the bar toward me, and grinned. He always acted that way when he was puzzled.

"One more brook to cross," I told him. "But it's wider than the Mississippi. What good does it do to know something if you can't prove it?"

"Well," he said, "what good does it do you if you can prove it?"

"Smiley," I said, "I reach the king-row, and I'm crowned. But this side of that last brook, I'm still a pawn, in pawn. What do you know about Alvin Carey?"

"Huh? He's a crackpot like you, Doc, but I don't like him. I think he's a sneak. But he's smart."

"Smiley," I said, "you surprise me. And for once I mean what I say. Some day I'll write an editorial about you, if I ever get a chance to write another editorial. What else do you know about Alvin, to his detriment? To his disadvantage, I mean."

"Well, he's yellow."

"I'm not sure of that," I said. "The draft board turned him down, if that's what you mean. Something about a trick knee. And—well, I know one stunt he pulled recently that took a lot of cool nerve."

"But don't you remember the time last year when a little chimney fire broke out at his place?" said Smiley, quickly. "A little smoke, that's all. But he ran out in his pajamas without waking anybody else up to tell 'em. He didn't stop till he reached the fire station, because he was too excited and scared to think there was a thing as a telephone."

"Smiley," I answered, "I bow before you. It's an outside chance. Pete's got his hands full right now, and is working like a Trojan to find somebody. Probably he hasn't called Alvin Carey yet. Shut up, sage, and let me think fast."

I closed my eyes and opened them again.

"I need three things, and I need them quick," I said. "I need a gun, and I need a candle stub, and I need a bottle of some kind of a cleaning fluid that smells like gasoline but is non-inflammable."

"Carbozol. I got a bottle of it, sure. And a candle, because once in a while the lights here go on the blink. But no gun."

"Smiley, this is in a desperate hurry, and I can't explain," I said. "But take a plain pint bottle, no label, and fill it with Carbozol for me. And get me a candle.

Cut it off short, to half an inch or so. A quarter of an inch, if you can cut it that fine. And have you got anything that looks like a gun?"

For a moment Smiley rubbed his chin thoughtfully. Then he grinned.

"I got an old thirty-two pistol I took away from a drunk in here one night when he got waving it around. But there ain't no bullets. I had the firing pin filed off so I could give it to my kid."

"That's the gun I want," I told him. "Quick, Smiley, get it and the other things for me. And I'll let you finish this game of solitaire for me. And it's going to play out, too."

I sat back in the chair and waited for him to return.

And then, with the stuff he gave me safely stowed in my pockets, I went out the back door and cut through alleys as fast as I could travel without getting out of breath. Pretty soon I got there.

There weren't any lights on, which was a good sign. It meant that maybe Pete Lane hadn't got around yet to notifying the nearest of kin. If I knew Pete, he'd try to get me first, so he'd have crime and criminal all in the same report and make a good impression on Carey. For, as Barnaby's heir, Al was going to be the richest guy in town. Unless my wild idea worked.

It was a warm evening and some of the downstairs windows were open, and that was good, too. The screens were put on with turnbolts from the outside and I took one off without making any noise.

I got inside, and I was quiet about it. I didn't kid myself that Al Carey might be asleep after the night's work he'd done. But he'd be in bed, playing possum, waiting for a telephone call.

Inside the window, I took off my shoes and left them. I sneaked into the hallway and up the stairs. Outside Al's door, which was an inch ajar, I took a deep breath.

Then I stepped inside and flicked on the light switch. I had the gun ready in my hand and I pointed it at Al Carey.

"Be quiet," I warned him.

The flick of the light switch had brought him bolt upright in the bed. He was in pajamas, all right, and his hair was tousled. But his eyes showed he hadn't been asleep.

I didn't give him a chance to think it over. I walked right up to the edge of the bed, keeping that broken pistol aimed smack between his eyes, and then before he could guess what I was going to do, I raised it and brought the butt down on top of his head.

CHAPTER 7
Test by Fire

'Twas brillig, and the slithy toves
Did gyre and gimble in the wabe:
All mimsy were the borogoves,
And the mome raths outgrabe.

That was the trickiest thing I had to do—to gauge that blow just right. I'd never hit a man over the head before.

And if this stunt I had in mind was going to work, it all depended on conking him out, not for too long, and without killing him. Just long enough for me to tie him up, because I couldn't have done that and held the gun on him at the same time.

If the blow killed him it wouldn't have hurt my conscience too much. Miles Harrison had been a nice guy. So had Yehudi Smith, whatever his real name was. But if the blow killed Carey, well, there'd be one more evidence of my homicidal mania for the police.

Al went out like a light, but his heart was still beating. And I worked fast at tying him. I used everything I could find, bathrobe cords, belts, neckties—he had almost a hundred of them—and I tore one sheet into strips.

He was swathed like a mummy when I got through, tied with his head and shoulders braced up against the head of the bed so he could see the bed itself. And a handkerchief inside his mouth held in by a scarf around the outside made a good gag. I used the strips of sheeting to tie him so he couldn't roll off the bed.

But I left his right arm free from the elbow down.

Then I slapped his face until his eyes opened. They looked groggy, at first, so I wet a washrag in the bathroom and sloshed him a few times with that. When he tried to get loose, I knew he knew what was going on.

I grinned at him. "Hello, Al," I said.

I took the pint bottle of non-inflammable cleaning fluid out of my pocket and took out the cork. Smiley had given me the right stuff.

It smelled like gasoline, all right.

I poured it over Al and over the bed, all around him.

Then, down by his knees, on a spot where the mattress was pretty wet with it, I put the half-inch stub of candle. I struck a match and held it to the wick.

"Better stop struggling, Al," I said. "You'll knock this over."

He stopped, all right. He lay as still as though he were dead, and his horrified eyes stared at that burning wick. Stared at it with the terrible fear of a pyrophobiac. For that's what Smiley's story of Al Carey and the chimney fire had reminded me of. Al had an abnormal, psychopathic fear of fire.

I took out of my pocket the notebook I always carry, and a stub of pencil, and put them down within reach of his free right hand.

"Any time you want to write, Al," I told him. Turning my back on him, I walked over to the window. I waited a minute and then looked back. I had to avoid looking at his eyes.

"It'll burn down in ten minutes," I said. "You'll just about have time if you start writing. I want it in full, the main details, anyway, addressed to Pete Lane. And tell him where to find the body you hid or buried. The actor. Tell him where to look for the glass-topped table, and the bottle that had the poison in it. You'll have to write fast. If you finish in time, I'll pick up the candle."

I said it calmly, as though it didn't matter.

Then I turned away again. Only seconds later, I heard the scratch of the pencil. . . .

It was nine o'clock when Jerry and I finished remaking the paper. We'd had to rip it wide open to make room. For three murders in one evening was the biggest thing that had ever happened in Carmel City.

It rushed us more than we had been rushed in years, but we didn't mind that. Nor the extra trouble. Hot news never seems like work.

The phone rang, and I answered it, and it was Jay Evers.

Jerry was staring at me in utter amazement when I put the receiver back after I finished talking.

"Who the devil were you talking to like that?" he asked me.

"Evers," I told him. "He wanted to buy the Courier, and I said no."

"But couldn't you have said no without that embroidery on it? Why insult him like you did? He'll never speak to you again."

"That was the idea," I told him. I grinned cheerfully. "Look, Jerry, if I didn't insult him, he might ask me again tomorrow."

"But what's that got to do with what you're telling me?"

"And tomorrow, Jerry, I'm going to have the ancestor of all hang-overs, and I'd sell the paper to him, and I don't want to sell it. I like the Courier, I like Carmel City. And I enjoy being free and not in the booby-hatch and the hoose-gow. So let the presses roll!"

"Doc, you better sit down before you fall down!"

But he was too late. Seconds too late.

VIRGINIA

THE AGE OF MIRACLES
by Melville Davisson Post

THE GIRL WAS standing apart from the crowd in the great avenue of poplars that led up to the house. She seemed embarrassed and uncertain what to do, a thing of April emerging into Summer.

Abner and Randolph marked her as they entered along the gravel road.

They had left their horses at the gate, but she had brought hers inside, as though after some habit unconsciously upon her.

But halfway to the house she had remembered and got down. And she stood now against the horse's shoulder. It was a black hunter, big and old, but age marred no beauty of his lines. He was like a horse of ebony, enchanted out of the earth by some Arabian magic, but not yet by that magic awakened into life.

The girl wore a long, dark riding skirt, after the fashion of the time, and a coat of hunter's pink. Her dark hair was in a great wrist-thick plait. Her eyes, too, were big and dark, and her body firm and lithe from the out-of-doors.

"Ah!" cried Randolph, making his characteristic gesture, "Prospero has been piping in this grove. Here is a daughter of the immortal morning! We grow old, Abner, and it is youth that the gods love."

My uncle, his hands behind him, his eyes on the gravel road, looked up at the bewitching picture.

"Poor child," he said; "the gods that love her must be gods of the valleys and not gods of the hills."

"Ruth amid the alien corn! Is it a better figure, Abner? Well, she has a finer inheritance than these lands; she has youth!"

"She ought to have both," replied my uncle. "It was sheer robbery to take her inheritance."

"It was a proceeding at law," replied the Justice. "It was the law that did the thing, and we cannot hold the law in disrespect."

"But the man who uses the law to accomplish a wrong, we can so hold," said Abner. "He is an outlaw, as the highwayman and the pirate are."

514

He extended his arm toward the great house sitting at the end of the avenue.

"In spite of the sanction of the law, I hold this dead man for a robber. And I would have wrested these lands from him, if I could. But your law, Randolph, stood before him."

"Well," replied the Justice, "he takes no gain from it; he lies yonder waiting for the grave."

"But his brother takes," said Abner, "and this child loses."

The Justice, elegant in the costume of the time, turned his ebony stick in his fingers.

"One should forgive the dead," he commented in a facetious note; "it is a mandate of the Scripture."

"I am not concerned about the dead," replied Abner. "The dead are in God's hands. It is the living who concern me."

"Then," cried the Justice, "you should forgive the brother who takes."

"And I shall forgive him," replied Abner, "when he returns what he has taken."

"Returns what he has taken!" Randolph laughed. "Why, Abner, the devil could not filch a coin out of the clutches of old Benton Wolf."

"The devil," said my uncle, "is not an authority that I depend on."

"A miracle of Heaven, then," said the Justice. "But, alas, it is not the age of miracles."

"Perhaps," replied Abner, his voice descending into a deeper tone, "but I am not so certain."

They had come now to where the girl stood, her back against the black shoulder of the horse. The morning air moved the yellow leaves about her feet. She darted out to meet them, her face aglow.

"Damme!" cried Randolph. "William of Avon knew only witches of the second order! How do you do, Julia? I have hardly seen you since you were no taller than my stick, and told me that your name was 'Pete-George,' and that you were a circus horse, and offered to do tricks for me."

A shadow crossed the girl's face.

"I remember," she said, "it was up there on the porch!"

"Egad!" cried Randolph, embarrassed. "And so it was!"

He kissed the tips of the girl's fingers and the shadow in her face fled.

For the man's heart was good, and he had the manner of a gentleman. But it was Abner that she turned to in her dilemma.

"I forgot," she said, "and almost rode into the house. Do you think I could leave the horse here? He will stand if I drop the rein."

Then she went on to make her explanation. She wanted to see the old house that had been so long her home. This was the only opportunity, today, when all the countryside came to the dead man's burial. She thought she might come, too, although her motive was no tribute of respect.

She put her hand through Abner's arm and he looked down upon her, grave and troubled.

"My child," he said, "leave the horse where he stands and come with me, for my motive, also, is no tribute of respect; and you go with a better right than I do."

"I suppose," the girl hesitated, "that one ought to respect the dead, but this man—these men—I cannot."

"Nor can I," replied my uncle. "If I do not respect a man when he is living, I shall not pretend to when he is dead. One does not make a claim upon my honor by going out of life."

They went up the avenue among the yellow poplar leaves and the ragweed and fennel springing up along the unkept gravel.

It was a crisp and glorious morning. The frost lay on the rail fence. The spiderwebs stretched here and there across the high grasses of the meadows in intricate and bewildering lacework. The sun was clear and bright, but it carried no oppressive heat as it drew on in its course toward noon.

The countryside had gathered to see Adam Wolf buried. It was a company of tenants, the idle and worthless mostly, drawn by curiosity. For in life the two old men who had seized upon this property by virtue of a defective acknowledgment to a deed, permitted no invasion of their boundary.

Everywhere the lands were posted; no urchin fished and no schoolboy hunted. The green perch, fattened in the deep creek that threaded the rich bottom lands, no man disturbed. But the quail, the pheasant, the robin and the meadow lark, old Adam pursued with his fowling-piece. He tramped about with it at all seasons. One would have believed that all the birds of heaven had done the creature some unending harm and in revenge he had declared a war. And so the accident by which he met his death was a jeopardy of the old man's habits, and to be looked for when one lived with a fowling-piece in one's hands and grew careless in its use.

The two men lived alone and thus all sorts of mystery sprang up around them, elaborated by the Negro fancy and gaining in grim detail at every storyteller's hand. It had the charm and thrilling interest of an adventure, then, for the countryside to get this entry.

The brothers lived in striking contrast. Adam was violent, and his cries and curses, his hard and brutal manner were the terror of the Negro who passed at night that way, or the urchin overtaken by darkness on his road home. But Benton got about his affairs in silence, with a certain humility of manner, and a mild concern for the opinion of his fellows. Still, somehow, the Negro and the urchin held him in a greater terror. Perhaps because he had got his coffin made and kept it in his house, together with his clothes for burial. It seemed uncanny thus to prepare against his dissolution and to bargain for the outfit, with anxiety to have his shilling's worth.

And yet, with this gruesome furniture at hand, the old man, it would seem, was in no contemplation of his death. He spoke sometimes with a marked savor and an unctuous kneading of the hands of that time when he should own the land, for he was the younger and by rule should have the expectancy of life.

There was a crowd about the door and filling the hall inside, a crowd that elbowed and jostled, taken with a quivering interest, and there to feed its maw of curiosity with every item.

The girl wished to remain on the portico, where she could see the ancient garden and the orchard and all the paths and byways that had been her wonderland of youth, but Abner asked her to go in.

Randolph turned away, but my uncle and the girl remained some time by the coffin. The rim of the dead man's forehead and his jaw were riddled with birdshot, but his eyes and an area of his face below them, where the thin nose came down and with its lines and furrows made up the main identity of features, were not disfigured. And these preserved the hard stamp of his violent nature, untouched by the accident that had dispossessed him of his life.

He lay in the burial clothes and the coffin that Benton Wolf had provided for himself, all except the gloves upon his hands. These the old man had forgot. And now when he came to prepare his brother for a public burial, for no other had touched the man, he must needs take what he could find about the house, a pair of old, knit gloves with every rent and moth hole carefully darned, as though the man had sat down there with pains to give his brother the best appearance that he could.

This little touch affected the girl to tears, so strange is a woman's heart. "Poor thing!" she said. And for this triviality she would forget the injury that the dead man and his brother had done to her, the loss they had inflicted, and her long distress.

She took a closer hold upon Abner's arms, and dabbed her eyes with a tiny kerchief.

"I am sorry for him," she said, "for the living brother. It is so pathetic."

And she indicated the old, coarse gloves so crudely darned and patched together.

But my uncle looked down at her, strangely, and with a cold, inexorable face.

"My child," he said, "there is a curious virtue in this thing that moves you. Perhaps it will also move the man whose handiwork it is. Let us go up and see him."

Then he called the Justice.

"Randolph," he said, "come with us."

The Justice turned about. "Where do you go?" he asked.

"Why, sir," Abner answered, "this child is weeping at the sight of the dead man's gloves, and I thought, perhaps, that old Benton might weep at them too, and in the softened mood return what he has stolen."

The Justice looked upon Abner as upon one gone mad.

"And be sorry for his sins! And pluck out his eye and give it to you for a bauble! Why, Abner, where is your common sense. This thing would take a miracle of God."

My uncle was undisturbed.

"Well," he said, "come with me, Randolph, and help me to perform that miracle."

He went out into the hall, and up the wide old stairway, with the girl, in tears, upon his arm. And the Justice followed, like one who goes upon a patent and ridiculous fool's errand.

They came into an upper chamber, where a great bulk of a man sat in a padded chair looking down upon his avenue of trees. He looked with satisfaction. He turned his head about when the three came in and then his eyes widened in among the folds of fat.

"Abner and Mr. Randolph and Miss Julia Clayborne!" he gurgled. "You come to do honor to the dead!"

"No, Wolf," replied my uncle, "we come to do justice to the living."

The room was big, and empty but for chairs and an open secretary of some English make. The pictures on the wall had been turned about as though from a lack of interest in the tenant. But there hung in a frame above the secretary— with its sheets of foolscap, its iron ink pot and quill pens—a map in detail, and the written deed for the estate that these men had taken in their lawsuit. It was not the skill of any painter that gave pleasure to this mountain of a man; nor fields or groves imagined or copied for their charm, but the fields and groves that he possessed and mastered. And he would be reminded at his ease of them and of no other.

The old man's eyelids fluttered an instant as with some indecision, then he replied, "It was kind to have this thought of me. I have been long neglected. A little justice of recognition, even now, does much to soften the sorrow at my brother's death." Randolph caught at his jaw to keep in the laughter. And the huge old man, his head crouched into his billowy shoulders, his little reptilian eye shining like a crum of glass, went on with his speech.

"I am the greater moved," he said, "because you have been aloof and distant with me. You, Abner, have not visited my house, nor you, Randolph, although you live at no great distance. It is not thus that one gentleman should treat another. And especially when I and my dead brother, Adam, were from distant parts and came among you without a friend to take us by the hand and bring us to your door."

He sighed and put the fingers of his hands together.

"Ah, Abner," he went on, "it was a cruel negligence, and one from which I and my brother Adam suffered. You, who have a hand and a word at every turning, can feel no longing for this human comfort. But to the stranger, alone, and without the land of his nativity, it is a bitter lack."

He indicated the chairs about him.

"I beg you to be seated, gentlemen and Miss Clayborne. And overlook that I do not rise. I am shaken at Adam's death."

Randolph remained planted on his feet, his face now under control. But Abner put the child into a chair and stood behind it, as though he were some close and masterful familiar.

"Wolf," he said, "I am glad that your heart is softened."

"My heart—softened!" cried the man. "Why, Abner, I have the tenderest heart of any of God's creatures. I cannot endure to kill a sparrow. My brother Adam was not like that. He would be for hunting the wild creatures to their death with firearms. But I took no pleasure in it."

"Well," said Randolph, "the creatures of the air got their revenge of him. It was a foolish accident to die by."

"Randolph," replied the man, "it was the very end and extreme of carelessness. To look into a fowling-piece, a finger on the hammer, a left hand holding the barrel halfway up, to see if it was empty. It was a foolish and simple habit of my brother, and one that I abhorred and begged him to forgo, again and again, when I have seen him do it.

"But he had no fear of any firearms, as though by use and habit he had got their spirit tamed—as trainers, I am told, grow careless of wild beasts, and jugglers of the fangs and poison of their reptiles. He was growing old and would forget if they were loaded."

He spoke to Randolph, but he looked at Julia Clayborne and Abner behind her chair.

The girl sat straight and composed, in silence. The body of my uncle was to her a great protecting presence. He stood with his broad shoulders above her, his hands on the back of the chair, his face lifted. And he was big and dominant, as painters are accustomed to draw Michael in Satan's wars.

The pose held the old man's eye, and he moved in his chair; then he went on, speaking to the girl.

"It was kind of you, Abner, and you, Randolph, to come in to see me in my distress, but it was fine and noble in Miss Julia Clayborne. Men will understand the justice of the law and by what right it gives and takes. But a child will hardly understand that. It would be in nature for Miss Clayborne in her youth, to hold the issue of this lawsuit against me and my brother Adam, to feel that we had wronged her; had by some unfairness taken what her father bequeathed to her at his death, and always regarded as his own. A child would not see how the title had never vested, as our judges do. How possession is one thing, and the title in fee simple another and distinct. And so I am touched by this consideration."

Abner spoke then.

"Wolf," he said, "I am glad to find you in this mood, for now Randolph can write his deed, with consideration of love and affection instead of the real one I came with."

The old man's beady eye glimmered and slipped about.

"I do not understand, Abner. What deed?"

"The one Randolph came to write," replied my uncle.

"But, Abner," interrupted the Justice, "I did not come to write a deed." And he looked at my uncle in amazement.

"Oh, yes," returned Abner, "that is precisely what you came to do."

He indicated the open secretary with his hand.

"And the grantor, as it happens, has got everything ready for you. Here are foolscap and quill pens and ink. And here, exhibited for your convenience, is a map of the lands with all the metes and bounds. And here," he pointed to the wall, "in a frame, as though it were a work of art with charm, is the court's deed. Sit down, Randolph, and write." And such virtue is there in a dominant command, that the Justice sat down before the secretary and began to select a goose quill.

Then he realized the absurdity of the direction and turned about.

"What do you mean, Abner?" he cried.

"I mean precisely what I say," replied my uncle. "I want you to write a deed."

"But what sort of deed," cried the astonished Justice, "and by what grantor, and to whom, and for what lands?"

"You will draw a conveyance," replied Abner, "in form, with covenants of general warranty for the manor and lands set out in the deed before you and given in the plat. The grantor will be Benton Wolf, esquire, and the grantee Julia Clayborne, infant, and mark you, Randolph, the consideration will be love and affection, with a dollar added for the form."

The old man was amazed. His head, bedded into his huge shoulders, swung about; his pudgy features worked; his expression and his manner changed; his reptilian eyes hardened; he puffed with his breath in gusts.

"Not so fast, my fine gentleman!" he gurgled. "There will be no such deed."

"Go on, Randolph," said my uncle, as though there had been no interruption, "let us get this business over."

"But, Abner," returned the Justice, "it is fool work, the grantor will not sign."

"He will sign," said my uncle, "when you have finished, and seal and acknowledge—go on!"

"But, Abner, Abner!" the amazed Justice protested.

"Randolph," cried my uncle, "will you write, and leave this thing to me?"

And such authority was in the man to impose his will that the bewildered Justice spread out his sheet of foolscap, dipped his quill into the ink and began to draw the instrument, in form and of the parties, as my uncle said. And while he wrote, Abner turned back to the gross old man.

"Wolf," he said, "must I persuade you to sign the deed?"

"Abner," cried the man, "do you take me for a fool?"

He had got his unwieldy body up and defiant in the chair.

"I do not," replied my uncle, "and therefore I think that you will sign."

The obese old man spat violently on the floor, his face a horror of great folds.

"Sign!" he sputtered. "Fool, idiot, madman! Why should I sign away my lands?"

"There are many reasons," replied Abner calmly. "The property is not yours. You got it by a legal trick, the judge who heard you was bound by the technicalities of language. But you are old, Wolf, and the next Judge will go behind the record. He will be hard to face. He has expressed Himself on these affairs. 'If the widow and the orphan cry to me, I will surely hear their cry.' Sinister words,

Wolf, for one who comes with a case like yours into the court of Final Equity."

"Abner," cried the old man, "begone with your little sermons!"

My uncle's big fingers tightened on the back of the chair.

"Then, Wolf," he said, "if this thing does not move you, let me urge the esteem of men and this child's sorrow, and our high regard."

The old man's jaw chattered and he snapped his fingers.

"I would not give that for the things you name," he cried, and he set off a tiny measure of his index finger with the thumb.

"Why, sir, my whim, idle and ridiculous, is a greater power to move me than this drivel."

Abner did not move, but his voice took on depth and volume.

"Wolf," he said, "a whim is sometimes a great lever to move a man. Now, I am taken with a whim myself. I have a fancy, Wolf, that your brother Adam ought to go out of the world barehanded as he came into it."

The old man twisted his great head, as though he would get Abner wholly within the sweep of his reptilian eye.

"What?" he gurgled. "What is that?"

"Why, this," replied my uncle. "I have a whim—'idle and ridiculous,' did you say, Wolf? Well, then, idle and ridiculous, if you like, that your brother ought not to be buried in his gloves."

Abner looked hard at the man and, although he did not move, the threat and menace of his presence seemed somehow to advance him. And the effect upon the huge old man was like some work of sorcery. The whole mountain of him began to quiver and the folds of his face seemed spread over with thin oil. He sat piled up in the chair and the oily sweat gathered and thickened on him. His jaw jerked and fell into a baggy gaping and the great expanse of him worked as with an ague.

Finally, out of the pudgy, undulating mass, a voice issued, thin and shaken.

"Abner," it said, "has any other man this fancy?"

"No," replied my uncle, "but I hold it, Wolf, at your decision."

"And, Abner," his thin voice trebled, "you will let my brother be buried as he is?"

"If you sign!" said my uncle.

The man reeked and grew wet in the terror on him, and one thought that his billowy body would never be again at peace. "Randolph," he quavered, "bring me the deed."

Outside, the girl sobbed in Abner's arms. She asked for no explanation. She wished to believe her fortune a miracle of God, forever—to the end of all things. But Randolph turned on my uncle when she was gone.

"Abner! Abner!" he cried. "Why in the name of the Eternal was the old creature so shaken at the gloves?"

"Because he saw the hangman behind them," replied my uncle. "Did you notice how the rim of the dead man's face was riddled by the bird-shot and the center of it clean? How could that happen, Randolph?"

"It was a curious accident of gunfire," replied the Justice.

"It was no accident at all," said Abner. "That area of the man's face is clean because it was protected. Because the dead man put up his hands to cover his face when he saw that his brother was about to shoot him.

"The backs of old Adam's hands, hidden by the gloves, will be riddled with bird-shot like the rim of his face."

WASHINGTON

THE HUNGER

by Charles Beaumont

Now, WITH THE sun almost gone, the sky looked wounded—as if a gigantic razor had been drawn across it, slicing deep. It bled richly. And the wind, which came down from High Mountain, cool as rain, sounded a little like children crying: a soft, unhappy kind of sound, rising and falling.

Afraid, somehow, it seemed to Julia. Terribly afraid.

She quickened her step. I'm an idiot, she thought, looking away from the sky. A complete idiot. That's why I'm frightened now; and if anything happens— which it won't, and can't—then I'll have no one to blame but myself.

She shifted the bag of groceries to her other arm and turned, slightly. There was no one in sight, except old Mr. Hannaford, pulling in his newspaper stands, preparing to close up the drugstore, and Jake Spiker, barely moving across to the Blue Haven for a glass of beer: no one else. The rippling red brick streets were silent.

But even if she got nearly all the way home, she could scream and someone would hear her. Who would be fool enough to try anything right out in the open? Not even a lunatic. Besides, it wasn't dark yet, not technically, anyway.

Still, as she passed the vacant lots, all shoulder-high in wild grass, Julia could not help thinking, He might be hiding there, right now. It was possible. Hiding there, all crouched up, waiting. And he'd only have to grab her, and—she wouldn't scream. She knew that suddenly, and the thought terrified her. Sometimes you *can't* scream. . . .

If only she'd not bothered to get that spool of yellow thread over at Younger's, it would be bright daylight now, bright clear daylight. And—

Nonsense! This was the middle of the town. She was surrounded by houses full of people. People all around. Everywhere.

(*He was a hunger; a need; a force. Dark emptiness filled him. He moved, when he moved, like a leaf caught in some dark and secret river, rushing. But mostly he slept now, an animal, always ready to wake and leap and be gone. . . .*)

523

The shadows came to life, dancing where Julia walked. Now the sky was ugly and festered, and the wind had become stronger, colder. She clicked along the sidewalk, looking straight ahead, wondering, Why, why am I so infernally stupid? What's the matter with me?

Then she was home, and it was all over. The trip had taken not more than half an hour. And here was Maud, running. Julia felt her sister's arms fly around her, hugging. "God, my God."

And Louise's voice: "We were just about to call Mick to go after you."

Julia pulled free and went into the kitchen and put down the bag of groceries.

"Where in the world have you been?" Maud demanded.

"I had to get something at Younger's." Julia took off her coat. "They had to go look for it, and—I didn't keep track of the time."

Maud shook her head. "Well, I don't know," she said, wearily. "You're just lucky you're alive, that's all."

"Now—"

"You listen! He's out there somewhere. Don't you understand that? It's a fact. They haven't even come close to catching him yet."

"They will," Julia said, not knowing why: she wasn't entirely convinced of it.

"Of course they will. Meantime, how many more is he going to murder? Can you answer me that?"

"I'm going to put my coat away." Julia brushed past her sister. Then she turned and said, "I'm sorry you were worried. It won't happen again." She went to the closet, feeling strangely upset. They would talk about it tonight. All night. Analyzing, hinting, questioning. They would talk of nothing else, as from the very first. And they would not be able to conceal their delight.

"Wasn't it awful about poor Eva Schillings?"

No, Julia had thought: from her sisters' point of view it was not awful at all. It was wonderful. It was priceless.

It was news.

Julia's sisters . . . Sometimes she thought of them as mice. Giant gray mice, in high white collars: groaning a little, panting a little, working about the house. Endlessly, untiringly: they would squint at pictures, knock them crooked, then straighten them again; they swept invisible dust from clean carpets and took the invisible dust outside in shining pans and dumped it carefully into spotless apple-baskets; they stood by beds whose sheets shone gleaming white and tight, and clucked in soft disgust, and replaced the sheets with others. All day, every day, from six in the morning until most definite dusk. Never questioning, never doubting that the work had to be done.

They ran like arteries through the old house, keeping it alive. For it had become now a part of them, and they part of it—like the handcrank mahogany Victrola in the hall, or the lion-pelted sofa, or the Boutelle piano (ten years silent, its keys yellowed and decayed and ferocious, like the teeth of an aged mule).

Nights, they spoke of sin. Also of other times and better days: Maud and

Louise—sitting there in the bellying heat of the obsolete but steadfast stove, hooking rugs, crocheting doilies, sewing linen, chatting, chatting.

Occasionally Julia listened, because she was there and there was nothing else to do; but mostly she didn't. It had become a simple thing to rock and nod and think of nothing at all, while *they* traded dreams of dead husbands, constantly relishing their mutual widowhood—relishing it!—pitching these fragile ghosts into moral combat. "Ernie, God rest him, was an honorable man." (So were they all, Julia would think, all honorable men; but we are here to praise Caesar, not to bury him . . .) "Jack would be alive today if it hadn't been for that trunk lid slamming down on his head: that's what started it all." Poor Ernie! Poor Jack!

(*He walked along the railroad tracks, blending with the night. He could have been young, or old: an age-hiding beard dirtied his face and throat. He wore a blue sweater, ripped in a dozen places. On the front of the sweater was sewn a large felt letter: E. Also sewn there was a small design showing a football and calipers. His gray trousers were dark with stain where he had fouled them. He walked along the tracks, seeing and not seeing the pulse of light far ahead; thinking and not thinking, Perhaps I'll find it there, Perhaps they won't catch me, Perhaps I won't be hungry any more. . . .*)

"You forgot the margarine," Louise said, holding the large sack upside down.

"Did I? I'm sorry." Julia took her place at the table. The food immediately began to make her ill: the sight of it, the smell of it. Great bowls of beans, crisp-skinned chunks of turkey, mashed potatoes. She put some on her plate, and watched her sisters. They ate earnestly; and now, for no reason, this, too, was upsetting.

She looked away. What was it? What was wrong?

"Mick says that fellow didn't die," Maud announced. "Julia—"

"What fellow?"

"At the asylum, that got choked. He's going to be all right."

"That's good."

Louise broke a square of toast. She addressed Maud: "What else did he say, when you talked to him? Are they making any progress?"

"Some. I understand there's a bunch of police coming down from Seattle. If they don't get him in a few days, they'll bring in some bloodhounds from out-of-state. Of course, you can imagine how much Mick likes *that!*"

"Well, it's his own fault. If he was any kind of a sheriff, he'd of caught that fellow a long time before this. I mean, after all, Burlington just isn't that big." Louise dismembered a turkey leg, ripped little shreds of the meat off, put them into her mouth.

Maud shook her head. "I don't know. Mick claims it isn't like catching an ordinary criminal. With this one, you never can guess what he's going to do, or where he'll be. Nobody has figured out how he stays alive, for instance."

"Probably," Louise said, "he eats bugs and things."

Julia folded her napkin quickly and pressed it onto the table.

Maud said, "No. Most likely he finds stray dogs and cats."

They finished the meal in silence. Not, Julia knew, because there was any lull in thought: merely so the rest could be savored in the living room, next to the fire. A proper place for everything.

They moved out of the kitchen. Louise insisted on doing the dishes, while Maud settled at the radio and tried to find a local news broadcast. Finally she snapped the radio off, angrily. "You'd think they'd at least keep us informed! Isn't that the least they could do?"

Louise materialized in her favorite chair. The kitchen was dark. The stove warmed noisily, its metal sides undulating.

And it was time.

"Where do you suppose he is right now?" Maud asked.

Louise shrugged. "Out there somewhere. If they'd got him, Mick would of called us. He's out there somewhere."

"Yes. Laughing at all of us, too, I'll wager. Trying to figure out who'll be next."

Julia sat in the rocker and tried not to listen. Outside, there was a wind. A cold wind, biting; the kind that slips right through window putty, that you can feel on the glass. Was there ever such a cold wind? she wondered.

Then Louise's words started to echo. "He's out there somewhere. . . ."

Julia looked away from the window, and attempted to take an interest in the lacework in her lap.

Louise was talking. Her fingers flashed long silver needles. ". . . spoke to Mrs. Schillings today."

"I don't want to hear about it." Maud's eyes flashed like the needles.

"God love her heart, she's about crazy. Could barely talk."

"God, God."

"I tried to comfort her, of course, but it didn't do any good."

Julia was glad she had been spared that conversation. It sent a shudder across her, even to think about it. Mrs. Schillings was Eva's mother, and Eva—only seventeen . . . The thoughts she vowed not to think, came back. She remembered Mick's description of the body, and his words: ". . . she'd got through with work over at the telephone office around about nine. Carl Jasperson offered to see her home, but he says she said not to bother, it was only a few blocks. Our boy must have been hiding around the other side of the cannery. Just as Eva passed, he jumped. Raped her and then strangled her. I figure he's a pretty man-sized bugger. Thumbs like to went clean through the throat. . . ."

In two weeks, three women had died. First, Charlotte Adams, the librarian. She had been taking her usual shortcut across the school playground, about 9:15 P.M. They found her by the slide, her clothes ripped from her body, her throat raw and bruised.

Julia tried very hard not to think of it, but when her mind would clear, there were her sisters' voices, droning, pulling her back, deeper.

She remembered how the town had reacted. It was the first murder Burlington had had in fifteen years. It was the very first mystery. Who was the sex-crazed killer? Who could have done this terrible thing to Charlotte Adams? One of her gentleman friends, perhaps. Or a hobo, from one of the nearby jungles. Or. . .

Mick Daniels and his tiny force of deputies had swung into action immediately. Everyone in town took up the topic, chewed it, talked it, chewed it, until it lost its shape completely. The air became electrically charged. And a grim gaiety swept Burlington, reminding Julia of a circus where everyone is forbidden to smile.

Days passed, uneventfully. Vagrants were pulled in and released. People were questioned. A few were booked, temporarily.

Then, when the hum of it had begun to die, it happened again. Mrs. Dovie Samuelson, member of the local P.T.A., mother of two, moderately attractive and moderately young, was found in her garden, sprawled across a rhododendron bush, dead. She was naked, and it was established that she had been attacked. Of the killer, once again, there was no trace.

Then the State Hospital for the Criminally Insane released the information that one of its inmates—a Robert Oakes—had escaped. Mick, and many others, had known this all along. Oakes had originally been placed in the asylum on a charge of raping and murdering his cousin, a girl named Patsy Blair.

After he had broken into his former home and stolen some old school clothes, he had disappeared, totally.

Now he was loose.

Burlington, population 3,000, went into a state of ecstasy: delicious fear gripped the town. The men foraged out at night with torches and weapons; the women squeaked and looked under their beds and . . . chatted.

But still no progress was made. The maniac eluded hundreds of searchers. They knew he was near, perhaps at times only a few feet away, hidden; but always they returned home, defeated.

They looked in the forests and in the fields and along the river banks. They covered High Mountain—a miniature hill at the south end of town—like ants, poking at every clump of brush, investigating every abandoned tunnel and water tank. They broke into deserted houses, searched barns, silos, haystacks, treetops. They looked everywhere, everywhere. And found nothing.

When they decided for sure that their killer had gone far away, that he couldn't conceivably be within fifty miles of Burlington, a third crime was committed. Young Eva Schillings' body had been found, less than a hundred yards from her home.

And that was three days ago. . . .

". . . they get him," Louise was saying, "they ought to kill him by little pieces, for what he's done."

Maud nodded. "Yes; but they won't."

"Of course they—"

"No! You wait. They'll shake his hand and lead him back to the bughouse and wait on him hand and foot—till he gets a notion to bust out again."

"Well, I'm of a mind the people will have something to say about that."

"Anyway," Maud continued, never lifting her eyes from her knitting, "what makes you so sure they *will* catch him? Supposing he just drops out of sight for six months, and—"

"You stop that! They'll get him. Even if he *is* a maniac, he's still human."

"I really doubt that. I doubt that a human could have done these awful things." Maud sniffed. Suddenly, like small rivers, tears began to course down her snowbound cheeks, cutting and melting the hard white-packed powder, revealing flesh underneath even paler. Her hair was shot with gray, and her dress was the color of rocks and moths; yet, she did not succeed in looking either old or frail. There was nothing whatever frail about Maud.

"He's a man," she said. Her lips seemed to curl at the word. Louise nodded, and they were quiet.

(*His ragged tennis shoes padded softly on the gravel bed. Now his heart was trying to tear loose from his chest. The men, the men . . . They had almost stepped on him, they were that close. But he had been silent. They had gone past him, and away. He could see their flares back in the distance. And far ahead, the pulsing light. Also a square building: the depot, yes. He must be careful. He must walk in the shadows. He must be very still.*

The fury burned him, and he fought it.

Soon.

It would be all right soon. . . .)

". . . think about it, this here maniac is only doing what every man would *like* to do but can't."

"Maud!"

"I mean it. It's a man's natural instinct—it's all they ever think about." Maud smiled. She looked up. "Julia, you're feeling sick. Don't tell me you're not."

"I'm all right," Julia said, tightening her grip on the chair-arms slightly. She thought, They've been married! They talk this way about men, as they always have, and yet soft words have been spoken to them, and strong arms placed around their shoulders. . . .

Maud made tiny circles with her fingers. "Well, I can't force you to take care of yourself. Except, when you land in the hospital again, I suppose you know who'll be doing the worrying and staying up nights—as per usual."

"I'll . . . go on to bed in a minute." But, why was she hesitating? Didn't she want to be alone?

Why didn't she want to be alone?

Louise was testing the door. She rattled the knob vigorously, and returned to her chair.

"What would he want, anyway," Maud said, "with two old biddies like us?"

"We're not so old," Louise said, saying, actually: "That's true; we're old."

But it wasn't true, not at all. Looking at them, studying them, it suddenly occurred to Julia that her sisters were ashamed of their essential attractiveness. Beneath the 'twenties hair-dos, the ill-used cosmetics, the ancient dresses (which did not quite succeed in concealing their still voluptuous physiques), Maud and

Louise were youthfully full and pretty. They were. Not even the birch-twig toothbrushes and traditional snuff could hide it.

Yet, Julia thought, they envy me.

They envy my plainness.

"What kind of a man would do such heinous things?" Louise said, pronouncing the word, carefully, heen-ious.

And Julia, without calling or forming the thought, discovered an answer grown in her mind: an impression, a feeling.

What kind of a man?

A lonely man.

It came upon her like a chill. She rose from the pillowed chair, lightly. "I think," she said, "I'll go on to my room."

"Are your windows good and locked?"

"Yes."

"You'd better make sure. All he'd have to do is climb up the drainpipe." Maud's expression was peculiar. Was she really saying, "This is only to comfort you, dear. Of the three of us, it's unlikely he'd pick on you"?

"I'll make sure." Julia walked to the hallway. "Good night."

"Try to get some sleep." Louise smiled. "And don't think about him, hear? We're perfectly safe. He couldn't possibly get in, even if he tried. Besides," she said, "I'll be awake."

(*He stopped and leaned against a pole and looked up at the deaf and swollen sky. It was a movement of dark shapes, a hurrying, a running.*

He closed his eyes.

> *"The moon is the shepherd,*
> *The clouds are his sheep . . ."*

He tried to hold the words, tried very hard, but they scattered and were gone. "No."

He pushed away from the pole, turned, and walked back to the gravel bed.

The hunger grew: with every step it grew. He thought that it had died, that he had killed it at last and now he could rest, but it had not died. It sat inside him, inside his mind, gnawing, calling, howling to be released. Stronger than before. Stronger than ever before.

> *"The moon is the shepherd . . ."*

A cold wind raced across the surrounding fields of wild grass, turning the land into a heaving dark-green ocean. It sighed up through the branches of cherry trees and rattled the thick leaves. Sometimes a cherry would break loose, tumble in the gale, fall and split, filling the night with its fragrance. The air was iron and loam and growth.

He walked and tried to pull these things into his lungs, the silence and coolness of them.

But someone was screaming, deep inside him. Someone was talking.

"What are you going to do—"

He balled his fingers into fists.

"Get away from me! Get away!"

"Don't—"

The scream faded.

The girl's face remained. Her lips and her smooth white skin and her eyes, her eyes . . .

He shook the vision away.

The hunger continued to grow. It wrapped his body in sheets of living fire. It got inside his mind and bubbled in hot acids, filling and filling him.

He stumbled, fell, plunged his hands deep into the gravel, withdrew fists full of the grit and sharp stones and squeezed them until blood trailed down his wrists.

He groaned, softly.

Ahead, the light glowed and pulsed and whispered, Here, Here, Here, Here, Here.

He dropped the stones and opened his mouth to the wind and walked on. . . .)

Julia closed the door and slipped the lock noiselessly. She could no longer hear the drone of voices: it was quiet, still, but for the sighing breeze.

What kind of a man. . . .

She did not move, waiting for her heart to stop throbbing. But it would not stop.

She went to the bed and sat down. Her eyes traveled to the window, held there.

"He's out there somewhere. . . ."

Julia felt her hands move along her dress. It was an old dress, once purple, now gray with faded gray flowers. The cloth was tissue-thin. Her fingers touched it and moved upward to her throat. They undid the top button.

For some reason, her body trembled. The chill had turned to heat, tiny needles of heat, puncturing her all over.

She threw the dress over a chair and removed the underclothing. Then she walked to the bureau and took from the top drawer a flannel nightdress, and turned.

What she saw in the tall mirror caused her to stop and make a small sound.

Julia Landon stared back at her from the polished glass.

Julia Landon, thirty-eight, neither young nor old, attractive nor unattractive, a woman so plain she was almost invisible. All angles and sharpnesses, and flesh that would once have been called "milky" but was now only white, pale white. A little too tall. A little too thin. And faded.

Only the eyes had softness. Only the eyes burned with life and youth and—

Julia moved away from the mirror. She snapped off the light. She touched the window shade, pulled it slightly, guided it soundlessly upward.

Then she unfastened the window latch.

Night came into the room and filled it. Outside, giant clouds roved across the moon, obscuring it, revealing it, obscuring it again.

It was cold. Soon there would be rain.

Julia looked out beyond the yard, in the direction of the depot, dark and silent now, and the tracks and the jungles beyond the tracks where lost people lived.

"I wonder if he can see me."

She thought of the man who had brought terror and excitement to the town. She thought of him openly, for the first time, trying to imagine his features.

He was probably miles away.

Or, perhaps he was nearby. Behind the tree, there, or under the hedge. . . .

"I'm afraid of you, Robert Oakes," she whispered to the night. "You're insane, and a killer. You would frighten the wits out of me."

The fresh smell swept into Julia's mind. She wished she were surrounded by it, in it, just for a little while.

Just for a few minutes.

A walk. A short walk in the evening.

She felt the urge strengthening.

"You're dirty, young man. And heartless—ask Mick, if you don't believe me. You want love so badly you must kill for it—but nevertheless, you're heartless. Understand? And you're not terribly bright, either, they say. Have you read Shakespeare's Sonnets? Herrick? How about Shelley, then? There, you see! I'd detest you on sight. Just look at your fingernails!"

She said these things silently, but as she said them she moved toward her clothes.

She paused, went to the closet.

The green dress. It was warmer.

A warm dress and a short walk—that will clear my head. Then I'll come back and sleep.

It's perfectly safe.

She started for the door, stopped, returned to the window. Maud and Louise would still be up, talking.

She slid one leg over the sill; then the other leg.

Softly she dropped to the frosted lawn.

The gate did not creak.

She walked into the darkness.

Better! So much better. Good clean air that you can breathe! The town was a silence. A few lights gleamed in distant houses, up ahead; behind, there was only blackness. And the wind.

In the heavy green frock, which was still too light to keep out the cold—though she felt no cold; only the needled heat—she walked away from the house and toward the depot.

It was a small structure, unchanged by passing years, like the Landon home and most of the homes in Burlington. There were tracks on either side of it.

Now it was deserted. Perhaps Mr. Gaffey was inside, making insect sounds on the wireless. Perhaps he was not.

Julia stepped over the first track, and stood, wondering what had happened and why she was here. Vaguely she understood something. Something about the yellow thread that had made her late and forced her to return home through the gathering dusk. And this dress—had she chosen it because it was warmer than the others . . . or because it was prettier?

Beyond this point there was wilderness, for miles. Marshes and fields overgrown with weeds and thick foliage. The hobo jungles: some tents, dead campfires, empty tins of canned heat.

She stepped over the second rail, and began to follow the gravel bed. Heat consumed her. She could not keep her hands still.

In a dim way, she realized—with a tiny part of her—why she had come out tonight.

She was looking for someone.

The words formed in her mind, unwilled: "Robert Oakes, listen, listen to me. You're not the only one who is lonely. But you can't steal what we're lonely for, you can't take it by force. Don't you know that? Haven't you learned that yet?"

I'll talk to him, she thought, and he'll go along with me and give himself up. . . .

No.

That isn't why you're out tonight. You don't care whether he gives himself up or not. You . . . only want him to know that you understand. Isn't that it?

You couldn't have any other reason.

It isn't possible that you're seeking out a lunatic for any other reason.

Certainly you don't want him to touch you.

Assuredly you don't want him to put his arms around you and kiss you, because no man has ever done that—assuredly, assuredly.

It isn't you he wants. It isn't love. He wouldn't be taking Julia Landon. . . .

"But what if he doesn't!" The words spilled out in a small choked cry. "What if he sees me and runs away! Or I don't find him. Others have been looking. What makes me think I'll—"

Now the air swelled with sounds of life: frogs and birds and locusts, moving; and the wind, running across the trees and reeds and foliage at immense speed, whining, sighing.

Everywhere there was this loudness, and a dark like none Julia had ever known. The moon was gone entirely. Shadowless, the surrounding fields were great pools of liquid black, stretching infinitely, without horizon.

Fear came up in her chest, clutching.

She tried to scream.

She stood paralyzed, moveless, a pale terror drying into her throat and into her heart.

Then, from far away, indistinctly, there came a sound. A sound like footsteps on gravel.

Julia listened, and tried to pierce the darkness. The sounds grew louder. And louder. Someone was on the tracks. Coming closer.

She waited. Years passed, slowly. Her breath turned into a ball of expanding ice in her lungs.

Now she could see, just a bit.

It was a man. A black man-form. Perhaps—the thought increased her fear—a hobo. It mustn't be one of the hobos.

No. It was a young man. Mick! Mick, come to tell her, "Well, we got the bastard!" and to ask, narrowly, "What the devil you doing out here, Julie?" Was it?

She saw the sweater. The ball of ice in her lungs began to melt, a little. A sweater. And shoes that seemed almost white.

Not a hobo. Not Mick. Not anyone she knew.

She waited an instant longer. Then, at once, she knew without question who the young man was.

And she knew that he had seen her.

The fear went away. She moved to the center of the tracks.

"I've been looking for you," she said, soundlessly. "Every night I've thought of you. I have." She walked toward the man. "Don't be afraid, Mr. Oakes. Please don't be afraid. I'm not."

The young man stopped. He seemed to freeze, like an animal, prepared for flight.

He did not move, for several seconds.

Then he began to walk toward Julia, lightly, hesitantly, rubbing his hands along his trousers.

When Julia was close enough to see his eyes, she relaxed, and smiled.

Perhaps, she thought, feeling the first drops of rain upon her face, perhaps if I don't scream he'll let me live.

That would be nice.

WEST VIRGINIA

COME DOWN FROM THE HILLS

by John F. Suter

ARLAN BOLEY EASED his backhoe down the ramp from the flatbed, cut the motor, and climbed off. It was early in the morning in the dry season of late August, but the dew was just starting to rise. Boley knew that the oppressiveness of the air would pass, but he hated it all the same.

"You want me to do the first one along about here?" he asked. He brushed at his crinkly blond hair where a strand of cobweb from an overhanging branch had caught.

Sewell McCutcheon, who was hiring Boley's services for the morning, walked to the edge of the creek and took a look. He picked up a dead sycamore branch and laid it perpendicular to the stream. "One end about here." He walked downstream about fifteen feet and repeated the act with another branch. "Other end here."

Boley glanced across the small creek and, without looking at McCutcheon, asked, "How far out?"

The older man grinned, the ends of his heavy brown moustache lifting. "We do have to be careful about that." He reached into a pocket of his blue-and-white coveralls and took out a twenty-five-foot reel of surveyor's tape. He laid it on the ground, stooped over to remove heavy shoes and socks, and rolled the coveralls to his knees.

He unreeled about a foot of tape and handed the end to Boley. "Stand right at the edge and hold that," he said, picking up a pointed stake about five feet long.

While Boley held the tape's end, McCutcheon stepped down the low bank and entered the creek. The dark brown hair on his sinewy legs was plastered against the dead-white skin from the knees down. When he reached the other side, he turned around. "She look square to you?"

"A carpenter couldn't do better."

McCutcheon looked down. "Fourteen and a quarter feet. Midway's seven feet, one and a half inches. I don't know about you, Boley, but I hate fractions."

He started back, reeling up tape as he came. "Seven feet, three inches from her side. I'll just give her a little more than half, then she can't complain. Not that she won't."

He plunged the stake in upright at the spot. Then he waded ashore, went to the other boundary, and repeated the performance.

"That's the first one. When you finish," he told Boley, "come down just opposite the house and we'll mark off the second one."

"How deep?" Boley asked.

"Take about two feet off the bottom," McCutcheon said. "Water's low now. When she comes back up, it'll make a good pool there. Trout ought to be happy with it."

"I'll be gettin' to 'er, then," Boley said, going back to his machine. He was already eyeing the spot where he would begin to take the first bite with the scoop. He began to work within minutes. He had moved enough dirt with his backhoe in the past to know what he was doing, even with the added presence of the water that soaked the muck. There was also an abundance of gravel in the piles he was depositing along the bank.

When he judged that he had finished the hole, he lifted the scoop until it was roughly level with the seat. Then he swung the machine around and ran it down the creek toward his next worksite.

The pebble-bottomed stream, one typical of West Virginia, was known as Squirrel Creek. It divided two farms of nearly flat land at an altitude between one and two thousand feet. On the eastern side was McCutcheon's well-kept eighty acres. McCutcheon, a recent widower, planned well and worked hard, aided by his son and daughter-in-law. Both sides of the stream were lined with trees whose root systems kept the banks from crumbling and silting the creek bed. This was deliberate on McCutcheon's part, happenstance on his neighbor's.

When Boley came down opposite McCutcheon's white frame two-story, he cut the motor and walked over to where the farmer was sitting on the steps of his porch. The house was on a small rise, with a high foundation that would protect it in the event of an unusually heavy flash flood. Because of this, Boley had to look up a few inches to talk to McCutcheon.

"See anything of her?" he asked.

"Not yet," the farmer answered.

"Maybe this isn't gonna bother her."

McCutcheon rubbed his moustache. *"Everything* about this stream bothers that woman, Arly. One of the biggest trout I ever hooked in there was givin' me one helluva fight one day. I was tryin' to play him over to this side, but I hadn't yet managed it. Then, all of a sudden, outa nowhere came the old woman, screechin' her head off. 'What d'you mean ketchin' *my* fish?' she squawks. And with that she wades right out into the water, grabs the line with both hands, and flops that trout out on the ground at her side of the creek. Whips out a knife I'da never guessed she had and cuts the line. Then off to the house with my catch."

"Well," said Boley, "it was on her half of the creek, wasn't it? Property line down the middle? That why you've been measurin'?"

"Oh, sure," the farmer replied. "I recognize that. But that's not the way she looks at it. Had the fish been over here, she'd still have done it."

"I'd better get at it while it's quiet," Boley said, mentally thankful for his own Geneva's reasonableness.

As he walked to his machine, he heard McCutcheon say, "She must be away somewhere."

Later, Boley finished piling the last of the scooped silt and rocks on the bank of the stream. McCutcheon would later sort out the rocks and use the silt in his garden.

Paid for his work, Boley put the backhoe on the flatbed and fastened it securely. He turned around to head out, when he glanced over the creek toward the brown-painted cottage on the other side. A battered red half-ton pickup was just pulling up to the front of the house, barely visible through the tangle of bushes between stream and house.

A rangy older woman with dyed jet-black hair jumped from the truck and began to force her way toward the creek.

"Arlan Boley!" she screamed. A crow's voice contained more music. "What're you doin' over there?"

Boley put the truck in gear and pushed down the accelerator. He had no wish to talk to Alice Roberts. Leave that to McCutcheon.

Six days later, Boley and his family went into town. While Geneva and the two children were making some minor purchases for the opening of school, Boley went to the courthouse to the sheriff's office.

He had just finished paying his first-half taxes and was pocketing the receipt when he was tapped on the shoulder.

"Guess I'll have to wait 'til spring now before I can get you for non-payment," a voice said.

Boley recognized the voice of his old friend, the sheriff. "Hi, McKee," he said, turning. "You want that place of mine so bad, make me an offer. I might surprise you."

"No, thanks," McKee replied. "More'n I could handle." He nodded toward the clerk's window. "You payin' with what you got from Sewell McCutcheon?"

"Some. It took a little extra." He looked at McKee with curiosity. "What's the big deal? All I did was scoop him two holes in the creek for trout to loll around in from now on."

"You did more than that, Boley. You might have provided him with a fortune. Or part of one."

Boley nudged McKee's shoulder with his fist, feeling the hardness still existing in McKee's spare frame. "Don't tell me he panned that muck and found gold."

"You're not far off the mark."

Boley's eyes widened. He noticed a tiny lift at the ends of McKee's lips and a small deepening of the lines in the sheriff's tanned face. "Well, get to it and tell me," he said.

"Maybe you heard and maybe you didn't," McKee said, "but a state geologist's been usin' a vacant office here in the courthouse for the last ten days. Been workin' in the lower end of the county tryin' to see if there's a coal seam worth explorin' by that company that owns some of the land. Anyway, today McCutcheon walked in lookin' for him. Said he needed an opinion on an object in his pocket."

"And he got his interview?"

McKee nodded. "It seems he pulled out a fair-sized rock. First glance, could have been quartz or calcite. Kinda dull—but somehow different. This state fellow thought at first it was another pebble, then he took a good look and found it wasn't."

"So what *did* he find it was?"

"A diamond."

Boley had been half anticipating the answer, but he had tried to reject it. His jaw dropped. "No kidding!"

"No kidding."

"McCutcheon's probably turning over every rock out of that stream."

The sheriff dipped his chin. "I'll bet. Geologist said it's what they call an alluvial diamond, and the probability of findin' more is very small. Said it was formed millions of years ago when these mountains were as high as the Himalayas or higher. Somewhere in all that time, water eroded away whatever surrounded this one, and it might have even washed down here from someplace else. Come down from the hills, you might say."

An odd feeling crossed Boley's mind. Several times in the past, fragments of an old ersatz folk song had made themselves recognizable at the fringe of an unpleasant situation. "Just come down from the hills" was in one of the verses.

"What's the matter?" McKee asked.

"Nothing. How big is this rock? What's it worth?"

"A little bigger than the last joint on my thumb, not as big as the whole thumb. Worth? The man told McCutcheon there's no way of knowin' until it's cut. And it might be flawed."

Boley stared into the distance. "I'd better get on home and start seein' what's in the bottom of that run that goes through my property. Everybody in the country'll be doin' the same thing wherever there's water." He paused. "Or does anybody else know?"

"Only McCutcheon, that geologist, and the two of us," McKee said. "There's sort of an agreement to keep our mouths shut. You never know who would get drawn in here, if the word got out. Don't you even tell Geneva."

"What's McCutcheon done with the thing?"

"I suggested that he should put it in a safety-deposit box."

"It's what I'd do. I hope he has," Boley said.

The quirk around McKee's mouth had gone. "You know Alice Roberts?"

"Miner's widow across the creek from McCutcheon?"

"That's the one."

"No. I've seen her. She evidently knows who I am. I don't think I want to know her."

"Not good company," McKee said. "I wonder if she's heard about this. Do me a favor, would you? Drop by McCutcheon's place before long. You have a good excuse—checkin' up on the job you did. See what you can find out, but don't let on what you know."

Boley gave him a thoughtful look. "Seems to me you know a lot already."

The following evening, Boley left home on the pretext that he wanted to look at some land where he might be asked to make a ditch for a farmer who wanted to lay plastic pipe from his well pump to a new hog house. Instead, Boley went to McCutcheon's.

He found the farmer sitting alone on his porch. The sun had not quite set. His son and daughter-in-law had gone into town.

"Hello, Sewell," Boley said, walking to the foot of the steps. "Water cleared yet where I dug 'er out?"

"If it ain't by now, it never will," McCutcheon said. "Come up."

Boley went up and sat in a cane-bottomed rocker like the farmer's. "Ever since I dug it out, I've been wonderin' why you did that," he said. "After all, you have a pretty good farm pond at the back. Fed by three springs, stocked with bass and blue gills, isn't it?"

McCutcheon smiled. "That's right. Bass and blue gills. But no trout. Running water's for trout. I like variety."

"You put all that gunk on your garden yet?"

"Oh, yeah. We just took a bunch of rakes and dragged all the rocks and pebbles out, let the muck dry some, then shoveled 'er into a small wagon, towed 'er to the garden, and that was it."

Boley looked at the gravel drive leading from the house to the main road. "I guess you can bust up the rocks and fill in some potholes when you get more."

McCutcheon seemed uninterested. "I suppose. I have a small rock pile out there. Don't know what I'll do with 'em."

Boley decided that the other man was keeping his secret. He wondered if the son and daughter-in-law knew. And if they could keep quiet. To change the subject, he said, "Anybody ever want to buy your land, Sewell?"

The farmer nodded. "Every now and then some developer comes by. Thing is, this isn't close to the lake and the recreation area, and they don't want to offer much."

"It's a good bit for the three of you to handle."

"Maybe it will be later," McCutcheon agreed. "That's when I'll think again."

Boley jerked his head toward the Roberts property. "I'd think they'd get that over there for the price they want."

"Funny old gal," McCutcheon said. "Her husband was a miner, died of black lung. No children. He never had time to work the property. Thirty-nine acres, came down from his old man. Alice like to wore herself out years ago, tryin' to make somethin' of it, then gave up. Except she thinks the place is worth like the middle of New York City—*and* that the creek belongs to her, clear to where it touches my land. You understand any better?"

"I see the picture," Boley answered, "but I don't understand the last part."

"Neither do I," McCutcheon admitted. "How about a cold beer?"

"Fine," Boley said.

McCutcheon went into the house to get it. He had been gone for several minutes when Boley heard footsteps coming around the house from the rear. He turned and saw Alice Roberts at the foot of the steps. She began to talk in a loud voice. "So. Both of you'll be here together—the two of you who took that diamond out've my crick. And how many more we haven't heard about yet."

Boley stood up. "What diamond? I don't know what you're talkin' about, Mrs. Roberts."

She continued up the steps. Boley guessed her to be in her early sixties, but her vigor was of her forties.

"Don't you lie to me, mister!" she growled, sitting in the chair he had just vacated. "You know all about it. I saw you here the day it came out of the water. What cut is he giving you?"

Boley leaned against a porch post. "I'm not gettin' any cut of any kind, lady. I've been paid for diggin' some dirt and rocks out of the water for McCutcheon. I don't see where any diamond comes into it."

McCutcheon reappeared at the door, carrying two cans of cold beer. He gave one to Boley. "Alice," he said, "I didn't know you were here. Could I get you some cola?"

"The only thing you can get me is the diamond you stole from my crick."

McCutcheon glanced quickly at Boley, who continued to look puzzled. "There's some mistake, Alice. I never took anything of yours. Did you lose a diamond in the water?"

"No, I did not lose *anything* in the water," she snapped. "You found out a big diamond was in my crick and your crony fished it out. I want it."

"I made two fishin' holes in my side of the water," McCutcheon said. "I got some rich dirt for my garden and a heap of rocks. You can have every rock in that pile, if you like."

She got to her feet. "I'll take you up on that. There might be more diamonds in there that you missed. I'll go get the pickup." She went down the steps at a speed that awed Boley.

He turned to McCutcheon. "What was that all about?"

The farmer began to talk in a low tone. "Water's down more and she can get across on steppin' stones, so she'll be back in a hurry." He proceeded to tell Boley the same story McKee had. Boley did not admit to its familiarity. Instead, he said, "How did she find out?"

"Beats me," McCutcheon answered. "But if you don't want a bad case of heartburn, you'd better leave right now. I'm used to it. It won't bother me."

"The diamond—"

"Is in the bank."

* * *

Boley was unable to tell McKee about this for several days. He had necessary work at home, getting in apples from his small orchard. He was also getting in field corn for a very sick neighbor.

After a little more than a week, he went to the courthouse. On the walk outside he was stopped by a friend. Harry Comstock, a quiet, balding man with thick glasses, drew maps for Border States, Inc. Border States harvested timber and was as efficient as the businesses that got everything from slaughtered pigs except the squeal. At times the company leased land for its operations; at others, it drew on its own land. Some of their holdings abutted the land owned by McCutcheon and Alice Roberts.

"Boley!" Comstock said. "Got a minute?"

"One or two."

"Won't keep you." Comstock squinted in the sun. "Didn't you do some work on Squirrel Creek for Sewell McCutcheon right recently?"

"Yeah. Scooped out a couple of fishin' holes for him," Boley said, hoping no more information was asked for.

"Well, you must have started something. Or maybe it's just coincidence. You know what happened yesterday? He came to the office and made a deal to buy fifty more acres from us to add to his land. All rights."

"Whereabouts?"

"Beginning at the creek and going east five acres, then back upstream."

"I'll bet it costs him," Boley said.

Comstock shook his head. "Not too much. Stuff in there's mostly scrub. Company's been wishing this sort of thing might happen."

Boley began to speak, but Comstock went on. "What makes it *real* interesting is that that wild old Alice Roberts came barging in about an hour later and bought twenty acres on the opposite side of the creek. Only hers is two acres west, the rest upstream. Again, all rights. What's goin' on?"

Boley looked blank. "Beats me. Did Alice Roberts pay for hers now?"

"In cash."

Boley studied the pavement. "That's the funny part, Harry. I can't give you any answers, most of all about that."

He went into the courthouse and sought McKee. The sheriff was in.

After McKee had closed his office door, Boley ran through all that had happened, including the recent land purchases.

"I figure what they're doin' is buyin' more land along that stream so they can hunt for more diamonds without Border States gettin' into it," he finished.

McKee's head was cocked to one side. "What it really sounds like is that Alice intended to go up there and buy up land on both sides of the water and cut Sewell off. He beat her to enough of it that she didn't want to push, or she would have stirred up Border States."

"Oh, well," said Boley. "It's none of our business."

"I hope you're right," said McKee, his voice dry and astringent. "I wish you'd keep your eyes and ears open, anyway. When there's somethin' in dispute that might be valuable, I always feel I might be on the hot seat. Somebody'll be in this jail out of this, is my guess."

The following morning, Boley had left home in his four-wheel-drive jeep to help an acquaintance assess the feasibility of gathering bittersweet from a difficult location in the man's woods. With autumn coming, the colorful plant was easily saleable for decorations to tourists passing through town.

He had completed the trip and was starting home after returning the man to his house. Looking down the long corridor of trees before him he couldn't see the highway. The lane swung to the right for a few hundred feet before meeting the paved road. He slowed and made the curve, then stopped abruptly. The lane was blocked by a familiar battered red pickup. Standing beside it was Alice Roberts.

He climbed from the jeep. "Mrs. Roberts. What do you want?"

The woman was expressionless. "Mornin', Boley. I want you to get back in your jeep and follow me."

Boley considered several replies. He answered evenly, "I'm afraid I can't do that. If you have work for me, there are some people ahead of you."

"I never said anything about that," she rasped. "How do you think I found where you were?"

"I suppose you called, and my wife told you."

"I didn't call, but she told me." She moved aside and opened the truck door.

Boley stared. Inside, very pale and very straight, sat Geneva.

There was a movement beside him and Boley's eyes dropped. Alice Roberts was holding a double-barrel shotgun in her hands.

"Woman," he said, "shotgun or no shotgun, if you've hurt Geneva, I'll stomp you to bits."

"Don't get excited, Boley," she replied. "Nobody's hurt—yet. Now, you get behind that wheel and follow me."

Forcing himself to be calm, Boley did as he was told. He watched Alice Roberts climb into the truck and prop the gun between the door and her left side. Then she started, turned, and drove out.

Boley followed, driving mechanically. He paid little attention to direction or time. Rage threatened to take control, but he refused to let it. He might need all of his wits.

He wasn't entirely surprised when he saw that they had reached McCutcheon's farm and were pulling into the drive leading to the front.

The truck stopped directly before the steps to the front porch. With her surprising agility, Alice Roberts came down from the driver's seat carrying the shotgun, darted around the front of the pickup, and opened the other door to urge Geneva out.

Boley pulled up behind the truck and got out. He walked over to his wife and put his arm around her quivering shoulders.

"Arly. What's this all about?" she whispered.

"I'm not sure I know," he murmured.

"Quit talkin'!" snapped the woman. "Just behave yourselves and nobody'll get hurt. Now get up there."

She followed them up to the porch and banged on the screen door. "Mc-Cutcheon! You in there? Come out!"

There was no answer. She repeated her demands.

Finally a voice came faintly through the house. "Come on around to the west side."

Boley took Geneva's arms and urged her down from the porch, Alice Roberts' footsteps impatient behind them. They went around the house to the right. Waiting for them, leaning against a beech tree, was Sewell McCutcheon.

The farmer's eyes rounded with surprise. "This is more than I expected," he said. "Why the gun, Alice?"

"To convince you I mean business. If I pointed it at *you*, you might think I was foolin'. I hear these folks got two kids, so you'll think a bit more about it. There's shells in both these chambers."

"What do you want, Alice?"

"I want to see that diamond. I want to look at it. I want to hold it."

"We'd have to go to the bank. It's in a safety-deposit box."

Alice lifted the gun. "You're a liar, Sewell McCutcheon. How do I know? I went to the bank yesterday and asked to rent a box the same size as yours. And what did the girl say? 'We don't have a box rented to Mr. McCutcheon.' Now you get that diamond out here."

McCutcheon looked from one to another of the three. "All right. You go sit on the porch. I have to go in the house. You can't ask me to give my hidin' place away to you."

"I could, but I won't," Alice answered. "And don't you try to call anybody or throw down on me with your own gun."

McCutcheon's only answer was a nod. He went rapidly up to the side door and into the house. Boley led Geneva up to a swing that hung near the front end of the porch and sat down on it with her.

Alice followed. "If you're thinkin' about those other two who live here, fergit it. They went off down to Montgomery earlier." She leaned against a stack of firewood McCutcheon had put up to season.

After what seemed to Boley to be an interminable time, the farmer reappeared. He carried a cylindrical plastic medicine container about two inches long and an inch in diameter.

"We'd best go down into the sun," he said. "You can get a better idea."

He led the way down into the yard toward the stream, out of the shade of the trees surrounding the house. He stopped, opened the container, and shook something into his right palm. He offered it to Alice.

"Here it is."

She plucked it from his hand and peered at it.

"Why, it looks just like a dirty quartz pebble or some of them other rocks," she muttered. "This is a diamond? An uncut one?"

"It is. It's real," McCutcheon answered. "I can prove it, too."

She stared at it, letting the sun shine on it. "Well, some ways you look at it—A real, honest-to-God diamond, pulled outa my crick! McCutcheon, all my life I've wanted one nice thing to call my own."

The farmer pulled at his moustache. "Well, Alice, I'm sorry for you, but it came off my property. It came outa my side."

She raised her eyes to his. "How about you get it cut? Cut in two parts. Let me have half."

McCutcheon reached over and removed the stone from her hand. "Alice, you've been too much trouble to me over the years. Threatenin' these people with a shotgun is just too much."

"Shotgun!" she yelled. "I'll give you shotgun!"

She raised the gun swiftly, reversing it, and grasping the barrels with both hands, she clubbed McCutcheon across the back of the head. He fell to the ground, bleeding.

Stooping, she pried his fingers open and took the stone from them. "I'm not gonna let you take it!" she cried, running to the creek. When she reached the bank, she drew back her arm and threw the diamond as hard as she could into the woods upstream from her house. "Now," she yelled, "it's where it belongs! I might be forever findin' it, but you ain't gonna get it!"

Boley retrieved the gun where she had dropped it. "Go inside and call the sheriff," he told Geneva. "Say we need paramedics for Sewell."

When the sheriff's car and the ambulance came, McCutcheon was unconscious. Alice Roberts sat by the creek, ignoring everything until they took her to the car in handcuffs.

Boley explained the morning's events to McKee, who had come with a deputy. The sheriff heard him out. "Sounds like we've got her for kidnaping and assault, at least."

Alice Roberts, in the police car, heard them. "Kidnaping?" she said. "They's only old empty shells in that gun."

McKee leaned in the window. "But they didn't know that, Alice." To Boley, he said, "And don't you back off on the charge."

"I won't," Boley promised. "I'm just glad it's over."

McKee gave him an odd look. "If you think that, you've got another think comin'. Let's do today's paperwork, then come see me late tomorrow afternoon."

When Boley arrived at his office late the next day, the sheriff closed the door and waved him to a seat. "Things are pretty much as I figured," he said.

"How's McCutcheon?" Boley asked. "And what about Alice?"

"Sewell's not too bad." McKee sat down. "He's gettin' a good goin' over for concussion, but that's about it. Alice is still locked up, which is where I want her." He leaned across the desk. "How's it feel to be a cat's-paw?"

Boley was startled. "There's some kind of set-up in this?"

McKee sat back. "I'll run it past you. Some of this I can't prove and we'll just have to wait and see what happens. Anyway, you know same as I do that one of this county's big hopes is to attract people with money to buy up some of this land. Build themselves a place where they can come weekends or for the summer. The trouble is, we have only one good-sized lake and one nice recreation area. There are lots of other good places, but developers want to pick 'em up for peanuts.

"Alice Roberts, poor soul, has a place that looks like the devil's back yard. But it wouldn't take a lot to make it presentable, and it lays well. Sewell's place looks good. Given the right price, he'd quit and retire."

"I'm beginning to get an idea," Boley said. "McCutcheon decided to start a diamond rush, is that it? Where'd he get the stone?"

"You dug it out for him," McKee replied. "Until then, everything was just what it seemed. You dug two fishin' holes. Then he did find the diamond, and all that hush-hush commenced.

"I'd say he called Alice over and had a talk. Showed her how they could put on an act, building things up to her sluggin' him, so his discovery would really hit the papers."

Boley said, "So they bought that land from Border States hoping to resell and clean up. But where did Alice get the money?"

"Maybe she had some put back. But I'd bet Sewell made her a loan."

"The diamond. Is it real?"

McKee grinned. "It's real. The state man wouldn't lie about that."

"You want me to press the kidnap charge."

"I do. And I've had the hospital keep McCutcheon sedated, partly to keep him from droppin' the assault charge. You hang on until I suggest you drop it."

Boley was still puzzled. "What about the diamond? She threw it into the woods. I saw her."

"You saw her throw something into the woods. Remember I said you might mistake it for dirty quartz or calcite? That's probably what Sewell let her throw away." McKee's amusement grew. "Another reason for keepin' her locked up— I want McCutcheon to have time to go over there and 'find' that stone again." He added a postscript. "Or maybe they'll leave it as an inducement for whoever buys Alice's place."

WISCONSIN

THE FIFTH GRAVE
by Jack Ritchie

WHEN RALPH CELEBRATED his twentieth wedding anniversary he invited me to the party and there I met his brother-in-law, Julius, a civil engineer.

"Well, well," Julius said, "Ralph's been telling me a lot about you, Henry. When you start deducting, the fur flies and nothing is sacred."

I smiled modestly. "I *do* try my best."

Ralph, Julius, and I were in the kitchen, where Ralph was making drinks for the crowd.

"I think I've got a problem for you to work on, Henry," Julius said. "It's about a missing body."

Naturally I became attentive.

Julius began. "Four years ago I was on a job up in Sheboygan County. We were rebuilding a country road—widening it and putting on a new topping. It was one of those roads that meanders all over the place, so while we were at it we decided to straighten it out as much as we could."

I nodded understandingly. If there is anything a civil engineer cannot endure it is a meandering road.

"Well, there was the country cemetery—just a little bit of a thing, maybe an acre or less. No buildings. And we needed a chunk off one end of the property for our road. That meant we had to move six graves.

"Getting permission to move graves is a delicate thing and you want to do it as quietly as you can. The last thing you want is a lot of publicity. So our firm's lawyers moved on tiptoe, so to speak, and we got the authorization.

"We moved six graves. But there were only *five* bodies. I mean there wasn't anything at all in the fifth grave—just the tombstone on top. I still remember the name. Lucas Martin. But no coffin, no body, no bones. You could see the spot hadn't even been dug up before."

"Hmm," I said wisely. "Did you note the date of death on the tombstone?"

"November 8, 1913."

November 8, 1913? Somehow that rang a bell in my memory. Where had I heard or seen that date before? "Did you call this matter of the missing body to the attention of the local authorities?"

"Hell, no. We were on a schedule. There's no telling how much time we'd have lost if we had to wait for some kind of an investigation. No, we just kept everything to ourselves and moved the five bodies and six tombstones to another part of the cemetery.

"And there were a couple of strange things about the sixth grave too. For one, the date of death was exactly the same as on the fifth tombstone—November 8, 1913. And for another, we found a body all right—a skeleton actually—but no coffin.

"I mean, after all those years you'd still expect to find enough scraps to show there had been one. But there was nothing. Just the skeleton. And Leslie Randolph—that was the name on the tombstone—must have been a woman, because there was enough left of the shoes she was buried in to tell us they were the high-button kind women wore in those days."

Julius and Ralph now regarded me expectantly.

"Well," I said, "First of all, since these two people evidently died on the same day I deduce that it might have been as a result of some kind of an epidemic. Typhus, perhaps, or diphtheria, both of which were rampant in those days. How old were they when they died?"

Julius thought a moment. "As I remember, both were about twenty-one or twenty-two."

I mulled the problem over for ten or fifteen seconds. "Or possibly they died in an automobile accident, with both of them in the same or conflicting vehicles. There were auto accidents, you know, even in 1913."

Ralph asked the pertinent question. "But why weren't both of them buried? Why just one?"

"I don't know yet, Ralph," I admitted. "However, I will give the matter thought. There is nothing that the deductive brain cannot unravel provided it is given all the facts. Have you forgotten anything, Julius?"

"No. That's it. The whole ball of wax."

What did I have to work with? Obviously, my starting point must be that date, November 8, 1913, but that would have to wait until tomorrow. I helped Ralph and Julius carry the trays of drinks into the living room.

The next day, after Ralph and I finished our shifts and signed out at headquarters, I went directly to the Journal Building where I got permission to consult the newspaper's back files.

The moment I saw the headlines for November 8, 1913, I had the solution for the entire conundrum. How simple it all was once you knew the facts.

I was so enthused I drove right over to Ralph's house where he was preparing to mow the lawn before supper.

"Ralph," I announced, "I have the solution to the problem of the unoccupied grave. The key to the entire matter is the date—November 8, 1913."

"What about November 8, 1913?"

"Between November seventh and the twelfth, in 1913, the Great Lakes experienced one of the worst storms in their history. Millions of dollars of damage was done and eight lake boats went down with all hands."

Ralph, who was born far inland, attempted to correct me. "Lake *ships*."

"No, Ralph. Lake *boats*. No matter what the size of a lake vessel, lake sailors traditionally refer to it as a boat." I returned to the main point. "Anyway, among the hundreds of lives lost were those of Leslie Randolph and Lucas Martin. They were either passengers, or possibly crewpersons, aboard one of those ill-fated lake boats."

"Crewperson? Leslie Randolph? In 1913?"

I was bulging with information. "Ralph, in those days the cooks on the lake boats were often women. As a matter of fact, on some of the boats they were husband-and-wife teams. Though not, evidently, in this case."

"What has all this got to do with the empty grave?"

"Ralph, when people are lost at sea—or in this case at lake—and their bodies are never recovered, it is often the custom to erect a tombstone over a blank plot in a cemetery to commemorate the event. And *that* is why there was no body beneath the tombstone of Lucas Martin. His body was never recovered. On the other hand, the body of Leslie Randolph *was* recovered—probably washed ashore—and it was buried under the sixth tombstone."

Ralph nodded to indicate that, so far, he went along with me. "But that still leaves something to explain, Henry. Why wasn't Leslie Randolph buried in a coffin?"

"I can only guess, Ralph. Perhaps Leslie Randolph's relatives decided to scrimp on funeral expenses. Or possibly she belonged to some stark religious sect that eschewed coffins."

But frankly I was not at all satisfied with either of those answers. The question remained, why *had* Leslie Randolph been buried without a coffin?

The subject continued to nag at the back of my mind, and so, three weeks later, when Captain Johnson sent Ralph and me up to Sturgeon Bay to pick up a fugitive I took the opportunity to detour, traveling through quite pleasant farm country liberally sprinkled with dairy herds. We arrived at the cemetery a little after eleven in the morning and parked at the side of the road.

The sun-dappled acre was surrounded on three sides by tall old trees, with the open side abutting the road. Across that road, perhaps a hundred yards back, stood a neat farm with its enclave of barn, silos, and outbuildings.

A large farm hound began barking and loping in our direction. I hesitated about getting out of the car until I saw him come to a halt, ready to defend his property but choosing not to venture across the road.

Ralph and I, with one eye on the hound, left the car and proceeded to stroll through the cemetery, reading tombstones, some of which dated back to the 1830s. Certain family names seemed to predominate—Randolph, Martin, Riley and Armstrong.

I found the transplanted graves of Leslie Randolph and Lucas Martin and verified the dates. Yes, November 8, 1913, and both of them had been twenty-two when they died.

I heard the slam of a screen door in the distance and turned to see a woman walking in our direction carrying a shotgun.

She closed the distance between us and I saw that she was perhaps in her middle twenties, with dark hair and violet eyes. She gave the hound the order to stop barking and then both of them crossed the road. At our car, she paused momentarily to stare at the license plate and then halted some fifteen feet from Ralph and me.

I smiled fully. "Do you always greet visitors to this cemetery with a double-barreled shotgun?"

She remained cautious. "That depends. If I don't recognize the car or the people I like to find out what's going on."

"Madam," I said joshingly, "we do not have the slightest intention of stealing bodies or tombstones."

"How about trees?" she asked, keeping the shotgun steady and aimed.

I thought the proper time had come for me to introduce myself. "My name is Detective-Sergeant Henry S. Turnbuckle," I said impressively. "Of the Milwaukee Police Department." I produced my wallet for identification purposes and held it at arm's length.

She came close enough to study my badge, my picture, and my face. She did the same for Ralph and then relaxed somewhat and the dog totally, his tail thumping.

"What in the world are two Milwaukee detectives doing in this part of the country?"

"Just passing through on our way up north on official business," I said. "And at the same time trying to solve a little mystery." I pointed to the headstones of Leslie Randolph and Lucas Martin. "I notice that both of these people seem to have died on the same day."

She looked at the stones. "Oh, yes. They died in the Great Lake Storm of 1913. Both of them were crewmen on one of the lake boats and it went down with all hands."

Ralph gazed at me with what I interpreted as great admiration for my deductive powers.

I chuckled. "And Leslie Randolph was undoubtedly a cook on the vessel?"

She shrugged. "I wouldn't know. He could have been a deck hand."

I blinked. He? "Leslie Randolph was a man?"

"But of course. As a matter of fact, both of them were my great-grandfather's best friends. The three of them had planned on working on the lake boats together, but then Great-grandfather's father died, so he decided to get married instead and take over the farm. Neither one of their bodies was ever recovered." She introduced herself. "Louise Armstrong. I'm baby-sitting the farm today. Everybody else is at the fair."

I rubbed my chin. Neither body was recovered? Then whose body was under Leslie Randolph's memorial stone? And, more important, why?

But then I had it. "Miss Armstrong," I said, pointing at Randolph's head-stone, "would it surprise you to learn that there is a woman's skeleton under that tombstone and that she was the victim of a murder that occurred nearly seventy years ago?"

She studied me doubtfully.

I turned to Ralph. "Where does one hide a tree? In a forest, of course. And where does one hide a body? In a cemetery." I frowned darkly.

"Ralph, I could have deduced all of this in Milwaukee had Julius but given me all the facts."

"What facts didn't he give you?"

"Ralph, if you are surreptitiously burying a body, especially in a semi-public place, you do not dig down the traditional six feet. You are anxious to get the matter over with as quickly as possible and leave the premises. Therefore you dig only as deep as you have to, which is perhaps three or four feet. And Julius failed to mention, or observe, that the grave must have been shallow."

Then I smiled confidently. "The individual who committed the murder *knew* that those tombstones were over empty plots. Now only two things remain to be ferreted out. Who was the victim and who was the murderer?"

I proceeded to think while they watched me respectfully and naturally I arrived at part of the solution in short order.

"Ralph," I said, "if you were going to bury a body in this cemetery and did not want to be observed while in the process, how would you go about it?"

"I'd wait until it got dark."

"But how could you see well enough to dig the grave? Would you bring a lantern? No, the light would gleam in the night like a terrestrial star and draw the curiosity of anyone who glimpsed it."

"All right, so I'd wait until there was moonlight."

"Ralph, I doubt that even moonlight would provide sufficient light for what you had to do."

"Why not?"

"Because you would want to *very* carefully conceal what you had done. After all, this is a functioning cemetery. People are bound to come here occasionally to pay their respects or to bury others. If the burying was done clumsily and there was evidence of digging it would draw immediate suspicion, especially from those who knew there was supposed to be no body under the tombstone.

"No, Ralph, in order to conceal the fact that one has buried a body one must go to a bit of trouble. First, one must spread out a tarpaulin upon which to deposit the raw earth one excavates. Then when the hole is dug and the body deposited one returns as much of the earth to the grave as one can and replaces the sod. Then one gathers up the soil displaced by the body and decompactation and carries it somewhere else for dispersal. And in order to be this painstaking I would venture to say that only daylight is suitable."

Ralph looked at the road. "Wouldn't that be taking pretty much of a chance, to dig by daylight? People would be bound to drive by and see what you were doing and wonder why. And what about the farm across the road? Anybody living there would certainly notice you."

"True, Ralph. Therefore I deduce that the body was buried early in the morning. *Very* early in the morning. This is dairy-farming country, Ralph, and farmers must remain home mornings to do the milking and adjacent chores before they can think of traveling anywhere. Therefore, our digger could count on the roads being deserted until at least mid-morning. And as for the farm across the road, while farmers rise early for milking—in the height of the summer when the sun rises at nearly four A.M.—they do not rise *that* early. They remain abed until their regular milking time, which is usually around six o'clock, summer, winter, spring, and fall.

"Hence, in that interval of daylight, say between four and six A.M. on a summer's day, when the occupants of the farm across the road were still asleep in their beds, the murderer came here with his body and buried it."

I did not exactly expect applause but a little appreciation would have been appropriate.

"What about the dogs?" Louise asked.

"What dogs?"

"Just about every farmer has a dog or two. And they bark. So even if this burying was done between four and six A.M., the dogs across the road would have barked their fool heads off until—" She stopped and became deeply thoughtful.

I attacked the problem of the dogs. "Ah ha," I said. "I have it. The *only* person who could have buried the body without having the dogs go crazy was actually—" I stopped and cleared my throat. "How long have Armstrongs lived on the farm across the road?"

"We are a Century Farm. Ever since 1842."

I thought about that some more and sighed. "Well, as long as I have gone this far I might as well finish it. As I deduce it, the only person who could have conducted the digging without raising a commotion would have had to be the *owner* of those dogs. And that, I am afraid to say, must have been one of your ancestors. Say your great-grandfather, perhaps?"

Louise said nothing.

I smiled magnanimously. "You may trust me to remain silent on this matter. I was merely indulging in the mental exercise presented by the problem, a veritable cerebral etude." I chuckled good-naturedly. "After all the murder is nearly seventy years old. History. So let sleeping murderers lie. The victim is dead, and, by now, so is the murderer."

Again Louise said absolutely nothing.

I frowned and then did some quick arithmetic. I was rather astounded. "Do you mean to say that your great-grandfather is still *alive?*"

She nodded reluctantly. "He's ninety-one. And Great-grandmother is ninety. They've been married sixty-seven years and they've retired to Florida."

Sixty-seven years? I did some more mental arithmetic and was again astounded. "That would mean he married her in about 1915. However—in the matter of Martin Lucas and Leslie Randolph—you distinctly said that your great-grandfather had planned to go with them on the lake boats, but he got married 'instead' and took over the farm. That would mean he married in 1913 or prior to that. In other words, he was married at least twice. What happened to his first wife?"

"She ran away with a traveling salesman," Louise said firmly.

"Ah ha," I said, wrapping it up, "so your great-grandfather told anyone who inquired. But did anyone ever see or hear from her again? Or from the mythical traveling salesman, for that matter?"

Louise had a remarkable way with silence.

Ralph rubbed his hands. "Well, congratulations, Henry. You've done it again. You've got your murderer and he's alive."

"Now Ralph, a lot of water has flowed under the bridge since—"

"It's your sworn duty to uphold the law," Ralph said solemnly. "You've got to go down there with extradition papers and drag that old man from the side of his wife and bring him back here for justice."

"Ralph, we've got to take into consideration the ages of both—"

"I can see the headlines now, Henry. *Detective Solves Seventy-year-old Murder. Collars Ninety-one-year-old Suspect*. Your picture will be in every newspaper and your name on everyone's lips. You might even get into the *Guinness Book of Records* for arresting the oldest murder suspect in the United States. Maybe the world."

"Ralph," I said, feeling a bit warm, "you don't seem to understand that my deductions, though undoubtedly correct, are all theoretical. In the world of practicality, we could meet with all kinds of stumbling blocks."

"What stumbling blocks, Henry?"

"Well, he might fight extradition, for instance. And then there's the body. Could we *positively* identify it as that of his first wife?"

"Science is marvelous, Henry. Face it, you've got him nailed."

My voice seemed a little higher than usual. "I do *not* have him nailed, Ralph. It is entirely possible that I may be wrong."

Strangely, Ralph seemed to be enjoying the situation. "But, Henry, your deduction about the dog was absolutely brilliant. It proves that Great-grandfather Armstrong was the only man who could have done the burying."

"About that dog," I said a trifle desperately, "we are *assuming* there was a dog. But Armstrong could have been an exception to the rule of dogs and farmsteads. Or, if he had a dog, this dog could have recently died and the burying of the unidentified body could have taken place between the time of the dog's death and the time the newly acquired puppy had learned how to bark. Great-grandfather Armstrong could have slept through the whole thing and any stranger with a body could have sneaked into the cemetery and buried her. Whoever she was."

Ralph was silent for a few moments and then he sighed dramatically. "Well, Henry, do you really and truly think we should forget about the whole thing?"

"I do, I do." I stared into the far distance. "Ralph, there are times when I think this entire universe is a put-on and I'm the only one who hasn't been told."

Louise's smile had been growing. "Would you like to come up to the house and have a cup of coffee or something?"

"Do you have any sherry?" Ralph asked. "At a time like this, Henry finds that nothing bucks him up like a glass of sherry."

We walked toward the house.

"Trees?" I said.

Louise nodded. "I thought you two might be timber cruisers. They ride about the countryside looking for valuable trees, mainly black walnut. There are about a half dozen in that grove around the cemetery and they're worth more than a thousand dollars each. Sometimes the cruisers make the farmer an offer, but other times they just make a note of the place and sneak back at night or when the farmer isn't home. Sam Riley down the road had two of his black walnuts cut down just a few weeks ago. They were at the other end of his pasture and he didn't hear or see a thing."

Inside the house, Louise found a half-empty bottle of sherry and dusted it off with a kitchen towel. She poured me a glass. "Why don't you come back some- time soon and solve the Mystery of the Purloined Black Walnut Trees?"

"I may," I said. I held my glass to the light. The *Guinness Book of Records*? I shook away the temptation and drank my sherry.

WYOMING

COUNTERPLOT
by Francis M. Nevins, Jr.

THE WEEKEND ICE storm made the motel cleaning women late for work on Monday morning. The woman assigned to the rooms at the end of the west wing gave a ritual tap on the door of 114, then used her passkey and stepped in. When she saw what lay on the green shag carpet she shrieked and went careening down the corridor in terror. The Cody police arrived ten minutes later. When the fingerprint report came back from F.B.I. headquarters the next day, they knew a part of the story. The rest they never learned, and would not have believed if someone had told them.

She followed instructions precisely. The Northwest jet touched down at Billings just before 5:00 P.M. on Friday, and by 5:30 she had rented a car from the Budget booth near the baggage-claim area. As the sun dropped over the awesomely close mountaintops she was crossing the Montana border into Wyoming. The two-lane blacktop rose and fell and wound among the magnificent mountains like a scenic railway, bringing her to the edge of Cody around 8:00.

She'd been told there would be a reservation for her at the Great Western Motel in the name of Ann Chambers. There was. She checked in, unpacked the two smaller suitcases, left the large gray Samsonite case at the back of the room closet, locked. Then she bathed, changed to a blue jumpsuit, turned on the TV, and settled in to wait. Until Monday morning if necessary. Those were the instructions.

Friday passed, and Saturday, and Sunday. She heard the harsh sound of frozen rain falling on the streets, the screech of brakes, the dull whine of car motors refusing to start. The storm didn't affect her. She stayed in the room, watching local television and reading a pile of paperback romances she had brought with her. Three times a day she would stride down the corridor to the coffee shop for a hasty meal. The only other customers were a handful of pickup-truck cowboys

553

who kept their outsized Stetsons on as they ate flamboyantly. None of them could be the man she was waiting for. She wondered if the storm would keep him from coming.

At 10:00 P.M. on Sunday, while she was sitting on the bed bundled in blankets, boredly watching a local TV newscast, a quick triple knock sounded on her door. She sprang up, smoothed the bedcovers, undid the chain bolt, and opened two inches. "Yes?"

"Software man." The words were exactly what she expected.

"Hardware's here," she replied as instructed, and cautiously drew back the door to let him in. He was heavy-set and rugged-looking, about 40, wearing a three-quarter-length tan suede jacket with sheepskin collar. When he took off his mitten cap she saw he was partially bald. He threw his jacket on the bed and inspected her.

"You sure ain't Frank Bolish," he said. "So who are you?"

"Arlene Carver. One of Frank's assistants." She held out her hand to him and took a chance. "If you read his columns you've probably seen my name mentioned. I do investigative work for him."

"Never read his columns," the man grunted. "I don't think newspapermen should be allowed to attack public officials the way Bolish does. Prove who you are." His accent was heavily Western, almost like Gary Cooper's but too soft and whispery as if he had a sore throat. Taking small steps, she backed toward the formica-topped round table at the room's far end where her oversized handbag lay.

"Hold it right there," the man ordered. "I'll find your ID myself." He strode long-legged across the room, passing her cautiously, reached for the bag, and shook its contents out on the bed.

"There's no gun," she told him, trying to control the irritation she was beginning to feel, "and the money's not there either. Do you think I'm a fool?"

He pawed through her alligator wallet, studying the array of plastic cards in their window envelopes. "Okay, so your name's Arlene Carver and you live in Bethesda, Maryland. That's close enough to Washington all right, but what tells me you're with Bolish?"

"How do I know you're Paxton?" she demanded. "I was told he was a skinny guy with thick gray hair. You're two hundred pounds and could use a toupee."

"I never claimed I was Paxton." He tugged a bulging pigskin wallet from his hip pocket and passed her a business card. "Ted Gorman, from Cheyenne. Private investigator. Paxton got cold feet Friday, hired me to drive up to Cody and make the delivery for him." He took a long careful breath. "He said either Bolish himself or his chief assistant Marty Lanning would pick it up."

"Frank has to be on a TV show tomorrow morning and Marty's down with flu," she said.

He gazed coldly at her. She knew he was trying to decide if she was genuine or an impostor. "Come on, man!" she told him impatiently. "I knew the stupid password and I knew what Paxton looks like. Give me the damn videotape!"

"Not yet." He perched himself on the round table and pointed a finger at her. "If you're with Bolish you'll know what's supposed to be on the tape. Tell me."

"The way Frank said Paxton described it over the phone," she answered slowly, "it's a videocassette made with a hidden camera at Vito Carbone's condo in Miami Beach. It shows Senator Vega taking a $100,000 payoff from Carbone and agreeing to sponsor some amendments to the Federal Criminal Code that the Mob wants." She paused and looked at him.

"More," he demanded.

"The videocassette was made for Angelo Generoso," she went on. "His family and the Carbones have been in an undeclared war for years. Paxton was the low-level torpedo the Generosos sent to Carbone's pad to dismantle the equipment and bring back the cassettes when it was all over. Only Paxton found out what was on that one tape, saw a chance to get rich, and disappeared with the thing instead. He'd grown up in rural Wyoming, so he came back out here to hole up till the heat died down. Then he phoned Frank in Washington and offered him the cassette for $25,000."

"Okay." The bald man nodded slightly. "That's the same story Paxton tells. You got the money?"

"Yes. You have the cassette?"

"Hold still a minute." He strode across the room and out into the corridor, leaving the door slightly ajar. She watched him enter the alcove down the hall that held the soft-drink machine. There was the sound of a lid being lifted, then the rumble of ice cubes being displaced. He re-entered the room rubbing the moist white protective jacket of the cassette against his shirt. "Ice machine didn't do it any harm," he said. "Let's see the money."

She bent over the bureau, pulled out the bottom drawer, and removed the Gideon Bible. Then she shook the Bible out over the bed. Twenty-five $1000 bills fluttered down from the pages onto the rumpled blanket. She picked them up and arranged them in a neat stack but did not hold them out to him.

"They could be counterfeit," the bald man muttered.

"Oh, for God's sake! This is throwaway money for Frank Bolish. Now give me the damn cassette!"

Hesitantly he placed it on the blanket beside the bills, then perched on the edge of the formica again, while she rebolted the chain lock. She then dragged the large gray Samsonite suitcase out of the closet, lifted it to the bed, and unlocked it. She took out the videocassette player, set it down on the bureau top, and used a tiny screwdriver to connect its wires with certain wires of the room television. When the player was ready she flipped the ON switch, took the cassette out of its protective jacket, and inserted it into the machine. Then she depressed the PLAY button and turned on the TV to watch the images from the cassette.

The tape ran for about twelve minutes. Its technical quality was poor, which was natural considering the secrecy in which it was made. It showed a quiet conference between two men in shirtsleeves. The older she recognized—Vito, lion of the Carbones. The younger—tall, slender, hypnotic-voiced—certainly looked like Senator Vega. The hidden camera caught the quick transfer of an envelope, the counting of the money, the careful repetition of what the senator must do in return for the gift.

She hit the STOP button before the scene had ended. "I don't like it," she said. "There's something staged-looking about that payoff. One of them's an actor, maybe both of them." She chewed her underlip nervously and turned her back for a second to switch off the TV.

When she faced him again, he was holding a small .25 aimed at her middle.

"You took a gamble and lost, lady," the bald man said. "It happens I do read Bolish's column every day, and I got a real good memory for names. He's never mentioned you in any of his material. Now, who the hell are you?"

She took another long deep breath to gain time. "All right," she told him then. "I—guess I gave myself away with what I said about that tape. My name is Arlene Carver but I don't work for Bolish. I'm a troubleshooter for Senator Vega. We heard rumors about a plot to smear him with a phony videotape, and then when Paxton offered the tape to Bolish one of Bolish's staff leaked the story to us. My partner managed to sidetrack the man Bolish sent out to make the pickup and I came on in his place. Look, what do you and Paxton care who pays you? The tape's a phony, but the media could crucify the senator with it, so we're willing to pay to keep it under wraps."

"Sure it's a phony. All you true believers who think Jorge Vega can pull together that good old Sixties coalition of the Hispanics and the blacks and the feminists and the Indians and the kids, you'll all swear till you're blue in the face the tape's a phony so your boy can become President in '84. Only if the tape gets out, it's Vega's finish, and you know it."

"It's no use talking politics with you," she said icily. "Take the money and leave this room, right now."

"Not quite yet." He waggled the .25 at her lazily. "You see, I still don't know who you are, lady, but I surely know who you're not. You don't work for Jorge Vega. *But I do.*"

Consternation flushed her face, and she jerked back as though he had struck her.

"Paxton didn't just make one long-distance call to Washington about that cassette," the man explained. "He offered it to Vega for the same price he wanted from Bolish. I'm a Wyoming boy, so the senator took me off my other work on his staff and asked me to get the tape from Paxton. I did. Didn't use money, just muscle. But then I decided to keep Paxton's date with Bolish, hoping I could find out what Bolish planned to print about the senator. Now, you're not with Bolish and you're not with Vega, so before I get angry and ask you the hard way, you tell me who you are and what your game is."

He took two slow steps toward her, his fingers tightening on the .25 as he moved.

"Put that toy away," she told him calmly, "before you find yourself in deep trouble." She reached inside her blouse with careful motions, pulled out a hinged leather cardholder, opened it, and held it out so he could see the gold shield and identification.

"Oh, hell," he mumbled, and gently set down the gun on the dresser top. "Why didn't you say you were F.B.I.?"

"Well, your loyalties weren't exactly displayed on a billboard," she told him. "The Bureau heard rumors about that cassette too, and my job was to run them down. A woman on Bolish's staff leaked it to the Bureau when Paxton made him the offer. I told the truth when I said my partner intercepted Bolish's messenger and I came on in his place. Another two minutes and I would have been reading you your rights. Depending on whether that tape is real or a phony, either Vega's going to be charged with taking a bribe or some big bananas in the Mob are going to face extortion charges. I don't think you broke any Federal laws by hijacking the cassette from Paxton, but I'll keep the tape from this point on."

"I'm not so sure of that." He grinned at her, reached down to his oversized cowboy belt buckle, and disconnected it from its leather strap. From the interior of the hollow buckle he extracted a leather cardholder of his own and flipped it at her. "Damndest thing I've seen in fifteen years with the Bureau," he laughed. "Two agents playing cat and mouse with each other like this. Yeah, I've been working the case from the other side. Picked up Paxton in Laramie on Friday night and decided to keep his appointment with Bolish's messenger on the off chance I'd get something we could use against Bolish. He's written a lot of columns the Bureau doesn't appreciate."

"Nice job," she said. "You fooled me all the way. I never would have guessed you were with the Bureau." She came toward him slowly, almost seductively, until she was two steps from the corner of the dresser that held his gun.

She leaped for the .25 at the same moment his hands leaped for her throat.

Late the next morning, when she entered to clean Room 114, the cleaning woman found the two intertwined bodies—the man shot with a .25 at point-blank range, the woman strangled to death. The police quickly determined what had happened but had no idea why they had killed each other, nor could they make sense of the inordinate number of artifacts of identity found in the room, all of them turning out to be spurious.

The F.B.I. report on the two sets of fingerprints, however, proved to be help-ful. The man was identified as a pistolero for the Carbone organized-crime fam-ily and the woman as an enforcer for the more progressive and affirmative-ac-tion-oriented Generosos.